W9-BFF-526

THE PENGUIN CLASSICS

FOUNDER EDITOR (1944-64): E. V. RIEU

COUNT LEO NIKOLAYEVICH TOLSTOY was born in 1828 at Yasnaya Polyana in the Tula province, and educated privately. He studied Oriental languages and law at the University of Kazan, then led a life of pleasure until 1851 when he joined an artillery regiment in the Caucasus. He took part in the Crimean war and after the defence of Sevastopol he wrote *The Sevastopol Stories*, which established his reputation. After a period in St Petersburg and abroad, where he studied educational methods for use in his school for peasant children in Yasnaya, he married Sophie Andreyevna Behrs in 1862. The next fifteen years was a period of great happiness; they had thirteen children, and Tolstoy managed his vast estates in the Volga Steppes, continued his educational projects, cared for his peasants and wrote *War and Peace* (1865-68) and *Anna Karenin* (1874-76). *A Confession* (1879-82) marked an outward change in his life and works; he became an extreme rationalist and moralist, and in a series of pamphlets after 1880 he expressed theories such as rejection of the state and church, indictment of the demands of the flesh, and denunciation of private property. His teaching earned him numerous followers in Russia and abroad, but also much opposition and in 1901 he was excommunicated by the Russian holy synod. He died in 1910, in the course of a dramatic flight from home, at the small railway station of Astapovo.

ROSEMARY EDMONDS was born in London and studied English, Russian, French, Italian and Old Church Slavonic at universities in England, France and Italy. During the war she was translator to General de Gaulle at Fighting France Headquarters in London and, after the liberation, in Paris. She went on to study Russian Orthodox Spirituality, and has translated Archimandrite Sophrony's *The Undistorted Image*. She has also translated Tolstoy's *Anna Karenin*, *The Cossacks*, *Resurrection* and *Childhood, Boyhood and Youth*; *The Queen of Spades* by Pushkin; and Turgenev's *Father and Sons*, all for the Penguin Classics. Her other translations include works by Gogol and Leskov. She is at present working in Spanish, and researching into Old Church Slavonic texts.

L · N · TOLSTOY

WAR AND PEACE

TRANSLATED AND
WITH AN INTRODUCTION
BY
ROSEMARY EDMONDS

VOLUME
I

PENGUIN BOOKS

Penguin Books Ltd, Harmondsworth, Middlesex, England
Penguin Books, 625 Madison Avenue, New York, New York 10022, U.S.A.
Penguin Books Australia Ltd, Ringwood, Victoria, Australia
Penguin Books Canada Ltd, 41 Steelcase Road West, Markham, Ontario, Canada
Penguin Books (N.Z.) Ltd, 182–190 Wairau Road, Auckland 10, New Zealand

—

First published 1869
This translation first published 1957
Reprinted 1961, 1963, 1965, 1967, 1968, 1969, 1970, 1971 (twice),
1972 (twice), 1973, 1974, 1975, 1977

—

Copyright © Rosemary Edmonds, 1957

—

Made and printed in Great Britain
by Hazell Watson & Viney Ltd,
Aylesbury, Bucks
Set in Monotype Bembo

CONTENTS

VOLUME ONE

INTRODUCTION

*'There is no greatness where simplicity, goodness and
truth are absent.'*

*In the year 1861 Tolstoy organized a school on his estate, where he taught
the children of his unlettered serfs. At the same time he was publishing a
magazine to 'educate the educated'. At first the twofold self-imposed task
seemed to progress well; but gradually the desire to teach and the necessity
for hiding the fact that he did not know what to teach brought him very near
despair, from which only the thought of marriage saved him. He had tried
everything but family life, and although in January 1862 he noted in his
Journal: 'All my teeth are coming out and I am still unmarried; it is likely
that I shall remain a bachelor for ever,' and the thought of a single life no
longer 'terrified' him, he decided to test the one remaining promise of happiness. Spiritually exhausted, discouraged, and worn down with a cough which
he was unable to throw off, at the age of thirty-four, in the autumn of 1862,
he married a girl sixteen years younger than himself.*

*In a letter to his cousin a year later Tolstoy writes: 'Never before have I
felt my intellectual and even all my moral faculties so unimpeded, so fit for
work. And I have work – a novel of the period 1810–1820, which has completely absorbed me since the beginning of the autumn.... Now I am an
author with all the powers of my soul, and I write and reflect as I have never
written or reflected before.' The novel was War and Peace, and Tolstoy
had entered on the third period of his life, the eighteen years during which he
lived what he called a 'sound, upright, family life.'*

*Tolstoy had read 'with relish' the history of Napoleon and Alexander I
of Russia, and immediately found himself 'enveloped in a cloud of joy. My
mind was filled with the possibility of doing a great thing – of writing a
psychological novel of Alexander and Napoleon, and of all the baseness, all
the empty phrases, the foolishness and the inconsistencies of their entourage
and of the pair themselves'. Eager and exhaustive research into his subject –
il lungo studio e il grande amore – and the writing of War and Peace
occupied him to the exclusion of all else for the next five years, until the
final proof sheets were corrected and the book appeared, first serially and*

then in six volumes in 1869. Emerging from his study after a day when the work of creation had gone well, Tolstoy would tell his family that a little more of his life-blood had gone into the inkwell. From beginning to end the Countess acted as his amanuensis, struggling with the often barely decipherable manuscript, parts of which Tolstoy drafted seven times before being satisfied. (The entry in her Journal for 12 November 1866 reads: 'I spend my whole time copying out Liova's novel. This is a great delight to me. As I copy, I live through a whole world of new ideas and impressions. Nothing has such an effect upon me as his ideas and his genius.' And two months later: 'All this winter L. has kept on writing, wrought up, the tears starting to his eyes and his heart swelling. I believe his novel is going to be wonderful.')

Tolstoy's subject is humanity – people moving in the strange delirium of war and war's chaos. The historic scenes are used as a foil and background for the personal dramas of those who took part in them. Interest is mainly concentrated in two households – the Rostovs, impoverished country squires, and the Bolkonskys, standing outside and higher than 'high' society – and Pierre Bezuhov. In the way Tolstoy has of walking through all his books, in War and Peace he may be identified with the two heroes, Pierre and Prince Andrei, in their passionate, unremitting strivings towards 'the infinite, the eternal and the absolute'. (He even anticipates his own maturer views when Pierre comes to the conclusion that 'to live with the sole object of avoiding doing evil so as not to have to repent is not enough. I used to do that – I lived for myself and I spoilt my life. And only now, when I am living for others – or at least trying to – only now do I realize all the happiness life holds.')

'The one thing necessary, in life as in art, is to tell the truth' was Tolstoy's doctrine, and his life was bound up with this anxiety, this search for the inward truthfulness which is reality. Tolstoy does not contrive: he records, recoiling from nothing and 'in the gutter seeing the image of the sky'. With him we watch his characters grow – Natasha running into the drawing-room with her doll in 1805 and Natasha going to church in 1812 is one and the same person at two different ages – not two ages fitted on to one person. We are conscious of family resemblances: Prince Andrei and his father are alike, only one is young and the other old. The Rostovs have in common some intangible quality which makes one conscious that Vera is a true Rostov while Sonya comes of different stock. In Pierre we can recognize his father, although old Prince Bezuhov appears only to die, and never utters a word.

Tolstoy knows his characters inside out – even to the way they walk. (Prince Vasili 'did not know how to walk on tiptoe and jerked his whole body awkwardly at each step'.) Revealing psychological pictures are conveyed with no less economy: 'Prince Andrei always showed particular energy when the chance occurred of taking a young man under his wing and furthering his ambitions. Under cover of obtaining assistance of this kind for another, which his pride would never let him accept for himself, he kept in touch with the circle which confers success and which attracted him.' Here is Julie Karagin, the wealthy heiress who succeeds in bringing Boris Drubetskoy to the point of proposing: 'There was no need to say more: Julie's face beamed with triumph and self-satisfaction; but she forced Boris to say all that is usually said on such occasions – to say that he loved her and had never loved any woman more. She knew that for her Penza estates and the Nizhni Novgorod forests she could demand that, and she received what she demanded.' And the French general Davoust who could have claimed better conditions than a peasant's hut with a tub for a seat: 'Better quarters could have been found for him, but Marshal Davoust was one of those men who purposely make the conditions of life as uncomfortable for themselves as possible in order to have an excuse for being gloomy. For the same reason they are always hard at work and in a hurry. "How can I think of the bright side of existence when, as you see, I sit perched on a barrel in a dirty shed, hard at work?" the expression of his face seemed to say.'

This penetrating observation is equally sure when applied to nations: 'A Frenchman's conceit springs from his belief that mentally and physically he is irresistibly fascinating both to men and women. The Englishman's self-assurance comes from being a citizen of the best-organized kingdom in the world, and because as an Englishman he always knows what is the correct thing to do, and that everything he does as an Englishman is undoubtedly right. An Italian is conceited because he is excitable and easily forgets himself and other people. A Russian is conceited because he knows nothing and does not want to know anything, since he does not believe that it is possible to know anything completely. A conceited German is the worst of them all, the most stubborn and unattractive, because he imagines that he possesses the truth in science – a thing of his own invention but which for him is absolute truth.'

Nothing could be simpler than the mass of incidents described in War and Peace. All the everyday happenings of family life – conversations between brother and sister, between mother and daughter, partings and reunions, hunting, Christmas holidays, dancing, card-playing (all the 'superbly rendered domesticity' over which Arnold Bennett was so enthusiastic) – are threaded on to the necklace with as much care as the account of the battle of Borodino. Each incident is vividly portrayed, each circumstance is real, as seen through the eyes of the various protagonists. An oak-tree standing by the highway, a moonlit night are *choses vues*, not by the author but by Prince Andrei driving by, and Natasha who cannot sleep. In the same way we live the battle of Austerlitz with Nikolai Rostov, share Petya's excitement over the Emperor Alexander's arrival in Moscow, and are one with Natasha as she interprets the solemn prayer for deliverance from the invader. It is never events themselves, however important and far-reaching, which interest Tolstoy, but the effect of the event on the individual and the latter's contribution to the event. In following the life of the spirit Tolstoy would have us seek out the spark of heroism, discover the poetry and dignity lying hidden in the human soul on its long progress in quest of the Kingdom of Heaven. But in his preoccupation with the ethical domain Tolstoy never loses sight of his aim as an artist, which, as he said in a letter to a friend, 'is not to resolve a question irrefutably but to compel one to love life in all its manifestations, and these are inexhaustible. If I were told that I could write a novel in which I could indisputably establish as true my point of view on all social questions, I would not dedicate two hours to such a work; but if I were told that what I wrote would be read twenty years from now by those who are children today, and that they would weep and laugh over it and fall in love with the life in it, then I would dedicate all my existence and all my powers to it.'

War and Peace is a hymn to life. It is the Iliad and the Odyssey of Russia. Its message is that the only fundamental obligation of man is to be in tune with life. In the words of a contemporary critic it is 'a complete picture of human life; a complete picture of the Russia of that day; a complete picture of everything in which people place their happiness and greatness, their grief and humiliation. That is War and Peace.... When the Russian Empire ceases to exist, new generations will turn to War and Peace to find out what sort of people were the Russians.' All the historians' accounts of the fateful year of 1812 ring hollow in comparison with the vitality, the actuality of Tolstoy's tableau of Russia during the great Napoleonic wars. And since Tolstoy's approach is always *sub specie aeternitatis*, he has created human beings working out their destiny in accordance with the eternal implacable laws of humanity. (In one place he even comments ironically: 'People of limited intelligence are fond of talking about "these days", imagining that they have discovered and appraised the peculiarities of "these days" and that human nature changes with the times.') He is deeply aware of the continuity of life. 'Life – actual everyday life,' he writes, 'with its essential concerns of health and sickness, work and recreation, and its intellectual preoccupations with philosophy, science, poetry, music, love, friendship, hatred, passion – ran its regular course, independent and heedless of political alliance or enmity with Napoleon Bonaparte and of all potential reforms.' And when the long chronicle draws to its end, nothing is finished. The last words are given to Prince Andrei's son, a child of fifteen, on the threshold of life. For Tolstoy, as for Pierre Bezuhov, 'Life is everything. Life is God. Everything changes and moves to and fro, and that movement is God. And while there is life there is joy in consciousness of the Godhead. To love life is to love God.' It is a pantheist philosophy, and Tolstoy is obsessed by the thought of man's greatest efforts and best hopes being defeated by death. (His own private tragedy was that having got to the gates of the Optinsky monastery, in his final flight, he could go no farther, and died.)

Tolstoy is a moralist, not a mystic. Christianity for him was a moral teaching, not a revelation. He loved the empirical, hated the transcendental. In his rationalism, in his luminous cleverness, he is a typical child of what Léon Daudet called 'le dix-neuvième siècle stupide'. His greatness lies in his extraordinary gift for psychological analysis and introspection – in his ability to capture and portray the flavour, the intimate quality of physical sensations (the little girl climbing down from the stove and feeling with her toes for the crevices between the bricks), and atmosphere (the feverish gaiety of Moscow in the weeks before the city fell to the French): this is not transient, this is immortal.

Tolstoy's realism drove him to strip war of its panache. 'Not to take prisoners ... that by itself would transform the whole aspect of war and make it less cruel. As it is we play at being magnanimous and all the rest of it. Such magnanimity and sensibility are like the magnanimity and sensibility of the lady who faints at the sight of a calf being killed: she is so tenderhearted that she can't look at blood – but fricassée of veal she will eat with gusto.... If there were none of this magnanimity-business in warfare, we should never go to war, except for something worth facing certain death for. ... And when there was a war ... it would be war! And then the spirit and determination of the fighting men would be something quite different.... War is not a polite recreation but the vilest thing in life, and we ought to understand that and not play at war. Our attitude towards the fearful necessity of war ought to be stern and serious. It boils down to this: we should have done with humbug, and let war be war and not a game. Other-wise, war is a favourite pastime of the idle and frivolous ... there is no profession held in higher esteem than the military.'

His attitude to history is the exact opposite of Carlyle's hero-worship. He sees the unconscious urges of mankind as the only agents of history, and applies to events the law of necessity that he observes operating in the lives of individuals. The note of philosophical fatalism sounds again and again. ('Hamlet should have been a Russian, not a Dane,' exclaimed William Morris after reading War and Peace in which every personage, every incident may echo Luther's cry, 'Ich kann nicht anders'.)

The second part of the famous Epilogue is entirely devoted to the problem of freewill versus this driving force of necessity. Tolstoy shows us what lay behind the epic conflict between Napoleon and the Russian people. For the first time since the beginning of history the Russian ideal manifested itself, and, confronted with this dynamic, the whole might of Napoleon and Napoleonic France crumbled and was eclipsed. The automatic interaction of cause and effect screened the awakening of forces which had not had to be reckoned with before: the spirit of simplicity, goodness, and truth – sim-plicity, the supreme beauty of man; goodness and truth, the supreme aims for which man should live and work. In 1812 simplicity, goodness, and truth overcame power, which ignored simplicity and was rooted in evil and falsity. This is the meaning of War and Peace. Tolstoy describes Kutuzov, the symbol of the Russian people (whose personal motto was 'Patience and Time'), as 'a simple, modest and therefore truly great figure who could not be cast in the lying mould invented by history'; and with Prince Andrei sees his importance in the fact that he 'will not introduce anything of his own. He will not scheme or start anything, but will listen, bear in mind all that he hears, put everything in its rightful place. He will not stand in the way of anything expedient or permit what might be injurious. He knows that there is something stronger and more important than his own will – the inevitable march of events, and he has the brains to see them and grasp their significance, and seeing that significance can abstain from meddling, from following his personal desires and aiming at something else.'

Kutuzov is complemented by Karatayev, the old soldier, 'qui accepte sa place dans la vie et dans la mort', and is the incarnation of the wisdom Pierre gropes for. 'Karatayev had no attachments, friendships, or loves, as Pierre understood them; but he felt affection for and lived on sympathetic terms with every creature with whom life brought him in contact, and especially with man – not any particular man but those with whom he *happened to be.... His life, as he looked at it, held no meaning as a separate entity. It had meaning only as part of a whole of which he was at all times conscious.' In Karatayev, 'the unfathomable, rounded-off, eternal personification of the spirit of simplicity and truth', we have the whole Russian people – the real heroes of the tremendous* épopée *of* War and Peace.

R. E.

FOUR NOTES

1. *Proper Names.* To ease the path of the Western reader I have often dispensed with the Russian patronymic, retaining only the first name and surname. To the same end the feminine termination of proper names has not been rendered into English.

2. *Passages in French.* French, the study of which was first encouraged in Russia by Catherine the Great, eventually became the language in which the educated classes thought and expressed themselves. In several of the various versions of *War and Peace* long passages appeared in French, but when Tolstoy undertook some revision in connexion with an edition of his collected works early in 1873 he excluded the French language. As there is no final, definitive, 'canonical' text of the novel, all but short remarks have been translated, though I have indicated where the original reads in French.

3. *Dates.* Apparent discrepancies in dates – for the French, for instance, the battle of Borodino occurred on 7 September, which for the Russians was 26 August – are explained by the fact that Russia, and Eastern Europe, generally, held to the old Julian calendar, and only adopted the new Gregorian calendar at the beginning of the present century.

4. *Sun-spots.* Tolstoy is guilty of various inaccuracies, of trifling importance in themselves but troubling to the translator. In 1805 Natasha appears as a child of thirteen; in 1809 she is sixteen. Her sister is seventeen in 1805 and twenty-four in 1809. Nikolai Rostov joined the army in September 1805 and returned in February 1806 – after an absence, that is, of five months. But in the memorable description of his home-coming we are told that he had been away 'a year and a half'.

Kutuzov is mentioned as having only one eye – but this does not prevent Tolstoy from referring to Kutuzov's 'eyes'.

When Prince Andrei left for the front his sister hung round his neck an antique silver icon on a finely wrought silver chain. But when he is picked up wounded on the battlefield the French remove from his neck the 'gold icon with its delicate gold chain' which had been put there by Princess Maria.

Old Prince Bolkonsky was well on 5 August, the day of the bombardment of Smolensk. He died on the 15th, after lying paralysed 'for three weeks'.

But where the spirit of life is concerned the alembic of Tolstoy's art is sure and unfailing.

R. E.

L. N. TOLSTOY

Born in 1828 (28 August, old style=9 September,
  new style)
Married in 1862

Began to write *War and Peace* in 1863
First part published in 1865
Last part published in 1869

Began to write *Anna Karenin* in 1873
Final parts published in 1877

Died in 1910 (7 November, old style=20 November,
  new style)

PRINCIPAL CHARACTERS

PIERRE (PIOTR KIRILLOVICH) BEZUHOV

COUNT ILYA ROSTOV
COUNTESS NATALIA ROSTOV
NIKOLAI (NICOLAS), their elder son
PIOTR (PETYA), their younger son
VERA, their elder daughter (*m.* Lieutenant Berg)
NATALIA (NATASHA), their younger daughter

SONYA, a niece of the Rostovs

PRINCE NIKOLAI ANDREYEVICH BOLKONSKY
ANDREI (ANDRÉ), his son
MARIA (MARIE), his daughter
LISA (LISE), Prince Andrei's wife
NIKOLAI, their son

MADEMOISELLE BOURIENNE, Princess Maria's French companion

PRINCE VASILI KURAGIN
HIPPOLYTE, his elder son
ANATOLE, his younger son
HÉLÈNE, his daughter

OTHER CHARACTERS

ALEXANDER I, Tsar of Russia
BAZDEYEV, OSIP ALEXEYEVICH, a prominent Freemason
DENISOV, VASSKA, friend of Nikolai Rostov
PRINCESS ANNA MIHALOVNA DRUBETSKOY, friend of the Rostovs
BORIS DRUBETSKOY, her son (*m.* Julie Karagin)
KUTUZOV, Commander-in-Chief of the Russian army
NAPOLEON
ROSTOPCHIN, Governor-General of Moscow

WAR AND PEACE

*

BOOK ONE

PART ONE

I

'*Eh bien, mon prince*, so Genoa and Lucca are now no more than private estates of the Bonaparte family. No, I warn you – if you are not telling me that this means war, if you again allow yourself to condone all the infamies and atrocities perpetrated by that Antichrist (upon my word I believe he is Antichrist), I don't know you in future. You will no longer be a friend of mine, or my "faithful slave", as you call yourself! But how do you do, how do you do ? I see I'm scaring you. Sit down and talk to me.'

It was on a July evening in 1805 and the speaker was the well-known Anna Pavlovna Scherer, maid of honour and confidante of the Empress Maria Fiodorovna. With these words she greeted the influential statesman Prince Vasili, who was the first to arrive at her *soirée*.

Anna Pavlovna had been coughing for some days. She was suffering from an attack of *la grippe* as she said – *grippe* being then a new word only used by a few people. That morning a footman in scarlet livery had delivered a number of little notes all written in French and couched in the same terms:

If you have nothing better to do, count (or prince), and if the prospect of spending an evening with a poor invalid is not too alarming, I shall be charmed to see you at my house between 7 and 10.

ANNETTE SCHERER.

'Mercy on us, what a violent attack !' replied the prince, as he came forward in his embroidered court uniform with silk stockings and buckled shoes. He wore orders on his breast and an expression of serenity on his flat face; he was not in the least disconcerted by such a reception. He spoke in the elegant French in which our forefathers not only spoke but also thought, and his voice had the quiet, patronizing intonations of a distinguished man who has spent a long life in

3

society and at court. He went up to Anna Pavlovna, kissed her hand, presenting to her view his perfumed, shining, bald head, and complacently seated himself on the sofa.

'First of all, *chère amie*, tell me how you are. Set my mind at rest,' said he, with no change of voice and tone, in which indifference and even irony were perceptible beneath the conventional sympathy.

'How can one feel well when one's moral sensibilities are suffering? Can anyone possessed of any feeling remain tranquil in these days?' said Anna Pavlovna. 'You are staying the whole evening, I hope?'

'What about the party at the English ambassador's? Today is Wednesday. I must put in an appearance there,' said the prince. 'My daughter is coming to fetch me.'

'I thought it had been put off. I must say, all these fêtes and firework displays are beginning to pall.'

'If they had known that it was your wish, the party would have been put off,' replied the prince mechanically, like a watch that has been wound up, saying things he did not even wish to be believed.

'Don't tease me! Well, and what has been decided in regard to Novosiltsov's dispatch? You know everything.'

'What is there to tell?' said the prince in a cold, listless tone. 'What has been decided? It has been decided that Bonaparte has burnt his boats, and it's my opinion that we are in the act of burning ours.'

Prince Vasili always spoke languidly, like an actor repeating his part in an old play. Anna Pavlovna Scherer, on the contrary, in spite of her forty years, was brimming over with vivacity and impulsiveness. To be enthusiastic had become her pose in society, and at times, even when she did not feel very like it, she worked herself up to the proper pitch of enthusiasm in order not to disappoint the expectations of those who knew her. The affected smile which constantly played round her lips, though it did not suit her faded looks, expressed her consciousness of having an amiable weakness which, like a spoilt child, she neither wished, nor could, nor considered it necessary to correct.

In the middle of a conversation about politics Anna Pavlovna burst out:

'Oh, don't speak to me of Austria. Of course I may know nothing about it, but Austria has never wanted, and doesn't want war. She is betraying us. Russia alone must save Europe. Our gracious benefactor realizes his lofty destiny and will be true to it. That is the one thing I have faith in. The noblest rôle on earth awaits our good and wonderful sovereign, and he is so virtuous and fine that God will not desert him. He will fulfil his mission and crush the hydra of revolution, which is more horrible than ever now in the person of this murderer and scoundrel. We alone must avenge the blood of the righteous one. On whom can we rely, I ask you? ... England with her commercial spirit will not and cannot comprehend all the loftiness of soul of the Emperor Alexander. She has refused to evacuate Malta. She wants to see – she looks for – some hidden motive in our actions. What answer did Novosiltsov get? None. The English have not understood, they're incapable of understanding the self-sacrifice of our Emperor, who desires nothing for himself and everything for the good of humanity. And what have they promised? Nothing! And what little they did promise they will not perform! Prussia has already intimated that Bonaparte is invincible and that all Europe is powerless before him. ... And I don't believe a word that Hardenberg says, or Haugwitz either. This famous Prussian neutrality is nothing but a snare. I have faith only in God and the high destiny of our beloved Emperor. He will save Europe!'

She broke off suddenly, with a smile of amusement at her own vehemence.

'I think,' said the prince, smiling, 'that if you had been sent instead of our dear Wintzingerode you would have captured the king of Prussia's consent by assault. You are so eloquent. Will you give me some tea?'

'In a moment. *A propos*,' she added, becoming calm again, 'I am expecting two very interesting men tonight, the vicomte de Mortemart, who is connected with the Montmorencys through the Rohans, one of the best families in France. He is one of the good *emigrés*, the genuine sort. And the Abbé Morio. You know that profound thinker? He has been received by the Emperor. Had you heard?'

'I shall be delighted to meet them,' said the prince. 'But tell me,' he went on with studied carelessness as if the matter had just occurred to him, whereas in fact the question he was about to put was the chief object of his visit, 'is it true that the Dowager Empress wants Baron Funke appointed first secretary at Vienna? The baron is a poor creature, by all accounts.'

Prince Vasili coveted for his son the post which others were trying to secure for the baron through the influence of the Empress Maria Fiodorovna.

Anna Pavlovna almost closed her eyes to signify that neither she nor anyone else could pass judgement on what the Empress might be pleased or see fit to do.

'Baron Funke was recommended to the Dowager-Empress by her sister,' was all she said, in a dry, mournful tone. As she named the Empress, Anna Pavlovna's face suddenly assumed an expression of profound and sincere devotion and respect, tinged with melancholy, and this happened whenever she mentioned her exalted patroness. She added that her Majesty had deigned to show Baron Funke *beaucoup d'estime*, and again her face clouded over with melancholy.

The prince preserved an indifferent silence. Having given him a rap for daring to refer in such terms to someone who had been recommended to the Empress, Anna Pavlovna, with the adroitness and quick tact natural in a woman brought up at court, now wished to console him, so she said:

'But *à propos* of your family – do you know that since your daughter came out she has won everyone's heart? People say she is as lovely as the day.'

The prince bowed in token of his respect and gratitude.

'I often think,' pursued Anna Pavlovna after a short pause, drawing a little closer to the prince and giving him an affable smile, as if to imply that nothing more was to be said about politics and social topics and that the time had come for a confidential chat – 'I often think how unfairly the good things of life are sometimes distributed. Why should fate have given you two such splendid children? I don't include Anatole, your youngest. I don't like him,' she added in a tone admitting of no rejoinder, and raising her eyebrows. 'Two such charming children. And really you appreciate them less than anyone – you don't deserve to have them.'

And she smiled her ecstatic smile.

'*Que voulez-vous?* Lavater would have said I lack the bump of paternity,' said the prince.

'Don't keep on joking. I mean to talk to you seriously. Do you know, I am displeased with your younger son. Between ourselves,' (and her face assumed its melancholy expression) 'they were talking about him in her Majesty's presence the other day and everyone was sorry for you ...'

The prince made no reply, but she was silent, looking at him significantly and waiting for him to answer. Prince Vasili frowned.

6

'What can I do about it?' he said at last. 'You know I did everything in a father's power for their education, and they have both turned out *des imbéciles*. Hippolyte is at least a quiet fool, but Anatole's a fool that won't keep quiet. That is the only difference between them,' he said, smiling in a more unnatural and animated way than usual, which brought out with peculiar prominence something surprisingly coarse and disagreeable in the lines about his mouth.

'And why is it that children are born to men like you? If you were not a father I could find no fault with you,' said Anna Pavlovna, looking up pensively.

'I am your faithful slave and to you alone I can confess that my children are the bane of my existence. They are the cross I have to bear. That is how I explain it to myself. *Que voulez-vous?*' He broke off with a gesture expressing his resignation to a cruel fate.

Anna Pavlovna meditated.

'Have you never thought of finding a wife for your prodigal son Anatole?' she asked. 'They say old maids have a mania for matchmaking. I am not yet conscious of that weakness in myself, but I know a little person who is very unhappy with her father. She is a relation of ours, the young Princess Bolkonsky.'

Prince Vasili said nothing, but with the rapidity of reflection and memory characteristic of a man of the world he signified by a motion of the head that he had taken in and was considering this information.

'Do you know that that boy Anatole is costing me forty thousand roubles a year?' he said, evidently unable to restrain the gloomy current of his thoughts. He paused. 'And what will it be in five years' time, if he continues at this rate? These are the advantages of being a father. Is she wealthy, this princess of yours?'

'Her father is very rich and miserly. He lives in the country. You know, he is the famous Prince Bolkonsky who was retired from the army when the late Emperor was still alive, and nicknamed the "king of Prussia". He is a very clever man but eccentric and difficult. The poor girl is as miserable as can be. She has a brother who recently married Lisa Meinen. He is an aide-de-camp of Kutuzov's. He'll be here this evening.'

'Listen, *chère* Annette,' said the prince, suddenly taking his companion's hand and for some reason bending it downwards. 'Arrange this affair for me and I am your most devoted slave – *slafe* with an f, as a bailiff of mine writes in his reports – for ever and ever. She is of good family and rich. That's all I want.'

And with the free and easy grace which distinguished him he raised the maid of honour's hand to his lips, kissed it, and having kissed it swung it to and fro as he sank back in his armchair and looked away.

'*Attendez*,' said Anna Pavlovna, reflectively. 'I will speak to Lisa, young Bolkonsky's wife, this very evening, and perhaps it can be arranged. It shall be in your family that I serve my apprenticeship as old maid.'

2

ANNA PAVLOVNA'S drawing-room was gradually filling. The cream of Petersburg arrived, people differing widely in age and character but alike in that they all belonged to the same class of society. Prince Vasili's daughter, the beautiful Hélène, came to take her father to the ambassador's party. She was wearing a ball dress and her maid of honour's badge. Then there was the youthful little Princess Bolkonsky, known as *la femme la plus séduisante de Pétersbourg*. She had been married during the previous winter, and now, owing to her condition, had ceased to appear at large functions but still went to small receptions. Prince Vasili's son, Prince Hippolyte, arrived with Mortemart, whom he introduced. The Abbé Morio and many others also came.

'You have not seen my aunt yet,' or 'You do not know my aunt?' Anna Pavlovna was saying to each new-comer, whom she then gravely conducted to a little old lady with tall stiff bows of ribbon in her cap, who had come sailing in from another room as soon as the guests began to arrive. Slowly switching her eyes from the visitor to her aunt, Anna Pavlovna presented them by name and then withdrew.

Everyone had to go through the same ceremony of greeting this old aunt whom not one of them knew or wanted to know or was interested in, while Anna Pavlovna in pensive silence solemnly observed and approved the exchange of formalities. *Ma tante* repeated the same words to each, asking after the visitor's health and reporting on her own and on that of her Majesty, 'who was better today, thank God'. Politely trying to betray no undue haste, her victims made their escape with a sense of relief at having performed a tiresome duty, and took care not to go near her again for the rest of the evening.

The young Princess Bolkonsky had brought some work in a gold-embroidered velvet bag. Her bewitching little upper lip, shaded with the faintest trace of down, was rather short and showed her teeth prettily, and was prettier still when she occasionally drew it down to meet the lower lip. As is always the case with a very charming woman, this little imperfection – the shortness of the upper lip and her half-open mouth – seemed to be a special form of beauty peculiarly her own. Everyone enjoyed seeing this lovely young creature so full of life and gaiety, soon to become a mother and bearing her burden so lightly. Old men and dull and dispirited young men felt as though they had caught some of her vitality after being in her company and talking to her for a little while. Whoever spoke to her and saw the bright little smile accompanying every word and the constant gleam of her white teeth was sure to go away thinking that he had been unusually amiable that day. And it happened the same with everyone.

Swaying slightly, the little princess tripped round the table, her work-bag on her arm, and gaily arranging the folds of her gown seated herself on a sofa near the silver samovar, as if all that she was doing was a *partie de plaisir* for herself and everyone around her.

'I have brought my work,' she said in French, opening her reticule and addressing the company generally. 'Mind you don't let me down, Annette,' she turned to her hostess. 'You wrote that it was to be an informal little evening, so you see what I have got on.'

And she spread out her arms to display her elegant grey dress trimmed with lace and girdled with a wide ribbon just below the bosom.

'*Soyez tranquille, Lise*, you will always be prettier than anyone else,' replied Anna Pavlovna.

'You know,' Lisa went on in French and in the same tone of voice, addressing a general, 'my husband is deserting me. He is going to get himself killed. Tell me what this nasty war is about,' she said, this time to Prince Vasili, and without waiting for an answer she turned to speak to his daughter, the beautiful Hélène.

'What an adorable creature the little princess is!' whispered Prince Vasili to Anna Pavlovna.

Shortly after the little princess, a stout, burly young man with close-cropped hair and spectacles appeared. He wore the light trousers then in fashion, a high starched jabot and a cinnamon-coloured jacket. This stout young man was the natural son of the celebrated grandee of Catherine's reign, Count Bezuhov, who now lay dying in Moscow.

The young man had not as yet entered any branch of the service, having only just returned from abroad, where he had been educated, and this was his first appearance in society. Anna Pavlovna greeted him with the nod she reserved for the lowest in the hierarchy of her drawing-room. But in spite of this welcome of the lowest grade a look of anxiety and dismay, as at the sight of something too huge and out of place, came over her face when she saw Pierre enter. He was indeed rather bigger than the other men in the room, but her dismay could only have reference to the clever, though diffident and at the same time observant and natural expression which distinguished him from everyone else in that drawing-room.

'It is very good of you, Monsieur Pierre, to come and visit a poor invalid,' said Anna Pavlovna, exchanging uneasy glances with her aunt to whom she conducted him.

Pierre muttered an unintelligible reply and continued to let his eyes wander round as if in search of something. He bowed to the little princess with a pleased and happy smile, as though she were an intimate acquaintance, and went up to the aunt. Anna Pavlovna's dismay was not unjustified, for Pierre turned away without waiting to hear the end of the old lady's speech about her Majesty's health. Anna Pavlovna stopped him in alarm with the words:

'Do you know the Abbé Morio ? He is a most interesting man ...'

'Yes, I have heard of his scheme for permanent peace, and it is very interesting but hardly practical ...'

'You think not ?' said Anna Pavlovna for the sake of saying something and in order to get back to her duties as hostess. But Pierre now committed a blunder in the reverse direction. First he had left a lady before she had finished speaking, and now he detained another who was wishing to get away from him. With head bent and long legs planted wide apart, he proceeded to explain to Anna Pavlovna why he considered the *abbé*'s plan an idle dream.

'We will discuss it by and by,' said Anna Pavlovna with a smile.

And having freed herself from the young man who did not know how to behave, she resumed her duties as mistress of the house and continued to listen and look on, ready to lend her aid wherever the conversation might happen to flag. Like the foreman of a spinning-mill who after settling his men to work walks up and down among the machinery noting here a stopped spindle or there one that squeaks or makes more noise than it should, and hastens to slow down the machine or set it running properly, so Anna Pavlovna moved about her drawing-room, approached some group that had fallen silent, or was talking too excitedly, and by a word or a slight rearrangement kept the conversational machine in smooth running order. But her singular apprehensions about Pierre were apparent all the time that she was occupied with these labours. She kept an anxious watch on him when he went to listen to what was being said in the circle around Mortemart, and then joined another group where the *abbé* was discoursing.

For Pierre, who had been educated abroad, this party at Anna Pavlovna's was the first he had attended in Russia. He knew that all the intellectual lights of St Petersburg were assembled there, and like a child in a toy-shop he did not know which way to look first, so fearful was he of missing any clever discussion that was to be heard. As he looked at the assured and refined expressions on the faces of all those present. he kept expecting something very profound. At last he came up to Morio. Here the talk seemed interesting and he stood waiting for a chance to air his own views, as young men are fond of doing.

3

ANNA PAVLOVNA'S *soirée* was in full swing. On all sides the spindles hummed steadily and without pause. With the exception of *ma tante*, beside whom sat only an elderly lady with a thin, careworn face who looked rather out of her element in this brilliant society, the company had settled into three groups. In one, composed chiefly of men, the *abbé* formed the centre. In another, young people were gathered round the beautiful Princess Hélène, Prince Vasili's daughter, and the very pretty, rosy-cheeked little Princess Bolkonsky, who was rather too plump for her years. In the third circle were Mortemart and Anna Pavlovna.

The *vicomte* was a pleasant-faced young man with soft features and nice manners who evidently considered himself a celebrity, though out of good breeding he modestly placed himself at the disposal of the company in which he found himself. Anna Pavlovna was obviously serving him up as a treat to her guests. Just as a clever *maître d'hôtel* offers as a particularly choice dish some piece of meat which no one who had seen it in the dirty kitchen would care to eat, so

Anna Pavlovna that evening served up to her guests first the *vicomte* and then the *abbé*, as peculiar delicacies. The circle round Mortemart immediately began discussing the execution of the duc d'Enghien. The *vicomte* said that the duc d'Enghien had fallen a victim to his own magnanimity, and that there were personal reasons for Bonaparte's resentment.

'Ah, yes! Do tell us all about it, *vicomte*,' said Anna Pavlovna, with a pleasant feeling that *Contez-nous cela, vicomte* had a Louis Quinze air.

The *vicomte* bowed and smiled urbanely, in token of his willingness to comply. Anna Pavlovna arranged a circle round him, inviting everyone to listen to his account.

'The *vicomte* knew the *duc* personally,' she whispered to one of the guests. 'The *vicomte* is a wonderful *raconteur*,' she said to another. 'How one sees the man of quality,' she exclaimed to a third; and the *vicomte* was handed round to the company in the most exquisite and advantageous light, like a well-garnished joint of roast beef on a hot platter.

The *vicomte* was ready to begin his story and a faint smile played about his lips.

'Come over here, *chère Hélène*,' said Anna Pavlovna to the lovely young princess who was sitting a little way off, the centre of another group.

The princess smiled. She rose with the same unchanging smile with which she had first entered the room – the smile of an acknowledged beauty. With a slight rustle of her white ball-dress trimmed with ivy lichen, with a gleam of white shoulders, glossy hair and sparkling diamonds, she made her way between the men who stood back to let her pass; and not looking at any one in particular but smiling on all, as it were graciously vouchsafing to each the privilege of admiring her beautiful figure, the shapely shoulders, back and bosom – which the fashionable low gown fully displayed – she crossed to Anna Pavlovna's side, the living symbol of festivity. Hélène was so lovely that not only was there no trace of coquetry in her, but on the contrary she even appeared a little apologetic for her unquestionable, all too conquering beauty. She seemed to wish but to be unable to tone down its effect.

'What a lovely creature!' remarked everyone who saw her. The *vicomte* lifted his shoulders and his eyes fell, as though he were overwhelmed by something quite out of the ordinary, when she took her seat opposite him and turned upon him the radiance of that unchanging smile.

'Madame, I doubt my ability in the face of such an audience,' said he, inclining his head with a smile.

The princess leaned her bare round arm on a little table and did not think it incumbent on her to say anything. She smiled and waited. All the time that he was telling his story she sat upright, glancing occasionally now at her beautiful rounded arm elegantly resting on the table, now at her still more beautiful bosom on which she readjusted a diamond necklace. Once or twice she smoothed the folds of her gown, and whenever the story was particularly exciting she would glance round at Anna Pavlovna and at once assume the very same expression that was on the maid of honour's face, and then relapse again into her radiant smile.

The little Princess Bolkonsky had also left the tea-table and followed Hélène.

'Wait a moment till I get out my work,' she exclaimed. 'Come, what are you thinking of?' she went on, turning to Prince Hippolyte. 'Fetch me my reticule, please.'

There was a general stir as the princess, smiling and having a word for everyone, sat down and gaily smoothed out her skirts.

'Now I am all right,' she said, and begging the *vicomte* to begin she took up her work.

Prince Hippolyte, having brought her the reticule, joined the circle, moving an armchair close to hers and seating himself beside her.

Le charmant Hippolyte struck one by his extraordinary likeness to his beautiful sister, and still more by the fact that in spite of this resemblance he was astoundingly ugly. His features were like his sister's, but in her case everything was illumined by the joyous, contented, unfailing smile of life and youth, and by the uncommonly classic proportions of her figure, while the same features in the brother were dulled by imbecility and looked conceited and sulky, and his body was thin and feeble. Eyes, nose, and mouth were all twisted into a vacant, bored grimace, while his arms and legs always fell into grotesque attitudes.

'It isn't a ghost story?' he said, sitting down beside the princess and hurriedly fixing his eye-glass in his eye, as though without this instrument he could not say a word.

'Why no, my dear fellow,' said the astonished *vicomte*, with a shrug.

13

'Because I detest ghost stories,' said Prince Hippolyte, in a tone which showed that he only understood the meaning of his words after he had uttered them.

He spoke with such self-confidence that no one could be sure whether his remark was very witty or very stupid. He wore a dark green frock-coat, knee-breeches of a shade that he called *cuisse de nymphe effrayée*, silk stockings and buckled shoes.

With much grace the *vicomte* recounted an anecdote then going the rounds, to the effect that the duc d'Enghien had secretly gone to Paris to visit Mademoiselle Georges, and there he came upon Bonaparte, who also enjoyed the favours of the famous actress, and that Napoleon, meeting the *duc*, had fallen into one of the swoons to which he was subject, and was thus at the *duc*'s mercy. The latter had taken no advantage of his position, and Bonaparte subsequently revenged himself for this magnanimous behaviour by having the *duc* executed.

The story was very neat and interesting, especially at the point where the rivals suddenly recognize each other, and the ladies appeared to be greatly excited by it.

'Charming!' said Anna Pavlovna with an inquiring glance at the little princess.

'Charming!' whispered the little princess, sticking her needle into her work as an indication that the interest and fascination of the tale prevented her from going on with her sewing.

The *vicomte* appreciated this silent homage and with a gratified smile was about to resume, but just then Anna Pavlovna, who had been keeping an eye on that dreadful young man, noticed that he was talking too loudly and heatedly with the *abbé*, and hurried to the rescue. Pierre had managed to start a conversation with the *abbé* about the balance of power, and the *abbé*, evidently interested by the young man's ingenuous fervour, was dilating at length on his pet theory. Both of them were talking and listening too eagerly and too naturally, and Anna Pavlovna did not like it.

'The means? The means are the balance of power in Europe and the rights of the people,' the *abbé* was saying. 'It is only necessary for one powerful nation like Russia – with all her reputation for barbarism – to place herself disinterestedly at the head of an alliance having for its object the maintenance of the balance of power in Europe – and the world would be saved!'

'But how would you establish that balance?' Pierre was beginning;

but at that moment Anna Pavlovna came up and, giving Pierre a stern glance, asked the Italian how he stood the Russian climate. The *abbé*'s face instantly changed and took on an offensively affected, sugary expression, evidently habitual to him when conversing with women.

'I am so enchanted by the wit and culture of the society – especially of the feminine members – into which I have had the honour to be received that there has been no time yet to think of the climate,' said he.

Making sure of the *abbé* and Pierre, Anna Pavlovna, the more conveniently to keep them under observation, brought them into the general circle.

At this point a new actor appeared on the scene: the young Prince Andrei Bolkonsky, husband of the little princess. Prince Bolkonsky was a very handsome youth of medium height, with firm, clear-cut features. Everything about him, from the weary, bored expression of his eyes to the measured deliberation of his step, presented the most striking contrast to his lively little wife. It was clear that he was not only acquainted with everyone in the room but found them so tedious that even to look at them and hear their voices was too much for him. And of all the faces of which he was so tired the face of his pretty little wife was apparently the one that bored him most. With a grimace that distorted his handsome countenance he turned away from her, kissed Anna Pavlovna's hand and screwing up his eyes scanned the whole company.

'Are you enlisting for the war, prince?' said Anna Pavlovna.

'General Kutuzov has been kind enough to make me his aide-de-camp.'

He spoke in French and stressed the last syllable of Kutuzov's name like a Frenchman.

'And what about Lise, your wife?'

'She is going into the country.'

'Don't you think it too bad of you to rob us of your charming wife?'

'*André*,' said the little princess, addressing her husband in the same coquettish tone which she employed with other men, 'you should have heard the story the *vicomte* has been telling us about Mademoiselle Georges and Bonaparte!'

Prince Andrei frowned and turned away. Pierre, who had been

watching him with glad, affectionate eyes ever since he came in, went up and took his arm. Without looking round, Prince Andrei twisted his face into a grimace of annoyance at being touched, but when he saw Pierre's beaming countenance he gave a smile that was unexpectedly cordial and pleasant.

'What, you here! You in gay society too!' he said to Pierre.

'I knew I should find you here,' Pierre answered. 'I'm coming to supper with you. May I?' he added in an undertone, not to disturb the *vicomte* who was proceeding with his story.

'No, impossible!' said Prince Andrei, laughing and pressing Pierre's hand to show that there was no need to ask. He was about to say something more but at that instant Prince Vasili and his daughter got up and the two young men rose to let them pass.

'You will excuse me, my dear *vicomte*,' said Prince Vasili to the Frenchman, affectionately holding him down by the sleeve to prevent him from rising. 'This wretched reception at the ambassador's deprives me of a pleasure and obliges us to interrupt you. I am very sorry to leave your delightful party,' said he, turning to Anna Pavlovna.

Lightly holding the folds of her gown, his daughter, Princess Hélène, made her way between the chairs, the smile on her lovely face more radiant than ever. Pierre gazed with rapturous, almost frightened eyes at this beautiful creature as she passed him.

'Very pretty,' said Prince Andrei.

'Very,' said Pierre.

As he went by, Prince Vasili seized Pierre by the arm and turned to Anna Pavlovna.

'Get this bear into shape for me!' he said. 'Here he's been staying with me a whole month and this is the first time I have seen him in society. Nothing is so necessary for a young man as the society of clever women.'

4

ANNA PAVLOVNA smiled and promised to take Pierre in hand. She knew that on his father's side he was related to Prince Vasili. The elderly lady who had been sitting with *ma tante* jumped up hastily and overtook Prince Vasili in the ante-room. The look of interest which her kindly, careworn face had affected till now had vanished, leaving nothing but anxiety and alarm.

'What have you to tell me, prince, concerning my Boris?' she said, hurrying after him into the ante-room. (She pronounced the name Boris with the accent on the *o*.) 'I cannot stay in Petersburg any longer. Tell me what news am I to take back to my poor boy.'

Although Prince Vasili's manner as he listened to the old lady was reluctant and almost uncivil, showing impatience even, she gave him an ingratiating, appealing smile and clung to his hand to detain him.

'It is nothing for you to say a word to the Emperor, and then he would be transferred to the Guards at once,' she implored.

'Princess, I am ready to do all I can,' answered Prince Vasili; 'but there are difficulties in the way of my proffering such a request to the Emperor. I should advise you to approach Rumyantsev, through Prince Golitsyn. That would be the wiser course.'

The elderly lady was a Princess Drubetskoy, belonging to one of the best families in Russia, but she was poor, and having long been living in retirement had lost touch with her former influential connexions. She had now come to Petersburg to get her only son into the Imperial Guards. It was, in fact, solely in order to see Prince Vasili that she had invited herself to Anna Pavlovna's party and sat listening to the *vicomte*'s story. She was dismayed at Prince Vasili's words, and her once handsome face expressed vexation, but only for a moment. She smiled again and clutched Prince Vasili's arm more tightly.

'Listen, prince,' she said. 'I have never asked you for anything before, and I never will again, nor have I ever reminded you of the friendship my father felt for you. But now I entreat you in God's name, do this for my son, and I shall always regard you as our benefactor,' she added hastily. 'No, don't be angry but promise me! I asked Golitsyn and he refused. Be the kind-hearted man you always were,' she said, trying to smile though tears were in her eyes.

'Papa, we shall be late,' said Princess Hélène, turning her beautiful head and looking over her statuesque shoulders as she waited at the door.

Influence in the world, however, is a capital which has to be used with economy if it is to last. Prince Vasili knew this and, having once realized that if he were to ask favours for everybody who petitioned him he would soon be unable to ask anything for himself, he rarely exerted his influence. But in Princess Drubetskoy's case, after her new appeal, he felt something like a qualm of conscience. She had reminded him of what was quite true: that he owed to her father his early advancement in his career. Moreover, he could see by her manner that she was one of those women – mostly mothers – who once having taken a notion into their heads will not rest until they have attained the desired object, and if opposed are ready to go on insisting day after day and hour after hour, even to the point of making scenes. This last reflection made him waver.

'My dear Anna Mihalovna,' he said with his habitual familiarity and the note of boredom in his voice, 'it is next to impossible for me to do what you ask; but to show how fond I am of you and how much I honour your father's memory I will do the impossible: your son shall be transferred to the Guards. Here is my hand on it. Now are you satisfied?'

'My dear friend, my dear benefactor! This is what I expected from you – I know how good you are.' He turned to go. 'Wait – one word more! When he has been transferred to the Guards ...' she hesitated. 'You are on good terms with Mihail Ilarionovich Kutuzov ... recommend Boris to him as adjutant. Then I shall be content, and never again ...'

Prince Vasili smiled.

'That I do not promise. You have no idea how Kutuzov has been besieged since his appointment as commander-in-chief. He told me himself that all the ladies in Moscow have conspired to surrender all their sons to him as adjutants.'

'No, no, you must promise! I will not let you go, my dear benefactor ...'

'Papa,' said his beautiful daughter again in the same tone as before, 'we shall be late.'

'Well, *au revoir*! Good-bye! You see how it is.'

'Tomorrow then you will speak to the Emperor?'

'Without fail; but I make no promises about Kutuzov.'

'Yes promise, do promise, *Basile*,' Anna Mihalovna called after him with a coquettish smile which in days long gone by, when she was a young girl, might have been becoming but which now ill suited her haggard face.

She had evidently forgotten her age and from habit was employing all the old feminine arts. But as soon as the prince had gone her face resumed its former cold, artificial expression. She returned to the group where the *vicomte* was still telling stories, and again pretended to listen, watching for the time when she could leave, now that her purpose was accomplished.

'And what do you think of this latest farce, the coronation at Milan?' asked Anna Pavlovna. 'And the new comedy of the people of Genoa and Lucca laying their petitions before Monsieur Bonaparte, and Monsieur Bonaparte sitting on a throne and granting the petitions of the nations! Delicious! No, but it's enough to turn one's brain! You would think the whole world had gone mad.'

Prince Andrei smiled ironically, looking straight into Anna Pavlovna's face.

' *"Dieu me la donne, gare à qui la touche,"* ' he said, (repeating Bonaparte's words at his coronation). 'They say he was very impressive when he pronounced that,' he remarked and he now repeated it in Italian: ' *"Dio mi la dona, guai a chi la tocca."* '

'I only hope that this will be the last drop that overflows the glass,' continued Anna Pavlovna. 'Really the sovereigns of Europe cannot continue to endure this man who is a living threat to them all.'

'The sovereigns?' echoed the *vicomte* in a polite but hopeless tone. 'The sovereigns, madame – I do not refer to Russia ... What did they do for Louis XVII, for the queen or Madame Elisabeth? Nothing!' and he became more animated. 'And believe me, they are reaping their rewards for having betrayed the cause of the Bourbons. The sovereigns! Why, they send ambassadors to present their compliments to the usurper!' And with an exclamation of contempt he again shifted his position.

Prince Hippolyte, who had been staring at the *vicomte* for some time through his eye-glass, at these words suddenly turned his whole body round to the little princess and asked her for a needle, with which he began tracing the arms of the Condé family on the table, expounding them to her with the utmost gravity, as if she had requested him to do so.

'*Bâton de gueules, engrêlé de gueules d'azur* – house of Condé,' he said.

The princess listened with a smile.

'If Bonaparte remains on the throne another year,' resumed the *vicomte* with the air of a man who, in a matter with which he is better acquainted than anyone else, is accustomed to pursue his own train of thought without heeding the reflections of others, 'things will have gone too far. By intrigue, violence, exile and executions French society – I mean good society – will have been destroyed for ever, and then …'

He shrugged his shoulders and spread out his hands. Pierre was about to put in a word, for the conversation interested him, but Anna Pavlovna, who had a watchful eye on him, interrupted.

'The Emperor Alexander,' said she, with the pathetic note which accompanied all her references to the Imperial family, 'has declared that he will leave it to the French people themselves to choose their own form of government. And I imagine it is certain that the whole nation, once delivered from the usurper, would throw itself into the arms of its rightful king,' she concluded, trying to be amiable to the royalist *émigré*.

'That is doubtful,' said Prince Andrei. '*Monsieur le vicomte* is quite right in thinking that matters have gone too far by now. In my opinion it would be difficult to return to the old régime.'

'From what I have heard,' remarked Pierre, blushing and again breaking into the conversation, 'almost all the aristocracy have already gone over to Bonaparte.'

'That is what the Bonapartists say,' replied the *vicomte* without looking at Pierre. 'At the present time it is not easy to find out what the public opinion of France really is.'

'Bonaparte has said so,' observed Prince Andrei with a sarcastic smile. (It was evident that he did not like the *vicomte* and was directing his remarks against him, though he did not look at him.)

'"I showed them the path of glory and they would have none of it,"' he continued, after a short silence, again quoting Napoleon's words. '"I opened my antechambers and they crowded in." I do not know what justification he had for saying that.'

'None,' retorted the *vicomte*. 'After the murder of the duc d'Enghien even his most partial supporters ceased to regard him as a hero. If indeed some people made a hero of him,' he went on, turning to Anna Pavlovna, 'since the murder of the *duc* there has been one martyr more in heaven and one hero less on earth.'

Before Anna Pavlovna and the others had time to smile their appreciation of the *vicomte*'s epigram Pierre again burst into the conversation, and though Anna Pavlovna had a presentiment that he would say something unseemly she was unable to stop him.

'The execution of the duc d'Enghien,' declared Pierre, 'was a political necessity, and I consider that Napoleon showed nobility of soul in not hesitating to assume full responsibility for it.'

'*Dieu! Mon Dieu!*' murmured Anna Pavlovna in dismay.

'What, Monsieur Pierre ... do you think murder a proof of nobility of soul?' said the little princess, smiling and drawing her work nearer to her.

'Oh! Oh!' exclaimed different voices.

'Capital!' said Prince Hippolyte in English, and began slapping his knee with the palm of his hand. The *vicomte* merely shrugged his shoulders.

Pierre looked solemnly at his audience over his spectacles.

'I say so,' he went on desperately, 'because the Bourbons fled from the Revolution, leaving the people to anarchy; and Napoleon alone was capable of understanding the Revolution, of quelling it, and so for the general good he could not stop short at the life of one man.'

'Won't you come over to the other table?' suggested Anna Pavlovna. But Pierre continued without heeding her.

'Yes,' he cried, growing more and more excited, 'Napoleon is great because he towered above the Revolution, suppressed its abuses, preserving all that was good in it – equality of citizenship and freedom of speech and of the press – and that was the only reason he possessed himself of power.'

'Yes, if when he had obtained power he had restored it to the lawful king, instead of taking advantage of it to commit murder,' said the *vicomte*, 'then I might have called him a great man.'

'He could not have done that. The people gave him power simply for him to rid them of the Bourbons and because they believed him to be a great man. The Revolution was a grand fact,' continued Monsieur Pierre, betraying by this desperate and challenging statement his extreme youth and desire to give full expression to whatever was in his mind.

'Revolution and regicide a grand fact! ... What next? ... But won't you come over to this table?' repeated Anna Pavlovna.

'Rousseau's *Contrat social*,' said the *vicomte* with a bland smile.

'I am not speaking of regicide, I am speaking of the idea.'

'Yes, the idea of plunder, murder, and regicide,' an ironical voice interjected again.

'Those were extremes, of course; but the whole meaning of the

Revolution did not lie in them but in the rights of man, in emancipation from prejudice, in equality; and all these principles Napoleon has preserved in all their integrity.'

'Liberty and equality,' exclaimed the *vicomte* scornfully, as though he had at last made up his mind to prove seriously to this young man how foolish his arguments were. 'All high-sounding words which have long been debased. Who does not love liberty and equality? Our Saviour Himself long ago preached liberty and equality. Have people been any happier since the Revolution? On the contrary. We wanted freedom, but Bonaparte has destroyed it.'

Prince Andrei with a smile on his face looked from Pierre to the *vicomte* and from the *vicomte* to the mistress of the house. In the first moment of Pierre's outburst Anna Pavlovna, in spite of her experience as a hostess, was appalled. However, when she saw that Pierre's sacrilegious utterances did not incense the *vicomte*, and had convinced herself that it was impossible to suppress them, she rallied her forces and joined the *vicomte* in falling on the orator.

'But, my dear Monsieur Pierre,' said Anna Pavlovna, 'what have you to say for a great man who was capable of executing a duke – or a commoner, for that matter – without cause and without trial?'

'I should like to ask how Monsieur explains the 18th Brumaire,' said the *vicomte*. 'Was not that a piece of trickery? It was chicanery in no way resembling the conduct of a great man.'

'And the prisoners he massacred in Africa?' said the little princess. 'That was horrible!' and she shrugged her shoulders.

'He's an upstart, whatever anyone says,' Prince Hippolyte threw in.

Monsieur Pierre, not knowing which to answer, gazed at them all and smiled. His smile was not like the half-smile of other people. When he smiled his serious and indeed rather morose look vanished in a flash and in its place appeared another – childlike, kindly, even rather foolish – which seemed to plead for indulgence.

The *vicomte*, who was meeting him for the first time, saw quite clearly that this young Jacobin was not nearly so terrible as his words suggested. Everyone was silent.

'How do you expect him to answer you all at once?' said Prince Andrei. 'Besides, in considering the actions of a statesman one has to distinguish between what he does as a private individual and as a general or an emperor. So it seems to me.'

'Yes, yes, of course!' caught up Pierre, delighted at the arrival of this reinforcement.

'One must admit,' continued Prince Andrei, 'that Napoleon on the bridge at Arcola, or in the hospital at Jaffa shaking hands with the plague-stricken, is great as a man; but ... but there are other things it would be difficult to justify.'

Prince Andrei, who had evidently wished to smooth over the awkwardness of Pierre's remarks, rose, making a sign to his wife that it was time to go.

Suddenly Prince Hippolyte started up and detaining the company with a wave of his hand and begging them to be seated began:

'Oh, I heard a delightful Moscow story today – I really must entertain you with it. You will excuse me, *vicomte* – I shall have to tell it in Russian, or the point will be lost.' And Prince Hippolyte began in Russian, speaking with the sort of accent a Frenchman has after spending some twelve months in Russia. Everyone stopped to listen, so eagerly and insistently did he demand their attention for his story.

'In Moscow there lives a lady, *une dame*. And she is very stingy. She must drive with two footmen behind her carriage. And very tall footmen. That was her style. And she had a lady's maid, also very tall. She said ...'

Here Prince Hippolyte paused and pondered, apparently having difficulty in collecting his thoughts.

'She said ... Oh yes! "Girl," she said to the maid, "put on livery and get up behind the carriage, and come with me while I make some calls."'

Prince Hippolyte burst into a loud guffaw, laughing long before any of his audience, which showed the narrator to disadvantage. A few persons, among them the elderly lady and Anna Pavlovna, did smile, however.

'They drove off. Suddenly there was a violent gust of wind. The girl lost her hat, and her long hair fell down ...' At this point he could contain himself no longer and between gasps of laughter concluded:

'And the whole town heard about it.'

This was the end of the anecdote. Although it was incomprehensible why he had told it, or why it had to be told in Russian, still Anna Pavlovna and the others appreciated Prince Hippolyte's good breeding in so agreeably putting a close to the unpleasant and ill-bred harangue of Monsieur Pierre. After the anecdote the conversation broke up into small talk of no import concerning balls past and to come, theatricals and when and where they should meet again.

5

THANKING Anna Pavlovna for her *charmante soirée*, the guests began to depart.

Pierre was ungainly, stout and uncommonly tall, with exceptionally large red hands; as the saying is, he had no idea how to enter a drawing-room and still less of how to get out of one. In other words, he did not know how to make some especially agreeable remark to his hostess before leaving. Moreover, he was absent-minded. He got up and, instead of his own, seized the plumed three-cornered hat of a general and stood holding it, pulling at the plume, until the general claimed it from him. But all his absent-mindedness and inability to enter a drawing-room and converse in it were redeemed by his kindly expression of modest simplicity. Anna Pavlovna turned to him, with an air of Christian meekness signifying her forgiveness for his misbehaviour, nodded and said:

'I hope to see you again, but I also hope you will change your opinions, my dear Monsieur Pierre.'

When she said this he made no reply but simply bowed and once more displayed to them all his smile, which said plainly as words: 'Opinions or no opinions, you see what a capital, good-hearted fellow I am.' And everyone, Anna Pavlovna included, could not help feeling this was so.

Prince Andrei had gone out into the hall, and presenting his shoulders to the footman for his cloak to be thrown over them was listening indifferently to the chatter of his wife and Prince Hippolyte, who had also come into the hall. Prince Hippolyte stood close to the pretty, pregnant princess and stared straight at her through his eyeglass.

'Go in, Annette, you will catch cold,' exclaimed the little princess, saying good-bye to Anna Pavlovna. 'It is settled,' she added in an undertone.

Anna Pavlovna had already managed to have a word with Lisa about the match she was plotting between Anatole and the little princess's sister-in-law.

'I rely on you, my dear,' said Anna Pavlovna, also in a low tone. 'You write to her and let me know how the father will view the matter. *Au revoir!*' and she went back out of the hall.

Prince Hippolyte approached the little princess and bending his face down close to her began saying something in a half whisper.

Two footmen, one the princess's, holding her shawl, the other his, with his *redingote*, stood waiting for them to finish talking. They listened to the unintelligible conversation in French with an air of understanding but not wishing to appear to do so. As usual, the little princess was smiling as she spoke, and she laughed as she listened.

'I am very glad I did not go to the ambassador's,' said Prince Hippolyte. 'So boring. It has been a delightful evening, hasn't it? Delightful!'

'They say the ball is to be a splendid one,' replied the princess, curling her downy lip. 'All the pretty women in society will be there.'

'Not all, since you won't be there; not all,' said Prince Hippolyte, tittering gleefully; and snatching the shawl from the footman, shoving him aside as he did so, he began to wrap it round the princess. Either from awkwardness or intentionally (no one could have said which), even after the shawl had been adjusted it was some time before he removed his arms: he almost seemed to be embracing the young woman.

Gracefully, but still smiling, she drew back and turning round glanced at her husband. Prince Andrei's eyes were closed; he appeared to be drowsy and tired.

'Are you ready?' he asked, looking past his wife.

Prince Hippolyte hastily flung on his cloak, which being in the latest fashion fell below his heels, and stumbling over it rushed out on to the steps after the princess, whom the footman was helping into the carriage.

'*Princesse, au revoir!*' he cried, his tongue as badly entangled as his feet.

Picking up her gown, the princess was taking her seat in the darkness of the carriage, her husband was arranging his sword; Prince Hippolyte, on the pretence of assisting, was in everyone's way.

'Ex-cuse me, sir,' said Prince Andrei drily and disagreeably in Russian to Prince Hippolyte, who was blocking his path.

'I shall expect you, Pierre,' the same voice called in warm affectionate tones.

The postilion whipped up the horses and the carriage rumbled away. Prince Hippolyte gave vent to a short, jerky guffaw as he stood on the steps waiting for the *vicomte* whom he had promised to take home.

*

'Well, *mon cher,* your little princess is very nice, very nice,' said the *vicomte,* seating himself in the carriage beside Hippolyte. 'Very nice indeed, quite French,' and he kissed the tips of his fingers.

Hippolyte burst into a laugh.

'And do you know, you are a terrible fellow for all that little innocent way of yours,' pursued the *vicomte.* 'I am sorry for the poor husband, that officer boy who gives himself the airs of a reigning monarch.'

Hippolyte spluttered again and through his laughter articulated:

'And you said that Russian ladies were not up to Frenchwomen. One must know how to set about things, that is all.'

Pierre, arriving first, went straight to Prince Andrei's study like one thoroughly at home, and at once, from habit, stretched himself out on a sofa, took from the shelf the first book that came to hand (it was Caesar's *Commentaries*) and leaning on his elbow began reading it in the middle.

'What have you done to Mademoiselle Scherer? She will be quite ill now,' said Prince Andrei, as he came into the study rubbing his small white hands together.

Pierre rolled his whole person over so that the sofa creaked, lifted his eager face to Prince Andrei, smiled and waved his hand.

'That *abbé* was very interesting, only he has got hold of the wrong end of the stick. To my thinking, permanent peace is possible but – I don't know how to put it … Not by means of a political balance of power.'

Prince Andrei was obviously not interested in such abstract conversation.

'My dear fellow, one can't everywhere and at all times say all one thinks. Come, tell me, have you made up your mind at last? Is it to be the cavalry or the diplomatic service?' he asked after a momentary silence.

Pierre sat up on the sofa with his legs crossed under him.

'Can you imagine it, I still don't know! Neither prospect smiles on me.'

'But you must decide on something! Your father's expecting it.'

At the age of ten Pierre had been sent abroad with an *abbé* as tutor, and had remained away till he was twenty. On his return to Moscow, his father had dismissed the *abbé* and said to the young man, 'Now you go to Petersburg, look round and make your choice. I agree to anything. Here is a letter to Prince Vasili, and here is money. Write and tell me all about everything, and I will help you in every way.' Pierre had already been three months trying to choose a career and had come to no decision. It was in regard to this choice of a career that Prince Andrei spoke to him now. Pierre rubbed his forehead.

'But he must be a freemason,' said he, meaning the *abbé* he had met at the party.

'That is all nonsense.' Prince Andrei pulled him up again. 'We'd better talk business. Have you been to the Horse Guards?'

'No, not yet, but here is an idea that occurred to me which I wanted to tell you. This war now is against Napoleon. If it were a war for freedom, I could have understood it, and I should have been the first to join the army; but to help England and Austria against the greatest man in the world – that is not right. ...'

Prince Andrei merely shrugged his shoulders at Pierre's childish talk. He assumed the air of one who really finds it impossible to reply to such nonsense; but it would in fact have been difficult to answer this naïve querying in any other way than Prince Andrei did answer it.

'If everyone would only fight for his own convictions, there would be no wars,' he said.

'And a very good thing that would be,' said Pierre.

Prince Andrei laughed.

'Very likely it would be a good thing, but it will never happen.'

'Well, what are *you* going to the war for?' asked Pierre.

'What for? I don't know. Because I have to. Besides, I am going ...' He stopped. 'I am going because the life I lead here – is not to my taste!'

6

THE rustle of a woman's dress was heard in the adjoining room. Prince Andrei gave a start, as though to pull himself together, and his face assumed the expression it had worn in Anna Pavlovna's drawing-room. Pierre removed his feet from the sofa. The princess came in. She had now changed her dress for another, a house gown to be sure but equally fresh and elegant. Prince Andrei rose and courteously pushed forward an easy-chair.

'I often wonder,' she began, speaking in French as usual and briskly and fussily settling herself in the arm-chair, 'how it is Annette never married. You are very foolish, all you men, not to have married her! Forgive me for saying so, but you really have no sense where women are concerned. What a contentious person you are, Monsieur Pierre!'

'Your husband and I were just at this moment having an argument: I can't make out why he wants to go to the war,' said Pierre, addressing the princess without any of the constraint so common between a young man and a young woman.

The princess jumped. Evidently Pierre's words touched her to the quick.

'Ah, that is exactly what I say. I don't understand – I simply do not understand why men cannot get on without war. Why is it we women want nothing of the kind? We don't care for it. Come, you shall be the judge. As I am always telling him: here he is uncle's adjutant, a most brilliant position. Everyone knows and esteems him. Only the other day at the Apraksins' I heard a lady asking, "Is that the famous Prince Andrei?" I did really!' She laughed. 'And it is the same wherever he goes. He might easily become aide-de-camp to the Sovereign. You know the Emperor spoke to him most graciously. Annette and I were saying it would be quite easy to arrange. What do you think?'

Pierre glanced at Prince Andrei and seeing that his friend did not like the conversation made no reply.

'When do you leave?' he asked.

'Oh, don't talk about his going, don't talk about it! I don't want to hear a word on the subject,' exclaimed the princess in the same capriciously playful tone that she had used to Hippolyte at the *soirée* and which was so obviously out of place in her own home circle, where Pierre was like one of the family. 'Today when I remembered that it would be the end of all these pleasant associations ... And then you know, André ...' (she gave her husband a meaning look) 'I am afraid, I am afraid,' she whispered, and a shudder ran down her back.

Her husband looked at her as though he were surprised to observe someone else in the room besides himself and Pierre. With frigid courtesy, however, he addressed an inquiry to his wife:

'What is it you are afraid of, Lise? I don't understand.'

'There, what egoists men are! Egoists, every one of you. Just for a whim of his own, goodness knows why, he deserts me and shuts me up alone in the country.'

'With my father and sister, don't forget that,' said Prince Andrei quietly.

'It comes to the same thing: I shall be alone, without *my* friends.... And he expects me not to be afraid.'

Her tone was querulous now and her drawn-up lip no longer suggested a smile but gave her face the look of a vicious little squirrel. She paused as though feeling it indecorous to speak of her condition before Pierre, though in that lay the whole gist of the matter.

'I still cannot imagine why you are afraid,' said Prince Andrei slowly, not taking his eyes off his wife.

The princess blushed and lifted her arms in a gesture of despair.

'No, André, I must say you have changed. Changed terribly....'

'Your doctor said that you were to go to bed earlier,' said Prince Andrei. 'It's time you were asleep.'

The princess said nothing and suddenly her short downy lip began to quiver. With a shrug of his shoulders Prince Andrei got up and walked about the room.

Pierre looked through his spectacles in naïve wonder from him to the princess, and made a movement as if he too would rise, but then thought better of it.

'Why should I mind if Monsieur Pierre is here!' suddenly exclaimed the little princess, and her pretty face contorted into a tearful grimace. 'I have been wanting to ask you for a long time, André, why you have changed towards me so? What have I done? You are going off to the war, you don't feel for me. Why is it?'

'Lise!' was all Prince Andrei said. But this one word conveyed entreaty and menace, and, most of all, conviction that she would herself regret her words; but she went on hurriedly:

'You treat me as though I were an invalid or a child. I see it all. You weren't like this six months ago, were you?'

'Lise, I beg you to stop,' said Prince Andrei, still more emphatically.

Pierre, who had been growing more and more agitated as this conversation proceeded, got up and went to the princess. He seemed unable to bear the sight of tears, and looked ready to weep himself.

'Please don't upset yourself, princess. All this is only your fancy because, I assure you, I know myself ... and so ... because ... No,

29

excuse me, an outsider has no business ... No, don't distress yourself ... Good-bye.'

Prince Andrei caught him by the arm.

'No, wait, Pierre. The princess is so kind, she would not wish to deprive me of the pleasure of your company for an evening.'

'Yes, he only thinks of himself,' muttered the princess, not attempting to restrain her tears of vexation.

'Lise!' said Prince Andrei coldly, raising his voice to a pitch which showed that he had come to the end of his patience.

All at once the angry squirrel-like expression on the princess's pretty little face changed to a moving and piteous look of fear. Her beautiful eyes gave a sidelong glance at her husband and her face assumed the timid, deprecating expression of a dog when it rapidly but feebly wags its drooping tail.

'*Mon Dieu, mon Dieu!*' she muttered and gathering the skirt of her dress with one hand she went up to her husband and kissed him on the forehead.

'*Bonsoir*, Lise,' said he, rising and courteously kissing her hand, as though she were a stranger.

*

The friends were silent. Neither felt inclined to be the first to speak. Pierre kept glancing at Prince Andrei; Prince Andrei rubbed his forehead with his small hand.

'Let us go and have supper,' he said with a sigh, getting up and walking to the door.

They went into the elegant, newly-decorated, luxurious dining-room. Everything, from the table-napkins to the silver, china, and glass, wore the peculiar stamp of newness characteristic of the establishments of newly-married couples. Half-way through supper Prince Andrei lent his elbow on the table and like a man who has had something on his mind for a long time and suddenly determines to speak out he began talking with a nervous irritation which was new to Pierre.

'Never, never marry, my dear fellow. That is my advice to you – don't marry until you can say to yourself that you have done all you are capable of doing, and until you cease to love the woman of your choice and see her plainly, as she really is; or else you will be making a cruel and irreparable mistake. Marry when you are old and good for nothing. Otherwise everything that is fine and noble in you will be thrown away. It will all be wasted on trifles. Yes, yes, yes! Don't look at me with such surprise. If you marry while you still have any hopes of yourself you will be made to feel at every step that for you all is over, every door closed but that of the drawing-room, where you will stand on the same level as the court lackey and the idiot. ... But what is the good ? ...'

He made a vigorous gesture with his arm.

Pierre took off his spectacles, which altered his face, making it look even more good-natured, and gazed wonderingly at his friend.

'My wife,' pursued Prince Andrei, 'is an excellent woman – one of those rare women with whom a man's honour is safe, but great heavens what wouldn't I give not to be married! You are the first and only person I say this to, because I hold an affection for you.'

As he said this, Prince Andrei was less than ever like the Bolkonsky who had lolled in Anna Pavlovna's easy-chairs with half-closed eyelids filtering French phrases through his teeth. Every muscle of his spare face now quivered with feverish excitement; his eyes, which had seemed lustreless and without life, now flashed with a fierce brilliancy. It was evident that however apathetic he might appear at ordinary times he more than made up for it by his vehemence in moments of irritation.

'You don't understand why I say this,' he went on, 'but it is the whole story of life. You talk of Bonaparte and his career,' said he (though Pierre had not mentioned Bonaparte). 'You talk of Bonaparte, but Bonaparte while he was working his way step by step towards his goal – he was free; there was nothing for him but his goal, and he reached it. But tie yourself up with a woman and like a convict in irons you lose all freedom! And all your aspirations, all the ability you feel within you is only a drag on you, torturing you with regret. Drawing-rooms, tittle-tattle, balls, idle conceits and futility – such is the enchanted circle that encloses me. I am setting off now to take part in the war, the greatest war there ever was, and I know nothing and am fit for nothing. I am an amiable fellow with a caustic wit,' continued Prince Andrei, 'and at Anna Pavlovna's they hang upon my words. And then think of that stupid set without which my wife cannot exist, and those women. ... If you only knew what all these fine ladies, indeed women in general, amount to! My father is right. Selfish, vain, humdrum, trivial in everything – that's what women are when they show themselves in their true colours! When you see them in society, you might fancy they had something in them, but there is nothing, nothing, nothing! No, don't marry, my dear chap, don't marry!' concluded Prince Andrei.

'It seems odd to me,' said Pierre, 'that you – you of all people – should consider yourself a failure, your life wrecked. You have everything before you, everything. And you ...'

He did not finish but his tone made it clear how highly he thought of his friend and how much he expected of him in the future.

'How can he talk like that?' thought Pierre, who considered the prince a model of perfection for the very reason that Bolkonsky possessed to the highest degree all those qualities that Pierre lacked, and which might best be summed up as will power. Pierre always admired Prince Andrei's easy demeanour with people in every walk of life, his extraordinary memory, his erudition (he had read everything, knew everything, had ideas on every subject), but above all he admired his capacity for work and study. And if Pierre was often struck by Andrei's lack of capacity for speculative philosophy (to which Pierre was particularly addicted), he regarded even this not as a defect but as a sign of strength.

Even in the best, most friendly and simple relations of life, praise and commendation are as indispensable as the oil which greases the wheels of a machine to keep them running smoothly.

'My day is done,' said Prince Andrei. 'What is there to say about me? Let us talk about you,' he added after a short silence, smiling at his own reassuring thoughts.

The smile was instantly reflected on Pierre's face.

'Why, what is there to say about me?' asked Pierre, his face relaxing into an easy-going, happy smile. 'What am I? Illegitimate!' He suddenly blushed purple. Obviously it cost him a great effort to bring out the word. 'Without name and without fortune ... and yet it is true....' But he did not say what was true. 'For the present I am free, and enjoying it. Only I haven't the least idea what to take up. I wanted to consult you seriously about it.'

Prince Andrei looked at him with kindly eyes. But his glance, friendly and affectionate as it was, still betrayed a consciousness of his own superiority.

'You are dear to me especially because you are the one live soul in all our circle of acquaintances. You are lucky. Choose as you will, the choice matters little. You will be all right anywhere. But look here: do break with the Kuragins and their kind of life. That sort of thing – all that junketing, dissipation and the rest of it so ill becomes you!'

'Can it be helped, my dear fellow?' said Pierre, shrugging his shoulders. 'Women, my dear fellow, women!'

'I don't understand it,' replied Prince Andrei. 'Women who are *comme il faut*, that is a different matter; but Kuragin's women – "women and wine" – I can't understand!'

Pierre was staying at Prince Vasili Kuragin's and taking part in the dissipated life of his son Anatole, the very young man whom his father and Anna Pavlovna were proposing to marry to Prince Andrei's sister in the hope of reforming him.

'Do you know what?' said Pierre, as if he had suddenly had a happy inspiration. 'Seriously, I have been thinking of it for a long time. ... Leading this sort of existence I can't decide or think properly about anything. One's head aches and one spends all one's money. He invited me this evening, but I won't go.'

'Give me your word of honour not to?'

'Word of honour.'

*

It was past one o'clock when Pierre left his friend. It was a luminous Petersburg midsummer night. Pierre took an open cab intending to drive straight home. But the nearer he got to the house the less he felt like sleep on such a night, which was more like evening or early morning. It was light enough to see far down the empty streets. On the way Pierre remembered that the usual set were to meet for cards at Anatole Kuragin's that evening, after which there was generally a drinking bout, finishing off with one of Pierre's favourite pastimes.

'It would be nice to go to Kuragin's,' he thought, but immediately recalled his promise to Prince Andrei not to go there again. Then, as happens to people with no strength of character, such a passionate desire came over him for one last taste of the familiar dissipation that he decided to go. And the thought immediately occurred to him that his word to Prince Andrei was not binding because before he had given it he had already promised Prince Anatole to come. 'Besides,' he reasoned, 'all these "words of honour" are mere convention and have no precise significance, especially if one considers that by tomorrow one may be dead, or some extraordinary accident may happen to sweep away all distinctions between honour and dishonour.' Arguments of this kind often occurred to Pierre, nullifying all his resolutions and intentions. He went to Kuragin's.

Driving up to the large house near the Horse Guards' barracks, where Anatole lived, Pierre ran up the lighted steps and went in at the open door. There was no one in the ante-room; empty bottles, cloaks and overshoes were scattered about; there was a smell of wine, and in the distance he heard talking and shouting.

Cards and supper were over but the company had not yet dispersed. Pierre threw off his cloak and entered the first room in which were the remains of supper, and a single footman, thinking himself unobserved, was surreptitiously drinking what was left in the glasses. From the third room came sounds of scuffling, laughter, familiar voices shouting, and the growl of a bear. Some eight or nine young men were crowding eagerly round an open window. Three others were romping with a bear cub, which one of their number was dragging by its chain and trying to set at his companions.

'I bet a hundred on Stevens!' shouted one.

'Mind, no holding on!' cried another.

'I back Dolohov!' cried a third. 'Kuragin, you come and see to the bets.'

'Let Bruin go now, here's a wager.'

'At one draught, or he loses!' shouted a fourth.

'Jacob, bring a bottle!' ordered the host, a tall, handsome fellow, standing in the midst of the group. He had taken off his coat and his fine cambric shirt was open over his chest. 'Wait a minute, gentlemen ... Here is our old Pierre! Good lad!' he cried, turning to Pierre.

A man of medium height, with clear blue eyes, whose voice was particularly striking among all those drunken voices for its tone of sobriety, called from the window:

'Come over here and look after the bets!'

This was Dolohov, an officer of the Semeonovsk regiment, a notorious gambler and dare-devil, who was making his home with Anatole. Pierre smiled, looking about him gaily.

'I don't understand. What's it all about?'

'Stop, he's not drunk! A bottle here!' cried Anatole; and taking a glass from the table he went up to Pierre.

'First of all, you must drink.'

Pierre proceeded to drain glass after glass, surveying from under his eyebrows the tipsy guests who were crowding round the window again, and lending an ear to their chatter. Anatole kept his glass filled while he explained that Dolohov had laid a wager with Stevens, an English sailor who was there, backing himself to drink a bottle of rum sitting on the sill of the third-floor window with his legs hanging down outside.

'Come on now, empty the bottle,' said Anatole, handing Pierre the last glass, 'or I shan't let you go!'

'No, I don't want any more,' said Pierre, pushing Anatole aside and going up to the window.

Dolohov was holding the Englishman's hand and clearly and explicitly repeating the terms of the wager, addressing himself more particularly to Anatole and Pierre.

Dolohov was a man of medium height, with curly hair and bright blue eyes. He was about five and twenty years old. Like all infantry officers he wore no moustache, so that his mouth, the most striking feature in his face, was not concealed. The lines of the mouth were remarkably finely drawn. The upper lip curved sharply in the middle and closed firmly over the strong lower one, and something in the nature of two smiles played continually, one on each side, round either corner of his mouth; and altogether, especially with the steady, insolent intelligence of his eyes, produced an effect which made it impossible to overlook his face. Dolohov had little fortune and no connexions. And yet through Anatole got through tens of thousands of roubles. Dolohov lived with him and had succeeded in so regulating the position that Anatole and all who knew them had a higher regard for him than for Anatole. Dolohov played every kind of game and almost always won. However much he drank he never lost his head. Both Kuragin and Dolohov were at that time notorious among the rakes and spendthrifts of Petersburg.

The bottle of rum was brought. Two footmen, evidently rather flustered and made nervous by the orders and shouts from all sides, were pulling at the sash-frame which prevented anyone from sitting on the outer sill.

Anatole with his swaggering air strode up to the window. He was longing to smash something. Pushing the footmen aside he tugged at the frame but it would not yield. He broke a pane.

'Now you have a try, Hercules,' said he, addressing Pierre.

Pierre seized hold of the cross bar, gave it a wrench and the oak frame came away with a crash.

'Take it right out, or they'll think I'm holding on,' said Dolohov.

'Is the Englishman bragging? ... Eh? ... Is it all right?' said Anatole.

'All right,' said Pierre, watching Dolohov, who had taken the bottle of rum and was going to the window through which the light of the sky was visible, the afterglow of sunset fading into dawn.

With the bottle of rum in his hand Dolohov jumped on to the window-sill.

'Listen!' he cried, standing there and speaking to those in the room. All were silent.

'I wager' – he spoke French so that the Englishman might understand him, and spoke it none too well – 'I wager fifty imperials ... or do you wish to make it a hundred?' he added, addressing the Englishman.

'No, fifty,' said the Englishman.

'Very well, fifty it is – that I will drink this whole bottle of rum without taking it from my lips, drink it sitting outside the window on this spot' (he stooped and pointed to the sloping ledge outside the window), 'and not holding on to anything. Is that understood?'

'Very well,' said Stevens.

Anatole turned to the Englishman and taking him by one of his coat buttons and looking down at him – the Englishman was short – began to repeat the terms of the wager in English.

'Wait!' cried Dolohov, knocking on the window-sill with the bottle to attract attention. 'Wait a minute, Kuragin, listen! If anyone else does the same thing I'll pay him a hundred imperials. Is that clear?'

The sailor nodded without making it plain whether he intended to take this new bet or not. Anatole still held him by the coat button and, though the Englishman kept nodding to show that he understood, went on translating Dolohov's words into English. A thin young hussar of the Life Guards, who had been out of luck all the evening, climbed up on to the window-sill, poked his head out and looked down.

'Oh-h-h!' he exclaimed, looking out of the window at the paving stones below.

'Shut up!' cried Dolohov, pulling him back so that the lad got his feet entangled in his spurs and jumped awkwardly into the room.

36

Placing the bottle on the window-sill so as to have it within reach, Dolohov climbed slowly and carefully through the casement and lowered his legs. Pressing with both hands against the sides of the frame he settled himself in a sitting position, let go his hands, shifted a little to the right, then to the left, and took up the bottle. Anatole brought a pair of candles and set them on the window-sill, although it was now quite light. Dolohov's back in his white shirt, and his curly head, were lighted up from both sides. Everyone crowded to the window, the Englishman in front. Pierre was smiling and silent. One of the party, rather older than the others, suddenly moved forward with a scared and angry face, and tried to clutch Dolohov by the shirt.

'Gentlemen, this is madness! He'll be killed!' said this man, less foolhardy than the rest.

Anatole stopped him.

'Don't touch him. You'll startle him and he'll fall and be killed. Eh? ... And what then, eh?'

Dolohov looked back, and again holding on with both hands arranged himself on his seat.

'If any one touches me again,' said he, articulating the words one by one through his thin compressed lips, 'I'll send him flying below. Now! ...'

Saying this he turned round again, let his hands drop, took the bottle and lifted it to his lips, threw his head back and raised his free hand to balance himself. One of the footmen who was stooping to pick up some broken glass remained in a half-bent attitude, his eyes fixed on the window and Dolohov's back. Anatole stood erect with staring eyes. The Englishman watched from one side, pursing his lips. The man who had tried to stop the proceedings ran to a corner of the room and flung himself on a sofa with his face to the wall. Pierre covered his eyes. A faint forgotten smile still hovered over his lips though horror and apprehension were written on his face. All were silent. Pierre took his hands from his eyes. Dolohov was still sitting in the same position, only his head was thrown farther back till the curly hair at the nape of his neck touched his shirt collar, and the hand holding the bottle was lifted higher and higher, trembling with the effort. The bottle was emptying visibly, rising almost perpendicularly over his head. 'Why does it take so long?' thought Pierre. It seemed to him as though more than half an hour had elapsed. Suddenly

Dolohov made a backward movement of the spine and his arm trembled nervously; this was sufficient to cause his whole body to slide as he sat on the sloping ledge. As he slipped, his head and arm wavered still more violently with the strain. One hand moved as if to clutch the window-sill but he brought it back. Pierre shut his eyes once more and declared to himself that he would never open them again. Suddenly he was conscious of a general stir. He looked up: Dolohov was standing on the window-sill, his face pale but triumphant.

'Empty!'

He tossed the bottle to the Englishman, who caught it neatly. Dolohov jumped down from the window. He smelt powerfully of rum.

'Capital! ... Bravo! ... That's something like a bet! You're a devil of a fellow!' rang the shouts from all sides.

The Englishman produced his purse and began counting out the money. Dolohov stood frowning and silent. Pierre dashed up to the window.

'Gentlemen, who wants to make a bet with me? I'll do the same!' he shouted suddenly. 'Or even without a bet, there! Give me a bottle. I'll do it ... bring a bottle!'

'Let him – let him!' said Dolohov, smiling.

'Are you mad? Who do you think would let you? Why, you turn giddy going downstairs,' protested several voices from various sides.

'I'll drink it! Let's have a bottle of rum!' shouted Pierre, pounding on a chair with drunken vehemence, and climbing out of the window.

They seized his arms; but he was so strong that everyone who touched him was sent flying.

'No, you'll never dissuade him like that,' said Anatole. 'Wait, let me fool him ... Listen! I'll take your bet, but for tomorrow; for now we are all going to —'s.'

'Come along then,' cried Pierre. 'Come along ... And we'll take Bruin with us.'

And he caught the bear up in his arms and began waltzing round the room with it.

7

PRINCE VASILI fulfilled the promise he had made to Princess Drubetskoy on the evening of Anna Pavlovna's *soirée*, when she had pleaded with him to help her only son Boris. A request had been preferred to the Emperor, an exception made, and Boris transferred to the Semeonovsk regiment of the Guards as ensign. But he was not appointed aide-de-camp, or attached to Kutuzov's staff, in spite of all Anna Mihalovna's endeavours and stratagems. Shortly after Anna Pavlovna's reception, Anna Mihalovna returned to Moscow and went straight to her rich relations, the Rostovs, with whom she always stayed when in Moscow. It was with these relations that her darling Bory, who had only recently entered a regiment of the line and was now being transferred to the Guards as ensign, had been brought up from childhood and lived for years at a time. The Guards had already left Petersburg on the 10th of August, and her son, delayed in Moscow for his equipment, was to overtake them on the march to Radzivilov.

The Rostovs were celebrating the *fête* day of the mother and the younger daughter, both called Natalia. Since morning an unceasing stream of six-horse carriages had been coming and going with visitors bringing their congratulations to the Countess Rostov's great mansion in Povarsky street, which all Moscow knew. The countess and her handsome elder daughter were in the drawing-room with the visitors, who were constantly followed by new arrivals.

The countess was a woman of about five and forty, with a thin oriental type of countenance, evidently worn out with child-bearing – she was the mother of a dozen children. Her languid movements and slow speech due to her frail health gave her an air of dignity which inspired respect. Princess Anna Mihalovna Drubetskoy, as an intimate friend of the family, also sat in the drawing-room, helping to receive and entertain the company. The young people were in the rooms behind the drawing-room, not considering it incumbent upon them to take part in receiving the visitors. The count met the guests and escorted them to the door again, inviting them all to dinner.

'Much obliged to you, much obliged, my dears' (he called everyone 'my dear' without exception, making not the slightest distinction between persons of higher or lower standing than his own). 'Much obliged for myself and my two dear ones whose name-day we are celebrating. Mind you come to dinner now, or I shall be offended. On behalf of the whole family I beg you to come, my dear.' This formula he repeated to all alike, without exception or variation, and with the same expression on his round jolly clean-shaven face, the same firm grip of the hand and repeated short bows. As soon as he had seen one visitor off, the count would return to one or another of those still in the drawing-room, pull forward a chair, and jauntily spreading out his legs and putting his hands on his knees with the air of a man who enjoys life and knows how to live, he would shake his head significantly and offer conjectures concerning the weather, or exchange confidences about health, sometimes in Russian and sometimes in execrable though self-confident French; and then again, looking weary but unflinching in the performance of duty, he would go to the door with still another departing guest, smoothing the scanty grey hairs over his bald patch and repeating his invitations to dinner. Now and then on his way back from the ante-room he would pass through the conservatory and the butler's pantry into the large marble dining-hall where covers were being laid for eighty people, and looking at the footmen who were bringing in the silver and china, moving tables and unfolding damask table-linen, he would call up Dmitri Vasilyevich, a man of good family who had charge of all his affairs, and say:

'Well, Mitenka, mind everything is all right. That's nice!' he would add, glancing with satisfaction at the enormous table extended to its full length. 'The great thing is the serving, you understand that.' And with a complacent smile he would return to the drawing-room.

'Maria Lvovna Karagin and her daughter!' announced the countess's colossal footman in his bass voice at the drawing-room door. The countess reflected for a second and took a pinch of snuff from a gold snuff-box with her husband's portrait on it.

'I'm worn out with callers,' she said. 'Well, this is the last one I'll see. She is so affected. Show her up,' she added to the footman in a dejected tone, as though she were saying, 'Finish me off and have done with it.'

A tall, stout woman with a haughty air, followed by a smiling round-faced girl, rustled into the drawing-room.

'Dear Countess, what an age ... She has been laid up, poor child... at the Razumovskys' ball ... and Countess Apraksin ... I was so delighted ...' The fragmentary phrases spoken by animated feminine voices broke in on one another and mingled with the hiss of silks and the scraping of chairs. The sort of conversation had begun which can be interrupted at the first pause for the visitor to rise and with a swish of her skirt murmur: 'I am so charmed … Mamma's health … and Countess Apraksin …' and then rustling again, make her way into the ante-room to put on pelisse or mantle and drive away.

The conversation touched on the chief topic of the day – the illness of the famous old Count Bezuhov, one of the richest and handsomest men of Catherine's time, and his illegitimate son Pierre, the young man who had behaved in such an unseemly manner at a *soirée* at Anna Pavlovna's.

'I am very sorry for the poor count,' declared the visitor. 'His health is so wretched, and now to have to suffer this anxiety about his son – it will be the death of him!'

'What is that?' asked the countess, pretending ignorance though she had already heard about the cause of Count Bezuhov's distress at least fifteen times.

'There's modern education for you!' exclaimed the visitor. 'Even when he was abroad as a child he was allowed to do as he liked, and now, so I hear, he has been behaving so atrociously in Petersburg that the police have ordered him out of the city.'

'You don't say so!' replied the countess.

'He got into bad company,' interposed Princess Anna Mihalovna. 'Prince Vasili's son, this Pierre and a certain young man named Dolohov, they say, have been up to heaven only knows what! And two of them have had to suffer for it – Dolohov has been reduced to the ranks, and Bezuhov's son sent back to Moscow. Anatole Kuragin's part in the affair, his father managed to hush up, but even so he has been ordered out of Petersburg.'

'But what did they do?' asked the countess.

'They are regular bandits, Dolohov especially,' replied the visitor. 'He is the son of Maria Ivanovna Dolohov, such a worthy woman, but there! Can you imagine it – the three of them somehow got hold of a bear, took it in a carriage with them and set off to visit some actresses. The police hurried to interfere, and they seized a police officer, tied him back to back to the bear and then threw the bear into the Moyka. And there was the bear swimming about with the police-man on his back!'

'What a figure the officer must have cut, my dear!' cried the count, helpless with laughter.

'Oh, how dreadful! What can you find to laugh at, count?'
But the ladies had to laugh in spite of themselves.

'It was all they could do to rescue the poor man,' pursued the visitor. 'And to think it is Kirill Vladimirovich Bezuhov's son who amuses himself in such a clever fashion! And he supposed to be so well-educated and intelligent! That shows what comes of educating young men abroad. I hope no one here in Moscow will receive him, in spite of his money. They wanted to bring him to my house but I absolutely declined: I have my daughters to consider.'

'What makes you say this young man is so rich?' asked the countess, leaning away from the girls, who immediately pretended not to be listening. 'Aren't all his children illegitimate, Pierre too?'

The visitor waved her hand.

'There are a score of them, I believe.'

Princess Anna Mihalovna intervened in the conversation, evidently burning to show her connexions and air her knowledge of what went on in society.

'The fact of the matter is,' said she significantly, speaking in a half-whisper, 'Count Kirill Vladimirovich's reputation is notorious.... He has lost count of the number of his children, but this Pierre was his favourite.'

'How handsome the old man was,' said the countess, 'only last year. I never saw a finer-looking man.'

'He is very much altered now,' said Anna Mihalovna. 'As I was saying, Prince Vasili is the next heir through his wife, but the count is very fond of Pierre: he took great pains with his education and has written to the Emperor about him, so that no one can tell, in the event of his death – and he is so ill that he may die at any moment, and Dr Lorrain has come from Petersburg – no one can tell, I say, who will come into his enormous fortune, Pierre or Prince Vasili. Forty thousand serfs and millions of roubles! I know it for a fact, Prince Vasili told me so himself. Besides, Kirill Vladimirovich is my mother's second cousin. He's also my Bory's godfather,' she added, as if she attached no importance to this circumstance.

'Prince Vasili arrived in Moscow yesterday. On some inspection business, I am told,' remarked the visitor.

'Yes, but between ourselves,' said the princess, 'that is a pretext. He has really come to see Count Kirill Vladimirovich, having heard how ill he is.'

'At all events, my dear, that was a capital joke,' said the count, and perceiving that the elder visitor was not listening he turned to the young ladies. 'I can just imagine how funny that policeman must have looked!'

And as he waved his arms in imitation of the police officer his portly form again shook with a deep ringing laugh, the laugh of one who always eats well and, in particular, drinks well. 'So, do come and dine with us,' he said.

8

A SILENCE ensued. The countess looked at her visitor, smiling affably but making no attempt to conceal the fact that she would not be in the least sorry if the guest were to get up and go. The visitor's daughter was already smoothing her dress and looking inquiringly at her mother, when suddenly from the next room came the sound of boys and girls running to the door and the noise of a chair falling over, and a girl of thirteen, holding something in the folds of her short muslin frock, darted in and stopped in the middle of the drawing-room. It was plain that her headlong flight had brought her farther than she had intended. Behind her in the doorway appeared a student with a crimson collar to his coat, a Guards officer, a girl of fifteen and a plump, rosy-cheeked little boy in a child's smock.

The count jumped up and opening his arms threw them round the little girl who had come running in.

'Ah, here she is!' he exclaimed, laughing. 'My little pet, whose name-day it is!'

'My dear child, there is a time for everything,' said the countess with feigned severity. 'You always spoil her, Ilya,' she added, addressing her husband.

'How do you do, my dear? Many happy returns of the day,' said the visitor. 'What a charming child,' she went on, turning to the mother.

The little girl with her black eyes and wide mouth was not pretty but she was full of life. In the wild dash her bodice had slipped from the bare childish shoulders and the black curls were tossed back in confusion. She had thin bare arms, little legs in lace-frilled drawers, and low shoes upon her feet. She was at the delightful age when a girl is no longer a child, though the child is not yet a young woman. Escaping from her father she ran to hide her flushed face in the lace of her mother's mantilla – paying no attention to her severe remarks and going into fits of laughter. Laughing and incoherent, she tried to

43

explain something about a doll which she produced from the folds of her frock.

'Do you see? ... It's my doll – Mimi.... You see ...'

And Natasha could not go on, it still seemed to her so funny. She leaned against her mother and burst into such loud, ringing laughter that even the prim visitor could not help joining in.

'Now run along and take that horrid object with you,' admonished her mother, pushing away her daughter with pretended sternness. 'She is my younger girl,' she added, turning to the visitor.

Natasha, raising her face for a moment from her mother's lace mantilla, glanced up through tears of laughter and hid her face again.

Obliged to contemplate this family scene, the visitor felt it incumbent upon her to take part in it.

'Tell me, my dear,' said she to Natasha, 'how did you come by Mimi? Is she your little girl?'

Natasha did not like the condescending tone, and looked at the visitor gravely, without speaking.

Meanwhile all the younger generation: Boris, the officer, Princess Anna Mihalovna's son; Nikolai, the undergraduate, the count's elder son; Sonya, the count's fifteen-year-old niece; and little Petya, his younger boy, had all settled down in the drawing-room, making conspicuous efforts to restrain within the bounds of decorum the glee and excitement which convulsed their faces. Evidently in the back part of the house, from which they had dashed out so impetuously, they had been engaged in much more entertaining conversation than town gossip, the weather and Countess Apraksin. Now and then they would glance at one another, hardly able to suppress their laughter.

The two young men, the student and the officer, friends from childhood, were of the same age and both good-looking, though not alike. Boris was tall and fair, and his calm, handsome face had regular, delicate features. Nikolai was a short, curly-haired young man with an open expression. The first dark down was already showing on his upper lip, and his whole face was expressive of impetuosity and enthusiasm. Nikolai had flushed crimson as soon as he entered the drawing-room, and could not find a word to say. Boris, on the contrary, at once found his footing and related quietly and humorously how he had known that doll Mimi before her nose had lost its beauty; how she had aged during the five years of their acquaintance, and how she was cracked right across the skull. As he said this he glanced at

Natasha, but Natasha turned away from him and looked at her little brother, who was screwing up his eyes and shaking with noiseless merriment, until, feeling she could control herself no longer, she jumped down and darted from the room as fast as her nimble little feet would carry her. Boris preserved his composure.

'You were meaning to go out, weren't you, mamma? Shall I order the carriage?' he smilingly asked his mother.

'Yes, yes, go and tell them, please,' she answered, returning his smile.

Boris quietly left the room and went in pursuit of Natasha. The plump little boy trotted crossly after them, as if vexed that their programme had been upset.

9

THE only young people remaining in the drawing-room – not counting the Karagin girl and the countess's elder daughter (who was four years older than her sister and already regarded herself as grown up) – were Nikolai and Sonya the niece. Sonya was a slender, tiny brunette with soft eyes shaded by long lashes, a thick braid of black hair coiled twice round her head, and a tawny tint to her skin especially noticeable on her neck and her bare, thin but shapely, muscular arms. The smooth grace of her movements, the soft elasticity of her small limbs and a certain wary artfulness in her manner suggested a beautiful, half-grown kitten which promises to develop into a lovely cat. She evidently considered it proper to show an interest in the general conversation and smile; but in spite of herself her eyes under their long thick lashes watched her cousin, who was soon to be off to his regiment, with such passionate girlish adoration that her smile could not for a single instant deceive anyone, and it was plain to see that the kitten had only crouched down the more energetically to spring up and play with her cousin the moment they, too, like Boris and Natasha could escape from the drawing-room.

'Yes, my dear,' said the old count, addressing the visitor and pointing to Nikolai, 'his friend Boris here has been given his commission, so for friendship's sake my Nikolai throws up the University and deserts his old father to go into the army. And to think there was a place and everything waiting for him in the Archives! There's friendship for you, eh?' said the count inquiringly.

'Yes, they say war has been declared,' remarked the visitor.

'They have been saying so for a long while,' replied the count, 'and they will say so again, and again after that, and that will be the end of it. My dear, there's friendship for you,' he repeated. 'He is going to join the Hussars.'

The visitor, not knowing what reply to make, shook her head.

'It is not out of friendship at all,' declared Nikolai, flaring up and spurning the accusation as though it were a shameful aspersion. 'It is not from friendship at all but simply because I feel that the army is my vocation.'

He glanced at his cousin and at the visitor's daughter, who were both looking at him with smiles of approbation.

'Colonel Schubert of the Pavlograd Hussars is dining with us today. He has been here on leave and is taking Nikolai back with him. What am I to say?' asked the count, shrugging his shoulders and speaking jestingly of a matter that had evidently occasioned him no little pain.

'I have already told you, papa,' said his son, 'that if you do not wish to let me go, I'll stay. But I know I am no use anywhere except in the army. I am not a diplomatist, or a government clerk – I'm not clever at disguising my feelings,' and as he spoke he kept glancing with the flirtatiousness of a handsome youth at Sonya and the young visitor.

The little kitten, feasting her eyes on him, seemed ready at a moment's notice to start her gambolling and display her kittenish nature.

'Well, well, very well!' said the old count. 'How he flares up at once! This Bonaparte has turned all their heads. They are all thinking of how he rose from ensign to emperor. Well, good luck to them,' he added, not noticing his visitor's amused expression.

While their elders began discussing Bonaparte, Julie Karagin turned to young Rostov.

'What a pity you weren't at the Arharovs' on Thursday. I missed you,' she said, smiling softly at him.

Flattered, the young man drew his chair closer to her with a flirtatious look and engaged the smiling Julie in a confidential conversation, entirely oblivious that his unconscious smile had stabbed the heart of Sonya, who flushed and tried to force a smile. In the midst of talking he glanced round at her. She gave him a passionate angry look and, scarcely able to hold back her tears and maintain the artificial

smile on her lips, she got up and left the room. All Nikolai's animation vanished. He waited for the first pause in the conversation and
then with a distressed face walked out of the room to find Sonya.

'How all these young people wear their hearts on their sleeves!'
remarked Anna Mihalovna, nodding in the direction of the departing
Nikolai. 'Cousinhood's a dangerous relationship,' she added.

'Yes,' said the countess, when the sunshine the young people had
brought into the room with them had disappeared. And then, as
though she were answering a question which no one had put but
which was constantly in her mind: 'How much suffering, how much
worry we go through before we can at last rejoice in them. And even
now there is really more anxiety than joy. One is apprehensive the
whole time, always apprehensive! This is the most perilous age for
girls as well as for boys.'

'It all depends on their upbringing,' said the visitor.

'Yes, you are right,' continued the countess. 'So far I have always,
thank God, been my children's friend and enjoyed their full confidence,' she declared, repeating the mistake of so many parents who
imagine that their children have no secrets from them. 'I know I shall
always be first in my daughters' confidence, and that if my dear
Nikolai with his impetuous nature does get into mischief (boys will
be boys), at any rate he will not behave like those Petersburg young
gentlemen.'

'Yes, they are splendid children, splendid,' confirmed the count,
who always settled all perplexing questions by finding everything
splendid. 'Just fancy – insisting on getting into the Hussars! What's
one to do, my dear?'

'What a charming creature your younger girl is!' said the visitor.
'Like a little bit of quicksilver!'

'Yes, that she is,' said the count. 'Takes after me! And what a voice
she has! Though she's my daughter, I dare to say that she'll be a
singer, a second Salomoni. We have engaged an Italian master to
teach her.'

'Isn't she too young still? I have heard it spoils the voice to train it
at that age.'

'Oh no, why should it be too soon!' replied the count. 'Didn't our
mothers get married at twelve or thirteen?'

'And she's in love with Boris already! What do you think of that!'
said the countess, looking at Boris's mother with a gentle smile, and

continued, evidently concerned with a thought that was always in her mind, 'Now you see, if I were to be too strict with her and forbid her ... goodness knows what they might get up to behind my back' (the countess meant that they might kiss in secret), 'but as it is I know every word she utters. She will come running to me of her own accord in the evening and tell me everything. Perhaps I spoil her, but really I believe it's the best way. I was stricter with her sister.'

'Yes, I was brought up quite differently,' remarked the elder daughter, the handsome Countess Vera, with a smile.

But the smile did not enhance Vera's beauty as smiles generally do: on the contrary it gave her face an unnatural and therefore unpleasing expression. Vera was good-looking, far from stupid, quick at learning, was well bred and had a pleasant voice. What she said was right and proper enough, yet, strange to say, everyone – countess and visitors alike – turned to look at her as if wondering why she had said it, and they all felt awkward.

'People are always too clever with their elder children: they try to make something exceptional of them,' said the visitor.

'What's the good of denying it, *ma chère*? Our dear countess tried to be too clever with Vera,' said the count. 'Well, what of that? She has turned out splendidly all the same,' he added, with a wink of approval to Vera.

The guests got up and took their leave, promising to return to dinner.

'What manners! I thought they were never going,' said the countess, when she had seen her visitors to the door.

10

WHEN Natasha ran out of the room she only went as far as the conservatory. There she paused and stood listening to the conversation in the drawing-room, waiting for Boris to come out. She was already beginning to grow impatient, and stamped her foot, on the verge of crying because he did not come at once, when she heard the young man's discreet steps, approaching neither too slowly nor too quickly. Natasha hastily flung herself among the flower-tubs and hid.

Boris paused in the middle of the conservatory, looked round, flicked a speck of dust from the sleeve of his uniform and going up to a mirror examined his handsome face. Natasha, not moving, peered out from her hiding-place, waiting to see what he would do. He stood for a little while in front of the glass, smiled and walked towards the opposite door. Natasha was on the point of calling to him but changed her mind. 'Let him look for me,' she said to herself. Boris had hardly left the conservatory before Sonya, flushed and in tears, came in at the other door, talking angrily to herself. Natasha restrained her first impulse to run out to her, and stayed in her hiding-place, watching (as though she wore a cap that made her invisible) what went on in the world. She was experiencing a novel and peculiar sort of enjoyment. Sonya, still murmuring to herself, kept looking round towards the door of the drawing-room. It opened and Nikolai made his appearance.

'Sonya, what is the matter? How can you?' said Nikolai, running up to her.

'Nothing, nothing; leave me alone!' sobbed Sonya.

'No, I know what it is.'

'Well, if you do, so much the better, and you can go back to her!'

'So-o-onya! Listen! How can you torture me and yourself like that over a mere fancy?' said Nikolai, taking her hand.

Sonya did not pull her hand away, and she left off crying.

Natasha, not stirring and scarcely breathing, watched from her hiding-place with sparkling eyes. 'What will happen now?' she wondered.

'Sonya, the whole world is nothing to me. You are my all,' said Nikolai. 'I'll prove it to you.'

'I don't like it when you talk like that.'

'Well then, I won't. Only forgive me, Sonya!' He drew her to him and kissed her.

'Oh, how nice,' thought Natasha; and when Sonya and Nikolai had left the conservatory she followed and called Boris to her.

'Boris, come here,' said she, with her face full of mischievous meaning. 'I want to tell you something. Here, come here!' and she led him into the conservatory, to the place among the tubs where she had been hiding.

Boris followed, smiling.

'What is the *something*?' he asked.

She grew confused, glanced round and seeing the doll she had thrown on one of the tubs picked it up.

'Kiss the doll,' said she.

Boris looked down with an attentive, friendly expression into her eager face, and made no reply.

'Don't you want to? Well, then, come here,' she said, and went deeper among the plants, tossing away the doll. 'Closer, closer!' she whispered. She seized the young officer by his cuffs, and a solemn, scared look appeared on her face.

'Then would you like to kiss me?' she whispered almost inaudibly, peeping up at him from under her brows, smiling and almost crying with agitation.

Boris reddened.

'How absurd you are!' he said, bending down to her and blushing still more but waiting and making no advance.

Suddenly she jumped up on to a tub, so that she stood taller than he, flung her thin little bare arms round him above his neck and, tossing back her curls, kissed him full on the lips.

Then she slipped down among the flower-pots on the other side of the tubs and stood, hanging her head.

'Natasha,' he said, 'you know that I love you, but ...'

'Are you in love with me?' Natasha interrupted him.

'Yes, I am, but please don't let us do this again. ... In another four years ... Then I shall ask for your hand.'

Natasha considered.

'Thirteen, fourteen, fifteen, sixteen,' she counted on her slender little fingers. 'All right! Then it's settled?' And her excited face beamed with a smile of delight and relief.

'Settled!' replied Boris.

'For ever and ever?' said the little girl. 'Till we die?'

And taking his arm, and with a happy face, she walked quietly beside him into the adjoining sitting-room.

II

THE countess was now so tired after receiving visitors that she gave orders not to admit anyone else, but the hall-porter was told to ask all further callers to be sure and return to dinner. The countess was longing for a *tête-à-tête* with the friend of her childhood, Princess Anna Mihalovna, whom she had not seen properly since her return from Petersburg. Anna Mihalovna, with her tear-worn, pleasant face, drew her chair nearer to the countess's.

'With you I will be quite frank,' said Anna Mihalovna. 'There are not many of us old friends left! That is why I value your friendship so.'

Anna Mihalovna looked at Vera and paused. The countess pressed her friend's hand.

'Vera,' she said to her elder and obviously not her favourite daughter, 'how is it you have no notion about anything? Can't you see that you are not wanted? Go and join your sister, or ...'

The handsome Vera smiled disdainfully, evidently not in the least mortified.

'If you had told me sooner, mamma, I should have gone immediately,' she replied as she rose to go to her own room.

But as she was passing through the sitting-room she noticed the two couples, a pair in each window-seat, and stopped to smile satirically. Sonya was sitting close up to Nikolai, who was copying out some verses for her, the first he had ever written. Boris and Natasha were at the other window and ceased talking when Vera came in. Sonya and Natasha looked up at Vera with guilty, happy faces.

It was both amusing and touching to see these two little girls so head over ears in love, but apparently the sight of them roused no pleasant feelings in Vera.

'How many times have I asked you not to touch my things,' she said. 'You have a room of your own,' and she took the inkstand from Nikolai.

'Just a minute, just a minute,' said he, dipping his pen in.

'You always succeed in doing things at the wrong time,' continued Vera. 'Just now you came tearing into the drawing-room so that everyone was ashamed of you.'

In spite or perhaps in consequence of the truth of her remark no one replied, and the four simply looked at one another. She lingered in the room with the inkstand in her hand.

'And what secrets can you have at your age, Natasha and Boris, or you two? It's all nonsense!'

'Now what does it matter to you, Vera?' said Natasha in defence, speaking very gently.

She was evidently even more than usually sweet and well-disposed to everyone that day.

'It is very silly,' said Vera. 'I am ashamed of you. Secrets indeed!...'

'Everyone has secrets. We don't interfere with you and Berg,' answered Natasha, beginning to get angry.

'I should think not,' said Vera, 'because there could never be any harm in anything I do. But I shall tell Mamma how you behave with Boris.'

'Natalia Ilyinishna behaves very well with me,' said Boris. 'I have nothing to complain of.'

'Stop, Boris, you are such a diplomat' – the word 'diplomat' was much in vogue among the children, who attached a special meaning to it – 'it is really tedious,' said Natasha in a hurt, trembling voice. 'Why is she always at me? You'll never understand, because you've never loved anyone,' she added, turning to Vera. 'You have no heart! You are just a Madame de Genlis,' (this nickname, which was considered very offensive, had been bestowed on Vera by Nikolai) 'and your greatest satisfaction is to make things unpleasant for people! Go and flirt with Berg as much as you like,' she finished quickly.

'Well, at all events, you won't see me running after a young man in the presence of visitors.'

'There now, she has gained her object!' interrupted Nikolai. 'Said something nasty to everyone and upset us all. Let's go to the nursery.'

All four rose like a flock of frightened birds and left the room.

'You said nasty things to me!' cried Vera. 'I never said a thing to anyone!'

'Madame de Genlis! Madame de Genlis!' shouted laughing voices through the door.

The handsome Vera, who had such an exasperating, unpleasant effect on everyone, smiled and, evidently unmoved by what had been said to her, went up to the glass and rearranged her sash and hair. Looking at her own handsome face she seemed to become colder and more composed than ever.

*

In the drawing-room the conversation continued.

'Ah, my dear,' said the countess, 'my life is not all roses either. Don't I see that if we go on at this rate our means can't last long? It's this club, and his easy-going nature. Even when we live in the country do we get any rest, with all the theatricals, hunting, shooting and heaven knows what else! But don't let us talk about me. Come, tell me how you managed it all? I often marvel at you, Annette – the way at your time of life you post off alone in a carriage, going to Moscow, to Petersburg, seeing all those ministers and important people and knowing how to deal with them all! I marvel at you! How in the world did you do it? I could never have managed it.'

'Ah, my love,' replied Princess Anna Mihalovna. 'God grant that you never know what it is to be left a helpless widow with a son you love to distraction! One learns a great many things then,' she went on with some pride. 'That lawsuit taught me much. When I wish to see one of the big-wigs I write a note: *Princess So-and-so desires an interview with Monsieur Un Tel*, and then I hire a cab and go two, three or four times, until I get what I want. I don't care what they think of me.'

'Well, tell me, whom did you interview for Boris?' asked the countess. 'Here's your boy an officer in the Guards, while my Nikolai is going as a cadet. There was no one to do anything for him. Whose help did you ask?'

'Prince Vasili's. He was most kind. Agreed to everything at once, and put the matter before the Emperor,' said Princess Anna Mihalovna enthusiastically, quite forgetting all the humiliation she had endured to gain her end.

'Prince Vasili, has he aged much?' inquired the countess. 'I have not seen him since we acted together in theatricals at the Rumyant-sevs', and I dare say he has forgotten me. He used to pay court to me in those days,' the countess recalled with a smile.

'He is just the same as ever,' replied Anna Mihalovna, 'amiable and overflowing with compliments. His head has not been turned at all. "I am only sorry that it is such a small thing to do for you, dear Princess. I am at your command," he said to me. Yes, he is a fine fellow and an extremely nice relation to have. But Nathalie, you know my love for my boy: there is nothing I would not do for his happiness. But my affairs are in such a bad way,' continued Anna Mihalovna sadly, lowering her voice, ' – such a bad way that I am in the most dreadful position. That wretched lawsuit is eating up my all, and making no progress. Would you believe it, I literally haven't a penny, and I don't know how I am going to get Boris his uniform.' She took out her handkerchief and began to cry. 'I must have five hundred roubles, and all I have is one twenty-five rouble note. I am in such straits. ... My only hope now is Count Kirill Vladimirovich Bezuhov. If he will not come forward to help his godson – he is Bory's godfather, you know – and make him some sort of allowance for his support, all my trouble will be thrown away. ... I shall not be able to equip him.'

The countess's eyes filled with tears and she pondered in silence.

'I often think,' said the princess, 'maybe it's a sin but I often think: There's Count Kirill Vladimirovich Bezuhov all alone ... that enormous fortune ... and what is he living for? Life's a burden to him, while Bory's life is just beginning.'

'Surely he will leave something to Boris,' said the countess.

'Heaven only knows, my dear! These rich grandees are such egoists. However, I shall take Boris and go and see him this minute and tell him straight out how things are. People may think what they choose of me, it is really all the same to me when my son's fate depends on it.' The princess rose. 'It is now two o'clock and you dine at four. I shall just have time.'

And in the manner of a practical Petersburg lady who knows how to make the best use of her time Anna Mihalovna sent for her son and with him went out into the ante-room.

'Good-bye, dearest,' said she to the countess, who accompanied her to the door, and added in a whisper so that her son should not hear, 'Wish me luck.'

'Are you going to Count Kirill Vladimirovich, my dear?' said the count coming out of the dining-room into the hall. 'If he is better, ask Pierre to come and dine with us. He used to come here and dance with the children, you know. Be sure to invite him, my dear. We will see how Tarass distinguishes himself today. He tells me Count Orlov never gave such a dinner as we are having today.'

12

'MY dear Boris,' said Princess Anna Mihalovna to her son as Countess Rostov's carriage in which they were seated drove along the straw-covered street and turned into the wide courtyard of Count Kirill Vladimirovich Bezuhov's house. 'My dear Boris,' said the mother, drawing her hand from beneath her old mantle and laying it timidly and tenderly on her son's arm, 'be affectionate and attentive to him. Count Kirill Vladimirovich is your godfather, after all, and your future depends on him. Remember that, my dear, and be nice to him, as you so well know how ...'

'If only I knew that anything would come of this except humiliation ...' replied her son coldly. 'However, I promised you, and I will do it for your sake.'

Though there was a visiting carriage standing at the steps, the hall-porter, after scrutinizing mother and son (who without asking to be announced had walked straight through the glass vestibule between the two rows of statues in niches) and eyeing the lady's threadbare mantle, asked whether they wished to see the princesses or the count, and hearing that they wanted the count he told them that his Excellency was worse and was not receiving anyone that day.

'We may as well go back,' said the son in French.

'My dear!' exclaimed his mother imploringly, again laying her hand on his arm, as if the touch might pacify or inspire him.

Boris said no more and looked inquiringly at his mother, without taking off his cloak.

'My good man,' said Anna Mihalovna ingratiatingly, addressing the hall-porter, 'I know Count Kirill Vladimirovich is very ill ... that is why I have come ... I am a relative of his ... I shall not disturb him, my good man ... I need only see Prince Vasili Sergeyevich: he is staying here, is he not? Kindly announce us.'

The hall-porter sullenly pulled the cord of a bell that rang upstairs, and turned away.

'Princess Drubetskoy to see Prince Vasili Sergeyevich,' he called to a footman in knee-breeches, slippers and a swallow-tail coat who ran to the head of the stairs and looked over from above.

The mother smoothed the folds of her dyed silk gown, glanced at herself in the massive Venetian mirror on the wall and briskly mounted the carpeted staircase in her down-at-heel shoes.

'My dear, you promised me,' she said to her son again, encouraging him with a touch of her hand.

The son, with eyes lowered, followed submissively after her.

They entered the large hall, one of the doors of which led to the apartments that had been assigned to Prince Vasili.

Just as the mother and son reached the middle of the hall and were about to ask the way of an elderly footman who had sprung to his feet at their approach, the bronze doorknob of one of the doors turned, and Prince Vasili, dressed in a velvet house jacket with a single star on his breast, came out, accompanying a handsome man with black hair. This was the celebrated Petersburg Doctor Lorrain.

'There is no doubt, then?' the prince was saying.

'Prince, *errare humanum est* – to err is human – but ...' replied the doctor, rolling his r's and pronouncing the Latin words with a French accent.

'Very well, very well. ...'

Seeing Anna Mihalovna and her son, Prince Vasili dismissed the physician with a bow and silently but with a look of inquiry came forward to meet them. The son noticed that an expression of profound grief suddenly appeared in his mother's eyes, and he smiled slightly.

'Ah, prince, in what melancholy circumstances we meet again! Well, how is our dear invalid?' said she, as though unaware of the frigid, offensive look fixed on her.

Prince Vasili stared at her, then at Boris with a look of inquiry that amounted to perplexity. Boris bowed politely. Ignoring the bow, Prince Vasili turned to Anna Mihalovna, replying to her question by a movement of his head and lips indicating very little hope for the patient.

'Is it possible?' cried Anna Mihalovna. 'Oh, how terrible! It is dreadful to think. ... This is my son,' she added, introducing Boris. 'He was anxious to thank you in person.'

Boris again bowed politely.

'Believe me, prince, a mother's heart will never forget what you have done for us.'

'I am glad I was able to be of service to you, my dear Anna Mihalovna,' said Prince Vasili, adjusting his shirt frill, and in tone and manner portraying here in Moscow before Anna Mihalovna who was under an obligation to him an even more consequential air than he had at Petersburg at Anna Pavlovna's *soirée*.

'Try to do your duty in the service, and prove yourself worthy of it,' he added, addressing Boris with severity. 'I am delighted. ... Here on leave, are you?' he asked indifferently.

'I am awaiting orders to join my new regiment, your Excellency,' replied Boris, betraying neither resentment at the prince's disagreeable manner nor any desire to pursue the conversation, but speaking so quietly and respectfully that the prince fixed an appraising glance on him.

'Are you living with your mother?'

'I am living at Countess Rostov's,' said Boris, again adding, 'your Excellency.'

'That is, with Ilya Rostov, who married Nathalie Shinshin,' said Anna Mihalovna.

'I know, I know,' returned Prince Vasili in his monotonous voice.

'I have never been able to understand how Nathalie could make up her mind to marry that raw cub! A completely stupid, ridiculous fellow, and a gambler into the bargain, so they say.'

'But a very good sort, Prince,' observed Anna Mihalovna with an affecting smile, as though she too knew that Count Rostov merited this view of himself but would ask him not to be too hard on the poor old man.

'What do the doctors say?' inquired the princess after a pause, her careworn face again assuming an expression of deep distress.

'They give very little hope,' said the prince.

'And I should so much have liked to thank *Uncle* once more for all his kindness to me and to Boris. Boris is his godson,' she added, her tone suggesting that this piece of information ought to give Prince Vasili extreme satisfaction.

Prince Vasili thought this over and frowned. Anna Mihalovna saw that he was afraid of finding in her a rival for Count Bezuhov's fortune, and hastened to reassure him.

'If it were not for my genuine love and devotion to *Uncle*' – she let the word drop with peculiar assurance and unconcern – 'I know his character – noble, upright ... but with only the young princesses about him ... they are still young....' She inclined her head and continued in a whisper: 'Has he performed his final duties, prince? These last moments are so precious. He is as bad as he could be, it seems; it is absolutely necessary to prepare him, if he is so ill. We women, prince,' she smiled sweetly, 'always know how to put these things. I absolutely must see him, however painful it may be for me; but then I am accustomed to suffering.'

Evidently the prince understood, and saw too, just as he had at Annette Scherer's, that he would have no little difficulty in getting rid of Anna Mihalovna.

'Would not such an interview be too much of an ordeal *chère* Anna Mihalovna?' said he. 'Let us wait till this evening. The doctors are expecting the crisis.'

'But one cannot delay, prince, at such a moment! Just think, his soul's salvation is at stake.... Oh, the duties of a Christian are a terrible thing....'

The door from the inner rooms opened, and one of the princesses, the count's nieces, entered. She had a cold, forbidding face and a long body strikingly out of proportion to her short legs.

Prince Vasili turned to her.

'Well, how is he?'

'Still the same. And what can you expect, with this noise? ...' said the princess, surveying Anna Mihalovna as though she were a stranger.

'Ah, my dear, I hardly recognized you,' exclaimed Anna Mihalovna with a happy smile, ambling lightly up to the count's niece. 'I have just arrived, and am at your service to help in nursing *mon oncle*. I can imagine what you must have gone through,' she continued, speaking in French and sympathetically turning up her eyes.

The count's niece made no reply, nor did she even smile, but immediately left the room. Anna Mihalovna drew off her gloves and, entrenched as it were in an arm-chair, beckoned Prince Vasili to sit down beside her.

'Boris,' she said to her son with a smile, 'I shall go in to see the count, to poor uncle, but meanwhile you, my dear, had better go and find Pierre, and don't forget to give him the Rostovs' invitation. They ask him to dinner. I suppose he won't go?' she continued, turning to the prince.

'On the contrary,' replied the latter, plainly cast down, 'I should be only too glad if you would relieve me of that young man. He sticks on here. The count has not once asked for him.'

He shrugged his shoulders. A footman conducted Boris down one flight of stairs and up another to Pierre's room.

13

PIERRE had not had time to choose a career for himself in Petersburg before being banished and sent back to Moscow for disorderly conduct. The story told about him at the Rostovs' was true. Pierre had assisted in tying a policeman on to the back of a bear. He had now been in Moscow for some days and was staying as usual at his father's house. Though he expected, of course, that his escapade would already be known in Moscow and that the ladies surrounding his father – who were never favourably disposed towards him – would have taken advantage of it to put the count against him, he still on the day of his arrival went to his father's part of the house. Entering the drawing-room, where the princesses spent most of their time, he greeted the ladies, two of whom were sitting at their embroidery-frames, while the third read aloud from a book. It was the eldest – the one who had come out to Anna Mihalovna – who was reading: a neat, prim, long-waisted maiden lady. The two younger ones, both rosy-cheeked pretty little creatures exactly alike except that one had a little mole on her lip which made her much prettier, were busy with embroidery. Pierre was received like a man risen from the dead or stricken with the plague. The eldest princess paused in her reading and stared at him in silence with eyes of dismay; the younger one without the mole assumed precisely the same expression; while the youngest – with the mole – who had a gay and lively disposition bent over her frame to hide a smile evoked, no doubt, by the amusing scene she saw coming. She drew her embroidery wool down through the canvas and lent over, pretending to be studying the pattern, scarcely able to suppress her laughter.

'How do you do, cousin?' said Pierre. 'Don't you recognize me?'

'I recognize you only too well, far too well.'

'How is the count? Can I see him?' asked Pierre awkwardly as usual but unabashed.

'The count is suffering both physically and morally, and your only anxiety, it seems, has been to increase his sufferings.'

'Can I see the count?' repeated Pierre.

'H'm! ... If you want to be the death of him, to kill him outright, of course you can. Olga, go and see whether uncle's beef-tea is ready – it is almost time,' she added, thus giving Pierre to understand that they were busy, and busy seeing after his father's comfort, while he was evidently only busy upsetting him.

Olga left the room. Pierre stood still a moment, looked at the sisters and said with a bow:

'Then I will go to my rooms. You will let me know when I can see him.'

He went out, followed by the low but ringing laugh of the sister with the mole.

Next day Prince Vasili had arrived and taken up his quarters in the count's house. He sent for Pierre and said to him:

'My dear fellow, if you behave here as you did in Petersburg, you will come to a bad end. That is all I have to say to you. The count is very, very ill: you really must not go near him.'

After that Pierre had been left alone, and he spent his days in solitude in his apartments upstairs.

When Boris appeared at his door Pierre was pacing up and down the room, stopping occasionally in the corners to make threatening gestures at the wall, as if running a sword through an invisible enemy, and glaring savagely over his spectacles, before resuming his promenade, muttering indistinct words, shrugging his shoulders and gesticulating.

'England's day is over,' said he, scowling and pointing his finger at some imaginary auditor. 'Mr Pitt, as a traitor to his country and the rights of man, is sentenced ...' But before Pierre – who at that moment was imagining himself to be his hero Napoleon, in whose person he had already effected the dangerous crossing of the Channel and captured London – could pronounce Pitt's sentence, he saw a well-built and handsome young officer entering his room. Pierre stopped short. Boris was a lad of fourteen when he had last seen him, and Pierre did not recognize him at all, but in spite of that, in his usual impulsive, cordial way, he took Boris by the hand and smiled affably.

'Do you remember me?' asked Boris quietly with a pleasant smile. 'I have come with my mother to see the count but it appears he is not well.'

'Yes, he is ill, so it seems. They do not give him a minute's peace,' answered Pierre, trying to think who this young man might be.

Boris perceived that Pierre failed to recognize him but he did not consider it necessary to introduce himself, and without the slightest embarrassment looked Pierre full in the face.

'Count Rostov begs you to come and dine today,' said he after rather a long silence which made Pierre feel uncomfortable.

'Ah, Count Rostov!' exclaimed Pierre joyfully. 'Then you are his son, Ilya? Fancy, I didn't recognize you at first! Do you remember how we used to drive to Sparrow Hills with Madame Jacquot? ... Ages ago.'

'You are mistaken,' said Boris in leisurely fashion with an assured and slightly derisive smile. 'I am Boris, Princess Anna Mihalovna Drubetskoy's son. It is Count Rostov, the father, who is called Ilya, and his son's name is Nikolai. And I never knew any Madame Jacquot.'

Pierre shook his head and waved his arms as if a swarm of mosquitoes or bees had attacked him.

'Oh dear, what am I thinking about? I have got everything mixed up. One has so many relatives in Moscow! You are Boris ... to be sure. Well, now we know where we are. And what do you think of the Boulogne expedition? It will go pretty hard with the English if Napoleon gets across the Channel. I think the expedition quite possible. So long as Villeneuve doesn't make a mess of things!'

Boris knew nothing about the Boulogne expedition; he did not read the papers and this was the first time he had ever heard of Villeneuve.

'Here in Moscow we are more occupied with dinner-parties and scandal than with politics,' he said in his quiet, ironical tone. 'I know nothing about it and have not given it a thought. Moscow is mainly busy with tittle-tattle,' he continued. 'Just now they are talking about you and the count.'

Pierre smiled his good-natured smile, as if afraid for his companion's sake that the latter might say something he would afterwards regret. But Boris spoke with circumspection, clearly and drily, looking straight into Pierre's eyes.

'Moscow has nothing else to do but gossip,' he went on. 'Everybody is wondering to whom the count will leave his fortune, though who can say, he may outlive the lot of us, as I sincerely hope he will ...'

'Yes, it is all very sad,' interrupted Pierre, 'very sad.'

Pierre was still apprehensive lest this young officer should inadvertently let fall some remark disconcerting to himself.

'And it must seem to you,' said Boris, flushing slightly but not changing his tone or attitude, 'it must seem to you that everybody's one idea is to get something from the rich man.'

'Exactly,' thought Pierre.

'And that's just what I want to tell you, to prevent misunderstandings, that you will be greatly mistaken if you reckon me and my mother among such people. We are very poor but, anyhow as far as I am concerned, just because your father is rich I don't regard myself as his relation, and neither I nor my mother would ever ask anything or take anything from him.'

For a long time Pierre did not understand, but when he did he jumped up from the sofa, seized Boris under the elbow with characteristic impetuosity and clumsiness, and, blushing far more than Boris, began to speak with a mixture of shame and vexation.

'Well, this is strange! Do you suppose I ... indeed who could think? ... I know very well ...'

But Boris again interrupted him.

'I am glad to have spoken freely. Perhaps you dislike it. You must forgive me,' said he, trying to put Pierre at ease instead of being put at ease by him, 'but I hope I have not offended you. It is a principle with me to speak out. ... Well, what message am I to take? Will you come to dinner at the Rostovs'?'

And Boris, with an obvious sense of relief at having discharged an onerous duty, extricating himself from an awkward situation and placing somebody else in one, became completely charming again.

'No, but I say,' said Pierre, regaining his composure, 'you are an amazing fellow! What you have just said is first-rate, first-rate. Of course you don't know me. We haven't seen each other for such a long time ... not since we were children. You might have thought I ... I understand you, understand you perfectly. I should never have done it, I should not have had the courage, but it's splendid. I am very glad to know you. A queer idea,' he added after a short pause, and smiling – 'a queer idea you must have had of me.' He began to laugh. 'Well, what of it! We must get better acquainted, I beg of you.' He pressed Boris's hand. 'Do you know, I have not once been in to the count. He has not asked for me ... I am sorry for him, as a man, but what can one do?'

'So you think Napoleon will succeed in getting his army across?' asked Boris with a smile.

Pierre saw that Boris wanted to change the subject and being of the same mind began to expound the advantages and disadvantages of the Boulogne expedition.

A footman came in to summon Boris to his mother – the princess was going. Pierre, in order to see more of Boris, promised to come to dinner and shook hands warmly, looking affectionately through his spectacles into Boris's eyes.

After Boris had gone, Pierre continued to walk up and down the room for some time, no longer piercing an imaginary foe with his sword but smiling at the recollection of that likeable, intelligent and resolute young man.

As often happens with young people, especially if they are leading a lonely existence, he felt an unaccountable affection for this youth and promised himself that they should become good friends.

Prince Vasili escorted the princess to the door. She was holding a handkerchief to her eyes, and her face was tearful.

'It is dreadful, dreadful!' she was saying. 'But whatever the cost, I shall do my duty. I will come back tonight and sit up with him. He can't be left like this. Every minute is precious. I can't think what the princesses are waiting for. God willing, I may perhaps find a way of preparing him! ... Adieu, prince! May God support you. ...'

'Good-bye, my dear,' replied Prince Vasili, turning away from her.

'Oh, he is in a dreadful state,' said the mother to her son when they were back in the carriage. 'He scarcely recognizes anyone.'

'I can't make out, mamma – what are his feelings towards Pierre?' asked the son.

'The will will make everything clear, my dear; our fate, too, hangs upon it ...'

'But what makes you think he will leave us anything?'

'Ah, my dear! He is so rich, and we are so poor!'

'Well, that's hardly a sufficient reason, mamma.'

'Oh, Heaven, how ill he is, how ill he is!' exclaimed the mother.

14

AFTER Anna Mihalovna had driven off with her son to visit Count Kirill Vladimirovich Bezuhov, Countess Rostov sat for a long time all alone, applying her handkerchief to her eyes. At last she rang.

'What is the matter with you, my dear?' she demanded crossly of the maid, who had kept her waiting a few minutes. 'Don't you care for attending on me, eh? I'll put you to other work, if that is the case.'

Her friend's anxieties and humiliating poverty had upset the countess and so she felt out of temper, a state of mind which always found expression in such remarks to her maid.

'I am very sorry, ma'am,' the girl apologized.

'Ask the count to come here.'

The count came waddling in to see his wife, looking, as usual, rather guilty.

'Well, my little countess! What a *sauté* of a game *au madère* we are going to have, *ma chère*! I've tried it; Tarass is well worth the thousand roubles I gave for him. It was money well spent.'

He sat down by his wife, jauntily planting his elbows on his knees, and ruffling up his grey hair.

'What are your commands, my little countess?'

'It's this, my dear – How did you get that stain there?' she said, pointing to his waistcoat. 'It's some of your *sauté*, no doubt,' she added with a smile. 'Well, you see, count, I want some money.'

Her face grew mournful.

'Oh, little countess!' ... And the count began fiddling to get out his pocket-book.

'I want a good deal, count! I want five hundred roubles.' And taking her cambric handkerchief she began to rub at her husband's waistcoat.

'You shall have it at once. Hey, there!' he shouted, as men only shout who are certain that those they summon will rush headlong to obey. 'Send Mitenka to me!'

Mitenka, a man of good family who had been brought up in the count's house and now had charge of all his affairs, stepped softly into the room.

'Listen, my dear boy,' said the count to the young man who came up respectfully. 'Bring me' – he thought for a moment – 'yes, bring me seven hundred roubles, yes. But mind, not tattered, dirty notes like last time but nice clean ones, for the countess.'

'Yes, Mitenka, clean ones, please,' said the countess, sighing deeply.

'When does your Excellency desire me to get them?' asked Mitenka. 'I must inform your Excellency ... However, do not be uneasy,' he added, perceiving that the count was already beginning to breathe heavily and rapidly, which was an unfailing sign of approaching wrath. 'I was forgetting ... Do you wish to have the money at once?'

'Yes, yes, that's right, bring it now. Give it to the countess.'

'What a treasure that Mitenka is,' added the count with a smile, when the young man had left the room. 'He doesn't know the meaning of the word "impossible". That's a thing I cannot stand. Everything is possible.'

'Ah, money, count, money! How much sorrow it causes in the world!' said the countess. 'But I am in great need of this sum.'

'You, my little countess, are a notorious spendthrift,' said the count, and having kissed his wife's hand he went back to his study.

When Anna Mihalovna returned from her visit to Bezuhov the money, all in crisp new notes, was lying ready under a handkerchief on the countess's little table, and Anna Mihalovna noticed that something was agitating the countess.

'Well, my dear?' asked the countess.

'Oh, what a terrible state he is in! One would not recognize him, he is so bad, so ill. I only stayed a minute, and did not say two words.'

'Annette, for heaven's sake don't refuse me,' the countess began suddenly, with a blush that looked strangely incongruous on her thin, dignified, elderly face, as she took the money out from under the handkerchief.

Anna Mihalovna instantly guessed what was coming and stooped to be ready to embrace the countess gracefully at the appropriate moment.

'This is for Boris from me, for his equipment. ...'

Anna Mihalovna was already embracing her and weeping. The countess wept too. They wept because they were friends, and because they were warm-hearted, and because they – friends from childhood – should have to think about anything so sordid as money, and because their youth was over. ... But the tears of both were sweet to them.

15

COUNTESS ROSTOV, with her daughters and already a considerable number of guests, was sitting in the drawing-room. The count had taken the gentlemen into his study and was showing them his choice collection of Turkish pipes. From time to time he would go out to inquire: 'Hasn't she come yet?' They were waiting for Maria Dmitrievna Ahrosimov, known in society as *le terrible dragon*, a lady distinguished not for her fortune or rank but for her direct mind and frank, unconventional behaviour. Maria Dmitrievna was known to the Imperial family as well as to all Moscow and Petersburg, and both capitals, while they marvelled at her, laughed up their sleeves at her brusqueness and told good stories about her; but at the same time everyone respected and feared her.

In the count's room, full of tobacco-smoke, the conversation turned on the war, which had just been announced by a manifesto, and on the subject of recruiting. As yet no one had read the manifesto, though all were aware of its appearance. The count was sitting on an ottoman couch with two of his guests smoking and talking on either side of him. He himself was neither smoking nor talking but with his head cocked first one way and then the other watched the smokers with evident satisfaction and listened to the arguments of his two neighbours, whom he had egged on against each other.

One of them was a sallow, clean-shaven civilian with a thin, wrinkled face, already advanced in years though dressed like a young man in the height of fashion. He sat with his legs up on the ottoman, as though he were at home, and having stuck the amber stem of his pipe far into the side of his mouth was spasmodically inhaling smoke and screwing up his eyes. This was an old bachelor, Shinshin, a cousin of the countess, famed in Moscow drawing-rooms for his biting tongue. He seemed supercilious as he talked to his companion, a fresh, rosy officer of the Guards, irreproachably groomed and buttoned, who held his amber mouth-piece in the middle of his handsome mouth, gently inhaling the smoke and letting it escape through his red lips in rings. This was Lieutenant Berg, an officer in the Semeonovsk regiment with whom Boris was to travel to join the army and concerning whom Natasha had teased her elder sister Vera, calling him her 'intended'. The count was sitting between these two, listening closely. His favourite occupation, next to playing boston, a card game of which he was very fond, was that of listener, especially when he succeeded in starting two good talkers on the opposite sides of an argument.

'Well then, old chap, *mon très honorable* Alphonse Karlovich,' said Shinshin, laughing ironically and mixing the most colloquial Russian expressions with exquisite French phrases (which lent peculiarity to his speech), 'you reckon you'll get an income from the Government, and your idea is to make a little something out of your company too ?'

'Not at all, Piotr Nikolayevich, I only want to show that the advantages of serving in the cavalry are few as compared with the infantry. Just consider my own position now, Piotr Nikolayevich.'

Berg always spoke quietly, politely and with extreme precision. His conversation invariably related entirely to himself: he always preserved a serene silence when a topic arose which was of no direct personal interest. He could remain silent for hours without feeling or causing others to feel the slightest embarrassment. But as soon as the conversation touched him personally he would begin to talk at length and with visible satisfaction.

'Consider my position, Piotr Nikolayevich: if I were in the cavalry I should not get more than a couple of hundred roubles every four months, even with the rank of lieutenant; while as it is I get two hundred and thirty,' said he, beaming happily at Shinshin and the count as though he had no doubt that his success must always be the chief desire of everyone else.

'Moreover, Piotr Nikolayevich, by transferring to the Guards I shall be to the fore,' pursued Berg. 'Vacancies occur so much more frequently in the Foot Guards. Then just think what can be done with two hundred and thirty roubles. I can even put a little aside, as well as sending to my father,' he went on, puffing out a smoke ring.

'True ... A German knows how to skin a flint, as the proverb says,' remarked Shinshin, shifting his pipe to the other side of his mouth and winking at the count.

The count chuckled. The other guests, seeing that Shinshin was in the vein, gathered round to listen. Berg, oblivious of irony or indifference, proceeded to explain how by transferring into the Guards he had already gained a step on his old comrades of the Cadet Corps; how in time of war the captain might get killed and he, as senior in the company, might easily succeed to the command; how popular he was with everyone in the regiment and how pleased his father was with him. Berg was evidently enjoying himself, and did not seem to suspect that other people also had their own interests. But all that he said was so prettily sedate, the naïveté of his youthful egotism so obvious, that he disarmed his hearers.

'Ah well, my boy, you will get on whether you are in the infantry or cavalry – that I'll warrant,' said Shinshin, patting him on the shoulder, and taking his feet off the ottoman.

Berg smiled with self-satisfaction. The count, followed by his guests, went into th e drawing-room.

*

It was that interval just before dinner when the assembled guests, expecting the summons to the dining-room, avoid embarking on any lengthy conversation; while they feel it incumbent on them to move about and say something, in order to show that they are in no wise impatient to sit down to table. The host and hostess look towards the door, and now and then exchange glances, while the visitors try to guess from these glances whom or what they are waiting for – is it some belated influential connexion, or a dish that is not quite done?

Pierre arrived just before the hour for dinner and awkwardly sat down in the middle of the drawing-room, on the first chair he came across, blocking the way for everyone. The countess tried to make him talk but he went on naïvely looking about through his spectacles, as though in search of somebody, answering all her inquiries in mono-

67

syllables. He was being very difficult, and he was the only person who did not notice the fact. Most of the guests, knowing of the affair with the bear, turned curious eyes on this big, stout, quiet-looking man, wondering how such an indolent, unassuming creature could have played such a prank on a policeman.

'You have only lately arrived in Moscow ?' the countess asked him.

'*Oui, madame,*' replied he, glancing round.

'You have not seen my husband yet ?'

'*Non, madame.*' He smiled quite inappropriately.

'You have been in Paris recently, I believe ? It must have been very interesting.'

'Very interesting.'

The countess exchanged glances with Anna Mihalovna, who realized that she was being asked to take charge of the young man, and crossing to a seat by his side she began to speak about his father; but, just as with the countess, he answered only in monosyllables. The other guests were all busily talking among themselves.

'The Razumovskys … It was delightful … You are very kind … Countess Apraksin …' were the broken phrases heard on all sides. The countess rose and went into the ante-room.

'Maria Dmitrievna ?' she was heard to ask there.

'Herself,' came the answer in a harsh female voice, and Maria Dmitrievna entered the room.

All the unmarried ladies and even the married ones, with the exception of the very oldest, rose. Maria Dmitrievna paused at the door. A woman of fifty, tall and stout, she wore her grey hair in ringlets and held her head erect. Under the pretext of turning back and adjusting the wide sleeves of her dress, she stood surveying the guests. Maria Dmitrievna always spoke in Russian.

'Health and happiness to our dear one whose name-day it is, and to her children,' she said in her loud, deep voice which drowned all other sounds. 'Well, you old sinner,' she went on, addressing the count who was kissing her hand, 'bored to tears in Moscow, I daresay ? No chance to go shooting with the dogs ? But what is to be done, old friend, these nestlings will grow up,' and she waved a hand towards the girls. 'You must look for husbands for them, whether you like it or not.

'Well, and how's my Cossack ?' she went on. (Maria Dmitrievna always called Natasha a Cossack.) And she stroked the child's hair as

Natasha came up, gaily and not at all shy, to kiss her hand. 'I know she's a scamp of a girl but I'm fond of her all the same.'

She got out of her huge reticule a pair of ear-rings of pear-shaped precious stones and giving them to the blushing Natasha, beaming with birthday happiness, turned away at once and addressed herself to Pierre.

'Ho, ho, sir! Come here to me,' said she, assuming a soft, gentle voice. 'Come here, sir ...' and she tucked her sleeve up higher in an ominous manner.

Pierre approached, ingenuously looking at her through his spectacles.

'Come along, come along, sir! I was the only person to tell your father the truth when he was in high favour, and in your case it's a sacred duty.'

She paused. All held their breath, waiting for what was to come, feeling that this was but the prologue.

'A pretty fellow, I must say! A pretty fellow! ... His father lies on his death-bed and he amuses himself setting a policeman astride a bear! For shame, sir, for shame! It would be better if you went to the war.'

She turned away and gave her hand to the count, who could scarcely keep from laughing.

'Well, I suppose it is time we were at table, eh?' said Maria Dmitrievna.

The count led the way with Maria Dmitrievna, followed by the countess on the arm of a colonel of hussars, a man to be made much of since Nikolai was to travel in his company to join the regiment. Then came Anna Mihalovna with Shinshin. Berg offered his arm to Vera. The smiling Julie Karagin walked in with Nikolai. A string of other couples followed, stretching the length of the dining-hall, and last of all, one by one, came the children with their tutors and governesses. The footmen bustled about, chairs scraped, the orchestra in the gallery struck up, and the guests took their places. The strains of the count's household band were succeeded by the clatter of knives and forks, the voices of the company and the subdued tread of the waiters. At one end of the table the countess presided, with Maria Dmitrievna on her right and Anna Mihalovna on her left, and the other ladies of the party. At the opposite end sat the count with the hussar colonel on his left and Shinshin and the other male guests on his right. On one side midway down the long table were the young people: Vera next to Berg, Pierre and Boris together; and on the other side the children with their tutors and governesses. From behind the crystal decanters and fruit-epergnes the count peeped across at his wife and her tall cap with its pale blue ribbons, and zealously filled his neighbours' glasses, not forgetting his own. The countess in turn, without neglecting her duties as hostess, threw significant glances from behind the pine-apples at her husband, whose rubicund face and bald forehead struck her as all the more conspicuous against his grey hair. At the ladies' end there was a rhythmic murmur of conversation; at the men's end the voices grew louder and louder, and loudest of all was the colonel of hussars who ate and drank so much, growing more and more flushed, that the count was already holding him up as an example to the rest. Berg with a tender smile was telling Vera that love was an emotion not of earth but of heaven. Boris was informing his new friend Pierre of the names of the guests, while he exchanged glances with Natasha, who was sitting opposite. Pierre spoke little, examined the new faces and ate with a will. Of the two soups he chose *à la tortue*, and from the savoury patties to the game he did not let a single dish pass or refuse any of the wines which the butler offered him, mysteriously poking a bottle wrapped in a napkin over his neighbour's shoulder and murmuring: 'Dry Madeira' ... 'Hungarian' ... or 'Rhine wine'. Pierre held up a wine-glass at random out of the four crystal glasses engraved with the count's monogram that stood before each guest, and drank with relish, gazing with ever-increasing amiability at the company. Natasha, who sat opposite, was looking at Boris as girls of thirteen gaze at the boy they have just kissed for the first time and are in love with. Sometimes she let this same look fall on Pierre, and the funny lively little girl's expression made him want to laugh, he could not tell why.

Nikolai was seated at some distance from Sonya, beside Julie Karagin, and was talking to her again with the same involuntary smile. Sonya wore a company smile on her lips but she was obviously in agonies of jealousy; first she turned pale, then blushed, and strained her ears to hear what Nikolai and Julie were saying. The governess kept looking round uneasily, as if preparing to resent any slight to the children. The German tutor was trying to fix in his memory all the different courses, desserts, and wines, in order to write a detailed description of the dinner to his folks in Germany; and he was greatly mortified when the butler with the bottle wrapped in a napkin passed him over. He frowned, trying to make it appear that he did not want any of that wine but was affronted because no one would believe that he did not want it to quench his thirst, or out of greediness, but simply from a conscientious desire for knowledge.

16

AT the men's end of the table the talk was growing more and more animated. The colonel was telling them that the manifesto on the declaration of war had already appeared in Petersburg, and that he had seen a copy of it which had that day been delivered by courier to the commander-in-chief.

'And why the deuce should we have to fight Bonaparte?' exclaimed Shinshin. 'He has already stopped Austria's cackle. I fear it may be our turn next.'

The colonel was a stout, tall German of sanguinary temperament, evidently devoted to the service and patriotically Russian. He resented Shinshin's remark.

'For ze reason, my goot sir,' said he, mispronouncing every word, 'for ze reason zat ze Emperor knows zat. He says in ze manifesto zat he cannot fiew wiz indeeference ze danger treatening Russia and zat ze safety and dignity of ze Empire as vell as ze sanctity of her *alliances...*' he spoke this last word with particular emphasis as though it contained the whole essence of the matter. Then with the infallible memory for official matters that was characteristic of him he quoted from the preamble to the manifesto:

'... and the desire which constitutes the Emperor's sole and immutable aim – to establish peace in Europe on lasting foundations – have now decided him to move part of his army across the frontier in a fresh effort towards the attainment of that purpose.'

'Zat, my dear sir, is ze reason,' he concluded, emptying his glass of wine with dignity and looking round at the count for encouragement.

'Do you know the saying, "Cobbler, cobbler, stick to your last!"?' returned Shinshin, knitting his brows and smiling. 'It fits us to a T. Even Suvorov was hacked to pieces, and where are we to find a Suvorov nowadays, may I ask?' said he, continually dropping from Russian to French and back again.

'Ve must fight to ze last tr-r-op of our plood!' said the colonel, thumping the table; 'und ve must be villing to tie for our Emperor, and zen all vill be vell. And ve must argue as leedle as po-o-ossible ...' (he lingered particularly on the word *possible*), 'as leedle as po-o-ossible,' he finished up, again turning to the count. 'Zat is ze vay ve old hussars look at it. But vat is your opinion, young man and young hussar?' he added, addressing Nikolai, who forsook his fair companion when he heard the talk on the war, and was eyes and ears intent on the colonel.

'I entirely agree with you,' replied Nikolai, colouring as red as a poppy, twisting his plate round and moving his wine-glasses about with a face as desperate and determined as though he were exposed to great danger at that actual moment. 'I am convinced that we Russians must die or conquer,' said he, feeling as soon as the words were out of his mouth, as did the others, that they were too impassioned and vehement for the occasion and therefore embarrassing.

'What you just said was splendid,' sighed Julie, who was sitting next to him. Sonya trembled all over and blushed to the ears and behind her ears and down her neck and shoulders while Nikolai was speaking.

Pierre listened to the colonel's speech and nodded approvingly.

'That is well spoken,' said he.

'You're a true hussar, young man!' cried the colonel, thumping the table again.

'What are you making such a noise about over there?' Maria Dmitrievna's deep voice suddenly inquired from the opposite end. 'Why do you pound the table?' she demanded of the hussar. 'What are you getting so heated about, pray? Do you imagine you have got the French here?'

'I am speaking the truth,' replied the hussar with a smile.

'We are talking about the war,' cried the count down the table. 'My son's going, you see, Maria Dmitrievna, my son's going.'

'Well, I have four sons in the army but still I don't fret. It is all in God's hands. You may die in your bed, or God may bring you safely out of a battle,' said Maria Dmitrievna, her deep voice easily carrying the whole length of the room.

'That is so.'

And the conversation was confined once more, among the ladies at one end and the men at the other.

'You wouldn't dare ask,' said her little brother to Natasha. 'I know you won't.'

'Yes, I will,' replied Natasha.

Her face suddenly glowed with a gay and desperate resolution. She half rose from her chair, with a glance inviting Pierre, who sat opposite, to listen to what was coming, and turned to her mother.

'Mamma!' rang the clear childish voice down the length of the table.

'What is it?' asked the countess in dismay; but seeing by her daughter's face that it was only mischief she shook a finger at her sternly and nodded her head in warning.

There was a sudden silence.

'Mamma, what sweets are we going to have?' cried Natasha's voice even more clearly and deliberately.

The countess tried to look severe but could not. Maria Dmitrievna shook a fat finger at the child.

'Cossack!' she said threateningly.

Most of the guests, uncertain what to make of this sally, looked at the parents.

'You will see what I'll do to you!' said the countess.

'Mamma, tell me what sweets we are going to have?' repeated Natasha boldly, with saucy gaiety, confident that her prank would not be taken amiss.

Sonya and fat little Petya were doubled up with laughter.

'There, you see, I *did* ask,' whispered Natasha to her little brother and to Pierre, glancing at him again.

'Ice-cream, only you will not be allowed any,' said Maria Dmitrievna.

Natasha saw there was nothing to be afraid of and so she braved even Maria Dmitrievna.

'Maria Dmitrievna! What sort of ice-cream? I don't like ice-cream.'

'Carrot-ices.'

'No, what kind, Maria Dmitrievna? What kind?' she almost shrieked. 'I want to know!'

Maria Dmitrievna and the countess burst out laughing, and all the guests joined in. They all laughed, not at Maria Dmitrievna's repartee but at the incredible audacity and smartness of this little girl who had the pluck and wit to tackle Maria Dmitrievna in this fashion.

Natasha only desisted when she was told that there would be pine-apple ice. Before the ices champagne was served. The orchestra struck up again, the count kissed his 'little countess' and the guests rose to drink her health, clinking glasses across the table with the count, the children, and one another. Again the footmen bustled about, chairs scraped, and in the same order in which they had entered, but with faces a little more flushed, the company returned to the drawing-room and to the host's study.

17

THE card-tables were brought out, partners selected for boston, and the count's guests distributed themselves about the two drawing-rooms, the sitting-room and the library.

Having spread his cards out fanwise, the count with difficulty kept himself from dropping into his usual after-dinner nap, and laughed at everything. The young people, at the countess's suggestion, gathered round the clavier and the harp. Julie first, by general request, played a little air with variations on the harp, and then joined the other young ladies in begging Natasha and Nikolai, who were noted for their musical talent, to sing something. Natasha, though much flattered at being treated like a grown-up person, at the same time felt shy.

'What are we to sing?' she asked.

'*The Fountain*,' suggested Nikolai.

'Well, then, let's be quick. Boris, come over here,' said Natasha. 'But where is Sonya?'

She looked round and seeing that her cousin was not there flew off in search of her.

Running into Sonya's room and not finding her, Natasha made for the nursery but Sonya was not there either. Natasha concluded that she must be on the chest in the passage. The chest in the passage was the spot consecrated to the woes of the younger female generation in the Rostov household. And there in fact was Sonya, lying face down-wards on Nanny's dirty striped feather-bed on top of the chest, crumpling her gauzy pink dress beneath her. Hiding her face in her slender fingers, she was sobbing so convulsively that her bare little shoulders shook. Natasha's face, which had been so radiant all through her name–day, changed at once: her eyes grew fixed, then her throat contracted and the corners of her mouth drooped.

'Sonya! What is the matter ? ... What has happened ? ... Oo–oo! ...'

And Natasha's large mouth widened, making her look quite ugly, and she began to wail like a baby, without knowing why except that Sonya was crying. Sonya tried to lift her head to answer but could not and buried her face still deeper in the bed. Natasha wept, sitting on the blue-striped feather-bed and hugging her friend. With an effort Sonya sat up and began to wipe away her tears and explain.

'Nikolai is going away in a week, his ... papers ... have come ... he told me himself ... But I should not have cried for that ...' (she showed Natasha a sheet of paper she was holding in her hand; on it were verses written by Nikolai), 'I should not have cried for that but you can't ... no one can understand ... how good and noble he is!'

And she began to cry again at the thought of how good and noble he was.

'It's all right for you ... I'm not envious ... I love you, and Boris, too,' she went on, gaining a little composure. 'He is a dear fellow ... there are no obstacles in your way. But Nikolai is my cousin ... the archbishop himself would have to ... else it would be impossible. And then if Mamma's told ...' (Sonya looked on the countess as her mother, and called her so) ... 'she'll say that I am spoiling Nikolai's career, that I am heartless and ungrateful, while truly ... God is my witness ... '(she crossed herself) 'I love her so much, too, and all of you, only Vera ... Why is she like that ? What have I done to her ? I am so grateful to you all that I would gladly make any sacrifice, only I have nothing to sacrifice. ...'

Sonya could say no more and again she buried her face in her hands and the feather-bed. Natasha set about consoling her but it was clear from her expression that she understood the full seriousness of her friend's trouble.

'Sonya!' she exclaimed suddenly, as though she had surmised the true reason for her cousin's misery. 'I'm sure Vera said something to you after dinner ? She did, didn't she ?'

'Yes, Nikolai wrote these verses himself, and I copied some others, and she found them on my table and said she'd show them to Mamma, and she says I am ungrateful and that Mamma will never let him marry me, but that he'll marry Julie. You saw how he devoted himself to her the whole day. ... Oh, Natasha, why is it ? ...'

And she started to sob again, more bitterly than ever. Natasha lifted her up, hugged her and smiling through her tears began to comfort her.

'Sonya, don't you believe her, darling! Don't believe her! Remember what we were saying, you and I and Nikolai, after supper in the sitting-room the other evening? We settled the way it should all be: I forget now exactly how it was, but you know it all came out right and quite possible to arrange. Why, Uncle Shinshin's brother is married to his first cousin, and we are only second cousins. And Boris said there would be no difficulty at all. You know I told him all about it. And he is so clever and so good!' said Natasha. 'Don't cry, Sonya, my pet, my darling!' and she kissed her, laughing. 'Vera's spiteful, never mind her! And it will all come right and she won't say anything to Mamma. Nikolai will tell her himself, and he's never thought of Julie.'

And Natasha kissed her head. Sonya sat up, and the little kitten revived; its eyes danced and it seemed ready to lift its tail, drop down on its soft paws and begin playing with the ball of wool again as a kitten should.

'Do you think so?... Really and truly?' she asked, quickly smoothing her frock and hair.

'Really and truly,' answered Natasha, tucking back a crisp lock that had strayed from under her cousin's plaits.

And they both laughed

'Well, let's go and sing *The Fountain.*'

'Come along then.'

'You know, that fat Pierre who sat opposite me is so funny,' said Natasha, stopping suddenly. 'I feel so happy!'

And Natasha set off at a run along the passage.

Sonya, shaking off some down that clung to her dress and slipping the verses inside her bodice next to her bony little chest, speeded after Natasha down the passage into the sitting-room with light, joyous steps and face aglow. At the company's request the young people sang the quartette *The Fountain*, which charmed everyone. Then Nikolai sang a new song he had just learnt.

> On a soft night beneath the moon,
> How joyous to feel and to know
> *That in this world there is someone*
> *Whose thoughts are thinking of thee!*

Her lovely fingers are straying
O'er the golden strings of the harp
Making passionate harmonies
Call and call to thee!
A day or two, then Paradise ...
But thy love on her death bed lies!

He was hardly at the end before the young people began to get ready for dancing in the large hall, and the musicians were heard clearing their throats and shuffling in the gallery.

*

Pierre was sitting in the drawing-room, where Shinshin had engaged him, as a man recently returned from abroad, in a political discussion in which others joined but which bored Pierre. When the music struck up, Natasha came into the drawing-room and walking straight up to Pierre said, laughing and blushing:

'Mamma told me to ask you to come and dance.'

'I am afraid of upsetting the figures,' Pierre replied, 'but if you will be my teacher ...' And he offered his large arm to the slender little girl, bending down to her level.

While the couples were arranging themselves and the musicians tuning up, Pierre sat down with his little partner. Natasha was blissful: she was dancing with a *grown-up* man come from *abroad*. She was sitting in view of everyone and talking to him like a grown-up lady. In her hand was a fan which one of the ladies had given her to hold, and assuming quite the air of a society woman (heaven knows when and where she had learnt it), she talked to her partner, fanning herself and smiling over the fan.

'Dear, dear! Look at her now!' exclaimed the countess as she crossed the ballroom, pointing to Natasha.

Natasha coloured and laughed.

'What do you mean, mamma? Why do you say that? It's quite natural – why shouldn't I?'

*

In the midst of the third *écossaise* there was the sound of chairs being pushed back in the sitting-room, where the count and Maria Dmitrievna had been playing cards with the majority of the more distinguished and older guests. Stretching their limbs which were cramped after sitting still so long, and putting away purses and pocket-books, they entered the ballroom. First came Maria Dmitrievna and the count, both in high good humour. With playful ceremony the count curved his arm after the style of a ballet dancer, and gave it to Maria Dmitrievna. He drew himself up, his face brightened into a debonair smile, and as soon as they had danced the last figure of the *écossaise* he clapped his hands to the musicians and called up to the first violin:

'Simeon! Do you know the *Daniel Cooper?*'

This was the count's favourite dance that he had danced in his youth. (*Daniel Cooper* was really one of the figures in the *anglaise*.)

'Look at papa!' cried Natasha at the top of her voice, quite forget-ting that she was dancing with a grown-up partner. She bent her curly head over her knees and made the whole room ring with her laughter.

Everyone present was, in fact, looking with a smile of pleasure at the jolly little old gentleman beside the stately Maria Dmitrievna, who was taller than her partner. Arms beating time to the music, shoulders back, toes turned out and tapping gently, and a broad smile on his round face, he prepared the onlookers for what was to follow. As soon as the gay irresistible strains of *Daniel Cooper* were heard (with a swift rhythm like that of a peasant dance) every door of the ballroom was suddenly filled with men on one side and women on the other beaming all over their faces – the servants had come to watch their master making merry.

'Just look at the master! Soaring about like an eagle!' an old nurse said out loud in one of the doorways.

The count danced well and knew that he did, but his partner could not dance at all and had no wish to excel at it. She held her portly figure erect, with her sturdy arms hanging by her sides (she had handed her reticule to the countess). It was only her stern but comely face that entered into the dance. What was expressed by the whole rotund person of the count, in Maria Dmitrievna found expression only in her increasingly radiant smile and the puckering of her nose. But if the count, getting more and more into his stride, captivated the spectators by his light-footed agility and unexpectedly graceful capers, Maria Dmitrievna with the slightest of exertions in moving her shoulders or curving her arms, when they turned or marked time with their feet, excited no less enthusiasm because of the contrast, which everyone appreciated, with her size and usual severity of demeanour. The dance grew livelier and livelier. The other couples could not attract a moment's attention to themselves, and did not even try to. All eyes were fastened on the count and Maria Dmitrievna. Natasha kept pulling everyone by the sleeve or dress urging them to *look at papa!* though as it was they needed no telling. They never took their eyes off the couple. In the intervals of the dance the count, stopping for breath, waved and shouted to the musicians to play faster. Faster, faster, and faster, lightly, more lightly, and ever more lightly whirled the count, flying round Maria Dmitrievna, now on his toes now on his heels, until at last he swung his partner back to her place, executed the final *pas*, lifting one fat leg in the air behind, bowing his perspiring head, smiling and making a wide sweep with his right arm amid a thunder of applause and laughter led by Natasha. Both partners stood still, out of breath and wiping their faces with cambric handkerchiefs.

'That's the way we used to dance in our time, *ma chère*,' said the count.

'That *was* a *Daniel Cooper*!' exclaimed Maria Dmitrievna, drawing a long breath and tucking back her sleeves.

18

AT the same time as the sixth *anglaise* was being danced in the Rostovs' ballroom, and while the musicians were playing out of tune from sheer tiredness, and the weary servants, footmen and cooks were getting the supper, Count Bezuhov had his sixth stroke. The doctors pronounced him past all hope. The form of confession was read over the dying man, the sacrament administered and preparations made for the final anointing, and the house was full of the bustle and thrill of suspense usual in such circumstances. Outside, a crowd of undertakers waited at the gates, eagerly anticipating a good order for the count's funeral and dodging behind the carriages that drove up. The military governor of Moscow, who had been assiduous in sending aides-de-camp to inquire after the count, this evening came himself to bid a last farewell to the renowned grandee of Catherine's court, Count Bezuhov.

The magnificent reception-room was crowded. Everyone stood up respectfully when the governor, after half an hour alone with the dying man, came out, bowing slightly in acknowledgement of their salutations and endeavouring to escape as quickly as possible from the glances fixed on him by doctors, clergy and relatives of the family. Prince Vasili, who had grown thinner and paler during the last few days, accompanied him to the door, repeating something several times in an undertone.

Having escorted the governor, Prince Vasili sat down on a chair alone in the ball-room, crossing one leg high over the other, leaning his elbow on his knee and covering his eyes with his hand. After sitting like this for some time he rose, looking about him with frightened eyes, and made his way with unwonted hurry down the long corridor leading to the back of the house, to the apartments of the eldest princess.

Those who remained in the dimly-lighted reception-room talked among themselves in jerky whispers and relapsed into silence, looking round inquiringly or expectantly whenever the door that led into the sick-room creaked as someone went in or came out.

'The limits of human life,' said a little old man, an ecclesiastic of some sort, to a lady who had taken a seat beside him and was listening naïvely to his words, 'the limits of human life are determined, one may not live beyond them.'

'I wonder, is it not too late for the last anointing?' inquired the lady, adding his clerical title, and apparently having no opinion of her own on the point.

'Ah, madam, it is a great sacrament,' replied the priest, passing a hand over the thin grizzled strands of hair combed across his bald head.

'Who was that? Was it the military governor himself?' someone asked at the other end of the room. 'What a youthful-looking man!'

'Yes, and he's well over sixty. I hear the count no longer recognizes anyone. Were they going to give him the final anointing?'

'I knew someone who received the last sacrament seven times.'

The second niece came out of the sick-room, her eyes red from weeping, and sat down by Doctor Lorrain, who had arranged himself gracefully under a portrait of the Empress Catherine, leaning his elbow on a table.

'Beautiful!' said the doctor in answer to a remark about the weather. 'Beautiful weather, princess; besides, in Moscow it is like being in the country.'

'It is, indeed,' replied the princess with a sigh. 'So he may have something to drink?'

Lorrain considered.

'He has taken his medicine?'

'Yes.'

The doctor glanced at his watch.

'Then give him a glass of boiled water containing a pinch of cream of tartar.' With his slender fingers he indicated what was meant by a pinch.

'Dere has neffer been a gase,' a German doctor was saying to an aide-de-camp, 'vere a mahn liffed after de dird sdroke.'

'What a constitution he had!' remarked the aide-de-camp. 'And who will inherit his fortune?' he added in a whisper.

'It vill not go begging,' replied the German with a smile.

They all looked round again at the door, which creaked as the second princess went in with the drink which Lorrain had prescribed for the sick man. The German doctor went over to Lorrain.

'Do you t'ink he can last till morning?' he asked in French which he pronounced vilely.

Lorrain, pursing his lips, waved a severely negative finger in front of his nose.

'Tonight, at latest,' said he in a low voice, and moved away with a decorous smile of self-satisfaction at being able so clearly to diagnose and state the patient's condition.

Meanwhile Prince Vasili had opened the door into the princess's apartment.

It was almost dark in the room; only two tiny lamps burned before the icons and there was a pleasant scent of flowers and burnt pastilles. Small articles of furniture, chiffoniers, cabinets and little tables, filled the room. The white quilt of a high feather-bed was visible behind a screen. A small dog began to bark.

'Ah, is that you, *mon cousin*?'

She rose and smoothed her hair which was, as usual, so extraordinarily smooth that it might have been made of one piece with her skull, and varnished.

'What is it, has anything happened?' she asked. 'I live in continual dread.'

'No, there is no change. I only came to have a little talk with you, Katishe – about business,' said the prince, wearily sinking into the

chair she had just vacated. 'I say, how warm you have got the room!'
he remarked. 'Well, come and sit here: let us have a talk.'

'I thought perhaps something had happened?' said the princess, and
sitting down opposite the prince she prepared to listen, her face stony
and obdurate as ever. 'I was trying to get a nap, *mon cousin*, but it's
no good.'

'Well, my dear?' said Prince Vasili, taking her hand and bending it
downwards, a habit of his.

It was plain that this 'well?' referred to a number of things which
they both understood without naming them.

The princess, who had a thin erect body quite incongruously long
for her legs, looked straight at the prince with no sign of emotion in
her prominent grey eyes. Then she shook her head and glanced up
at the icons with a sigh. The gesture might convey grief and devotion,
or it might imply weariness and hope of a speedy respite. Prince
Vasili interpreted it as an expression of weariness.

'And what about me?' he said. 'Do you suppose it's any easier for
me? I am as played out as a post-horse, but still I must have a talk
with you, Katishe, and a very serious one.'

Prince Vasili paused, and his cheeks began to twitch nervously, first
on one side, then on the other, giving his face an unpleasant expression such as it never had when he was in company. His eyes, too, were
different from usual: at one moment they gleamed impudently sly,
at the next they looked round furtively.

The princess, holding the little dog on her lap with her thin bony
hands, gazed intently into Prince Vasili's eyes, but it was plain that
she was resolved not to be the first to break the silence, even though
she sat till morning.

'Don't you see, my dear princess and cousin, Katerina Semeonovna,'
pursued Prince Vasili, evidently having to brace himself to go on with
what he wanted to say, 'at such a moment as the present, one must
think of everything. One must think of the future, of all of you. ...
I love the three of you as if you were my own children; you know
that.'

The princess continued to regard him with the same dull unwaver-
ing eye.

'And then of course my family also has to be considered,' Prince
Vasili resumed, testily pushing back a little table and not looking at
her. 'You know, Katishe, that you three Mamontov sisters and my

wife are the count's only direct heirs. I know – I quite understand how painful it is for you to talk or think about such things. And it is no easier for me; but, my dear, I am getting on for sixty, I must be ready for anything. You know that I have sent for Pierre? The count pointed directly to his portrait, signifying that he wanted to see him.'

Prince Vasili looked inquiringly at the princess but could not make out whether she was considering what he had just said or merely staring at him.

'One thing, cousin, I never cease praying God to be merciful to him, and grant his noble soul a peaceful passage from this …'

'Yes, yes. of course,' interrupted Prince Vasili impatiently, rubbing his bald forehead and angrily pulling towards him the little table that he had just pushed away. 'But … in short the fact is … you yourself are aware that last winter the count made a will passing over his direct heirs and us, and bequeathing all his property to Pierre.'

'He has made many a will!' remarked the princess placidly. 'But Pierre can't be his heir. Pierre is illegitimate.'

'*Ma chère*,' said Prince Vasili suddenly, clutching the little table in his excitement and speaking more rapidly, 'but what if a letter has been written to the Emperor begging him to have Pierre declared legitimate? You understand that the count's services would make his petition carry weight?'

The princess smiled as people smile when they think they know more about the subject under discussion than those with whom they are talking.

'I will tell you another thing,' Prince Vasili went on, clasping her hand. 'That letter was written, though it was not despatched, and the Emperor has heard about it. The only question is – has it been destroyed or not? If not, then as soon as *all is over*,' and the prince sighed, thereby intimating what he meant by the words *all is over*, 'and the count's papers are opened, the will and the letter will be delivered to the Emperor, and the petition will certainly be granted. Pierre, as the legitimate son, will get everything.'

'What about our share?' demanded the princess, smiling ironically, as if anything were possible except that.

'Why, my poor Katishe, it is as clear as daylight! He will be the sole legal heir to everything and you won't get a penny. You must know, my dear, whether the will and letter were written, and whether they have been destroyed or not. And if they have somehow been overlooked, you must know where they are and ought to find them because …'

'What next!' interrupted the princess, smiling sardonically, with no change in the expression of her eyes. 'I am a woman and according to you all women are idiots, but I do know that an illegitimate son cannot inherit … *un bâtard!*' she added, as if the word *bastard* would effectively prove to Prince Vasili the invalidity of his argument.

'Well, really, Katishe, can't you understand? You are so intelligent, how is it you don't see that if the count has written a letter to the Emperor begging him to recognize Pierre as legitimate, it follows that Pierre will not be Pierre any longer but Count Bezuhov, and will then inherit everything under the will? And if the will and the letter are not destroyed, all you will have will be the consolation of knowing that you were dutiful and the rest of it. That's certain.'

'I know the will was made, but I also know that it is invalid; and it seems to me, *mon cousin*, that you take me for a perfect fool,' said the princess with the air women assume when they suppose they have said something clever and stinging.

'My dear Princess Katerina Semeonovna!' began Prince Vasili impatiently. 'I came here not to squabble with you but to talk about your own interests as with a kinswoman, a kind, good, true kinswoman. I tell you for the tenth time that if this letter and the will in Pierre's favour are among the count's papers, then you, my dear little friend, are not an heiress, nor are your sisters. If you don't believe me then believe an expert. I have just been talking to Dmitri Onufrich' (this was the family solicitor), 'and he says the same.'

At this a sudden alteration evidently took place in the princess's ideas; her thin lips grew white (though her eyes did not change) and her voice when she began to speak came in jerks which obviously surprised even her.

'That would be a fine thing!' said she. 'I never wanted anything and I don't now.'

She pushed the little dog off her lap and smoothed the folds of her dress.

'That's his gratitude – that's the recognition people get who have sacrificed everything for him!' she cried. 'Very nice! Excellent! I want nothing, prince.'

'Yes, but you are not alone. There are your sisters,' replied Prince Vasili. But the princess did not heed him.

'Yes, I have known it for a long time but I had forgotten ... I knew I had nothing to expect in this house except meanness, deceit, envy, intrigue, and ingratitude – the blackest ingratitude ...'

'Do you or do you not know where that will is?' asked Prince Vasili, his cheeks twitching more than ever.

'Yes, I was a fool! I still believed in people, cared for them and sacrificed myself. But only the base, the vile succeed! I know whose work this is!'

The princess started to her feet but the prince stayed her. She looked like one who has suddenly lost faith in the whole human race. She gave her relative a vicious glance.

'There is still time, my dear. You must remember, Katishe, that it was all done without thinking, in a moment of anger, of illness, and afterwards forgotten. Our duty, my dear, is to rectify his mistake, to ease his last moments by not letting him commit this injustice. We must not let him die feeling that he was making unhappy those who ...'

'Those who have sacrificed everything for him,' caught up the princess, who would have risen again but the prince still held her fast, 'though he never had the good sense to appreciate it. No, *mon cousin*,' she added with a sigh, 'I shall live to learn that in this world one can expect no reward, that in this world there is no such thing as honour or justice. In this world one has to be cunning and wicked.'

'Come, come now! Calm yourself. I know your good heart.'

'No, I have a wicked heart.'

'I know your heart,' repeated the prince. 'I prize your friendship and I could wish that you had as high an opinion of me. Don't upset yourself, and let us talk sensibly while there is still time – be it a day or be it but an hour. ... Tell me all you know about the will, and above all where it is: you must know. We will take it at once and show it to the count. No doubt he has forgotten all about it and will wish it to be destroyed. You understand that my sole desire is to carry out his wishes religiously; that is my only reason for being here – I came simply to be of use to him and you.'

'Now I see it all! I know who has been intriguing – I know who it is!' cried the princess.

'That is not the point, my dear.'

'It's that protégée of yours, that precious Princess Drubetskoy, that

85

Anna Mihalovna of yours whom I would not take for my housemaid – the infamous, vile creature!'

'Let us not lose time,' said the prince in French.

'Ah, don't talk to me! Last winter she wormed her way in here and told the count such a pack of nasty, mean tales about all of us, especially Sophie – I can't repeat them – that it made the count really ill and for two whole weeks he would not see any of us. It was then, I know, that he wrote that horrid, vile document, but I thought it was of no consequence.'

'We've got to it at last – why ever did you not tell me about it sooner?'

'It's in the inlaid portfolio which he keeps under his pillow,' said the princess, ignoring his question. 'Now I know! Yes, if I have a sin, a heavy sin on my conscience, it is hatred of that horrible woman!' the princess almost shrieked, altogether different now. 'And what does she come worming herself in here for? But I will give her a piece of my mind! The time will come!'

19

WHILE all these various conversations were taking place in the reception-room and in the princess's apartment the carriage with Pierre (who had been sent for) and Anna Mihalovna (who found it necessary to accompany him) was driving into the courtyard of Count Bezuhov's house. As the wheels rolled softly over the straw spread beneath the windows Anna Mihalovna turned to her companion with words of consolation, discovered that he was asleep in his corner, and roused him. Waking up, Pierre followed Anna Mihalovna out of the carriage, and began to think for the first time of the interview before him with his dying father. He noticed that they had drawn up not at the main entrance but at a back door As he was leaving the carriage two men who looked like tradespeople shrank back from the doorway into the shadow of the wall. Pausing for a moment, Pierre observed several other similar figures in the shadow on both sides of the house. But neither Anna Mihalovna nor the footman nor the coachman, who could not have helped seeing these people, paid any attention to them. 'So I suppose it must be all right,' Pierre argued to himself, and he followed Anna Mihalovna.

With hurried steps Anna Mihalovna tripped up the narrow dimly-lit stone staircase, calling to Pierre, who was loitering behind. Though he could not see why he had to go to the count at all, and still less why he had to go by the back stairs, yet judging by Anna Mihalovna's air of assurance and haste Pierre concluded that it was all absolutely necessary. Half-way up the stairs they were almost knocked over by some men, who came running down carrying pails, their boots clattering. These men pressed close to the wall to let Pierre and Anna Mihalovna pass, and showed not the slightest surprise at seeing them there.

'Is this the way to the princesses' apartments?' inquired Anna Mihalovna of one of them.

'Yes,' replied the footman in a loud, bold voice, as if anything were permissible now. 'The door on the left, ma'am.'

'Perhaps the count did not ask for me,' said Pierre, when he reached the landing. 'I had better go to my own room.'

Anna Mihalovna waited till Pierre came up.

'Ah, my friend!' she said, laying her hand on his arm just as she had done earlier in the day to her son. 'Believe me, I suffer no less than you do, but be a man!'

'Really, hadn't I better go to my own room?' asked Pierre, looking benignly at her through his spectacles.

'Ah, my dear friend, forget the wrongs that may have been done you. Remember only that he is your father ... and in his death agony, perhaps.' She sighed. 'I have loved you like a son from the very first. Trust in me, Pierre. I shall not forget your interests.'

Pierre did not understand a word but it came over him with even more force that all this had to be, and so he meekly followed Anna Mihalovna, who was already opening a door.

The door led into the ante-room of the rear apartments. In one corner sat an old manservant of the princesses, knitting a stocking. Pierre had never been in this part of the house and had no idea of the existence of these rooms. Addressing a maid who was hurrying by with a carafe of water on a tray, and calling her 'my dear' and 'my good girl', Anna Mihalovna inquired after the princesses' health, and beckoned Pierre to follow her along the stone passage. The first door on the left led into the princesses' apartments. In her haste the maid with the carafe had not closed the door (at this time everything in the house was done in haste), and as Pierre and Anna Mihalovna passed by they involuntarily glanced into the room where the eldest niece was sitting in close conference with Prince Vasili. Seeing them pass, Prince Vasili made a movement of annoyance and drew back, while the princess sprang to her feet and, exasperated, slammed the door with all her might.

This action was so unlike the princess's habitual composure, and the dismay depicted on Prince Vasili's face so out of keeping with his usual air of importance, that Pierre stopped short and looked inquiringly through his spectacles at his guide. Anna Mihalovna manifested no surprise; she merely smiled faintly and sighed, as much as to say that all this was no more than she had expected.

'Be a man, my friend. I am here to watch over your interests,' said she in reply to his glance, and went tripping along the passage even faster than before.

Pierre could not make out what it was all about, and still less what 'watching over his interests' meant, but he decided that all these things had to be. From the passage they went into a large dimly-lit chamber adjoining the count's reception-room. It was one of those cold sumptuous apartments which Pierre had previously only entered from the front. But even in this room, right in the middle, there now stood an empty bath tub, and water had been spilt on the carpet. They were met by a servant coming towards them on tiptoe, and a deacon carrying a censer, neither of whom paid any attention to Pierre and Anna Mihalovna, who went into the reception-room familiar to Pierre, with its two Italian windows opening into the conservatory and the large bust and full-length portrait of Catherine. The same people were still sitting here in almost the same attitudes as before, whispering to one another. As Anna Mihalovna entered they all fell silent and turned to look at her pale, careworn face and at the stout, burly Pierre who followed her submissively, hanging his head.

Anna Mihalovna's face expressed consciousness that the critical moment was at hand. With the bearing of a Petersburg lady of experience, keeping Pierre close at her side, she marched into the room even more boldly than she had that afternoon. She felt that as she was bringing the person whom the dying man wished to see her own admission was assured. Casting a rapid glance at all those in the room and noticing the count's spiritual adviser there, she glided up to him with a mincing gait, not exactly bowing but suddenly diminishing her stature, and respectfully received the blessing first of the one and then of another ecclesiastic.

'Thank God we are in time,' said she to one of the priests. 'All of us, his kinsfolk, have been so anxious. This young man is the count's son,' she added in a lower tone. 'What a terrible moment!'

After this she went over to the doctor.

'My dear doctor,' she said to him, speaking in French. 'This young man is the count's son. ... Is there any hope?'

The doctor cast his eyes upwards and silently shrugged his shoulders. With just the same gesture Anna Mihalovna raised her shoulders and eyes, almost closing her eyelids, gave a sigh and moved away from the doctor to Pierre. She addressed Pierre with peculiar deference and a tender melancholy.

'Have faith in His mercy,' and pointing out a small sofa where he should sit and wait for her, she noiselessly directed her steps towards the door which was the centre of attention and which creaked faintly as it closed behind her.

Pierre, having made up his mind to obey his monitress in all things, moved towards the little sofa she had indicated. As soon as Anna Mihalovna had disappeared he noticed that the eyes of everyone in the room were fastened on him with something more than curiosity and sympathy. He noticed that they whispered together, casting significant looks at him with a kind of awe and even obsequiousness. He was shown a degree of respect such as he had never been shown before. A lady whom he did not know, the one who had been talking to the priests, rose and offered him her place; an aide-de-camp picked up and handed to him a glove Pierre had dropped; the doctors became respectfully silent as he passed by them, and moved to make way for him. Pierre's first impulse was to sit somewhere else so as not to disturb the lady, to pick up his own glove and to walk round the doctors who were not really at all in his way; but all at once he felt that this would not do, that tonight he was a person obliged to go through some terrible ceremony which everyone expected of him, and that he was bound to accept their services. He took the glove from the aide-de-camp in silence, and sat down in the lady's chair, placing his large hands on his squarely planted knees in the naïve attitude of an Egyptian statue, fully decided in his own mind that all was as it should be, and that in order not to lose his head and commit some folly he must not follow his own notions but must yield himself up entirely to the will of those who had assumed direction of him.

Two minutes had not elapsed before Prince Vasili entered, carrying his head high and wearing his long frock-coat with three stars on his breast. He seemed to have grown thinner since the morning; his eyes looked larger than usual when he glanced round the room and caught sight of Pierre. He went up to him, took his hand (a thing he had never done before) and drew it downwards as if wishing to test whether it were firmly fixed on.

'*Courage, courage, mon ami.* He has asked to see you. *C'est bien ...*' and he turned to go.

But Pierre thought it necessary to ask: 'How is ...' He hesitated, not knowing whether it would be proper to call the dying man 'the count', yet blushing to call him 'father'.

'He had another stroke half an hour ago. Another stroke. *Courage, mon ami ...*'

Pierre was in such a confused state of mind that at the word 'stroke' he imagined a blow of some kind. He stared at Prince Vasili in perplexity, and only later grasped that a stroke meant an attack of illness. Prince Vasili said a few words to Lorrain in passing and went through the door on tiptoe. He did not know how to walk on tiptoe and jerked his whole body awkwardly at each step. The eldest princess followed him, and after them went the priests and deacons, and some of the servants of the house. Through the door was heard a stir of movement, and finally Anna Mihalovna, still with the same expression – pale but resolute in the discharge of duty – came running out and touching Pierre on the arm said:

'The goodness of God is inexhaustible. The office of the last anointing is about to begin. Come.'

Pierre went through the door, treading on the soft carpet, and noticed that the aide-de-camp, and the lady he did not know, and some more of the servants all followed him in, as though it were now no longer necessary to ask permission to enter that room.

20

PIERRE well knew this vast room divided by columns and an arch, its walls hung with Persian tapestries. The part of the room behind the columns, where on one side stood a tall mahogany bedstead with silken hangings and on the other a huge case containing icons, was brightly illuminated with a red light like a church for evening service. Under the shining icons Pierre saw a long invalid chair, and in this chair, propped up by smooth, snowy-white pillows, the slips obviously just changed, lay the majestic form of his father, Count Bezuhov, covered to the waist by a bright green quilt, with the familiar mane of grey hair above his lofty forehead, reminding one of a lion, and the deep typically aristocratic wrinkles on his handsome brick-coloured face. He was lying directly under the icons, both his great stout arms outside the quilt. A wax taper had been thrust between the forefinger and thumb of his right hand which lay palm downwards, and an old servant was bending over from behind the chair to hold the candle in position. Around the chair stood the clergy, their long hair falling over their magnificent glittering vestments, with lighted tapers in their hands, performing their office with slow solemnity. A little behind them stood the two younger princesses holding handkerchiefs to their eyes, and just in front of them their eldest sister, Katishe, fixing a vicious and determined look on the icons, as though declaring to all that she would not answer for herself if she were to look round. Anna Mihalovna, with a meek and mournful all-forgiving expression on her face, stood by the door with the unknown lady. Prince Vasili, on the other side of the door, near the invalid chair, was leaning his left arm on the carved back of a velvet chair which he had turned round for the purpose. He held a wax taper in his left hand and was crossing himself with his right, raising his eyes each time his fingers touched his forehead. His face wore a calm look of piety and resignation to the will of God. 'If you cannot comprehend such sentiments, so much the worse for you,' he seemed to be saying.

Behind him stood the aide-de-camp, the doctors and the menservants: just as in church, the men and women had separated to opposite sides. All were silently crossing themselves; the only sounds were the reading of the Scriptures, the subdued chanting of deep bass voices and during the intervals of silence profound sighing and the restless movement of feet. Anna Mihalovna, with an air of importance to show that she knew what she was about, walked right across the room to where Pierre was standing and gave him a taper. He lit it, and then, confused under the glances of those around him, began to cross himself with the hand that held the candle.

The youngest of the sisters, the rosy, fun-loving Princess Sophie, the one with the mole, was watching him. She smiled, hid her face in her handkerchief and remained with it hidden for some time; but looking up and seeing Pierre she began to laugh again. She was evidently unable to look at him without laughing but could not resist looking at him, so to be out of temptation she crept away behind one of the columns. In the middle of the service the voices of the clergy suddenly ceased; the priests whispered together and the old servant who was holding the candle in the count's hand straightened himself and turned to the ladies. Anna Mihalovna stepped forward and bending over the sick man beckoned behind her back to Lorrain. The French doctor had been standing without a candle, leaning against one of the pillars in the respectful attitude of a foreigner conveying that in spite of belonging to a different faith he appreciates all the solemnity of the rite being performed and even approves of it. He now approached the sick man with the noiseless step of one in the prime of life, with his delicate white fingers lifted the hand that lay on the green quilt and turning sideways began to feel the pulse, considering for a moment. The sick man was given something to drink, there was a stir around him, then once more they all resumed their places and the service continued. During this interval Pierre noticed that Prince Vasili left his position behind the carved chair and, with an air which intimated that he knew what he was doing and if others failed to understand it was so much the worse for them, went not to the dying man but past him to the eldest princess, and together they retired to the depths of the alcove where the high bedstead stood with its silken hangings. From there both the prince and the princess disappeared through the farther door, but before the end of the service returned, one after the other, to their places. Pierre paid no more attention to this occurrence than to the rest of what went on, having made up his mind once for all that everything he saw happening around him that evening was in some manner essential.

The chanting ceased, and the voice of the priest was heard respectfully felicitating the sick man on having received the sacrament. The dying man lay as lifeless and immobile as before. Around him there was a general stir: footsteps were audible and whispers, of which Anna Mihalovna's was the most distinct.

Pierre heard her say:

'He positively must be carried to the bed; here it would be impossible. ...'

The sick man was so surrounded by doctors, princesses and servants that Pierre could no longer see the reddish-yellow face with the mane of grey hair which, though he saw other faces as well, he had not lost sight of for an instant throughout the whole service. He surmised by the cautious movements of those who crowded round the invalid chair that they had lifted the dying man and were carrying him across to the bed.

'Catch hold of my arm or you'll drop him,' he heard one of the servants say in a frightened whisper. 'Lower down ... once more,' exclaimed other voices, and the laboured breathing and shuffling steps of the bearers grew more hurried, as if the weight they carried was beyond their strength.

As the bearers, among their number Anna Mihalovna, passed the young man he caught a momentary glimpse over their heads and backs of the dying man's high, fleshy bare chest and powerful shoulders, raised by those who were holding him under the armpits, and of his leonine head with the mane of grey curls. This head, with its extraordinarily wide brow and cheekbones, its fine handsome voluptuous mouth and cold, majestic expression, was not disfigured by the approach of death. It was just the same as Pierre remembered it three months previously, when the count had sent him to Petersburg. But now this head was rolling helplessly with the uneven steps of the bearers, and the cold listless eyes gazed unseeing.

After a few minutes' bustle around the high bedstead the little party who had been carrying the sick man broke up. Anna Mihalovna touched Pierre on the arm and said, 'Come.' Pierre went with her over to the bed on which the sick man had been arranged, limbs piously disposed in keeping with the rites which had just been performed. He lay with his head propped high on the pillows. His hands had been symmetrically placed on the green silk quilt, palms downwards. When Pierre approached, the count was looking straight at him but with a gaze the intent and significance of which no mortal man could fathom. Either this look had simply nothing to say and merely fastened upon him because those eyes must needs look at something, or it had too much to say. Pierre hesitated, not knowing what to do, and glanced inquiringly at his guide. Anna Mihalovna made a hurried sign with her eyes towards the sick man's hand and moved her lips as though sending it a kiss. Carefully craning his neck to avoid disturbing the quilt, Pierre did as he was bid, and pressed his lips to the broad-boned fleshy hand. Neither the hand nor a single muscle of the count's face quivered. Once more Pierre looked questioningly at Anna Mihalovna to see what he was to do now. She indicated with her eyes a chair that stood beside the bed. Pierre obediently sat down in the chair, his eyes inquiring whether he had done the right thing. Anna Mihalovna nodded approvingly. Pierre again assumed the naïvely symmetrical pose of an Egyptian statue, obviously troubled that his ungainly person took up so much room, and doing his utmost to appear as small as possible. He looked at the count. The count was still gazing at the spot where Pierre's face had been before he sat down. Anna Mihalovna's expression conveyed that she appreciated the affecting solemnity of this last meeting between father and son. Two minutes went by, which seemed like an hour to Pierre. Suddenly the powerful muscles and lines of the count's face began to twitch. The twitching increased, the handsome mouth was drawn to one side (only now did Pierre realize how near death his father was), and from the distorted mouth issued an unintelligible, hoarse sound. Anna Mihalovna looked intently into the sick man's eyes, trying to make out what he wanted, pointing first at Pierre, then at the tumbler; then she said Prince Vasili's name in an inquiring whisper, then pointed to the quilt. The eyes and face of the sick man showed impatience. With an effort he looked at the servant who never left his master's bedside.

'Wants to be turned over on the other side, the master does,' whispered the servant, and got up to turn the count's heavy body towards the wall.

Pierre rose to help the man.

While the count was being turned over, one of his arms fell back helplessly and he in vain endeavoured to pull it after him. Perhaps he noticed the look of horror on Pierre's face at the sight of that lifeless arm, or some other thought may have flitted across his dying brain at that moment, in any case he glanced at the refractory arm, at Pierre's horror-stricken face and at the arm again, and on his lips a feeble piteous smile appeared, quite out of character with his features, seeming to deride his own helplessness. Suddenly, at the sight of that smile, Pierre felt a lump in his throat and a tickling in his nose, and tears dimmed his eyes. The sick man was turned on to his side with his face to the wall. He gave a sigh.

'He is dozing,' said Anna Mihalovna, observing one of the nieces approaching to take her turn by the bedside. 'Come ...'

Pierre left the room.

21

THERE was no one in the reception-room now except Prince Vasili and the eldest princess, who were sitting under the portrait of Catherine the Great in eager conversation together. As soon as Pierre and his companion appeared they fell silent, and Pierre fancied he saw the princess hide something as she whispered:

'I cannot abide that woman.'

'Katishe has had tea served in the small drawing-room,' said Prince Vasili to Anna Mihalovna. 'Go and have something to eat, my poor Anna Mihalovna, or you will collapse.'

To Pierre he said nothing, merely giving his arm a sympathetic squeeze just below the shoulder. Pierre and Anna Mihalovna went into the small drawing-room.

'There is nothing so refreshing after a night without sleep as a cup of this excellent Russian tea,' Lorrain was saying with an air of restrained briskness as he sipped tea from a delicate Chinese cup without a handle. He was standing before a table on which tea and a cold supper had been laid in the small circular room. Around the table all who were at Count Bezuhov's house that night had gathered with a view to fortifying themselves. Pierre well remembered this little circular drawing-room with its mirrors and tiny tables. In the days when balls were held at the house, Pierre, who did not dance, had liked to sit in this little room of mirrors and watch the ladies as they passed through in their ball dresses with diamonds and pearls on their bare shoulders glance at themselves in the brilliantly lighted glasses with their repeating reflections. Now this same room was dimly lighted by a pair of candles and, in the middle of the night, on one small table stood a disorderly array of tea things and supper dishes, and a motley crowd of people who were anything but festive sat talking in whispers, every gesture, every word betraying that not one of them was oblivious to what was happening and what was about to happen in the bedroom. Pierre did not eat anything, though he very much wanted to. He looked round inquiringly at his monitress, and saw that she was tiptoeing back to the reception-room, where they had left Prince Vasili and the eldest princess. Pierre supposed this also was as it should be, and after a short interval followed her. Anna Mihalovna was standing beside the princess, and both were speaking at once in angry undertones.

'Allow me, madam, to know what is and what is not to be done,' the Princess Katishe was saying, evidently in the same angry temper as when she had slammed the door of her room.

'But, my dear princess,' answered Anna Mihalovna in a bland persuasive manner, barring the way to the bedroom and preventing the other from passing, 'would this not be too great a tax on our poor uncle at such a moment, when he needs quiet? To discuss worldly matters when his soul has already been prepared. ...'

Prince Vasili was seated in an easy chair, one leg crossed high above the other, in his familiar posture. His cheeks, which were so flabby that they seemed to hang in pouches, were twitching violently; but he wore the air of a man little concerned with what the two ladies were saying.

'Come, my dear Anna Mihalovna, let Katishe have her way. You know how fond the count is of her.'

'I have no idea what is in this document even,' said the younger of the two ladies, turning to Prince Vasili and pointing to the inlaid portfolio which she held in her hand. 'I only know that the real will is in his writing-table, and this is a paper that has been forgotten. ...'

She tried to pass Anna Mihalovna, but the latter sprang forward to bar her way again.

'I know, my dear, good princess,' said Anna Mihalovna, grabbing the portfolio so firmly that it was plain she would not readily let go of it again. 'Dear princess, I beg of you, I implore you, spare him! I implore you!'

The princess did not reply. All that was heard was the sound of a scuffle for possession of the portfolio, but there could be no doubt that if the princess did open her mouth to speak what she said would not be flattering for Anna Mihalovna. Though the latter clung on tightly, her voice lost none of its soft firmness.

'Pierre, my dear, come here. I imagine he will not be one too many in this family council, eh, prince?'

'Why don't you speak, cousin?' suddenly shrieked Katishe, so loud that those in the drawing-room heard her and were startled. 'Why do you keep silent while heaven knows who takes upon herself to interfere and make a scene on the very threshold of a dying man's room? Scheming creature, you!' she hissed viciously, and tugged with all her might at the portfolio, but Anna Mihalovna took two or three steps forward to keep her hold on it, and succeeded in changing her grip.

Prince Vasili rose. 'Oh!' said he with reproach and surprise. 'This is preposterous. Come, let go, I tell you.'

The Princess Katishe let go.

'You too!'

But Anna Mihalovna paid no heed.

'Let go, I tell you. I will assume the whole responsibility. I will go and ask him myself. I ... will that satisfy you?'

'But, prince,' said Anna Mihalovna, 'after such a solemn sacrament, let him have a moment's peace. Here, Pierre, tell us your opinion,' said she, turning to the young man who had come close to them and was looking with astonishment at the princess's angry face, which had lost all dignity, and at Prince Vasili's twitching cheeks.

'Remember that you will answer for all the consequences,' said Prince Vasili severely. 'You don't know what you are doing.'

'You vile woman!' screamed the princess, darting unexpectedly at Anna Mihalovna and snatching the portfolio from her.

Prince Vasili bowed his head and spread out his hands.

At this point the door, the dreadful door which Pierre had watched so long and which usually opened so gently, burst open noisily, banging back against the wall, and the second of the three sisters rushed out wringing her hands.

'What are you thinking of?' she cried frantically. 'He is dying and you leave me alone!'

Her sister dropped the portfolio. Anna Mihalovna swiftly stooped and, snatching up the object of contention, ran into the bedroom. The eldest princess and Prince Vasili, recovering themselves, followed her. A few minutes later the eldest sister emerged again with a pale, hard face, biting her underlip. At the sight of Pierre her face expressed uncontrollable dislike.

'Yes, now you can rejoice!' said she. 'This is what you have been waiting for.'

And breaking into sobs she hid her face in her handkerchief and ran from the room.

The next to come out was Prince Vasili. Reeling slightly, he dropped down on to the sofa where Pierre was sitting, and covered his face with his hand. Pierre noticed that he was pale, and that his lower jaw trembled and shook as though he had an attack of ague.

'Ah, my friend,' said he, taking Pierre by the elbow, and there was a sincerity and softness in his voice which Pierre had never heard before. 'We sin and we deceive, and all for what? I am getting on for sixty, my dear boy ... I too ... Everything ends in death, everything! Death is awful ...' and he burst into tears.

Anna Mihalovna was the last to come out. She went up to Pierre with slow, quiet steps.

'Pierre!' she said.

Pierre looked at her inquiringly. She kissed the young man on the forehead, wetting him with her tears. Then after a pause she said:

'He is no more. ...'

Pierre gazed at her through his spectacles.

'Come, I will take you away. Try to weep. Nothing relieves like tears.'

She led him into the dark drawing-room and Pierre was glad that no one was there to see his face. Anna Mihalovna left him, and when she returned he was fast asleep with his head on his arm.

Next morning Anna Mihalovna said to Pierre:

'Yes, my dear, it is a great loss for us all. I do not speak of you. But God will uphold you, you are young and now, I hope, in command of an immense fortune. The will has not been opened yet. I know you well enough to rest assured that this will not turn your head, but it will impose new duties on you, and you must be a man.'

Pierre was silent.

'Perhaps later on I will tell you, my dear boy, that if I had not been here, God only knows what might have happened. You know, uncle promised me only the day before yesterday not to forget Boris. But he did not have time. I hope, my dear friend, that you will carry out your father's wish.'

Pierre did not understand a word of all this and colouring shyly looked dumbly at Princess Anna Mihalovna. After this talk with Pierre Anna Mihalovna returned to the Rostovs' and went to bed. On waking later in the morning she began to tell the Rostovs and all her acquaintances the details of Count Bezuhov's death. She declared that the count had died as she would wish to die herself, that his end had been not simply affecting but edifying; that the last meeting between father and son had been so touching that she could not recall it without tears, and that she did not know which had borne himself the more admirably in those awful moments – the father who had had a thought for everything and everybody during those last hours, and had spoken such moving words to his son, or Pierre, whom it had been pitiful to see, so stricken was he though he struggled to control his grief so as not to distress his dying father. 'Such scenes are painful, but they do one good. It uplifts the soul to see such men as the old count and his worthy son,' said she. The behaviour of the eldest princess and Prince Vasili she also reported, in disapproving terms but under the seal of secrecy and in a whisper.

22

AT Bald Hills, Prince Nikolai Andreyevich Bolkonsky's estate, the arrival of the young Prince Andrei and his wife was expected daily, but this did not upset the ordered routine which regulated life in the old prince's household. General-in-chief Prince Nikolai Andreyevich (nicknamed in society 'the king of Prussia'), having been banished to his country estates in the reign of the Emperor Paul, had remained at Bald Hills ever since, with his daughter Princess Maria and her companion, Mademoiselle Bourienne. Though in the new reign he was free to return to the capitals he still continued to live in the country, saying that anyone who wanted to see him could come the hundred miles from Moscow to Bald Hills, while so far as he himself was concerned he needed nothing and nobody. He was in the habit of remarking that there are only two sources of human vice, idleness and superstition; and only two virtues, energy and intelligence. He had personally undertaken his daughter's education, and to develop in her these two cardinal virtues gave her lessons in algebra and geometry up to her twentieth year, and mapped out her life into an uninterrupted schedule of occupations. He himself was constantly engaged in writing his memoirs, solving problems in higher mathematics, turning snuff-boxes on his lathe or working in the garden and superintending the building ever in progress on his estate. As the prime condition of successful activity is order, order in his household was exacted to the utmost. He always appeared at meals in precisely the same circumstances, and not only at the same hour but at the same minute. With those about him, from his daughter to his serfs, the prince was sharp and inflexible, so that without being a cruel man he inspired a degree of fear and respect such as a really brutal man would have found difficult to obtain. Although he was living in retirement and now had no influence in matters of state, every high official in the province where the prince's estates lay felt obliged to pay his respects, and waited in the lofty antechamber just like the architect, the gardener or Princess Maria, till the prince made his appearance punctually at the regular hour. And everyone waiting in this antechamber knew the same feeling of deference and even awe when the enormously high door of the study swung open and the figure of the little old man appeared, in his powdered wig, with his small dry hands and bushy grey eyebrows, which sometimes when he frowned hid the gleam of his shrewd, youthfully bright eyes.

On the day when the young couple were to arrive, Princess Maria as usual came down into the antechamber at the hour appointed to wish her father good morning, crossing herself in trepidation and repeating a silent prayer. This happened every morning, and every morning she prayed that the daily interview might pass off felicitously.

An old manservant in a powdered wig who was sitting in the antechamber got up quietly and greeted her in a whisper.

Through the door came the steady hum of a lathe. The princess timidly opened the door, which moved easily and noiselessly on its hinges, and stood still on the threshold. The prince was working at his lathe, and after glancing round went on with what he was doing.

The great room was full of objects evidently in constant use. The huge table covered with books and plans, the tall, glass-fronted bookcases with keys in the locks, the high desk for the prince to write at while standing up, on which was an open manuscript-book, and the carpenter's lathe with tools laid ready to hand and shavings scattered around – all suggested continuous, varied, and regulated activity. The motion of the small foot shod in a Tartar boot embroidered in silver, and the firm pressure of the lean sinewy hand showed that the prince still possessed the tenacious strength and vigour of a green old age. After a few more turns of the lathe he removed his foot from the treadle, wiped his chisel, dropped it into a leather pouch attached to the lathe, and going to the table called his daughter to him. He never wasted blessings on his children, so he simply held out his bristly cheek (as yet unshaven for the day) and said, with a severe and at the same time tenderly attentive look:

'Quite well? All right then, sit down.'

He took the exercise-book containing lessons in geometry which he had written out himself, and drew up a chair with his foot.

'For tomorrow!' said he, briskly finding the page and marking from one paragraph to another with his horny nail.

The princess leaned over the table towards the exercise-book.

'Wait, here's a letter for you,' said the old man abruptly, pulling out from a pocket fastened to the table an envelope addressed in a feminine hand and tossing it on to the table.

The princess's face coloured in blotches at the sight of the letter. She hastily picked it up and bent her head over it.

'From your Héloïse?' asked the prince with a cold smile that showed his still sound but yellowing teeth.

'Yes, it's from Julie,' replied the princess with a timid glance and a timid smile.

'I shall allow two more letters to pass, but the third I shall read,' said the prince sternly. 'You write much nonsense, I'll be bound. I shall read the third.'

'Read this one if you like, father,' replied the princess, flushing still more and holding out the letter.

'The third, I said, the third,' cried the prince shortly, pushing the letter away; then, leaning his elbows on the table, he drew towards him the exercise-book with the geometrical figures.

'Well, madam,' began the old man, stooping over the book close to his daughter and laying one arm on the back of her chair, so that she felt herself surrounded on all sides by the acrid odour of tobacco and old age which she had so long associated with her father. 'Now, madam, these triangles are equal; if you will observe the angle a-b-c...'

The princess glanced up in dismay into her father's eyes glittering so close to her. The red patches on her face came and went, and it was plain that she understood nothing and was so frightened that her fear would prevent her understanding any of her father's explanations, however clear they might be. Whether it was the teacher's fault or the pupil's, the same thing recurred every day: the princess's eyes grew dim, she could not see or hear anything and was only conscious of her father's stern withered face close to her, his breath and the smell of him, and her one thought was to get away as quickly as possible to work out the problem in peace in her own room. The old man would lose all patience, noisily push back the chair on which he was sitting and then draw it forward again, make efforts to control himself and not fly into a rage, but he almost always did break out into a fury, storming and sometimes flinging down the exercise-book.

The princess made a wrong answer.

'What an idiot the girl is!' roared the prince, pushing the book aside and turning away sharply; but rising immediately he paced up and down, touched his daughter's hair and seated himself again.

He drew up his chair and proceeded to explain.

'This won't do, young lady. It won't do,' said he, as the princess took and closed the exercise-book with the next day's lessons and made to leave. 'Mathematics are a most important subject, madam. And I don't want you to be like all the other silly women. Persevere and you will get to like it.' He patted her on the cheek. 'Mathematics will drive all the nonsense out of your head.'

She turned to go but he stopped her by a gesture and took a book with pages uncut from the high desk.

'Here, your Héloise has sent you something else: some *Key to the Mystery*. A religious book. I don't interfere with anyone's belief. ... I have glanced at it. Take it. Now, be off, be off.'

He patted her on the shoulder, closing the door after her himself.

Princess Maria returned to her room with the sad, scared expression that rarely left her and made her plain, sickly face still less attractive. She sat down at her writing-table on which were some miniatures and a litter of books and papers. The princess was as untidy as her father was tidy. She put down the geometry book and eagerly broke the seal of her letter. It was from the most intimate of her childhood friends, none other than Julie Karagin, who had been at the Rostovs' name-day party.

Julie wrote entirely in French:

Chère et excellente amie,

How terrible and frightful a thing separation is! Though I tell myself that half my life and half my happiness are bound up in you, that in spite of the distance separating us our hearts are united by indissoluble bonds, mine rebels against fate and in spite of all the pleasures and distractions that surround me I cannot overcome a certain secret sorrow which has lurked in the depths of my heart ever since we parted. Why are we not together as we were last summer, in your big study, on the blue sofa – the confidences sofa? Why can I not, as I did three months ago, draw fresh moral strength from your eyes, so sweet, so calm, so penetrating, the eyes which I loved so much and seem to see before me as I write.

Having read thus far, Princess Maria sighed and glanced into the pier-glass which stood on her right. It reflected a slight, homely figure and thin features. Her eyes, always melancholy, now looked with particular hopelessness at her reflection in the mirror. 'She flatters me,' thought the princess, turning away and continuing to read. Julie, however, had not flattered her friend: indeed, the princess's eyes – large, deep and luminous (it sometimes seemed as if whole shafts of warm light radiated from them) – were so lovely that very often in spite of the plainness of her face they gave her a charm that was more attractive than beauty. But the princess never saw the beautiful expression of her own eyes – the expression they had when she was not thinking of herself. Like most people's, her face assumed an affected, unnatural expression as soon as she looked in a glass. She went on with the letter:

All Moscow talks of nothing but war. One of my two brothers is already abroad, the other is with the Guards, just about to march for the frontier. Our beloved Emperor has left Petersburg and intends, they say, to expose his precious person to the hazards of war. God grant that the Corsican monster who is destroying the peace of Europe may be brought low by the angelic being whom the Almighty in His mercy has sent to rule over us. To say nothing of my brothers, this war has deprived me of one most dear to my heart: I mean young Nikolai Rostov, whose ardour could not endure inaction and who has left the University to go and join the army. Yes, my dear Marie, I will own to you that notwithstanding his extreme youth his departure for the army has been a great grief to me. This young man – I told you about him last summer – has so much nobility, so much of that genuine youthfulness which we meet with so rarely in this age of ours, when every lad of twenty is an old man. Above all he has so much candour and heart. He is so pure and poetic that my acquaintance with him, transient as it was, must be counted one of the sweetest enjoyments of my poor heart, which has already suffered so deeply. Some day I will tell you about our parting and what passed between us. All that is still too recent. Ah, dear friend, how happy you are not to know these poignant joys and sorrows! You are fortunate, because the keenest are usually the latter! I know very well that Count Nikolai is too young ever to be anything more than a friend, but this sweet friendship, this intimacy, so poetic and pure, were what my heart needed. But enough of this. The chief news of the day, and the talk of all Moscow, is the death of old Count Bezuhov, and his will. Just fancy – the three princesses get very little, Prince Vasili nothing, and it is Monsieur Pierre who inherits all. He has, into the bargain, been recognized as legitimate, and is therefore Count Bezuhov and possessor of the finest fortune in Russia. They say Prince Vasili played a very ugly part in the whole affair and has gone back to Petersburg quite out of countenance.

I confess I understand very little to do with bequests and wills; but I do know that since the young man whom we all knew as plain Monsieur Pierre has become Count Bezuhov and master of one of the largest fortunes in Russia, I am greatly amused to observe the change in tone and behaviour of mammas burdened with daughters to marry – and of the young ladies themselves – towards this individual, who, between you and me, has always seemed to be a poor specimen. As people have amused themselves for the past two years by marrying me off (generally to men I don't even know), the matrimonial gossip of Moscow now speaks of me as the future Countess Bezuhov. But I need not tell you that I have no ambition for the post. *A propos* of marriages, do you know that quite recently that *universal aunt*, Anna Mihalovna, confided to me, under seal of strictest secrecy, a marriage project for you – neither more nor less than with Prince Vasili's son, Anatole, whom they want to reform by marrying him to someone rich and *distinguée*, and it is on you that his relations' choice has fallen. I don't know what you will think of it, but I felt it my duty to warn you. He is said to be very handsome and very wild. That is all I have been able to find out about him.

But enough of this gossip. I am at the end of my second sheet of paper, and mamma has sent for me to go and dine at the Apraksins'. Read the mystical book I am sending you: it is all the rage here. Although there are things in it difficult for the feeble mind of man to fathom, it is an admirable book which soothes and elevates the soul. Adieu! Give my respects to your father and my compliments to Mademoiselle Bourienne.

Fond love,   JULIE

P.S. Let me have news of your brother and his charming little wife.

The princess sat thinking, a pensive smile playing over her lips; her face, lighted up by her luminous eyes, was completely transformed. Then suddenly jumping up she walked over to the table, treading heavily. She got out a sheet of paper and her hand began to fly rapidly over it. This is the reply she wrote, also in French:

Chère et excellente amie,

Your letter of the 13th was a great joy to me. So you still love me, my romantic Julie? And separation, of which you say such hard things, has not had its usual effect upon you. You complain of our separation – what should I have to say if I ventured to complain, bereft as I am of all who are dear to me? Ah, if we had not religion to console us life would be very sad. Why should you suspect me of looking stern when you speak of your affection for that young man? In such matters, I am only severe with myself. I understand such feelings in others, and if I cannot actually approve them, never having experienced them, neither do I condemn them. Only it seems to me that Christian love, love of one's neighbour, love of one's enemies, is more meritorious, sweeter and more beautiful than the feelings inspired in a romantic and affectionate young girl like you by a young man's beautiful eyes.

The news of Count Bezuhov's death reached us before your letter, and affected my father deeply. He says that the count was the last representative but one of the *grand siècle*, and that now it is his turn, but that he will do his best to put it off as long as possible. God preserve us from that terrible misfortune! I cannot agree with you about Pierre, whom I knew when he was a boy. He always seemed to me to have an excellent heart, and that is the quality I value most in people. As to his inheritance and the *rôle* played by Prince Vasili, it is very sad for both of them. Ah, my dear friend, our divine Saviour's words, that it is easier for a camel to go through the eye of a needle than for a rich man to enter into the kingdom of God, are terribly true; I pity Prince Vasili but I am sorrier still for Pierre. So young, and burdened with such riches – what temptations he will be exposed to! If I were asked what I wished most in the world it would be to be poorer than the poorest beggar. A thousand thanks, dear friend, for the volume you sent me and which is all the rage with you in Moscow. Yet since you tell me that along with many good things it contains others which the weak intellect of man cannot fathom, it seems to me rather useless to spend time in reading what is unintelligible and can therefore bear no good fruit. I have never been able to understand the mania some people have for confusing their judgement by devoting themselves to mystical books which only arouse their doubts and excite their imaginations, giving them a bent for exaggeration utterly contrary to Christian simplicity. Let us rather read the Epistles and the Gospels. Let us not seek to penetrate the mysteries they contain, for how should we, miserable sinners that we are, presume to inquire into the awful and holy secrets of Providence so long as we wear the garment of this mortal flesh which forms an impenetrable veil between us and the Eternal? Let us rather confine ourselves to studying the sublime principles which our divine Saviour has left for our guidance here below; let us seek to conform to them and follow them, and let us be persuaded that the less we allow our feeble human minds to roam, the more pleasing it will be to God, Who rejects all knowledge that does not proceed from Him; and the less we strive to search out what He has been pleased to conceal from us, the sooner will He discover it to us through His divine Spirit.

My father has said nothing to me of any suitor: he only told me that he had received a letter and is expecting a visit from Prince Vasili. In regard to this project of marriage for me, I may say to you, *chère et excellente amie*, that I regard marriage as a divine institution to which we are bound to conform. However painful it may be, should the Almighty ever impose upon me the duties of wife and mother I shall endeavour to fulfil them as faithfully as I am able, without disquieting myself by inquiring into the nature of my feelings towards him whom He may bestow on me for husband.

I have had a letter from my brother, announcing his speedy arrival at Bald Hills with his wife. This pleasure will be of brief duration, for he is leaving us again to take part in this unhappy war into which we have been drawn, God knows how or why. Not only where you are – at the heart of affairs and of the world – is the talk all of war: even here amid the labours of the countryside and nature's peace – which townsfolk consider typical of the country – rumours of war are heard and make themselves painfully felt. My father can talk of nothing but marches and countermarches, things of which I understand nothing; and the day before yesterday during my usual walk through the village I witnessed a heartrending scene ... a convoy of recruits conscripted from our estate and on their way to the army. You should have seen the state of the mothers, wives and children of the men who were going, and heard them sobbing. It seems as though humanity has forgotten the precepts of its divine Saviour, Who preached love and forgiveness of injuries, and that men ascribe the greatest merit to the art of killing one another.

Adieu, chère et bonne amie. May our divine Saviour and His most holy Mother keep you in their holy and all-powerful care!

MARIE

'Ah, you are finishing a letter, princess. I have already sent mine. I wrote to my poor mother,' said the smiling Mademoiselle Bourienne in her full sweet voice, speaking rapidly and rolling her *r*'s, and altogether bringing into Princess Maria's intense, melancholy and overcast atmosphere what seemed like the breath of another world, carefree, gay, and self-sufficient.

'Princess, I must warn you,' she added, lowering her voice and listening to herself with pleasure as she rolled her r's, 'the prince has been rating Mihail Ivanov. He is in a very bad humour, very morose. Be prepared, you know ...'

'Ah, *chère amie*,' replied Princess Maria. 'I have asked you never to call my attention to the humour in which my father happens to be. I do not allow myself to criticize him, and would not have others do so either.'

The princess glanced at her watch and seeing that already she was five minutes late in starting her practice on the clavier hurried into the sitting-room, a look of alarm on her face. Between noon and two o'clock, in accordance with the time-table mapped out for each day, the prince took his siesta while the princess practised the clavier.

23

THE grey-haired valet was sitting in the study dozing and listening to the snoring of the prince, who was in his large study. From a distant part of the house, through the closed doors, came the sound of difficult passages – twenty times repeated – of a Dussek sonata.

Just then a carriage and a gig drove up to the porch. Prince Andrei got out of the carriage, helped his little wife to alight and stood back for her to pass in front of him. Old Tikhon in his wig, popping his head out of the door of the ante-room, reported in a whisper that the prince was asleep and then hastily closed the door. Tikhon knew that not even the arrival of the son of the house, nor any other unusual event, must be allowed to disturb the appointed order of the day. Prince Andrei apparently knew this as well as Tikhon; he looked at his watch as if to ascertain whether his father's habits had changed since he had last seen him and having satisfied himself that they had not he turned to his wife.

'Twenty minutes and he will get up. Let us go along to Princess Maria's room,' he said.

The little princess had grown stouter during this time but her eyes and her short downy smiling lip lifted just as gaily and prettily as ever when she began to speak.

'Why, this is a palace,' she said to her husband, looking around with the expression with which people compliment their host at a ball. 'Come along, quick – quick!' And she glanced with a smile at Tikhon and her husband and the footman who was leading the way.

'Is that Marie practising? Let's go quietly and take her by surprise.'

Prince Andrei followed her with a courteous but melancholy expression.

'You're looking older, Tikhon,' he said in passing to the old man-servant, who kissed his hand.

Just as they reached the room from which the sounds of the clavi-chord were coming, the pretty, fair-haired Frenchwoman tripped out from another door. Mademoiselle Bourienne seemed overwhelmed with delight.

'Oh, what happiness for the princess!' she cried. 'I must go and tell her.'

'No, no, please.... You are Mademoiselle Bourienne,' said the little princess, kissing her. 'I know of you already as my sister-in-law's friend. She is not expecting us!'

They went up to the door of the sitting-room, from which came the notes of the oft-repeated passage of the sonata. Prince Andrei stopped and made a grimace, as if expecting something disagreeable.

The little princess entered the room. The passage broke off in the middle, a cry was heard, then Princess Maria's heavy tread and the sound of kissing. When Prince Andrei went in the two princesses, who had only met once before for a short time at his wedding, were clasped in each other's arms, warmly pressing their lips to whatever place they happened to touch. Mademoiselle Bourienne stood near them pressing her hand to her heart, with a beatific smile and appar-ently as ready to cry as to laugh. Prince Andrei shrugged his shoulders and frowned just as lovers of music do when they hear a wrong note. The two women let go of one another; then once again, as though time were precious, seized each other's hands and began kissing them and pulling them away, and took to kissing each other's face again, and to Prince Andrei's complete surprise they both burst into tears and began to kiss again. Mademoiselle Bourienne started to cry, too. Prince Andrei obviously felt uncomfortable but to the two women it seemed perfectly natural that they should weep: it evidently never entered their heads that it could have been otherwise at this meeting.

'Ah, *chère!* ...' 'Ah! Marie ...' both suddenly exclaimed and then laughed. 'I dreamed last night ...' 'Weren't you expecting us? ... Ah, Marie, you have got thinner! ...' 'And you have grown stouter! ...'

'I recognized the princess at once,' put in Mademoiselle Bourienne.

'And I had no idea! ...' exclaimed Princess Maria. 'Ah, André, I did not see you.'

Prince Andrei kissed his sister, took her hand in his, and told her that she was as great a cry-baby as ever. Princess Maria had turned towards her brother and through her tears her large eyes, now beautiful and luminous, rested on him with a fond expression, gentle and sweet.

The little princess chattered incessantly. Her short downy upper lip danced up and down, lightly touching the rosy lower one then curling into a smile that showed off her glistening teeth and sparkling eyes. She was describing an accident that had occurred to them on Spassky hill and might have been serious for her in her condition, and immediately went on to tell them that she had left all her clothes in Petersburg and heaven knew what she would have to wear here, and that Andrei had quite changed, and that Kitty Odyntsov had married an old man, and that she had a suitor for Princess Maria, who was in earnest but that they would talk about that by-and-by. Princess Maria was still looking silently at her brother, and her beautiful eyes were full of love and melancholy. It was clear her thoughts were following a train of her own, regardless of her sister-in-law's prattle. In the middle of the latter's description of the latest fête at Petersburg she addressed her brother:

'And are you really going to the war, André ?' she asked with a sigh.

Lisa sighed too.

'Yes, and I must be off tomorrow,' he replied.

'He abandons me here, and the Lord knows why, when he might have had promotion ...'

Princess Maria did not listen to the end of this remark but following the thread of her thoughts turned to her sister-in-law with a tender glance at her figure.

'Is it certain ?' she asked.

The little princess's face altered. She sighed.

'Quite,' said she. 'Oh, I am so frightened....'

Her lip went down. She brought her face close to her sister-in-law's, and unexpectedly again burst into tears.

'She needs rest,' said Prince Andrei with a frown. 'Don't you, Lise ? Take her to your room, while I go to father. How is he ? The same as ever ?'

'Yes, just the same. But perhaps your eyes will see some change,' replied the princess cheerfully.

'The same regular time-table, the same walks in the garden, the lathe?' asked Prince Andrei with a scarcely perceptible smile, showing that in spite of all his love and respect for his father he was not blind to his foibles.

'Yes, the same time-table, and the lathe, and mathematics and my geometry lessons,' replied the princess merrily, as though her geometry lessons were among the greatest delights of her life.

When the twenty minutes had elapsed and the time had come for the old prince to get up, Tikhon appeared to summon the young prince to his father. The old man made a departure from his usual routine in honour of his son's arrival: he gave orders to admit him to his apartments while he dressed before dinner. The prince kept to the old fashion and wore a caftan and powdered hair. And when Prince Andrei entered his father's room (not with the peevish face and manners which he assumed in society but with the lively expression he had when talking with Pierre), the old man was sitting in a large leather-covered arm-chair, wrapped in a powdering mantle, while he entrusted his head to Tikhon.

'Ah, here's the warrior! Out to conquer Bonaparte, are you?' cried the old man, shaking his powdered head as far as the pigtail which Tikhon was busy plaiting would allow. 'Mind you set about him good and true, or as things are he'll soon be putting us on the list of his subjects! How are you?' and he held out his cheek.

The old man was in a good humour after his nap before dinner. (He was accustomed to say that a nap after dinner was silver but one before dinner was gold.) He cast happy, sidelong glances at his son from under his thick beetling brows. Prince Andrei went up and kissed his father on the spot indicated to him. He made no reply on his father's favourite topic – quizzing the military men of the day and Bonaparte in particular.

'Yes, here I am, father, and I have brought my wife who is with child,' said Prince Andrei, watching every movement of his father's features with eager and respectful eyes. 'How is your health?'

'Only fools and rakes ever need to be ill, my boy, and you know me – abstemious, and busy from morning till night, so of course I am well.'

'Thank God for that,' said his son smiling.

'God has nothing to do with it. Come now.' he continued, going back to his favourite hobby, 'tell us how the Germans have taught you to fight Bonaparte according to this new science you call "strategy"?'

Prince Andrei smiled.

'Give me time to collect my wits, father,' said he with a smile which showed that his father's foibles did not prevent his honouring and loving him. 'Why, I haven't had time to settle down yet!'

'Nonsense, nonsense!' cried the old man, pulling at his pigtail to assure himself that it was firmly plaited, and grasping his son by the arm. 'The quarters for your wife are all ready. Princess Maria will take her over and show her round, and they'll chatter nineteen to the dozen. That's the way of all women! I am glad to have her here. Sit down and talk to me. Mikhelson's army I understand, and Tolstoy's too ... a simultaneous attack.... But what's the southern army going to do? Prussia remains neutral, I know that. How about Austria?' said he, rising from his chair and pacing up and down the room with Tikhon running behind to hand him various articles of clothing. 'What's Sweden going to do? How will they get across Pomerania?'

Seeing that his father insisted, Prince Andrei – at first reluctantly but gradually warming up and from force of habit unconsciously dropping from Russian into French – began to expound the plan of operation for the coming campaign. He explained how an army, ninety thousand strong, was to threaten Prussia and force her to abandon her neutrality and take part in the war; how a portion of this army was to go to Stralsund and unite with some Swedish forces; how two hundred and twenty thousand Austrians with a hundred thousand Russians were to operate in Italy and on the Rhine; how fifty thousand Russians and as many English were to land at Naples; and how this total force of some five hundred thousand men was to attack the French from different sides. The old prince did not manifest the slightest interest in this description – in fact he might not have been listening: he continued to dress as he walked about, and three times unexpectedly interrupted. Once he held up the story by shouting: 'The white one, the white one!'

This meant that Tikhon was not handing him the waistcoat he wanted. Another time he stopped to ask:

'And is she to be confined soon?' and reproachfully shaking his head said, 'That's too bad! Go on, go on!'

The third interruption came when Prince Andrei was nearing the end of his discourse. The old man began to sing in a cracked old voice: '*Malbrook s'en va-t-en guerre. Dieu sait quand reviendra.*'

His son merely smiled.

'I'm not saying it's a plan I approve of,' he remarked. 'I was just stating it. Napoleon has certainly one of his own by now, which is probably as good as ours.'

'Well, you've told me nothing new.' And meditatively the old man repeated to himself quickly: '*Dieu sait quand reviendra.* Now go to the dining-room.'

24

A T the appointed hour the prince, powdered and shaven, entered the dining-room where his daughter-in-law, Princess Maria and Mademoiselle Bourienne were awaiting him together with his architect, who by a strange caprice of his employer's was allowed at table though his subordinate position gave him no claim to that honour. The prince, who was a great stickler for distinctions of rank and rarely admitted even the local bigwigs to his table, had suddenly selected Mihail Ivanovich (who always went into a corner to blow his nose on a checked pocket handkerchief) to illustrate the theory that all men are equal, and had more than once impressed on his daughter that the architect was every whit as good as themselves. At table the prince was wont to address his conversation mainly to the tongue-tied Mihail Ivanovich.

In the dining-room, which like all the other rooms in the house was tremendously lofty, the members of the household, and the footmen – one behind each chair – stood waiting for the prince to enter. The head butler, napkin on arm, was scanning the table to see that it was properly set, beckoning the waiters and anxiously glancing from the clock on the wall to the door through which the prince was to appear. Prince Andrei was staring at a huge gilt frame, new to him, containing the genealogical tree of the princes Bolkonsky, opposite which was a similar frame with a badly-executed portrait (evidently painted by an artist belonging to the estate) of a ruling prince in a crown – an alleged descendant of Rurik and ancestor of the Bolkonskys. Prince Andrei was looking at this genealogical tree, and shaking his head and laughing, as a man laughs at a portrait so like the original as to be comical.

'That's father all over!' he said to Princess Maria as she came up to him.

Princess Maria looked at her brother in surprise. She did not understand what he was laughing at. Everything her father did inspired her with a reverence that did not admit of criticism.

'To everyone his Achilles' heel,' continued Prince Andrei. 'Fancy, with *his* tremendous intellect, indulging in such nonsense!'

Princess Maria could not understand how her brother could be so audacious, and was about to object when the awaited footsteps were heard coming from the study. The prince walked in briskly, jauntily, in his usual manner, as though he meant his precipitate movements to contrast with the strict formality of the house. Just at that moment the great clock struck two, and was echoed in shriller tones by another clock in the drawing-room. The prince paused. His keen, flashing eyes from under their thick, overhanging brows sternly scanned all present and came to rest on the little princess. As courtiers do when the Tsar enters, she experienced the sensation of fear and respect which the old man inspired in all around him. He stroked her hair and then patted her awkwardly on the back of the neck.

'I am glad, glad to see you,' he said, looking her steadily in the eyes again, and quickly turned away to take his seat. 'Sit down, sit down! Mihail Ivanovich, sit down!'

He pointed his daughter-in-law to a place beside him. A footman pushed the chair forward for her.

'Oho!' said the old man, casting an eye on her rounded figure. 'You've been in a hurry. Too bad!'

He laughed a dry, cold, disagreeable laugh, laughing as he always did, with his lips but not with his eyes.

'You must take plenty of exercise – walk as much as possible, as much as possible,' he said.

The little princess did not, or did not wish to, hear his words. She sat silent and appeared agitated. The prince asked after her father, and she began to smile and talk. He asked about mutual acquaintances, and she grew still more animated and chattered away, giving him greetings from various people and retailing the gossip of the town.

'Countess Apraksin, poor thing, has lost her husband. She cried her eyes out,' said she, growing more and more lively.

The livelier she became the more sternly the prince looked at her, and suddenly, as though he had studied her sufficiently and had formed a clear idea of her, he turned away and addressed Mihail Ivanovich.

'Well, Mihail Ivanovich, our friend Bonaparte is in for a bad time. Prince Andrei' (he always spoke of his son in the third person) 'has been telling me of the forces being massed against him! And to think that you and I have always considered him a man of straw!'

Mihail Ivanovich did not at all know when 'you and I' had ever said any such thing about Bonaparte, but realizing that he was wanted as a peg on which to hang his employer's favourite topic he glanced wonderingly at the young prince, not quite sure what was coming next.

'He is a capital tactician!' said the prince to his son, indicating the architect.

And the conversation turned again on the war, on Bonaparte, and the generals and statesmen of the day. The old prince seemed convinced not only that all these men were mere schoolboys ignorant of the a b c of war and politics, and that Bonaparte was a trumpery little Frenchy successful only because there were no longer any Potemkins or Suvorovs to stand up to him; but he was also persuaded that no political complications existed in Europe, and that the war did not amount to anything but was merely a sort of puppet-show at which the authorities were playing while pretending to be doing something serious. Prince Andrei gaily bore with his father's sarcasm at the expense of the new men, and drew him on and listened to him with obvious pleasure.

'The past always seems good,' said he, 'but did not Suvorov himself fall into the trap Moreau laid for him, and not know how to get out?'

'Who told you that? Who said so?' cried the prince. 'Suvorov!' And he flung away his plate, which Tikhon caught very neatly. 'Suvorov! ... Consider, Prince Andrei! Frederick and Suvorov were a pair.... Moreau! – Moreau would have been taken prisoner if Suvorov's hands had been free; but he was saddled with the Hofs-kriegs-wurst-schnapps-rath. The devil himself could not have done anything. You'll see – you'll find out what those Hof-kriegs-wurst-raths are like! Suvorov was no match for them, so what chance do you suppose Mihail Kutuzov will have? No, my dear young friend,' he continued, 'you and your generals won't make any progress against Bonaparte: you'll have to call in Frenchmen – set a thief to catch a thief! The German, Pahlen, has been sent to New York in America to fetch the Frenchman Moreau,' he said, referring to the overtures that had been made that year to Moreau to enter the Russian service. 'It's marvellous! Were the Potemkins, Suvorovs and Orlovs Germans, pray? No, my lad, either you fellows have all lost your wits, or I have outlived mine. May God help you, but we shall see. They call Bonaparte a great general now! Ha!'

'I don't at all say that our plans are perfect,' remarked Prince Andrei. 'Only I can't understand how you can have such an opinion of Bonaparte. Laugh as much as you please, but all the same Bonaparte is a great general!'

'Mihail Ivanovich!' cried the old prince to the architect, who was giving his attention to the roast and hoping that they had forgotten him. 'Didn't I tell you Bonaparte was a great tactician? And here he says the same thing.'

'To be sure, your Excellency,' replied the architect.

The prince again laughed his chilling laugh.

'Bonaparte was born with a silver spoon in his mouth. His soldiers are first-rate. Besides, he began by attacking Germans and one would have to be half asleep not to beat the Germans. From the very beginning of the world everyone has beaten the Germans. They never beat anyone – except one another. He made his reputation fighting against them.'

And the prince began to expatiate on all the blunders which in his opinion Bonaparte had committed in his wars, and even in politics. His son made no rejoinder, but it was evident that whatever arguments were advanced he was as little able as his father to change his opinion. Prince Andrei listened, refraining from reply and involuntarily wondering how a solitary old man having for so long lived in retirement in the country could know and discuss in such detail and so acutely all the military and political events in Europe of recent years.

'You think, do you, that I am too old to understand the present state of affairs?' concluded his father. 'But my mind's full of them. I can't sleep of a night. Tell me now, this great commander of yours – where and how has he proved his skill?'

'That would be a long story,' answered his son.

'Well, then, you go along to your Bonaparte! Mademoiselle Bourienne, here is another admirer of your powder-monkey of an emperor!' he cried in excellent French.

'You know I am no Bonapartist, prince.'

'*Dieu sait quand reviendra …*' hummed the prince out of tune, and with a still more discordant laugh he quitted the table.

The little princess had sat silent all through the discussion and the rest of the meal, looking in alarm now at Princess Maria, now at her father-in-law. When they left the table she took her sister-in-law's arm and drew her into another room.

'What a clever man your father is,' said she. 'Perhaps that is why I am afraid of him.'

'Oh, he is so kind!' answered Princess Maria.

25

PRINCE ANDREI was to leave the following evening. The old prince, not making any alteration in his habits, retired as usual after dinner. The little princess was with her sister-in-law. Prince Andrei in a travelling coat without epaulets was in his suite packing with the help of his valet. After inspecting the carriage himself and seeing the trunks put in, he ordered the horses to be harnessed. Only the things he always carried with him remained in his room: a dressing-case, a large canteen fitted with silver plate, two Turkish pistols, and a sabre – a present from his father who had brought it from the siege of Ochakov. All these travelling effects of Prince Andrei's were in the most perfect order: everything was new and clean, in cloth covers carefully tied with tapes.

People who are given to deliberating on their actions generally find themselves in a serious frame of mind when it comes to embarking on a journey or changing their mode of life. At such moments one reviews the past and forms plans for the future. Prince Andrei looked very thoughtful and tender. With his hands behind his back he paced briskly from corner to corner of the room, looking straight before him and meditatively shaking his head. Did he dread going to the war, or was he sad at leaving his wife? Both perhaps, but evidently he had no wish to be seen in such a mood, for catching the sound of footsteps in the passage he hurriedly unclasped his hands, stopped at the table as if fastening the cover of the dressing-case, and assumed his usual serene and impenetrable expression. It was the heavy tread of Princess Maria that he heard.

'They told me you had ordered the carriage to be brought round,' she cried, panting (she had apparently been running), 'and I did so want to have another little talk alone with you. God knows how long we may be parted again. You are not vexed with me for coming? You have changed so, Andrusha,' she added, as though to explain the question.

She smiled as she called him by his pet name. It was obviously strange to her to think that this stern, handsome man should be the same Andrusha, the slender mischievous boy who had been the play-mate of her childhood.

'And where is Lise?' he asked, answering her question only by a smile.

'She was so tired that she fell asleep on the couch in my room. Oh, Andrei, what a treasure of a wife you have,' she said, sitting down on the sofa facing her brother. 'She is quite a child: such a sweet, merry-hearted child. I have grown so fond of her.'

Prince Andrei was silent, but the princess noticed the ironical, con-temptuous expression which appeared on his face.

'But one must be indulgent to little weaknesses – who is free from them, Andrei? She was brought up and has grown up in society, don't forget. And then her position now is not a rosy one. We ought to put ourselves in other people's places. *Tout comprendre, c'est tout pardonner*. Just think what it must be like for her, poor little thing, after the life she has been used to, to part from her husband and be left alone in the country, and in her condition too! It's very hard.'

Prince Andrei smiled as he looked at his sister, in the way we smile at those we fancy we can see through.

'You live in the country and don't find the life so terrible,' said he.

'I? – but that's different. Why speak of me? I have no desire for any other life – I couldn't have because I have never known any other. But you think, Andrei: for a young society woman to be buried in the country during the best years of her life, all alone too, for papa is always busy and I ... well, you know what poor company I am for a woman accustomed to the best society. There is only Mademoiselle Bourienne ...'

'I don't like your Mademoiselle Bourienne at all,' said Prince Andrei.

'Oh no! She is very kind and good, and, what is more, much to be pitied. She has nobody, nobody at all. To tell you the truth, I don't need her – she's even in my way. I have always been rather a solitary creature, you know, and now I am more so than ever. I like to be alone. ... Father likes her very much. She and Mihail Ivanovich are the two people to whom he is always gentle and kind, because both of them are under an obligation to him. As Sterne says: "We don't love men so much for the good they have done us as for the good we have done them." *Mon père* took her in when she was a homeless orphan, and she is very good-natured. And father likes her way of reading. She reads to him in the evenings. She reads aloud beautifully.'

'Tell me the truth, Marie. I expect father's temper must make things trying for you sometimes, doesn't it?' Prince Andrei asked suddenly.

Princess Maria was first surprised, then aghast at this question.

'For me? ... Me? ... Trying for me?' she stammered.

'He has always been harsh; and now I should think he's getting very difficult,' said Prince Andrei, speaking slightingly of their father either in order to disconcert his sister or to see what she would say.

'You are a good man, André, except for a sort of intellectual pride,' said the princess, following her own train of thought rather than the thread of the conversation – 'and that is a great sin. Have we any right to judge father? And even if it were possible, what feeling but *vénération* could such a man as my father inspire? And I am so contented and happy with him. I only wish that you were all as happy as I am.'

Her brother shook his head incredulously.

'The only thing that worries me – I will tell you the truth, André – is father's attitude to religion. I cannot understand how a man of his tremendous intellect can fail to see what is as clear as daylight, and can go so far astray. That is the only thing that makes me unhappy. But even in this I have begun to notice a shade of improvement. His satire has been a little less biting of late, and there was a monk whom he received and had a long talk with.'

'Ah, my dear, I am afraid you and your monk are wasting your powder,' said Prince Andrei banteringly but affectionately.

'Ah, *mon ami*, I can only pray and hope that God will hear me. André,' she said timidly, after a moment's silence, 'I have a great favour to ask of you.'

'What is it, my dear?'

'No – promise you won't refuse. It will be no trouble to you, and there is nothing beneath you in it. Only it will be a comfort to me. Promise, Andrusha,' said she, thrusting her hand in her reticule and taking hold of something but not bringing it out, as if what she held were the subject of her request and must not be shown until she were assured of his promise to do what she desired.

She looked at her brother with a humble, beseeching glance.

'Even if it cost me a great sacrifice ...' answered Prince Andrei, as if guessing what it was about.

'Think whatever you will! I know you are just like father. Think as you choose, but do this for my sake! Please do! Father's father, our grandfather, wore it in all the battles he fought.' (She still did not take out what she was holding in the reticule.) 'So you promise?'

'Of course, what is it?'

'André, I will bless you with this icon and you must promise me you will never take it off. ... Do you promise?'

'If it does not weigh half a hundredweight and won't break my neck. ... To please you ...' said Prince Andrei, but immediately seeing the pained expression that came over his sister's face at this jest he repented and added: 'I shall be very glad to, my dear – really very glad.'

'He will save you in spite of yourself, and have mercy on you and bring you to Himself, for in Him alone is truth and peace,' she said in a voice trembling with emotion, solemnly holding up in both hands before her brother a small old-fashioned oval icon of the Saviour with a dark face in a silver setting, on a little silver chain of delicate workmanship.

She crossed herself, kissed the icon and handed it to Andrei.

'Please, André, for my sake ...'

Her large timid eyes shone with kindly light. Those eyes lighted up the whole of her thin, sickly face and made it beautiful. Her brother put out his hand for the icon but she stopped him. Andrei understood, crossed himself and kissed the icon. His face was both tender (for he was touched) and at the same time ironical.

'Thank you, my dear.'

She kissed him on the brow and sat down again on the sofa. Both were silent.

'As I was saying to you, André, be kind and generous-hearted as you always used to be. Don't judge Lise harshly,' she began. 'She is so sweet, so good, and her position just now is a very hard one.'

'Come, Masha, I don't think I have complained of my wife to you, or found fault with her. Why do you say all this to me?'

Red patches appeared on Princess Maria's face and she was dumb as though she felt guilty.

'I have said nothing to you, but you have been *talked to*. And that makes me sad.'

The red patches flamed still deeper on her forehead, neck and cheeks. She tried to say something but could not get a word out. Her brother had guessed right: the little princess had cried after dinner, and spoken of her forebodings about her confinement, and of how she dreaded it, and had complained of her lot, of her father-in-law and her husband. After her tears she had fallen asleep. Prince Andrei felt sorry for his sister.

'Let me tell you one thing, Masha, I have no fault to find with *my wife*, I never had and never shall have, nor have I any cause for self-reproach in regard to her; and this will always be so in whatever circumstances I find myself. But if you want to know the truth ... if you want to know whether I am happy? The answer is No. Is she happy? No. Why is this so? I do not know. ....'

As he said this he got up, went over to his sister and, stooping, kissed her forehead. His fine eyes shone with a thoughtful, kindly, unwonted gleam though he was not looking at his sister but over her head towards the dark aperture of the open door.

'Let us go to her, it is time to say good-bye. No, you go ahead and wake her, and I will follow. Petrushka!' he called to his valet. 'Come here and take these things. That goes under the seat, and this on the right.'

Princess Maria rose and started towards the door. Then she stopped and said in French:

'André, if you had faith you would have turned to God and implored Him to give you the love you do not feel, and your prayer would have been granted.'

'Well, maybe!' said Prince Andrei. 'Go on, Masha, I'll come immediately.'

On the way to his sister's room, in the gallery which connected one house with the other, Prince Andrei encountered Mademoiselle Bourienne smiling sweetly. It was the third time that day that she had thrown herself in his path in a secluded corridor, with the same ecstatic and artless smile.

'Oh, I thought you were in your room,' said she, for some reason blushing and casting down her eyes.

Prince Andrei looked at her severely, and his face suddenly showed irritation. He did not speak but stared at her forehead and hair, not looking at her eyes, with such contempt that the Frenchwoman flushed scarlet and turned away without a word. When he reached his sister's room his wife was awake and her blithe voice could be heard through the open door babbling away. She was chattering on in French, as though anxious to make up for lost time after long repression.

'No, but imagine the old Countess Zubov with her false curls and a mouth full of false teeth, as though she would defy the years. ... Ha, ha, ha, Marie!'

It was at least the fifth time that Prince Andrei had heard his wife tell the same story about Countess Zubov, with the same laugh. He entered the room quietly. The little princess, plump and rosy was sitting in an easy-chair with her work in her hands, pouring out Petersburg reminiscences and even the catch-phrases of Petersburg. Prince Andrei went up to her, stroked her hair and asked if she felt rested after the journey. She answered him and continued with her chatter.

The coach with six horses was waiting at the porch. It was an autumn night, so dark that the coachman could not see the pole of the carriage. Servants with lanterns bustled about on the steps. The great mansion was brilliant with lights shining through the lofty windows. The domestic serfs crowded in the outer hall, waiting to say good-bye to the young prince. The members of the household were collected in the big hall: Mihail Ivanovich, Mademoiselle Bourienne, Princess Maria and the little princess. Prince Andrei had been summoned to his father's study, where the old prince wished to bid him a private farewell. All were waiting for them to come out.

When Prince Andrei went into the study the old man, the spectacles of old age on his nose and wearing a white dressing-gown in which he never received anyone except his son, was sitting at the table writing. He glanced round.

'Are you off?' And he went on writing.

'I have come to say good-bye.'

'Kiss me here,' and he indicated his cheek. 'Thank you, thank you!'

'Why do you thank me?'

'Because you don't dilly-dally, because you aren't tied to your wife's apron-strings. The service before everything. Thank you, thank you!' And he went on writing so vigorously that his quill spluttered and squeaked. 'If you have anything to say, say it. I can attend to these two things at once,' he added.

'About my wife. ... I am so sorry to leave her on your hands ...'

'Why talk nonsense? Say what it is you want.'

'When the time comes, send to Moscow for an *accoucheur*. ... Get him here.'

The old prince stopped writing and pretending not to understand fixed his son with stern eyes.

'I know that if nature does not do her work no one can help,' said Prince Andrei, obviously embarrassed. 'I know that not more than one in a million cases goes amiss, but this is her whim and mine. People have been telling her things, she has had a dream, and she's frightened.'

'H'm ... H'm ...' growled the old man, taking up his pen again. 'I'll see to it.'

He signed his name with a flourish, and suddenly turned to his son with a laugh.

'It's a bad business, eh?'

'What is, father?'

'Your wife!' said the old prince with blunt significance.

'I don't understand,' said Prince Andrei.

'Yes, there's nothing to be done about it, my young friend,' said the prince. 'They're all alike; and there's no getting unmarried again. Never fear, I won't tell anyone; but you know yourself it's the truth.'

He grasped his son's hand with his small bony fingers, shook it, looked him straight in the face with keen eyes which seemed to see through a person, and again laughed his chilly laugh.

The son sighed, thereby admitting that his father had read him correctly. The old man continued to fold and seal his letters, snatching up and throwing down wax, seal and paper with his habitual rapidity.

'What can you do? She's a beauty. I'll see to everything. Make your mind easy,' said he abruptly, as he sealed the last letter.

Andrei was silent. It was both pleasant and painful that his father understood him. The old man got up and handed the letter to his son.

'Come,' said he, 'don't worry about your wife. Whatever can be done shall be done. Now listen. Give this letter to Mihail Ilarionovich.'

(This was Kutuzov.) 'I have asked him to make use of you in proper places, and not keep you too long as an adjutant: it's a nasty job! Tell him that I remember him with affection. Write and let me know how he receives you. If he gives you a proper welcome, stay with him. The son of Nikolai Andreich Bolkonsky need serve no one on sufferance. Now come here.'

He spoke so rapidly that half his words were left unfinished, but his son was used to understanding him. He led him to a desk, threw back the lid, pulled open a drawer and drew out a manuscript-book filled with his own bold, angular, close handwriting.

'I am sure to die before you. So remember, these are my memoirs to be given to the Emperor after my death. Now here is a bank-note and a letter: it is a prize for anyone who writes a history of Suvorov's campaigns. Send it to the Academy. Here are some jottings for you to read after I am gone. You will find them worth your while.'

Andrei did not tell his father that he would no doubt live a long time yet. He felt it better not to say that.

'I shall carry out your wishes, father,' he said.

'Well, now, good-bye.' He gave his hand to be kissed, and embraced his son. 'Remember one thing, Prince Andrei: if you get killed, it will be a grief to me in my old age ...' He paused abruptly and then in a scolding voice suddenly cried: 'But if I were to hear that you had not behaved like the son of Nikolai Bolkonsky, I should be – ashamed!'

'You need not have said that to me, father,' replied the son with a smile.

The old man did not speak.

'There's another thing I wanted to ask you,' continued Prince Andrei. 'If I am killed and if I have a son, keep him here with you, as I was saying yesterday. Let him grow up under your roof.... Please.'

'Not let your wife have him?' said the old man, and he laughed.

They stood in silence, facing one another. The old man's keen eyes gazed straight into his son's. There was a tremor in the lower part of the old prince's face.

'We have said good-bye ... now go!' said he suddenly. 'Go!' he shouted in a loud, angry voice, opening the study door.

'What is it? What has happened?' asked Prince Andrei's wife and sister as Prince Andrei came out and they caught a momentary glimpse of the old man in his white dressing-gown, without his wig and wearing his spectacles, as he appeared at the door shouting irately.

Prince Andrei sighed and made no reply.

'Well!' said he, turning to his wife. And this 'Well!' sounded like a cold sneer, as though he were saying: 'Now go through your little performance.'

'André, already?' said the little princess, turning pale and fixing terror-stricken eyes on her husband.

He embraced her. She shrieked and fell swooning on his shoulder.

He warily released the shoulder she leant on, glanced into her face and carefully laid her in an armchair.

'Adieu, Marie,' said he gently to his sister, taking her by the hand and kissing her, and hastened out of the room.

The little princess lay in the armchair, Mademoiselle Bourienne chafing her temples. Princess Maria, supporting her sister-in-law, continued to look with her beautiful eyes dim with tears at the door through which Prince Andrei had disappeared, and she made the sign of the cross after him. From the study came the sounds of the old man blowing his nose with sharp angry reports like pistol shots. Hardly had Prince Andrei left the room before the study door was flung open and the stern figure of the old man in his white dressing-gown looked out.

'Gone, has he? Well, and a good thing too!' said he, and looking furiously at the fainting little princess he shook his head reprovingly and slammed the door.

PART TWO

I

In the October of 1805 a Russian army was cantoned in the villages and towns of the Archduchy of Austria, and fresh regiments kept arriving from Russia and encamping about the fortress of Braunau, making a heavy burden for the inhabitants on whom they were billeted. Braunau was the headquarters of the commander-in-chief, Kutuzov.

On the 11th of October 1805 one of the infantry regiments that had just reached Braunau halted about half a mile from the city, waiting to be reviewed by the commander-in-chief. Despite the un-Russian appearance of the locality and surrounding landscape – orchards, stone walls, tiled roofs and distant hills – and the fact that the peasants gazing with curiosity at the soldiers were not Russians, the regiment looked exactly like every Russian regiment when it is getting ready for an inspection anywhere in the heart of Russia.

In the evening, on the last stage of the march, an order had been received that the commander-in-chief would review the regiment on the march. Though the wording of the order had not seemed altogether clear to the commanding officer, and the question arose whether the troops were to be in marching order or not, it was decided at a consultation between the battalion commanders to present the regiment in parade formation, on the principle that it is always better 'to bow too low than not bow low enough'. So the soldiers, after a twenty-mile march, did not get a wink of sleep but were up all night cleaning and polishing, while the adjutants and company commanders calculated and reckoned; and by morning the regiment – instead of the straggling disorderly mob it had been on the last stage of its march the day before – presented a compact array of two thousand men, each of whom knew his place and his duty, and had every button and strap shining and in position. Not only externally was all correct – if the commander-in-chief should think fit to look beneath the uniforms he would see on every man alike a clean shirt, and in every knapsack he would find the regulation number of articles, 'awl, soap and all' as the soldiers put it. There was only one detail concerning which no one could be at ease. This was their foot-gear. The boots of more than half the men were worn out. But this was not the fault of the commanding officer since, notwithstanding his repeated demands, supplies had not been issued by the Austrian commissariat, and the men had marched some seven hundred miles.

The commander of the regiment was a florid-looking general past middle age, with grizzled eyebrows and whiskers, stout, and thick-set: the depth of his chest was greater than the breadth of his shoulders. Wearing a brand-new uniform showing the creases where it had been folded, and heavy gold epaulets which seemed to stand up rather than lie on his massive shoulders, he had the air of a man happily perform-ing one of the most solemn functions in life. He walked up and down in front of the line, throwing his leg out at every step and slightly arching his back. It was plain that the commander was proud of his regiment, delighted in it and was heart and soul wrapped up in it. His pompous gait, however, seemed to suggest that his military interests left plenty of room in his thoughts for the attractions of society and the fair sex.

'Well, my dear Mihail Mitrich,' said he, addressing one of the battalion commanders, who stepped forward with a smile (it was clear that both were in excellent spirits), 'we had a tough night of it, didn't we? However, everything seems all right. The regiment doesn't look at all bad, eh?'

The battalion commander understood the jovial irony and laughed.

'No, we shouldn't even be turned off the Petersburg Parade Ground.'

'What's that?' asked the commander.

At that moment two figures on horseback appeared on the road from the town, along which signallers had been posted. They were an aide-de-camp and a Cossack riding behind him.

The aide-de-camp had been sent from headquarters to confirm the order not clearly worded the day before, and make it plain that the commander-in-chief wished to inspect the regiment in exactly the condition in which it had arrived – wearing greatcoats and carrying packs, and without any polishing up.

A member of the Hofkriegsrath from Vienna had been with

Kutuzov the previous day, with proposals and demands for Kutuzov to join up in all haste with the allied armies under the Archduke Ferdinand and General Mack; and Kutuzov, not considering this junction advisable, intended, as one of the arguments in support of his view, to show the Austrian general the pitiable state in which the troops from Russia had arrived. With this object he was anxious to go out to meet the regiment, so that the worse the condition of the men the better pleased the commander-in-chief would be. Though the aide-de-camp did not know these ins-and-outs, he nevertheless delivered the urgent order that the men should be in their greatcoats and carrying packs, and insisted that if it were otherwise the commander-in-chief would be ill pleased.

On hearing this the commanding officer's head sank; he shrugged his shoulders in silence and testily spread out his arms.

'A fine mess!' he cried. 'Didn't I tell you, Mihail Mitrich, that "marching order" meant greatcoats?' said he, turning reproachfully to the battalion commander. 'Oh, my God!' he added, stepping resolutely forward. 'Company commanders!' he shouted in a voice accustomed to giving orders. 'Sergeant-majors! ... How soon will his Excellency be here?' he asked the aide-de-camp with respectful deference evidently proportioned to the dignity of the personage to whom he was referring.

'In about an hour, I fancy.'

'Shall we have time to make the change?'

'I can't say, general ...'

The commanding officer, hastening among the ranks himself, arranged for the men to change back into their greatcoats. The company commanders ran off to their companies, the sergeant-majors began bustling about (the greatcoats were not quite up to the mark), and in an instant the solid squares which till then had been standing silent and motionless, stirred, stretched out and began to hum with talk. Soldiers ran this way and that, throwing up their knapsacks with a jerk of their shoulders and pulling the straps over their heads, unfastening their greatcoats and lifting their arms high in the air, trying to get them into the sleeves.

Half an hour later everything was in the same good order as before, only the square had been transformed from black to grey. The general strutted out to the front of the regiment again and examined it from a distance.

'Whatever does this mean? What is that?' he shouted, stopping short. 'Captain of the 3rd company!'

'Captain of the 3rd company wanted by the general! ... captain to the general ... 3rd company to the captain! ...' the command passed along the lines and an adjutant ran to look for the missing officer.

When the eagerly but wrongly-repeated summons reached its destination in a cry of: 'The general to the 3rd company!' the missing officer emerged from behind his men and, though well on in years and not in the habit of running, came towards the general, trotting awkwardly on his toes. The captain's face showed the uneasiness of a schoolboy called upon to repeat a lesson he has not learnt. Patches of deeper colour appeared on his red face (the redness of which was obviously due to intemperance), and his mouth twitched nervously. The general looked the captain up and down as he approached panting, slackening pace as he drew nearer.

'You'll soon be dressing your men in petticoats! What does that mean?' shouted the commanding officer, thrusting out his lower jaw and pointing to a soldier in the ranks of the 3rd company who wore a greatcoat a different colour from the other greatcoats. 'And where have you been? The commander-in-chief is expected and you leave your post? Eh? I'll teach you to rig your men out in dressing-gowns for inspection! ... Eh? ...'

The captain, never taking his eyes off his superior, pressed two fingers more and more rigidly to his cap, as if in this pressure lay his only hope of salvation.

'Well, why don't you speak? Who's that you've got dressed up there like a Hungarian?' demanded the commander with grim facetiousness.

'Your Excellency ...'

'Well, "your Excellency" what? Your Excellency! Your Excellency! What about your Excellency? ... Nobody knows.'

'Your Excellency, it's the officer Dolohov, who was reduced to the ranks,' the captain said softly.

'Well? Was he degraded into a field-marshal, or into the ranks? If he's a soldier, then he must be dressed like the others, in regulation uniform.'

'Your Excellency, you yourself authorized him to wear that, on the march.'

'Authorized? Authorized? That's just like you young men,' said the commanding officer, cooling down a little. 'Authorized indeed ... We give you an inch, and you take ...' The general paused. 'We give you an inch, and you – Well!' said he with a fresh access of temper. 'Be good enough to dress your men properly....'

And the general glanced at the adjutant and directed his jerky steps towards the regiment. It was obvious that he was pleased with his display of anger and hoped to find a further pretext for wrath as he progressed along the ranks. Having berated one officer for an un-polished badge and another because his line was not straight, he reached company three.

'Ho-o-o-w are you standing? Where's your leg? Your leg – where is it?' shouted the commanding officer with a note of anguish in his voice, while there were still half a dozen men between him and Dolohov in his bluish greatcoat.

Dolohov slowly straightened his bent knee staring the general in the face with his bright, insolent eyes.

'Why that blue coat? Off with it! ... Sergeant-major! Strip this man ... the rasc ...' He did not have time to finish.

'General, I am bound to obey orders, but I am not bound to put up with ...' said Dolohov quickly.

'No talking in the ranks! ... No talking, no talking!'

'Not bound to put up with insults,' Dolohov concluded in a loud, ringing voice.

The eyes of the general and the private met. The general stopped silent, angrily pulling down his tight muffler.

'Have the goodness to change your coat, I beg of you,' said he as he turned away.

2

'HE's coming!' shouted one of the signalmen at that moment.

The commanding officer, flushing, ran to his horse, seized the stir-rup with trembling hands, threw his body across the saddle, righted himself, drew his sabre and with a radiant, resolute face, opening his mouth sideways, prepared to shout the word of command. The regi-ment fluttered like a bird preening its wings, and became still.

'Atten – tion!' roared the general in a soul-shaking voice, express-ing at once gladness on his own account, severity towards the regi-ment and welcome as regards the approaching chief.

Along the broad country road, shaded with trees on both sides, came a high Viennese calèche painted light blue, slightly creaking on its springs and drawn by six horses at a brisk trot. Behind the calèche galloped the suite and an escort of Croats. Beside Kutuzov sat an Austrian general in a white uniform which made a strange contrast with the Russian black. The calèche drew up in front of the regiment. Kutuzov and the Austrian general were talking in low voices and Kutuzov smiled slightly as, treading heavily, he stepped down from the carriage, exactly as though the two thousand men breathlessly gazing at him and at their general did not exist.

The word of command rang out, and again the regiment quivered and with a jingling sound presented arms. The dead silence was broken by the feeble voice of the commander-in-chief, and the regiment roared 'Long life to your Ex ... len ... len ... lency!' And again all was still. At first Kutuzov stood where he was, while the regiment moved; then he and the general in white, accompanied by the suite, started to walk down the line.

From the way the general in command of the regiment saluted the commander-in-chief, drawing himself up obsequiously and devouring him with his eyes, and from the way he followed the two generals through the ranks, bending forward and hardly able to restrain his jerky gait, and from the way he darted forward at Kutuzov's every word or gesture, it was plain that he performed his duties as a subordinate with even greater enjoyment than he did those of a commander. The regiment, thanks to the stern discipline and strenuous endeavours of its general, was in splendid condition compared to others that had reached Braunau at the same time. The number of sick and stragglers left behind was only two hundred and seventeen. And everything was in excellent order, with the exception of the soldiers' boots.

Kutuzov proceeded down the ranks, stopping now and then to say a few friendly words to officers or even privates whom he had known in the war against Turkey. Glancing at their boots he more than once shook his head mournfully, pointing them out to the Austrian general with an expression implying that he blamed no one but could not help noticing what a bad state of things it was. Each time this happened the commanding officer ran forward, afraid of missing a single word the commander-in-chief might utter in regard to the regiment. Behind Kutuzov, at a distance that allowed every softly-spoken word to be heard, followed some twenty personages of his suite. These gentlemen were talking among themselves and occasionally laughing. Nearest of all to the commander-in-chief walked a handsome adjutant. This was Prince Bolkonsky. Beside him was his comrade Nesvitsky, a tall, excessively stout staff-officer with a kind, smiling, handsome face and liquid eyes. Nesvitsky could hardly keep from laughing at the antics of a swarthy officer of the Hussars walking near him. This hussar, with a grave face and without a smile or a change in the fixed expression of his eyes, watched the commanding officer's back and mimicked his every movement. Each time the commander tottered and leaned forward, the hussar officer would totter and lean forward in precisely the same manner. Nesvitsky was laughing and nudging the others to look at the wag.

Kutuzov walked slowly and languidly past thousands of eyes that were almost falling out of their heads in the effort to watch him. On reaching the third company he suddenly stopped. His suite, not anticipating this halt, involuntarily crowded up close to him.

'Ah, Timohin!' said the commander-in-chief, recognizing the red-nosed captain who had been in trouble over the blue greatcoat.

Timohin, who, one would have said, had drawn himself up to his fullest height when he was reprimanded by his commanding officer, now when addressed by the commander-in-chief stood so rigidly erect that it seemed the strain must prove too much should the commander-in-chief continue looking at him; and accordingly Kutuzov, evidently realizing the position and wishing the captain nothing but good, quickly turned away, a scarcely perceptible smile flitting over his puffy, scarred face.

'Another Ismail comrade,' said he. 'A brave soldier! Are you satisfied with him?' he asked of the commanding officer.

And the latter – unconscious that he was being reflected in the hussar as in a looking-glass – started, stepped forward and replied:

'Highly satisfied, your Excellency!'

'We all have our little weaknesses,' said Kutuzov, smiling and walking away. 'He used to have a predilection for Bacchus.'

The commanding officer was afraid that he might be held responsible for this, and did not answer. The hussar at that moment noticed the face of the red-nosed captain with his stomach drawn in, and imitated his expression and attitude so exactly that Nesvitsky laughed outright. Kutuzov turned round. The officer evidently possessed perfect control of his features: while Kutuzov was turning round he managed to replace the grimace by the most serious, deferential and innocent of expressions.

The third company was the last and Kutuzov paused, apparently trying to remember something. Prince Andrei moved forward from the suite and said in an undertone, in French:

'You ordered me to remind you of the officer Dolohov, reduced to the ranks in this regiment.'

'Where is Dolohov?' asked Kutuzov.

Dolohov, attired by now in the grey greatcoat of an ordinary soldier, did not wait to be summoned. The well-proportioned figure of the fair-haired soldier with clear blue eyes stepped forward from the ranks, went up to the commander-in-chief and presented arms.

'A complaint to make?' Kutuzov asked with a slight frown.

'This is Dolohov,' said Prince Andrei.

'Ah!' said Kutuzov. 'I hope you will profit by this lesson. Do your duty. The Emperor is gracious. And I shan't forget you if you deserve well.'

The bright blue eyes looked at the commander-in-chief just as boldly as they had looked at the general of his regiment, their expression seeming to rend the veil of convention that so widely separates commander-in-chief from private.

'I only beg one favour, your most high Excellency,' said Dolohov in his firm, ringing, deliberate voice. 'I ask for an opportunity to atone for my offence, and prove my devotion to his Majesty the Emperor and to Russia!'

Kutuzov turned away. For a second there was a gleam in his eyes of the same smile with which he had turned from Captain Timohin. He frowned, as though to declare that everything Dolohov had said to him, and everything he could possibly say, he had known long ago and was weary of, and that it was all so much wasted breath. He moved away and went back to the carriage.

The regiment broke up into companies and set off for their appointed quarters not far from Braunau, where they hoped to find boots and clothes, and to rest after their hard marches.

'You won't bear me a grudge, Prohor Ignatich?' said the commanding officer, overtaking the third company and riding up to Captain Timohin who was marching in front. The commanding officer's face now that the inspection was successfully over beamed with delight he could not suppress. 'In the Emperor's service ... one can't help ... one sometimes flies off the handle on parade. ... I am the first to apologize, you know me! ... He was very pleased!' And he held out his hand to the captain.

'Upon my word, general, as if I'd make so bold! ...' answered the captain, his nose growing plum-colour as he gave a smile which showed where two front teeth were missing that had been knocked out by the butt-end of a gun at Ismail.

'And assure Dolohov that I shall not forget him – he may rest easy on that score. By the way, tell me, pray, how is he behaving himself? I've been meaning to inquire. ...'

'He's most punctilious in the discharge of his duties, your Excellency; but his temper ...' said Timohin.

'What about his temper?' asked the general.

'It varies with the day, your Excellency,' said the captain. 'One day he is sensible, intelligent and quiet. And the next he's like a wild beast. In Poland, if you please, he all but killed a Jew.'

'Yes, yes,' remarked the commanding officer. 'Still, one must be easy on a young man in misfortune. He has influential connexions, you know. ... So you would be wise to ...'

'Exactly so, your Excellency,' said Timohin, showing with a smile that he understood his chief's wishes.

'Quite, quite.'

The commanding officer sought out Dolohov in the ranks and reining in his horse said to him:

'The first engagement may bring you your epaulets!'

Dolohov looked round and said nothing. There was no change in the ironical smile that curled his lips.

'Well, that's all right then,' continued the commanding officer. 'A round of vodka for the men from me,' he added loud enough to be heard by the soldiers. 'I thank you all! God be praised!' And he rode past that company and overtook the next one.

'After all, he's really a good fellow and not difficult to serve under,' said Timohin to the subaltern beside him.

'"King of hearts", in fact,' said the subaltern, laughing. (The commanding officer was nicknamed the 'king of hearts'.)

The happy mood of their officers after the inspection infected the men. The company marched along cheerfully. Soldiers' voices could be heard on all sides chatting away.

'Who invented the story that Kutuzov's blind in one eye?'

'Well so he is! Quite blind.'

'Nay, lad, he can see better than what you can. Boots and leg-bands ... he didn't miss a thing.'

'I say, mate, when he looked at my feet ... well, thinks I ...'

'And that other one with him, that there Austrian – looked as if 'e was smeared with chalk – white as flour, 'e was. I bet they polish 'im up like us rubs the guns!'

'Hey, Fedeshou! ... Did he say when the fighting would start? You were near him. They did say Bonaparte himself was at Braunau.'

'Bonaparte here! ... That's fool talk! What won't you know next! The Prussians are up in arms now. The Austrians, you see, are laying theirs down. When they're out of it, then the war will begin with Bonaparte. And here you go saying Bonaparte's in Braunau! Shows you're a fool! Why not keep your ears open?'

'Plague take these quartermasters! See, there's the fifth company turning off into the village already. ... They'll have their buckwheat cooked before we get in.'

'Give us a biscuit, old man.'

'And yesterday did you give me a plug of baccy? Not a bit of it. Still, all right, here you are.'

'They might call a halt here – the idea of another four miles on an empty stomach!'

'Wasn't it fine when those Germans gave us carts? Sitting easy and going alone – that was something like!'

'But hereabouts, my friend, the folk look half daft. Back there the Poles at any rate were our Emperor's people, but here they're all regular Germans.'

'Singers to the front!' shouted an officer.

And a score of men broke from different ranks and ran to the head of the column. The drummer, who led the singing, faced about, flourished his arm and struck up an interminable soldier's song beginning: *Morning dawned, the sun was rising* and ending *On then, boys, on to glory, led by old Father Kamensky*. This song had been composed in Turkey and now was sung in Austria, the only variation being the words *Father Kutuzov* in place of *Father Kamensky*.

Jerking out the last words in military style and waving his arms as if he were hurling something to the ground, the drummer, a lean, handsome soldier of about forty, looked sternly at the singers and screwed up his face. Then, satisfied that all eyes were fixed on him, he raised both arms as though he were carefully lifting some invisible but precious object above his head and, holding it there for several seconds, suddenly flung it down with a despairing gesture:

'Oh, my bower, oh, my bower! ...'

'Oh, my bower new! ...' chimed in twenty voices, and the kitchen orderly, disregarding the weight of his equipment, frisked out in front and walking backwards before the company twitched his shoulders and made gestures of defiance with his ladles. The soldiers, swinging their arms in time with the music, marched with long steps, involuntarily keeping to the beat. Behind the company was heard the rattle of wheels with the creaking of springs and the tramp of horses. Kutuzov and his suite were returning to town. The commander-in-chief made a sign for the men to continue marching at ease, and he and all his staff showed pleasure at the singing and the spectacle of the dancing soldier and the gay and lively appearance of troops as they marched. Conspicuous in the second file of the right flank, the side on which the carriage was passing the company, was Dolohov, the blue-eyed private, who was jauntily swinging along with particular grace, keeping time to the song and looking into the faces of those driving by with an expression that seemed to smack of pity for all who were not at that moment marching with the company. The hussar cornet in Kutuzov's suite who had mimicked the commanding officer fell behind the carriage and rode up to Dolohov.

Hussar cornet Zherkov had at one time belonged to the same wild set in Petersburg of which Dolohov had been the leader. Meeting Dolohov abroad as a common soldier, Zherkov had not found it expedient to recognize him. But now that Kutuzov had spoken to the gentleman-ranker he addressed him with the cordiality of an old friend.

'My dear fellow, how are you?' said he through the singing, walking his horse abreast of the company.

'How am I?' Dolohov repeated coldly. 'As you see.'

The lively song gave a special flavour to the tone of easy good fellowship in which Zherkov spoke and to the studied coolness of Dolohov's reply.

'And how do you get on with your officers?' inquired Zherkov.

'All right. They are good fellows. How did you manage to wriggle on to the staff?'

'I was attached: I'm on duty.'

Neither spoke.

She let the hawk fly upward from out of her right sleeve, rang out the song, the very sound of it inspiring a bold, blithe sensation. Their conversation would probably have been different but for the influence of the song.

'Is it true that the Austrians have been beaten?' asked Dolohov.

'The devil only knows. They say so.'

'I'm glad,' answered Dolohov briefly and clearly, as the song demanded.

'I say, come round one evening. We'll have a game of faro,' said Zherkov.

'Why, have you too much money?'

'Do come.'

'Can't. I've sworn off. I'm neither drinking nor playing cards till I get reinstated.'

'Well, that's only till after the first engagement.'

'We shall see.'

They were silent again.

'Look in if you need anything. One can at least be of use on the staff ...' said Zherkov.

Dolohov grinned.

'Don't worry yourself. If I want anything, I shan't beg for it – I'll take it myself.'

'Well, I only meant ...'

'And I only meant ...'

'Good-bye.'

'Good-bye to you. ...'

> And high in the air, and far away,
> The hawk flew off to her native land.

Zherkov put spurs to his horse, which pranced excitedly from foot to foot uncertain which to move first, then steadied itself and galloped forward, outstripping the company and catching up with the carriage, all in time to the song.

3

ON his return from the review Kutuzov took the Austrian general into his private room and calling his adjutant asked for certain papers relating to the state of the troops on their arrival, and the letters that had been received from the Archduke Ferdinand, who was in command of the advanced army. Prince Andrei Bolkonsky came in with the required documents. Kutuzov and the Austrian member of the Hofkriegsrath were sitting over a map which was spread on the table.

'Ah! ...' said Kutuzov, glancing at Bolkonsky and by this exclamation as it were inviting his adjutant to wait while he went on with the conversation in French.

'All I can say, general,' proceeded Kutuzov with a pleasing elegance of expression and intonation which constrained one to listen to each deliberately uttered word. It was evident that Kutuzov took pleasure in listening to himself. 'All I can say, general, is that if the matter depended on my personal wishes the desire of his Majesty the Emperor Francis would have been fulfilled long ago. I should long since have joined the Archduke. And upon my honour I assure you that for me personally it would be a relief to hand over the supreme command of the army to a general better informed than myself, and more expert – of whom Austria possesses an abundance – and so throw off all this weighty responsibility. But circumstances are sometimes too strong for us, general.'

And Kutuzov smiled in a way that seemed to say: 'You are quite at liberty not to believe me, and indeed I don't care whether you believe me or not, but you have no grounds for telling me so. And that is the whole point.'

The Austrian general looked dissatisfied, but had no choice but to reply in the same tone.

'On the contrary,' said he, in a querulous, irritated manner that contrasted with the flattering intention of the words he uttered, 'on the contrary, his Majesty highly appreciates the part that your Excellency has played in the common cause; but we consider that the present delay robs the glorious Russian troops and their generals of the laurels which they are accustomed to win in their battles,' he concluded, with a phrase evidently prepared beforehand.

Kutuzov bowed, still with the same smile.

'That is my conviction, however, and judging by the last let'er with which his Highness the Archduke Ferdinand has honoured me, I have no doubt that the Austrian troops, under the direction of so skilful a leader as General Mack, have by now already gained a decisive victory and no longer need our aid,' said Kutuzov.

The general frowned. Though there was no definite news of an Austrian defeat, there was too much circumstantial evidence confirming the unfavourable rumours that were rife; and so Kutuzov's assumption of an Austrian victory sounded very much like a sneer. But Kutuzov continued to smile blandly with the same expression, which seemed to say that he had a right to make this assumption. And in fact the last letter he had received from General Mack informed him of a victory and of the very favourable strategic position of the army.

'Let me have that letter,' said Kutuzov turning to Prince Andrei. 'Here, listen to this' – and Kutuzov with an ironical smile hovering about the corners of his mouth read out to the Austrian general the following passage in German from the Archduke Ferdinand's letter:

'We have fully concentrated forces of nearly seventy thousand men with which to attack and defeat the enemy should he cross the Lech. Since we are already masters of Ulm, we cannot be deprived of the advantage of commanding both banks of the Danube, and therefore should the enemy not cross the Lech we can at any moment cross the Danube, throw ourselves on his line of communication, recross the river lower down and frustrate his intention should he think of turning the main body of his forces against our faithful ally. We shall wait confidently therefore until the Imperial Russian army is ready to join us, when we shall easily find an opportunity in common to prepare for the enemy the fate he deserves.'

Kutuzov drew a long breath on coming to the end of this paragraph, and looked with an attentive, affable expression at the member of the Hofkriegsrath.

'But you know the wise maxim, your Excellency, which bids us be prepared for the worst,' said the Austrian general, evidently anxious to have done with jests and to get to business.

He cast a displeased glance at the adjutant.

'Excuse me, general,' interrupted Kutuzov, also turning to Prince Andrei. 'Look here, my dear fellow, get from Kozlovsky all the reports from our scouts. Here are two letters from Count Nostitz, and here's one from his Highness the Archduke Ferdinand – and these,' he said, handing him several papers. 'Make out a neat memorandum in French showing all the information we have had of the movements of the Austrian army. When you have finished, give it to his Excellency.'

Prince Andrei inclined his head in token of having understood from the first not only what had been said but also what Kutuzov would have liked to tell him. He gathered up the papers and with a bow to include both men stepped softly over the carpet and went out into the waiting-room.

Though not much time had elapsed since Prince Andrei had left Russia, he had changed greatly during that period. In the expression of his face, in his movements, in his gait, scarcely a trace was left of his former affected languor and indolence. He now looked like a man who has no time to think of the impression he is making on others, and is absorbed in work, both agreeable and interesting. His face showed more satisfaction with himself and those around him; his smile and glance were brighter and more attractive.

Kutuzov, whom he had joined in Poland, had received him very kindly and promised not to forget him. He had singled him out from among the other adjutants, taken him with him to Vienna and entrusted him with the more important duties. From Vienna Kutuzov had written to his old comrade, Prince Andrei's father:

'Your son', he wrote, 'bids fair to become an officer distinguished by his industry, energy and ability. I count myself fortunate to have such a subaltern.'

On Kutuzov's staff, among his fellow-officers and in the army generally, Prince Andrei had, as he had had in Petersburg society, two diametrically opposed reputations. Some, a minority, recognized Prince Andrei as being in a way different from themselves and everyone else, expected great things of him, listened to him, admired and imitated him; and with them Prince Andrei was natural and pleasant. Others, the majority, disliked him and considered him conceited, cold and disagreeable. But Prince Andrei had known what line to take with them too, so that they respected and were even afraid of him.

Coming out of Kutuzov's room into the waiting-room with the papers in his hand Prince Andrei went up to his comrade, the aide-de-camp on duty, Kozlovsky, who was sitting at the window with a book.

'Well, prince?' asked Kozlovsky.

'We are to draw up a memorandum to account for our not moving forward.'

'And why is it?'

Prince Andrei shrugged his shoulders.

'Any news from Mack?' asked Kozlovsky.

'No.'

'If it were true that he has been defeated news would have come.'

'Probably,' said Prince Andrei moving towards the outer door. But at that instant a tall Austrian general in a greatcoat with a black bandage round his head and the order of Maria Theresa on his collar, who had evidently just arrived, hurried into the room, slamming the door behind him. Prince Andrei stopped short.

'Commander-in-chief Kutuzov?' demanded the newly-arrived general, speaking quickly with a harsh German accent. He looked about him, and then made straight for the door of the private room.

'The commander-in-chief is engaged,' said Kozlovsky, hurrying towards the unknown general and barring his way to the door. 'Whom shall I announce?'

The unknown general looked down disdainfully at the short figure of Kozlovsky, as if surprised that anyone should not know him.

'The commander-in-chief is engaged,' repeated Kozlovsky calmly.

The general's face contracted, his lips twitched and trembled. He took out a notebook, hurriedly scribbled something in pencil, tore out the leaf, handed it to Kozlovsky, stepped quickly over to the window and threw himself into a chair, surveying those in the room as if asking what they were looking at him for. Then he lifted his head, stretched his neck as though intending to say something but immediately, with affected indifference, began to hum to himself, producing a strange sound which he instantly broke off. The door of the private room opened and Kutuzov appeared on the threshold. The general with the bandaged head bent forward as though running away from some danger, and with long, swift strides of his thin legs hastened up to Kutuzov.

'You see before you the unfortunate Mack,' he articulated in a broken voice.

Kutuzov's face as he stood in the open doorway remained perfectly immobile for several seconds. Then a frown ran over it, like a wave, leaving his forehead smooth again. He bowed his head respectfully, shut his eyes, ushered Mack in before him without a word, and himself closed the study door behind them.

The report which had already circulated of the defeat of the Austrians and the surrender of their entire army at Ulm proved to be correct. Within half an hour adjutants had been despatched in various directions with orders to the effect that the Russian troops, who had hitherto been inactive, would soon have to meet the enemy.

Prince Andrei was one of those rare staff-officers whose chief interest was centred on the general progress of the war. When he saw Mack and heard the details of the disaster he realized that half the campaign was lost, appreciated to the full the difficult situation of the Russian army, and vividly imagined what awaited it and the part he would have to play. He could not help feeling a thrill of delight at the thought of arrogant Austria's humiliation, and that perhaps within a week he would have a chance to witness and take part in the first Russian encounter with the French since the days of Suvorov. But he feared that Bonaparte's genius might outweigh all the valour of the Russian troops, and at the same time he could not bear to entertain the idea of his hero suffering disgrace.

Agitated and upset by these thoughts, Prince Andrei started for his room to write to his father, to whom he wrote every day. In the corridor he fell in with Nesvitsky, the comrade who shared quarters with him, and Zherkov, the comic man. They were, as usual, laughing at some joke.

'Why are you looking so glum?' asked Nesvitsky, noticing Prince Andrei's pale face and glittering eyes.

'There's nothing to be cheerful about,' answered Bolkonsky.

Just as Prince Andrei met Nesvitsky and Zherkov there came towards them from the other end of the corridor Strauch, an Austrian general who was attached to Kutuzov's staff to look after the provisioning of the Russian army. He was with the member of the Hofkriegsrath who had arrived the previous evening. There was plenty of room in the wide corridor for the generals to pass the three officers but Zherkov, giving Nesvitsky a push, exclaimed in a breathless voice:

'They're coming! ... they're coming! ... Stand aside, make way! Make way, please!'

The generals came along, looking as if they wished to avoid embarrassing demonstrations of respect. A silly smile of glee which he seemed unable to suppress spread over the face of Zherkov, the comic man.

'Your Excellency,' said he in German, stepping forward and addressing the Austrian general, 'I have the honour to congratulate you.'

He bowed, and awkwardly, like a child at a dancing lesson, scraped first with one foot and then with the other.

The member of the Hofkriegsrath looked at him severely; but seeing the earnestness of his silly smile could not refuse him a moment's attention. He screwed up his eyes and showed that he was listening.

'I have the honour to congratulate you. General Mack has arrived, quite safe and sound but for a slight bruise just here,' he added, pointing with a beaming smile to his head.

The general frowned, turned and went on his way.

'Good God, what a fool!' said he angrily, when he was a few steps away.

Nesvitsky with a chuckle threw his arms round Prince Andrei, but Bolkonsky, paler than ever and with an angry look on his face, pushed him aside and turned to Zherkov. The nervous irritability induced by the appearance of Mack, the news of his defeat and the thought of what lay before the Russian army found vent in wrath at Zherkov's untimely jest.

'If you, sir,' he began cuttingly, with a slight trembling of his lower jaw, 'choose to set up as a clown, I can't prevent you; but I warn you, if you dare a second time to play the fool in my presence I'll teach you how to behave.'

Nesvitsky and Zherkov were so astounded at this outburst that they gazed at Bolkonsky in silence, with wide-open eyes.

'Why, I only congratulated them,' said Zherkov.

'I am not trifling with you; be good enough to hold your tongue!' cried Bolkonsky, and taking Nesvitsky by the arm he walked off, leaving Zherkov who could find nothing to say.

'Come, what's the matter, old fellow?' said Nesvitsky soothingly.

'What's the matter?' exclaimed Prince Andrei, standing still in his excitement. 'Don't you understand, either we are officers serving our Tsar and our country, rejoicing in the successes and grieving at the misfortunes of our common cause, or we're hirelings caring nothing for our master's concerns! Forty thousand men massacred and the army of our allies destroyed, and you find it something to laugh at!'

he said in French, as if the use of this language added to the effect of what he was saying. 'It's all very well for a twopenny-halfpenny individual like that young man of whom you have made a friend, but not for you, not for you. Only a *whipper-snapper* could amuse himself in this fashion,' added Prince Andrei in Russian but pronouncing the word *whipper-snapper* with a French accent, when he noticed that Zherkov was still within hearing.

He waited to see if the cornet had any answer to make. But Zherkov turned on his heel and walked out of the corridor.

4

THE Pavlograd Hussars were encamped two miles outside Braunau. The squadron in which Nikolai Rostov was serving as a cadet was quartered in the German village of Zalzeneck, and the best billet in the village had been assigned to the squadron-commander, Cavalry-Captain Denisov, known to the entire cavalry division as 'Vasska' Denisov. Ensign Rostov had been sharing the squadron-commander's quarters ever since he had joined the regiment in Poland.

On October the 11th, the very same day when the news of Mack's defeat had raised a stir at headquarters, the camp life of the officers of the squadron was quietly proceeding as usual. Denisov, who had been losing at cards all night, had not yet come in when Rostov returned early in the morning from a foraging expedition. Rostov in his cadet uniform rode up to the porch, checked his horse, swung his leg over the saddle with the supple dexterity of youth, paused a moment in the stirrup as though sorry to dismount and at last sprang down and called to his orderly.

'Ah, Bondarenko, my dear fellow,' he cried to the hussar who rushed forward to attend to the horse. 'Walk him up and down for a bit, my friend,' he continued with that fraternal cordiality with which handsome young men are apt to treat everybody when they are happy.

'Right, your Excellency,' answered the Ukrainian with a gay toss of his head.

'Mind now, walk him up and down properly!'

Another hussar also rushed towards the horse but Bondarenko had already thrown the reins of the snaffle over the horse's head. It was evident that the ensign was liberal with his tips and that it paid to serve him. Rostov stroked the animal's neck and then its flank, and lingered for a moment on the step.

'Splendid! He'll make a fine charger!' he said to himself with a smile, and lifting his sabre he ran up the steps, his spurs rattling. The German on whom they were billeted, wearing a jerkin and a pointed cap, looked out from the cowshed where he was clearing manure with a pitchfork. At the sight of Rostov the German's face immediately lit up with a jolly smile.

'*Schön gut Morgen! Schön gut Morgen!*' he repeated, giving a wink, evidently pleased to greet the young man.

'Busy already?' said Rostov with the same gay brotherly smile that was constantly on his face. 'Hurrah for the Austrians! Hurrah for the Russians! Hurrah for the Emperor Alexander!' he went on, quoting the German's often repeated cry.

The German laughed, came right out of the cowshed, pulled off his cap and waving it over his head cried:

'And hurrah for the whole world!'

Rostov, following the German's example, waved his cap above his head and with a laugh shouted: 'And hurrah for the whole world!' Though neither the German cleaning his cowshed nor Rostov back with his platoon from foraging for hay had any reason for rejoicing, both looked at each other with happy enthusiasm and brotherly love, wagged their heads in token of mutual affection, and parted with smiles, the German returning to his cowshed and Rostov going into the cottage which he occupied with Denisov.

'Where's your master?' he asked Lavrushka, Denisov's orderly, whom the whole regiment knew for a rogue.

'He hasn't been in since last night. He must have been losing,' answered Lavrushka. 'I know by now, if he wins he comes home early, blowing his own trumpet; but if he's not back before morning it means he's lost and will come in in a rage. Will you have some coffee?'

'Yes, make haste.'

Ten minutes later Lavrushka brought the coffee.

'Here he comes!' said he. 'Now for trouble!'

Rostov glanced out of the window and saw Denisov returning home. Denisov was a little man with a red face, sparkling black eyes, and tousled black moustache and hair. He wore a hussar's cloak, which was unfastened, wide, sagging pantaloons, and a crumpled shako on the back of his head. He came up to the porch gloomily hanging his head.

'Lavwuska!' he shouted loudly and angrily. 'Take this off, idiot!'

'I *am* taking it off,' replied Lavrushka's voice.

'Ah, you're up already,' said Denisov, entering the room.

'Long ago,' replied Rostov. 'I have already been after the hay, and seen Fraülein Mathilde.'

'Oho! And I've been losing, bwother, losing all night like a son of a dog!' cried Denisov, not pronouncing his *r*'s. 'Such howid bad luck! Such howid bad luck! The moment you left, so it began. Hey there! Tea!'

Puckering up his face in a sort of smile and showing his short strong teeth, he began to run the stubby fingers of both hands through his thick black hair which stood up like a forest.

'The devil himself must have dwiven me to that wat' (an officer nicknamed 'the rat'), he said, rubbing his forehead and face with both hands. 'Just fancy! He didn't give me a single cahd, not one, not a single one!'

Denisov took the lighted pipe that was offered to him, gripped it in his fist and tapped it on the floor, making the sparks fly, while he continued to shout.

'Gives you the singles but collahs the doubles!'

He scattered the burning tobacco, smashed the pipe and threw it down. Then, after a short silence, he suddenly looked up at Rostov, his glittering black eyes full of merriment.

'If only we had some women here. But there's nothing for one to do but dwink. If only we could soon start the fighting. Hey, who's there?' he called, turning to the door as he heard the tread of heavy boots and the clatter of spurs followed by a respectful cough.

'The quartermaster!' said Lavrushka.

Denisov scowled even more.

'W'etched business!' he exclaimed, flinging down a purse containing a few gold pieces. 'Wostov, deah fellow, see how much is left, and shove the puhse undah the pillow,' said he, and went out to see the quartermaster.

Rostov took the money and mechanically arranging the old and new coins in separate piles began counting them.

'Ah, Telyanin! How d'ye do? I got a dwubbing last night,' Denisov was heard saying in the next room.

'Where was that? At Bykov's, at the rat's? ... I heard about it,' said a second piping voice, and thereupon Lieutenant Telyanin, a small man, an officer of the same squadron, entered the room.

Rostov thrust the purse under the pillow and shook the damp little hand that was held out to him. Telyanin had for some reason been transferred from the Guards shortly before the present campaign. He conducted himself very properly in the regiment but was not liked, and Rostov especially could neither conquer nor conceal his groundless aversion for the man.

'Well, my young horseman, how do you like my Rook?' he asked. (Rook was a saddle horse that Telyanin had sold Rostov.)

The lieutenant never looked the person he was speaking to in the face: his eyes were continually flitting from one object to another. 'I saw you out riding this morning ...'

'Oh, he's all right, a good horse,' replied Rostov, though the animal for which he had given seven hundred roubles was not worth half that sum. 'He's begun to go a bit lame on the left foreleg,' he added.

'Cracked hoof! That's nothing. I'll tell you what to do, and show you what kind of a rivet to put on.'

'Yes, please do,' said Rostov.

'I'll show you, I'll show you! There's no secret about it. And you'll be thanking me for that horse.'

'Then I'll have him brought round,' said Rostov, anxious to get away from Telyanin, and he went out to give the order.

In the passage Denisov with a pipe in his mouth was squatting on the threshold facing the quartermaster who was reporting to him. When he saw Rostov, Denisov screwed up his face and, pointing with his thumb over his shoulder to the room where Telyanin was sitting, frowned and shuddered with loathing.

'Ugh, I don't like that fellow!' said he, regardless of the quartermaster's presence.

Rostov shrugged his shoulders as much as to say: 'Nor do I, but what's to be done about it?' And having given his order, he returned to Telyanin.

Telyanin was still sitting in the same indolent attitude in which Rostov had left him, rubbing his small white hands.

'There certainly are disgusting people about,' thought Rostov as he went into the room.

146

'Well, have you told them to bring the horse round?' asked Telyanin, getting up and looking carelessly about him.

'I have.'

'Let's go ourselves. I only came over to ask Denisov about today's orders. Have you got them, Denisov?'

'Not yet. Where are you off to?'

'I want to teach this young man how to shoe a horse,' said Telyanin. They went out down the front steps to the stable. The lieutenant explained how to rivet the hoof and went away to his own quarters.

When Rostov returned there was a bottle of vodka and a sausage on the table. Denisov was sitting at the table scratching with his pen on a sheet of paper. He looked gloomily into Rostov's face and said:

'I am w'iting to her.'

He leaned his elbows on the table, with the pen in his hand, and evidently delighted at the chance of saying what he had in mind faster than he could put it on paper he related to Rostov the contents of his letter.

'Don't you see, my fwiend,' said he, 'we are asleep until we love. We are childwen of dust ... but when we fall in love we are gods, puah again as the day we were cweated.... Who's that now? Send him to the devil! I'm busy!' he shouted to Lavrushka who, not in the least daunted, came up to him.

'Who should it be? You told him to come yourself. It's the quartermaster for the money.'

Denisov scowled, opened his mouth to shout something but stopped.

'W'etched business,' he muttered to himself. 'I say, Wostov, how much is left in the puhse?' he asked, turning to Rostov.

'Seven new, three old.'

'Oh, w'etched! Well, what are you standing there foh, you sca'-cwow? Fetch in the quahtehmasteh!' he shouted to Lavrushka.

'Please, Denisov, let me lend you some money. I've got plenty, you know,' said Rostov, reddening.

'I don't like bowowing fwom my own fellows, I don't like it,' growled Denisov.

'But if you won't let me lend you some like a comrade I shall be offended. Really I've got it,' repeated Rostov.

'No, I tell you.'

And Denisov went over to the bed to get the purse from under the pillow.

'Where did you put it, Wostov?'

'Under the bottom pillow.'

'It isn't here.'

Denisov flung both pillows on the floor. There was no purse.

'That's stwange.'

'Hold on, didn't you throw it out?' said Rostov, picking up the pillows one at a time and shaking them.

He pulled off the quilt and shook it. There was no purse.

'I couldn't have forgotten, could I? No, I remember thinking how you kept it under your pillow like a secret treasure,' said Rostov. 'I put it just here. Where is it?' he demanded, turning to Lavrushka.

'I haven't been in the room. It must be where you put it.'

'But it isn't!'

'That's just like you. You throw a thing down anywhere and forget all about it. Look in your pockets.'

'No, if I hadn't thought about treasure,' said Rostov, 'but I remember putting it there.'

Lavrushka tore the whole bed apart, looked under it and under the table, searched everywhere and then stood still in the middle of the room. Denisov watched him in silence, and when Lavrushka spread out his hands in amazement, saying that the purse was nowhere to be found, he glanced at Rostov.

'Wostov, none of your schoolboy twicks …'

Rostov, conscious of Denisov's gaze fixed upon him, raised his eyes and instantly dropped them again. All the blood which had seemed congested somewhere below his throat rushed to his face and eyes. He could hardly draw his breath.

'And no one's been in the room 'cept the lieutenant and yourselves. It must be here somewhere,' said Lavrushka.

'Now then, you devil's puppet, fly awound, hunt for it!' shouted Denisov suddenly, turning purple and starting towards the valet with a threatening gesture. 'Find that puhse or I'll horsewhip you. I'll horsewhip the lot of you!'

Rostov, avoiding Denisov's glance, began buttoning up his jacket, buckled on his sabre and put on his cap.

'I must have that puhse, I tell you,' roared Denisov, shaking the orderly by the shoulders and knocking him against the wall.

'Denisov, let him be; I know who has taken it,' said Rostov, going towards the door without raising his eyes.

Denisov paused, considered a moment and evidently understanding the meaning of Rostov's remark clutched him by the arm.

'Wubbish!' he cried, and the veins on his forehead and neck stood out like cords. 'I tell you, you're mad; I won't allow it. The puhse is here. I'll have the hide off this wascal, and it'll be found.'

'I know who has taken it,' repeated Rostov in an unsteady voice, and went to the door.

'And I tell you, don't you dahe to do it!' shouted Denisov, rushing at the cadet to hold him back.

But Rostov wrenched his arm free and with as much fury as though Denisov were his worst enemy fixed his eyes firmly and directly on his face.

'Do you realize what you are saying?' he said in a trembling voice. 'Except for myself no one else has been in the room. So that if it was not he, then...'

He could not finish and ran from the room.

'Oh, may the devil take you and evewybody else!' were the last words Rostov caught.

Rostov made for Telyanin's quarters.

'The master is not in, he's gone to the staff,' Telyanin's orderly told him. 'Has something happened?' he added, wondering at the cadet's agitated face.

'No, nothing.'

'You've only just missed him,' said the orderly.

The staff quarters were some two miles from Zalzeneck, and Rostov, without returning home, mounted his horse and headed in that direction. In the village was an inn which the officers frequented. Rostov rode up to this inn and at the porch saw Telyanin's horse.

In the second room of the tavern the lieutenant was sitting over a dish of sausages and a bottle of wine.

'Ah, so you've come here too, young man!' said he, smiling and raising his eyebrows.

'Yes,' said Rostov, as if it cost him a great effort to utter this monosyllable: and he sat down at the next table.

Both were silent. There were two Germans and a Russian officer in the room. No one spoke and the only sounds were the clatter of knives against plates and the lieutenant's munching. When Telyanin had finished his lunch he pulled out of his pocket a double purse and, pushing the rings apart with his small white, curved-up fingers, drew out a gold piece and with a lift of his eyebrows gave it to the waiter.

'Make haste, please,' he said.

The coin was a new one. Rostov stood up and went over to Telyanin.

'Allow me to look at your purse,' he said in a low, almost inaudible voice.

With shifting eyes but eyebrows still raised, Telyanin handed him the purse.

'Yes, it's a pretty little purse, isn't it ? ... Yes ... yes ...' said he, and suddenly turned pale. 'Look at it, young man,' he added.

Rostov took the purse in his hand and examined it, and the money in it, and looked at Telyanin. The lieutenant was glancing around in his usual way and seemed suddenly to have grown very good-humoured.

'If we ever get to Vienna, I shall leave it all there, but here in these rubbishy little towns there's nowhere to spend it,' said he. 'Well, let me have it, young man, I must be going.'

Rostov said nothing.

'What about you ? Going to have lunch too ? They feed one quite decently here,' continued Telyanin. 'Give it to me now.'

He stretched out his hand and took hold of the purse. Rostov let go of it. Telyanin took the purse and began slipping it into the pocket of his riding breeches, while his eyebrows lifted carelessly and his mouth half opened, as much as to say, 'Yes, yes, I am putting my purse in my pocket, and that's a very simple matter and no one else's business.'

'Well, young man ?' he said, sighing and glancing into Rostov's eyes from under his raised brows. A flash darted with the swiftness of an electric spark from Telyanin's eyes into Rostov's, and was shot back again, and again and again, all in a single instant.

'Come over here,' said Rostov, catching hold of Telyanin by the arm and almost dragging him to the window. 'That money is Denisov's! You took it ...' he whispered just above Telyanin's ear.

'What ? ... What ? ... How dare you ? What ? ...' exclaimed Telyanin.

But the words sounded like a piteous cry of despair and an appeal for forgiveness. As soon as Rostov heard this note in his voice a great weight of suspense fell from him. He was rejoiced and in the very same instant began to feel sorry for the miserable creature standing before him; but he had to carry the thing through to the end.

'There are people here, heaven knows what they will think,' muttered Telyanin, snatching up his forage-cap and moving towards a small empty room. 'We must clear this up ...'

'I know it, and I shall prove it,' said Rostov.

'I ...'

Every muscle of Telyanin's pale terrified face began to twitch, his eyes still shifted from side to side though they looked down and never once rose to Rostov's face, and his sobs were audible.

'Count! ... Don't ruin a young man ... here's the wretched money, take it ...' He threw it on the table. 'I have an old father, a mother!'

Rostov took the money, avoiding Telyanin's gaze and without a word made to leave the room. But at the door he paused and turned back.

'My God,' he said, with tears in his eyes, 'how could you have done it?'

'Count ...' said Telyanin, moving towards the cadet.

'Don't touch me,' cried Rostov, drawing back. 'If you are in need, take the money.'

He flung the purse at him and ran out of the inn.

5

IN the evening of the same day an animated discussion was taking place in Denisov's quarters between some of the officers of the squadron.

'And I tell you, Rostov, that it's your business to apologize to the commanding officer,' a tall grizzly-haired staff-captain with enormous moustaches and a large-featured furrowed face was saying to Rostov, who was crimson with excitement.

This staff-captain Kirsten had twice been reduced to the ranks for affairs of honour and had twice regained his commission.

'I will not allow anyone to call me a liar!' cried Rostov. 'He told me I was lying and I told him he was lying. And there the matter will rest. He can put me on duty every day, or place me under arrest, but no one can force me to apologize, because if he, as the colonel, thinks it beneath his dignity to give me satisfaction, then ...'

'Yes, but wait a bit, old man, and listen to me,' interrupted the staff-captain in his deep bass, calmly stroking his long moustaches.

'In the presence of other officers you tell the colonel that an officer has stolen ...'

'It wasn't my fault that the conversation took place in the presence of other officers. Maybe I ought not to have spoken before them, but I am not a diplomat. That's why I went into the Hussars – I thought that here I should have no need of such finicky considerations – and he tells me I am lying – so let him give me satisfaction ...'

'That's all very fine, no one imagines you're a coward; but that isn't the point. Ask Denisov if it isn't out of the question for a sub-altern to demand satisfaction of his commanding officer ?'

Denisov sat gloomily chewing his moustache and listening to the conversation, evidently with no desire to take part in it. In reply to the staff-captain's question he shook his head.

'In the presence of other officers you speak to the colonel about this unsavoury business, and Bogdanich' (Bogdanich was the colonel) 'shuts you up.'

'He did not shut me up, he said I was lying.'

'Well, have it your own way, but you talked a lot of rubbish to him and you ought to apologize.'

'Not on your life!' shouted Rostov.

'I did not expect this of you,' said the staff-captain gravely and sternly. 'You don't want to apologize, but, man, you're in the wrong all round – not only with him but with the whole regiment and all of us. Look here: if only you'd thought the matter over, and taken advice before acting – but no, you go and blurt it all out before the officers. What was the colonel to do ? Have the officer court-martialled and disgrace the whole regiment ? Bring shame on the whole regiment on account of one scoundrel ? Is that your idea ? Well, it isn't ours! And Bogdanich was a brick: he told you you were telling an untruth. It's not pleasant, but what's to be done, my dear fellow ? You brought it on yourself. And now, when we want to smooth things over, you're so high and mighty you won't apologize, and insist on making the whole affair public. You're huffy at being put on extra duty but why can't you apologize to an old and honourable officer ? Whatever Bogdanich may be, he's an honourable and gallant old colonel. You're quick at taking offence but you don't mind dis-gracing the whole regiment!' The staff-captain's voice began to tremble. 'You have been in the regiment next to no time, my lad, you're here today and gone tomorrow, transferred somewhere as adjutant. Much you'll care if it's said there are thieves among the Pavlograd officers! But we do care. Am I not right, Denisov? We do care!'

Denisov had kept silent all this time, and did not move though he occasionally glanced at Rostov with his glittering black eyes.

'Your pride is so dear to you that you aren't willing to apologize,' continued the staff-captain, 'but we old fellows who have grown up and, God willing, hope to die in the regiment – we have the honour of the regiment at heart, and Bogdanich knows it. Oh yes, we have its honour at heart all right! And this is wrong, wrong, I tell you! You may take offence if you choose, but I shall never mince words. It's all wrong!'

And the staff-captain got up and turned away from Rostov.

'That's twue, devil take it!' shouted Denisov, jumping up. 'Now then, Wostov, now then!'

Rostov, alternately flushing and growing pale, looked first at one officer and then at the other.

'No, gentlemen, no ... you mustn't think ... I see, you are quite mistaken to think that of me ... I ... for me ... for the honour of the regiment I'd ... Ah well, I'll prove that in action, and for me the honour of the flag.... Well, never mind, you're right, I am to blame!' The tears stood in his eyes. 'I was to blame, to blame all round. Now what more do you want?'

'Well done, count,' cried the staff-captain, turning round and clapping Rostov on the shoulder with his large hand.

'I tell you,' shouted Denisov, 'he's a capital fellow.'

'That's better, count,' repeated the staff-captain, beginning to address Rostov by his title, as though in acknowledgement of his confession. 'Go and apologize, your Excellency, yes, sir, go and apologize!'

'Gentlemen, I'll do anything. No one shall hear another word from me,' Rostov protested in an imploring voice, 'but I cannot apologize. By God I can't, say what you will! How can I go and apologize, like a little boy begging pardon?'

Denisov burst out laughing.

'It'll be the worse for you, if you don't. Bogdanich is vindictive: he'll make you pay for your obstinacy,' said Kirsten.

'No, on my word it's not obstinacy! I can't describe my feeling. I can't ...'

'Well, it's as you like,' said the staff-captain. 'By the way, where has the scoundrel hidden himself?' he asked Denisov.

'He weported sick. He's to be stwuck off the list tomowow,' muttered Denisov.

'It is an illness, there's no other way of explaining it,' said the staff-captain.

'Illness or not, he'd better not cwoss my path – I'd kill him!' cried Denisov in a bloodthirsty tone.

At this point Zherkov came into the room.

'What brings you here?' demanded the officers turning to the new-comer.

'We're going into action, gentlemen! Mack and his whole army have surrendered.'

'What a story!'

'I've seen him myself.'

'What, seen Mack alive, in the flesh?'

'Into action! We're going into action! He must have a good drink for such news. But how is it you're here?'

'I've been sent back to my regiment again, on account of that devil Mack. An Austrian general complained of me. I congratulated him on Mack's arrival.... What's the matter, Rostov? You look as if you'd just come out of a hot bath.'

'Oh, my dear fellow, we've been in such a mess here the last couple of days.'

The regimental adjutant came in and confirmed the news brought by Zherkov. They were under orders to march next day.

'Active service, gentlemen!'

'Well, thank God! We've been sitting here too long!'

6

KUTUZOV fell back towards Vienna, destroying behind him the bridges over the rivers Inn (at Braunau) and Traun (near Linz). On October the 23rd the Russian army was crossing the river Enns. At noon the Russian baggage-wagons, the artillery and columns of troops stretched through the town of Enns on both sides of the bridge.

It was a warm, showery autumnal day. The wide view that opened out from the heights where the Russian batteries stood guarding the bridge was at times narrowed by a diaphanous curtain of slanting rain, then suddenly widened out so that distant objects shone distinct in the sunlight, as though they were varnished. Down below, the little town could be seen with its white, red-roofed houses, its cathedral, and the bridge, on both sides of which jostling masses of Russian troops poured past. At the bend of the Danube, vessels, an island and a castle with a park surrounded by the waters of the two rivers, where the Enns flowed into the Danube, all became visible, as well as the rocky left bank of the Danube covered with pine forests, with a mysterious background of green summits and bluish gorges. The turrets of a convent rose up beyond a wild apparently virgin pine forest, and far away on the other side of the Enns could be discerned the mounted patrols of the enemy.

Among the field-guns on the brow of the hill the general in command of the rearguard stood with an officer of his staff scanning the countryside through field-glasses. A little behind them Nesvitsky, who had been sent to the rearguard by the commander-in-chief, was sitting on the tail of a gun-carriage. His Cossack who accompanied him had handed him over a knapsack and a flask, and Nesvitsky was treating some officers to little pies with genuine *doppel-kümmel* to wash them down. The officers were gathered round him, in a delighted circle, some on their knees, some squatting Turkish fashion on the wet grass.

'Yes, the Austrian prince who built that castle over there was no fool. It's a magnificent spot! You are not eating anything, gentlemen?' Nesvitsky was saying.

'Thank you very much, prince,' answered one of the officers, pleased to be talking to such an important member of the staff. 'Yes, it's a lovely spot. We passed close to the park and saw a couple of deer ... and what a wonderful house!'

'Look, prince,' said another, who would dearly have liked to take a further pie but felt shy, and therefore affected to be examining the landscape. 'Look over there, our infantry have gone in already. Over there, do you see, in the meadow behind the village, three of our men are dragging something along. They'll ransack that little palace quick enough!' he remarked with evident approval.

'That they will,' said Nesvitsky. 'Ah, but what I should like,' he added, munching a pie in his handsome mouth with its dewy lips, '– would be to slip in yonder!'

He pointed to the turreted convent which could be seen on the mountain-side. He smiled, and his eyes narrowed and gleamed. 'That would be something like, gentlemen!'

The officers laughed.

'Just to flutter the little nuns a bit. Italians, they say, and some of them young and pretty. Upon my word, I'd give five years of my life for it!'

'They must be bored to death, too,' laughed an officer bolder than the rest.

Meanwhile the staff-officer standing on the brow of the hill was pointing out something to the general, who looked through his field-glasses.

'Yes, so it is, so it is,' said the general angrily, lowering the glasses and shrugging his shoulders. 'So it is, they'll be fired on at the crossing. And why are they dawdling so?'

On the opposite side the enemy could be seen by the naked eye, and a milk-white puff of smoke arose from their battery, followed immediately by a distant report, and our troops could be seen hurrying to get across the river.

Nesvitsky dismounted from the cannon with a grunt and went up to the general, smiling.

'Wouldn't your Excellency like to eat something?' he asked.

'It's a bad business,' said the general, without answering him. 'Our men were too slow.'

'Shall I ride down to them, your Excellency?' asked Nesvitsky.

'Yes, please do,' said the general, and he repeated the orders that had already once before been given in detail. 'And tell the hussars that they are to cross last and set fire to the bridge, as I ordered; and check over the inflammable material on the bridge.'

'Very good,' replied Nesvitsky.

He called the Cossack to bring up his horse, told him to put away the knapsack and flask, and lightly swung his heavy body into the saddle.

'I'm away to pay a visit to those little nuns,' said he to the officers who were watching him with smiles, and he rode off by the path that wound down the hill.

'Now then, captain, let's try the range,' said the general, turning to an artillery officer. 'Have a little fun to relieve the monotony!'

'To the guns!' commanded the officer, and in a moment the gunners came running cheerfully from their camp fires and began to load.

'One!' rang the command.

Number one recoiled nimbly. There was a deafening metallic roar from the cannon and a shell whistled over the heads of our men under the hillside and fell a long way short of the enemy, a little spurt of smoke showing where it burst.

The faces of officers and men lit up at the sound. They leaped to their feet and began busily watching the movements of our troops below and, farther off, of the approaching enemy – all of which could be seen as in the hollow of a hand. At the same instant the sun came out fully from behind the clouds and the fine note of the solitary cannon-shot and the brilliance of the bright sunshine merged into a single inspiriting impression of light-hearted gaiety.

7

Two of the enemy's shots had already flown over the bridge, where there was a crush of men. Half-way across stood Prince Nesvitsky, who had dismounted from his horse and whose stout person was jammed against the parapet. He looked laughingly back at his Cossack who was a few steps behind, holding the two horses by their bridles. Each time Prince Nesvitsky tried to move forward, soldiers and baggage-wagons forced him back, crowding him against the side of the bridge, and all he could do was to smile.

'Look out there, my boy!' cried the Cossack to a convoy soldier who was driving his wagon into the press of infantrymen round his wheels and almost under the horses' hooves. 'Look out there! No, you wait a tick! Can't you see the general wants to pass?'

But the convoyman, paying no heed to the title of general, shouted at the soldiers who blocked his way. 'Hi there, boys! Keep to your left! Wait now!'

But the 'boys', shoulder to shoulder with their bayonets interlocking, pushed on over the bridge in one dense mass. Looking down from the parapet, Prince Nesvitsky saw the rapid, noisy little ripples of the Enns chasing each other along as they bubbled and eddied around the piles of the bridge. Looking along the bridge, he saw equally lively waves of soldiery, shoulder-knots, covered shakos, knapsacks, bayonets, long muskets, and under the shakos faces with broad cheek-bones, sunken cheeks, and listless tired expressions, and feet moving through the sticky mud that coated the planks of the bridge. Sometimes among the monotonous waves of infantry, like a fleck of white foam on the ripples of the Enns, an officer in a riding-cloak, with a different type of face from the men's, squeezed his way through; sometimes, like a chip of wood whirling along in the river, a hussar on foot, an orderly or a civilian would be carried across the bridge by the tide of troops; and sometimes, like a log floating downstream, an officers' or company's baggage-wagon, loaded high and covered with leather, would roll across the bridge, hemmed in on all sides.

'Why, it's like a burst dam,' said the Cossack, hopelessly blocked. 'Are there many more of you to come?'

'A million minus one!' replied a cheerful soldier in a torn great-coat, winking as he passed out of sight. After him came an old soldier.

'If *he*' (*he* was the enemy) 'begins popping at the bridge now,' said the old soldier glumly to a comrade, 'you won't stop to scratch yourself.'

And the soldier passed on. Following him came another, riding on a cart.

'Where the devil did you put the leg-bands?' said an orderly, running behind the cart and rummaging in the back of it.

And he in turn was borne past with the wagon.

Then came some hilarious soldiers who had evidently been drinking.

'And then, my old chum, he ups with the butt of his gun and hits him one in the teeth ...' one of the soldiers was saying gaily, with a wide swing of his arm. He wore his greatcoat tucked up round his waist.

'Yes – that ham was a bit of all right,' answered another with a loud laugh.

And they, too, passed on, so that Nesvitsky did not find out who had been struck in the teeth, or what the ham had to do with it.

'Bah! How they scurry! *He's* only got to fire a blank, and one would think they were all in danger of being killed,' said a sergeant in an angry, reproachful tone.

'When it flew past me – that round shot, I mean,' said a young soldier with an enormous mouth, 'I thought I was done for. It's a fact, 'pon my word, I was that scared!' he added, almost laughing, as if he were proud of having been frightened.

And he, too, tramped by. Next followed a cart unlike any that had gone before. It was a German *Vorspann* drawn by a pair of horses

158

driven by a German, and was loaded with what appeared to be the effects of an entire household. A fine brindled cow with an enormous udder was fastened to the cart behind. On a pile of feather beds sat a woman with a baby at the breast, an old granny, and a healthy young German girl with bright red cheeks. The little party of refugees had no doubt obtained a special permit to pass. The eyes of all the soldiers turned towards the women, and as the cart moved forward at walking pace their remarks were all related to the two young women. Every face wore a practically identical smile born of unseemly thoughts concerning the pair.

'Look, the German sausage is making tracks, too!'

'Sell us the missis,' cried another soldier, addressing the German, who strode along with downcast eyes, angry and frightened.

'See how smart she's made herself! Oh, the little hussies!'

'There now, Fedotov, you ought to be billeted on them!'

'No such luck, old fellow!'

'Where are you off to?' asked an infantry officer who was eating an apple, also half smiling as he looked at the handsome girl.

The German shut his eyes, signifying that he did not understand.

'Have one if you like,' said the officer, giving the girl an apple. She accepted it with a smile.

Nesvitsky, like the rest of the men on the bridge, did not take his eyes off the women till they had passed. When they had gone by, the same stream of soldiers followed, with the same interchange of repartee, until at last they all came to a halt. As often happens, the horses attached to some company's baggage-wagon became restive at the end of the bridge, and the whole crowd was obliged to wait.

'What are we stopping for? There's no proper order!' said the soldiers. 'Where are you shoving to? What the devil! Have patience, can't you? It'll be worse than this when the bridge is set fire to. Look, there's an officer hemmed in too,' different voices were saying in the crowd, as the men looked about them and kept trying to press forward to get off the bridge.

Looking down under the bridge at the waters of the Enns, Nesvitsky suddenly heard a sound that was new to his ears – the sound of something swiftly approaching ... something that splashed into the water.

'I say, look where that one went!' a soldier near by observed gravely, looking round at the sound.

'Encouraging us to get along quicker!' said another uneasily.

The crowd moved on again. Nesvitsky realized it had been a cannon-ball.

'Hey, Cossack, my horse!' he said. 'Now then, you there! Out of the way! Make way there!'

With great difficulty he managed to get to his horse. Shouting continually, he moved forward. The soldiers squeezed back to let him pass, but immediately after pressed on him again so that his leg was jammed, and those nearest him could not help themselves for they were pushed on still more violently from behind.

'Nesvitsky! Nesvitsky! you old fwight!' cried a hoarse voice from the rear.

Nesvitsky looked round and saw, some fifteen paces away but separated from him by the living mass of moving infantry, Vasska Denisov, red, black and shaggy, with his cap on the back of his head and his hussar's cloak jauntily flung over his shoulder.

'Tell these devils, these demons, to give us woom,' shouted Denisov, evidently in a paroxysm of excitement, his coal-black eyes with their bloodshot whites flashing and rolling while he brandished his sheathed sabre in a small bare hand as red as his face.

'Ah, Vasska!' replied Nesvitsky, delighted, 'but what are you doing here?'

'The squadwon can't get thwough!' roared Vasska Denisov, showing his white teeth fiercely and spurring his raven thoroughbred Bedouin. The horse twitched his ears as he brushed against bayonets, and snorted, spurting white foam from his bit, pawing the planks of the bridge with his hooves, and apparently ready to leap over the parapet, if his rider would let him.

'What is this? They're like sheep! Just like sheep! Out of the way! ... Make woom! Stop there, you devil with the cart! I'll cut you to pieces!' he shouted, actually drawing his sword from its scabbard and beginning to flourish it.

The soldiers crowded closer together with terrified faces, and Denisov joined Nesvitsky.

'How's it you're not drunk today?' said Nesvitsky when Denisov had ridden up to him.

'They don't give us time to get dwunk,' replied Vasska Denisov. 'The wegiment is dwagged to and fwo all day long. If they mean us to fight, let's fight. But as it is, the devil only knows what we're doing!'

'What a beau you are these days!' said Nesvitsky, looking at Denisov's new cloak and saddle-cloth.

Denisov smiled, pulled out of his sabretache a handkerchief that diffused a smell of scent and thrust it under Nesvitsky's nose.

'Of course! I'm going into action! I've shaved, bwushed my teeth and scented myself!'

Nesvitsky's imposing figure, with his Cossack in attendance, and Denisov's determination as he flourished his sword and shouted at the top of his voice, enabled them to squeeze through to the farther end of the bridge and halt the infantry. At the end of the bridge Nesvitsky found the colonel to whom he had to deliver the command and his errand accomplished he rode back.

Having cleared the way, Denisov reined in his horse at the end of the bridge. Carelessly holding in his stallion who was neighing and pawing the ground, anxious to join his fellows, he watched the squadron approaching him. The hooves rang hollow on the planks of the bridge, sounding like several horses galloping, and the squadron, with the officers riding in front and the men four abreast, spread across the bridge and began to pour off at the other end.

The infantry who had been halted, packed together, in the trampled mud gazed with that peculiar aloof feeling of ill-will and derision with which troops of different arms usually encounter one another at the neat jaunty hussars riding by in regular order.

'Smart, tidy lads! Only fit for a circus!'

'What's the use of them? They're led about just for show!' remarked another.

'Don't kick up the dust, you infantry!' jested a hussar whose prancing horse had spattered a foot soldier with mud.

'I'd like to put you on a two-days' march with a knapsack! Your gold lace would soon get a bit tarnished,' said the infantryman, wiping the mud off his face with his sleeve. 'Perched up there, you're more like a bird than a man.'

'There now, Zikin, they ought to put you on a horse. You'd look fine,' said a corporal, chaffing a thin little soldier stooping under the weight of his knapsack.

'Put a broomstick between your legs and ride-a-cock-horse,' the hussar shouted back.

8

THE rest of the infantry hurriedly crossed the bridge, squeezing together into a funnel at the end. At last all the baggage-wagons were
across, the crush became less and the last battalion marched on to the
bridge. Only Denisov's squadron of hussars were left on the farther
side of the river facing the enemy. The enemy, though plainly visible
from the heights opposite, could not as yet be seen from the level of
the bridge, since from the valley through which the river flowed the
horizon was bounded by rising ground only half a mile away. At the
foot of the hill lay waste land dotted here and there with bands of
Cossack patrols. Suddenly, on the road at the top of the high ground
troops appeared in blue uniform, accompanied by artillery. It was the
French. The Cossack patrol retired down the hill at a trot. All the
officers and men of Denisov's squadron, though they tried to talk of
other things and to look in other directions, thought only of what was
there on the hill-top and their eyes constantly turned to the patches
coming into sight on the skyline, which they knew to be the enemy's
troops. The weather had cleared again since noon, and a brilliant sun
was moving westward over the Danube and the dark surrounding
hills. There was no wind, and at intervals from that hill-top floated
the sound of bugle-calls and the shouts of the enemy. Except for a few
scattered skirmishers there was no one now between the squadron and
the enemy. An open space of some seven hundred yards was all that
separated them. The enemy had ceased firing, and that rigid, ominous
gap, unapproachable and intangible, which divides two hostile armies
was all the more keenly felt.

'One step beyond that line, which is like the bourne dividing the
living from the dead, lies the Unknown of suffering and death. And
what is there? Who is there? There beyond that field, beyond that
tree, that roof gleaming in the sun? No one knows, but who does not
long to know? You fear to cross that line, yet you long to cross it; and
you know that sooner or later it will have to be crossed and you will
find out what lies there on the other side of the line, just as you will
inevitably have to learn what lies the other side of death. But you are
strong, healthy, cheerful and excited, and surrounded by other men
just as full of health and exuberant spirits.' Such are the sensations, if

not the actual thoughts of every man who finds himself confronted by the enemy, and these feelings lend a singular vividness and happy distinctness of impression to everything that takes place at such moments.

A puff of smoke rose from the high ground occupied by the enemy, and a cannon-ball whistled over the heads of the squadron of hussars. The officers, who had been standing together, scattered to their posts. The hussars began carefully aligning their horses. The whole squadron subsided into silence. All looked intently at the enemy in front and at the squadron commander, awaiting the word of command. Another cannon-ball flew by them, and a third. There was no doubt that the enemy was aiming at the hussars but the balls whizzing regularly and rapidly passed over the heads of the horsemen and struck the ground somewhere in the rear. The hussars never looked round but every time they heard the whizz of a ball as though at the word of command the whole squadron with its rows of faces so alike yet so different, holding its breath until the cannon-shot had passed over, rose in the stirrups and sank back again. Without turning their heads the soldiers glanced at one another out of the corners of their eyes, curious to see the effect on their comrades. Every face, from Denisov's to the bugler's, showed around lips and chin one common expression of conflict, excitement and agitation. The quartermaster frowned, and glared at the men as though meditating punishment for them. Cadet Mironov ducked every time a ball flew over. On the left flank Rostov on his Rook – a handsome beast despite its unsound legs – had the happy air of a schoolboy called up before a large audience for an examination in which he feels sure he will distinguish himself. He was glancing round at everyone with a serene, radiant expression, as if asking them to notice how calmly he sat under fire. But into his face too there crept, against his will, that line about the mouth that betrayed something novel and stern.

'Who's bobbing up and down there? Cadet Miwonov? That's not wight! Look at me!' cried Denisov who could not keep still in one place and kept riding to and fro before the squadron.

Vasska Denisov, with his snub nose and black hair, his short stocky figure, his sinewy hands with the stumpy, hairy fingers grasping the hilt of his drawn sword, looked just the same as always, or rather, as he was apt to look especially towards evening after he had emptied his second bottle. He was only a trifle redder in the face than usual, and tossing back his shaggy head, as birds do when they drink, his little legs pitilessly plunging the spurs into the sides of his good Bedouin, he galloped to the other flank of the squadron, sitting as though he were falling backwards in the saddle, and shouted to the men in a husky voice to look to their pistols. He rode up to Kirsten. The staff-captain, on his sedate, broad-backed charger, came at a walking-pace to meet him. The staff-captain's face with its long whiskers was as grave as ever, only his eyes flashed with unwonted brilliance.

'Well,' said he to Denisov, 'it won't come to a fight. You'll see – we shall retire.'

'The deuce knows what they're about!' muttered Denisov. 'Ah, Wostov!' he cried, noticing the cadet's beaming face, 'you've not had long to wait.'

And he smiled approvingly, unmistakably pleased at the sight of the cadet. Rostov felt perfectly happy. Just then the colonel appeared on the bridge. Denisov galloped up to him.

'Your Excellency! Let us attack 'em. I'll dwive them back!'

'Attack indeed!' said the colonel in a peevish voice, puckering up his face as if to shake off a persistent fly. 'And why are you delaying here? Don't you see the scouts are withdrawing? Lead your squadron back.'

The squadron crossed the bridge and passed out of range of the enemy's guns without losing a single man. The second squadron that had been in the line followed them across and the last Cossacks quitted the farther side of the river.

The two squadrons of the Pavlograd regiment after crossing the bridge rode one after the other up the hill. Their colonel, Karl Bogdanich Schubert, had joined Denisov's squadron and was riding at a foot-pace not far from Rostov but without taking the slightest notice of him, though this was the first time they had met since the incident in connexion with Telyanin. Rostov, feeling himself at the front in the power of the man with whom he now admitted that he had been to blame, did not lift his eyes from the colonel's athletic shoulders, the light hair at the back of his head, and his red neck. It seemed to Rostov that Bogdanich was only pretending not to notice him, and that his whole aim now was to test the cadet's courage, so he drew himself up and looked around gaily. Then he fancied that Bogdanich was riding close to him in order to display his own valour.

Next it occurred to him that his opponent would send the squadron into some desperate attack on purpose to punish him, Rostov. And then again, he imagined how after the attack Bogdanich would come up to him as he lay wounded, and magnanimously extend the hand of reconciliation.

Zherkov, whose high shoulders were well known to the Pavlograd Hussars as he had not long left their regiment, rode up to the colonel. After his dismissal from the general staff Zherkov had not remained in the regiment, saying that he was not such a fool as to slave at the front when he could get more pay for doing nothing on the staff, and had succeeded in attaching himself as an orderly-officer to Prince Bagration. He now came to his former chief with a message from the commander of the rearguard.

'Colonel,' said he, with his melancholy air of gravity, addressing Rostov's enemy and glancing round at his comrades, 'there's an order to halt and fire the bridge.'

'An order, *who to*?' asked the colonel grimly.

'Well, I don't know, colonel, *who to*,' replied the cadet gravely, 'only the prince told me to "go and tell the colonel that the hussars are to make haste back and burn the bridge".'

Zherkov was followed by an officer of the suite, who rode up to the colonel of the hussars with the same order. After the officer of the suite Nesvitsky came galloping up on a Cossack horse that could scarcely carry his weight.

'How's this, colonel?' he shouted, while still at a distance. 'I told you to fire the bridge, and now someone has gone and blundered. They're all out of their minds over there, and one can't make head or tail of anything.'

The colonel took his time in halting the regiment, and turned to Nesvitsky.

'You spoke to me about inflammable material,' said he, 'but you never said a word about firing it.'

'But, my dear sir,' exclaimed Nesvitsky as he reined in his horse, taking off his forage-cap and passing his plump hand over his hair which was wet with perspiration, 'wasn't I telling you to fire the bridge when the inflammable material had been put in position?'

'I am not your "dear sir", Mr Staff-officer, and you did not tell me to burn the bridge! I know my duty, and it is my habit orders strictly to obey.' (Bogdanich was a Russo-German who spoke very poor

Russian.) 'You said the bridge would be burnt, but who would burn it, by the Holy Ghost I could not tell ...'

'Ah, that's always the way!' cried Nesvitsky with a wave of the hand. 'What are you doing here?' he asked, turning to Zherkov.

'I am on the same errand. But you *are* wet! Let me give you a wipe.'

'You were saying, Mr Staff-officer ...' pursued the colonel in an aggrieved tone.

'Colonel,' interrupted the officer of the suite, 'there is need of haste, or the enemy will be pouring grape-shot into us.'

The colonel looked dumbly at the officer of the suite, at the stout staff-officer, at Zherkov, and scowled.

'I will the bridge fire,' said he in a solemn voice, as if to announce that in spite of everything they might do to annoy him he would still do his duty.

Spurring his horse with his long, muscular legs, as though the animal were to blame for it all, the colonel moved forward and ordered the second squadron, the one in which Rostov was serving under Denisov, to return to the bridge.

'There, it's just as I thought,' said Rostov to himself. 'He wants to test me!' His heart contracted and the blood rushed to his face. 'Let him see whether I am a coward!' he thought.

Once more, over all the light-hearted faces of the men in the squadron the same serious expression appeared that they had worn when under fire. Rostov, not taking his eyes from his enemy, the colonel, tried to discover in his face confirmation of his conjectures; but the colonel never once glanced at Rostov but gazed ahead solemn and stern as he always was at the front. The word of command rang out.

'Lively now, lively!' several voices repeated around him.

Their sabres catching in the bridles and their spurs jingling, the hussars hastily dismounted, not knowing what they were to do. The soldiers crossed themselves. Rostov no longer looked at the colonel: he had no time for that. He was afraid of falling behind the hussars, so much afraid that his heart stood still. His hand trembled as he turned his horse over to an orderly, and he felt the blood rushing back to his heart with a thud. Denisov rode past him, leaning back and shouting something. Rostov saw nothing save the hussars running by his side, their spurs catching and their sabres clattering.

'Stretchers!' shouted a voice behind him.

Rostov did not think what this call for stretchers meant; he ran on, striving only to be ahead of the others; but just at the bridge, not looking where he was going, he came on some slimy, trodden mud, stumbled, and fell on his hands. The others outstripped him.

'On boss zides, captain,' he heard the voice of the colonel who, having ridden ahead, had reined in his horse not far from the bridge and sat looking on with a triumphant, cheerful face.

Rostov, wiping his muddy hands on his breeches, glanced at his enemy and was about to run on, imagining that the farther forward he went the better. But Bogdanich, though without looking at him, or recognizing that it was Rostov, shouted to him:

'Who is that in the middle of the bridge? Get to the right! Cadet, come back!' he cried angrily, and turned to Denisov, who with swaggering bravado had ridden on to the planks of the bridge.

'Why you run risks, captain? You had better dismount,' said the colonel.

'Oh, every bullet finds its billet,' replied Denisov, turning in his saddle.

*

Meanwhile, Nesvitsky, Zherkov and the officer of the suite were standing together out of range of the enemy's fire, watching now the little band of hussars in yellow shakos, dark green jackets braided with gold lace, and blue riding-breeches, who were swarming about the bridge, and then what was approaching in the distance from the opposite side – the blue uniforms and the groups with horses, easily recognizable as artillery.

'Will they be able to burn the bridge or not? Who'll get there first? Will they be in time to fire the bridge, or will the French train their grape-shot on them and wipe them out?'

These were the questions every man in the main body of troops on the high ground above the bridge involuntarily asked himself with sinking heart, as he watched the bridge and the hussars in the bright evening light, and the blue tunics advancing from the other side with their bayonets and guns.

'Ugh! The hussars will catch it hot!' exclaimed Nesvitsky. 'They're within grape-shot range now.'

'He shouldn't have taken so many men,' said the officer of the suite.

167

'That's true,' said Nesvitsky. 'Two smart young fellows would have done the job just as well.'

'Ah, your Excellency,' put in Zherkov, his eyes fixed on the hussars though he still spoke with that naïve air of his that made it impossible to guess whether he was in jest or in earnest. 'Ah, your Excellency! What an idea! Send two men? And then who would give us the Vladimir medal and ribbon? But now, even if they do get a peppering, the squadron may be recommended for honours and the colonel receive a ribbon for himself. Our Bogdanich knows a thing or two.'

'There now,' said the officer of the suite. 'Here comes the grape-shot.'

He pointed to the French field-pieces, which were being unlimbered and hurriedly brought into action.

On the French side, amid the groups with cannon, a puff of smoke arose, then a second and a third, almost simultaneously; and by the time the report of the first had reached their ears, the smoke of a fourth was seen. Then two reports, one after another, and a third.

'Oh! Oh!' moaned Nesvitsky, as if in excruciating pain, clutching at the staff-officer's arm. 'Look, a man has fallen! One is down, one fallen!'

'Two, I think?'

'If I were Tsar I would never make war,' said Nesvitsky, turning away.

The French guns were speedily reloaded. The infantry in their blue uniforms advanced towards the bridge at a run. Smoke appeared again, but at irregular intervals, and grape-shot pattered and rattled on the bridge. But this time Nesvitsky could not see what was happening there. A dense cloud of smoke poured from the bridge. The hussars had succeeded in setting fire to it, and the French batteries were now firing at them, no longer to hinder them but because the guns were trained and there was someone to shoot at.

The French had time to send three charges of grape-shot before the hussars got back to their horses. Two were misdirected and the shot went high, but the last round fell in the midst of the group of hussars and hit three of them.

Rostov, preoccupied by his relations with Bogdanich, had paused on the bridge, not knowing what to do. There was no one to hew down (which had always been his idea of a battle), nor could he help to fire the bridge, because he had not provided himself with burning straw like the other soldiers. He was standing there looking about him when suddenly he heard a rattling on the bridge as though some-one were scattering hazel nuts, and the hussar nearest him fell against the parapet with a groan. Rostov ran up to him with the others. Again there was a cry of 'Stretchers!' Four men seized the hussar and began lifting him.

'O-o-o-h! For Christ's sake let me be!' shrieked the wounded man, but nevertheless he was lifted and laid on a stretcher.

Nikolai Rostov turned away and, as if searching for something, started to gaze into the distance, at the waters of the Danube, at the sky, at the sun. How beautiful the sky looked, how blue and calm and deep! How brilliant and majestic was the setting sun! How tenderly shone the distant waters of the Danube! And fairer still were the purpling mountains stretching far away beyond the river, the convent, the mysterious gorges, the pine forests veiled in mist to their summits. ... There all was peace and happiness. 'I should wish for nothing, wish for nothing, for nothing in the world, if only I were there,' thought Rostov. 'In myself alone and in that sunshine there is so much happi-ness, while here ... it is groans, suffering and confusion, hurry. ... Now they are shouting again, and all running back somewhere, and I shall run with the rest, while death, death is all above me and around me. ... A moment more and I shall never see this sun, this river, that gorge again. ...'

At that instant the sun began to hide behind the clouds, and more stretchers came into view ahead of Rostov. And the fear of death and of the stretchers, and love of the sun and of life all merged into one sickening agitation.

'O Lord God! Thou Who art in this heaven, save, forgive and pro-tect me!' Rostov whispered.

The hussars ran back to the men holding their horses. Their voices grew louder and more confident; the stretchers disappeared from sight.

'Well, fwiend? So you've smelt powdah?' shouted Vasska Denisov just above his ear.

'It's all over; but I am a coward – yes, I am a coward,' thought Rostov, and with a heavy sigh he took Rook, who was standing rest-ing one foot, from the orderly and prepared to mount.

'Was that grape-shot?' he asked Denisov.

'It was, and no mistake!' cried Denisov. 'You worked like hewoes.

But it is wascally work! An attack is ware sport, you hew down the dogs! But this sort of thing is the vewy devil, being shot at like a tahget.'

And Denisov rode up to a group that had stopped near Rostov, composed of the colonel, Nesvitsky, Zherkov and the staff-officer.

'I believe no one noticed,' thought Rostov. And this was true: no one had noticed anything, for everyone was familiar with the sensation which the cadet under fire for the first time experienced.

'This will make a fine despatch to send in!' said Zherkov. 'They'll be promoting me sub-lieutenant before I know where I am, eh?'

'Inform the prince that I the bridge fired!' said the colonel triumphantly and gaily.

'And if he inquires about the losses?'

'Not worth mentioning,' growled the colonel in his bass voice. 'A couple of hussars wounded, and one knocked out on the spot,' he added with undisguised cheerfulness, unable to restrain a smile of satisfaction as he sonorously enunciated the words *knocked out*.

9

PURSUED by the French army of a hundred thousand men under the command of Bonaparte, encountering a population that was unfriendly to it, losing confidence in its allies, suffering from shortness of supplies, and forced into action under conditions of war unlike anything that had been foreseen, the Russian army of thirty-five thousand men commanded by Kutuzov was hurriedly retiring along the Danube, stopping when overtaken by the enemy, and fighting rearguard skirmishes only so far as was necessary to ensure their retreat without the loss of their heavy equipment. There had been actions at Lambach, Amstetten and Melk; but despite the courage and endurance – which even the enemy acknowledged – with which the Russians fought, the only consequence of these engagements was a yet more rapid retreat. Austrian troops that had escaped capture at Ulm and had joined Kutuzov at Braunau, now parted from the Russian army, and Kutuzov was left with only his own weak and exhausted forces. It was no longer possible to think of defending Vienna. Instead of an offensive, the plan of which, carefully elaborated in accordance with the new science of strategics, had been communicated to Kutuzov by the Austrian Hofkriegsrath when he was in Vienna, the only thing that remained to him now, unless he were to sacrifice his army as Mack had done at Ulm, was to effect a junction with the fresh troops arriving from Russia, and even this was almost an impossibility.

On the 28th of October Kutuzov and his army crossed to the left bank of the Danube and, for the first time, halted, having now put the river between himself and the main body of the French. On the 30th he attacked and defeated the division under Mortier, which was stationed on the left bank. In this engagement for the first time some trophies were captured: a standard, some cannon, and two enemy generals. For the first time, after retreating for a fortnight, the Russians had halted and at the end of the battle not only held the field but had driven off the French. Though the troops were exhausted and in rags, and the dead, the wounded and sick, and stragglers had reduced their numbers by a third; though some of the sick and wounded had been abandoned on the other side of the Danube with a letter from Kutuzov commending them to the humanity of the enemy; though the big hospitals and the houses of Krems which had been converted into *lazaretti* were unable to accommodate all the sick and wounded remaining – still, in spite of all this, the stand made at Krems and the victory over Mortier raised the spirits of the troops considerably. Throughout the whole army and at headquarters the most gratifying though erroneous reports were rife of the imaginary approach of columns from Russia, of some victory won by the Austrians, and of the panic retreat of Bonaparte.

Prince Andrei during the battle had been in attendance on the Austrian general Schmidt, who was killed in action. He himself had had his horse wounded under him and his hand slightly grazed by a bullet. As a mark of especial favour the commander-in-chief sent him with news of this victory to the Austrian court, now no longer at Vienna (which was threatened by the French) but at Brünn. In spite of his apparently delicate constitution Prince Andrei could endure physical fatigue far better than many very strong men, and on the night of the battle, having arrived at Krems, excited but not weary, with despatches from Dokhturov to Kutuzov, he was sent on immediately with a special despatch to Brünn. Such an errand not only ensured a decoration for the courier but was an important step towards promotion.

The night was dark and starry: the road made a black line across the snow that had fallen the previous day – the day of the engagement.

Now reviewing his impressions of the recent battle, now picturing pleasantly the effect he would create with his news of the victory, or recalling the farewells of the commander-in-chief and his fellow-officers, Prince Andrei drove swiftly along in his post-chaise, enjoying the feelings of a man who has at last attained the first instalment of some long-coveted happiness. As soon as he closed his eyes the roar of musketry and cannon filled his ears, mingling with the rumble of wheels and the sensation of victory. He began to dream that the Russians were flying and that he himself was slain. Then he would awake with a start, happy in the realization that nothing of the sort had happened and that, on the contrary, it was the French who had run away. He would again recall all the details of the victory and his own calm courage during the battle and, reassured, doze off again. ... The bright, starlit night was followed by a bright, cheerful morning. The snow was melting in the sunshine, the horses sped swiftly along past varying forests, fields and villages on both sides of the road.

At one of the post-houses he overtook a convoy of Russian wounded. The Russian officer in charge of the transport was lolling in the foremost cart, shouting and berating a soldier with coarse abuse. Six or more white-faced, bandaged, dirty men were being jolted over the stony road in each of the long German wagons. Some of them were talking (Prince Andrei caught the sound of their Russian speech), others were eating their bread, while the more severely wounded gazed dumbly, with the languid interest of sick children, at the courier hurrying past them.

Prince Andrei ordered his driver to stop, and asked one of the soldiers in what action they had been wounded.

'Day before yesterday, on the Danube,' answered the soldier. Prince Andrei took out his purse and gave the man three gold pieces.

'That's for them all,' he said to the officer who came up. 'Get well soon, lads!' he continued, turning to the soldiers. 'There's plenty to do still.'

'What news, sir ?' asked the officer, evidently anxious to start a conversation.

'Good news! ... Forward!' he cried to his driver, and they galloped on.

It was quite dark when Prince Andrei reached Brünn and found himself surrounded by lofty buildings, the lighted windows of shops and houses, by street lamps, by fine carriages rumbling over the cobbled streets and all that atmosphere of a large and lively city which is always so fascinating to a soldier after camp life. Despite his hurried journey and sleepless night, Prince Andrei drove up to the palace feeling even more excited and alert than he had the evening before. Only his eyes glittered feverishly, and his thoughts followed one another with extraordinary clearness and rapidity. Vividly, all the details of the battle came into his mind, no longer confused but in due sequence, word for word, as he saw himself stating them to the Emperor Francis. Vividly he imagined the casual questions that might be put to him and the answers he would give. He expected to be presented immediately to the Emperor. But at the principal entrance to the palace an official came running out to meet him and, learning that he was a courier, conducted him to another door.

'To the right at the end of the corridor, your Excellency! There you will find the adjutant on duty,' said the official. 'He will take you to the minister of war.'

The adjutant on duty came to meet Prince Andrei and asked him to wait, and went on to the minister of war. Five minutes later he returned and, bowing with marked courtesy, ushered Prince Andrei before him along a corridor into the room where the minister of war was at work. The adjutant by his extravagant politeness appeared to wish to ward off any attempt at familiarity on the part of the Russian courier. Prince Andrei's exultant feelings were considerably impaired by the time he approached the door of the minister's room. He felt affronted, and this sense of wounded pride instantly and without his noticing it changed into one of disdain for which there was no foundation. His fertile brain at the same moment suggested to him a point of view which gave him the right to despise both the adjutant and the minister of war. 'Gaining victories probably seems easy to them, when they don't know the smell of gunpowder!' he said to himself. His eyes narrowed contemptuously, and he walked into the minister's office with deliberately slow steps. His feeling was still further intensified when he caught sight of the minister of war seated at a large table and for the first two minutes taking no notice of his arrival. The minister's bald head with its fringe of grey hair was bent over some papers which he was reading and marking with a lead pencil. There was a wax candle on each side of the papers, which he finished reading without raising his eyes at the opening of the door and the sound of footsteps.

'Take this and deliver it,' said the minister to his adjutant, handing him the papers and still taking no notice of the courier.

Prince Andrei felt that of all the matters that preoccupied the minister of war the feats of Kutuzov's army either interested him the least, or else he felt obliged to give this impression to the Russian courier. 'Well, it's all the same to me,' he thought. The minister pushed the remaining papers aside, arranged them neatly and looked up. He had an intelligent head full of character but the instant he turned to Prince Andrei the firm, intelligent expression of the minister's face changed in a manner which was evidently habitual and deliberate, and took on the stupid, artificial smile – which does not even attempt to hide its artificiality – of a man who is continually receiving many petitioners one after another.

'From General Field-Marshal Kutuzov?' he queried. 'I hope it is good news? There has been an encounter with Mortier? A victory? It is high time.'

He took the despatch, which was addressed to him, and began to read it with a melancholy expression.

'Ach, my God, my God! Schmidt!' he exclaimed in German. 'What a misfortune! What a misfortune!'

Having skimmed through the despatch he laid it on the table and raised his eyes to Prince Andrei, evidently meditating something.

'Ach, what a misfortune! The affair, you say, was decisive? But Mortier was not taken.' He pondered. 'I am very glad you have brought good news, though the death of Schmidt is a heavy price to pay for the victory. His Majesty will no doubt wish to see you, but not today. I thank you. Go and get rested. Be at the levée tomorrow after the review. However, I will have you informed.'

The stupid smile, which had disappeared while he was speaking, reappeared on the minister's face.

'*Au revoir*. I thank you indeed. His Majesty will probably wish to see you,' he repeated, and inclined his head.

Prince Andrei left the palace feeling that he had abandoned all the interest and happiness afforded him by the victory into the indifferent hands of the minister of war and the polite adjutant. The whole tenor of his thoughts changed instantaneously: the battle figured in his mind as a remote, far-away memory.

10

PRINCE ANDREI put up at Brünn with a Russian acquaintance of his, Bilibin, the diplomat.

'Ah, my dear prince! I could not have a more welcome visitor,' said Bilibin, as he came out to greet Prince Andrei. 'Franz, put the prince's things in my bedroom,' said he to the servant who was ushering Bolkonsky in. 'So you're the messenger of victory, eh? Splendid! For my part, I am kept indoors ill, as you see.'

Having washed and changed, Prince Andrei walked into the diplomat's luxurious study and sat down to the dinner which had been prepared for him. Bilibin settled himself comfortably beside the fire.

After his journey and the whole campaign during which he had been deprived of all the conveniences of cleanliness and all the refinements of life, Prince Andrei experienced an agreeable feeling of repose among luxurious surroundings such as he had been accustomed to from childhood. Moreover, it was pleasant after his reception by the Austrians to talk, not indeed in Russian, for they were speaking French, but at least with a Russian who would, he supposed, share the general Russian aversion (which was then particularly strong) for the Austrians.

Bilibin was a man of five-and-thirty, a bachelor, who belonged to the same set as Prince Andrei. They had known each other previously in Petersburg, but had become more intimate during Prince Andrei's last stay in Vienna with Kutuzov. Just as Prince Andrei was a young man who gave promise of rising high in the military profession, so Bilibin promised to do even better in the diplomatic service. He was still a young man but no longer a young diplomat, since he had begun his career at the age of sixteen, had served in Paris and Copenhagen, and now held a fairly important post in Vienna. Both the chancellor and our ambassador in Vienna knew him and prized him highly. He was not one of that great multitude of diplomats whose merits are limited to the possession of negative qualities, who have only to avoid doing certain things, and to speak French in order to be considered good diplomats. He was one of those who like and know how to work, and notwithstanding his natural indolence would sometimes spend the whole night at his writing-table. He put in equally good work whatever the nature of the matter in hand. It was the question

'How?' that interested him, not the question 'What for?' He did not care what the diplomatic business was about, but found the greatest satisfaction in preparing a circular, memorandum or report skilfully, pointedly and elegantly. Bilibin's services were valued not only for the labours of his pen but also for his talent for dealing and conversing with those in the highest spheres.

Bilibin enjoyed conversation, just as he enjoyed work, only when it could be made elegantly witty. In society he was always on the watch for an opportunity to say something striking, and took part in a conversation only when this was possible. His talk was always plentifully sprinkled with amusingly original and polished phrases of general interest. These sayings were elaborated beforehand in the alembic of his mind as if intentionally in a portable form easy for even the dullest member of society to remember and carry from salon to salon. And in fact Bilibin's witticisms were hawked round the Viennese drawing-rooms and were often not without influence on matters that were considered important.

His thin, worn, sallow face was covered with deep wrinkles, which always looked as clean and well-washed as the tips of one's fingers after a bath. The movement of these wrinkles made up the principal play of expression of his countenance. Sometimes it was his forehead that would pucker into deep folds and his eyebrows lift, sometimes his eyebrows would drop and heavy furrows crease his cheeks. His deep-set little eyes always looked out frankly and twinkled.

'Well, now, tell us about your exploits,' said he.

Bolkonsky, very modestly and without once mentioning himself, described the engagement and his reception by the minister of war.

'I got as much welcome as a dog in a game of skittles,' he said in conclusion.

Bilibin smiled and the wrinkles on his face relaxed.

'However, my dear fellow,' he remarked, examining his nails at a distance and wrinkling the skin above his left eye, 'with all my respect for the *Orthodox Russian army*, I must say that your victory was not particularly victorious.'

He continued in this fashion, talking in French and introducing Russian words only when he wished to give scornful emphasis

'Come now! With all your weight of numbers you fell on the unfortunate Mortier and his one division, and even then Mortier slips through your fingers! Where's the victory?'

'No, but seriously,' said Prince Andrei, 'at least we may say without boasting that it was rather better than at Ulm ...'

'Why didn't you capture one, just one, marshal for us?'

'Because things don't always turn out as forecast or go with the smoothness of a parade. We had expected, as I told you, to be at their rear by seven o'clock in the morning, but we did not arrive there until five of the afternoon.'

'And why didn't you reach them at seven in the morning? You ought to have reached them at seven in the morning,' said Bilibin, smiling. 'You ought to have been there at seven in the morning.'

'Why didn't you succeed in impressing on Bonaparte through diplomatic channels that he had better leave Genoa alone?' retorted Prince Andrei in the same tone.

'I know,' interrupted Bilibin, 'you're thinking that it's very easy to capture marshals, sitting on a sofa by one's fireside. That is true, but still why didn't you take him? And don't be surprised if not only the minister of war but also the most august Emperor and King Francis is not particularly jubilant over your victory. Why, even I, a poor secretary of the Russian Embassy, feel no especial joy ...'

He looked straight at Prince Andrei and suddenly the wrinkled skin on his forehead smoothed out.

'Now it is my turn to ask "why?", *mon cher*,' said Bolkonsky. 'I confess I cannot understand – perhaps there are diplomatic subtleties here beyond my feeble intellect, but I can't make it out: Mack loses a whole army, while the Archduke Ferdinand and the Archduke Karl give no sign of life and make one blunder after another. Kutuzov alone at last gains a real victory and breaks the French spell, and the minister of war is not even interested enough to inquire after the details!'

'That's just it, my dear fellow! Don't you see – it's hurrah for the Tsar, for Russia, for the Faith! All very fine and good, but what do we, the Austrian court, I mean, care for your victories? Bring us nice news of a victory by the Archduke Karl or Ferdinand – one archduke's as good as another, as you know – if it's only a victory over a fire-brigade of Bonaparte's, and it will be quite another story, to be proclaimed by a salute of guns! But this sort of thing can only annoy. The Archduke Karl does nothing, the Archduke Ferdinand covers himself with disgrace; you abandon Vienna, give up its defence, as much as to say, God is on our side and the devil take you and your capital! The one general we all loved – Schmidt – you put in the way of a bullet, and then expect compliments on a victory! ... Confess that more exasperating news than yours could not have been conceived. It's as if it had been done on purpose, on purpose. Besides, even if you had won the most brilliant victory, supposing even the Archduke Karl had won a victory, what difference would it make to the general course of events? It's too late now, with Vienna occupied by the French army.'

'What? Occupied? Vienna occupied?'

'Not only occupied, but Bonaparte is at Schönbrunn, and the count, our dear Count Vrbna, goes to him for orders.'

After the fatigues and impressions of his journey, after his reception and especially after having dined, Bolkonsky felt that he could not take in the full significance of the words he heard.

'This morning Count Lichtenfels was here,' continued Bilibin, 'and showed me a letter containing a circumstantial account of the parade of the French in Vienna, with Prince Murat and the whole bag of tricks. ... So you see, your victory is not such a great matter for rejoicing, and you can't be received as a saviour ...'

'Really I don't care about that, I don't care at all!' said Prince Andrei, beginning to understand that his news of the battle before Krems was in fact of small importance in view of such events as the fall of Austria's capital. 'However did Vienna come to be taken? What of the bridge and the famous bridge-head, and Prince Auersperg? We heard reports that Prince Auersperg was defending Vienna,' said he.

'Prince Auersperg is on this, on our side of the Danube, and is defending us – doing it pretty badly, I think, but still defending us. But Vienna is on the other side. No, the bridge has not yet been taken, and I hope it will not be, for it is mined and orders have been given to blow it up. Otherwise, we should long ago have been in the mountains of Bohemia, and you and your army would have spent an unpleasant quarter of an hour between two fires.'

'But still this does not mean that the campaign is over,' said Prince Andrei.

'Well, I believe it is. And so do the bigwigs here, though they dare not say so. It will be just as I foretold at the beginning of the campaign: your skirmish at Dürenstein will not settle the affair, nor will gunpowder decide the matter, but those who invented it,' said Bilibin, quoting one of his own *mots*, releasing the wrinkles on his forehead and pausing. 'The only question is what the meeting in Berlin between the Emperor Alexander and the King of Prussia may bring forth. If Prussia joins the alliance, Austria's hand will be forced and there will be war. But if not, it will merely be a matter of settling where the preliminaries of a second Campo Formio are to be drawn up.'

'But what an extraordinary genius!' Prince Andrei suddenly exclaimed, clenching his small fist and pounding the table with it. 'And what luck the man has!'

'Buonaparte?' said Bilibin inquiringly, knitting his brow to indicate that he was about to say something witty. 'Buonaparte?' he repeated, accentuating the *u*. 'I certainly think now that he is laying down laws for Austria from Schönbrunn we must relieve him of that *u*. I am firmly resolved on an innovation, and call him simply Bonaparte!'

'No, joking apart,' said Prince Andrei. 'Do you really think the campaign is over?'

'This is what I think. Austria has been made a fool of, and she is not used to that. And she will retaliate. And she has been fooled in the first place because her provinces have been pillaged – they say the *Orthodox Russian troops* are terrible looters – her army is beaten, her capital taken, and all this for the beautiful eyes of his Sardinian majesty. And therefore – this is between ourselves, *mon cher* – my instinct tells me that we are being deceived; my instinct tells me of negotiations with France and projects for peace, a secret peace, concluded separately.'

'Impossible!' cried Prince Andrei. 'That would be too base.'

'Time will show,' said Bilibin, letting the creases run off his forehead again as a sign that the conversation was at an end.

When Prince Andrei went to the room prepared for him and stretched himself in a clean nightshirt on the feather bed with its warmed and fragrant pillows he began to feel that the battle of which he had brought tidings was far, far away. The alliance with Prussia, Austria's treachery, Bonaparte's new triumph, tomorrow's parade and levée, and his audience with the Emperor Francis occupied his mind.

He closed his eyes, but instantly the roar of cannon, of musketry, and the rattling of carriage wheels sounded in his ears, and now once more the musketeers were descending the hill-side in a thin line, and the French were firing, and he felt his heart palpitating as he rode forward beside Schmidt with the bullets merrily whistling all around, and he experienced tenfold the joy of living, as he had not done since childhood.

He woke up. ...

'Yes, that all happened!' he said, and smiling happily to himself like a child he fell into a deep, youthful slumber.

II

NEXT morning he woke late. Recalling his recent impressions, the first thought that came into his mind was that today he was to be presented to the Emperor Francis; he remembered the minister of war, the extravagantly polite Austrian adjutant, Bilibin, and last night's conversation. Having dressed for his attendance at court in full parade uniform, which he had not worn for a long time, he went down to Bilibin's study fresh, full of spirits and handsome, with his arm in a sling. In the study were four gentlemen of the diplomatic corps. With Prince Hippolyte Kuragin, who was a secretary at the embassy, Bolkonsky was already acquainted. Bilibin introduced him to the others.

The gentlemen assembled at Bilibin's were wealthy, gay young society men, who here, as in Vienna, formed an exclusive circle which Bilibin, their leader, called *les nôtres*. This set, consisting almost without exception of diplomats, evidently had its own interests having nothing to do with war or politics but related to the doings of society, their intimacies with certain women, and to the official side of the service. These gentlemen received Prince Andrei as one of themselves, (an honour they did not extend to many). Out of politeness and to break the ice, they asked him a few questions about the army and the battle, and then the conversation quickly drifted back into inconsequential, merry sallies of wit and gossip.

'But the best of it was,' said one, relating a disaster that had befallen a fellow diplomat, 'the best of it was that the chancellor told him flatly that his appointment to London was a promotion, and that he was to regard it so. Can you imagine his face at that?'

'Worse than that, gentlemen – I am giving Kuragin away to you – here is this Don Juan going to profit by his misfortune: he's a shocking fellow!'

Prince Hippolyte was lolling in an easy chair, his legs thrown over the arm. He laughed.

'Come, come!' said he.

'Oh, you Don Juan! Oh, you serpent!' cried various voices.

'You don't know, Bolkonsky,' said Bilibin turning to Prince Andrei, 'that all the atrocities committed by the French army (I almost said the Russian army) are nothing compared to what this man has been doing among the women!'

'Woman is the companion of man,' announced Prince Hippolyte, and began staring through his eyeglass at his raised legs.

Bilibin and *les nôtres* roared with laughter as they looked in Hippolyte's eyes. Prince Andrei saw that this Hippolyte, of whom – he could not disguise it from himself – he had so nearly been jealous on his wife's account, was the butt of the circle.

'Oh, I must give you a treat with Kuragin,' Bilibin whispered to Bolkonsky. 'He's exquisite when he discusses politics – you should see his gravity!'

He sat down beside Hippolyte and wrinkling his forehead began talking about politics. Prince Andrei and the others gathered round the pair.

'The Berlin cabinet cannot express its opinion concerning an alliance,' began Hippolyte, gazing round with importance from one to the other, 'without expressing ... as in its last note ... you understand ... you understand ... and then if his Majesty the Emperor does not waive the principle of our alliance ...

'Wait, I have not finished ...' said he to Prince Andrei, seizing him by the arm. 'I believe that intervention will be stronger than non-intervention. And ...' he paused. 'The non-receipt of our despatch of November the 28th cannot be counted conclusive. That is how it will all end.'

And he let go of Bolkonsky's arm to indicate that he had now quite finished.

'Demosthenes, I know thee by the pebble thou secretest in thy golden mouth!' said Bilibin, his thick thatch of hair moving forward on his head with satisfaction.

Everybody laughed, and Hippolyte louder than any of them. He was visibly distressed, and breathed painfully, but could not restrain the wild laughter that convulsed his usually impassive features.

'Now then, gentlemen,' said Bilibin. 'Bolkonsky is my guest here in Brünn, and I want to entertain him, to the best of my ability, with all the attractions of our life here. If we were in Vienna it would be easy enough, but in this beastly Moravian hole it is more difficult, and I beg you all to help me. We must do him the honours of Brünn. You can undertake the theatre, I will introduce him to society, and you, Hippolyte, the women, of course.'

'We ought to let him see Amélie, she's a charmer!' said one of *les nôtres*, kissing his finger-tips.

'Altogether, this bloodthirsty soldier must have his attention turned to more humane interests,' said Bilibin.

'I shall scarcely be able to avail myself of your hospitality, gentlemen: it is already time I was off,' replied Bolkonsky, glancing at his watch.

'Where to ?'

'To the Emperor.'

'Oh! Oh! Oh!'

'Well, *au revoir*, Bolkonsky! *Au revoir*, prince! Come back early to dinner,' cried several voices. 'We are taking you in hand.'

'Try to extol the work of the commissariat and the planning of routes when you are speaking to the Emperor,' said Bilibin, accompanying Bolkonsky as far as the hall.

'I should like to say flattering things of them, but as far as I know the facts I can't,' replied Bolkonsky with a smile.

'Well, do as much of the talking as you can, anyway. Audiences are his passion but he doesn't like talking himself and never has a word to say, as you will find out.'

12

AT the levée the Emperor Francis merely looked intently into Prince Andrei's face and nodded his long head to him as he stood in the place assigned to him among the Austrian officers. But after the levée the adjutant he had seen the previous day ceremoniously informed Bolkonsky of the Emperor's desire to grant him an audience. The Emperor Francis received him standing in the middle of the room. Prince Andrei was struck by the fact that before beginning the conversation the Emperor seemed embarrassed and did not know what to say, and was blushing.

'Tell me, when did the battle begin?' he asked hurriedly.

Prince Andrei told him. This question was followed by others no less simple: 'Was Kutuzov well? How long was it since he left Krems?' and so on. The Emperor spoke as though his sole aim were to put a given number of questions – the answers to which, as was only too evident, could have no interest for him.

'At what o'clock did the engagement begin?' asked the Emperor.

'I cannot inform your Majesty at which o'clock the fighting began in the front lines, but at Dürenstein, where I happened to be, our army made the first attack after five in the afternoon,' replied Bolkonsky, growing more animated and supposing that now he would have a chance to enter into the accurate account, which he had ready in his mind, of all he knew and had seen. But the Emperor smiled and interrupted him.

'How many miles is it?'

'From where to where, your Majesty?'

'From Dürenstein to Krems.'

'Three and a half miles, your Majesty.'

'The French abandoned the left bank?'

'According to our scouts, the last of them crossed on rafts during the night.'

'Have you enough forage at Krems?'

'Forage had not been supplied to the extent ...'

The Emperor interrupted him.

'At what o'clock was General Schmidt killed?'

'At seven o'clock, I believe.'

'At seven o'clock? Very sad! Very sad!'

The Emperor said that he thanked him, and bowed. Prince Andrei withdrew and was immediately surrounded by courtiers on all sides. Everywhere he saw friendly eyes gazing at him and heard friendly voices addressing him. Yesterday's adjutant reproached him for not having stayed at the palace, and offered him his own house. The minister of war came up and congratulated him on the Maria Theresa Order of the third class, with which the Emperor was presenting him. The Empress's chamberlain invited him to wait upon her Majesty. The Archduchess, too, wished to see him. He did not know whom to answer and it took him several seconds to collect his wits. The Russian ambassador put a hand on his shoulder, drew him to the window and began to talk to him.

Contrary to Bilibin's prognostications, the news brought by Bolkonsky was hailed with rejoicing. A thanksgiving service was arranged, the Grand Cross of Maria Theresa was conferred on Kutuzov, and the whole army received awards. Bolkonsky was overwhelmed with invitations and had to spend the whole morning calling on the principal dignitaries of Austria. Between four and five in the afternoon, having paid all his visits, he was returning homewards to Bilibin's mentally composing a letter to his father about the battle and his reception at Brünn. At the steps of Bilibin's house stood a vehicle half full of luggage, and Franz, Bilibin's man, with some difficulty dragging a travelling-trunk was coming out of the door. (On his way back to Bilibin's Prince Andrei had stepped into a bookshop to provide himself with some books for the campaign, and had spent some time there.)

'What's this?' asked Bolkonsky.

'Ach, your Excellency!' said Franz, struggling to tumble the trunk into the cart. 'We are to move on. The scoundrel is at our heels again!'

'Eh? What?' queried Prince Andrei.

Bilibin came out to meet Bolkonsky. His ordinarily composed face betrayed excitement.

'There now, you must confess that this is a pretty business,' said he. 'This affair of the Tabor bridge – the bridge at Vienna. They are across, and not a shot fired!'

Prince Andrei could not understand.

'But where have you been that you don't know what every coachman in town has heard by now?'

'I come from the Archduchess. I heard nothing there.'

'And didn't you see that people are packing up everywhere?'

'No, I didn't. ... What is it all about?' inquired Prince Andrei impatiently.

'What is it all about? Why, the French have crossed the bridge that Auersperg was defending, and the bridge was not blown up: so Murat is at this moment rushing along the road to Brünn, and today or tomorrow they'll be here.'

'What do you mean – here? And how is it the bridge wasn't blown up, since it was mined?'

'That's what I ask you. No one – not Bonaparte himself – knows why.'

Bolkonsky shrugged his shoulders.

'But if the bridge is crossed it means it's all over with the army: it will be cut off,' said he.

'That's just it,' replied Bilibin. 'Listen! The French enter Vienna, as I told you. Very well. Next day, which was yesterday, *messieurs les maréchaux* Murat, Lannes, and Belliard get on their horses and ride down to the bridge. (Observe that all three are Gascons.) "Gentlemen," says one, "you are aware that the Tabor bridge is mined and counter-mined, and is protected by formidable fortifications and fifteen thousand troops with orders to blow up the bridge and not let us cross? But our Sovereign Emperor Napoleon will be pleased if we take this bridge. So let the three of us go and take the bridge." "Yes, let's!" say the others. And off they go and take the bridge, cross it and now with their whole army are on this side of the Danube, marching on us, on you, and on your lines of communication.'

'Stop jesting,' said Prince Andrei sadly and gravely.

The news grieved him and yet it gave him pleasure. As soon as he heard that the Russian army was in such a hopeless situation, the idea occurred to him that it was he who was destined to extricate it from that situation – that this was his Toulon that would lift him from the ranks of obscure officers and open to him the path to glory! As he listened to Bilibin he was already picturing himself arriving at the camp, and there, at a council of war, giving an opinion that alone could save the army, and how he would be entrusted personally to execute the plan.

'Stop jesting,' said he.

'I am not jesting,' Bilibin went on. 'Nothing could be truer or more melancholy. These gentlemen ride on to the bridge without escort, and wave white handkerchiefs. They assure the officer on duty that it's a truce and that they, the marshals, are come for a parley with Prince Auersperg. The officer on duty lets them enter the *tête de pont*. They spin him a thousand Gascon absurdities, saying that the war is over, that the Emperor Francis has arranged a meeting with Bona-parte, that they desire to see Prince Auersperg, and so on. The officer sends for Auersperg; these gentlemen embrace the officers, crack jokes, sit about on the cannons, while a French battalion meantime advances unnoticed on to the bridge, flings the bags with the incen-diary material into the river, and marches up to the fortifications. Finally the lieutenant-general, our dear Prince Auersperg von Mau-tern himself, appears on the scene. "My dear enemy! Flower of

Austrian chivalry, hero of the Turkish wars! Hostilities are at an end, we can take each other's hands. ... The Emperor Napoleon burns with impatience to make Prince Auersperg's acquaintance." In short, these gentlemen, who are not Gascons for nothing, so bewilder Auersperg with fair words – he is so flattered by this speedy intimacy with French marshals, so dazzled by the spectacle of their cloaks and Murat's ostrich plumes – that their fire gets into his eyes and he quite forgets that he ought to be firing away at the enemy.' (In spite of the *élan* of his remarks, Bilibin did not omit to pause after this witticism, to allow Bolkonsky time to appreciate it.) 'The French battalion rushes to the bridge-head, spikes the guns and the bridge is taken! But this is the best of all,' he went on, his excitement subsiding under the fascination of his own story, '– the sergeant in charge of the cannon which was to give the signal for firing the mines and blowing up the bridge, this sergeant seeing the French troops running on to the bridge was on the point of firing when Lannes pulled his arm away. The sergeant, who seems to have had more sense than his general, goes up to Auersperg and says: "Prince, you are being deceived, here are the French!" Murat sees the game is up if the sergeant is allowed to have his say. With feigned astonishment (he is a true Gascon) he turns to Auersperg and observes: "Is this your world-famous Austrian discipline – do you permit a man from the ranks to address you like that?" It was a stroke of genius. Prince Auersperg feels his dignity at stake and has the sergeant put under arrest. Come, you must own that all this story of the Tabor bridge is sheer delight. It was not exactly stupidity, nor was it dastardly ...'

'Perhaps it is treason, though,' said Prince Andrei, vividly seeing in his imagination the grey greatcoats, the wounds, the smoke of gunpowder, the sounds of firing and the glory that awaited him.

'Not that either. This puts the court into a sorry pickle,' continued Bilibin. 'It's not treason, or dastardliness, or stupidity: it's the same as at Ulm ... it is ...' – he seemed to be trying to find a suitable expression. 'It's ... *c'est du Mack.* We've been Macked,' he concluded, feeling that he had coined a word, a new word that would be repeated. His hitherto puckered brow became smooth in token of his satisfaction, and with a faint smile on his lips he fell to contemplating his finger-nails.

'Where are you going?' he said, suddenly turning to Prince Andrei, who had risen and was making for his room.

'I'm off.'

'Where to?'

'To the army.'

'But you meant to stay another couple of days, didn't you?'

'Yes, but now I am off at once.'

And Prince Andrei, after giving directions about his departure, went to his room.

'Do you know, my dear fellow,' said Bilibin, coming into his room, 'I have been thinking about you. What are you going for?'

And in support of the irrefutability of his argument all the creases ran off his face.

Prince Andrei looked inquiringly at him and made no reply.

'Why are you going? I know you think it is your duty to gallop back to the army now that the army is in danger. I understand that, my dear fellow, it's heroic.'

'Nothing of the kind,' said Prince Andrei.

'But you are *un philosophe*, so be a complete one: look at things from the other side, and you will see that your duty, on the contrary, is to take care of yourself. Leave it to others who are not fit for anything else. ... You have had no orders to return and you have not been dismissed from here; therefore you can stay and go with us wherever our unhappy lot carries us. They say we are going to Olmütz. And Olmütz is a very decent little town. And you and I can make the journey very comfortably in my calèche.'

'Do stop jesting, Bilibin,' cried Bolkonsky.

'I am speaking to you sincerely, as a friend. Consider. Where and why are you going, when you might remain here? One of two things will happen' (here he puckered the skin over his left temple): 'either peace will be concluded before you can reach your regiment, or else defeat and disgrace await you with the rest of Kutuzov's army.'

And Bilibin let his brow go smooth again, feeling that his logic was incontestable.

'I cannot argue about it,' replied Prince Andrei coldly, but he was thinking: 'I am going to save the army.'

'My dear fellow, you are a hero!' said Bilibin.

THAT same night, after taking leave of the minister of war, Bolkonsky set off to rejoin the army, though he did not know where he would find it and was fearful of being captured by the French on the way to Krems.

In Brünn everybody attached to the court was packing up, and the heavy baggage was already being despatched to Olmütz. Near Etzelsdorf Prince Andrei struck the high road along which the Russian army was moving with the utmost haste and in the greatest disorder. The road was so encumbered with carts that progress by carriage was impossible. Prince Andrei procured a horse and a Cossack from the officer in command of the Cossacks, and hungry and weary, threading his way past the baggage-wagons, rode in search of the commander-in-chief and of his own luggage. He heard the most sinister reports of the position of the army as he went along, and the appearance of the troops fleeing in disorder confirmed these rumours.

'As for that Russian army which English gold has brought from the ends of the universe – we shall see that it meets the same fate as met the army at Ulm.' He remembered these words from Bonaparte's address to his army at the opening of the campaign, and they inspired in him admiration for the man's genius, together with a feeling of wounded pride and a hope of glory. 'And should there be nothing left but to die?' he said to himself. 'Well, I shall know how to die, and no worse than the next man, if I must.'

Prince Andrei looked disdainfully at the endless confusion of detachments, baggage-wagons, field-pieces, artillery, baggage-wagons again, and still more baggage-wagons and carts of every possible description, overtaking one another and jamming the muddy road, three and four abreast. On every side, behind and before, as far as the ear could hear there was the creaking of wheels, the rumble of wagons, carts, and gun-carriages, the tramp of hooves, the cracking of whips, the shouts of drivers urging on their horses, the cursing of soldiers, orderlies and officers. Lying by the sides of the road were the carcases of dead horses, some flayed, some not, and broken-down carts beside which solitary soldiers sat waiting for something; then again he saw soldiers straying from the main column and hastening in bands to the neighbouring villages or returning from them dragging fowls, sheep, hay or bulging sacks. At each slope, up or down, of the road the crowds packed closer and the din of shouting was more incessant. Soldiers floundering knee-deep in mud pulled at the guns and wagons themselves. Whips cracked, hooves slipped, traces gave way and lungs were split with yelling. The officers directing the retreat rode back and forth among the wagons. Their voices were but feebly audible amid the general uproar and their faces betrayed their despair of being able to check the chaos.

'*Voilà* our precious Orthodox Russian army,' thought Bolkonsky, remembering Bilibin's words.

Wishing to find out where the commander-in-chief was, he rode up to a convoy. Directly opposite him came a strange one-horse vehicle, evidently rigged up by soldiers out of any available materials and looking like a cross between a cart, a cabriolet and a calèche. A soldier was driving it, and a woman enveloped in shawls sat behind the apron under the leather hood of the conveyance. Prince Andrei rode up and was just putting his question to the soldier when his attention was diverted by the desperate shrieks of the woman sitting in the vehicle. An officer in charge of the convoy was beating her driver for trying to pass ahead of the others, and the blows of his whip lashed the apron of the equipage. The woman screamed piercingly. Seeing Prince Andrei she leaned out from behind the apron, and waving her thin arms from under the woollen shawls cried:

'Aide-de-camp. Mr Aide-de-camp! ... For God's sake. ... Protect me. ... Whatever will become of us? ... I am the doctor's wife – the doctor of the 7th Chasseurs. ... They won't let us through: we have been left behind and have lost our party ...'

'I'll flatten you flatter than a pancake!' shouted the angry officer to the soldier. 'Turn back with your slut!'

'Mr Aide-de-camp, help me! What are they going to do with us?' screamed the doctor's wife.

'Kindly let this cart pass. Don't you see there's a woman in it?' said Prince Andrei riding up to the officer.

The officer glanced at him and without replying addressed the soldier again. 'I'll teach you. ... Back!'

'Let them pass, I tell you!' repeated Prince Andrei, compressing his lips.

'And who are you?' cried the officer, suddenly turning upon him in a drunken fury. 'Who do you think *you* are? Are *you*' (he put a peculiarly offensive intonation into the word) 'in command, pray? I am commander here, not you! Back there, or I'll flatten you flatter'n a pancake,' he repeated, the expression having evidently taken his fancy.

'A proper snub for the little adjutant,' said a voice behind.

Prince Andrei saw that the officer was in one of those paroxysms of drunken fury in which a man does not recollect what he says. He realized that his championship of the doctor's wife in her odd trap might expose him to what he dreaded more than anything in the world – ridicule – but instinct urged him on. Before the officer had time to finish what he was saying, Prince Andrei, his face distorted with rage, rode up to him and raised his riding-whip.

'Kind – ly – let – them – pass!'

The officer flourished his arm in an angry gesture and hastily rode away.

'It's all because of these staff-officers that there's all this disorder,' he muttered. 'Have it your own way.'

Prince Andrei, without lifting his eyes, made haste to escape from the doctor's wife, who was hailing him as her deliverer, and dwelling with disgust on the minutest details of this humiliating scene he cantered on towards the village where he was told that he would find his commander-in-chief.

On reaching the village he dismounted and went to the nearest house, intending to rest, if only for a minute, eat something, and try to sort out the mortifying thoughts that tormented his mind. 'This is a mob of scoundrels, not an army,' he thought, going up to the window of the first house, when a familiar voice called him by name.

Looking round, he saw Nesvitsky's handsome face thrust out of a little window. Nesvitsky, chewing something between his moist lips, was waving and calling him in.

'Bolkonsky! Bolkonsky! Can't you hear? Come on in quickly!' he shouted.

Entering the house, Prince Andrei found Nesvitsky and another adjutant having a meal. They turned round eagerly asking if he had any news. He read agitation and alarm on their familiar features, particularly on Nesvitsky's usually laughing face.

'Where is the commander-in-chief?' asked Bolkonsky.

'Here, in that house over there,' answered the adjutant.

'Tell us, is it true about the peace and capitulation?' asked Nesvitsky.

'I was going to ask you that. I know nothing except that it was all I could do to get here.'

'And look at the plight we're in! Awful! I own it was wrong – we laughed at Mack, but here we are doing even worse,' said Nesvitsky. 'But sit down and have some food.'

'You won't find your baggage or anything else now, prince. And God only knows what has become of your man Piotr,' said the other adjutant.

'Where are headquarters?'

'We are to spend the night in Znaim.'

'Well, I've got all I need into packs for two horses,' said Nesvitsky; 'and capital packs they made for me – I could cross the mountains of Bohemia with them. We're in a bad way, brother. But, I say, you must be ill, shivering like that,' he added, noticing Prince Andrei wince violently.

'It's nothing,' replied Prince Andrei. He had just remembered his recent encounter with the doctor's wife and the convoy officer.

'What is the commander-in-chief doing here?' he asked.

'I haven't the least idea,' said Nesvitsky.

'Well, all I can make out is that everything is abominable, absolutely abominable,' said Prince Andrei, and started for the house where the commander-in-chief was.

Passing by Kutuzov's carriage and the exhausted saddle-horses of his suite, with their Cossacks vociferating loudly together, Prince Andrei entered the passage. Kutuzov himself, he was told, was inside with Prince Bagration and Weierother. Weierother was the Austrian general who had succeeded Schmidt. In the passage little Kozlovsky was squatting on his heels in front of a copying-clerk. The clerk, with cuffs rolled back, was writing rapidly, using a tub turned bottom upwards as a table. Kozlovsky's face looked worn – he too had evidently not slept all night. He cast a glance at Prince Andrei and did not even nod to him.

'Second line. ... Have you written that?' he continued dictating to the clerk. 'The Kiev Grenadiers, the Podolian ...'

'Not so fast, your Honour,' said the clerk, glancing up at Kozlovsky in a rude, surly fashion.

Through the door came the sound of Kutuzov's voice, excited and impatient, interrupted by another, an unfamiliar voice. The sound of these two voices, the preoccupied way in which Kozlovsky had glanced at him, the disrespectful manner of the harassed clerk, the fact that the clerk and Kozlovsky were sitting round a tub on the floor at so little distance from the commander-in-chief, and the noisy laughter of the Cossacks holding the horses outside the window – all made Prince Andrei feel that some grave calamity was hanging over them.

He turned to Kozlovsky with urgent questions.

'In a moment, prince,' said Kozlovsky. 'These are the dispositions for Bagration.'

'But the capitulation?'

'There is no such thing. Orders are issued for a battle.'

Prince Andrei moved towards the door of the room from which the voices were heard. But just as he was going to open it there was silence, the door opened and Kutuzov with his aquiline nose and puffy face appeared on the threshold. Prince Andrei was standing directly in front of Kutuzov but the expression of the commander-in-chief's one sound eye showed him to be so absorbed by his thoughts and anxieties that he did not see anything at all. He looked straight into his adjutant's face without recognizing him.

'Well, have you finished?' he inquired of Kozlovsky.

'In one second, your Excellency.'

Bagration, a gaunt middle-aged man of medium height with firm impassive features like an oriental, came out after the commander-in-chief.

'I have the honour to present myself,' repeated Prince Andrei rather loudly, holding out an envelope to Kutuzov.

'Ah, from Vienna? Very good. Presently, presently!'

Kutuzov went out into the porch with Bagration.

'Well, good-bye, prince,' said he to Bagration. 'Christ be with you. My blessing on you in your great endeavour.'

Kutuzov's face suddenly softened, and tears came into his eyes. With his left hand he drew Bagration to him, while with his right, on which he wore a ring, he made the sign of the cross over him with a gesture evidently habitual, and offered him his podgy cheek, but Bagration kissed him on the neck instead.

'Christ be with you!' repeated Kutuzov, and went towards his carriage. 'Get in with me,' said he to Bolkonsky.

'Your Excellency, I could wish to be of use here. Allow me to remain in Prince Bagration's division.'

'Get in,' said Kutuzov, and noticing that Bolkonsky hesitated he added: 'I have need of good officers myself, need them myself.'

They took their seats in the carriage and drove for some minutes in silence.

'There is still much, much before us,' said he as though with an old man's keenness of perception he understood all that was passing in Bolkonsky's mind. 'If a tenth part of his division returns tomorrow, I shall thank God,' he went on, as if speaking to himself.

Prince Andrei glanced at Kutuzov and his eyes were involuntarily attracted by the deep scar with its clear-cut edges on Kutuzov's temple, where a bullet had pierced his skull at Ismail, and the empty eye-socket, less than eighteen inches from him. 'Yes, he has a right to speak so calmly of the death of so many men,' thought Bolkonsky.

'That is why I beg to be sent to that division,' he said.

Kutuzov made no reply. He seemed to have forgotten what he had just said, and sat plunged in thought. Five minutes later, gently swaying on the easy springs of the carriage, he turned to Prince Andrei. There was no trace of emotion on his face. With delicate irony he began to question Prince Andrei on the details of his interview with the Emperor, on the remarks he had heard at court concerning the Krems affair, and about certain ladies they both knew.

14

ON November the 1st Kutuzov had received information from one of his spies that showed the army he commanded to be in an almost hopeless position. The spy reported that the French, after crossing the bridge at Vienna, were advancing in considerable strength upon Kutuzov's line of communication with the troops arriving from Russia. If Kutuzov decided to remain at Krems, Napoleon's army of a hundred and fifty thousand men would cut him off completely and surround his exhausted army of forty thousand, and he would find himself in the same predicament as Mack at Ulm. If Kutuzov decided to abandon the road connecting him with the reinforcements arriving from Russia, he would have to march into the unknown and pathless regions of the Bohemian mountains, defending himself against superior forces and giving up all hope of effecting a junction with Buxhöwden. If Kutuzov decided to retreat along the road from Krems to Olmütz, to unite with the troops from Russia, he ran the risk of finding himself forestalled on that road by the French who had crossed the Danube at Vienna, and having to accept battle while on the march, encumbered by his baggage and transport, against an enemy three times as numerous and hemming him in from both sides.

Kutuzov chose this last course.

The French, the spy reported, having crossed the bridge at Vienna, were advancing by forced marches towards Znaim, which lay about sixty-six miles away on the line of Kutuzov's retreat. To reach Znaim before the French offered the best hopes of saving the army. To let the French get to Znaim first would mean exposing his entire army to a disgrace like that of the Austrians at Ulm, or to total destruction. But to forestall the French with his whole army was impossible. The road for the French from Vienna to Znaim was shorter and better than the road for the Russians from Krems to Znaim.

On the night he received this information Kutuzov despatched Bagration's vanguard, four thousand strong, to the right across the hills from the Krems-Znaim to the Vienna-Znaim road. Bagration was to effect this march without resting, and to halt facing Vienna with Znaim to his rear, and if he succeeded in arriving before the French he was to delay them as long as he could. Kutuzov himself with all his transport took the road to Znaim.

Marching thirty miles that stormy night across the roadless hills, with his famished, ill-shod soldiers, and losing a third of his men in stragglers by the way, Bagration came out at Hollabrünn on the Vienna-Znaim road a few hours ahead of the French who were approaching Hollabrünn from Vienna. It would take Kutuzov with all the transport fully another twenty-four hours to reach Znaim, and so to save the army Bagration with his four thousand hungry exhausted men would have to engage the entire force of the enemy confronting him at Hollabrünn for four-and-twenty hours, which was manifestly impossible. But a freak of fate made the impossible possible. The success of the trick that had placed the bridge at Vienna in the hands of the French without a blow inspired Murat to try to trick Kutuzov too. Meeting Bagration's feeble detachment on the Znaim road he supposed it to be Kutuzov's whole army. In order to make sure of crushing this army absolutely he decided to await the arrival of all the forces that had started out from Vienna, and with this end in view he proposed a three days' truce, on condition that both armies should remain where they were without moving. Murat declared that negotiations for peace were already proceeding and that therefore, to avoid unnecessary bloodshed, he proposed this truce. The Austrian general, Count Nostitz, occupying the advanced posts, believed Murat's emissary and retired, leaving Bagration's division exposed. Another emissary rode to the Russian line to make the same assurances about peace negotiations and to offer the Russian army the three days' truce. Bagration replied that he was not authorized either to accept or decline a truce, and sent his adjutant to Kutuzov to report the proposition he had received.

A truce was Kutuzov's sole chance of gaining time, of giving Bagration's exhausted troops some rest, and letting the transport and heavy convoys (the movements of which were concealed from the French) advance if but one stage nearer Znaim. The offer of a truce gave the only – and quite unexpected – opportunity of saving the army. On the receipt of the news Kutuzov promptly despatched Adjutant-General Wintzingerode, who was in attendance on him, to the enemy camp. Wintzingerode was instructed not merely to agree to the truce but to propose terms of capitulation, and meanwhile Kutuzov sent his aides back to hasten to the utmost the movements of the baggage-trains of the entire army along the road from Krems to Znaim. Bagration's weary, famished contingent, alone covering this operation of the baggage-trains and of the whole army, was to remain stationary in face of an enemy numerically eight times as strong.

Kutuzov's anticipations that the proposals of capitulation, which bound him to nothing, would give time for part of the transport to come up, and also that Murat's blunder would very soon be discovered, proved correct. As soon as Bonaparte, who was at Schönbrunn, sixteen miles from Hollabrünn, received Murat's despatch and the proposal for a truce and capitulation he detected a ruse and wrote the following letter to Murat:

> Schönbrunn, 25th Brumaire, 1805,
> at eight o'clock in the morning.

To Prince Murat.

I cannot find words to express to you my displeasure. You only command my advance-guard and have no right to arrange an armistice without my orders. You are causing me to lose the fruits of a campaign. End the armistice immediately and march up on the enemy. Inform him that the general who signed this capitulation had no right to do so – that no one but the Emperor of Russia has that right.

If, however, the Emperor of Russia should ratify the said convention, I will ratify it; but it is only a trick. Advance, destroy the Russian army. ... You are in a position to capture their baggage and artillery.

The Russian Emperor's aide-de-camp is an impostor. Officers are of no account when they have no powers. This one had none. The Austrians let themselves be tricked about the crossing of the bridge at Vienna; you are letting yourself be tricked by one of the Emperor's aides-de-camp.   NAPOLEON

Bonaparte's adjutant dashed off at full gallop with this menacing letter to Murat. Bonaparte himself, not trusting to his generals, with all the Guards moved towards the field of battle, afraid of being cheated of his prey, while Bagration's four thousand men merrily lighted camp fires, dried and warmed themselves, cooked their porridge for the first time in three days, and not one of them knew or dreamed of what was in store for him.

15

BETWEEN three and four o'clock in the afternoon Prince Andrei, who had persisted in his request to Kutuzov, arrived at Grunth and reported to Bagration. Bonaparte's adjutant had not yet reached Murat's detachment and the battle had not yet begun. In Bagration's division nothing was known of the general course of events: some talked of a peace but did not believe in its possibility; others of a battle, but neither did they believe in the imminence of an engagement.

Knowing Bolkonsky to be a favourite and trusted adjutant, Bagration received him with distinction and special marks of favour, explaining to him that that day or the next would probably see action, and giving him full liberty to be present with him during the battle or to join the rearguard and superintend the retreat, 'which is also very important'.

'However, I hardly think there will be an engagement today,' said Bagration, as if to reassure Prince Andrei. At the same time he thought, 'If this is one of the common run of little staff dandies out to win a medal, he will get it just as well by staying in the rear; but if he wants to be with me, let him. ... He will be useful if he is a brave officer.'

Making no reply, Prince Andrei asked permission to reconnoitre the position and learn the disposition of the forces, so as to know his bearings should he be sent to execute an order. The officer on duty, a handsome, elegantly-attired man with a diamond ring on his forefinger, who was fond of speaking French though he spoke it badly, offered to be Prince Andrei's guide.

On all sides they saw rain-soaked officers with dejected faces, who appeared to be looking for something, and soldiers dragging doors, benches and fencing from the village.

'See that, prince! We can't stop those fellows,' said the staff-officer pointing to the soldiers. 'The officers let them get out of hand. And look there,' he pointed to a sutler's tent, 'there they gather and there they sit. This morning I drove them all out and now look, it's full again. I must go and scare them a bit, prince. One moment.'

'Let us go together, and I'll get myself some cheese and a loaf of bread,' said Prince Andrei, who had not yet had time for a meal.

'Whyever didn't you mention it, prince? I would have offered you something.'

They got off their horses and went into the sutler's tent, where several officers with flushed and weary faces were sitting at a table eating and drinking.

'Now what does this mean, gentlemen?' said the staff-officer in the reproachful tones of a man who has repeated the same thing more than once. 'You know it won't do to leave your posts like this. The prince gave orders forbidding this sort of thing. Really, captain,' and he turned to a thin, muddy little artillery officer who without boots (he had given them to the sutler to dry) stood up in his stockinged feet as they entered, smiling not altogether comfortably.

'Now, aren't you ashamed of yourself, Captain Tushin?' pursued the staff-officer. 'One would think that you as an artillery officer would set a good example, yet here you are with your boots off! If the alarm sounded, you'd cut a pretty figure without boots!' (The staff-officer smiled.) 'Have the goodness to return to your posts, gentlemen, all of you, all!' he added in a tone of authority.

Prince Andrei could not help smiling as he looked at Captain Tushin, who, silent and grinning, shifted from one stockinged foot to the other, and looked inquiringly with his large, intelligent, good-natured eyes from Prince Andrei to the staff-officer.

'The soldiers say it's easier barefoot,' said Captain Tushin smiling shyly, evidently anxious to carry off his awkward predicament by assuming a jocular tone. But before he had uttered the words he sensed that his jest was not appreciated and would not be a success. He grew confused.

'Kindly go to your posts,' said the staff-officer, trying to preserve his gravity.

Prince Andrei glanced again at the diminutive figure of the artillery officer. There was something peculiar about it, quite unsoldierly, rather comical but extraordinarily attractive.

The staff-officer and Prince Andrei mounted their horses and rode on.

Riding out beyond the village, continually overtaking or meeting soldiers and officers of various divisions, they came in sight on their left of some new entrenchments being thrown up, the freshly-dug clay showing red. Several battalions of soldiers, in their shirt-sleeves despite the cold wind, swarmed in these earthworks like white ants; unseen arms kept tossing up shovelsful of red clay, behind the breast-works. Prince Andrei and his guide rode up to the entrenchment, examined it and went on. Just behind it they came upon some dozens of soldiers all running to and fro to take their turns in the entrenchment. They were obliged to hold their noses and put their horses to a trot to escape the pestilential atmosphere.

'The pleasures of camp life, prince,' remarked the staff-officer.

They rode up the opposite hill. From the top of it they could see the French. Prince Andrei reined in his horse and began to look around.

'That's where our battery stands,' said the staff-officer, indicating the highest point. 'It's commanded by that queer fellow we saw without his boots. You can see everything from over there: shall we go, prince?'

'A thousand thanks, I can find my way alone now,' said Prince Andrei, to be rid of his escort. 'Please do not trouble yourself further.'

The staff-officer turned back, and Prince Andrei rode on alone.

The farther forward and nearer the enemy he went, the more orderly and cheerful he found the men. The greatest disorder and despondency had been in the baggage-train he had passed that morning on the road to Znaim and seven miles from the French. In Grunth too a certain apprehension and alarm could be felt. But the nearer Prince

Andrei rode to the French lines the more confident was the appearance of our troops. The soldiers in their greatcoats stood drawn up in line, and a sergeant-major and a captain were calling over the men, poking the last man in each section in the chest and telling him to hold up his hand. Soldiers were dotted all over the plain, dragging logs and brushwood, and constructing rude huts, laughing good-humouredly and chatting together; around the bivouac fires sat others, some dressed, some stripped, drying their shirts and leg-bands, or mending boots or greatcoats, and crowding round the cauldrons and porridge pots. In one company dinner was ready and the soldiers gazed with eager eyes at the steaming boiler, waiting while the quartermaster-sergeant carried a wooden bowlful to be tasted by an officer who sat on a log in front of his shanty.

In another company – a fortunate one since not all were provided with vodka – the men stood in a group round a pock-marked, broad-shouldered sergeant-major who was tilting a keg and filling one after another the canteen-lids held out to him. The soldiers with reverent faces lifted the canteen-lids to their mouths, drained them, and licking their lips and wiping them on the sleeves of their greatcoats walked away from the sergeant-major with brightened expressions. Every face was as serene as if all this were happening at some quiet halting-place at home in Russia, instead of within sight of the enemy on the eve of an action in which at least half of the detachment must be left on the field. After riding past a regiment of chasseurs Prince Andrei reached the lines of the Kiev Grenadiers – stalwart fellows engaged in similar peaceful pursuits – and not far from the regimental commander's hut, distinguished by its height from the others, came out in front of a platoon of grenadiers before whom a man was stretched, naked, on the ground. Two soldiers held him down while two others were flourishing their switches and bringing them down at measured intervals on his bare back. The victim shrieked unnaturally. A stout major was pacing up and down the line and regardless of the screams kept repeating:

'It's a disgrace for a soldier to steal. A soldier should be honest, honourable and brave, but if he robs his comrades there is no honour in him, he's a scoundrel. Go on! Go on!'

So the swishing of the canes and the despairing but exaggerated screaming continued.

'Go on, go on!' repeated the major.

A young officer with a bewildered expression of compassion on his face stepped away from the scene of punishment and looked round inquiringly at the aide-de-camp as he rode by.

Prince Andrei, having reached the front line, rode along by the outposts. Our line and that of the enemy were separated by a considerable distance at both flanks but in the centre where the truce envoys had crossed that morning the lines came so close that the pickets of the two armies could see each other's faces and exchange remarks. Besides the soldiers who formed the picket line many inquisitive onlookers had gathered from both sides who laughed and jested as they scrutinized their strange foreign enemies.

Since early morning, in spite of orders not to approach the picket line, the officers had been unable to keep off the local townspeople. The soldiers whose post was in that part of the line, like showmen exhibiting something unusual, no longer paid any attention to the French but made observations on the sightseers while they wearily waited to be relieved. Prince Andrei pulled up to study the French.

'Look – look there!' one soldier was saying to his comrade, pointing to a Russian musketeer who had gone up to the lines with an officer and was talking rapidly and excitedly to a French grenadier. 'Hark at him jabbering away! The Frenchie can't get a word in! What d'ye say to that, Sidorov?'

'Wait – listen. Ah, that's good, that is!' answered Sidorov, who considered himself a scholar at French.

The soldier they were laughing about was Dolohov. Prince Andrei recognized him and stopped to hear what he was saying. Dolohov together with his captain had come from the left flank where his regiment was stationed.

'Now then, go on, go on!' urged the captain, leaning forward and trying not to miss a word, though it was all unintelligible to him. 'Go on, keep it up! What's he saying?'

Dolohov did not answer his captain: he had been drawn into a heated dispute with the French grenadier. They were talking, as was to be expected, about the campaign. The Frenchman, confusing the Austrians with the Russians, contended that it was the Russians who had surrendered and fled from Ulm, while Dolohov maintained that the Russians had never been defeated but had beaten the French.

'Our orders are to clear you out of here, and we shall too,' said Dolohov.

'Better mind you aren't taken prisoner and all your Cossacks with you!' retorted the French grenadier.

Spectators and listeners on the French side laughed.

'We'll make you dance, the way Suvorov did ... *on vous fera danser,*' said Dolohov.

'What's he prating about?' asked a Frenchman.

'Ancient history,' said another, guessing that Dolohov was referring to a former war. 'The Emperor will show your Suvara, the same as he did the others ...'

'Bonaparte ...' Dolohov was beginning, but the Frenchman interrupted him.

'Not Bonaparte. He is the Emperor! *Sacré nom ...*!' he cried angrily.

'The devil skin your Emperor!' And Dolohov swore coarse soldier's oaths at him in Russian, and shouldering his musket walked away.

'Let us be going, Ivan Lukich,' he said to his captain.

'Ah, that's how they talk French-language,' said the picket soldiers. 'Now you have a try, Sidorov!'

Sidorov winked and turning to the French began to gabble a stream of meaningless syllables as fast as his tongue would move:

'*Kari – mala – tafa – safi – muter – kaska,*' he rattled out, trying to throw expression into his voice.

'Ho! ho! ho! Ha! ha! ha! ha! Ouh! ouh!' Peals of such hearty, jovial laughter rang out from the soldiers, in which the French across the line could not help joining, that it would seem as though after that they could only fire off their muskets in the air, explode the ammunition and all hurry back to their homes as fast as possible.

But the guns remained loaded, the loop-holes in blockhouses and entrenchments looked out as threateningly as ever, and the unlimbered cannon confronted one another as before.

16

HAVING ridden along the entire line, from the right flank to the left, Prince Andrei made his way to the battery from which, according to the staff-officer, he could get a view of the whole field. Here he dismounted, and leaned against the end one of the four field-pieces, which had been taken off their platforms. An artilleryman on sentinel duty in front of the guns was about to stand to attention before the officer but at a sign from Prince Andrei resumed his measured, mono-tonous pacing. Behind the cannon were their limbers, and still farther back picket-ropes and the gunners' bivouac fires. To the left at a short distance from the farthest piece was a new little hut made of wattles, from which came the sound of officers' voices in lively conversation.

It was in fact true that a view over the whole Russian disposition and the greater part of the enemy's opened out from this battery. Directly facing it, on the crest of the opposite hill, could be seen the village of Schön Graben and in three places, farther to the left and to the right, Prince Andrei could distinguish through the smoke of their camp-fires the mass of the French troops, of whom the greater number were undoubtedly in the village itself and behind the hill. To the left of the houses something resembling a battery was discernible in the smoke but it was impossible to see it clearly with the naked eye. Our right flank was distributed along a rather steep incline which dominated the French position. Our infantry were here, with the dragoons at the very ridge. In the centre, where Tushin's battery stood and from which Prince Andrei was surveying the position, there was a sharp drop towards the brook separating us from Schön Graben. On the left our troops were close to a copse where bonfires smoked and the infantry were felling wood. The French line was wider than ours and it was plain that they could easily outflank us on both sides. To our rear was a steep and precipitous ravine which would make it difficult for artillery and cavalry to retire. Prince Andrei took out his pocket-book and, leaning an elbow on the cannon, sketched a plan of the disposition of the armies. In two places he pencilled certain observations to which he intended to draw Bagration's attention. His idea was firstly to concentrate all the artillery in the centre, and secondly to remove the cavalry back to the other side of the ravine. Prince Andrei, who was constantly in attendance on the commander-in-chief, concerned with the movements of masses of men and organization in general, and always studying historical accounts of battles, now found himself involuntarily trying to imagine in broad outline the course of the coming action. He pictured eventualities somewhat as follows: 'If the enemy makes the right flank the point of attack,' he said to himself, 'the Kiev Grenadiers and the Podolsky Chasseurs must hold their position till reserves from the centre come up. In that case the dragoons could make a successful flank counter-attack. If they attack our centre we place the centre battery on this high ground and under its cover withdraw the left flank and retire to the ravine by echelons.' So he reasoned. ...

All this time while he stood beside the cannon he could hear the voices of the officers talking in the hut but, as often happens, he had not taken in a single word of what they were saying. Suddenly, however, he was so struck by the earnestness of their tones that he began to listen.

'No, my dear friend,' said a pleasant voice which Prince Andrei seemed to recognize, 'what I say is – if one could know what will happen after death, then not one of us would be afraid of death. That is true, my dear fellow.'

Another and younger voice interrupted.

'Well, afraid or not, it's all the same, there's no escaping it.'

'It makes no difference, one's afraid! Oh you clever people who know all about it!' said a third lusty voice, breaking in upon them both. 'You artillerymen are so cocksure because you can carry everything along with you – you have your tipples of vodka and snacks wherever you go.'

And the owner of the lusty voice, evidently an infantry officer, laughed.

'Yes, one is afraid,' pursued the first speaker, the one with the familiar voice. 'One's afraid of the unknown, that's what it is. It is all very well saying the soul goes up to heaven ... don't we know that up yonder it's not heaven but just space.'

Again the manly voice interrupted.

'Well, give us a taste of your herb-vodka, Tushin,' it said.

'Why, that's the captain who stood in the sutler's hut with his boots off,' thought Prince Andrei, pleased to recognize the agreeable philosophizing voice.

'Some herb-vodka? Certainly!' said Tushin. 'But now, about understanding the life to come ...' He did not finish. At that instant there was a hiss in the air: nearer and nearer, swifter and louder, louder and swifter, and a cannon-ball, as though it had not completed all it wanted to say, smacked into the ground not far from the hut, tearing up the soil with superhuman violence. The ground seemed to groan with the terrible impact.

Little Tushin immediately rushed out of the hut ahead of the rest, his stumpy pipe stuck in the corner of his mouth and his kind intelligent face looking rather pale. He was followed by the owner of the lusty voice, a dashing infantry officer who hurried off to his company, buttoning his jacket as he ran.

17

MOUNTING his horse Prince Andrei lingered to watch the puff of smoke from the cannon that had fired the ball. His eyes rapidly scanned the wide landscape but all he could see was that the hitherto motionless masses of the French were beginning to stir, and that there really was a battery to the left. The smoke still clung about it. Two Frenchmen on horseback, adjutants probably, were galloping on the hill. A small but clearly distinguishable enemy column was moving downhill, apparently for the purpose of strengthening the front line. Before the smoke of the first shot had drifted away a fresh puff appeared, followed by a report. The battle had begun. Prince Andrei turned his horse and spurred back to Grunth to look for Prince Bagration. Behind him he heard the cannonade growing louder and more frequent. Evidently our guns were beginning to reply. From the bottom of the slope, where the lines were closest, came the crack of musketry.

Lemarrois had just arrived at a gallop with Bonaparte's angry letter, and Murat, humiliated and anxious to retrieve his blunder, had immediately moved his forces to attack the centre and outflank both the Russian wings, hoping before nightfall and the arrival of the Emperor to demolish the insignificant division that stood opposite.

'It has begun! Here it is!' thought Prince Andrei, feeling the blood rush to his heart. 'But where – what form will my Toulon take?'

Passing between the companies that only a quarter of an hour before had been eating kasha-gruel and drinking vodka, he saw soldiers hastily moving about everywhere, falling into line and getting their muskets ready, and on every face he recognized the same eagerness that filled his own heart. 'It has begun! Here it is! Terrible but glorious!' said the face of every private and officer.

Before he reached the earthworks still in process of construction, he saw in the twilight of the dull autumn evening mounted men coming towards him. The foremost, wearing a Cossack cloak and lambskin cap and riding a white horse, was Prince Bagration. Prince Andrei stopped and waited for him to come up. Prince Bagration reined in his horse and recognizing Prince Andrei nodded to him. He continued to gaze ahead while Prince Andrei reported what he had seen.

The thought, *It has begun! Here it is!* could be read even on Prince Bagration's strong brown face with its half-closed, dim, sleepy eyes. Prince Andrei glanced with uneasy curiosity at that impassive countenance and wished he could tell what, if anything, the man was thinking and feeling at this moment. 'Is there anything at all behind those dispassionate features?' Prince Andrei wondered. Prince Bagration nodded his head in approval of what Prince Andrei told him, and said, 'Good!' in a tone seeming to imply that all that was taking place and all that was reported to him was exactly what he had anticipated. Prince Andrei, out of breath from galloping, spoke rapidly. Prince Bagration pronounced his words with an oriental accent, letting them drop very slowly, as if to impress that there was no need for haste. However, he put his horse to the trot in the direction of Tushin's battery. Prince Andrei followed with the suite. The party consisted of an officer of the suite, Bagration's personal adjutant, Zherkov, an orderly officer, the staff-officer on duty riding a fine bobtailed horse, and a civilian official – an auditor who had asked out of curiosity to be present at the battle. The auditor, a fat man with a fat face, kept looking about him with a naïve smile of delight, cutting a queer figure among the hussars, Cossacks and adjutants, in his camlet coat as he jolted along on his horse with a convoy-officer's saddle.

'He wants to see a battle,' said Zherkov to Bolkonsky, pointing to the auditor, 'but the pit of his stomach's turning already.'

'Come, that's enough!' exclaimed the auditor with a beaming smile that was at once artless and artful, as if he were flattered at being made the butt of Zherkov's jokes and was purposely trying to appear more stupid than he really was.

'It's very amusing, *mon monsieur prince*,' said the staff-officer. (He remembered that in French there was some peculiar way of addressing a prince, but could not get it quite right.)

By this time they were all nearing Tushin's battery, and a ball struck the ground in front of them.

'What was that that fell?' asked the auditor with his naïve smile.

'A French pancake,' said Zherkov.

'So that's what they send over?' asked the accountant. 'How awful!'

And he seemed to swell with enjoyment. The words were hardly out of his mouth when there was another sudden violent whistling noise which ended abruptly in a thud into something soft ... f-f-flop! and a Cossack, riding a little behind and to the right of the auditor, crashed off his horse to the ground. Zherkov and the staff-officer crouched down in their saddles and turned their horses away. The auditor stopped, facing the Cossack, and examined him with curiosity. The Cossack was dead but the horse was still struggling.

Prince Bagration screwed up his eyes, glanced back over his shoulder and seeing the cause of the confusion turned his head again indifferently, as much as to say: 'Is it worth while bothering with trifles?' He reined in his horse with the ease of a good rider, and slightly bending over disengaged his sabre which had caught in his cloak. It was an old-fashioned one, of a kind no longer in general use. Prince Andrei remembered the story of how Suvorov had presented his sabre to Bagration in Italy, and the recollection was particularly agreeable to him at this moment. They reached the battery from which Prince Andrei had surveyed the field of battle.

'Whose company?' asked Prince Bagration of an artilleryman standing by the ammunition-wagon.

He asked, 'Whose company?' but really he meant: 'Got cold feet here, haven't you?' and the gunner understood him.

'Captain Tushin's, your Excellency!' shouted the freckled, red-headed artilleryman in a cheerful voice, standing to attention.

'Good, good,' muttered Bagration absent-mindedly, and he rode past the limbers to the end cannon.

As he approached, a shot boomed from the cannon, deafening him and his suite, and in the smoke that suddenly enveloped the gun they could see the artillerymen seizing and straining to get it quickly back into position. A huge broad-shouldered soldier, Gunner Number One, holding the sponge, his legs wide apart, sprang to the wheel; while Number Two with a shaking hand rammed the charge into the cannon's mouth. The short, round-shouldered Captain Tushin, stumbling over the tail of the gun-carriage, hastened forward without noticing the general and gazed into the distance, shading his eyes with his small hand.

'Two points up and that'll do it,' he cried in a thin little voice to which he tried to impart a swaggering note that did not go with his appearance. 'Number Two!' he piped. 'Let 'em have it, Medvedev!'

Bagration called to him, and Tushin, raising three fingers to his cap with a shy awkward gesture more like a priest giving a benediction than a soldier saluting, came up to the general. Though it had been intended for Tushin's field-pieces to sweep the valley, he was throwing fire-balls at the village of Schön Graben, visible just opposite, in front of which large masses of the French were concentrating.

No one had given Tushin any orders where to fire and what ammunition to use, and so, having consulted his sergeant-major Zaharchenko, for whom he had great respect, he had decided that it would be a good thing to set fire to the village. 'Very well!' said Bagration when he had listened to the officer's report, and he began to scan the battlefield extended before him, as if he were deliberating something. The French had advanced closest on our right. Below the height on which the Kiev regiment was stationed, in the hollow where the brook flowed, could be heard the soul-shaking roll and rattle of musketry, and much farther to the right, behind the dragoons, the officer of the suite pointed out to Bagration a column of French that was outflanking us. To the left the horizon was bounded by the adjacent wood. Prince Bagration ordered two battalions from the centre to go to the right to reinforce the flank. The officer of the suite ventured to remark to the prince that if these battalions were withdrawn the artillery would be exposed. Prince Bagration turned to the officer and with his lifeless eyes looked at him in silence. It seemed to Prince Andrei that the officer's observation was a very true one, and was, in fact, irrefutable. But at that moment an adjutant galloped up with a message from the colonel of the regiment in the hollow reporting that enormous masses of the French were marching down upon them, that his regiment was in disorder and was falling back upon the Kiev Grenadiers. Prince Bagration inclined his head in token of assent and approval. He rode off at walking pace to the right and sent an adjutant to the dragoons with orders to attack the French. But the adjutant returned half an hour later to say that the commander of the dragoons had already retired beyond the ravine to escape heavy fire and useless loss of life, and had hurried his sharpshooters into the wood.

'Very good!' said Bagration.

As he was leaving the battery, firing was also heard to the left in the wood. It was too far for him to reach the left flank in time so Prince Bagration despatched Zherkov to tell the senior general (the one who had paraded his regiment before Kutuzov at Braunau) to retreat as quickly as possible beyond the ravine, as the right flank would probably not be able to hold the enemy for long. Tushin and the battalion that had been covering his battery were forgotten. Prince Andrei listened carefully to Bagration's colloquies with the commanding officers and to the orders he gave them and remarked to his astonishment that in reality no orders were given but that Prince Bagration merely tried to make it appear as though everything that was being done of necessity, by accident or at the will of individual commanders, was performed if not exactly by his orders at least in accordance with his design. Prince Andrei noticed, however, that though what happened was due to chance and independent of the general's will, the tact shown by Bagration made his presence extremely valuable. Officers who rode up to him with distracted faces regained their composure; soldiers and officers saluted him gaily, recovered their spirits in his presence, and unmistakably took pride in displaying their courage before him.

18

HAVING ridden up to the highest point of our right flank, Prince Bagration began to make the descent to the spot where there was a continual racket of musketry and nothing could be seen for the smoke. The nearer they got to the hollow the less they could see but the more they felt the proximity of the actual battlefield. They began to meet wounded men. One man with a bleeding head and no cap was being dragged along by two soldiers who supported him under the arms. There was a rattle in his throat and he vomited blood: the bullet must have hit him in the mouth or throat. Another whom they met was walking sturdily along by himself, without his musket, groaning aloud and shaking his arm which had just been injured, while the blood streamed down over his greatcoat as from a bottle. He looked more scared than hurt: he had been wounded only a moment ago. Crossing a road they descended a steep incline and saw a number of men lying on the ground; they also met a crowd of soldiers, some of whom were not wounded. The soldiers were climbing the hill, breathing heavily and, despite the general's presence, talking loudly and gesticulating. Farther forward in the smoke rows of grey cloaks were now visible, and an officer catching sight of Bagration rushed after the retreating throng of men shouting to them to come back.

Bagration rode up to the ranks along which shots crackled out swiftly, now here, now there, drowning the sound of voices and the shouts of command. The whole atmosphere reeked with burnt explosives. The men's excited faces were black with powder. Some were using their ramrods, others putting powder on the touch-pans or taking charges from their pouches, while still others were firing, though what they were firing at could not be seen for the fog which there was no wind to carry away. Quite often there was a pleasant buzz and whistle. 'What is going on here?' wondered Prince Andrei, riding up to the crowd of soldiers. 'It can't be the line, for they are all crowded together. It can't be a charge because they are not moving. It cannot be a square for they are not drawn up for that.'

The commander of the regiment, a rather thin, frail-looking old man with an amiable smile and eyelids that drooped more than half-way over his old eyes, giving him a mild expression, rode up to Bagration and welcomed him as a host welcomes an honoured guest. He explained to Prince Bagration that his regiment had had to face a cavalry attack of the French, that though the attack had been repulsed he had lost more than half his men. The colonel said that the attack had been repulsed, supposing this to be the proper military term for what had happened; though in point of fact he did not know himself what had taken place during that half-hour to the forces entrusted to his command, and was unable to say with certainty whether the attack had been thrown back or whether his regiment had been worsted. All he knew was that at the beginning of the engagement balls and shells began flying all about his regiment and hitting his men, then someone had shouted 'Cavalry!' and our side had started to fire. And they were still firing, not now at the cavalry which had disappeared, but at the French infantry who had shown themselves in the hollow and were shooting at our men. Prince Bagration inclined his head, to signify that this was all he could wish and just what he had foreseen. Turning to his adjutant he ordered him to bring down the two battalions of the 6th Chasseurs whom they had just passed. Prince Andrei was struck at that instant by the change that had come over Bagration's face, which now wore the concentrated, happy look of determination of a man taking a final run before plunging into the water on a hot day. The dull lethargic expression was gone, together with the affectation of profound thought: the round, steady, hawk's eyes looked before him eagerly and somewhat disdainfully, apparently not resting anywhere although his movements were as slow and deliberate as before.

The regimental commander turned to Prince Bagration urging him to go back as it was too dangerous where they were. 'Please, your Excellency, for God's sake!' he kept repeating, glancing for support to the officer of the suite, who looked away from him. 'There, you see!' and he drew attention to the bullets perpetually buzzing, singing, and whistling around them. He spoke in a tone of entreaty and protest such as a joiner might use to a gentleman picking up an axe: 'We're used to it, sir, but you'd blister your fine hands.' He spoke as if those bullets could not kill him, and his half-closed eyes lent still more persuasiveness to his words. The staff-officer joined his entreaties to those of the colonel but Prince Bagration made no reply and merely gave an order to cease firing and re-form, so as to give room for the two battalions approaching to join them. While he was speaking a breeze sprang up and like an invisible hand drew the curtain of smoke hiding the hollow from right to left, and the hill opposite with the French moving about on it opened out before them. All eyes instinctively fastened on this French column advancing against them and winding down over the rough ground. Already the soldiers' shaggy caps could be seen; already the officers could be distinguished from the men, and the standard flapping in folds against the staff.

'They march well,' remarked someone in Bagration's suite.

The head of the column had already descended into the hollow. The clash then would take place on this side of the dip. ...

The remains of our regiment which had already been in action hastily re-formed and moved to the right; from behind it, dispersing the laggards, came the two battalions of the 6th Chasseurs in fine order. They had not yet reached Bagration but the heavy measured tread could be heard of a whole body of men marching in step. On their left flank, nearest to Bagration, marched the captain, a stately figure with a foolish happy expression on his round face – the same man who had followed Tushin when they rushed out of the wattle-hut. It was clear that his one idea at this moment was to march past the commander with a swagger.

With the self-complacency of a man in the front line on parade he stepped springily by on his muscular legs, almost sailing along, stretching himself to his full height without the smallest effort, his ease contrasting with the heavy tread of the soldiers who were keeping step with him. He wore hanging by his leg a slender unsheathed sword (it was small and curved, and not like a real weapon), and looked round now at the superior officers now back at his men, not once losing step, with supple turns of his powerful body. It seemed as though his whole soul was concentrated on marching past the commander in the best possible style, and feeling that he was doing it well he was happy. 'Left ... left ... left ...' he seemed to repeat to himself at each alternate step; and in time with him, every face different but every face grave, the moving wall of soldiers marched by, burdened with knapsacks and muskets, as though each one of these hundreds of soldiers was repeating to himself at every other step: 'Left ... left ... left. ...' A stout major, puffing and falling out of step, skirted a bush in his path; a straggler, out of breath and frightened at his defection, ran at the double to catch up with his company. A cannon-ball cleaving the air flew over the heads of Bagration and his suite and fell into the column to the accompaniment of 'Left ... left!'

'Close the ranks!' rang out the jaunty voice of the captain. The soldiers passed in a semicircle round something on the spot where the ball had fallen, and an old trooper on the flank, a warrant-officer who had lingered behind near the dead regained his line, skipped into step, and looked sternly about him. *Left! left! left!* seemed to resound from the ominous silence and the regular monotonous tramp of feet beating the ground in unison.

'Well done, lads!' said Prince Bagration.

'For your your Ex ... slen ... slen – slency!' came a confused shout from the ranks. A surly-looking soldier marching on the left looked up at Bagration as he shouted, with an expression that seemed to say: 'We know that without telling!' Another, opening his mouth wide, shouted and marched on without looking round, as though fearful of letting his attention stray.

The order was given to halt and down knapsacks.

Bagration rode round the ranks that had just marched past him, and dismounted. He gave the reins to a Cossack, took off and handed over his cloak, stretched his legs and set his cap straight. The head of the French column, with its officers leading, appeared at the foot of the hill.

'Forward, and God with us!' cried Bagration in a firm, ringing voice, turning for a moment to the front line, and swinging his arms a little went forward himself, almost stumbling over the rough field, with the awkward gait of a man always on horseback. Prince Andrei felt that some irresistible power was impelling him on, and he knew a great happiness.*

Already the French were at hand: Prince Andrei, walking beside Bagration, could distinguish without difficulty their bandoliers, the red epaulets, even the faces of the French. (He saw quite clearly one bandy-legged old French officer wearing Hessian boots who was struggling up the hill, catching hold of the bushes.) Prince Bagration gave no further orders, and continued to march in silence at the head of his forces. Suddenly one shot, then another, then a third snapped out from among the French, smoke appeared all along their uneven ranks and there was the rattle of musketry. Several of our men fell, among them the round-faced officer who had marched so gaily and diligently. But at the very instant the first report was heard Bagration turned round and shouted: 'Hurrah!'

'Hurrah-ah-ah!' rang a long-drawn shout from our ranks, and out-stripping Bagration and one another our men dashed down the slope in a broken but joyous eager crowd on to the disordered foe.

19

THE charge of the 6th Chasseurs secured the retreat of our right flank. In the centre Tushin's forgotten battery, which had succeeded in set-ting fire to the village of Schön Graben, held up the French advance. The French stopped to put out the fire, which the wind was spreading, and thus gave us time to retreat. The withdrawal of the centre through the hollow to the other side was effected with much haste and noise, though in good order. But the left flank, which consisted of the Azov and Podolsky infantry and the Pavlograd Hussars, was simultaneously attacked and outflanked by the cream of the French forces under Lannes, and was thrown into confusion. Bagration had sent Zherkov to the general commanding that left flank with orders to retreat immediately.

Zherkov, not removing his hand from his cap, dug his spurs into his horse and dashed off. But no sooner had he left Bagration than his

*This was the attack of which Thiers says : 'The Russians behaved val-iantly and, a rare occurrence in war, two bodies of infantry were seen to march resolutely upon each other, neither giving way until they met in head-on collision.' And Napoleon said at St Helena: 'Some of the Russian battalions showed complete fearlessness.'

courage failed. He was seized with panic and could not persuade himself to go to where there was danger.

Having reached the left flank, instead of continuing to the front where the firing was, he began to look for the general and his staff where they could not possibly be, and so it was he did not deliver the message.

The command of the left wing belonged by right of seniority to the general of the regiment Kutuzov had reviewed at Braunau and in which Dolohov was serving as a private. But the command of the extreme left flank had been assigned to the colonel of the Pavlograd Hussars in which Rostov was serving, and this led to a misunderstanding. The two commanders were exceedingly irritated with one another and, long after the right flank had gone into action and the French were already advancing, the pair were engaged in discussions having the sole object of giving offence to one another. Both regiments, cavalry and infantry alike, were by no means in readiness for the work before them. No one, from private to general, expected a battle and they were all calmly engaged in peaceful pursuits – the cavalry feeding their horses and the infantry collecting fire-wood.

'He higher dan I in rank iss,' said the German colonel of the hussars, flushing and addressing an adjutant who had ridden up, 'so let him do vhat he vill, but I my hussars cannot sacrifice. ... Bugler, sount ze retreat!'

But matters were becoming urgent. Cannon and musketry roared and rattled in unison on the right and in the centre, while the capotes of Lannes' sharpshooters were already seen crossing the mill-dam and forming up on this side hardly out of range. The infantry general walked over to his horse with his jerky step, clambered into the saddle and, drawing himself up very erect and tall, rode to the Pavlograd colonel. The two commanders met with polite bows and secret malevolence in their hearts.

'Once again, colonel,' said the general, 'I cannot leave half my men in the wood. I *beg* of you, I *beg* of you,' he repeated, 'to occupy the *position* and prepare for an attack.'

'And I peg of you not to mix in vot iss not your pusiness!' replied the colonel heatedly. 'If you vere a cavalryman ...'

'I am not a cavalryman, colonel, but I am a Russian general, and if you are unaware of the fact ...'

'I am quite avare, your Excellency,' suddenly shouted the colonel, touching up his horse and turning purple with rage. 'Vill you be so goot to come to ze front and you vill see dat dis position iss no goot. I haf no vish to massacre my men for your gratification.'

'You forget yourself, colonel. I am not considering my own satisfaction and I will not permit such a thing to be said.'

Accepting the colonel's invitation as a challenge to his courage, the general squared his chest and, frowning, rode forward beside him to the front line, as if all their differences were to be settled there among the bullets. They reached the outposts, a few shots flew over them, and they halted in silence. There was nothing fresh to be seen from the line, for the impossibility of cavalry manoeuvring among the bushes and gullies was equally obvious from the spot where they had been standing before, as was the fact that the French were outflanking our left. The general and the colonel glared sternly and significantly at one another like two game-cocks about to fight, each seeking in vain for signs of cowardice in the other. Both stood the test. As there was nothing for them to say, and neither wished to give occasion for it to be alleged that he had been the first to retire from the range of fire, they might have remained there indefinitely, mutually testing each other's courage, if just then they had not heard the snap of musketry and a muffled shout in the wood almost behind them. The French had fallen on the men gathering fire-wood in the copse. It was no longer possible for the hussars to withdraw along with the infantry. They were cut off from the line of retreat on the left by the French. Now, however inconvenient the position, they would have to attack in order to force their way through.

The squadron in which Rostov was serving had scarcely time to mount before they found themselves face to face with the enemy. Again, as on the bridge at Enns, there was no one between the squadron and the enemy, and once more that terrible dividing line of uncertainty and fear – like a line separating the living from the dead – lay between them. All were conscious of this invisible line, and the question whether they would cross it or not, and how they would cross it, filled them with excitement.

The colonel rode up to the front, angrily gave some reply to questions put to him by his officers, and like a man desperately insisting on his own rights thundered out an order. No one said anything definite but the rumour of an attack spread through the squadron. The command to fall in was given, and there was the scrape of sabres being drawn from scabbards. But still no one stirred. The troops of the left flank, infantry and hussars alike, felt that the command itself did not know what to do, and this hesitation communicated itself to the men.

'If only they would be quick,' thought Rostov, feeling that at last the time had come to experience the intoxication of a charge, of which he had heard so much from his fellow hussars.

'Fo'ard, and God be with you, lads!' rang out Denisov's voice. 'At a twot, fo'ward!'

The horses' rumps in the front rank began to sway. Rook pulled at the reins and started of his own accord.

On the right Rostov could see the foremost rows of his own hussars and still farther ahead there was a dark streak which he could not make out distinctly but assumed to be the enemy. Shots were heard, but in the distance.

'Charge!' came the word of command, and Rostov felt the droop of Rook's hindquarters as he broke into a gallop.

Anticipating his horse's movements, Rostov became more and more elated. He had noticed a solitary tree ahead. At first this tree had been in the very centre of the line that had seemed so terrible. But now they had crossed that line and not only had nothing terrible happened but on the contrary it was all jollier and more exciting every moment. 'Oh, won't I slash at them!' thought Rostov, gripping the hilt of his sabre.

'Hurr-a-a-ah!' roared cheering voices.

'Let anyone come my way now,' thought Rostov, driving his spurs into Rook and allowing him to go at full gallop so that they outstripped the others. Ahead the enemy were already visible. Suddenly something like a wide birch-broom seemed to sweep over the squadron. Rostov lifted his sabre ready to strike, but at that instant Nikitenko, the trooper who was riding in front of him, veered aside, and Rostov felt himself as in a dream being carried forward at an unnatural pace yet not moving from the spot. A hussar he knew, Bandarchuk, bumped into him and looked at him angrily. Bandarchuk's horse swerved and dashed past.

'What's the matter? I am not moving? Have I fallen? Am I dead? ...' Rostov asked and answered himself all in one breath. He was alone in the middle of a field. Instead of galloping horses and hussars' backs he saw around him nothing but the still earth and the stubble. There was warm blood under him. 'No, I am wounded and my horse is killed.' Rook tried to rise on his forelegs but fell back, pinning his rider's leg. Blood was flowing from the horse's head. Rook struggled but could not rise. Rostov tried to get to his feet but he too fell back: his sabretache had caught in the saddle. Where our men were, where the French were, he did not know. There was not a soul to be seen.

Having disentangled his leg, he stood up. 'Where, in which direction now was the line that had so sharply divided the two armies?' he asked himself and could not answer. 'Can something have gone wrong with me? Is this the regular way of things, and what do I do?' he wondered as he scrambled to his feet; and at that moment he began to feel as though there were something unusual about his benumbed left arm. The wrist felt as if it did not belong to it. He examined his hand carefully but could find no sign of blood. 'Ah, here's someone coming,' he thought joyfully, seeing men running towards him. 'They will help me!' The foremost was wearing a strange shako and a blue cloak. He was dark and sunburnt, and had a hooked nose. Two others were running at his heels and there were many more behind. One of them said something in a strange language that was not Russian. Surrounded by similar figures in the same sort of shakos, behind the others, stood a lone Russian hussar. They were holding him by the arms, and his horse was being led behind him.

'It must be one of our men, taken prisoner. ... Yes, that's it. Surely they couldn't take me prisoner too. Who are these men?' thought Rostov, unable to believe his own eyes. 'Can they be the French?' He looked at the approaching Frenchmen, and in spite of the fact that only a moment before he had been dashing forward solely for the purpose of getting at these same Frenchmen to hack them to pieces their proximity now seemed so awful that he could not believe his eyes. 'Who are they? Are they coming at me? Can they be running at me? And why? To kill me? Me whom everyone is so fond of?' He thought of his mother's love for him, of his family's and his friends', and the enemy's intention of killing him seemed impossible. 'But perhaps they will!' For over ten seconds he stood rooted to the spot, not realizing the situation. The foremost Frenchman, the one with the hook nose, was already so close that he could see the expression on his face. And the excited, alien features of the man who was bearing so swiftly down on him with fixed bayonet and bated breath terrified Rostov. He snatched up his pistol and instead of firing flung it at the Frenchman and tore with all his might towards the bushes. He did not now run with the feeling of doubt and conflict with which he had trodden the Enns bridge but like a hare fleeing from the hounds. A single unmixed instinct of fear for his young and happy life possessed his whole being. Leaping over the furrows, he fled across the field with the urgency with which he used to run when playing tag in his boyhood, now and then turning his pale, kindly, youthful face to look back, while a chill of horror shivered down his spine. 'No, better not look,' he thought, but as he got near the bushes he glanced round once more. The Frenchmen had slackened their pace and just as he looked round the first man slowed down to a walk and turned to shout something in a loud voice to a comrade farther back. Rostov paused. 'No, there's some mistake,' thought he. 'They can't have meant to kill me.' But meanwhile his left arm felt as heavy as though it weighed an extra half hundredweight. He could not run another step. The Frenchman stopped too and took aim. Rostov shut his eyes and ducked. One bullet, then another whistled past his head. He mustered his last remaining strength, and carrying his left wrist in his right hand he reached the bushes. In the bushes there were Russian sharpshooters.

20

THE infantry regiments that had been caught unawares in the wood rushed out, men from different companies getting mixed up, and retired in a disorderly mob. One soldier in his panic shouted the meaningless words 'Cut off!' that are so terrible to hear in battle, and the cry infected the whole throng.

'Surrounded! Cut off! We're lost!' shouted the fugitives.

The moment he heard the firing and the cry from behind, the general realized that something dreadful was happening to his regiment, and the thought that he, an exemplary officer of many years' service, never guilty of any breach, might now be accused of negligence or inefficiency, so staggered him that, forgetting the recalcitrant cavalry colonel, his own dignity as a general, and, above all, quite forgetting the danger and all regard for self-preservation, he clutched the saddle-bow and spurring his horse galloped to the regiment under a hail of bullets falling all around but fortunately missing him. His one desire was to find out what was wrong and at any cost remedy or correct the blunder, if he had made one, so that he, an exemplary officer with twenty-two years' service who had never incurred a reprimand, should not be held to blame.

Having galloped unharmed between the French, he reached a field behind the wood through which our men were running, deaf to orders, and scattering down the hill. This was the critical moment of moral vacillation which decides the fate of battles: would this disorderly mob of soldiers heed the voice of their commander, or would they merely look at him and continue their flight? Despite his despairing yells – and hitherto their general had always been such a redoubtable figure – despite his infuriated, purple countenance distorted out of all likeness to itself, and despite his brandished sword, the soldiers all continued to run, shouting, shooting into the air and not listening to the word of command. The moral see-saw which decides the fate of battles was evidently coming down on the side of panic.

The general coughed and nearly choked with shouting and powder-smoke, and stood still in despair. All seemed lost. But at that moment the French, who had been attacking, suddenly and for no apparent reason turned and fled, disappearing from the outskirts of the wood, and in the wood, Russian sharpshooters showed themselves. It was Timohin's company, the only one to have maintained its order in the wood, and having lain in ambush in a ditch they now attacked the French unexpectedly. Timohin, armed only with his short sword, had dashed at the enemy with such a frantic cry and such mad drunken determination that the French, unable to collect their wits, had thrown down their muskets and run. Dolohov, running beside Timohin, shot and killed one Frenchman at close quarters, and was the first to seize a surrendering French officer by his collar. Those who were running away returned, battalions re-formed, and the French, who had been on the verge of splitting our left flank in half, were for the moment repulsed. Our reserve units were able to reunite and men stopped deserting. The general was standing at the bridge with Major Ekonomov, letting the retreating companies file past them, when a soldier came up, caught hold of his stirrup and almost leaned against him. The soldier was wearing a bluish coat of broadcloth, he had no knapsack or cap, his head was bandaged, and over his shoulder was slung a French cartridge pouch. In his hand he held an officer's sword. The soldier was pale, his blue eyes looked impudently into the general's face while a smile parted his lips. Although the general was engaged in giving orders to Major Ekonomov, he could not help noticing this soldier.

'Your Excellency, here are two trophies,' said Dolohov, pointing to the French sword and cartridge pouch. 'An officer was taken prisoner by me. I stopped the company.' Dolohov breathed hard from exhaustion and spoke in broken sentences. 'The whole company can bear me witness. I beg you will remember this, your Excellency!'

'Very good, very good,' replied the general, and he turned to Major Ekonomov.

But Dolohov did not go away; he untied the handkerchief round his head, pulled it off and called attention to the blood congealed on his hair.

'A bayonet wound. I kept in the front. Please remember, your Excellency!'

★

Tushin's battery had been forgotten, and it was only at the very end of the action that Prince Bagration, still hearing the cannonade in the centre, sent a staff-officer, and later Prince Andrei, to order the battery to retire as speedily as possible. The supporting columns attached to Tushin's battery had been withdrawn in the middle of the engagement, in obedience to someone's order, but the battery continued to blaze away, and was not taken by the French simply because the enemy could not conceive of the temerity of firing from four quite unprotected guns. On the contrary, the energetic activity of this battery led the French to suppose that the main Russian forces must be concentrated here in the centre. Twice they had attempted to storm this point but on each occasion had been driven back by grape-shot from the four isolated guns on the hillock.

Shortly after Prince Bagration's departure Tushin had succeeded in setting fire to Schön Graben.

'Look at them scattering! It's burning! Just look at the smoke! A fine job! My word! See that smoke – there's smoke for you!' exclaimed the artillerymen, their spirits reviving.

All the cannon, without waiting for orders, were directed on the conflagration. Every shot was hailed with shouts of 'Bravo! That's the way to do it! Look there! Capital!', as if the soldiers were urging each other on. The fire, fanned by the breeze, was spreading rapidly. The French columns that had marched out beyond the village went back, but as though in revenge for this reverse the enemy mounted ten guns to the right of the village to return Tushin's fire.

In their childlike glee at the conflagration of the village and at their success in cannonading the French our gunners did not notice this battery until two balls, followed immediately by four more, fell among our guns, one knocking over two horses and another tearing off the leg of the powder-wagon driver. The men's ardour once roused was not cooled, however, but only changed character. The horses were replaced by others from a reserve gun-carriage, the wounded were carried away, and the four cannon were turned against the ten-gun battery. Tushin's companion officer had been killed at the beginning of the engagement and within an hour seventeen of the forty men making up the crew had been disabled, but the gunners were still as cheerful and as eager as ever. Twice they noticed the French appearing down below, close to them, and they sent volleys of grape-shot at them.

Little Tushin, with his soft, awkward movements, kept calling on his orderly to 'refill my pipe for that one!' and then, scattering sparks from it, sprang forward shading his eyes under his small hand to look at the French.

'Smack at 'em, lads!' he would exclaim, and seizing the cannon by the wheel would work the screws himself.

In the smoke, deafened by the incessant discharges which made him shudder every time, Tushin ran from one gun to another with his pipe between his teeth, adjusting the aim here, counting the charges there, seeing to the replacing of dead or wounded horses, and shouting orders in his shrill, high-pitched, undecided voice. His face grew more and more excited. Only when a man was killed or wounded did he frown and turn away from the sight, calling out angrily to the others who, as is always the case, hesitated about lifting the injured or dead. The soldiers, for the most part handsome fellows (and, as they always are in the artillery, a head and shoulders taller than their officer and twice as broad in the chest), all looked at their commander with the inquiring look of children in trouble, and the expression which happened to be on his face was invariably reflected on theirs.

Owing to the terrible din and uproar, and the necessity for concentration and diligence, Tushin did not experience the slightest qualm of fear, and the idea that he might be killed or badly wounded never entered his head. On the contrary, he grew more and more elated. It seemed to him that it was a very long time ago – almost as far back as the day before – when he had first caught sight of the enemy and fired the first shot, and that the little scrap of field where he stood was well-known, familiar ground. Though he forgot nothing, thought of everything, did everything the best of officers could have done in his position, he was in a state akin to feverish delirium or intoxication.

The deafening roars of his own guns on every side, the whistle and thud of the enemy's cannon-balls, the sight of the flushed, perspiring faces of the crews bustling round the guns, the sight of the blood of men and horses, of the little puffs of smoke on the enemy's side (always followed by a ball flying over to hit the earth, a man, a cannon or a horse) – all these sights and sounds formed into a fantastic world which took possession of his brain and at this moment afforded him sheer delight. The enemy's guns were in his imagination not guns but pipes from which an invisible smoker occasionally puffed out wreaths of smoke.

'There, he's having another puff,' muttered Tushin to himself as a curling cloud of smoke leaped from the hill and was borne off to the left in a ribbon by the wind. 'Now look out for the ball – we'll toss it back!'

'What is it, your Honour?' asked an artilleryman who stood near him and heard him muttering.

'Nothing ... a shell ...' he replied.

'Come along now, our Matvevna,' he said to himself. 'Matvevna' was the name his fancy gave to the large, old-fashioned gun at the far end. The French swarming round their artillery reminded him of ants. In his dream-world the Number One gunner of the second field-piece, a handsome fellow too much given to drink, was 'uncle'; Tushin looked at him oftener than at the others, and delighted in his every movement. The noise of musketry at the foot of the hill, now dying away now quickening again, seemed like someone's breathing. He listened intently to the ebb and flow of these sounds.

'Ah, she's taking another breath again!' he soliloquized.

He imagined himself as a powerful giant of monstrous stature hurling cannon balls at the French with both hands.

'Now then, Matvevna, my little one, don't disappoint me!' he was saying as he moved away from the gun when a strange unfamiliar voice called above his head:

'Captain Tushin! Captain!'

Tushin looked round in alarm. It was the staff-officer who had turned him out of the hut at Grundth. He was shouting and out of breath.

'I say, are you mad? Twice you've been ordered to retreat, and you ...'

'Now what are they pitching into me for?' Tushin wondered, looking with apprehension at his superior.

'I ... I don't ...' he stammered, putting two fingers to the peak of his cap. 'I ...'

But the staff-officer did not finish all he meant to say. A cannon-ball flying close made him duck down over his horse. He paused and just as he was about to continue another ball stopped him. He wheeled the animal round and galloped off.

'Retire! Everyone is to retire!' he shouted back from a distance.

The soldiers laughed. A moment later an adjutant arrived with the same order.

This was Prince Andrei. The first thing he saw as he rode up to the space occupied by Tushin's guns was an unharnessed horse with a broken leg, that lay screaming beside the harnessed horses. Blood was gushing from its leg as from a fountain. Among the limbers a number of the killed were lying. One cannon-ball after another flew over as he approached, and he was conscious of a nervous tremor running down his spine. But the mere thought of being afraid roused his courage again. 'I cannot be afraid,' he said to himself, and dismounted slowly among the guns. He delivered his message but did not leave the battery. He decided to have the guns removed from their positions and withdrawn in his presence. Together with Tushin, stepping over dead bodies, and under terrible fire from the French, he attended to the limbering of the guns.

'A staff-officer was here a minute ago, but he soon made himself scarce,' remarked an artilleryman to Prince Andrei. 'Not like your Honour.'

Prince Andrei said nothing to Tushin. They were both so busy that they hardly seemed to see each other. When they had limbered up two of the four field-pieces and were moving downhill (one gun that had been smashed and a howitzer were left behind) Prince Andrei went up to Tushin.

'Well, good-bye till we meet again ...' he said, holding out his hand.

'Good-bye, my dear fellow,' said Tushin. 'Dear, good soul! Fare-well, my dear fellow,' said Tushin, and for some unknown reason tears suddenly filled his eyes.

21

THE wind had dropped and black clouds hung low over the field of battle, mingling on the horizon with the smoke of gunpowder. It was growing dark and the glow of conflagrations showed all the more distinctly in two places. The cannonade was dying down but the rattle of musketry in the rear and on the right sounded oftener and nearer. As soon as Tushin with his field-pieces, continually driving round or coming upon wounded men, was out of range of fire, and had descended into the ravine, he was met by some of the staff, among them the officer and Zherkov, who had twice been sent to Tushin's battery but had never reached it. Interrupting one another they all gave orders and counter-orders as to how and where to proceed, loading him with blame and criticism. In silence Tushin rode behind on his artillery nag, fearing to open his mouth because at every word he felt, he could not have said why, ready to burst into tears. Though the orders were to abandon the wounded, many of them dragged themselves after the troops and begged for a seat on the gun-carriages. The jaunty infantry officer – the one who had darted out from Tushin's hut just before the battle – lay stretched on 'Matvevna's' carriage with a bullet in his stomach. At the foot of the hill a pale hussar cadet supporting one hand with the other came up to Tushin and pleaded for a place.

'Captain, for God's sake, I've hurt my arm,' he said timidly. 'For God's sake ... I can't walk. For God's sake!'

It was plain that this cadet had more than once repeated the request for a lift and been refused. He asked in a hesitating, piteous voice.

'Tell them to let me get on, for God's sake.'

'Give him a place,' said Tushin. 'Put a coat under him, you, uncle,' he said, addressing his favourite soldier. 'But where is the wounded officer?'

'We set him down. He was dead,' replied someone.

'Help him up. Sit there, sit there, my dear fellow. Spread out the cloak, Antonov.'

The cadet was Rostov. With one hand he supported the other; he was pale and his lower jaw trembled and his teeth chattered with fever. He was helped on to 'Matvevna', the gun from which they had removed the dead officer. There was blood on the cloak they spread out which stained his breeches and hands.

'What, you wounded, lad?' said Tushin, going up to the gun on which Rostov sat.

'No, only a sprain.'

'But this blood on the gun-carriage?' asked Tushin.

'That was the officer, your Honour, stained it,' replied a gunner, wiping away the blood with his coat-sleeve as if apologizing for the state of his cannon.

By main force and with the help of the infantry the guns were dragged up the rise, and having reached the village of Guntersdorf they halted. By this time it was so dark that it was impossible to distinguish the soldiers' uniforms ten paces away, and the firing had begun to subside. Suddenly shouts and the rattle of shots were heard again near by on the right. The darkness was lit by flashes. This was the last attack on the part of the French, and the soldiers were replying to it as they entrenched themselves in the houses of the village. Once more they all rushed out but Tushin's guns were stuck, and the artillerymen, Tushin and the cadet exchanged silent glances, awaiting their fate. The firing began to die down, and soldiers talking eagerly streamed out of a side street.

'Safe and sound, Petrov?' asked one.

'We gave it 'em hot, mate! They won't stick their noses out again now,' said another.

'It's too dark to see a thing. How they shot up their own fellows! It's as dark as pitch, mate! I say, isn't there something to drink?'

The French had been driven back for the last time. And once more through the impenetrable darkness Tushin's field-pieces moved forward, surrounded by the rumbling infantry as by a frame.

In the dark it seemed as though a sombre invisible river flowed on and on in one direction, murmuring with whispers and the droning of voices, the sound of hooves and wheels. Amid the general hum, clearer than all the other noises in the blackness of the night, rose the groans of the wounded. The gloom that enveloped the army was filled with their cries. Their groaning was one with the blackness of the night. A little later a wave of excitement ran through the moving

224

mass. Someone followed by a suite had ridden by on a white horse, and had said something in passing.

'What did he say? Where do we go now? Is it a halt? Thanked us, what?' were the eager questions heard on all sides, and the whole moving mass compressed into itself (evidently those in front had stopped) and a report spread that there were orders to halt. All stood still where they were, in the middle of the muddy road.

Fires were lighted, and voices were heard more audibly. Captain Tushin, after giving orders to his battery, sent one of his men to look for a dressing-station or a surgeon for the cadet, and sat down by the bonfire his soldiers had kindled by the roadside. Rostov too dragged himself to the fire. Feverish shivering caused by pain, cold and damp shook his whole body. Sleep almost overpowered him but he was kept awake by the agony of his arm for which he could find no satisfactory position. Sometimes he closed his eyes for a moment or two, then he would gaze at the fire which seemed to him a burning glare, or turn and look at the slender round-shouldered figure of Tushin sitting cross-legged like a Turk beside him. Tushin's large, kindly, intelligent eyes were fastened upon him with sympathy and commiseration. Rostov saw that Tushin wished with all his soul to help him but could not.

On all sides they could hear the footsteps and chatter of the infantry moving about, driving by and settling down around them. The sounds of voices, of tramping feet, of horses' hooves stamping in the mud, the crackling of wood fires far and near – all merged into one pulsating uproar.

Now it was no longer an invisible river rolling on in the darkness but the swell of a glowering sea, subsiding and still agitated after a storm. Rostov in a dazed fashion saw and heard what was going on around him. A foot-soldier came up to the fire, squatted on his heels, held his hands to the blaze and turned his face.

'No objection, your Honour?' he asked Tushin. 'I've got lost from my company, your Honour. I don't know where I am. It's the devil!'

At the same time as the soldier an infantry officer with a bandaged cheek came up to the fire, and addressing Tushin requested to have the guns moved a trifle to let a baggage-wagon go past. The company commander was followed by a couple of soldiers, quarrelling and fighting desperately over a boot each was trying to snatch from the other.

'What, you picked it up? I should say so! A smart one, you are!' one of them was shouting hoarsely.

Then a thin, pale soldier, his neck bandaged with a bloodstained leg-band, came up and angrily asked the artillerymen for water.

'Must one be left to die like a dog?' said he.

Tushin told them to give the man some water. Then a cheery soldier ran up to beg for some red-hot embers for the infantry.

'Fire, fire all hot for the infantry! Good luck to you, lads, and thanks for the fire. We'll pay it back with interest,' said he, bearing the flaming brand away into the darkness.

Next came four soldiers carrying something heavy on a cloak, and passed by the blaze. One of them stumbled.

'Oh the devils, they've spilled logs on the road,' snarled he.

'He's dead, what's the use of dragging him along?' said another of the four.

'Shut up!'

And they disappeared into the darkness with their burden.

'I say, does it hurt?' Tushin asked Rostov in a whisper.

'Yes, it does ache.'

'Your Honour, the general wants you. He's in the hut here,' said a gunner, coming up to Tushin.

'Right, my boy.'

Tushin rose and walked away from the fire, buttoning his great-coat and setting himself straight.

Not far from the artillery camp-fire, in a hut that had been made ready for him, Prince Bagration sat at dinner, talking with a number of high officers who had gathered at his quarters. The little old colonel with the half-closed eyes was there, greedily gnawing at a mutton-bone, and the general of twenty-two years' irreproachable service, his face flushed with a glass of vodka and dinner, and the staff-officer with the signet-ring, and Zherkov stealing uneasy glances at them all, and Prince Andrei, pale, with compressed lips and feverishly glittering eyes.

In a corner of the hut stood a standard captured from the French, and the auditor with the naïve face was fingering the stuff it was made of and shaking his head doubtfully, possibly because the banner really interested him, possibly because it was hard to look on at a dinner where no place had been laid for him when he was so hungry. In the next hut there was the French colonel who had been taken prisoner by the dragoons. Our officers were flocking round to have a look at him. Prince Bagration was thanking the commanders of the various divisions and inquiring into details of the engagements and our losses. The general whose regiment had been inspected at Braunau was telling the prince that as soon as the action began he had withdrawn from the woods, mustered the men engaged in felling trees and, allowing the French to go by, had then made a bayonet charge with two battalions and routed them.

'As soon as I saw that their first battalion was disorganized, your Excellency, I stood in the road and said to myself: "I'll let them get through and then open fire on them"; and that's what I did.'

The general had so longed to do this, and was so regretful that he had not succeeded in doing it, that it seemed to him now that this was what had happened. Indeed, might it not actually have been so? How could anyone tell in all that confusion what did or did not happen?

'By the way, your Excellency, I ought to inform you,' he continued, remembering Dolohov's conversation with Kutuzov, and his own late interview with the gentleman-ranker, 'that Private Dolohov, who was reduced to the ranks, took a French officer prisoner before my eyes and notably distinguished himself.'

'It was there I saw the charge of the Pavlograd Hussars, your Excellency,' chimed in Zherkov, looking around uneasily. He had not seen a single hussar the whole day, and had only heard about them from an infantry officer. 'They broke up two squares, your Excellency.'

Hearing Zherkov, several of those present smiled, expecting one of his usual sallies, but perceiving that what he was saying also redounded to the glory of our arms and of the day's work they looked grave again, though many of them were very well aware that what Zherkov was saying had no foundation in fact. Prince Bagration turned to the elderly colonel.

'I thank you all, gentlemen. All branches of the service behaved heroically: infantry, cavalry, and artillery. How was it two field-pieces were abandoned in the centre?' he inquired, searching with his eyes for someone. (Prince Bagration did not ask about the cannon on the left flank: he knew that all the cannon there had been abandoned at the very beginning of the action.) 'I believe I sent you, didn't I?' he said, turning to the staff-officer on duty.

'One was damaged,' answered the staff-officer, 'but the other I can't explain. I was there all the time myself, giving orders, and had only just left.... It was pretty hot, it's true,' he added modestly.

Someone remarked that Captain Tushin was bivouacking close by in the village and had already been sent for.

'Ah, but you were there, were you not?' said Prince Bagration, addressing Prince Andrei.

'Yes, indeed, we just missed each other,' said the staff-officer, giving Bolkonsky an affable smile.

'I had not the pleasure of seeing you,' declared Prince Andrei, coolly and abruptly. Everyone was silent.

Tushin appeared in the doorway, timidly edging in behind the backs of the generals. Making his way past the high-ranking officers in the crowded hut, abashed as he always was before his superiors, he did not notice the staff of the banner and stumbled over it. Several of those present laughed.

'How is it that a gun was abandoned?' asked Bagration, frowning not so much at the captain as at those who were laughing, among whom Zherkov's voice was distinguished above the rest.

Only now, when confronted by stern authority, did Tushin realize the full horror of his crime and the disgrace of still being alive after having lost two guns. He had been so wrought up that until that moment he had not thought about it. The officers' laughter confused him still more. He stood before Bagration, his lower jaw trembling, and was hardly able to stammer out:

'I ... I don't know ... your Excellency ... I hadn't the men ... your Excellency.'

'You could have got them from the covering troops.'

Tushin did not say that there had been no covering troops, although actually this was the truth. He was afraid of getting some other officer into trouble, so he stood in silence with his eyes fixed on Bagration in the way a bewildered schoolboy stares at the face of an examiner.

The silence lasted some time. Prince Bagration, evidently not wishing to be severe, found nothing to say, and the others did not venture to intervene. Prince Andrei looked at Tushin from under his brows and his fingers twitched nervously.

'Your Excellency!' Prince Andrei broke the silence in his curt voice. 'You were pleased to send me to Captain Tushin's battery. I went there and found two-thirds of his men and horses knocked out, two guns disabled, and no covering forces whatever.'

Prince Bagration and Tushin now looked with equal intensity at Bolkonsky who spoke with suppressed emotion.

'And if your Excellency will permit me to express my opinion,' he went on, 'we owe today's success mainly to the action of this battery and the heroic endurance of Captain Tushin and his company.' And without waiting for a reply Prince Andrei rose and walked away from the table.

Prince Bagration looked at Tushin and, apparently reluctant to evince any mistrust of Bolkonsky's outspoken judgement yet unable to put complete faith in it, inclined his head and told Tushin that he could go. Prince Andrei followed him out.

'Thanks, my dear fellow, you got me out of a scrape,' said Tushin.

Prince Andrei gave him a look but said nothing, and went away. His heart was heavy and full of melancholy. It was all so strange, so unlike what he had hoped.

★

'Who are they? Why are they here? What do they want? And when will all this end?' Rostov asked himself, as he watched the changing shadows. The pain in his arm grew steadily worse. He ached with sleep, crimson circles danced before his eyes, and the impression of those voices and faces and a sense of loneliness merged with the physical pain. It was they, those soldiers, wounded, not wounded – it was they who were pressing upon him, crushing him, twisting the sinews and scorching the flesh of his shattered arm and shoulder. To get rid of them he closed his eyes.

For a moment he dozed off but in that brief interval of oblivion he dreamed of innumerable things: he saw his mother and her large white hand, Sonya's thin shoulders, Natasha's eyes and her laugh, Denisov with his voice and his whiskers, and Telyanin, and all the affair with Telyanin and Bogdanich. All that affair was inextricably mixed up with this soldier with the harsh voice, and it was that affair and this soldier that were so agonizingly, so ruthlessly pulling and squeezing his arm and dragging it always in the same direction. He was trying to free himself but they would not let go of his shoulder for a single second, or relax their hold a hair's breadth. It would not have hurt, it would have been all right, if only they would stop pulling at it; but there was no escape from them.

He opened his eyes and looked up. The black canopy of night hung less than a yard above the glow of the charcoal fire. Powdery snow fluttered down through the glow. Tushin had not returned, the surgeon did not come. He was alone except for some poor soldier sitting naked at the other side of the fire, warming his thin, sallow body.

'Nobody cares about me!' thought Rostov. 'There is no one to help me or take pity on me. Yet once I was at home, strong, happy and loved.' He sighed, and the sigh unconsciously became a groan.

'In pain, eh?' asked the little soldier, shaking his shirt out over the fire, and not waiting for an answer he gave a grunt and added: 'Shocking number of fellows done for today!'

Rostov did not heed the soldier. He gazed at the snowflakes fluttering above the fire and thought of winter at home in Russia, the warm, bright house, his soft fur coat, the swiftly-gliding sledge, his healthy body, and all the love and affection of his family. 'And what did I come here for?' he wondered.

Next day the French did not renew their attack and the remnant of Bagration's division was reunited with Kutuzov's army.

PART THREE

I

PRINCE VASILI was not a man to plan and look ahead. Still less did he ever plot evil with a view to his own advantage. He was merely a man of the world who had got on and to whom success had become a matter of habit. Circumstances and the people he encountered were allowed to shape his various schemes and devices, which he never examined very closely though they constituted his whole interest in life. Of such plans he had not just one or two but dozens in train at once, some at their initial stage, others nearing achievement, still others in course of disintegration. He never said to himself, for instance: 'So-and-so now has influence, I must gain his confidence and friendship and through him secure a special grant'; or 'There's Pierre, a rich fellow: I must entice him to marry my daughter and lend me the forty thousand I need.' But when he came across a man of position instinct immediately whispered to him that this person might be useful, and Prince Vasili would strike up an acquaintance and at the first opportunity, without any premeditation, led by instinct, would flatter him, treat him with easy familiarity, and finally make his request.

He had Pierre ready at hand in Moscow and procured for him an appointment as gentleman of the bedchamber, which at that time conferred the same status as the rank of privy councillor, and insisted on the young man's travelling with him to Petersburg and staying at his house. With an absent-minded air, yet at the same time taking it absolutely for granted that it was the right thing, Prince Vasili was doing everything to get Pierre to marry his daughter. Had he thought out his ideas beforehand he could not have been so natural in his behaviour, and so simple and unaffected in his relations with everybody, both above and below him in social standing. Something always drew him to men richer or more powerful than himself, and he was endowed with the rare art of being able to hit on exactly the right moment for making use of people.

Pierre, on unexpectedly becoming Count Bezuhov and a wealthy man, after his recent life of loneliness and inaction found himself so busy and beset that only when he was in bed could he have a moment to himself. He had to sign papers, to appear at Government offices for reasons which were not clear to him, to catechize his chief steward, to visit his estate near Moscow and to receive a great number of persons who had hitherto not cared even to be aware of his existence but now would be offended and hurt if he refused to see them. All these various individuals – business men, relations and acquaintances alike – were with one accord disposed to treat the young heir in the most kindly, friendly manner: they were all evidently firmly persuaded of Pierre's noble qualities. He was continually hearing such phrases as: 'With your extraordinary kindness,' or 'Thanks to your generous heart,' or 'You who are so upright, count …' or 'If he were as clever as you are,' and so on, until he actually began to believe in his exceptional kindness and remarkable intelligence, the more so as at the bottom of his heart it had always seemed to him that he really was very good-natured and very intelligent. Even people who before had been spiteful and openly hostile now became gentle and affectionate. The cross-grained eldest princess with the long waist and the hair plastered down like a doll's had come into Pierre's room after the funeral. With lowered eyes and crimson cheeks she told him how sincerely she regretted the misunderstandings that had arisen between them in the past, and asked him – she felt that that was all she had the right to ask – to be allowed, after the blow that had befallen her, to remain for a few weeks longer in the house she was so fond of and where she had made such sacrifices. She could not restrain her tears and wept freely at these words. Touched by such a change in this statue-like princess, Pierre took her hand and begged forgiveness, though he did not know for what. Later that day the princess began to knit Pierre a striped comforter, and from that time was quite different to him.

'Do this for her, *mon cher*. After all, she had to put up with a great deal from the deceased,' said Prince Vasili, handing him some deed to sign for the princess's benefit.

Prince Vasili had decided that this bone – a note of hand for thirty thousand – had better be thrown to the poor princess lest it enter her head to gossip about the part he had played in the matter of the inlaid portfolio.

Pierre signed the deed, and after that the princess became even more amiable. The other sisters became equally affectionate, especially the youngest, the pretty one with the mole, who often embarrassed him with her smiles and her confusion at the sight of him.

It seemed so natural to Pierre that everyone should like him, it would have seemed so unnatural had anybody disliked him, that he could not help believing in the sincerity of those around him. Besides, he had no time to ask himself whether these people were sincere or not. He never had a moment of leisure: he felt as if he were living in a constant state of mild and agreeable intoxication. He was the centre of some important social mechanism and something was for ever expected of him, which he must perform or people would be grieved and disappointed; but if he did this and that all would be well; and he did whatever was required of him, but still the happy result remained in the future.

More than anyone else in these early days Prince Vasili took control of Pierre's affairs and of Pierre himself. On the death of Count Bezuhov he did not let Pierre slip out of his hands. He went about with the air of a man weighed down by affairs, weary, worn out, but too tender-hearted to abandon this helpless youth, who after all was the son of his old friend, and the possessor of such an enormous fortune, to the vagaries of fate and the designs of scoundrels. During the few days he stayed on in Moscow after Count Bezuhov's death he would invite Pierre, or go to him himself, and advise him on what ought to be done in a tone of such weariness and assurance as to imply each time: 'You know that I am overwhelmed with business and that it is out of pure charity that I concern myself with you; and of course you realize too that the suggestions I make are the only possible ones.'

'Well, my dear fellow, tomorrow we are off at last,' said Prince Vasili one day, closing his eyes and drumming his fingers on Pierre's elbow, speaking as if he were saying something that had long since been decided and could not now be altered. 'We start tomorrow and I'm giving you a place in my carriage. I am very glad. We have got through everything that was pressing here, and I ought to have been back long ago. Here, I received this from the chancellor. I put in an application for you, and you have been entered in the diplomatic corps and made a gentleman of the bedchamber. Now a diplomatic career lies open to you.'

Notwithstanding the effect produced on him by the tired, confident tone with which these words were pronounced, Pierre, who had thought long about his career, tried to protest. But Prince Vasili broke in on his protest in a cooing bass which precluded all possibility of interrupting the flow of his words and which he employed in cases where extreme measures of persuasion were needed.

'*Mais, mon cher*, I did it for my own sake, to satisfy my conscience, and there is no need to thank me. No one ever yet complained of being too well loved; and besides, you are not tied down, you could throw it up tomorrow. You'll see for yourself in Petersburg. And it is high time you got away from these painful associations.' Prince Vasili sighed. 'So that's all arranged, my dear boy. And my valet can go in your carriage. Ah, yes, I was almost forgetting,' he added. 'You know, *mon cher*, your father had a little account to settle with me, so as I have received some monies from the Ryazan estate I'll keep them; you don't want them. We'll make it all square by and by.'

What Prince Vasili called 'some monies from the Ryazan estate' meant several thousand roubles quit-rent from Pierre's peasants, which sum he retained for himself.

In Petersburg Pierre found himself surrounded by the same atmosphere of tenderness and affection as in Moscow. He could not decline the post, or rather the dignity (for he did nothing), that Prince Vasili had procured for him, and acquaintances, invitations and social obligations were so numerous that he felt even more conscious than he had in Moscow of a sense of bewilderment, bustle and continual expectation of some future good which was always near but never attained.

Of his old circle of bachelor friends many were no longer in Petersburg. The guards had gone on active service. Dolohov had been reduced to the ranks, Anatole was in the army somewhere in the provinces, Prince Andrei was abroad, and so Pierre had no opportunity of spending his nights in the way he used to enjoy them, or of opening his mind in intimate talks with some friend older than himself and whose opinions he respected. His whole time went in dinners and balls, or, more often than all, at Prince Vasili's in the company of the portly princess, his wife and his beautiful daughter Hélène.

Like everyone else, Anna Pavlovna Scherer made Pierre aware of the change that had taken place in society's attitude towards him.

In Anna Pavlovna's presence of old, Pierre had always felt that what he was saying was unseemly, tactless and not the right thing, that remarks which were sensible while they were forming in his mind became idiotic as soon as he spoke them aloud, whereas Hippolyte's feeblest utterances had the effect of being clever and endearing. Now everything that Pierre said was *charmant*. Even if Anna Pavlovna did not say so he could see that she was longing to and only refrained out of regard for his modesty.

At the beginning of the winter in this year 1805 Pierre received one of Anna Pavlovna's customary pink notes of invitation to which was added the postscript: '*La belle Hélène* will be here, whom one is never tired of feasting one's eyes on.'

As he read this it struck Pierre for the first time that a certain link which other people recognized had been formed between himself and Hélène, and the thought both alarmed him as though an obligation were being laid on him which he could not fulfil, and at the same time pleased him as an entertaining idea.

Anna Pavlovna's party was exactly like the former one, except that the novelty she offered her guests on this occasion was not Mortemart but a diplomat newly arrived from Berlin and bringing the very latest details of the Emperor Alexander's visit to Potsdam, and of how the two august friends had there pledged themselves in an indissoluble alliance to uphold the cause of justice against the enemy of the human race. Pierre was welcomed by Anna Pavlovna with a shade of melancholy, evidently relating to the recent loss which the young man had sustained in the death of Count Bezuhov. (Everyone constantly felt it their duty to assure Pierre that he was greatly afflicted by the passing away of the father he had hardly known.) Her melancholy was of precisely the same kind as the exalted melancholy she always manifested at any allusion to Her Most August Majesty the Empress Maria Fiodorovna. Pierre was flattered. Anna Pavlovna had arranged the groups in her drawing-room with her habitual skill. The large circle, in which Prince Vasili and some generals were conspicuous, were enjoying the benefit of the diplomat. Another group was gathered about the tea-table. Pierre would have liked to join the former but Anna Pavlovna – who was in the state of nervous excitement of a commander on the battlefield whose head is full of a thousand new and brilliant ideas which he has hardly time to put into execution – on seeing Pierre laid a finger on his coat-sleeve and said:

'Wait, I have designs on you for this evening.' She glanced at Hélène and smiled at her. 'My dear Hélène, be charitable to *ma pauvre tante* who adores you. Go and keep her company for ten minutes. And that you may not find it too tiresome, here is our dear count who certainly won't refuse to escort you.'

The beauty moved away towards *ma tante*, but Anna Pavlovna detained Pierre, with the air of still having some last and indispensable arrangement to complete with him.

'Isn't she exquisite?' she said to Pierre, indicating the stately beauty as she glided away. 'And how she carries herself! For such a young girl what tact, what finished perfection of manner! It comes from the heart. Happy the man who wins her! With her the most unworldly of men could not fail to occupy the most brilliant position in society. Don't you think so? I only wanted to know your opinion,' said Anna Pavlovna, and released Pierre.

Pierre was perfectly sincere when he agreed with Anna Pavlovna as to Hélène's perfection of manner. If he ever thought of Hélène it was of her loveliness and of this extraordinary ability of hers to appear silently serene and dignified in society.

The old aunt received the two young people in her corner but seemed desirous of hiding her adoration for Hélène and more inclined to show her fear of Anna Pavlovna. She looked at her niece as though to inquire what she was to do with the pair. As Anna Pavlovna turned away, she again laid a finger on Pierre's sleeve, remarking:

'I hope you will never say in future that people find it dull in my house,' and she glanced at Hélène.

Hélène smiled in a way which implied that she could not admit the possibility of anyone seeing her and not feeling enchanted. The aunt coughed, swallowed the phlegm, and said in French that she was very glad to see Hélène; then she addressed Pierre with the same greeting and the same grimace. In the middle of a halting and tedious conversation Hélène looked at Pierre and smiled with the beautiful radiant smile she gave to everyone. Pierre was so used to this smile, and it had so little meaning for him, that he paid no attention to it. The aunt was just speaking of a collection of snuff-boxes that had belonged to Pierre's father, Count Bezuhov, and she showed them her own box. Princess Hélène asked to see the portrait of the aunt's husband on the lid.

'The work of Vines, probably,' said Pierre, alluding to a celebrated miniature-painter, and he leant over the table to take the snuff-box, all the time trying to hear what was being said at the other table.

He half rose, meaning to go round, but the aunt handed him the snuff-box, passing it across Hélène's back. Hélène bent forward to make room, and looked round with a smile. She was, as she always did for evening parties, wearing a gown cut in the fashion of the day, very low back and front. Her bosom, which always reminded Pierre of marble, was so close to him that his short-sighted eyes could not but perceive the living charm of her neck and shoulders, so near to his lips that he need only stoop a little to have touched them. He was conscious of the warmth of her body, the faint breath of perfume and the slight creak of her corset as she moved. He saw not her marble beauty forming a single whole with her gown, but all the fascination of her body, which was only veiled by her clothes. And once having seen this, his eyes refused to see her in any other way, just as we cannot reinstate an illusion that has been explained.

'So you have never noticed before how beautiful I am?' Hélène seemed to say. 'You had not noticed that I am a woman? Yes, I am a woman, who might belong to anyone – might belong to you,' said her eyes. And at that moment Pierre was conscious that Hélène not only could but must become his wife, and that it must be so.

He was aware of this at that moment as surely as if he were standing at the altar with her. How and when it would be, he could not tell. He did not even know if it would be a good thing (indeed, he had a feeling that for some reason it would not), but he knew that it was to be.

Pierre dropped his eyes, then lifted them and tried to see her again as a distant beauty removed from him, the way he had seen her every day until then, but found it no longer possible. He could not do it any more than a man who has been staring through the mist at a tuft of steppe grass and taking it for a tree can see it as a tree once he has recognized it for a tuft of grass. She was terribly close to him. Already she had power over him. And between him and her there existed no barrier now save the barrier of his own will.

'Well, I will leave you in your little corner,' came Anna Pavlovna's voice. 'I can see you are very comfortable here.'

And Pierre, frantically trying to think whether he had been guilty of anything reprehensible, crimsoned and looked about him. it seemed to him that everyone knew as well as he did what had happened to him.

After a little while, when he had joined the large circle, Anna Pavlovna said to him: 'I hear you are having your Petersburg house redecorated.'

This was true. The architect had told him it was necessary, and Pierre, without knowing why, was having the huge Petersburg mansion done up.

'That is an excellent idea, but don't give up your quarters at Prince Vasili's. It is good to have a friend like the prince,' said she, smiling at Prince Vasili. 'I know something about that, do I not? And you are still so young. You need someone to advise you. You mustn't be angry with me for exercising an old woman's privilege.'

She paused, as women always do after talking about their age, expecting some comment. 'If you marry, it's a different matter,' she continued, uniting the pair in one glance. Pierre did not look at Hélène, nor she at him. But she was still as terribly close to him. He stammered something and coloured.

Back at home Pierre could not get to sleep for a long while for thinking of what had happened. What had happened? Nothing. He had merely discovered that a woman he had known as a child, a woman of whom he had been able to say indifferently, 'Yes, she's nice-looking' when anyone told him that Hélène was a beauty, might be his.

'But she's brainless, I have always said so,' he thought. 'There is something nasty, something not right in the feeling she excites in me. Didn't I hear that her own brother Anatole was in love with her and she with him, that there was a regular scandal and that was the reason he was sent away? Her brother is – Hippolyte. Her father – Prince Vasili. That's not good,' he reflected, but while he was thus musing (the reflections were not followed to their conclusion) he caught himself smiling and was conscious that another line of thought had sprung up and while meditating on her worthlessness he was also dreaming of how she would be his wife, how she would love him, how she might become quite different, and how all he had heard and thought about her might be untrue. And he again saw her not as Prince Vasili's daughter but visualized her whole body only veiled by her grey gown. 'But no, why did this idea never enter my mind before?' and again he told himself that it was impossible, that there would be something nasty and unnatural in this marriage, something which seemed dishonourable. He recalled past words and glances of hers, and the words and looks of people who had seen them together. He remembered Anna Pavlovna's words and looks when she had spoken about his house, recalled a thousand similar hints on the part of Prince Vasili and others, and was seized with terror lest he had already in some way bound himself to do a thing which was obviously wrong and not what he ought to do. But at the very time he was expressing this conviction to himself, in another part of his mind her image rose in all its womanly beauty.

2

In November 1805 Prince Vasili was obliged to go on a tour of inspection through four provinces. He had secured this commission for himself so as to call in on his neglected estates at the same time. He intended to pick up his son Anatole on the way (where his regiment was stationed) and take him to visit Prince Nikolai Andreyevich Bolkonsky, in the hope of marrying him to the rich old man's daughter. But before setting out on these new ventures Prince Vasili wanted to settle matters with Pierre, who had, it was true, of late spent whole days at home, that is in Prince Vasili's house where he was staying, and was absurd, agitated and foolish in Hélène's presence (the proper condition of a man in love), but still had not made his declaration.

'This is all very fine, but matters must come to a head,' said Prince Vasili to himself with a melancholy sigh one morning, feeling that Pierre, who was under such obligations to him ('but never mind that'), was not behaving very well in the circumstances. 'Youth ... frivolity ... well, God bless him,' thought he, relishing his own goodness of heart. '*Mais il faut que ça finisse.* The day after tomorrow is my little Hélène's name-day. I will invite a few friends in and then, if he does not see what he ought to do, it will be my affair. Yes, my affair. I'm her father.'

Six weeks after Anna Pavlovna's 'At Home' and the sleepless agitated night when he had decided that to marry Hélène would be a calamity and that he must escape her and go away, Pierre, in spite of this decision, had not moved from Prince Vasili's and felt with horror that in people's eyes he was committing himself more every day, that he could not go back to his former ideas of her, that he could not

239

break away from her even, and though it would be an awful thing he would have to unite his life to hers. Perhaps he might have been able to hold back, but not a day passed without a party at Prince Vasili's (where parties had hitherto been the exception), and Pierre had to be present unless he wished to spoil the general pleasure and disappoint everyone. Prince Vasili in the rare moments when he was at home would take Pierre's hand in passing and, drawing him down absent-mindedly, present his wrinkled, clean-shaven cheek for a kiss, saying: 'Till tomorrow,' or 'Be in to dinner or I shan't see you,' or 'I am staying in on your account,' and the like. But though when Prince Vasili did stay at home for Pierre (as he said) he barely exchanged a couple of words with him, Pierre did not feel equal to disappointing him. Every day he repeated one and the same thing to himself: 'It is time I understood her and made up my mind what she really is. Was I mistaken before, or am I mistaken now? No, she is not stupid. No, she's a fine girl!' he would say to himself sometimes. 'She never does the wrong thing, never makes silly remarks. She does not talk much but what she does say is always clear and simple, so she cannot be stupid. She has never been disconcerted and is never out of countenance, so she cannot be a bad woman!' It often happened that he began to argue or think aloud in her company and every time she had replied either by some brief but appropriate remark that showed she was not interested, or by a mute smile and glance which to Pierre proved her superiority more palpably than anything else. She was right in regarding all reflections as nonsense in comparison with that smile.

She always turned to him now with a radiantly confiding smile meant for him alone, in which there was something more significant than in the smile which she wore for the world in general. Pierre knew that everyone was waiting for him to speak the one word needful, to cross a certain boundary, and he knew that sooner or later he would cross it; but an unaccountable horror seized him at the mere thought of this fearful step. A thousand times in the course of those six weeks, during which he felt himself being drawn nearer and nearer to that dreadful abyss, Pierre said to himself: 'What am I doing? I must act with determination. Can it be that I haven't any?'

He was anxious to come to a decision but felt with dismay that in this matter he lacked the strength of will which he had known in himself and really did possess. Pierre belonged to the category of people who are strong only when their consciences are absolutely clean. But since that day when he had been overpowered by a feeling of desire while stooping over the snuff-box at Anna Pavlovna's an unacknowledged sense of the sinfulness of that impulse paralysed his will.

On Hélène's name-day a small party of friends and relatives – 'Our nearest and dearest,' as his wife called them – met for supper at Prince Vasili's. All these friends and relatives had been given to understand that the evening was to be a momentous one for the young girl's future. The guests were seated at supper. Princess Kuragin, a portly, imposing woman who had once been handsome, was sitting at the head of the table. On either side of her were the most honoured guests – an old general and his wife, and Anna Pavlovna Scherer. At the other end of the table sat the younger and less important guests, and there too were placed as members of the family Pierre and Hélène, side by side. Prince Vasili was not having supper: he walked round in high good humour, sitting down beside one friend after another. He had a light-hearted pleasant word for everybody, except Pierre and Hélène, whose presence he seemed to ignore. He was the life of the whole party. The wax candles burned brightly, the silver and crystal gleamed, as did the ladies' finery and the gold and silver of the men's epaulets; footmen in scarlet livery moved round the table; and the clatter of plates mingled with the clink of knives and glasses and the hum of various animated conversations. At one end of the assembly an old chamberlain was heard assuring an aged baroness of his ardent love for her, while she laughed; at the other someone was relating the misfortunes of a certain Maria Viktorovna. In the centre Prince Vasili focused attention on himself. With a playful smile on his lips he was telling the ladies about the previous Wednesday's session of the privy council at which Sergei Kuzmich Vyazmitinov, the new military governor-general of Petersburg, had received and read a rescript – much talked of at the time – from the Emperor Alexander Pavlovich. The Emperor, writing from the army to Sergei Kuzmich, had said that he was the recipient of declarations of loyalty from all sides, that the testimony from Petersburg afforded him particular pleasure, that he was proud to be at the head of such a nation and would endeavour to prove himself worthy. This rescript began with the words: 'Sergei Kuzmich, From all sides reports reach me,' etc.

'So he never got further with it than "Sergei Kuzmich"?' asked one of the ladies.

'No, no, not a syllable,' answered Prince Vasili, laughing. '"Sergei Kuzmich ... From all sides." "From all sides ... Sergei Kuzmich ..." Poor Vyazmitinov could not get any further. He started again and again but no sooner did he utter "*Sergei*" – than a sniff ... "*Kuz-mi-ch*" – tears ... and "*From all sides*" is smothered in sobs, and he could not go on. And out came the handkerchief again, and again we heard "Sergei Kuzmich, From all sides," ... and more tears, until at last somebody else was asked to read it for him.'

'"Kuzmich ... From all sides" ... and tears,' someone repeated, laughing.

'Don't be unkind,' cried Anna Pavlovna from her end of the table, holding up a threatening finger. 'He is such a worthy, excellent man, our good Vyazmitinov....'

All the company laughed heartily. At the head of the table, in the places of honour, everyone seemed to be in high spirits and under the influence of various enlivening tendencies. Only Pierre and Hélène sat mutely side by side almost at the bottom of the table, a radiant smile hovering on both their faces, a smile which had nothing to do with Sergei Kuzmich – a smile of bashfulness at their own feelings. But gaily as the others all talked, laughed and joked, much as they enjoyed their Rhine wine, the *sauté* and the ice cream, carefully as they avoided glancing at the young couple, and heedless and un-observant as they seemed of them, yet it was somehow perceptible from the occasional glances they gave that the anecdote about Sergei Kuzmich, the laughter and the food were all affectation, and that the whole attention of all the party was in reality concentrated on the two young people, Pierre and Hélène. Prince Vasili mimicked the sniffs of Sergei Kuzmich and at the same time ran a searching eye over his daughter, and while he laughed the expression on his face said: 'Yes, yes, it's going on all right, it will be settled this evening.' Anna Pavlovna shook her finger at him for laughing at 'our good Vyaz-mitinov' and in her eyes which flashed for a moment in Pierre's direction Prince Vasili read congratulation on his future son-in-law and his daughter's felicity. Old Princess Kuragin, offering her neigh-bour some wine with a melancholy sigh, looked resentfully at her daughter, her sigh seeming to say: 'Yes, there is nothing left for you and me but to sip sweet wine, my dear, now that it is the turn of the young ones to be so flauntingly, clamorously happy.' 'And what stupid stuff it all is that I am saying, as though it interests me,' thought a diplomat, glimpsing the glad faces of the lovers. 'That's happiness!'

Into the petty trivialities, the conventional interests that united the company, there had entered the simple feeling of attraction felt by handsome and healthy young creatures for each other. And this human emotion dominated everything else and triumphed over all their artificial chatter. Jests fell flat, news was not interesting, the animation was unmistakably forced. Not only the guests but the very footmen waiting at table appeared to feel the same and they forgot their duties as they looked at the beautiful Hélène with her radiant face and at Pierre's broad, red, happy and uneasy countenance. Even the light from the candles seemed to focus on those two happy faces.

Pierre was conscious that he was the centre of all this, and his position both pleased and embarrassed him. He was like a man absorbed in some occupation. He had no clear sight nor hearing; no understanding of anything. Only now and then disconnected ideas and impressions from the world of reality flashed through his mind.

'So it is all over,' he thought. 'How on earth did it all happen? And so quickly! Now I know that not for her sake alone, nor for my own sake, but for everyone *it* must inevitably come to pass. They are all expecting *it*, they are so sure that it will happen that I cannot, I cannot, disappoint them. But how will it be? I do not know; but it certainly will happen!' thought Pierre, glancing at those dazzling shoulders so close to his eyes.

Or he would suddenly feel a vague shame. It made him uncomfortable to be the object of general attention and considered a lucky man and with his homely face to be looked on as a sort of Paris in possession of his Helen of Troy 'But no doubt it's always like this, and must be so,' he tried to console himself. 'And yet what have I done to bring it about? When did it begin? I travelled from Moscow with Prince Vasili. That was nothing. Next, I stayed in his house, and why not? Then I played cards with her and picked up her reticule and drove out with her. When did it begin, how had it all come about?' And here he was sitting by her side as her betrothed, hearing, seeing, feeling her nearness, her breathing, her movements, her beauty. Then all at once it would seem to him that it was not she but he who was so extraordinarily beautiful that they all had to look at him; and made happy by this universal admiration he would expand his chest, raise his head high and rejoice at his good fortune. Suddenly he heard a familiar voice addressing him for the second time. But

Pierre was so absorbed that he did not take in what was said to him.

'I'm asking you when you last heard from Bolkonsky,' repeated Prince Vasili a third time. 'How absent-minded you are, my dear boy.'

Prince Vasili smiled, and Pierre noticed that everyone in the room was smiling at him and Hélène. 'Well, what of it, since you all know?' said Pierre to himself. 'What of it? It's the truth,' and he himself smiled his gentle, childlike smile, and Hélène smiled too.

'When did you get the letter? Was it from Olmütz?' repeated Prince Vasili, who pretended that he wanted to know in order to settle some argument.

'How can people consider or talk of such trifles?' thought Pierre. 'Yes, from Olmütz,' he answered with a sigh.

After supper Pierre led his partner into the drawing-room in the wake of the others. The guests began to disperse, some without taking leave of Hélène. Others as if unwilling to distract her from serious concerns came up for a minute and then hurried away, refusing to let her see them off. The diplomat preserved a mournful silence as he left the drawing-room. What was his futile career compared with Pierre's happiness? The old general snapped at his wife when she asked him how his leg was. 'Oh, the old fool,' he thought. 'That Hélène now will be just as much of a beauty when she's fifty.'

'I believe I may congratulate you,' whispered Anna Pavlovna to Hélène's mother and kissed her warmly. 'But for this sick headache I would stay longer.'

The princess made no reply: she was tormented by jealousy of her daughter's happiness.

While the guests were taking their leave Pierre was left for a long while alone with Hélène in the little drawing-room where they were sitting. Often before during the past six weeks he had been alone with her, but he had never spoken to her of love. Now he felt that it was inevitable but he could not make up his mind to the final step. He felt ashamed: it seemed to him that he was occupying some other man's place at Hélène's side. 'This happiness is not for you,' whispered a voice within him. 'This happiness is for those who have not in them what you have within you.'

But he had to say something and so he began by asking whether she had enjoyed the evening. She replied with customary directness that this name-day had been one of the pleasantest she had ever had.

One or two of the nearest relatives were still lingering on. They were sitting in the big drawing-room. Prince Vasili walked up to Pierre with languid steps. Pierre rose and observed that it was getting late. Prince Vasili levelled upon him a look of stern inquiry, implying that Pierre's remark was so strange that he could not believe his ears. But the expression of severity was immediately replaced by another, and taking Pierre's hand Prince Vasili drew him down into a seat and smiled affectionately.

'Well, my little girl?' he said at once, addressing his daughter in the careless tone of consistent tenderness which comes natural to parents who have petted their children from babyhood, but which Prince Vasili had only acquired through imitating other parents.

And he turned to Pierre again.

'"*Sergei Kuzmich, From all sides –*"' he began, unbuttoning the top button of his waistcoat.

Pierre smiled, but his smile showed that he knew it was not the anecdote about Sergei Kuzmich that interested Prince Vasili at that moment, and Prince Vasili knew that Pierre knew it. He suddenly muttered something and went away. It seemed to Pierre that even Prince Vasili was embarrassed, and this elderly man of the world's discomfiture touched Pierre: he glanced at Hélène and fancied that she too was disconcerted, and her look seemed to say: 'Well, it's your own fault.'

'It is inevitable – the step must be taken – but I can't, I can't!' thought Pierre, and once more he began to talk about irrelevant matters, of Sergei Kuzmich, inquiring what was the point of the story, as he had not heard it properly. Hélène with a smile answered that she did not know either.

When Prince Vasili returned to the drawing-room his wife was talking in low tones to an elderly lady about Pierre.

'Of course it is a very brilliant match, but happiness, my dear ...'

'Marriages are made in heaven,' responded the elderly lady.

Prince Vasili walked over and sat down on a sofa in the far corner of the room, pretending not to have heard the ladies. He closed his eyes and appeared to be dozing. His head began to droop and he roused himself.

'Aline,' he said to his wife, 'go and see what they are doing.'

The princess went up to the door, walked past it with a dignified, nonchalant air and glanced into the little drawing-room. Pierre and Hélène still sat talking as before.

'Just the same,' she said in reply to her husband.

Prince Vasili frowned, twisting his mouth to one side, and his cheeks began to twitch with the disagreeable, brutal expression characteristic of him. He shook himself, got up, threw back his head and with resolute steps walked past the ladies into the little drawing-room. Swiftly and with an assumption of delight he went up to Pierre. His face was so extraordinarily solemn that Pierre rose in alarm.

'Thank God!' said Prince Vasili. 'My wife has told me!' He put one arm round Pierre, the other round his daughter. 'My dear boy. ... My little girl.... I am very, very pleased.' His voice trembled. 'I loved your father ... and she will make you a good wife.... God bless you both!'

He embraced his daughter, then Pierre again, and kissed him with his malodorous mouth. Real tears moistened his cheeks.

'Princess, come here!' he called.

The princess came in, and she too wept. The elderly lady also put her handkerchief to her eye. Pierre was kissed, and several times he kissed the hand of the lovely Hélène. After a while they were left alone again.

'All this had to be and could not have been otherwise,' thought Pierre, 'so it's no use wondering whether it is a good thing or not. It is good at least in that it's definite and I am no longer tortured by doubts.' Pierre held his betrothed's hand in silence, watching her beautiful bosom as it rose and fell.

'Hélène!' he said aloud, and stopped.

'Something special is said on these occasions,' he thought, but could not for the life of him remember what it was. He glanced into her face. She bent forward closer to him. Her face flushed rosy-red.

'Oh, take off those ... those ...' she said, pointing to his spectacles.

Pierre took them off, and his eyes, besides the strange look people's eyes have when they remove their spectacles, held a look of dismay and inquiry. He was about to bend over her hand and kiss it, but with a quick, rough movement of her head she intercepted his lips and pressed them with her own. Pierre was struck by the transformed, unpleasantly distorted expression of her face.

'Now it's too late, it's all over; and besides I love her,' thought Pierre.

'*Je vous aime!*' he said, remembering what had to be said on these

246

occasions; but the words sounded so thin that he felt ashamed for himself.

Six weeks later he was married and settled in the enormous newly-decorated Petersburg mansion of the Counts Bezuhov, the fortunate possessor, as people said, of a beautiful wife and millions of money.

3

In the December of 1805 old Prince Nikolai Bolkonsky received a letter from Prince Vasili, announcing that he intended to visit him with his son. ('I am setting out on a journey of inspection and of course seventy miles is only a step out of the way for me to come and see you, my honoured benefactor,' wrote Prince Vasili. 'My son Anatole is accompanying me, *en route* for the army, and I hope you will allow him the opportunity of expressing in person the deep respect that, following his father's example, he entertains for you.')

'Well, there's no need to bring Marie out, it seems, if suitors come to us of their own accord,' incautiously remarked the little princess when she heard about this.

Prince Nikolai frowned and said nothing.

A fortnight after the letter Prince Vasili's servants arrived in advance of him one evening, and on the next day he and his son appeared.

Old Bolkonsky had never had much of an opinion of Prince Vasili's character, and the high position and honours to which Kuragin had risen of late, in the new reigns of Paul and Alexander, had increased his distrust. And now from the letter and the little princess's hints he saw what was in the wind, and his poor opinion altered into a feeling of contemptuous ill-will. He snorted whenever he mentioned him, and on the day that Prince Vasili was expected was particularly testy and bad-tempered. Whether he was out of humour because Prince Vasili was coming or particularly annoyed at Prince Vasili's visit because he was out of humour did not alter the fact that he was in a bad temper, and early in the morning Tikhon was already advising the architect not to go to the prince with his report.

'Listen to him tramping up and down,' said he, drawing the architect's attention to the sound of the prince's footsteps. 'Stepping flat on his heels, and we all know what that means. ...'

However, at nine o'clock the prince went out for his usual walk, wearing his velvet fur-lined coat with the sable collar and a sable cap.

There had been a fall of snow on the previous evening. The path to the orangery which the prince was in the habit of taking had been swept clear: the marks of a broom were still visible in the snow and a spade had been left sticking in one of the banks of loose snow that bordered the path on both sides. The prince continued on through the conservatories, the serfs' quarters and the out-buildings, frowning and silent.

'Could one get through in a sleigh?' he asked his overseer, a venerable man resembling his master in looks and manner, who was escorting him back to the house.

'The snow is deep, your Excellency. I am having the avenue swept.'

The prince nodded and went up to the porch. 'God be praised,' thought the overseer, 'the cloud has blown over!'

'It would have been difficult to drive up, your Honour,' he added. 'So I hear, your Honour, there's a minister coming to visit your Honour?'

The prince turned round to the overseer and fixed him with scowling eyes.

'What's that? A minister? What minister? Who gave you orders?' he began in his shrill, harsh voice. 'For the princess, for my daughter, you don't sweep the road, but for a minister –! I don't recognize ministers!'

'Your Honour, I thought ...'

'You thought!' shouted the prince, his words tumbling out with more and more haste and incoherence. 'You thought! ... Brigands! Blackguards! ... I'll teach you to think!' and raising his stick he swung it and would have hit the overseer had not Alpatych instinctively avoided the blow. 'You thought! ... Blackguards! ...' shouted the prince rapidly. But although Alpatych, shocked at his own temerity in dodging the blow, moved closer to the prince and bowed his bald head submissively, or perhaps for that very reason, the prince, while he continued to shout: 'Blackguards! ... Shovel the snow back again!' did not lift his stick a second time but hurried into the house.

Princess Maria and Mademoiselle Bourienne stood waiting for the old prince before dinner, well aware that he was in a bad temper – Mademoiselle Bourienne with a radiant face that said: 'I am aware of nothing, I am just the same as usual,' Princess Maria, pale and terrified, with downcast eyes. What made it harder for Princess Maria was that she knew she ought to act like Mademoiselle Bourienne at such times,

248

but she could not manage it. 'If I pretend not to notice his ill-humour he will think I have no sympathy with him,' she would think to herself. 'If I appear depressed and out of spirits myself, he will accuse me (as he has done before) of being sulky,' and so on.

The prince glanced at his daughter's scared face and snorted.

'Little idiot!' he muttered under his breath. 'And the other one not here! So they've been tittle-tattling to her already,' he thought, when he saw that the little princess was not in the dining-room.

'And where is the princess?' he asked. 'In hiding?'

'She is not very well,' answered Mademoiselle Bourienne with a bright smile. 'She won't come down. It is natural in her condition.'

'H'm! H'm! Kh! Kh!' grunted the prince, and sat down to table.

His plate seemed to him not quite clean; he pointed to a spot and flung it away. Tikhon caught it and handed it to the butler. The little princess was not ill but she went in such overwhelming terror of the prince that on hearing he was in a bad temper she decided not to appear.

'I am afraid for the baby,' she said to Mademoiselle Bourienne. 'Heaven knows what a fright might do.'

The little princess, in fact, lived at Bald Hills in a continual state of fear of her father-in-law, for whom she also felt an antipathy, though she did not realize it because the fear was so much the stronger feeling. The prince reciprocated this antipathy but in his case it was swallowed up in contempt. As she settled down at Bald Hills the little princess took a special fancy to Mademoiselle Bourienne, spent her days with her, sometimes begged her to sleep in her room, and often talked about the old prince with her and criticized him.

'So we are to have company, *mon prince*?' remarked Mademoiselle Bourienne, as she unfolded her white napkin with her rosy fingers. '*Son excellence* Prince Kuragin and his son, I hear?' she said in a tone of inquiry.

'H'm! His *excellence* is a young puppy. ... I got him his appointment in the service,' said the prince disdainfully. 'And why the son should come is more than I can make out. Perhaps Princess Lisa and Princess Maria can tell us. I don't know what he's bringing his son here for. I don't want him.' And he looked at his daughter who had blushed crimson. 'Aren't you well? Eh? In awe of the "minister", I suppose, as that blockhead Alpatych called him this morning?'

'No, *mon père*.'

Unsuccessful as Mademoiselle Bourienne had been in her choice of a topic she did not desist but prattled on about the conservatories and the beauty of some flower that had just opened, and after the soup the prince became more genial.

Dinner over, he went to see his daughter-in-law. The little princess was sitting at a small table gossiping with Masha, her maid. She turned pale on seeing her father-in-law.

The little princess had altered very much. She was now more plain than pretty. Her cheeks were sunken, her lip was drawn up and there were sagging folds of skin under her eyes.

'Yes, I feel a sort of heaviness,' she replied to the prince's inquiry as to how she was.

'Is there anything you want?'

'No, *merci, mon père*.'

'Very well then, very well.'

He went out and into the butler's pantry, where Alpatych stood with downcast head.

'Filled up the road again?'

'Yes, your Honour. Forgive me for heaven's sake. ... It was only my stupidity.'

'All right, all right,' the prince interrupted him, and laughing in his unnatural way he stretched out his hand for Alpatych to kiss, and then proceeded to the study.

In the evening Prince Vasili arrived. He was met in the avenue by coachmen and footmen, who with much shouting dragged his carriages and sledges up to one wing of the house, over snow which had purposely been shovelled back on the driveway.

Prince Vasili and Anatole were conducted to separate apartments.

Taking off his tunic, Anatole sat with his arms akimbo before a table on a corner of which he fixed his large, handsome eyes, smiling absent-mindedly. His whole life he regarded as one unbroken round of gaiety which someone or other was for some reason bound to provide for him. So now he looked on this visit to a churlish old man and a rich and ugly heiress in just the same way. It might all, he thought, turn out very jolly and amusing. 'And why not marry her if she really has such a lot of money? Money never comes amiss,' reflected Anatole.

He shaved and scented himself with the care and elegance which had become habitual to him, and with his characteristic air of all-conquering good humour walked into his father's room, holding his head high. Two valets were busily engaged in dressing Prince Vasili, who was looking about him with lively interest. He gave his son a cheerful nod as the latter entered, as much as to say: 'Good, that's how I want to see you looking.'

'I say, father, joking apart, is she very hideous? Eh?' he asked in French, as though reverting to a subject more than once discussed in the course of their journey.

'That'll do. What nonsense! The great thing is for you to try and be respectful and cautious with the old prince.'

'If he gets nasty, I'm off,' said Anatole. 'I can't stand these old gentlemen. What?'

'Remember that for you everything depends on this.'

Meanwhile, in the feminine part of the household not only was it known that the minister and his son had arrived but every detail of their personal appearance had been inventoried. Princess Maria was sitting alone in her room vainly trying to master her agitation.

'Why did they write? Why did Lise tell me about it? Of course it can never be!' she said aloud, looking at herself in the glass. 'How am I to go into the drawing-room? Even if I like him I could never be natural with him now.' The mere thought of her father's look filled her with terror.

The little princess and Mademoiselle Bourienne had by this time received all the intelligence they needed from Masha, the lady's maid, who told them what a handsome young man the minister's son was, with his rosy cheeks and black eyebrows; how his papa had dragged his legs upstairs with difficulty while the son had flown up like an eagle, three steps at a time. With these items of information the little princess and Mademoiselle Bourienne hastened to Princess Maria's room, the lively sound of their chatter preceding them along the corridor.

'You know they've come, Marie?' said the little princess, waddling in and sinking heavily into an arm-chair.

She was no longer in the loose gown she generally wore in the mornings but had put on one of her best dresses. Her hair had been carefully arranged and her face was full of animation, which did not, however, conceal its flabby, pasty contours. In the finery in which she was accustomed to appear in Petersburg society it was still more noticeable how much plainer she had become. Mademoiselle Bourienne, too, had taken pains to add some subtle finishing touches which rendered her fresh, pretty face still more attractive.

'What! Aren't you going to change, *chère princesse*?' she exclaimed. 'They'll be coming in a minute to tell us the gentlemen are in the drawing-room and we shall have to go down, and you aren't doing a thing to smarten yourself up!'

The little princess got up from the arm-chair, rang for the maid, and hastily and merrily began to think out what her sister-in-law should wear and to put her ideas into effect. Princess Maria's self-respect was wounded by the fact that the arrival of a suitor could perturb her, and it was still more mortifying that both her friends took her agitation as a matter of course. To tell them that she felt ashamed for herself and for them would be to betray her agitation, while to decline to dress up as they suggested would prolong their banter and insistence. She flushed, her lovely eyes lost their brilliance, red blotches appeared on her face, which took on the unbeautiful victimized expression it so often wore, as she surrendered herself to Mademoiselle Bourienne and Lisa. Both women laboured with *perfect sincerity* to make her look pretty. She was so homely that it could never have entered the head of either of them to think of her as a rival. Consequently it was with perfect sincerity, in the naïve, unhesitating conviction women have that dress can make a face pretty, that they set to work to attire her.

'No, really, *ma bonne amie*, that dress is not becoming,' said Lisa, looking sideways at Princess Maria from a distance. 'Tell her to bring out your maroon velvet. Yes, really! Why, you know, this may be the turning-point of your life. That one's too light, it doesn't suit you. No, it's all wrong!'

It was not the dress that was wrong, but the face and whole figure of the Princess Maria, but neither Mademoiselle Bourienne nor the little princess realized this: they still fancied that if they put a blue ribbon in her hair and combed it up high, and arranged the blue sash lower on the maroon velvet, and so on, all would be well. They forgot that the frightened face and the figure could not be altered, and therefore, however much they might vary the setting and adornment, the face itself would remain pitiful and plain. After two or three changes to which Princess Maria submitted meekly, when her hair had been arranged on the top of her head (a style which quite altered and spoilt her looks) and she had put on the maroon velvet with the blue sash, the little princess walked round her twice, with her small hand smoothing out a fold here and pulling down the sash there, and then gazed at her with head first on one side and then on the other.

'No, it won't do,' she said decidedly, clasping her hands. 'No, Marie, this dress really does not suit you at all. I like you better in your little grey everyday frock. Please, for my sake. Katya,' she said to the maid, 'bring the princess her grey dress, and you'll see, Mademoiselle Bourienne, how I'll arrange it,' she added, smiling in anticipation of artistic enjoyment.

But when Katya brought the required garment Princess Maria still sat motionless before the glass looking at her face, and in the mirror she saw that there were tears in her eyes and her mouth was quivering and she was on the point of breaking into sobs.

'Come, *chère princesse*,' said Mademoiselle Bourienne, 'just one more little effort.'

The little princess, taking the dress from the maid, went up to Princess Maria.

'Now, we'll try something simple and nice,' she said.

The three voices – hers, Mademoiselle Bourienne's and Katya's, who was laughing at something – blended into a sort of gay twitter like the chirping of birds.

'No, leave me alone,' said Princess Maria.

And there was such seriousness and such suffering in her tone that the twitter of the birds was silenced at once. They looked at the great beautiful eyes, full of tears and brooding, turned on them imploringly, and realized that it would be useless and even cruel to insist.

'At least alter your coiffure,' said the little princess. 'Didn't I tell you,' she added reproachfully to Mademoiselle Bourienne, 'Marie has one of those faces which that style never suits. Never. Do please re-arrange it.'

'Leave me alone, leave me alone. I don't care in the least,' answered a voice scarcely able to keep back the tears.

Mademoiselle Bourienne and the little princess were obliged to acknowledge to themselves that Princess Maria in this guise looked very plain, far more so than usual, but it was too late. She was staring at them with an expression they both knew, thoughtful and sad. It did not frighten them (Princess Maria never inspired fear in anyone). But they knew that when this expression appeared on her face she became mute and inflexible.

'You will alter it, won't you?' said Lisa, and when Princess Maria made no answer Lisa went out of the room.

Princess Maria was left alone. She did not comply with Lisa's request, and not only did not rearrange her hair but did not even look at herself in the glass. Letting her arms drop helplessly, she sat with downcast eyes, and day-dreamed. She imagined a husband, a man, a strong, commanding and mysteriously attractive being, suddenly carrying her off into a totally different happy world that was his. She pictured a child, *her own* – like the baby she had seen the day before in the arms of her old nurse's daughter – at her own breast, with her husband standing by and gazing fondly at her and the child. 'But no, it can never be, I am too ugly,' she thought.

'Tea is served. The prince will be out in a moment,' said the maid's voice at the door.

She started up and was horrified at what she had been thinking. And before going downstairs she went into the little prayer-room hung with icons, and fixing her eyes on the blackened countenance of a large icon of the Saviour, in front of which burned a lamp, stood before it for several moments with folded hands. Princess Maria's soul was full of an agonizing doubt. Could the joy of love, of earthly love for a man, be for her? In her reveries of marriage Princess Maria dreamed of happiness with a home and children of her own, but her strongest and most secret craving was for earthly love. The more she tried to conceal this feeling from others and even from herself, the stronger it grew. 'O God,' she cried, 'how am I to stifle in my heart these temptings of the devil? How am I to renounce for ever these vile fancies, so as to fulfil Thy will in peace?' And scarcely had she put this question than God's answer came to her, in her own heart: 'Desire nothing for thyself, seek nothing, be not anxious or envious. Man's future and thy destiny too must remain hidden from thee, but live to be ready for whatever may come. If it be God's will to prove thee in the duties of marriage, be ready to obey His will.' With this consoling thought (though still she hoped for the fulfilment of that forbidden earthly longing) Princess Maria sighed, crossed herself and went downstairs, without thinking of her gown or her hair, or of how she would make her entrance or of what she would say. What could all that signify in comparison with God's ordering for her, without Whose will not one hair falls from the head of man?

4

WHEN Princess Maria came down, Prince Vasili and his son were already in the drawing-room talking to the little princess and Mademoiselle Bourienne. When she walked in with her heavy step, treading on her heels, the gentlemen and Mademoiselle Bourienne stood up and the little princess, with a gesture indicating her to the gentlemen, said: *'Voilà, Marie!'* Princess Maria saw them all and saw them in detail. She saw Prince Vasili's face look grave for a second at the sight of her but instantly smile again, and the little princess watching with curiosity to see the impression 'Marie' produced on the visitors. She saw Mademoiselle Bourienne too, with her ribbon and pretty face more eager than she had ever noticed it turned towards *him*. But *him* she could not see, she only saw something large, brilliant and handsome moving towards her as she entered the room. Prince Vasili was the first to greet her, and she kissed the bald forehead bent over her hand and in reply to his words said that, on the contrary, she remembered him very well. Then Anatole came up to her. She still could not see him. She was only conscious of a soft hand taking hers firmly, while she lightly brushed with her lips a white forehead beneath beautiful fair hair smelling of pomade. When she looked at him she was dazzled by his beauty. Anatole stood with the thumb of his right hand hooked round a button of his uniform, chest thrust out and spine drawn in, slightly swinging one foot which rested on his heel, as with head a little on one side he looked blithely at the princess without speaking and obviously not thinking at all about her. Anatole was not quick-witted, nor ready or eloquent in conversation, but he had the faculty, so invaluable for social purposes, of composure and imperturbable assurance. If a man lacking in self-confidence remains dumb on being introduced, and betrays a consciousness of the impropriety of such dumbness and an anxiety to find something to say, the effect will be bad. But Anatole was dumb and swung his foot as he cheerfully observed the princess's coiffure. It was clear that he could be silent in this way for any length of time. 'If anyone finds this silence awkward, let him talk, but I have no desire to,' his demeanour suggested. Moreover, in Anatole's manner with women there was that air of supercilious consciousness of his own superiority which does more than anything else to excite curiosity, awe and even love. His manner made it seem as if he were saying to them: 'I know you, yes; but why should I let you bother me? You'd be only too pleased, of course.' Perhaps he did not really think this when he met women (it is probable, indeed, that he did not, for he thought very little at any time), but that was the effect conveyed by his look and manner. The princess felt it and as though to show him that she did not venture to expect to interest him she turned to his father. The conversation was general and animated, thanks to Lisa's voice and the little downy lip that flew up and down over her white teeth. She met Prince Vasili with that playful tone so often adopted by voluble lively people, which consists in the assumption that between the person so addressed and oneself there are some semi-private long-established jokes and amusing reminiscences, even where no such reminiscences really exist – just as none existed in the present case. Prince Vasili readily fell in with this tone and the little princess drew Anatole too, whom she hardly knew, into these recollections of ridiculous incidents that had never happened. Mademoiselle Bourienne also joined in, and Princess Maria was pleased to find that even she was being made to share in their gaiety.

'Well, anyway, here we shall have your company all to ourselves, dear prince,' said the little princess (in French, of course) to Prince Vasili. 'Not like at Anna Pavlovna's receptions, where you always escape. Do you remember, *cette chère Annette*?'

'Ah, but you don't talk politics to me like Annette!'

'And our little tea-table?'

'Oh yes!'

'Why were you never at Annette's?' the little princess asked Anatole. 'Ah, I know, I know,' she said with a sly glance. 'Your brother Hippolyte has told me fine tales of your doings. Oh!' and she shook her finger at him. 'I know about your pranks in Paris too.'

'But Hippolyte didn't tell you, did he –' said Prince Vasili, addressing his son and seizing the little princess's arm as though she would have run away and he were just in time to catch her, '– he didn't tell you how he himself was breaking his heart over our sweet princess and how she showed him the door? Oh, she is a pearl among women,' he added, turning to Princess Maria.

For her part, Mademoiselle Bourienne, at the mention of Paris, did not let the chance slip to join in the general stream of recollections. She ventured to inquire if it were long since Anatole had left Paris and how he had liked that city. Anatole answered the Frenchwoman very readily, and smiling and staring at her he talked to her about her native land. When he saw the pretty little Bourienne Anatole decided that it would not be so very dull at Bald Hills after all. 'Not half bad-looking!' he thought, watching her. 'Not half bad-looking, this *demoiselle de compagnie*. I hope she'll bring her along when we're married,' he mused. '*La petite est gentille.*'

The old prince in his room was taking his time about dressing, frowning and ruminating on what course to adopt. The visit annoyed him. 'What are Prince Vasili and that son of his to me ? The father is an empty-headed braggart and the son must be a fine specimen,' he growled to himself. What angered him was that the visit revived in his mind an unresolved and constantly avoided question, concerning which the old prince was never honest with himself. The problem was whether he could ever decide to part with his daughter and let her marry. The prince could never make up his mind to put this squarely to himself, knowing beforehand that if he did he would have to answer it truthfully, and truth conflicted not only with his feelings but with the whole possibility of existence for him. Life without Princess Maria, little as he appeared to care for her, was unthinkable. 'And why should she get married ?' he thought. 'No doubt to be un-happy. Look at Lisa with Andrei – a better husband one would fancy could hardly be found nowadays – but is she contented with her lot ? And who would marry Maria for love ? She's plain, ungraceful. They'd take her for her connexions, her money. And don't old maids get on well enough ? They are happier really.' So mused Prince Bol-konsky while he dressed, yet the question he was always putting off demanded immediate attention. Prince Vasili had brought his son obviously with the intention of making an offer and probably that day or the next would ask for a definite reply. His name and position in society were quite all right. 'Well, I've no objection,' the prince kept saying to himself. 'Only he must be worthy of her. And that is what we shall see. Yes, that is what we shall see, that is what we shall see,' he repeated aloud, and with his habitual alert step he walked into the drawing-room, taking in the whole company at a rapid glance. He noticed that the little princess had changed her dress, noticed Mademoiselle Bourienne's ribbon and the hideous way in which Princess Maria's hair was done, noticed the smiles that Mademoiselle Bourienne and Anatole were exchanging and his daughter's isolation amid the general conversation. 'She's decked herself out like a fool!' he thought, looking vindictively at Princess Maria. 'No shame in her; and he ignores her!'

He went up to Prince Vasili.

'Well, how d'ye do, how d'ye do, glad to see you.'

'Friendship laughs at distance,' began Prince Vasili rapidly, speaking in his accustomed self-confident, familiar tone. 'This is my younger son. I beg you to favour him with your friendship.'

Prince Bolkonsky surveyed Anatole.

'A fine young fellow, a fine young fellow!' he said. 'Well, come and give me a kiss,' and he offered his cheek.

Anatole kissed the old man and looked at him curiously and with perfect composure, waiting for some instance of the eccentricity his father had told him to expect.

Prince Bolkonsky sat down in his usual place in the corner of the sofa, drew up an arm-chair for Prince Vasili, pointed to it and began inquiring about political affairs and news. He listened with apparent attention to what Prince Vasili had to say but he glanced continually at Princess Maria.

'So they are writing from Potsdam already, are they?' he said, repeating Prince Vasili's last words. Then he suddenly got up and went over to his daughter.

'Was it for our guests that you got yourself up like that, eh?' he said. 'Nice of you, very nice! You have done your hair in some new fashion for visitors, and before visitors I tell you, never dare in future to change your style of dressing without my consent.'

'It was my fault, *mon père*,' interceded the little princess, flushing.

'*You* may do as you please,' said Prince Bolkonsky, with an exaggerated bow to his daughter-in-law, 'but she need not make a guy of herself, she's plain enough without that.'

And he sat down on the sofa again, paying no further attention to his daughter, whom he had reduced to tears.

'On the contrary, that coiffure suits the princess very well,' said Prince Vasili.

'Well, my young prince, and what's your name?' said Prince Bolkonsky, turning to Anatole. 'Come here and talk to me, let us get acquainted.'

'Now the fun begins,' thought Anatole, and with a smile he took a seat by the old prince.

'Well, my dear boy, I hear you've been educated abroad, not taught to read and write by the parish clerk like your father and myself. Tell me, my dear boy, you are serving in the Horse Guards now, are you not?' asked the old man, scrutinizing Anatole intently.

'No, I have transferred into the line,' replied Anatole, scarcely able to keep from laughing.

'Ah, excellent! So you want to serve your Tsar and country, do you? These are times of war. A fine young fellow like you ought to see service. Ordered to the front, eh?'

'No, prince, our regiment has gone to the front but I am attached ... what is it I am attached to, papa?' asked Anatole, turning to his father with a laugh.

'A credit to the service, I must say. "What is it I am attached to!" Ha-ha-ha!' laughed the old prince, and Anatole laughed still louder. Suddenly the old prince frowned.

'Well, you may go,' he said to Anatole.

With a smile Anatole rejoined the ladies.

'So you had him educated abroad, eh, Prince Vasili?' said the old prince to Kuragin.

'I did what I could, and I assure you the education there is far better than ours.'

'Yes, everything is different nowadays, everything is newfangled. The lad's a fine fellow, a fine fellow! Well, come along to my room.'

He took Prince Vasili's arm and led him away to the study. As soon so they were alone Prince Vasili promptly made known his hopes and desires.

'Do you suppose I keep her chained up, that I can't part with her?' said the old prince indignantly. 'What an idea! It can be tomorrow as far as I'm concerned. Only let me tell you I shall want to be better acquainted with my future son-in-law. You know my principles – everything above-board! Tomorrow I will ask her in your presence: if she wants it, then he can stay on. He can stay on and I'll see.' The old prince snorted. 'Let her marry, it's all the same to me,' he screamed in the piercing voice in which he had said good-bye to his son Andrei.

'I will be frank with you,' said Prince Vasili in the tone of a crafty man convinced of the futility of being crafty with so sharp-eyed a sparring partner. 'I know you see through people. Anatole is no genius, but he is an honourable, good-hearted lad; an excellent son and kinsman.'

'Very well, very well, we shall see.'

As is always the case with women who have led secluded lives without masculine society for any length of time, with Anatole's appearance all three of the women in Prince Bolkonsky's household felt that life had not been life till this moment. Their powers of thinking, of feeling, of observation immediately increased tenfold, so that their existence which till now had been passed as it were in darkness was suddenly lit by a new light that was full of significance.

Princess Maria did not give another thought to her face and coiffure. The frank handsome countenance of the man who might perhaps become her husband absorbed all her attention. He seemed to her good, brave, resolute, manly and high-minded. She was convinced of this. A thousand dreams of a future family life continually rose in her imagination. She did her best to drive them away and strove to conceal them.

'But am I not too cold with him?' wondered the princess. 'I try to hold myself in check because in my heart of hearts I feel too close to him already; but then of course he cannot be aware of what I think of him, and may imagine I don't like him.'

And Princess Maria endeavoured and yet did not know how to be cordial to her new guest.

'Poor girl, she's devilish plain!' was what Anatole was thinking.

Mademoiselle Bourienne's reflections – she too had been thrown into a great state of excitement by Anatole's arrival – were of a different nature. Naturally, a pretty young woman with no stated position in society, no relations or friends and far from her native land did not intend to devote her life to waiting on Prince Bolkonsky, to reading aloud to him and playing the part of companion to Princess Maria. Mademoiselle Bourienne had long been looking out for the Russian prince who would immediately appreciate how superior she was to the ugly, badly dressed, ungainly Russian princesses, would fall in love with her and carry her off. And now this Russian prince was here at last. Mademoiselle Bourienne knew a little story her aunt had told her and to which her fancy supplied a sequel. The story, which she loved to go over in her imagination, was about a young girl who had been seduced, and her poor mother (*sa pauvre mère*) had appeared to her and reproached her for yielding to a man without being married. Mademoiselle Bourienne was often touched to tears as in imagination she told *him*, her seducer, this tale. Now this *he*, a real Russian prince, had arrived. He would elope with her, then *ma pauvre mère* would come on the scene, and he would marry her. This was how her future shaped itself in Mademoiselle Bourienne's brain all the while she was talking to him about Paris. Not that Mademoiselle Bourienne was calculating (not for a moment did she think out beforehand what she should do) but it had all been ready within her long ago and now simply fell into place round Anatole, whom she was anxious and determined to please as much as possible.

The little princess, like an old war-horse that hears the trumpet, instinctively and quite oblivious of her condition prepared for the familiar flirtatious gallop, without any *arrière-pensée* or particular effort, but with a naïve and light-hearted gaiety.

Although in feminine society Anatole generally affected the attitude of a man weary of being run after by women his vanity was flattered by the spectacle of the effect he produced on these three ladies. Moreover, he was beginning to feel for the pretty and provocative Mademoiselle Bourienne that passionate animal attraction which was apt to come upon him with extreme rapidity and prompt him to the coarsest and most reckless actions.

After tea the company moved into the sitting-room and Princess Maria was invited to play on the clavichord. Anatole leaned on his elbows facing her, near Mademoiselle Bourienne, and fixed his sparkling, laughing eyes on Princess Maria, who with painful and joyous agitation felt his gaze resting on her. Her favourite sonata bore her away into the most intimate of poetic worlds, and the feeling of his eyes upon her added still more poetry to that world. In reality, however, though he was gazing in her direction, Anatole was not thinking of her but was occupied with the movements of Mademoiselle Bourienne's little foot, which he was at that moment touching with his own under the clavichord. Mademoiselle Bourienne, too, was looking at Princess Maria, and in her fine eyes there was an expression of uneasy joy and hope, also new to the princess.

'How fond she is of me!' thought Princess Maria. 'How happy I am now, and how happy I may be with such a friend and such a husband! Husband? Can it be possible?' she asked herself, not daring to look at his face but still feeling his eyes fastened upon her.

When the party broke up after supper to retire for the night Anatole kissed Princess Maria's hand. She did not know how she found the courage but she looked straight into his handsome face as it came near her short-sighted eyes. After the princess he bent over the hand of Mademoiselle Bourienne (this was not etiquette but then he did everything with such assurance and simplicity) and Mademoiselle Bourienne flushed and glanced in dismay at the princess.

'*Quelle délicatesse* – how considerate of him,' thought the princess. 'Can Amélie' (this was Mademoiselle Bourienne's name) 'suppose I could be jealous of her, and fail to appreciate her tenderness and devotion to me?' She went up to Mademoiselle Bourienne and kissed her warmly. Anatole made to kiss the little princess's hand.

'No, no, no! When your father writes and tells me that you are behaving well, I will give you my hand to kiss. Not before!' And smiling and shaking a finger at him she left the room.

5

THEY all went to their apartments and, except Anatole who fell asleep the moment he got into bed, all lay awake a long time that night.

'Is he really to be my husband, this handsome stranger who is so kind? Yes, above all, kind,' thought Princess Maria, and a feeling of terror such as she had almost never experienced before came upon her. She was afraid to look round: it seemed to her that there was someone standing there behind the screen in the dark corner. And this someone was *he* – the devil – and *he* was this man with the white forehead, black eyebrows and red lips.

She rang for her maid and asked her to come and sleep in her room.

Mademoiselle Bourienne walked up and down the winter garden for a long while that evening in vain expectation of someone, now smiling at that someone, now working herself up to tears by imagining her *pauvre mère*'s reproaches after her fall.

The little princess scolded her maid because her bed was not comfortable. She could neither lie on her side nor on her face. Every position was awkward and unrestful. Her burden oppressed her – oppressed her now more than ever because Anatole's presence had so vividly recalled the time when she was not like that and had felt light and gay. She sat in a low chair, in dressing-jacket and night-cap, while Katya, sleepy and dishevelled, beat and turned the heavy feather-bed for the third time, muttering to herself.

'I told you it was all humps and hollows,' repeated the little princess. 'I should be glad enough to go to sleep, so it's not my fault.' And her voice quivered like a child's about to cry.

The old prince was awake too. Tikhon, half asleep, heard him stamping angrily up and down and snorting. The old prince felt as though he had been affronted through his daughter. The affront was the more bitter because it concerned not himself but another, his daughter, whom he loved better than himself. He told himself that he would think the whole matter over thoroughly and decide what was right and what must be done, but instead of doing so he only further worked up his irritation.

'The first man that turns up – and she forgets her father and everything else. Flies upstairs, combs her hair high in the air and wags her tail and makes herself generally unrecognizable! She's glad to throw over her father! And she knew I should notice it. Frr ... frr ... frr ... And don't I see that young tomfool had no eyes for anyone but the little Bourienne (must get rid of her)! And where is her pride that she doesn't realize for herself? If not for her own sake she might at least show some for mine. I must make her see that this fool doesn't give her a thought but only gapes at Bourienne. No, she has no pride, but I'll make her see. ...'

The old prince knew that if he were to tell his daughter she was labouring under a delusion, that Anatole was bent on a flirtation with Mademoiselle Bourienne, he would wound her self-respect and his case (not to part with her) would be won. Pacifying himself with this reflection he summoned Tikhon and began to undress.

'What devil brought them here?' he thought while Tikhon was slipping the night-shirt over his master's shrivelled old body and the chest furred with grey hairs. 'I never invited 'em. They come and upset my life. And there's not much of it left.'

'Damn them!' he muttered, while his head was still hidden in the night-shirt.

Tikhon was used to the prince's habit of expressing his thoughts aloud, and so it was with unmoved countenance that he met the wrathful inquiring face that emerged from the shirt.

'Have they gone to bed?' asked the prince.

Tikhon, like all good valets, knew by instinct the direction of his master's thoughts. He guessed that the inquiry referred to Prince Vasili and his son.

'Their Honours have gone to bed and put out their lights, your Excellency.'

'Never mind, never mind ...' exclaimed the prince briskly, and thrusting his feet into his slippers and his arms into the sleeves of his dressing-gown he went to the couch on which he always slept.

Although nothing had been said between Anatole and Mademoiselle Bourienne they understood one another perfectly so far as the first part of their romance was concerned, up to the appearance on the scene of the *pauvre mère*. They felt that they had a great deal to say to each other in private, and so from early morning they sought an opportunity of meeting alone. While Princess Maria went to her father's room at the usual hour, Mademoiselle Bourienne and Anatole met in the winter garden.

On this particular day Princess Maria made her way to the study door with more trepidation than ever. It seemed to her that not only was everyone aware that her fate was about to be decided but they also knew what she was feeling about it. She read it in Tikhon's face, and in that of Prince Vasili's valet who made her a low bow when she encountered him in the passage carrying hot water.

The old prince's manner to his daughter was extremely affectionate and careful that morning. That expression of restraint Princess Maria knew very well: it was the look his face wore while his withered hands clenched with vexation because she could not grasp a problem in arithmetic, and he would get up and walk away from her repeating the same words in a low voice several times over.

He came to the point at once, speaking formally.

'A proposal has been made to me on your behalf,' he said with an unnatural smile. 'You guessed, I presume, that Prince Vasili did not come here and bring his *protégé* (for some unknown reason Prince Bolkonsky elected to refer thus to Anatole) 'for the sake of my charms. Last night a proposition was made to me on your account. And as you know my principles, I refer the matter to you.'

'How am I to understand you, *mon père* ?' said the princess, turning pale and then blushing.

'How understand me!' cried her father angrily. 'Prince Vasili finds you to his taste as a daughter-in-law and makes you a proposal for his *protégé*. That is how and what you are to understand! And I am asking you.'

'I do not know what you think, *mon père*,' the princess articulated in a whisper.

'I? I? What have I to do with it? Leave me out of the question. *I* am not going to be married. What is *your* opinion? That is what I should be glad to learn.'

The princess saw that her father regarded the project with disfavour but at the same instant the thought occurred to her that now or never the destiny of her whole life hung in the balance. She lowered her eyes so as to avoid his gaze which she felt would deprive her of all power of thought and make her incapable of anything but her habitual compliance.

'I only want to carry out your wishes,' she said, 'but if I had to express my own desire ...'

She had not time to finish. The old prince interrupted her.

'Admirable!' he shouted. 'He will take you with your dowry and hook on Mademoiselle Bourienne into the bargain. She'll be the wife, while you ...'

The prince stopped. He noticed the effect of these words on his daughter. She bowed her head and was ready to burst into tears.

'There, there, I was joking, I was joking,' he said. 'Remember one thing, princess: I hold to the principle that a girl has a perfect right to choose for herself. I give you complete freedom. But remember one thing: your life's happiness depends on your decision. Never mind about me.'

'But I don't know ... father.'

'There's no need for discussion. He will do as he's told, whether it's to marry you or anyone else, but you are at liberty to choose. ... Go to your room, think it over and come back to me in an hour's time and in his presence tell me your decision, yea or nay. You will pray over it, I know. Well, pray if you like, only you'd do better to exercise your judgement. Now go.

'Yea or nay, yea or nay!' he still shouted, after the princess, reeling as if in a trance, had left the study.

Her fate was decided, and decided for happiness. But what her father had said about Mademoiselle Bourienne – that insinuation was horrible. It was not true, of course, but still it was horrible and she could not get it out of her mind. She walked on straight through the

265

winter garden, neither seeing nor hearing, when all of a sudden she was roused by the familiar voice of Mademoiselle Bourienne. She lifted her eyes and two steps away saw Anatole clasping the French-woman in his arms and whispering something in her ear. With a horrified expression on his handsome face Anatole looked round at Princess Maria but did not immediately let go of Mademoiselle Bourienne's waist, who had not yet seen her.

'Who's there? What do you want? Wait a moment!' was what Anatole's face seemed to say. Princess Maria gazed blankly at them. She could not believe her eyes. At last Mademoiselle Bourienne uttered a scream and fled. Anatole bowed to Princess Maria with an amused smile, as though inviting her to join in a laugh at this peculiar incident, and then shrugging his shoulders went to the door that led to his apartment.

An hour later Tikhon came to summon Princess Maria to the old prince, and added that Prince Vasili was with him. When Tikhon came for her, Princess Maria was sitting on a sofa in her room holding the weeping Mademoiselle Bourienne in her arms and gently stroking her hair. The princess's beautiful eyes had regained their serenity and radiance, and were directed with fond and tender pity on Mademoiselle Bourienne's pretty little face.

'Oh, princess, I must have lost your affection for ever!' said Mademoiselle Bourienne.

'Why? I love you more than before,' replied Princess Maria, 'and I will try to do everything in my power for your happiness.'

'But you despise me. You who are so pure – you could never understand being carried away by passion. Oh, if only my poor mother ...'

'I understand everything,' answered Princess Maria, smiling mournfully. 'Calm yourself, my dear. I am going to my father,' she said, and went out.

When Princess Maria entered, Prince Vasili was sitting with one leg crossed high over the other and a snuff-box in his hand. There was a smile of emotion on his face, as if he were so deeply moved that he could only regret and laugh at his own sensibility. He took a hasty pinch of snuff.

'Ah, my dear, my dear!' he began, getting up and taking her by both hands. He heaved a sigh and went on: 'My son's fate is in your hands. Decide, my good, dear, sweet Marie, whom I have always loved like a daughter.'

He drew back. A real tear appeared in his eye.

'Huh! ... Huh! ...' snorted Prince Bolkonsky.

'The prince on behalf of his *protégé* – I mean his son – makes you a proposal. Are you or are you not willing to be the wife of Prince Anatole Kuragin? Say Yes or No!' he shouted. 'And then I reserve for myself the right to state my opinion too. Yes, my opinion, and merely my opinion,' added the old prince in response to Prince Vasili's beseeching expression. 'Yes or no?'

'My desire, *mon père*, is never to leave you, never to part my life from yours. I do not wish to marry,' she said firmly, glancing with her beautiful eyes at Prince Vasili and at her father.

'Nonsense! Fiddlesticks! Stuff and nonsense!' cried Prince Bolkonsky, frowning. He took his daughter's hand and drawing her towards him did not kiss her but only leaned his forehead to hers, just touched it, and squeezed the hand he held, so violently that she winced and uttered a cry.

Prince Vasili rose.

'My dear, let me tell you that this is a moment I shall never forget, never; but my dear, can you give us no hope, however small, of touching this heart of yours, which is so kind and generous? Say that perhaps ... The future is so vast. Say "Perhaps".'

'Prince, what I have told you is all that my heart can say. I thank you for the honour, but I shall never be your son's wife.'

'Well, there's an end of it, my dear fellow. Very glad to have seen you, very glad! Go back to your rooms, princess, go along now,' said the old prince 'Most glad to have seen you,' he reiterated, embracing Prince Vasili.

'My vocation is a different one,' Princess Maria was thinking to herself. 'My vocation is to be happy in the happiness of others, in the happiness of love and self-sacrifice. And cost what it may, I will make poor Amélie happy. She loves him so passionately. She is so passionately penitent. I will do all I can to bring about a match between them. If he is not rich I will give her means, I will beg my father, I will ask Andrei. I shall be so happy when she is his wife. She is so unfortunate, a stranger, alone and helpless. And, oh God, how passionately she must love him if she could so far forget herself! Perhaps I might have done the same! ...' thought Princess Maria.

THE Rostovs had received no news of their Nikolai for a long time when one day in the middle of winter the count was handed a letter addressed in his son's handwriting. Anxious and in haste to escape notice, he ran off on tiptoe to his study, shut himself in and began to read. Anna Mihalovna, hearing of the arrival of a letter – she always knew everything that happened in the house – went softly into the room and found the count with the missive in his hand, sobbing and laughing at once. Though her circumstances had improved, Anna Mihalovna was still living at the Rostovs'.

'My dear friend?' she brought out with a note of melancholy inquiry in her voice prepared to sympathize in any direction.

The count sobbed more violently.

'Our little Nikolai ... letter ... wa ... a ... s ... wounded, *ma chère* ... wounded ... my darling boy ... the little countess ... promoted to be an officer ... thank God ... how are we to tell the little countess?'

Anna Mihalovna sat down beside him, with her own handkerchief wiped the tears from his eyes and from the page, then having dried her own eyes read the letter, soothed the count and decided that before dinner and before tea she would prepare the countess, and then, after tea, with God's help break the news to her.

All during dinner Anna Mihalovna talked about the war and dear Nikolai, inquired twice when his last letter had been received, though she knew already, and remarked that they might well be getting a letter from him this very day. Every time the countess began to look uneasy under these hints, and glance in trepidation from the count to Anna Mihalovna, the latter adroitly turned the conversation to insignificant topics. Natasha, who of the whole family was the one most keenly alive to shades of intonation, look and expression, pricked up her ears from the beginning of the meal and was certain that there was some secret between her father and Anna Mihalovna, that it had something to do with her brother and that Anna Mihalovna was paving the way for it. For all her recklessness she did not venture to ask any questions at dinner (she knew how sensitive her mother was where news of Nikolai was concerned); but she was too excited to eat anything and wriggled about on her chair regardless of the protests of her governess. As soon as dinner was over she rushed headlong after Anna Mihalovna and catching up with her in the sitting-room flung herself on her neck.

'Auntie darling, do tell me what it is!'

'Nothing, my dear.'

'Yes, there is, you darling sweet precious pet, I won't leave off – I am sure you know something.'

Anna Mihalovna shook her head.

'You are a sly puss, *mon enfant*,' she said.

'Is it a letter from Nikolai? It is!' cried Natasha, reading confirmation in Anna Mihalovna's face.

'But for heaven's sake be careful: you know what a shock it may be to your mamma.'

'It will be, it will be, only tell me about it. You won't? Then I shall go right away and tell her this minute.'

Anna Mihalovna gave her a brief account of what was in the letter, on condition that she did not breathe a syllable to anyone.

'No, I won't, word of honour,' promised Natasha, crossing herself, 'I won't tell a soul!' and she ran off at once to Sonya.

'Nikolai ... wounded ... a letter,' she proclaimed in gleeful triumph.

'*Nicolas!*' was all Sonya could articulate, instantly turning white.

Natasha, seeing the effect the tidings of her brother's wound produced on Sonya, felt for the first time the distressing aspect of the news.

She rushed over to Sonya, hugged her and began to cry.

'It's only a little wound, but he has been made an officer; he's all right now, he wrote himself,' she said through her tears.

'One can see what regular cry-babies all you women are,' said Petya, stalking up and down the room with determined strides. 'Now I'm very glad, very glad indeed that my brother has distinguished himself so. You're all of you blubberers! You don't understand a thing.'

Natasha smiled through her tears.

'You haven't seen the letter?' asked Sonya.

'No, but she said it was all over, and that he's an officer now.'

'Thank God!' said Sonya, crossing herself. 'But perhaps she didn't tell you the truth. Let us go to *maman*.'

Petya had been strutting up and down in silence.

'If I'd been in Nikolai's place I would have killed a lot more of

269

those Frenchman,' he said 'They're such beasts! I'd have killed so many there would have been a pile of them.'

'Be quiet, Petya, what a silly you are!'

'I'm not a silly – you're sillies to cry about nothing,' retorted Petya.

'Do you remember him?' Natasha asked suddenly, after a moment's silence.

Sonya smiled. 'Do I remember *Nicolas*?'

'I mean, Sonya, do you remember him properly so that you can recall every single detail about him?' said Natasha with an emphatic gesture, evidently trying to put into her words the most earnest meaning. 'I do Nikolai, I remember him,' she said. 'But not Boris. I don't remember him a bit.'

'What? You don't remember Boris!' exclaimed Sonya in amazement.

'It's not that I don't remember – I know what he's like, but it's not the way it is with Nikolai: if I shut my eyes I can see *him*. But not Boris' (she shut her eyes), 'no, there's nothing there.'

'Oh, Natasha!' said Sonya, looking solemnly and earnestly at her friend as though she considered her unworthy to hear what she had in mind to say, and was saying it to someone else with whom joking was out of the question. 'I fell in love with your brother once and for all, and whatever may happen to him, and to me, I shall never cease to love him as long as I live.'

Natasha gazed at Sonya with wondering inquisitive eyes, and did not speak. She felt that what Sonya had said was true, that there was love such as Sonya was speaking of. But Natasha had never experienced anything like it. She believed that it could exist but she did not understand it.

'Shall you write to him?' she asked.

Sonya was thoughtful. The question of how to write to *Nicolas*, and whether she ought to write, was one that worried her. Now that he was an officer and a wounded hero, would it be nice on her part to remind him of herself and, as it were, of the obligations he had taken on himself in regard to her?

'I don't know. I suppose if he writes to me I shall write back,' she said, blushing.

'And you wouldn't feel shy to write to him?'

Sonya smiled. 'No.'

'Well, I should blush to write to Boris. I'm not going to.'

'But what is there to blush about?'

'Oh, I don't know. I just feel awkward, ashamed.'

'Well, I know why she'd be ashamed,' said Petya, who had been offended by Natasha's remark to him. 'It's because she was in love with that fat man in glasses' (this was how Petya described his namesake, the new Count Bezuhov); 'and now she's in love with that singing fellow' (he meant Natasha's Italian singing-master), 'that's why she's ashamed.'

'Petya, you are a stupid,' said Natasha.

'No stupider than you are, madam,' said the nine-year-old Petya with the air of an elderly brigadier.

The countess had been prepared by Anna Mihalovna's hints during dinner. Retiring to her room, she sat down in a low chair and riveted her gaze on a miniature of her son painted on the lid of a snuff-box, while the tears kept coming into her eyes. Anna Mihalovna, with the letter in her hand, tiptoed to the countess's door and paused.

'Don't come in,' she said to the old count who was following her; 'later,' and she closed the door behind her.

The count put his ear to the keyhole and listened.

At first he heard the sound of vague conversation, then Anna Mihalovna's voice alone, uttering a long speech, then a shriek, then silence, then both voices talking at once with joyful intonations, and finally footsteps and Anna Mihalovna opened the door. Her face wore the proud expression of a surgeon who has performed a difficult amputation and invites the public in to admire his skill.

'It is done!' she said to the count, pointing triumphantly to the countess, who sat holding in one hand the snuff-box with the portrait and in the other the letter, and pressing her lips first to one and then to the other.

When she saw the count she held out her arms to him, embraced his bald head, looking over the top of it at the letter and the portrait again, and in order to press them to her lips once more she gently pushed the bald head away. Vera, Natasha, Sonya and Petya came into the room, and the reading of the letter began. After a brief description of the march and the two engagements in which Nikolai had taken part, and his promotion to officer's rank, Nikolai said that he kissed the hands of *maman* and papa, begging their blessing, and sent kisses to Vera, Natasha and Petya. Then he sent greetings to Monsieur Schelling and Madame Schoss and to his old nurse, and finally asked them to kiss for him his dear Sonya, whom he still loved and thought of the same as ever. When she heard this Sonya blushed so that the tears came into her eyes, and unable to bear the looks turned upon her she ran into the ballroom, whirled and spun round till her skirts puffed out like a balloon, and, flushing and smiling, she plumped down on the floor. The countess was crying.

'What are you crying about, *maman*?' asked Vera. 'From all he writes you ought to be glad instead of crying.'

This was perfectly true, but the count and the countess and Natasha all looked at her reproachfully. 'Who is it that she takes after?' thought the countess.

Nikolai's letter was read over a hundred times, and those who were considered worthy to hear it had to come to the countess, for she would not let it out of her hands. The tutors went in, the nurses, Mitenka, and several acquaintances, and the countess read the letter each time with new delight and each time discovered in it fresh proofs of Nikolai's virtues. How strange, how extraordinary and joyful it was to her to think that her son – the little son whose tiny limbs had faintly stirred within her twenty years ago, the son over whom she had so often quarrelled with the count who would spoil him, the son who had learnt to say 'pear' before he could say 'nanny' – should now be away in a foreign land, in strange surroundings, a gallant warrior, alone, without help or guidance, busy doing his proper work. All the universal experience of the ages, showing that imperceptibly children do grow from the cradle to manhood, did not exist for the countess. Her son's progress towards manhood at each of its stages had seemed as extraordinary as though there had not been millions upon millions of human beings who had gone through exactly the same process. Just as twenty years before she could not believe that the little creature that was lying somewhere under her heart would one day wail and suck her breast and begin to talk, so now it was incredible that that little creature could be this strong, brave man, the paragon of sons and of men, that judging by this letter he was now.

'What *style*, how charmingly he describes everything!' said she, reading over the descriptive parts of the letter. 'And what nobility of soul! Not a word about himself ... not a word! He mentions some Denisov or other, though he himself, I dare say, was braver than any of them. Nothing at all about his sufferings. What a heart! How like him it is! And how he has remembered everybody! No one forgotten. I always said – I said when he was only so high, I used to say ...'

For over a week they were all hard at work preparing a letter to Nikolai from the entire household, writing out rough drafts and making fair copies; while under the watchful eye of the countess and the fussy solicitude of the count all sorts of necessaries were collected into a parcel, together with money for the new uniform and equipment of the recently commissioned officer. Anna Mihalovna, a practical woman, had succeeded in obtaining special patronage for herself and her son among the army authorities that even extended to their correspondence. She had opportunities of sending her letters to the Grand Duke Konstantin Pavlovich, who commanded the Guards. The Rostovs assumed that 'The Russian Guards Abroad' was quite a sufficiently definite address, and that if a letter reached the Grand Duke in command of the Guards there was no reason why it should not reach the Pavlograd regiment which was no doubt in the immediate vicinity. And so it was decided to send the letters and the money by the Grand Duke's courier to Boris, and Boris must see that they were forwarded to Nikolai. The letters were from the old count, the countess, Petya, Vera, Natasha and Sonya, and finally there was a sum of six thousand roubles for his equipment, and various other things which the count was sending to his son.

7

ON the 12th of November Kutuzov's campaigning army, encamped near Olmütz, was preparing to be reviewed on the following day by the two Emperors – the Russian and the Austrian. The Guards, who had only just arrived from Russia, spent the night ten miles from Olmütz and next morning were to proceed straight to the review, reaching the parade-ground at Olmütz by ten o'clock.

That day Nikolai Rostov had received a note from Boris telling him that the Ismailov regiment was quartered for the night ten miles from Olmütz, and that he wanted to see him to give him a letter and some money. The money Rostov was particularly in need of now that the troops, after their active service, were stationed near Olmütz and the camp swarmed with well-provisioned canteen-keepers and Austrian Jews offering all kinds of attractions. The Pavlograds held banquet after banquet to celebrate honours won in the field, and made expeditions into town to a certain Caroline the Hungarian who had recently opened a restaurant there with girls as waiters. Rostov, who had just celebrated his promotion to cornet and had bought Denisov's horse Bedouin, was in debt all round, to his comrades and the sutlers. On receipt of the note from Boris, Rostov rode into Olmütz with a fellow-officer, dined there, drank a bottle of wine, and then set off alone to the Guards' camp to find the companion of his childhood. Rostov had not yet had time to get his new uniform. He was wearing a shabby cadet's jacket with a private's cross, equally shabby riding-breeches with the leather seat all worn, and an officer's sabre with a sword-knot. The Don horse he was riding was one he had bought from a Cossack during the campaign. A crumpled hussar's cap was stuck jauntily back on one side of his head. As he rode up to the camp of the Ismailov regiment he was thinking of how he would impress Boris and all his comrades in the Guards by looking so thoroughly a hussar who has been under fire and suffered the rigours of the front.

The Guards had made their whole march as though it were a pleasure excursion, showing off their smartness and discipline. They had come by easy stages, their knapsacks transported on baggage-wagons, and at every halt the Austrian authorities had provided excellent dinners for the officers. The regiments had made their entry into towns and their exit from them with bands playing, and, by the Grand Duke's orders, the men had marched all the way in step (a point on which the Guards prided themselves), the officers on foot and in their proper places.

Boris had marched and shared quarters throughout with Berg, who was already in command of a company. Berg, who had received his captaincy during the march, had succeeded in gaining the confidence of his superiors by his zeal and exactitude, and had established his financial affairs on a very satisfactory basis. Boris during the same period had made the acquaintance of many persons who might prove useful to him, and among their number, through a letter of introduction from Pierre, was Prince Andrei Bolkonsky, through whom he had hopes of obtaining an appointment on the staff of the commander-in-chief. Berg and Boris, both as neat and smart as new pins and quite recovered from the fatigues of the previous day's march, were playing draughts at a round table in the clean quarters that had been assigned to them. Berg held a smoking pipe between his knees. Boris in the precise manner characteristic of him was piling the draughts into a little pyramid with his slim white fingers while he waited for Berg's move, watching his opponent's face and obviously thinking only of the game, his attention concentrated, as it always was, on what he was engaged on.

'Well, how are you going to get out of that?' he remarked.

'We'll do our best,' replied Berg, touching his king and taking his hand away again.

At that moment the door opened.

'Here he is at last!' shouted Rostov. 'And Berg too! *Ah, petisongfong, allay cushay dormir!*' he cried, imitating the French of his old Russian nurse which he and Boris used once upon a time to make fun of.

'Goodness, how you have altered!' Boris got up to greet Rostov, not forgetting as he did so to hold on to the board and replace some falling pieces. He was about to embrace his friend but Nikolai drew back. With the dread of beaten tracks peculiar to youth, the desire to avoid imitation and express one's feelings in some new and original way, and shun the conventional forms employed by one's elders, Nikolai wanted to do something singular on meeting his friend. He wanted to pinch Boris, or give him a shove – anything rather than the customary kiss, which was what everybody did. Boris, on the contrary, embraced Rostov in a composed and friendly fashion and kissed him three times.

They had not met for nearly six months, and being at the age when young men take their first steps along life's road each saw immense changes in the other, quite new reflections of the different circumstances in which those first steps had been taken. Both had changed greatly since they were last together, and both were in a hurry to show the changes they had undergone.

'Ah, you damned dandies! Cool and trim as if you'd just come in from a stroll! Not like us poor devils from the line,' exclaimed Rostov, with martial swagger and baritone notes in his voice that were new to Boris, pointing to his own mud-stained riding-breeches.

The German landlady popped her head out of a door at Rostov's loud voice.

'Rather pretty, what?' cried Nikolai with a wink.

'Why do you shout so? You'll scare the wits out of them,' said Boris. 'I wasn't expecting you today,' he added. 'I only sent the note off to you yesterday – through Bolkonsky, an adjutant of Kutuzov's, who's a friend of mine. I didn't think he would get it to you so quickly. ... Well, how are you? Been under fire already?' asked Boris.

Without answering, Rostov fidgeted with the soldier's cross of St George suspended from the gold lace of his uniform and indicating his bandaged arm glanced smiling at Berg.

'As you see,' he said.

'So you have, to be sure!' said Boris with a smile. 'And we had a capital march here too. You know his Imperial Highness kept all the while with our regiment, so that we had every convenience and comfort. In Poland the receptions, the dinners, the balls! I can't tell you. And the Tsarevich was very gracious to all our officers.'

And the two friends related their experiences: the one describing gay revels with the hussars and life in the fighting line, the other the charms and advantages of service under the command of royalty.

'Oh, you Guards!' said Rostov. 'But I say, send for some wine.'

Boris made a grimace.

'If you really think so,' he said.

And going to his bed he took a purse from under the clean pillows and ordered wine to be brought.

'Oh, and I have some money and a letter to give you,' he added.

Rostov took the letter and tossing the money on the sofa put both elbows on the table and began to read. He read a few lines and then looked daggers at Berg. Meeting Berg's eyes, he hid his face behind the letter.

'Well, they've sent you a tidy sum,' said Berg, looking at the heavy purse that sank into the sofa. 'And here are we, count, having to scrape along on our pay. I can tell you in my own case ...'

'I say, Berg, my dear fellow,' began Rostov, 'when you get a letter from home and meet one of your own people whom you want to talk everything over with, and I'm on the scene, I'll clear out at once so as not to be in your way. Do you hear, be off, please, anywhere, anywhere ... to the devil!' he cried, and immediately seizing him by the shoulder and looking amiably into his face, evidently anxious to mitigate the rudeness of his words, he added, 'Don't be angry, my dear fellow. You know I speak straight from the heart to an old friend like you.'

'Why, of course, count, I quite understand,' said Berg, getting up and speaking in a muffled throaty voice.

'You might go and see the people of the house: they did invite you,' suggested Boris.

Berg put on the cleanest of coats, without a spot or speck of dust, stood in front of a mirror and brushed his lovelocks upwards, after the style of the Emperor Alexander Pavlovich, and having assured himself from Rostov's expression that his coat had been observed left the room with a bland smile.

'Oh dear, what a beast I am, though!' muttered Rostov, as he read the letter.

'Why is that?'

'Oh dear, what a brute I've been not once to have written and to have given them such a fright! Oh, what a brute I am!' he repeated, flushing suddenly. 'Well, did you send Gabriel for some wine? All right, let's have a drink!'

Among the letters from home was enclosed a note of recommendation to Prince Bagration which the old countess, on Anna Mihalovna's advice, had obtained through acquaintances and sent to her son, urging him to present and make use of it.

'What nonsense! What do I want with that?' exclaimed Rostov, flinging the letter under the table.

'What did you throw that away for?' asked Boris.

'It's some letter of recommendation ... what the deuce do I want with a letter like that!'

'What the deuce do you want with it?' said Boris, picking it up and reading the inscription. 'This letter might be very useful to you.'

'I'm not in need of anything, and I won't be adjutant to anybody.'

'Why not?' inquired Boris.

'It's a lackey's job.'

'You are still the same old idealist, I see,' remarked Boris, shaking his head.

'And you're still the same diplomatist. But that's not the point. . . . Well, tell me, how are you?' asked Rostov.

'Just as you see. So far everything's all right; but I don't mind confessing I should be very glad to be made an adjutant and not always have to stick in the line.'

'Why?'

'Why, because once a man goes in for a military career he ought to try to make it as brilliant a career as he can.'

'Oh, so that's it!' said Rostov, clearly thinking of something else.

He looked intently and inquiringly into his friend's eyes, searching vainly, it seemed, for the solution to some question.

Old Gabriel brought in the wine.

'Shouldn't we send for Berg now?' suggested Boris. 'He'll drink with you, but I can't.'

'Send for him, do! Well, and how do you get on with the Hun?'

'He's an extremely nice, straightforward, pleasant fellow,' said Boris.

Again Rostov looked narrowly into Boris's eyes and sighed. Berg returned, and over the bottle of wine conversation between the three officers grew lively. The Guardsmen told Rostov about their march and how they had been fêted in Russia, in Poland, and abroad. They recounted the sayings and doings of their commander, the Grand Duke, together with anecdotes of his kind-heartedness and his irascibility. Berg, as usual, kept silent when the subject did not concern him personally, but à propos of the Grand Duke's quick temper he related with gusto how in Galicia he had been successful in speaking to him when His Highness had inspected the regiments and had flown into a rage over some irregularity in the way the men marched. With a satisfied smile on his face he described how the Grand Duke had ridden up to him in a violent passion shouting: 'Pack of mercenaries!' (*mercenary* was the Tsarevich's favourite term of abuse when he was in a rage), and called for the company commander.

'Would you believe it, count, I wasn't in the least alarmed, because I knew I was right. Without boasting, you know, count, I may say I know the regimental drill-book by heart, and the standing orders, too, as well as I know the Lord's Prayer. So you see, count, there's never the slightest detail neglected in my company, and so my conscience was easy. I came forward.' (Berg stood up and showed how he had come forward with his hand to the peak of his cap. It would certainly have been difficult for a face to express more respectfulness and self-complacency than his did.) 'Well, he boiled over, as you might say, and stormed and stormed at me until it was more a matter of death than life, as the saying is, shouted "Mercenary!" and threatened me with the devil and Siberia,' proceeded Berg with a knowing smile. 'I was certain I was right, so I held my tongue – wasn't that best, count? ... "You dumb, are you?" he shouted. Still I held my tongue. And what do you think, count? Next day it was not mentioned even in the order of the day! That's the result of keeping one's head. Yes, indeed, count,' said Berg, lighting his pipe and sending up smoke rings.

'Yes, that was capital,' said Rostov smiling.

But Boris saw that Rostov was preparing to make fun of Berg, so he skilfully changed the subject, begging Rostov to tell them how and where he got his wound. This pleased Rostov, and he began a circumstantial account, growing more and more animated as he went on. He described the Schön Graben affair exactly as men who have taken part in battles always do describe them – that is, as they would like them to have been, as they have heard them described by others, and as sounds well, but not in the least as they really had been. Rostov was a truthful young man and would never had told a deliberate lie. He began his story with the intention of telling everything exactly as it happened, but imperceptibly, unconsciously and inevitably he passed into falsehood. If he had told the truth to his listeners who, like himself, had heard numerous descriptions of cavalry charges and had formed a definite idea of what a charge was like and were expecting a precisely similar account from him, either they would not have believed him or, worse still, would have thought Rostov himself to blame if what generally happens to those who describe cavalry charges had not happened to him. He could not tell them simply that they had all set out at a trot, that he had fallen off his horse, sprained his arm and then run from the Frenchmen into the woods as fast as his legs would carry him. Besides, to tell everything exactly as it had been would have meant the exercise of considerable self-control to confine himself to the facts. It is very difficult to tell the truth and young people are rarely capable of it. His listeners expected to hear how, forgetful of himself and all on fire with excitement, he had rushed down like a hurricane on the enemy's square, hacked his way in, slashing the French right and left; how his sabre had tasted flesh, and he had fallen exhausted, and so on. And that was what he told them.

In the middle of his tale, just as he was saying: 'You can't imagine the strange frenzy one experiences during a charge,' Prince Andrei Bolkonsky, whom Boris was expecting, walked into the room. Prince Andrei, who liked playing patron to young men and was flattered at being applied to for his influence, had taken a fancy to Boris (who had succeeded in making a favourable impression on him the day before), and was disposed to do for the young man what he desired. Having been sent with papers from Kutuzov to the Tsarevich, he had looked up his young *protégé*, hoping to find him alone. When he came in and saw a hussar of the line recounting his military exploits (Prince Andrei could not endure that type of person), he smiled cordially to Boris but scowled and dropped his eyelids as he made Rostov a slight bow before wearily and languidly sitting down on the sofa, disgusted at finding himself in such uncongenial society. Perceiving this, Rostov seethed. But he did not care, the man was nothing to him. Glancing, however, at Boris he saw that he too seemed ashamed of the valiant hussar. In spite of Prince Andrei's disagreeable, ironical manner, in spite of the disdain with which Rostov from his point of view as a *fighting* soldier, regarded all these little staff-adjutants in general, of whom the new-comer was evidently one, Rostov felt uncomfortable; he reddened and subsided into silence. Boris inquired what news there was at headquarters, and what, without indiscretion, one might ask about our plans.

'We shall probably advance,' replied Bolkonsky, obviously reluctant to say more in the presence of a stranger.

Berg seized the opportunity to inquire with great deference whether the report was true that the allowance of forage-money to captains of companies was to be doubled? To this Prince Andrei replied with a smile that he could not presume to offer an opinion on state questions of such gravity, and Berg laughed with delight.

'In regard to that business of yours,' Prince Andrei continued, addressing Boris again, 'we will have a word about it later,' and he looked round at Rostov. 'Come to me after the review and we'll do what we can.'

And having glanced about the room, Prince Andrei turned to Rostov, whose childish, uncontrollable embarrassment, now changing to anger, he did not condescend to notice, and said: 'You were talking, I believe, of the Schön Graben affair? Were you there?'

'I was,' said Rostov in a curt tone apparently intended as an insult to the adjutant.

Bolkonsky observed the hussar's temper, and it amused him. With a faintly contemptuous smile he said:

'Ah, there are a great many stories now about that affair!'

'Yes, stories!' exclaimed Rostov loudly, looking from Boris to Bolkonsky with eyes full of sudden fury. 'A great many stories, I dare say, but the stories we tell are the accounts of men who have been under the enemy's fire. *Our* stories carry some weight, they're not the tales of little staff upstarts who get decorations for doing nothing.'

'The race to which you assume I belong?' said Prince Andrei with a quiet and particularly amiable smile.

A strange feeling of exasperation was mingled in Rostov's heart at that moment with respect for this man's self-possession.

'I am not talking about you,' he said. 'I don't know you, and frankly I don't want to. I'm speaking of staff-officers in general.'

'And I will tell you this much,' Prince Andrei interrupted in a tone of quiet authority, 'you are bent on insulting me, and I am ready to agree that it would be very easy to do so if you haven't sufficient respect for yourself; but you must admit that the time and place are ill chosen for this squabble. In a day or two we shall all have to take part in a great and more serious duel, and besides, Drubetskoy here, who tells me he is an old friend of yours, is in no way to blame that my physiognomy has the misfortune to displease you. However,' he added as he got up, 'you know my name and where to find me; but remember, I do not regard either myself or you as having been insulted, and my advice, as an older man, is to let the matter drop. Well, Drubetskoy, I shall expect you on Friday after the review. Good-bye till then,' he concluded, and with a bow to them both he went out.

Only when Prince Andrei was gone did Rostov bethink him of the answer he ought to have given, and not having thought of it in time made him more furious still. He ordered his horse at once and, coldly taking leave of Boris, rode home. Should he go to headquarters to-morrow and challenge that conceited adjutant, or in fact let the matter drop, was the question that worried him all the way back. At one moment he pictured vindictively how he would enjoy seeing the fright the feeble, bumptious little fellow would be in, facing his pistol; at the next he was feeling with surprise that of all the men he knew there was none he would be more glad to have for his friend than that detestable little adjutant.

8

THE day after Rostov's visit to Boris the review took place of the Austrian and Russian troops, including the reinforcements freshly arrived from Russia as well as those who had been campaigning with Kutuzov. Both Emperors, the Russian with his heir the Tsarevich and the Austrian with the Archduke, were to inspect the allied forces which together made up an army of eighty thousand men.

From early morning the troops, scoured and polished, had been shifting about the plain, lining up in front of the fortress. Thousands of legs and bayonets moved and halted at the word of command, turned with banners flying, formed up in detachments, and wheeled round other similar masses of infantry in different uniforms. Farther off, with measured hoof beats and the jingling of trappings, rode the cavalry, elegant in blue, red and green laced uniforms, mounted on black, roan or grey horses, bandsmen in front, their jackets covered with lace. Yonder, the artillery was crawling slowly into place between infantry and cavalry, the long line of polished shining cannon quivering on the gun-carriages, which made a heavy, brazen din and left behind the smell of linstocks. Not only the generals in full-dress uniform, wearing scarves and all their decorations, with slender waists or thick waists pinched in to the uttermost, and red necks squeezed into stiff collars; not only the flamboyant pomaded officers, but every soldier with face newly washed and shaven and weapons clean and rubbed up to the final glitter, every horse groomed till its coat shone like satin and every hair of its mane had been damped to lie smoothly – all alike felt that something grave, important, and solemn was happening. From general to private, every man was conscious of his own insignificance, aware that he was but a grain of sand in that ocean of humanity, and yet at the same time had a sense of power as a part of that vast whole.

By dint of strenuous exertion and bustle since early morning, by ten o'clock everything was in the required order. The ranks were drawn up on the huge parade-ground. The whole army was arranged in three lines: the cavalry in front, next the artillery, and behind them the infantry.

A lane was left between each two ranks of soldiery. The army was sharply divided into three sections: Kutuzov's veterans (with the Pavlograd Hussars on the right flank in front), the Guards and regiments of the line recently arrived from Russia, and the Austrian troops. But they all stood in line, under one command and in similar order.

Like wind rustling through leaves ran an excited whisper: 'They're coming! They're coming!' Alarmed voices were heard, and a stir of final preparation swept through the troops.

From the direction of Olmütz in front of them, a group of horsemen came into sight. And at that moment, though the air was still, a gentle breeze blew overhead, fluttering the streamers on the lances and worrying at the unfurled standards which flapped against their staffs. It seemed as though by this slight tremor the army itself was expressing its joy at the advent of the Emperors. A single voice was heard shouting: 'Eyes front!' Then, like cocks at sunrise, other voices at different extremities of the plain caught up and repeated the command. And all fell silent.

In the deathlike stillness the only sound was the tramp of horses' hooves. It was the Emperors' suites. The two monarchs rode towards the flank, and the trumpets of the first cavalry regiment began to play the assembly march. But it seemed less as though the notes came from the buglers than as if the entire army, in its delight at the Emperors' approach, had spontaneously burst into music. Through the flourish of trumpets the youthful gracious voice of the Emperor Alexander was distinctly heard, uttering some words of greeting, and the first regiment's roar of 'Hurrah' was so deafening, so prolonged, so joyful that the men themselves felt awestruck at the multitude of their numbers and the immense strength they constituted.

Rostov, standing in the foremost ranks of Kutuzov's army, which the Tsar approached first, was possessed by the same feeling as every other man there present – a feeling of self-forgetfulness, a proud consciousness of might, and passionate devotion to the man round whom this solemn ceremony was centred.

One word, he thought, from this man and this vast mass (myself, an insignificant atom, with it) would plunge through fire and water, ready to commit crime, to face death or perform the loftiest deeds of heroism. And so he could not but tremble and feel his heart stand still at the imminence of the Emperor who was the embodiment of that word.

'Hurrah! hurrah! hurrah!' thundered from all sides, one regiment after another greeting the Tsar with the strains of the march, and then 'Hurrah! ...' and the assembly march again, followed by 'Hurrah! hurrah!' swelling louder and louder and merging into one deafening roar.

Until the Sovereign reached it each waiting regiment in its silent immobility appeared like a lifeless body; but as soon as the Sovereign came abreast of it the particular regiment woke to life and its thunder joined the roar extending down the whole line past which he had ridden. In the terrible overwhelming tumult of those voices, amid the square masses of troops standing as if turned to stone, a few hundred men on horseback, the suites, moved with careless ease, yet symmetrically and above all freely, and in front of them two figures – the Emperors. Upon them was concentrated the undivided raptly-passionate attention of all that mass of soldiery.

The handsome, youthful Emperor Alexander, in the uniform of the Horse Guards, in a cocked hat worn point forward, with his pleasant face and low resonant voice, was the focus of all eyes.

Rostov was not far from the trumpeters, and with his keen sight he recognized the Tsar from a distance and watched him approaching. When the Emperor had come to within twenty paces of him and Nikolai could distinguish quite clearly every detail of his handsome, happy young face, he experienced a feeling of tenderness and ecstasy such as he had never known before. Everything about the Sovereign – every trait, every movement – seemed to him entrancing.

Pausing in front of the Pavlograd regiment, the Tsar said something in French to the Austrian Emperor and smiled.

Seeing that smile, Rostov unconsciously began to smile himself and felt a still stronger surge of love for his Sovereign. He longed to express this love in some way, and knowing that this was impossible was ready to weep. The Tsar called the colonel of the regiment to him and said a few words.

'Oh God, what would happen if the Emperor were to speak to me!' thought Rostov. 'I should die of happiness!'

The Tsar also addressed the officers.

'I thank you all, gentlemen (to Rostov every word sounded like a voice from heaven). 'I thank you from the bottom of my heart.'

How gladly would Rostov have died there and then for his Tsar!

'You have earned the standards of St George and will be worthy of them.'

'Oh, to die, to die for him!' thought Rostov.

The Tsar said something more which Rostov did not catch, and the soldiers, bursting their lungs, roared 'Hurrah!'

Rostov cheered too, leaning forward in his saddle and cheering with all his might, beside himself with enthusiasm and willing to do himself any injury to express it.

The Tsar stopped for several seconds facing the hussars, as if he were undecided.

'How could the Emperor be undecided?' wondered Rostov, but immediately even this hesitation appeared to him majestic and captivating, like everything else the Tsar did.

The Sovereign's hesitation lasted only an instant. The Tsar's foot, in the narrow pointed boot of the day, touched the belly of the bobtailed bay mare he was riding; the Tsar's hand in a white glove gathered up the reins, and he moved off accompanied by an irregularly swaying sea of aides-de-camp. Farther and farther he rode away, stopping in front of other regiments, until at last all that Rostov could see of him was the white plume of his cocked hat waving above the heads of the suite that encircled the Emperors.

Among the gentlemen of the suite Rostov noticed Bolkonsky, sitting his horse in an indolent careless fashion. Rostov recalled their quarrel of the previous day, and the question presented itself whether he ought or ought not to challenge Bolkonsky. 'Of course not!' he now thought. 'Is it worth thinking or speaking of it at a moment like this? At a time of such devotion, such rapture, such self-sacrifice, what do any of our squabbles and affronts matter? I love all men now, and forgive everyone.'

When the Emperor had inspected almost all the regiments, the ceremonial march past began, and Rostov on Bedouin, recently purchased from Denisov, brought up the rear of his squadron – that is, he rode alone and in full view of the Emperor.

Before he reached the Tsar, Rostov, who was a splendid horseman, twice dug his spurs into Bedouin's flanks and succeeded in forcing him into the spectacular trot to which the animal had recourse when excited. Bending his foaming muzzle to his chest, arching his tail, and seeming to fly along without touching the ground, Bedouin, as if he, too, were conscious of the Emperor's eye upon him, passed by in superb style, daintily lifting his feet high in the air.

Rostov himself, legs well back and stomach drawn in, feeling all of a piece with his horse, rode past the Emperor with a frowning but blissful face 'like a vewy devil', as Denisov expressed it.

'Bravo Pavlograds!' exclaimed the Tsar.

'Oh God, shouldn't I be happy if he bade me fling myself into fire this instant!' thought Rostov.

When the review was over the officers fresh from Russia and those of Kutuzov's army collected into groups and began to discuss the honours that had been conferred, the Austrians and their uniforms, the front line, Bonaparte and the bad time in store for him now, especially when the Essen corps arrived and Prussia took our side.

But the main topic of conversation everywhere was the Emperor Alexander. His every word and gesture were expatiated upon with ecstasy.

Each had but one and the same desire: under the Emperor's command to advance with all speed against the enemy. Led by the Emperor himself, none could deny them victory: so thought Rostov and most of the officers after the inspection.

The occasion produced in them all more confidence of success than the winning of a couple of decisive engagements would have done.

9

THE day after the review Boris put on his best uniform and, armed with his comrade Berg's good wishes, rode off to Olmütz to see Bolkonsky, in the hope of profiting by his friendliness to obtain for himself the best possible post – preferably that of adjutant to some important personage, a position in the service which seemed to him particularly alluring. 'It's all very well for Rostov, whose father sends him ten thousand roubles at a time, to talk about not caring to cringe or be anyone's lackey, but I have nothing except my own brains so I must pursue my career and not let opportunities slip but must make the most of them.'

He did not find Prince Andrei in Olmütz that day. But the sight of the town where the headquarters and the diplomatic corps were established, and the two Emperors were living with their suites, their households and their courts only strengthened his desire to belong to this upper world.

He knew no one, and in spite of his dashing Guardsman's uniform all these exalted beings driving about the streets in their elegant carriages, with their plumes, ribbons and decorations, courtiers and military alike, seemed so immeasurably above him, a little officer in the Guards, that they not only would not but could not recognize his existence. At the quarters of the commander-in-chief Kutuzov, where he inquired for Bolkonsky, all the adjutants and even the orderlies looked at him as though they wished to impress the fact that there were a great many officers of his sort hanging about the place and they were heartily sick of seeing them. In spite of this, or rather because of it, he went to Olmütz again on the following day, the 15th, after dinner, and going into the house occupied by Kutuzov asked for Bolkonsky. Prince Andrei was in and Boris was shown into a large room, probably at some time used for dancing but which now held five bedsteads and various pieces of furniture: a table, chairs and a clavier. One adjutant was sitting in a Persian smoking-jacket writing at a table near the door. Another, the stout, red-faced Nesvitsky, lay on a bed with his arms clasped behind his head, laughing with an officer who had sat down beside him. A third was playing a Viennese waltz on the clavier, while a fourth, leaning on the instrument, hummed the tune. Bolkonsky was not there. None of these gentlemen made any move on seeing Boris. The one who was writing, in reply to Boris's inquiry, turned round crossly, saying that Bolkonsky was on duty and that he should go through the door on the left, into the reception-room, if he wanted to see him. Boris thanked him and went to the reception-room, where he found some ten officers and generals.

When Boris entered, Prince Andrei, his eyelids drooping disdainfully (with that peculiar air of polite weariness which says as plainly as words: 'If it were not my duty I should not think of wasting a minute talking to you'), was listening to an old Russian general with many decorations, who stood rigidly erect, almost on the tips of his toes, reporting some matter to Prince Andrei with the obsequious expression of a common soldier on his purple face.

'Very well, then, be so kind as to wait a while,' said Prince Andrei to the general in Russian with the French accent he affected when he wanted to speak contemptuously, and noticing Boris, Prince Andrei paid no further heed to the general (who ran after him begging to be allowed to say one thing more), but nodded to Boris and turned to him with a bright smile.

At that moment Boris realized clearly something of which he had already had an inkling – that in the army, quite apart from the subordination and discipline prescribed in the military code and recognized by him and the others in his regiment, there existed another and more actual form of subordinancy, one which compelled this tight-laced, purple-faced general to wait respectfully while Captain Prince Andrei chose to chat with Lieutenant Drubetskoy. More than ever was Boris determined to follow in future the guidance not of the written code laid down in regulations but of this unwritten code. He felt now that simply by having been recommended to Prince Andrei he immediately took precedence over the general, who in other circumstances, at the front, had the power to annihilate a mere lieutenant in the Guards. Prince Andrei came up to him and shook hands.

'Very sorry you did not find me in yesterday. I was fussing about with Germans the entire day. Went with Weierother to look over the dispositions. When a German starts being accurate there's no end to it!'

Boris smiled, as though he understood as a matter of common knowledge what Prince Andrei was referring to. But it was the first time he had heard the name of Weierother, or even the term 'dispositions'.

'Well now, my dear fellow, so you still want to be an adjutant? I have been thinking about you since I saw you.'

'Yes, I was considering' – for some reason Boris could not help blushing – 'asking the commander-in-chief. He has had a letter about me from Prince Kuragin. I only wanted to ask him because I fear the Guards won't be in action,' he added as though excusing himself.

'Very well, very well, we will talk it over presently,' said Prince Andrei. 'Only let me report on this gentleman's business and I am at your disposal.'

While Prince Andrei was away reporting the business of the purple-faced general, that gentleman, evidently not sharing Boris's conception of the advantages of the unwritten code of subordinacy, glared so fiercely at the presumptuous lieutenant who prevented him having his say to the adjutant that Boris began to feel uncomfortable. He moved away and waited impatiently for Prince Andrei's return from the commander-in-chief.

'Well, my dear fellow, as I said, I have been thinking about you,' resumed Prince Andrei, when they had gone into the large room with the clavichord. 'It's no use your going to the commander-in-chief. He would be extremely civil and polite, ask you to dine with him' ('That wouldn't be so bad as regards that unwritten code,' thought Boris), 'but nothing more would come of it: there will soon be enough of us aides-de-camp and staff-officers to form a battalion! But I tell you what we will do: I have a friend, an adjutant-general and an excellent fellow, Prince Dolgorukov; and though you may not know it, the fact is now that Kutuzov and his staff and the rest of us are of mighty little account. Everything at present is centred round the Emperor. So let us go to Dolgorukov. I have to call on him anyhow, and I have already spoken to him about you. We shall see whether he can't attach you on his own staff or find you a post somewhere nearer the sun.'

Prince Andrei always showed particular energy when the chance occurred of taking a young man under his wing and furthering his ambitions. Under cover of obtaining assistance of this kind for another, which his pride would never have let him accept for himself, he kept in touch with the circle which confers success and which attracted him. He most readily took up Boris's cause and went with him to Prince Dolgorukov.

It was already quite late in the evening when they made their way into the palace at Olmütz occupied by the Emperors and their retinues.

That same day there had been a council of war in which all the members of the Hofkriegsrath and both Emperors had been present. At the council it had been decided – against the advice of the elder generals, Kutuzov and Prince Schwartzenberg – to advance at once and give battle to Bonaparte. The sitting was only just over when Prince Andrei, accompanied by Boris, arrived at the palace to seek out Prince Dolgorukov. Everyone at headquarters was still under the spell of the day's council which had resulted in a triumph for the younger party. The voices of those who favoured delay and advised further postponement of the attack had been so unanimously drowned, and their arguments confuted by such conclusive evidence of the advantages of attacking, that the subject of their deliberations – the impending engagement and the victory certain to follow it – already seemed to be a thing of the past rather than of the future. All the advantages were on our side. Our immense forces, undoubtedly superior to those of Napoleon, were concentrated in one place; the armies were inspired by the presence of their Emperors and eager for action; the strategic position on which the battle must be fought was known in the minutest detail to the Austrian general, Weierother, who was in command of the troops (a lucky accident had ordained that the previous year the Austrian army had chosen for their manoeuvres the very field where they now had to fight the French); every feature of the locality was familiar and marked down on maps, while Bonaparte's present inaction argued a state of weakness.

Dolgorukov, one of the warmest advocates of an immediate offensive, had only just returned from the council, weary and exhausted but full of excitement and proud of the victory he had obtained. Prince Andrei introduced his *protégé* but Prince Dolgorukov, though he pressed his hand politely and firmly, said nothing to Boris, and evidently unable to suppress the thoughts which were uppermost in his mind addressed Prince Andrei in French.

'Ah, my dear fellow, what a battle we have won! God grant that the victory to follow may be equally brilliant. However, my dear fellow,' he said brusquely and eagerly, 'I must confess to having been unjust to the Austrians and particularly to Weierother. What accuracy and meticulousness! What knowledge of the locality! What foresight for every eventuality, every contingency down to the minutest detail! No, my dear boy, anything more propitious than present circumstances could not have been devised. The combination of Austrian precision with Russian valour – what more could one wish for?'

'So it has been definitely decided to attack?' said Bolkonsky.

'And do you know, I fancy Bonaparte has completely lost his head. You know that a letter came from him today addressed to the Emperor?' Dolgorukov smiled significantly.

'You don't say so! What does he write?' asked Bolkonsky.

'What can he write? Bubble and froth and so forth ... all simply to gain time. I tell you he's in our hands, that's certain! But the most amusing thing of all,' he continued with a sudden good-natured laugh, 'is that we couldn't for the life of us think how to address the reply! If not "Consul" – and of course not "Emperor" – it would have to be "General Bonaparte", it seemed to me.'

'But there is a considerable difference between not recognizing him as Emperor and calling him General Bonaparte,' remarked Bolkonsky.

'That's just the point,' interrupted Dolgorukov quickly, laughing. 'You know Bilibin – he's a very clever fellow. He suggested writing "To the Usurper and Enemy of the Human Race".' Dolgorukov broke into a hearty peal of laughter.

'And nothing more?' observed Bolkonsky.

'All the same, in the end it was Bilibin who found a suitable form of address. He's a shrewd clever fellow.'

'What was it?'

'"To the Head of the French Government ... *Au chef du gouvernement français*,"' said Dolgorukov with grave satisfaction. 'Good, don't you think?'

'Yes, but it won't please him at all,' observed Bolkonsky.

'Not one bit! My brother knows him, he's dined with him – with this self-styled Emperor – more than once in Paris, and tells me he's never met a subtler or more cunning diplomatist – French finesse plus Italian play-acting, you know! You've heard the anecdotes about him and Count Markov? Count Markov was the only person who could meet him on his own ground. The story of the handkerchief's a gem!'

And the loquacious Dolgorukov, turning now to Boris now to Prince Andrei, told them the story of how Bonaparte, to try out Markov, our ambassador, purposely dropped his pocket-handkerchief at Markov's feet and stood still to see if he would pick it up for him, and how Markov promptly dropped his own beside Bonaparte's and picked it up again, leaving Bonaparte's where it lay.

'Delicious!' said Bolkonsky. 'But prince, I have come to you as a supplicant on behalf of this young man. You see ...' But, before Prince Andrei could finish, an aide-de-camp came in to summon Dolgorukov to the Emperor.

'Oh, how annoying!' said Dolgorukov, hurriedly rising and shaking hands with Prince Andrei and Boris. 'You know I should be very glad to do all in my power either for you or for this charming young man.' He pressed Boris's hand again with a sincere good-natured expression of careless gaiety. 'But you see how it is ... another time!'

Boris was greatly excited by the thought of being so close to the higher powers as he felt himself to be at that moment. He was conscious that here he was in contact with the springs that set in motion all those vast movements of the mass, of which he in his regiment felt himself a tiny, humble and insignificant atom. They followed Prince Dolgorukov out into the corridor and met (emerging from the door of the Emperor's room at which Dolgorukov went in) a short man in civilian clothes with an intelligent face and sharply projecting jaw which, far from being a disfigurement, lent peculiar energy and mobility to his expression. This short man nodded to Dolgorukov as to an intimate friend, and fixed Prince Andrei with a cold stare, walking straight towards him and apparently expecting him to bow or step out of his way. Prince Andrei did neither: a look of animosity crossed his features and the short young man turned away and walked down the side of the corridor.

'Who was that ?' asked Boris.

'That is one of the most remarkable but to me most unpleasant of men – the minister of foreign affairs, Prince Adam Czartoryski. It is such men as he who decide the fate of nations,' added Bolkonsky with a sigh he could not suppress as they left the palace.

Next day the armies took the field, and up to the time of the battle of Austerlitz Boris found no opportunity of seeing either Prince Andrei or Dolgorukov again, and remained for the time being with the Ismailov regiment.

IO

AT dawn on the 16th Denisov's squadron, in which Nikolai Rostov was serving and which formed part of Prince Bagration's detachment, marched out from its bivouac into action, so it was said, and after proceeding for about three-quarters of a mile behind other columns was halted on the highway. Rostov saw the Cossacks and then the first and second squadrons of hussars, and infantry battalions and artillery pass by and go forward; and then Generals Bagration and Dolgorukov ride past with their adjutants. As before, all the panic he had felt at the prospect of battle, all the struggle he had had with himself to overcome that fear, all his dreams of distinguishing himself in true hussar style in this battle went for nothing. His squadron was held back in reserve, and Nikolai Rostov spent a tedious and wretched day. Soon after eight in the morning he heard firing ahead of him and shouts of *hurrah*, and saw wounded being carried back (there were not many of them), and finally beheld a whole detachment of French cavalry being brought in, conducted by a unit of a hundred Cossacks. Evidently it was all over and, though only a small affair, had been attended with success. The returning men and officers spoke of a brilliant victory, of the occupation of the town of Wischau and the capture of a whole French squadron. The morning was bright and sunny after a sharp night frost, and the cheerful glitter of the autumn day was in keeping with the news of victory, which was conveyed not only by the accounts of those who had taken part in it but by the happy faces of soldiers, officers, generals and adjutants passing this way and that before Rostov. And Nikolai felt all the more depressed that he should have suffered to no purpose all the dread that precedes a battle, and then been obliged to spend this glorious day in inactivity.

'Wostov, come here. Let's dwink to dwown our gwief!' shouted Denisov, who had settled by the roadside with a flask and some food.

The officers gathered in a ring round Denisov's canteen, eating and chatting.

'Here they come, bringing in another prisoner!' cried one of the officers, pointing to a captive French dragoon being escorted in on foot by two Cossacks.

One of them was leading by the bridle a fine large French horse taken from the prisoner.

'Sell us that horse!' Denisov called out to the Cossacks.

'If you like, your Honour.'

The officers sprang up and crowded round the Cossacks and their prisoner. The dragoon was a young Alsatian lad who spoke French with a German accent. He was breathless with agitation, his face was red, and when he heard French spoken he at once turned to the officers, addressing first one then another of them. He said he would not have been captured, and it was not his fault but the corporal's who had sent him to seize some horse-cloths, though he had told him the Russians were there. And at every word he added: 'But don't let any harm come to my little horse!' and stroked the animal. It was plain that he did not quite grasp where he was. At one moment he was finding excuses for having been taken prisoner, at the next imagining himself before his own officers and insisting on his soldierly discipline and zeal for the service. He brought with him into our reduced in all its freshness the very atmosphere of the French army, which was so alien to us.

The Cossacks sold the horse for two gold pieces, and Rostov, being the richest of the officers now that he had received his money, became its owner.

'But don't hurt my little horse,' said the Alsatian good-naturedly to Rostov, when the animal was handed over to the hussar.

Rostov reassured the dragoon with a smile and gave him some money.

'Alley! Alley!' said the Cossack, touching the prisoner's arm to make him go on.

'The Emperor! The Emperor!' was suddenly heard among the hussars.

All was stir and bustle, and down the road behind Rostov saw a number of horsemen with white plumes in their hats riding towards them. In a moment everyone was in his place, waiting.

Rostov did not remember and had no consciousness of how he ran to his place and mounted. Instantly his regret at not having taken part in the action and his humdrum mood among men he saw every day had gone – instantly every thought of himself had vanished. He was entirely absorbed by happiness at the nearness of the Emperor. This nearness by itself, he felt, made up to him for the morning's disappointment. He was happy as a lover is happy when the moment arrives for the longed-for rendezvous. Not daring to look down the line, and not glancing round, he was conscious by an ecstatic instinct of *his* approach. And he felt it not only from the sound of the tramping hooves of the approaching cavalcade, but because as *he* drew nearer everything around him grew brighter, more joyous and full of meaning, more festive. Nearer and nearer moved this sun, as he seemed to Rostov, shedding around him rays of blissful and majestic light, until Rostov felt himself enfolded in that radiance and heard *his* voice, caressing, serene, regal and yet so simple. A deathly silence ensued, just as Rostov felt ought to be the case, and in this silence the Sovereign's voice was heard.

'The Pavlograd Hussars?' he inquired.

'The reserves, sire!' replied some other voice, a very human voice compared with the one that had asked in French: 'The Pavlograd Hussars?'

The Emperor came level with Rostov and reined in his horse. Alexander's face was even more beautiful than it had been at the review three days before. It shone with such gaiety and youth – such innocent youthfulness that it suggested the high spirits of a boy of fourteen – and yet it was still the face of the majestic Emperor. Casually glancing up and down the squadron, the Sovereign's eyes met Rostov's and for upwards of two seconds rested on them. Whether or no the Tsar realized what was going on in Rostov's soul (it seemed to Rostov that he saw everything), at any rate for the space of two seconds his blue eyes gazed into Rostov's face. A soft, mild light poured from them. Then all at once he raised his eyebrows, and with a sharp movement of his left foot touched his horse and galloped on.

The young Emperor had not been able to restrain his desire to be present at the battle and, in spite of the expostulations of his courtiers, at noon had left the third column under whose escort he had been moving and had spurred off towards the vanguard. But before he could come up with the hussars several adjutants met him with news of the successful issue of the skirmish.

The action, which had consisted merely in the capture of a French squadron, was represented as a brilliant victory over the enemy. Consequently the Emperor and the whole army, especially while the smoke still hung over the battlefield, believed that the French had been defeated and forced to retreat. A few minutes after the Tsar had passed, the Pavlograd division was ordered to advance. In Wischau itself, a little German town, Rostov saw the Emperor once more. In the market-place, which just before the Sovereign's arrival had been the scene of a fairly lively interchange of shots, lay a number of dead and wounded whom there had not been time to move. The Emperor, surrounded by his suite of officers and courtiers, was mounted on a bob-tailed chestnut mare, a different horse from the one he had ridden at the review. Leaning over and gracefully holding a gold lorgnette to his eye, he was looking at a soldier lying on his face with blood on his bare head. The wounded soldier was so dirty, coarse and revolting that Rostov was shocked that he should be so close to the Sovereign. Rostov saw how the Tsar's stooping shoulders contracted as though a cold shiver had run across them, how his left foot began convulsively tapping the horse's side with the spur, and how the well-trained animal looked round indifferently and did not stir. An adjutant, dismounting, lifted the soldier under the arms to lay him on a stretcher that had been brought up. The soldier groaned.

'Gently, gently, can't you be more gentle ?' exclaimed the Emperor, apparently suffering more than the dying soldier, and he rode away.

Rostov saw that his eyes were full of tears, and heard him say in French to Tchartorizhsky as they moved off:

'What a terrible thing war is, what a terrible thing! *Quelle terrible chose que la guerre!*'

The troops of the vanguard were posted before Wischau, in sight of the enemy's lines, which all day long had yielded ground to us at the first shot. The Emperor's gratitude was conveyed to the van-guard, rewards were promised and a double ration of vodka was served out to the men. Camp-fires crackled and soldiers' songs rang out even more merrily than on the previous night. Denisov was cele-brating his promotion to the rank of major, and Rostov, who had already drunk quite enough, at the end of the carousal proposed a toast to the health of the Emperor. 'Not "Our Sovereign the Emperor", as they say at official dinners,' he explained, 'but to the health of our Sovereign, that good, enchanting, great man! Let us drink to his health, and to the certain defeat of the French! If we fought before,' said he, 'and gave no quarter to the French, as at Schön Graben, what shall we not do now when *he* is at our head. We will all die – die gladly for him. Is that not so, gentlemen? Perhaps I am not expressing myself very well, I have drunk a good deal – but that's how I feel, and so do all of you. To the health of Alexander the First! Hurrah!'

'Hurrah!' rang the hearty voices of the officers.

And the old cavalry captain Kirsten shouted no less heartily and sincerely than the twenty-year-old Rostov.

When the officers had drunk the toast and smashed their glasses, Kirsten filled others and in shirt-sleeves and riding breeches went glass in hand to the soldiers' camp-fires and with his long grey whis-kers, his white chest visible under his unbuttoned shirt, stood in a stately pose in the light of the camp-fire, waving his uplifted arm.

'Lads! here's to the health of our Sovereign Emperor, and to vic-tory over our enemies! Hurrah!' he roared in his dashing old soldier's baritone.

The hussars crowded round and responded with a loud shout in unison.

Late that night, when they had all separated, Denisov with his stubby hand slapped his favourite, Rostov, on the shoulder.

'No one to fall in love with in the field, so he's fallen in love with the Tsar,' he said.

'Denisov, don't joke about that,' cried Rostov. 'It's such a lofty, such a sublime feeling, so ...'

'I agwee, I agwee, fwiend, and I share and appwove ...'

'No, you don't understand!'

And Rostov got up and took himself off to wander about among the camp-fires, dreaming of what happiness it would be to die, not saving the Emperor's life (of that he did not even dare dream), but simply to die before his eyes. He really was in love with the Tsar and the glory of the Russian arms and the hope of coming victory. And he was not the only one to experience this feeling during those memorable days that preceded the battle of Austerlitz: nine-tenths of the men in the Russian army were at that moment in love, though perhaps less ecstatically, with their Tsar and the glory of the Russian arms.

II

THE following day the Emperor remained in Wischau. His physician, Villier, was several times summoned to him. At headquarters and among the troops near by the news circulated that the Emperor was unwell. He was eating nothing and had slept badly that night, so those about him reported. The cause of this indisposition was said to be the painful impression produced upon his sensitive nature by the sight of the killed and wounded.

At daybreak on the 17th a French officer with a flag of truce was conducted from our outposts into Wischau. This officer was Savary.

The Tsar had only just fallen asleep, and so Savary had to wait. At midday he was admitted to the Emperor and an hour later he rode off with Prince Dolgorukov to the advanced post of the French army.

It was rumoured that Savary had been sent to propose a meeting between the Emperor Alexander and Napoleon. To the rejoicing and pride of the whole army a personal interview was refused and, instead of the Sovereign, Prince Dolgorukov, the victor at Wischau, was dispatched with Savary to negotiate with Napoleon, if, contrary to expectations, these negotiations were founded on a genuine desire for peace.

Towards evening, Dolgorukov returned, went straight to the Tsar and remained closeted with him for a long time.

On the 18th and 19th of November the army moved forward two days' march, and the enemy's outposts, after a brief interchange of shots, retired. In the highest army circles from noon on the 19th an intense, bustling excitement and activity began which lasted until the morning of the 20th, when the famous battle of Austerlitz was fought.

Up to midday of the 19th the activity, the eager talk, the running to and fro and the dispatching of adjutants was confined to the head-quarters of the Emperors. But on the afternoon of that day the excitement communicated itself to Kutuzov's headquarters and the staffs of the divisional commanders. By evening the adjutants had spread it in every direction and to every part of the army, and in the night of the 19th the eighty thousand men comprising the allied forces arose from their bivouacs with a hum of voices, and swayed forward in one enormous mass six miles long.

The concentrated activity, which had begun in the morning at the headquarters of the Emperors and had given the impetus to all the activity that followed, was like the first movement of the centre wheel of a great tower-clock. One wheel moved slowly, another was set in motion, then a third, and wheels began to revolve faster and faster, levers and cogwheels to work, chimes to play, figures to pop out and the hands to advance in measured time, as a result of that activity.

Just as in the mechanism of a clock, so in the mechanism of the military machine, an impetus once given leads on to the final result; and the parts of the mechanism which have not yet been started into action remain as indifferently stationary. Wheels creak on their axles as the cogs engage, the revolving pulleys whirr in rapid motion, while the next wheel stands as apathetic and still as though it would stay so for a hundred years; but the momentum reaches it – the lever catches and the wheel, obeying the impulse, creaks and joins in the common movement, the result and aim of which are beyond its ken.

Just as in the clock the result of the complex action of innumerable wheels and pulleys is merely the slow and regular movement of the hand marking the time, so the result of all the complex human activities of these 160,000 Russians and French – of all their passions, hopes, regrets, humiliations, sufferings, outbursts of pride, fear and enthusiasm – was only the loss of the battle of Austerlitz, the battle of the three Emperors, as it was called; that is to say, a slow movement of the hand on the dial of human history.

Prince Andrei was on duty that day, in constant attendance on the commander-in-chief.

At six in the evening Kutuzov visited the headquarters of the Emperors and after a brief audience with the Tsar went to see the earl marshal, Count Tolstoy.

Bolkonsky took advantage of this interval to drop in on Dolgorukov to try and learn details of the coming action. He felt that Kutuzov was upset and disgruntled about something, and that they were displeased with him at headquarters; also that at imperial headquarters everyone adopted the tone with him of men who know something other people are not aware of; and for that reason he was anxious to have a talk with Dolgorukov.

'Well, how d'you do, *mon cher*,' said Dolgorukov, who was sitting at tea with Bilibin. 'The fête comes off tomorrow. How is your old fellow? Out of sorts?'

'I should not say he was out of sorts, but I fancy he would like to get a hearing.'

'But he did get a hearing at the council of war, and will again when he is willing to talk sense. But to delay and hang about now when Bonaparte fears nothing so much as a combined attack is impossible.'

'Yes, you've seen him, haven't you?' said Prince Andrei. 'Well, what did you think of Bonaparte? How did he impress you?'

'Yes, I saw him, and I'm convinced he fears nothing on earth so much as a general engagement,' repeated Dolgorukov, evidently setting great store by this all-round conclusion drawn from his interview with Napoleon. 'If he weren't afraid of battle, why did he ask for that interview? Why propose negotiations, and, above all, why retreat when retreat is so entirely contrary to his whole method of conducting warfare? Believe me, he is afraid, afraid of a large-scale offensive. His hour has come. Mark my words!'

'But tell me, what is he like, eh?' asked Prince Andrei again.

'He's a man in a grey overcoat, very anxious to be called "Your Majesty", but to his chagrin he got no title from me! That is the sort of man he is – and that's all I can say,' replied Dolgorukov, looking round at Bilibin with a smile.

'In spite of my profound respect for old Kutuzov,' he continued, 'we should be a pretty set of fools to wait about and give him the chance to escape, or trick us, just when he's right in our hands. No, we mustn't forget Suvorov and his maxim: "It is better to attack than be attacked". I assure you, the energy of young men is often a safer guide in warfare than all the experience of old slow-coaches.'

'But in what position are we going to attack him? I have been at the outposts today and there was no making out where his main forces are concentrated,' said Prince Andrei.

He was longing to explain to Dolgorukov a plan of attack of his own that he had devised.

'Oh, that's of no consequence whatever,' Dolgorukov said quickly, getting up and spreading a map out on the table. 'Every contingency has been provided for. If he is at Brünn ...'

And Prince Dolgorukov gave a rapid and vague account of Weierother's plan for a flanking movement.

Prince Andrei began to point out objections and to expound his own plan, which may have been as good as Weierother's but for the disadvantage that Weierother's had already been accepted. As soon as Prince Andrei began to demonstrate the defects of the latter and the merits of his own scheme, Prince Dolgorukov ceased to attend and gazed absent-mindedly not at the map but at Prince Andrei's face.

'In any case, there is to be a council of war at Kutuzov's tonight: you can say all this then,' remarked Dolgorukov.

'I intend to,' said Prince Andrei, moving away from the map.

'Whatever are you bothering about, gentlemen?' said Bilibin, who till then had been listening with an amused smile to their conversation and now was evidently ready with a joke. 'Whether tomorrow brings victory or defeat the glory of our Russian arms is assured. Except your Kutuzov there is not a single Russian in command of a column! The commanders are: *Herr General* Wimpfen, *le comte de* Langeron, *le prince de* Lichtenstein, *le prince de* Hohenlohe, and finally Prshprsh-plus-every-letter-in-the-alphabet-to-follow, like all those Polish names.'

'Be quiet, you slanderer!' said Dolgorukov. 'It's not true, there are a couple of Russians now, Miloradovich and Dokhturov, and there would have been a third, Count Arakcheyev, but for his weak nerves.'

'However, I think General Kutuzov has come out,' said Prince Andrei. 'I wish you good luck and success, gentlemen!' he added, and having shaken hands with Dolgorukov and Bilibin he left them.

On the way back Prince Andrei could not refrain from asking Kutuzov, who sat in moody silence beside him, what he thought of tomorrow's battle.

Kutuzov looked sternly at his adjutant and after a pause replied:
'I think the battle will be lost, and I said so to Count Tolstoy and

asked him to tell the Emperor. What do you think was his answer?
"My dear general, rice and cutlets are my affair, military matters
you must look after yourself." Yes ... that was the answer I got!'

12

SHORTLY after nine o'clock that evening Weierother with his plans
drove over to Kutuzov's quarters, where the council of war was to be
held. All the commanders of columns had been summoned to the
commander-in-chief and with the exception of Bagration, who declined to come, all appeared at the appointed hour.

Weierother, who had the arranging of the proposed engagement,
by his urgent eagerness presented a sharp contrast to the ill-pleased,
sleepy-looking Kutuzov who reluctantly played the part of chairman and president of the council of war. Weierother evidently felt
himself to be at the head of a movement that already there was no
stopping. He was like a horse in harness running downhill with a
heavy cart-load behind him. Whether he was pulling it or it was
pushing him, he did not know – but he was borne along, helter-
skelter, with no time to consider where this movement might land
him. Weierother had been twice that evening to the enemy's picket-
line to reconnoitre personally, had made two visits to the Emperors,
Russian and Austrian, to report and expound, and between whiles
had called at his own headquarters to dictate the dispositions for the
German troops. Now, exhausted, he arrived at Kutuzov's.

He was evidently so deeply engrossed that he even forgot to be
respectful to the commander-in-chief: he interrupted him, talked
rapidly and indistinctly, without looking at the person he was addressing, and failed to answer questions that were put to him. He was
bespattered with mud and had a woe-begone, haggard, distracted
air, and at the same time he was haughty and self-confident.

Kutuzov was occupying a nobleman's castle of modest dimensions
near Ostralitz. In the large drawing-room, which had become the
commander-in-chief's office, were gathered Kutuzov himself,
Weierother and the members of the council of war. They were
drinking tea, and only awaited Prince Bagration before opening the
council. Shortly after seven Bagration's orderly rode over with the
message that the prince was unable to attend. Prince Andrei came in to
inform the commander-in-chief of this and, availing himself of

permission previously granted by Kutuzov to be present at the meeting, remained in the room.

'Well, since Prince Bagration is not coming, we can begin,' said Weierother, hastily jumping up from his seat and going over to the table on which an enormous map of the environs of Brünn was spread out.

Kutuzov, with his uniform unbuttoned so that his fat neck bulged over his collar as if escaping from bondage, was sitting in a low chair with his podgy old hands laid symmetrically on the arms. He was almost asleep. At the sound of Weierother's voice he opened his solitary eye with an effort.

'Yes, yes, pray do, it's late as it is,' he exclaimed, and nodding his head he let it droop and again closed his eye.

If at first the members of the council believed Kutuzov was pretending to be asleep, the nasal sounds to which he gave vent during the subsequent reading were sufficient proof that the commander-in-chief was absorbed by a vastly more serious matter than the desire to show his contempt for the dispositions or anything else – he was engaged in satisfying the irresistible human need for sleep. He was, in point of fact, sleeping soundly. Weierother, with the gesture of a man too busy to lose a moment, glanced at Kutuzov and, persuaded that he was asleep, took up a paper and in a loud, monotonous voice began reading the dispositions for the impending battle, under a heading which he also read out:

'Dispositions for an attack on the enemy position behind Kobelnitz and Sokolnitz, 20th November, 1805.'

The disposals were very intricate and obscure. They began as follows (in German):

'Whereas the enemy's left wing rests on wooded hills and his right extends along Kobelnitz and Sokolnitz behind the ponds that are there, while we on the other hand with our left wing far outflank his right, it will be to our advantage to attack this last-named wing, especially if we occupy the villages of Sokolnitz and Kobelnitz, whereby we can fall on his flank and pursue him over the plain between Schlapanitz and the Thuerassa forest, avoiding the defiles of Schlapanitz and Bellowitz which cover the enemy's front. To this end it will be necessary ... The first column will proceed ... The second column will proceed ... The third column will proceed ...'

and so on, read Weierother.

The generals appeared to listen grudgingly to these complicated instructions. The tall fair-haired General Buxhöwden stood leaning his back against the wall and, staring at a burning candle, he seemed not to be listening, or even wishing it to be supposed that he was listening. Directly opposite Weierother, with his brilliant wide-open eyes fixed upon him, sat the ruddy Miloradovich in martial attitude, hands on knees with elbows bent outwards, moustache twisted upwards and shoulders raised. He preserved a stubborn silence, gazing at Weierother's face and only taking his eyes off him when the Austrian chief-of-staff finished speaking. Then Miloradovich looked round significantly at the other generals. But it was quite impossible to tell from this knowing glance whether he agreed or disagreed, was satisfied or not with the arrangements. Next to Weierother sat Count Langeron, who all through the reading, with a subtle smile that never left his typically southern French face, watched his own delicate fingers twirling by its corners a gold snuff-box adorned with a miniature portrait. In the middle of one of the longest sentences he stopped the rotary motion of the snuff-box, lifted his head and with polite hostility lurking in the corners of his thin lips interrupted Weierother to make some remark. But the Austrian general, continuing to read, frowned angrily and jerked his elbows as much as to say: 'You can tell me your ideas later, but now be so good as to look at the map and listen.' Langeron threw up his eyes with an expression of perplexity, glanced at Miloradovich as though seeking enlightenment but, meeting the latter's impressive gaze that meant nothing, looked away gloomily and fell to revolving the snuff-box again.

'A geography lesson!' he muttered as if to himself but loud enough to be heard.

Przhebyzhewski, with respectful but dignified courtesy, held one hand to the ear nearest Weierother, with the air of one all attention. Dokhturov, a little man, sat opposite Weierother with an assiduous and modest mien, and bending over the outspread map conscientiously studied the dispositions and the unfamiliar locality. Several times he asked Weierother to repeat words he had not caught or the difficult names of villages. Weierother complied and Dokhturov noted them down.

When the reading, which lasted more than an hour, was ended, Langeron again brought his snuff-box to rest and, without looking at Weierother or at anyone in particular, began to discourse on the difficulties of carrying out a plan depending on hypothetical knowledge of the enemy's position, which might well be uncertain, seeing that he was in movement. Langeron's objections were valid but it was obvious that their principal aim was to show General Weierother – who had read out his dispositions with as much self-confidence as though he were addressing a pack of schoolboys – that he had to do not with fools but with men who could teach him a thing or two about the art of waging war.

When the monotonous sound of Weierother's voice ceased Kutuzov opened his eye, as a miller wakes up at any interruption in the soporific drone of the mill-wheel. He listened to Langeron, and then as though saying to himself: 'So you are still at the same silly nonsense!' quickly closed his eye again and let his head sink still lower.

Langeron, doing his utmost to sting Weierother's military vanity as author of the plan, argued that Bonaparte might easily attack instead of waiting to be attacked, and consequently render the whole plan completely futile. Weierother met all objections with a firm and contemptuous smile that was evidently prepared beforehand against any piece of criticism, whatever it might be.

'If he could attack us, he would have done so today,' said he.

'So you think he isn't strong enough?' said Langeron.

'I doubt if he has as many as forty thousand men,' replied Weierother with the smile of a doctor to whom an old wife tries to explain how to treat a patient.

'In that case he is courting destruction by waiting for us to attack him,' said Langeron with a subtly ironical smile, again looking round to his neighbour, Miloradovich, for support.

But Miloradovich was obviously miles from the discussion.

'*Ma foi!*' said he, 'tomorrow we shall see all that on the field of battle.'

Weierother again indulged in that smile which said that it was absurd and strange for *him* to meet with objections from Russian generals, and to have to prove to them what he had not only thoroughly convinced himself of but had convinced their majesties the Emperors of too.

'The enemy has extinguished his fires and a continual noise is heard from his camp,' said he. 'What does that mean? Either he is retreating, which is the only thing we need fear, or he is changing his position.' (He smiled sardonically.) 'But even if he should take up a position in the Thuerassa, it would only be saving us a great deal of trouble, and all our arrangements to the minutest detail remain the same.'

'How can that be? ...' began Prince Andrei, who had for some time been watching for an opportunity to express his doubts.

Kutuzov woke up at this point, cleared his throat huskily and looked round at the generals.

'Gentlemen, the dispositions for tomorrow – or rather for today, since it is past midnight – cannot be altered now,' said he. 'You have heard them, and we shall all do our duty. But before a battle there is nothing more important' – he paused – 'than a good night's rest.'

He made a show of rising from his chair. The generals bowed and retired. It was after midnight. Prince Andrei went out.

*

The council of war at which Prince Andrei was not given a chance to express his opinion, as he had hoped to do, left him doubtful and uneasy. He did not know who was right – Dolgorukov and Weierother, or Kutuzov and Langeron and the others who did not approve of the plan of attack. 'But had it really been impossible for Kutuzov to state his views directly to the Emperor? Could it really not have been managed differently? Must court and personal considerations be allowed to imperil tens of thousands of lives, and my life, *mine* too?' he wondered.

'Yes, I may very likely be killed tomorrow,' he reflected. And suddenly at this thought of death a whole chain of most remote, most intimate memories rose up in his imagination: he recalled his last parting from his father and his wife; he remembered the early days of his love for her; thought of her approaching motherhood, and began to feel sorry for her and for himself, and in a nervously overwrought and softened mood he went out of the hut in which he and Nesvitsky were billeted and walked up and down outside.

The night was foggy and the moonlight gleamed mysteriously through the mist. 'Yes, tomorrow, tomorrow!' he thought. 'Tomorrow, maybe, all will be over for me, all these memories will be no more – all these memories will have no more meaning for me.

Tomorrow perhaps – indeed, tomorrow for sure – I have a presentiment that for the first time I shall at last have to show what I can do.' And his fancy painted the battle, the loss of it, the concentration of the fighting at one point and the hesitation of all the commanders. And then the happy moment – the Toulon for which he had been waiting so long – presenting itself to him at last! Firmly and clearly he speaks his opinion to Kutuzov and Weierother, to the Emperors. All are struck by the truth of his arguments but no one offers to put them into execution, so he takes a regiment, a division – stipulates that no one is to interfere with his arrangements – leads his division to the critical spot and wins the victory alone. 'What about agony and death?' said another voice. Prince Andrei, however, does not answer this voice but continues to dream of his triumphs. The dispositions for the next battle are planned by him alone. Nominally he is only an adjutant on Kutuzov's staff, but he does everything alone. He wins the next battle by himself. Kutuzov is removed, he is appointed. ... 'Well, and then?' asks the other voice again. 'Supposing a dozen times you escape being wounded or killed or betrayed – well, what then?' 'Why, then ...' Prince Andrei answered himself, 'I don't know what will happen then. I can't know, and have no wish to; but if I want glory, want to be famous and beloved, it's not my fault that I want it, that it's the only thing I care for, the only thing I live for. Yes, the only thing! I shall never tell anyone, but, oh God, what am I to do if all I care for is fame and the affections of my fellow-men? Death, wounds, the loss of my family – nothing holds any terrors for me. And precious and dear as many people are to me – father, sister, wife – those I cherish most – yet dreadful and unnatural as it seems, I would exchange them all immediately for a moment of glory, of triumph over men, of love from men I don't know and never shall know, for the love of those men there,' he thought, as he listened to voices in Kutuzov's courtyard. They came from the orderlies who were packing up; one voice, probably a coachman's, was teasing Kutuzov's old cook, whom Prince Andrei knew and who was called Tit.

'Tit, I say, Tit?' he called.

'What?' answered the old man.

'Tit, go thresh a tit-bit,' said the wag.

'Pshaw! you go to the devil!' growled the old man, his voice smothered by the laughter of the orderlies and servants.

'All the same, the only thing I love and prize is triumph over all of them. I care for nothing but this mysterious power and glory which I seem to feel in the haze that hangs above my head!'

13

ROSTOV that same night was with a platoon on picket duty to the line of outposts in front of Bagration's detachment. His hussars were posted along the line in couples; he himself rode up and down, struggling to overcome an irresistible inclination to drowsiness. Behind him could be seen an immense expanse of ground with our army's camp-fires glowing dimly in the fog; in front of him was misty darkness. Peer as he would into this foggy distance, Rostov could see nothing: at one moment it seemed to lighten up a little, at the next it looked black; did tiny lights glimmer over there where the enemy ought to be, or had the glimmer been only in his own eyes? His eyes kept closing and the image now of the Emperor, now of Denisov or of memories of Moscow floated across his mind, until he hurriedly opened his eyes again and saw right in front of him the head and ears of the horse he was riding and sometimes, when he came within half a dozen paces of them, the black figures of hussars, but in the distance still the same misty darkness. 'Why not? ... It might easily happen,' mused Rostov. 'The Emperor might meet me and give me some order as he would to any other officer. "Go and find out what's over there," he will say. I have heard a lot of stories of his getting to know an officer quite by chance and attaching him to his person. What if he were to take me into his service? Oh, how I would watch over him, how I would tell him the whole truth and unmask those who deceive him!' And, in order to give greater colour to his picture of his love and devotion to the Sovereign, Rostov imagined some enemy or treacherous German whom he would delight not only in killing but in slapping in the face in the presence of the Emperor. Suddenly a shout in the distance roused him. He started and opened his eyes.

'Where am I? Oh yes, in the picket line ... the pass and watch-word: *draught-bar, Olmütz*. What bad luck that our squadron will be in reserve tomorrow ...' he thought. 'I'll ask to go to the front. It may be my only chance of seeing the Emperor. It won't be long now before I'm relieved. I'll take another turn up and down and when I get back I'll go to the general and ask him.' He adjusted himself in the saddle and touched up his horse to ride once more round his hussars. It seemed to him that it was getting lighter. To the left he could see the gleam of a slope and facing it a black knoll that looked as steep as a wall. On the top of this knoll was a white patch which Rostov could not account for. Was it a clearing in the woods lit up by the moon, or the remains of snow, or white houses? He even thought something moved on the white patch. 'It must be snow, that patch ... a patch – *une tache*,' he thought, half in French, half in Russian. 'There now, it's no *tache*. ... Na-tash-a, my sister, black eyes. Na-tash-a ... (won't she be surprised when I tell her I've seen the Emperor!) Na-tash-a ... take my *sabretache*. ...' 'Keep to the right, your Honour, there are bushes here,' said the voice of a hussar past whom Rostov was riding, in the very act of falling asleep. Rostov lifted his head, which had almost dropped on to his horse's mane, and pulled up beside the hussar. He could not shake off the youthful, childish drowsiness that overcame him. 'But, I say, what was I thinking? I mustn't forget. How I shall speak to the Emperor? No, that's not it – that's for tomorrow. Oh yes! Na-tash-a ... *sabretache* ... sabre them. ... Whom? The hussars. ... Ah, the hussars with moustaches. Along the Tversky boulevard rode the hussar with the moustaches, and I was thinking about him just opposite Guryev's house. ... Old man Guryev. ... Oh, but Denisov's a fine fellow! No, but that's all nonsense. The great thing now is that the Emperor's here. How he looked at me and longed to say something but dared not. ... No, it was I who did not dare. But that's nonsense, the great thing is not to forget the important thing I was thinking of. Yes, Na-tash-a, *sabretache* ... oh yes, yes. That's it.' And again his head sank forward on to his horse's neck. All at once it seemed to him that he was being fired at. 'What? What? What? ... Cut them down! What? ...' said Rostov, waking up. At the instant that he opened his eyes he heard in front of him, in the direction of the enemy, the long-drawn shouts of thousands of voices. His horse and the horse of the hussar near him pricked up their ears at these shouts. Over where the shouting came from a light flared up and died again, followed by another and another, and all along the French line on the hillside lights flared, while the clamour grew louder and louder. Rostov heard that it was French but could not distinguish the words in the roar of voices. All he could hear was 'a ha ah!' and 'rrrr!'

'What's that? What do you make of it?' said Rostov to the hussar beside him. 'It must be in the enemy's camp, surely?'

The hussar did not reply.

'Why, don't you hear it?' Rostov asked again, after waiting some time for a reply.

'Who can tell, your Honour?' the hussar answered reluctantly.

'From the direction it must be the enemy,' Rostov repeated.

'Maybe 'tis, and maybe 'tisn't,' muttered the hussar. 'It's dark. There now, steady!' he cried to his fidgeting horse.

Rostov's horse, too, was getting restive and pawed the frozen ground as it listened to the noise and looked at the lights. The shouting increased in volume and merged into a general roar that only an army of several thousand could produce. The lights spread farther and farther until no doubt they stretched all along the line of the French camp. Rostov was no longer sleepy. The gay, triumphant huzzas of the enemy army had a stimulating effect on him. *'Vive l'Empereur! l'Empereur!'* he now heard distinctly.

'They can't be far off – probably just beyond the brook, don't you think?' he said to the hussar beside him.

The man only sighed without replying, and cleared his throat angrily. The sound of horse's hooves was heard approaching at a trot along the line of hussars, and out of the foggy darkness the figure of a sergeant suddenly loomed huge as an elephant.

'Your Honour, the generals!' said the sergeant, riding up to Rostov.

Rostov, still looking round towards the fires and the shouts, joined the sergeant and rode to meet several horsemen who were moving along the line. One was mounted on a white horse. Prince Bagration and Prince Dolgorukov with their adjutants had come to investigate the curious phenomenon of lights and shouts in the enemy's camp. Rostov rode up to Bagration, made his report and fell in with the adjutants, who were listening to what the generals were saying.

'Take my word for it,' said Prince Dolgorukov, addressing Bagration, 'this is nothing but a trick! He has retreated and ordered the rearguard to light fires and make a noise to deceive us.'

'I hardly think so,' said Bagration. 'I saw them this evening on that knoll; if they had retreated they would have withdrawn from there too. ... Officer!' said Bagration to Rostov. 'Are the enemy's pickets still there?'

'They were there this evening, but I can't be sure now, your Excellency. Shall I take some hussars and find out?' replied Rostov.

Bagration hesitated and before answering tried to see Rostov's face in the mist.

'Well, go and see,' he said, after a brief pause.

'Yes, sir.'

Rostov put spurs to his horse, called to Sergeant Fedchenko and two other hussars to follow him, and trotted off down the slope in the direction of the shouting, which still continued. He felt a mixture of trepidation and excitement at riding alone with three hussars into that mysterious and dangerous, misty distance where no one had been before him. Bagration shouted to him from the hill not to go beyond the stream but Rostov pretended not to hear and rode on and on without stopping, continually mistaking bushes for trees and gullies for men, and continually discovering his mistakes. Descending the hill at a trot, he lost sight both of our own and the enemy's fires, but the shouts of the French were louder and more distinct. In the valley he saw ahead of him something that looked like a river but when he reached it he found it was a road. Having come out on to this road, he reined in his horse, hesitating whether to go along it or cut across and ride over the black field up the hillside. To keep to the highway which gleamed white in the mist would have been less dangerous because it would be easier to see people coming along it. 'Follow me!' he said, as he crossed the road and began galloping up the hill towards the point where the French pickets had been that evening.

'Your Honour, there he is!' cried one of the hussars behind him.

And before Rostov had time to make out what the black thing was that suddenly loomed up in the fog there was a flash followed by a report, and a bullet whizzed high in the mist, with a plaintive sound, and sped out of hearing. Another musket missed fire but flashed in the pan. Rostov turned his horse and rode back at a gallop. Four more shots followed at varying intervals, and the bullets whistled past each in a different pitch somewhere in the fog. Rostov pulled at his horse, exhilarated like himself by the firing, and brought him to a walk. 'More! Go on, fire again!' a light-hearted voice was saying inside himself. But no more shots came.

Only as he approached Bagration did Rostov put his horse to the gallop again, and with his hand at the salute rode up to the general.

Dolgorukov was still insisting that the French had retreated and the lighted fires were merely to deceive us. 'What does that prove?' he was saying as Rostov rode up. 'They might retreat and leave pickets.'

'It's plain they have not all gone yet, prince,' said Bagration. 'We must wait till morning. We'll find out about everything tomorrow.'

'The picket's still on the hill, your Excellency, just where it was in the evening,' reported Rostov, bending forward, his hand to his cap, and unable to repress the smile of delight induced by his expedition and especially by the whizz of the bullets.

'Very good, very good,' said Bagration. 'Thank you, officer.'

'Your Excellency,' said Rostov, 'may I ask a favour?'

'What is it?'

'Tomorrow our squadron is to be in reserve. May I beg to be attached to the first squadron?'

'What's your name?'

'Count Rostov.'

'Ah, very well! You may stay in attendance on me.'

'Count Ilya Rostov's son?' asked Dolgorukov.

But Rostov made him no reply.

'Then I may reckon on it, your Excellency?'

'I will give the order.'

'Tomorrow very likely I may be sent with some message to the Emperor,' thought Rostov. 'Hallelujah!'

*

The lights and shouting in the enemy's camp had been occasioned by the fact that while Napoleon's proclamation was being read to the troops the Emperor himself came on horseback to ride round the bivouacs. The soldiers on seeing him lighted wisps of straw and ran after him shouting, '*Vive l'Empereur!*' Napoleon's proclamation was as follows:

Soldiers! The Russian army is advancing against you to avenge the Austrian army of Ulm. They are the same battalions you broke up at Hollabrünn* and have been pursuing ever since, up to this place. The position we occupy is a strong one, and while they are marching to outflank me on the right they will be exposing their own flank. Soldiers! I myself will lead your battalions. I will keep out of fire, if you, with your habitual valour, carry disorder and confusion into the

* The battle which Tolstoy calls Schön Graben. (Tr.)

enemy's ranks, but should victory for one instant be in doubt you will see your Emperor exposing himself to the foremost fire of the enemy, for victory must not tremble in the balance, especially on a day when the honour of the French infantry, on which rests the honour of our nation, is at stake.

Do not, on the plea of removing the wounded, break your ranks! Let each man be animated by the thought that we must subdue these hirelings of England who are inspired with such hatred of our nation. This victory will conclude our campaign and we can return to winter quarters, where we shall be joined by fresh troops now mobilizing in France; and then the peace I shall conclude will be one worthy of my people, of you, and of myself.

NAPOLEON.

14

AT five in the morning it was still quite dark. The troops of the centre, of the reserves, and of Bagration's right flank had not yet moved; but on the left flank the columns of infantry, cavalry and artillery, destined to be the first to descend from the heights to attack the French right flank and drive it into the Bohemian mountains, according to plan, were already up and astir. The smoke from the camp-fires, into which they were throwing everything that was not wanted, made the eyes smart. It was cold and dark. The officers were hurriedly drinking tea and breakfasting; the soldiers, munching biscuit and beating a tattoo with their feet to warm themselves, were crowded round the fires, throwing into the flames the remains of huts, chairs, tables, wheels, tubs and everything else they did not want or could not carry away with them. Austrian column guides were moving in and out among the Russian troops, serving as heralds of the advance. As soon as an Austrian officer showed himself near the quarters of a regimental commander the regiment began to rouse itself: the soldiers ran from the fires, thrust their pipes into the tops of their boots, bags into the baggage-wagons, got their muskets ready and fell into line. The officers buttoned their jackets, buckled on their swords and pouches, and strode up and down the ranks shouting. The orderlies and men in charge of the baggage-train harnessed the horses and packed and tied up the wagons. The adjutants, battalion commanders and colonels mounted their chargers, crossed themselves, gave final orders, exhortations and commissions to men remaining behind with the baggage, and the monotonous tramp of thousands of feet began. The columns moved forward, not knowing where they were going and, because of the throngs around them, the smoke and the thickening fog, unable to see either the place they were leaving or the one to which they were advancing.

A soldier on the march is as much shut in and borne along by his regiment as a sailor is by his ship. However far he goes, however strange, unknown and dangerous the regions to which he penetrates, all about him – just as the sailor sees the same decks, masts and rigging – he has always and everywhere the same comrades and ranks, the same sergeant-major Ivan Mitrich, the same regimental dog Nigger, and the same officers. The soldier rarely cares to find out the latitude in which his ship is sailing; but on the day of battle – heaven knows why or how – a stern note, of which all are conscious, sounds in the moral atmosphere of an army, announcing the approach of something decisive and solemn, and rousing the men to a curiosity unusual in them. On the day of battle soldiers make excited efforts to get beyond the interests of their regiment, they become all ears and eyes and ask eager questions about what is going on around them.

The fog had become so dense that though it was growing light they could not see ten paces ahead of them. Bushes looked like gigantic trees, and level ground like cliffs and slopes. Anywhere, on any side, they might stumble upon the enemy who, ten paces away, would be invisible. But for a long while the columns advanced always in the same fog, marching downhill and up, skirting gardens and orchards, in new and unfamiliar country, and nowhere encountering the enemy. On the other hand, the soldiers became aware that in front and behind and on all sides of them other Russian columns were all moving in the same direction. Every soldier felt cheered to know that where he was going, to that unknown spot were also going many many more of our men.

'See there, the Kurskies have gone on too,' said various voices in the ranks.

'Stupendous lot of our troops here, chum! 'Ad a look at the camp-fires last night – no end to 'em. Good as Moscow!'

Though none of the column commanders rode up to the ranks or talked to the soldiers (the commanding officers, as we saw at the council of war, were out of humour and disapproving of the affair, and so they merely carried out their orders without exerting themselves to encourage the men), yet the troops marched gaily, as troops always do when advancing into action, especially on the offensive. But, after they had been marching for about an hour, all the time in thick fog, the greater part of the army had to halt, and an unpleasant impression of confusion and mismanagement spread through the ranks. How such a feeling communicates itself is very difficult to explain; but there is no doubt that it is transmitted with extraordinary accuracy and rapidity and spreads, imperceptible and irresistible, like water along a mountain valley. Had the Russian army been acting alone, without allies, it might possibly still have taken a considerable time for this impression of mismanagement to become a general conviction; but as things were, there was a keen and natural satisfaction in ascribing the mix-up to the stupid Germans, and everyone was convinced that the German sausage-makers were responsible for a dangerous muddle.

'What are we stopping for? Is the way blocked? Or have we already run up against the French?'

'No, we should have heard from them. They'd have started firing.'

'They were in hurry enough to start us, and now here we stand without rhyme or reason in the middle of a field. It's those damned Germans making a muddle of everything! Silly devils!'

'Yes, I'd have sent them on in front. But no fear, they keep behind. And here we are stuck with nothing to eat.'

'I say, are we to be planted here all day? The cavalry's blocking the road, I'm told,' exclaimed an officer.

'Ach, those damned Germans! They don't know their own countryside!' said another.

'What division are you?' shouted an adjutant, riding up.

'Eighteenth.'

'Then what are you doing here? You ought to have been in front long ago. Now you won't get there before nightfall.'

'What fool arrangements, they don't know themselves what they're about,' said the officer, and rode off.

Next a general trotted by, shouting something angrily in a foreign tongue.

'Jabber-jabber! Can't make out a word of it,' said a soldier, mimicking the general who had ridden away. 'I'd like to shoot the lot of them, the blackguards!'

'We were ordered to be in position before nine, but we're not half-way yet. Fine orders!' was being repeated on different sides.

And the feeling of energy with which the army had started out began to curdle into vexation and anger at the stupid arrangements, and at the Germans.

The muddle originated when, with the Austrian cavalry moving towards the left flank, the higher command discovered that our centre was too far separated from our right flank, and ordered all the cavalry to switch to the right. Several thousand cavalry crossed in front of the infantry, and the infantry had to wait till they had passed.

Ahead of the troops an altercation had arisen between an Austrian guide and a Russian general. The general shouted a demand that the cavalry should be halted; the Austrian argued that not he but the higher command was responsible. Meanwhile the troops were at a standstill, growing listless and dispirited. After an hour's delay they moved on at last and found themselves going downhill. The fog that was dispersing on the heights lay as thick as ever on the low ground to which they were descending. In front in the fog a shot was heard and then another, at first erratic, at varying intervals – tratta ... tat, and then the firing became more frequent and regular, and the skirmish of the little stream, the Holdbach, began.

Not having expected to come on the enemy down by the stream, and suddenly stumbling on him in the fog, not hearing a word of encouragement from their commanders, with a general sense of being too late, and, worst of all, unable to see a thing before or about them in the thick mist, the Russians fired back slowly and languidly at the enemy, advancing and then halting again, never receiving a command in time from the officers and adjutants, who wandered about in the fog over unfamiliar ground, searching vainly for their own units. This was how the action began for the first, the second and the third columns, who had gone down into the valley. The fourth column, with which Kutuzov was, stayed on the Pratzen heights.

Below, where the engagement was beginning, the fog lay dense; higher up it was clearing but still nothing could be seen of what was going on in front. Whether all the enemy forces were, as we had assumed, six miles away, or whether they were close by in that sea of mist, no one knew till after eight o'clock.

Nine o'clock came. The fog stretched, an unbroken sea, over the plain below, but at the village of Schlapanitz on the high ground where Napoleon stood surrounded by his marshals it was quite light. Overhead was a clear blue sky and the sun's vast orb quivered like a huge, hollow, purple float on the surface of the milky sea of mist. Not only the whole French army but Napoleon himself with his staff were – not on the far side of the streams and hollows of the villages of Sokolnitz and Schlapanitz, beyond which we had intended to take up our position and begin the attack – but on this side, so close indeed that Napoleon could distinguish a cavalryman from a foot soldier in our army with the naked eye. Napoleon, in the blue cloak he had worn throughout the Italian campaign, sat on his small grey Arab horse a little in front of his marshals. He gazed in silence at the hills which seemed to rise out of the sea of mist, and the Russian troops moving across them in the distance, and he listened to the sounds of firing in the valley. Not a muscle of his face – still thin in those days – moved; his glittering eyes were fixed intently on one spot. His forecasts were proving correct. Part of the Russian force had already descended into the valley towards the ponds and lakes, part were abandoning the Pratzen heights which he had intended to attack and which he regarded as the key to the position. He saw through the fog, in a hollow between two hills near the village of Pratzen, Russian columns, their bayonets gleaming, moving continuously in one direction, towards the valleys, and disappearing one after another into the mist. From information he had received overnight, from the sounds of wheels and footsteps heard by the outposts during the dark hours, from the slack formation of the Russian columns, from all the evidence he thought it plain that the allies believed him to be a long way in front of them, that the columns moving in the vicinity of Pratzen constituted the centre of the Russian army, and that this centre was now sufficiently extenuated for him to attack with success. But still he did not begin the battle.

That day was a high-day and holiday for him – it was the anniversary of his coronation. He had slept for a few hours up to dawn, and waking refreshed, vigorous and in good spirits, he mounted his horse and rode out into the field in that happy mood in which everything seems possible and success certain. He sat motionless, looking at the heights rising out of the mist, and his cold face wore that peculiar look of confident, self-complacent happiness sometimes seen on the face of a young lad happily in love. His marshals were grouped behind him, not venturing to distract his attention. He looked now at the Pratzen heights, now at the sun floating up out of the mist.

When the sun had completely emerged from the fog, and fields and mist were a dazzling brilliance – as though he had only been waiting for this to begin the action – he drew the glove from his shapely white hand, made a sign with it to the marshals and gave the order for battle. The marshals, accompanied by their adjutants, galloped off in different directions, and a few minutes later the main body of the French army was making rapidly for those Pratzen heights which the Russian troops were fast abandoning as they filed down the valley to their left.

15

AT eight o'clock that morning Kutuzov rode up to Pratzen at the head of Miloradovich's fourth column, the one that was to take the place of Przhebyzhewski's and Langeron's columns, which were now on their way down into the valley. He greeted the men of the foremost regiment and gave them the order to march, thereby indicating that he intended to lead that column in person. When he reached the village of Pratzen, he halted. Prince Andrei stood just behind him, one of the immense number of his staff. Prince Andrei was in a state of excitement, of nervous irritability and at the same time of repressed calm, as a man often is at the approach of a long-awaited moment. He was firmly convinced that this day was to be his Toulon, or his bridge of Arcola. How it would come about he did not know, but he felt sure it would do so. He was as familiar with the locality and the position of our troops as anyone could be in our army. His own strategic plan, which obviously could not conceivably be carried out now, was forgotten. Now, entering into Weierother's plan, Prince Andrei was deliberating over possible contingencies and inventing new combinations in which his rapidity of resource and decision might be called for.

To the left, below in the mist, the musketry fire of unseen forces could be heard. There, it seemed to Prince Andrei, the fight would be concentrated. 'That is where we shall encounter difficulties,' he thought, 'and that is where I shall be sent with a brigade or a division, and there, standard in hand, I shall march forward and sweep everything before me.'

317

Prince Andrei could not look unmoved upon the standards of the passing battalions. Seeing them he kept thinking: 'Perhaps that is the very standard with which I shall lead the army.'

Towards morning nothing was left of the night mist on the heights but a hoar-frost now turning to dew; in the valleys however it still lay like a milk-white sea. Nothing was visible in the valley on the left into which our troops had descended and from whence came the sounds of firing. Above the heights stretched a dark clear sky, and to the right the vast orb of the sun. In the distance in front, on the farther shore of that sea of mist, some wooded hills were discernible, and it was there that the enemy should have been, and something could be descried there. On the right the Guards plunged into the region of mist with a tramp of hooves and rumble of wheels, and an occasional glint from a bayonet. To the left, beyond the village, similar masses of cavalry came up and disappeared into the sea of fog. In front and behind were the marching infantry. The commander-in-chief was standing at the end of the village, letting the troops pass by him. Kutuzov seemed worn and irritable that morning. The infantry filing past him came to a halt without any command being given, apparently obstructed by something in front.

'Do tell them to form into battalion columns and go round the village!' he said angrily to a general who had ridden up. 'How is it you don't understand, your Excellency, my dear sir, that it's out of the question to have them defile through narrow village streets when we are advancing to meet the enemy?'

'I intended to re-form them beyond the village, your Excellency,' replied the general.

Kutuzov laughed sourly.

'A fine thing that'll be, deploying in sight of the enemy! A fine thing!'

'The enemy is a long way off yet, your Excellency. According to the dispositions ...'

'The dispositions!' cried Kutuzov bitterly. 'Who told you that? ... Kindly do as you are commanded.'

'Yes, sir.'

'Mon cher,' Nesvitsky whispered to Prince Andrei, 'the old man's in a vile temper.'

An Austrian officer in a white uniform with green plumes in his hat galloped up to Kutuzov and asked him in the Emperor's name: Had the fourth column started?

Kutuzov turned away without answering, and his eye fell casually upon Prince Andrei, standing beside him. Seeing him, Kutuzov let his malevolent and caustic expression soften, as though acknowledging that his adjutant was not to blame for what was being done. And, still not answering the Austrian adjutant, he addressed Bolkonsky.

'Go and see, my dear fellow, whether the third division has passed the village. Tell them to stop and await my orders.'

No sooner had Prince Andrei set off than he called him back.

'And ask whether the sharpshooters have been posted,' he added. 'What are they about? What are they about?' he murmured to himself, still making no reply to the Austrian.

Prince Andrei galloped off to do his bidding.

Overtaking all the advancing battalions, he stopped the third division and satisfied himself that actually there were no sharpshooters in front of our columns. The colonel at the head of the foremost regiment was greatly amazed at the commander-in-chief's order to post sharpshooters forward. He had been resting in the full conviction that there were other troops in front of him and that the enemy could not be less than six miles away. There was really nothing to be seen ahead except a barren stretch of ground sloping downhill and shrouded in dense mist. Having given orders in the commander-in-chief's name to rectify this omission, Prince Andrei galloped back. Kutuzov, still in the same place, his bulky frame slumped in the saddle with the lassitude of age, sat yawning wearily with closed eyes. The troops were not moving now but stood with the butts of their muskets on the ground.

'Good, very good,' he said to Prince Andrei, and turned to a general who, watch in hand, was saying it must be time they started, since all the columns of the left flank had gone down already.

'Plenty of time, your Excellency,' muttered Kutuzov in the midst of a yawn. 'Plenty of time!' he repeated.

At that moment in the distance behind Kutuzov there were sounds of regiments cheering, and the cheers came rapidly nearer, as they swept along the whole extended line of the advancing Russian columns. Evidently the object of these greetings was riding quickly. When the soldiers of the regiment in front of which Kutuzov was standing began to shout, he rode off a little to one side and looked round with a frown. Along the road from Pratzen galloped what appeared to be a squadron of horsemen in different-coloured uniforms. Two of them rode side by side ahead of the others, at full gallop. One was in a black uniform with white plumes in his hat, on a bob-tailed chestnut horse, the other in a white uniform on a black charger. These were the two Emperors followed by their suites. Kutuzov, affecting the style of an old soldier in the line, gave the command 'Atten – tion!' and rode up to the Emperors, saluting. His whole appearance and manner were suddenly transformed. He put on the air of a subordinate who obeys without question. With a pretence of respectfulness, which unmistakably struck Alexander unpleasantly, he rode up and saluted.

This unpleasant impression merely flitted across the young and happy face of the Emperor, like traces of haze in a clear sky, and vanished. After his indisposition he looked a trifle thinner that day than on the field at Olmütz, where Bolkonsky had seen him for the first time abroad, but there was the same bewitching combination of majesty and gentleness in his fine grey eyes, and on his delicate lips the same capacity for varying expression and the same predominating look of noble-hearted, innocent youth.

At the Olmütz review he had been more majestic, here he was livelier and more energetic. He was a little flushed from the two-mile gallop, and reining in his horse he drew a long breath and looked round at the faces of his suite, all as young and eager as his own. Tchartorizhsky, Novosiltsov, Prince Volkonsky, Stroganov and the others, all richly attired, gay young men on splendid, well-groomed, fresh, only slightly heated horses, chatting and laughing together, had pulled up behind the Emperor. The Emperor Francis, a ruddy, long-faced young man, sat bolt upright on his handsome black horse, looking about him in a leisurely preoccupied way. He beckoned to one of his white-uniformed adjutants and asked him some question. 'Most likely at what o'clock they started,' thought Prince Andrei, observing his old acquaintance with a smile, which he could not repress, as he recalled his reception at Brünn. In the Emperors' suite were the pick of the young orderly-officers of the Guards and the regiments of the line, Russian and Austrian. Among them were grooms leading extra horses, beautiful beasts from the Tsar's stables, covered with embroidered saddle-cloths.

Like a fresh breeze from the fields blowing into a stuffy room through an open window so a breath of youthfulness, energy and confidence in victory reached Kutuzov's dispirited staff with the advent of this cavalcade of brilliant young people.

'Why don't you begin, Mihail Ilarionovich?' the Emperor Alexander impatiently addressed Kutuzov, while he glanced courteously towards the Emperor Francis.

'I was waiting, your Majesty,' Kutuzov answered, bowing deferentially.

The Emperor bent his ear forward, with a slight frown and an air of not having quite caught his words.

'I was waiting, your Majesty,' repeated Kutuzov (Prince Andrei noticed that Kutuzov's upper lip twitched unnaturally when he repeated the word 'waiting'). 'Not all the columns have formed up yet, sire.'

The Emperor heard him but it was obvious that the answer did not please him. He shrugged his rather sloping shoulders and glanced at Novosiltsov, who stood near, with a look that seemed to complain of Kutuzov.

'We are not on the Empress Field, you know, Mihail Ilarionovich, where the parade is not begun until all the regiments are present,' said the Tsar with another look at the Emperor Francis as though inviting him, if not to take part, at least to listen to what he was saying. But the Emperor Francis continued to gaze about him and paid no heed.

'That is the very reason I do not begin, sire,' said Kutuzov in a ringing voice, apparently to preclude the possibility of not being heard, and again something in his face twitched. 'That is the very reason I do not begin, sire, because we are not on parade and not on the Empress Field,' he articulated clearly and distinctly.

All those in the Tsar's suite exchanged swift looks and their faces expressed disapproval and reproach. 'However old he may be, he ought not – he certainly ought not – to speak like that,' said their glances.

The Tsar stared steadily and attentively into Kutuzov's eyes, waiting to hear what more he might have to say. But Kutuzov for his part, with respectfully bowed head, also seemed to be waiting. The silence lasted nearly a minute.

'However, if it be your Majesty's command,' said Kutuzov, lifting his head and again affecting to be the dull-witted, unreasoning general who obeys orders.

He touched his horse and calling Miloradovich, the commander of the column, gave him the command to advance.

The troops began to move again, and two battalions of the Novgorod and one of the Apsheron regiment filed forward past the Emperor.

While the Apsheron battalion was marching by, the florid Miloradovich, without his greatcoat, his uniform covered with orders, and wearing his cocked hat with its enormous tuft of plumes on one side and with the points front and back, galloped forward with a flourish and, saluting jauntily, reined up his horse in front of the Emperor.

'God be with you, general!' said the Tsar.

'Indeed, sire, we shall do everything it is possible to do, sire,' he answered gaily, arousing none the less ironic smiles among the gentlemen of the Tsar's suite by his execrable French.

Miloradovich wheeled his horse round sharply and stationed himself a little behind the Emperor. The Apsheron men, excited by the presence of the Tsar, marched past the Emperors and their suites at a vigorous pace, keeping perfect step.

'Lads!' shouted Miloradovich in a loud, self-confident and cheery voice, obviously so elated by the sound of firing, the prospect of battle and the sight of the intrepid Apsherons, who had been his comrades in the campaigns under Suvorov and were now swinging so gallantly past the Emperors, that he forgot his Majesty's presence. 'Lads, it's not the first village you've had to take!'

'We're ready!' roared the soldiers.

The Emperor's horse started at the sudden shout. This horse, who had carried the Sovereign at reviews in Russia, also bore her rider here on the field of Austerlitz, patiently enduring the careless thrusts of his left heel and pricking up her ears at the sound of musketry just as she had done on the Empress Field, not understanding the significance of the volleys nor of the nearness of the Emperor Francis's black cob, nor of all that was being said, thought and felt that day by the man upon her back.

The Tsar turned with a smile to one of his immediate suite and, pointing to the Apsheron lads, made some remark.

16

Kᴜᴛᴜᴢᴏᴠ, accompanied by his adjutants, rode behind the carabineers at a walking pace.

After continuing for half a mile at the tail of the column he stopped at a solitary, deserted house – it had probably once been an inn – almost at the fork of two roads, both of which led downhill and were crowded with marching troops.

The fog was beginning to clear and about a mile and a half away on the opposite heights the enemy troops were dimly visible. Down below, on the left, the firing was becoming more distinct. Kutuzov had stopped and was in conversation with an Austrian general. Prince Andrei, who was a little behind, watching them, turned to an adjutant to ask him for a field-glass.

'Look! Look!' exclaimed this adjutant, pointing not at the troops in the distance but down the hill before him. 'It's the French!'

The two generals and the adjutants reached for the field-glass, trying to snatch it from one another. The expression on all their faces suddenly changed to horror. The French were supposed to be a mile and a half away, and all of a sudden here they were right in front of us.

'The enemy? ... No, it can't be! ... Yes, look, it is! ... It certainly is! ... But how can it be?' cried different voices.

With the naked eye Prince Andrei saw below them to the right, not more than five hundred paces from where Kutuzov was standing, a dense column of French soldiers moving up to meet the Apsherons.

'Here it is! The decisive moment is at hand! My moment has come,' thought Prince Andrei, and striking his horse he rode up to Kutuzov.

'The Apsherons must be halted, your Excellency,' he shouted.

But at that very instant a pall of smoke spread over everything, firing was heard close by and barely a couple of steps from Prince Andrei a voice in naïve terror cried: 'Hey, mates, it's all up with us!' And at this voice, as if at a command, they all started to run.

Ever-increasing masses of men rushed back in confusion to where five minutes before they had marched past the Emperors. Not only would it have been difficult to check the mob; it was impossible not to be carried back with it oneself. Bolkonsky only tried not to lose touch with it, and gazed round bewildered and unable to grasp what was taking place under his eyes. Nesvítsky with an angry crimson face, utterly unlike himself, was shouting to Kutuzov that if he didn't get away at once he would be taken prisoner for a certainty. Kutuzov remained in the same spot and without answering drew out a handkerchief. Blood was flowing from his cheek. Prince Andrei forced his way up to him.

'You are wounded?' he asked, with difficulty controlling the trembling of his lower jaw.

'The wound is not here, it is there!' said Kutuzov, pressing the handkerchief to his wounded cheek and pointing to the fleeing soldiers.

'Stop them!' he shouted, and at the same time, realizing probably that there was no stopping them, he lashed at his horse and rode off to the right.

A fresh wave of fugitives caught him up and carried him away with them.

The troops were pouring back in such a dense mass that once surrounded by them it was difficult to extricate oneself. A soldier was shouting: 'Get on! What are you waiting for?' Another in the same spot turned round to fire in the air. A third struck the very horse on which Kutuzov was mounted. Having succeeded with the greatest effort in struggling through the torrent of men to the left, Kutuzov, his suite diminished by more than half, rode towards the sound of nearby artillery fire. Freeing himself from the racing multitude, Prince Andrei, trying to keep near Kutuzov, saw on the side of the hill amid the smoke a Russian battery still firing away while the French came running towards it. Higher up stood some Russian infantry, neither moving forward to protect the battery nor back in the same direction as the runaways. A general on horseback detached himself from this brigade of infantry and approached Kutuzov. Of Kutuzov's suite only four were left. They were all pale and looking at one another dumbly.

'Stop those wretches!' Kutuzov gasped to the regimental commander, pointing to the flying soldiers; but at that instant, as though in revenge for the words, a shower of bullets, like a flock of little birds, flew buzzing over the heads of the regiment and Kutuzov's suite.

The French were attacking the battery and, catching sight of

Kutuzov, were shooting at him. With this volley the regimental commander clapped his hand to his leg; several soldiers fell and a second lieutenant who was holding the flag let it drop from his hands. The flag tottered and caught on the muskets of the nearest soldiers. The soldiers started to load and fire without orders.

With a groan of despair Kutuzov looked round. 'Bolkonsky,' he whispered in a voice shaking with the consciousness of his age and helplessness. 'Bolkonsky,' he whispered, pointing to the demoralized battalion and the enemy, 'what's this?'

But before he had uttered the words, Prince Andrei, feeling tears of shame and rancour choking him, had already leaped from his horse and run to the standard.

'Forward, lads!' he shouted in a voice shrill as a child's.

'This is my hour!' thought Prince Andrei, seizing the staff of the standard and exulting as he heard the whistle of bullets unmistakably aimed at him. Several soldiers fell.

'Hurrah!' shouted Prince Andrei, and scarcely able to hold up the heavy standard he ran forward in the unhesitating conviction that the whole battalion would follow him.

And it was indeed only for a few steps that he ran alone. One soldier started after him, then another, until the whole battalion with a shout of 'Hurrah' had dashed forward and overtaken him. A sergeant of the battalion darted up and grasped the standard which was swaying from its weight in Prince Andrei's hands, but he was immediately shot down. Prince Andrei snatched up the standard again and dragging it along by the staff ran on with the battalion. In front he saw our artillerymen, some of whom were fighting, while others had deserted their guns and were running towards him. He also saw French infantry pouncing on the artillery horses and reversing the field-pieces. Prince Andrei and the battalion were now within twenty paces of the cannon. He heard the incessant whizz of bullets overhead, and to right and left of him soldiers continually groaned and dropped. But he did not look at them: he kept his eyes fixed on what was going on in front of him – on the battery. He could now see distinctly the figure of a red-haired gunner, with his shako knocked awry, pulling one end of a mop while a French soldier tugged at the other. He could see distinctly the distraught yet furious faces of these two men, who were obviously quite unconscious of what they were doing.

'What are they about?' wondered Prince Andrei as he looked at them. 'Why doesn't the red-haired gunner make off, since he is unarmed? Why doesn't the Frenchman finish him off? He wouldn't get far, though, before the Frenchman remembered his bayonet and ran him through.'

In point of fact another Frenchman, with his musket at the ready, hurried up to the struggling pair, and the fate of the red-haired gunner, who had no idea of what was coming to him and had just triumphantly secured the mop, was probably sealed. But Prince Andrei did not see how it ended. It seemed to him as though one of the nearby soldiers, brandishing a heavy cudgel, dealt him a violent blow on the head. It hurt a little but the worst of it was that the pain distracted his attention and prevented him from seeing what he was looking at.

'What's this? Am I falling? My legs are giving way,' he thought, and fell on his back. He opened his eyes, hoping to see how the struggle between the Frenchmen and the gunners ended, and anxious to know whether the red-haired artilleryman was killed or not, whether the cannon had been captured or saved. But he saw nothing. Above him there was now only the sky – the lofty sky, not clear yet still immeasurably lofty, with grey clouds creeping softly across it. 'How quiet, peaceful and solemn! Quite different from when I was running,' thought Prince Andrei. 'Quite different from us running and shouting and fighting. Not at all like the gunner and the Frenchman dragging the mop from one another with frightened, frantic faces. How differently do these clouds float across that lofty, limitless sky! How was it I did not see that sky before? And how happy I am to have found it at last! Yes, all is vanity, all is delusion except these infinite heavens. There is nothing, nothing but that. But even it does not exist, there is nothing but peace and stillness. Thanks be to God! ...'

17

ON our right flank, commanded by Bagration, at nine o'clock the battle had not yet begun. Not caring to assent to Dolgorukov's demand that he should advance into action, and anxious to be rid of all responsibility, Prince Bagration proposed to Dolgorukov to send to inquire of the commander-in-chief. Bagration knew that as the distance separating the two flanks was almost seven miles the messenger, even if he were not killed (which he very likely would be), and even if he found the commander-in-chief (which would be extremely difficult), he could hardly succeed in making his way back before evening.

Bagration cast his large, expressionless, sleepy eyes round his suite, and the boyish face of Rostov, breathless with excitement and hope, was the first to catch his eye. He sent him.

'And if I should meet his Majesty before I find the commander-in-chief, your Excellency?' asked Rostov, with his hand to his cap.

'You can give the message to his Majesty,' said Dolgorukov, anticipating Bagration.

After being relieved at the outposts Rostov had managed to get a few hours' sleep before daybreak, and felt cheerful, bold and resolute, brimming with elasticity of movement and confidence in his luck, and in that state of mind which makes everything seem possible, pleasant and easy.

All his hopes were being fulfilled that morning: there was to be a general engagement, and he was taking part in it; more than that, he was in attendance on the bravest of generals; and, still more, he was being sent with a message to Kutuzov, perhaps even to the Sovereign himself. It was a fine morning, he had a good mount under him. His heart was full of joy and happiness. Having received his instructions, he gave his horse the rein and galloped off along the line. At first he rode along the line of Bagration's troops, which had not yet advanced into action but were standing motionless; then he came out into the region occupied by Uvarov's cavalry, and here he noticed activity and signs of preparation for battle. Once past Uvarov's cavalry he could clearly hear the sound of musketry and gunfire ahead of him. The firing grew louder and louder.

The sound that now reached him in the fresh morning air was not of two or three musket shots at irregular intervals as before, followed by one or two cannon shots; down the slopes of the hills before Pratzen he could hear volleys of musketry, interspersed with such frequent thunder from the cannon that sometimes there was no distinguishing them apart and they merged into one general roar. He could see puffs of musketry smoke chasing one another down the hillsides, while smoke from the cannon rolled up in clouds, spread and became one. He could see, from the glint of bayonets in the smoke, moving masses of infantry and narrow lines of artillery with green caissons.

Rostov stopped his horse on a hillock for a moment to try and make out what was going on, but strain his attention as he would he could not understand or interpret anything of what was happening: there were men of some sort moving about in the smoke, lines of troops were hurrying this way and that – but what they were doing, who they were, where they were going, it was impossible to tell. This spectacle and these sounds, so far from exciting any feeling of depression or fearfulness, only stimulated his energy and determination.

'Go on, give it them! Go on!' was his mental response to the sounds he heard, and he resumed his gallop along the line, penetrating farther and farther into the area where the army was already in action.

'How it is going to turn out there, I don't know, but it will all be all right!' thought Rostov.

After passing some Austrian troops he noticed that the next part of the line (the Guards) were already engaged.

'So much the better! I shall see it at close quarters,' he thought.

He was riding almost along the front line. A handful of horsemen came galloping towards him. They were our Uhlans returning in disorder from the attack. Rostov passed them, not without noticing that one of them was covered with blood, and galloped on.

'That's no affair of mine!' he thought.

He had not ridden many hundred yards after that before he saw to his left, across the whole width of the field, an immense body of cavalry in dazzling white uniforms and mounted on coal-black chargers, trotting straight towards him, across his path. Rostov urged his horse to its utmost to get out of their way, and would have succeeded had they continued at the same speed but they kept increasing their pace so that some of the horses broke into a gallop. Rostov heard the thud of hooves and the clatter of arms coming nearer and nearer; in a minute they were close enough for him to distinguish their horses, their figures and even their faces. They were our Horse Guards about to charge the French cavalry, who were advancing to meet them.

The Horse Guards were galloping, though still holding in their horses. Rostov could see their faces now, and heard the command 'Charge!' shouted by an officer as he pressed his thoroughbred forward. Fearing to be crushed or swept into the attack on the

French, Rostov spurred along the front as hard as his horse could go, but still was not in time to escape them.

The last rider in the line, a huge pock-marked fellow, scowled viciously on seeing Rostov just in front of him, where they must inevitably collide. This Guardsman would certainly have overturned Rostov and his Bedouin with him (Rostov felt how small and slight he was compared to these gigantic men and horses), had it not occurred to Rostov to flourish his whip in the eyes of the Guardsman's horse. The heavy, coal-black charger shied and laid back its ears; but the pock-marked Guardsman drove his great spurs in violently and the horse, lashing its tail and stretching its neck, flew on faster than ever. Hardly had the Horse Guards passed Rostov before he heard their shout of 'Hurrah!' and looking back saw their foremost ranks mixed up with some foreign cavalry, probably French, with red epaulets. After that it was impossible to see anything, for cannon began to belch forth smoke which enveloped everything.

At the moment that the Horse Guards dashed past him and disappeared in the smoke Rostov hesitated whether to gallop after them or continue on his errand. This was the brilliant charge of the Horse Guards which filled the French themselves with so much admiration. Rostov was appalled to hear later that of all that mass of fine enormous men, of all those splendid, wealthy young officers and cadets who had galloped past him on horses worth thousands of roubles, only eighteen survived the charge.

'I have no need to envy them. My turn will come, and maybe I shall see the Emperor any minute now!' thought Rostov, and he sped on.

When he came up to the Foot Guards he realized that cannon-balls were flying over and about them – not so much because he heard the sounds of the missiles as because of the uneasy looks of the men and the unnatural martial solemnity of the officers.

As he was passing behind one of the lines of a regiment of Foot Guards he heard a voice calling him by name.

'Rostov!'

'Eh?' he called back, not recognizing Boris.

'I say, we've been in the front line! Our regiment went in to attack!' said Boris with the happy smile seen on the faces of young men who have been under fire for the first time.

Rostov stopped.

'Have you indeed!' said he. 'Well, how was it?'

'We drove them back!' said Boris eagerly, and becoming talkative. 'Fancy ...'

And Boris began describing how the Guards having taken up their position and seeing troops in front of them thought they were Austrians, and all at once discovered from the cannon-balls aimed at them by those same troops that they themselves were in the front line and had quite unexpectedly to go into action. Rostov set his horse moving, without waiting to hear Boris to the end.

'Where are you off to?' asked Boris.

'To his Majesty with a message.'

'There he is!' said Boris, thinking Rostov had said 'his Highness' and pointing to the Grand Duke with his high shoulders and frowning brows standing a hundred paces from them, wearing a helmet and Horse Guards' jacket, and shouting something to a pale, white-uniformed Austrian officer.

'No, that's the Grand Duke, and my errand is to the commander-in-chief or the Emperor,' said Rostov, and was about to spur his horse again.

'Count! Count!' shouted Berg, running up on the other side, no less excited than Boris. 'Count! I was wounded in my right hand' (he pointed to his blood-stained wrist bound up with a pocket-handkerchief), 'and I kept my place at the front. Count, I had to hold my sword in my left hand. All our family – the von Bergs – have been true knights.'

He was still talking but Rostov did not wait to hear any more, and rode on.

Passing the Guards and across a vacant space, Rostov – to avoid getting into the front line again as he had when the Horse Guards charged – followed the line of reserves, making a wide circuit round the place from whence came the hottest musket-fire and cannonade. Suddenly, quite close in front of him and behind our troops, where he could never have expected the enemy to be, he heard musketry-firing.

'What can it be?' wondered Rostov. 'The enemy in the rear of our troops? Impossible!' And all at once he was overwhelmed by panic for himself and for the issue of the whole battle. 'But whatever it is,' he reflected, 'there's no riding round it now. I must look for the commander-in-chief here, and if all is lost it will be my duty to perish with the rest.'

The foreboding of evil that had suddenly come upon Rostov was more and more confirmed the farther he advanced into the region behind the village of Pratzen, which was full of troops of all kinds.

'What does it mean? What is it? Who are they firing at? Who's doing the firing?' Rostov kept asking as he met Russian and Austrian troops running in confused crowds across his path.

'The devil only knows! We're all massacred! Everything's lost!' he was told in Russian, in German, in Czech by the fleeing rabble, who understood what was happening as little as he did.

'Hang the Germans!' shouted one.

'To hell with them – the traitors!'

'Damn these Russians!' muttered a German.

A number of wounded were among the crowds on the road. Oaths, cries and groans mingled in a general hubbub. The firing subsided, and Rostov learned later that Russian and Austrian soldiers had been firing at one another.

'Great heavens!' thought Rostov, 'and the Emperor may be here at any moment and see this rout. ... But no, these can only be a handful of scoundrels. It will soon be over, it's not the real thing, it *can't* be! I must make haste and get past them as fast as I can.'

The idea of defeat and flight could not enter Rostov's head. Though he saw French cannon and French troops on the Pratzen heights, the very spot where he had been told to look for the commander-in-chief, he could not and would not believe *that*.

18

ROSTOV had been directed to seek out Kutuzov and the Emperor in the vicinity of the village of Pratzen. But neither they nor even a single commanding officer were there – only disordered mobs of the rank and file. He urged on his now weary horse to get quickly past these crowds but the farther he went the more demoralized they were. The high road on which he had come out swarmed with calèches, carriages and vehicles of all kinds, with Russian and Austrian soldiers of every corps, wounded and unwounded. The whole rabble droned and jostled in confusion under the sinister whizz of cannon-balls from the French batteries stationed on the Pratzen heights.

'Where is the Emperor? Where is Kutuzov?' Rostov kept asking of everyone he could stop, but nobody could vouchsafe him any answer.

At last, seizing a soldier by the collar, he forced him to reply.

'Aye, brother! They've all bolted long ago!' said the soldier, laughing for some reason and shaking himself free.

Releasing this soldier, who was evidently drunk, Rostov held up the horse of a batman or groom to some important personage, and began to question him. The man declared that the Tsar had been driven in a carriage at full speed about an hour before along that very road, and that he was dangerously wounded.

'It can't be!' exclaimed Rostov. 'It must have been someone else.'

'I saw him with my own eyes,' said the man with a self-satisfied smirk. 'I ought to know the Emperor by now, after the times I've seen him in Petersburg. He was leaning back in the carriage as white as anything. My goodness, the way those four black horses thundered past! It's time I knew the imperial horses and Ilya Ivanich – why, I don't believe Ilya ever drives anyone but the Tsar.'

Rostov let go of the horse and was about to ride on when a wounded officer passing by addressed him.

'Who is it you want?' asked the officer. 'The commander-in-chief? Oh, he was killed by a cannon-ball – it got him in the chest. He was in front of our regiment when it happened.'

'Not killed – wounded,' another officer corrected him.

'Who? Kutuzov?' asked Rostov.

'Not Kutuzov, but what's his name – oh well, it's all the same ... there are not many left alive. If you go that way, to the village over there, all the commanders are there together,' said the officer, pointing to the village of Gostieradeck, and he walked on.

Rostov rode on at a foot-pace, not knowing to whom he was going, or why. The Emperor was wounded, the battle lost. It was impossible to doubt it now. Rostov rode in the direction indicated to him, and where he saw turrets and a church in the distance. What need to hurry? What was he to say now to the Tsar or to Kutuzov, even supposing they were alive and unwounded?

'Take this road, your Honour, that way you'll be killed straight off!' a soldier shouted to him. 'That way you'll get killed!'

'What are you talking about?' said another. 'Where is he to go? That way's nearest.'

Rostov considered, and then went in the direction where they said he would be killed.

'Nothing matters now. If the Emperor's wounded, am I to try and save my skin?' he thought. He rode on into the sector where there had been the heaviest slaughter of men escaping from Pratzen. The French had not yet occupied this ground, and the Russians – those, that is, who were unhurt or only slightly wounded – had long before abandoned it. All about the field, like heaps of manure on well-kept plough-land, lay the dead and wounded, a dozen or fifteen bodies to each couple of acres. The wounded had crawled together in twos and threes, and their cries and groans were distressing to hear (though it seemed to Rostov that sometimes they were simulated). He put his horse to a trot, to avoid the sight of all this suffering, and he felt afraid – afraid not for his life but for the courage he needed and which would not stand the spectacle of these unfortunates.

The French had ceased firing at this field strewn with dead and wounded where there was no one left to kill, but seeing an adjutant riding across they trained a gun on him and fired several shots. The sensation caused by those terrible whistling sounds and the spectacle of the corpses around him merged in Rostov's mind into a single feeling of terror and self-commiseration. He recalled his mother's last letter. 'How would she feel,' he thought, 'if she could see me now here on this field, with the cannon aimed at me?'

At the village of Gostieradeck there were Russian troops retiring from the field of battle, who though in some confusion were less disordered. Here they were out of range of the French cannon, and the musketry-fire sounded far away. Here everyone clearly saw and openly said that the battle was lost. No one to whom Rostov applied could tell him where the Emperor was, or Kutuzov. Some said that the rumour was true that the Emperor had been wounded, others said not and explained the widely-spread false report by the fact that the Emperor's carriage had dashed from the field of battle with the pale and terrified Grand Marshal Count Tolstoy, who had ridden out to the battle-field with others of the Emperor's suite. One officer told Rostov that he had seen someone from headquarters behind the village to the left, and thither Rostov rode, with no hope now of finding anyone but simply to satisfy his conscience. After going a couple of miles and passing the last of the Russian troops, he saw, near a kitchen-garden with a ditch round it, two mounted men facing the ditch. One with a white plume in his hat somehow seemed a familiar figure to Rostov; the other, a stranger on a beautiful chestnut (which Rostov fancied he had seen before) rode up to the ditch, put spurs to his horse and giving it its head leaped lightly over and into the garden. Only a little earth from the bank crumbled off under the animal's hind hooves. Turning sharply, he jumped the ditch again and deferentially addressed the horseman with the white plume, apparently urging him to do the same. The rider, whose figure Rostov seemed to know and which somehow riveted his attention, shook his head and made a gesture of refusal with his hand, and by that gesture Rostov immediately recognized his lamented, his idolized Sovereign.

'But it can't be he, alone in the middle of this empty field!' thought Rostov. At that moment Alexander turned his head and Rostov saw the beloved features that were so deeply engraved on his memory. The Emperor was pale, his cheeks looked sunken and his eyes hollow, but the charm, the gentleness of his face, was all the more striking. Rostov felt happy in the certainty that the rumours about the Emperor being wounded were false. He was happy to be seeing him. He knew that he might, that indeed he ought to go straight to him and deliver the message Dolgorukov had commanded him to deliver.

But as a youth in love trembles and turns faint and dares not utter what he has spent nights in dreaming of, and looks around in terror, seeking aid or a chance of delay and flight, when the longed-for moment arrives and he is alone with *her*, so Rostov, now that he had attained what he had longed for beyond everything in the world, did not know how to approach the Emperor, and a thousand reasons occurred to him why it would be untimely, improper and impossible to do so.

'Why, it's as though I were glad to take advantage of his being alone and despondent! It might be disagreeable or painful for him to see a strange face at this moment of sorrow. Besides, what could I say to him now, when my heart fails me and my mouth feels dry at the mere sight of him?' Not one of the innumerable speeches he had addressed to the Tsar in his imagination could he recall now. Those speeches were for the most part framed for quite different conditions: to be spoken pre-eminently at moments of victory and triumph, above all, on his death-bed, as he lay dying of wounds and the Sovereign thanked him for his heroic exploits, while he gave expression as he died to the love he had proved by his conduct.

334

'Besides, how am I to ask the Emperor for his instructions to the right flank when it's four o'clock in the afternoon and the battle is lost? No, I certainly ought not to ride up to him, I must not intrude on his melancholy. Better die a thousand deaths than meet with an angry look, or give him a bad opinion of me,' Rostov decided, and with grief and despair in his heart he rode away, continually looking back at the Tsar, who still stood in the same attitude of indecision.

While Rostov was thus arguing with himself and riding sadly away, Captain von Toll chanced to ride up to the same spot, and seeing the Emperor went straight up to him, offered his services and assisted him to cross the ditch on foot. The Emperor, feeling unwell and in need of rest, sat down under an apple-tree, and von Toll remained beside him. Rostov from a distance saw with envy and heart-burning how von Toll talked long and ardently to the Emperor and how the Emperor, apparently weeping, covered his eyes with one hand and with the other pressed von Toll's hand.

'And I might have been in his place,' thought Rostov, and with difficulty restraining his tears of pity for the Emperor he rode away in utter despair, not knowing where he should go or for what reason.

His despair was all the more bitter because he felt that his own weakness was the cause of his unhappiness.

He might ... not only might but ought to have gone up to the Sovereign. It was a unique chance of showing his devotion to the Emperor and he had not made use of it.... 'What have I done?' he thought. And he turned his horse about and galloped back to the spot where he had seen the Emperor; but there was no one on the other side of the ditch now. A train of baggage-wagons and carriages was winding along. From one of the drivers he learnt that Kutuzov's staff were not far off, in the village the vehicles were bound for. Rostov followed them.

In front of him walked Kutuzov's groom, leading horses in horse-cloths. Then came a cart, and behind that went an old bandy-legged domestic serf in a peaked cap and jacket.

'Tit! I say, Tit!' cried the groom.

'What?' responded the old man absent-mindedly.

'Go, Tit, thresh a tit-bit!'

'Ugh, fool you!' said the old man, spitting angrily. A short interval of silence followed, and then the same joke was repeated.

*

Before five o'clock that evening the battle had been lost at every point. More than a hundred cannon were already in the possession of the French.

Przhebyzhewski and his corps had laid down their arms. Other columns, after losing half their strength, were retreating in confused, disorderly masses.

All that were left of Langeron's and Dokhturov's forces were crowded together around the pools and sluices of the village of Augest.

By six o'clock the only firing still to be heard was a heavy cannonade directed at the dam of Augest by the French who had established numerous batteries on the slopes of the Pratzen and were trying to cut down our men as they retreated.

In the rearguard Dokhturov and others, rallying their battalions, kept up a musketry-fire at the French cavalry who were pursuing our troops. It was growing dark. On the narrow Augest dam where for so many years the old miller in his tasselled cap had sat peacefully angling, while his grandson, with shirt-sleeves rolled up, plunged his arms into the water-can among the wriggling silvery fish; on that dam where for so many years the Moravians in their shaggy caps and blue jackets had peacefully driven their two-horse teams, loaded with wheat, to the mill, and returned dusty with flour that whitened their carts – on that narrow dam amid army vans and field-pieces, under the horses' hooves and between the wagon-wheels, men with faces distorted with fear of death now crowded together, crushing one another, expiring, trampling on the dying and killing each other, only to move on a few steps and be killed themselves in the same way.

Every ten seconds a cannon-ball flew over, lashing the air, or a shell burst in the midst of that dense throng, slaying some and spurting their blood on those who were near.

Dolohov, wounded in the arm, with ten men of his company on foot (he was an officer again now), and the regimental commander on horseback, represented all that remained of an entire regiment. Carried along by the press, they had got wedged in the approach to the dam and stood, jammed in on all sides, because a horse in front had fallen under a cannon and the crowd were dragging it out. A cannon-ball killed someone behind them, another fell in front, and Dolohov was splashed with blood. The mob, pushing forward desperately, squeezed together, moved a few steps and stopped again.

'A hundred paces more and I shall be safe; but another couple of minutes here is certain death,' each man was thinking.

Dolohov, standing in the centre of the crowd, forced his way to the edge of the dam, knocking down two soldiers, and ran on to the slippery ice that covered the mill-pool.

'Turn this way!' he shouted, leaping over the ice, which creaked under him. 'Turn this way!' he cried to the men with the gun. 'It holds!'

The ice bore him but it swayed and cracked, and clearly, far from supporting a cannon or a number of people, it would very shortly give way under his weight alone. The others looked at him and crowded to the bank, unable to bring themselves to step on to the ice. The general on horseback at the entry to the dam raised his hand and opened his mouth to speak to Dolohov. Suddenly a cannon-ball hissed so low overhead that everyone ducked. There was a flop as though the ball had struck something soft, and the general fell from his horse in a pool of blood. No one gave him a look, or thought of picking him up.

'On to the ice! Go over the ice! Get on! Turn round! Don't you hear? Go on!' quickly shouted innumerable voices, after the ball had struck the general, though they knew not what nor why they were shouting.

One of the guns in the rear that was just moving on to the dam turned off on to the ice. A crowd of soldiers from the dam began running on to the frozen pond. The ice cracked under one of the first of them, and his leg slipped into the water. He tried to right himself and floundered in up to the waist. The soldiers nearest shrank back, the gun-driver pulled up his horse, but from behind still came the shouts: 'Take to the ice! What are you stopping for? Get on! Get on!' And screams of terror were heard in the crowd. The soldiers near the cannon waved their arms and lashed the horses to make them turn and move forward. The horses started off the bank. The ice that held under the foot-soldiers broke in a huge sheet and some forty men dashed, some forward, some back, pushing each other under water.

All the time the cannon-balls whizzed regularly by, smacking on to the ice, into the water and oftenest of all into the crowd that covered the dam, the ponds and the bank.

ON the Pratzen heights, at the spot where he had fallen with the flagstaff in his hand, lay Prince Andrei Bolkonsky, losing blood and, without realizing it, moaning a soft, plaintive moan like a child.

Towards evening his complaining ceased and he became quite still. He did not know how long his unconsciousness lasted. Suddenly he felt again that he was alive and suffering from a burning, lacerating pain in his head.

'Where is it, that lofty sky I saw today and had never seen before?' was his first thought. 'And this agony I did not know either,' he thought. 'Yes, I knew nothing, nothing till now. But where am I?'

He listened, and heard the sound of approaching hooves and voices speaking French. He opened his eyes. Above him again was the same lofty sky with clouds floating higher than ever and between them stretches of blue infinity. He did not turn his head and did not see those who, judging from the voices and the clatter of hooves, had ridden up to him and stopped.

The horsemen were Napoleon escorted by two aides-de-camp. Bonaparte, making a tour of the field of battle, had been giving final orders to strengthen the batteries firing at the Augest dam, and was now inspecting the dead and wounded left on the field.

'Fine men!' remarked Napoleon, looking at a dead Russian grenadier who lay on his belly with his face half buried in the soil, his neck turned black and one arm flung out and stiffened in death.

'The field-guns have exhausted their ammunition, sire,' said an adjutant arriving that moment from the batteries that were firing at Augest.

'Have more brought from the reserve,' said Napoleon, and having gone on a few yards he stopped by Prince Andrei, who lay on his back with the flagstaff that he had dropped beside him. (The flag had been carried off by the French as a trophy.)

'That's a fine death!' said Napoleon, looking down at Bolkonsky.

Prince Andrei grasped that this was said of him, and that it was Napoleon saying it. He heard the speaker addressed as *Sire*. But he heard the words as he might have heard the buzzing of a fly. Not only did they not interest him – they made no impression upon him, and were immediately forgotten. There was a burning pain in his head;

he felt that his life-blood was ebbing away, and he saw far above him the remote, eternal heavens. He knew it was Napoleon – his hero – but at that moment Napoleon seemed to him such a small, insignificant creature compared with what was passing now between his own soul and that lofty, limitless firmament with the clouds flying over it. It meant nothing to him at that moment who might be standing over him, or what was said of him: he was only glad that people were standing near, and his only desire was that these people should help him and bring him back to life, which seemed to him so beautiful now that he had learned to see it differently. He made a supreme effort to stir and utter some sound. He moved his leg feebly and gave a weak, sickly groan which aroused his own pity.

'Ah, he is alive!' said Napoleon. 'Pick up this young man – *ce jeune homme* – and carry him to the dressing-station.'

Having said this, Napoleon passed on to meet Marshal Lannes, who, hat in hand, rode smiling up to the Emperor to congratulate him on the victory.

Prince Andrei remembered nothing more: he became insensible from the excruciating pain of being lifted on to the stretcher, the jolting while he was being moved, and the probing of his wound at the dressing-station. He did not regain consciousness till late in the day, when with the other wounded and captured Russian officers he was being taken to the hospital. During this transfer he felt a little stronger and was able to look about him, even to speak.

The first words he heard on coming to himself were those of a French convoy officer who was saying hurriedly:

'We must halt here: the Emperor will be coming this way directly. He will like to see these gentlemen-prisoners.'

'There are so many prisoners today – practically the whole Russian army – that I should think he's sick of them,' said another officer.

'All the same! They say this one was the commander of all the Emperor Alexander's Guards,' said the first speaker, pointing to a wounded Russian officer in the white uniform of the Horse Guards.

Bolkonsky recognized Prince Repnin whom he had met in Petersburg society. Next to him stood another officer of the Horse Guards, a lad of nineteen, also wounded.

Bonaparte rode up at a gallop and reined in his horse.

'Who is the senior officer here?' he asked, on seeing the prisoners.

They named the colonel, Prince Repnin.

'Were you the commander of the Emperor Alexander's regiment of Horse Guards?' asked Napoleon.

'I commanded a squadron,' replied Repnin.

'Your regiment did its duty honourably,' said Napoleon.

'Praise from a great general is the highest reward a soldier can have,' said Repnin.

'I bestow it upon you with pleasure,' said Napoleon. 'And who is that young man beside you?'

Prince Repnin named Lieutenant Suhtelen.

Napoleon looked at him and smiled. 'He is very young to try odds with us.'

'Youth is no bar to courage,' muttered Suhtelen in a choked voice.

'A fine answer!' said Napoleon. 'Young man, you will go far!'

Prince Andrei, who had also been thrust forward under the Emperor's eyes to complete the array of prisoners, could not fail to attract his attention. Napoleon apparently remembered seeing him on the battlefield, and addressing him he used the same epithet '*jeune homme*' with which his first sight of Bolkonsky was associated in his memory.

'Well, and you, young man,' said he. 'How do you feel, *mon brave*?'

Although five minutes previously Prince Andrei had been able to say a few words to the soldiers who were carrying him, now with his eyes fixed steadily on Napoleon he was silent.... So trivial seemed to him at that moment all the interests that engrossed Napoleon, so petty did his hero with his paltry vanity and delight in victory appear, compared to that lofty, righteous and kindly sky which he had seen and comprehended, that he could not answer him.

Everything did indeed seem so futile and insignificant in comparison with the stern and solemn train of thought induced in him by his lapsing consciousness, as his life-blood ebbed away, by his suffering and the nearness of death. Gazing into Napoleon's eyes, Prince Andrei mused on the unimportance of greatness, the unimportance of life which no one could understand, and the still greater unimportance of death, the meaning of which no one alive could understand or explain.

The Emperor, after pausing in vain for an answer, turned away and said to one of the officers as he moved on:

'See that these gentlemen are looked after and taken to my bivouac. Let my surgeon, Dr Larrey, attend to their wounds. *Au revoir*, Prince Repnin!' and he spurred his horse and galloped away.

His face was radiant with happiness and self-satisfaction.

The soldiers who had been carrying Prince Andrei had removed from him the little gold icon Princess Maria had placed round her brother's neck, but when they saw the friendly manner with which the Emperor treated the prisoners they hastened to restore the holy image.

Prince Andrei did not see how or by whom it was replaced but the little icon with its delicate gold chain suddenly appeared on his chest outside his uniform.

'How good it would be,' thought Prince Andrei, letting his eyes rest on the icon which his sister had hung round his neck with such emotion and reverence, 'how good it would be if everything were as clear and simple as it seems to Marie. How good it would be to know where to seek help in this life, and what to expect after it, beyond the grave! How happy and at peace I should be if I could say now: "Lord, have mercy on me! …" But to whom am I to say that? Is it to the great Power, indefinable, incomprehensible, which I not only cannot turn to but which I cannot even express in words – the great All or Nothing,' said he to himself, 'or is it to that God who has been sewn into this amulet by Marie? Nothing, nothing is certain, except the unimportance of everything within my comprehension and the grandeur of something incomprehensible but all-important.'

The stretchers started off. At every jolt he felt intolerable pain again; his fever increased and he sank into delirium. The visions of his father, his wife, his sister and his unborn son, and the tenderness he had felt on the night before the battle, the figure of the insignificant little Napoleon, and over all these the lofty sky, formed the chief substance of his delirious fancies.

The quiet home life and peaceful happiness of Bald Hills passed before his imagination. He was enjoying that happiness when that little Napoleon suddenly appeared with his indifferent, narrow look of satisfaction at the misery of others, and was followed by doubts and torments, and only the heavens promised peace. Towards morning all these dreams ran together and slid into the chaos and obscurity of unconsciousness and oblivion, the outcome of which in the opinion of Napoleon's surgeon, Dr Larrey, was far more likely to be death than recovery.

'A nervous, spleeny subject,' said Larrey, 'he won't recover.'

And Prince Andrei, together with the other hopeless cases, was handed over to the care of the inhabitants of the district.

WAR AND PEACE

*

BOOK TWO

PART ONE

I

EARLY in the year 1806 Nikolai Rostov returned home on leave. Denisov, too, was going home to Voronezh and had been persuaded by Rostov to travel with him as far as Moscow and there pay the Rostovs a visit. Denisov met his comrade at the last posting-station but one, emptied three bottles of wine with him, and after that, in spite of the ruts on the road to Moscow, slept soundly, lying at the bottom of the sledge beside Rostov, who grew more and more impatient as they got nearer to Moscow.

'Is it much farther? Is it much farther? Oh, these insufferable streets, these shops and bakers' signs, street-lamps and sledges!' thought Rostov, when they had presented their leave-permits at the town gates and were driving into Moscow.

'Denisov, we're here! Asleep!' he exclaimed, leaning forward with his whole body as if by that position he hoped to hasten the progress of the sledge.

Denisov made no response.

'There's the corner at the cross-roads, where Zahar the cabman has his stand – and there's Zahar himself, and still the same horse. And here's the little shop where we used to buy gingerbread! Oh, when shall we be there? Hurry!'

'Which house is it?' asked the driver.

'Why, that one over there at the end – the big one, don't you see? That's our house,' said Rostov. 'That's our house, of course! Denisov, Denisov, we shall be there in a minute!'

Denisov raised his head, cleared his throat, and said nothing.

'Dimitri,' said Rostov to his valet on the box, 'those lights are in our house, aren't they?'

'To be sure, sir; and there's a light in your father's study.'

'So they haven't gone to bed yet? What do you think? Mind now, don't forget to put out my new Hungarian tunic,' added Rostov, fingering his new moustache. 'Now then, get on,' he shouted to the driver. 'And do wake up, Vasska,' he continued, turning to Denisov, whose head was nodding again. 'Come on, get along – you shall have three roubles for vodka, but do get on!' Rostov shouted, when the sledge was only three doors away. It seemed to him that the horses were not moving. At last the sledge bore to the right and drew up at the steps. Rostov saw the familiar cornice with the bit of broken plaster overhead, the porch, the kerb-stone. He sprang out while the sledge was still moving, and ran into the vestibule. The house stood cold and silent, as though it were not concerned that he had come home. There was no one in the hall. 'Oh, God, is everything all right?' he thought, stopping for a moment with a sinking heart and then immediately starting to run through the vestibule and up the familiar crooked steps. There was the same old door-handle, which always annoyed the countess when it was not properly cleaned, as loose and as much askew as ever. A solitary tallow candle burned in the ante-room.

Old Mihail was asleep on his perch. Prokofy, the footman, who was so strong that he could lift the back of the carriage off the ground, sat plaiting bast shoes out of odd strips of cloth. He looked up as the door opened, and his expression of sleepy indifference was suddenly transformed into one of delighted amazement.

'Merciful heavens! The young count!' he cried, recognizing his young master. 'Is it possible? Me darlin'!' And Prokofy, trembling with excitement, rushed towards the drawing-room door, probably with the intention of announcing him; but apparently he changed his mind, for he came back and fell on his young master's neck.

'All well?' asked Rostov, drawing away his arm.

'Yes, yes, God be praised! They've just finished supper! Let us have a look at you, your Excellency!'

'Everything quite all right?'

'Yes, praise be!'

Rostov had entirely forgotten Denisov. Not wishing anyone to forestall him and announce his arrival, he pulled off his fur coat and ran on tiptoe into the great dark ballroom. Everything was the same: the same old card tables and the same chandelier with a cover over it; but someone had already seen the young master, and before he could reach the drawing-room something swooped out of a side door like a tornado and began hugging and kissing him. A second and a third figure sprang in from a second and a third door; more hugging, more kissing, more outcries and tears of joy. He could not distinguish which was Papa, which Natasha, which Petya. Everyone shouted and talked and kissed him at the same time. Only his mother was not there, he noticed that.

'And to think I never knew.... My little Nikolai ... dear boy!'

'Here he is ... our Nikolai.... How he's changed! ... Where are the candles? Let us have some tea!'

'And me, kiss me!'

'Darling Nikolai ... me too!'

Sonya, Natasha, Petya, Anna Mihalovna, Vera and the old count were all hugging him; and the men-servants and maids flocked into the room, exclaiming and oh-ing and ah-ing.

Petya, clinging to his legs, kept shouting, 'And me too!'

Natasha, after pulling him down to her and covering his face with kisses, skipped back and keeping hold of his jacket pranced up and down like a goat in the same spot, uttering shrill shrieks.

On all sides were loving eyes glistening with tears of joy, and on all sides were lips seeking a kiss.

Sonya too, as red as turkey twill, clung to his arm and radiant with bliss looked eagerly into the eyes she had been so longing to see. Sonya was turned sixteen now and very pretty, especially at this moment of happy, rapturous excitement. She gazed, unable to take her eyes off him, smiling and holding her breath. He gave her a grateful glance, but was still expectant and looking for someone else. The old countess had not yet made her appearance. But now footsteps were heard at the door, steps so rapid that they could hardly be his mother's.

Yet she it was, in a new gown which he did not know, made during his absence. The others all let him go, and he ran to her. When they came together she fell on his breast sobbing. She could not lift her face but only pressed it to the cold braiding of his hussar's jacket. Denisov, who had come into the room unnoticed by anyone, stood there looking at them and rubbing his eyes.

'Vasili Denisov, your son's fwiend,' he said, introducing himself to the count who looked at him inquiringly.

'Welcome! I know, I know,' said the count, kissing and embracing him. 'Nikolai wrote us. ... Natasha, Vera, look – here is Denisov!'

The same happy ecstatic faces were turned to Denisov's shaggy figure, surrounding him.

'Darling Denisov!' squealed Natasha, and beside herself with delight she darted up, threw her arms round him and kissed him. Everyone was embarrassed at this. Denisov too blushed, but smiled and taking Natasha's hand kissed it.

Denisov was conducted to the room prepared for him, while the Rostovs all gathered round Nikolai in the sitting-room.

The old countess, not letting go of his hand, which she kept kissing every minute, sat beside him. The rest, crowding round, caught his every movement, word, look, and could not take their blissfully adoring eyes off him. His brother and sisters quarrelled and disputed with each other for the places nearest to him, and fought with one another as to who should bring him tea, a handkerchief or his pipe.

Rostov was very happy in the love they showed him; but the first moment of meeting had been so blissful that his happiness now seemed a little tame, and he kept expecting something more and more, and yet more.

Next morning, after their journey, the travellers slept on till ten o'clock.

The adjoining room was littered with sabres, bags, sabretaches, open portmanteaux and dirty boots. Two pairs of clean boots with spurs had just been placed by the wall. Servants were bringing in wash-basins, hot water for shaving and clothes well-brushed. There was a masculine odour and a smell of tobacco.

'Hey, Gwishka – my pipe!' shouted Vasska Denisov in his husky voice. 'Wostov, get up!'

Rostov, rubbing his eyes that seemed glued together, lifted his tousled head from the warm pillow.

'Why, is it late?'

'Late! It's getting on for ten o'clock,' answered Natasha's voice, and in the next room they heard the rustle of starched petticoats and girlish whispering and laughter. The door was opened a crack, to reveal a glimpse of something blue, of ribbons, black hair and merry faces. It was Natasha, with Sonya and Petya, come to see whether their brother was up.

'Nikolai! Do get up!' Natasha's voice was heard at the door again.

'Directly!'

Meanwhile Petya in the outer room had espied and seized upon the sabres with the rapture small boys feel at the sight of a military elder brother, and forgetting that it was hardly correct for his sisters to see the young men undressed pushed upon the bedroom door.

'Is this your sabre?' he shouted.

The girls skipped back. Denisov hid his hairy legs under the counterpane, looking with a scared face to his comrade for help. The door admitted Petya and closed after him. A giggle was heard from outside.

'Nikolai darling, come out in your dressing-gown,' cried Natasha's voice.

'Is this your sabre?' asked Petya. 'Or is it yours?' he said, addressing the black-moustached Denisov with slavish respect.

Rostov hurriedly put something on his feet, threw his dressing-gown over his shoulders and went out. Natasha had got one spurred boot on and was just slipping her foot into the other. Sonya when he came in was spinning round to make her skirts into a balloon and then duck down. They were dressed alike in new pale-blue frocks, and both were fresh, rosy and full of spirits. Sonya ran away, but Natasha, taking her brother's arm, led him into the sitting-room, where they began talking. They hardly gave one another time to ask and answer all the questions in regard to a thousand and one trifles which could only be of interest to themselves. Natasha laughed at every word he said and at every word she said herself, not because what they were saying was amusing but because she felt happy and was unable to contain her joy which brimmed over into laughter.

'Oh, how nice, how splendid!' she said to everything.

Rostov felt that, under the influence of the warm sunshine of love, for the first time for eighteen months his soul and his face were expanding into the childlike smile which had not once appeared on his countenance since he left home.

'No, but listen,' she said, 'you're a grown-up man now, aren't you? I'm awfully glad you're my brother.' She touched his moustache. 'I want to know what men are really like. Are you like us? Yes? No?'

'Why did Sonya run away?' asked Rostov.

'Oh, that is a whole long story! How are you going to speak to Sonya – shall you call her "thou" or "you"?'

'I don't know – just as it happens,' said Rostov.

'Call her "you", please. I'll tell you why afterwards.'

'But why?'

'All right, I'll tell you now. You know Sonya's my dearest friend – so much my friend that I would burn my hand off for her. Here, look!'

She pulled up her muslin sleeve and showed him a red scar on her long, thin, soft arm, well above the elbow, near the shoulder (in a place where it would be covered even in a ball-gown).

'I did that to prove how much I loved her! I just heated a ruler in the fire and pressed it there.'

Sitting in his old schoolroom on the sofa with the little cushions on its arms, and looking into Natasha's wildly excited eyes, Rostov was carried back into that world of home and childhood which had no meaning for anyone else but gave him some of the sweetest joys of life. And burning one's arm with a ruler as a proof of love did not seem pointless to him: he understood, and was not surprised.

'So that was what you did? No more?' he asked.

'We are such friends, such great friends! All that with the ruler is nothing, but we are friends for ever and ever. If she loves anyone, it's for ever; but I don't understand that, I forget so quickly.'

'Well, what then?'

'Well, she loves me and you like that.' Natasha suddenly flushed. 'Well, you remember before you went away? ... Well, she says you are to forget all that. ... She said, "I shall always love him, but let him be free." Isn't that lovely and noble now? Yes, yes, very noble! It is, isn't it?' asked Natasha so seriously and with such feeling that evidently what she was saying now she had talked of before with tears.

Rostov was silent.

Then, 'I never go back on my word,' he said. 'And besides, Sonya is so charming that only a fool would refuse such happiness.'

'No, no!' cried Natasha. 'She and I have already talked it over. We knew you'd say that. But it won't do, because, don't you see, if you say that – if you consider yourself bound by your promise – it would look as if she had said it on purpose? It makes it as though you were marrying her because you were obliged to, and that wouldn't do at all.'

Rostov saw that they had considered the whole question thoroughly. He had already been struck the evening before by Sonya's beauty; in the glimpse he had caught of her today she seemed even lovelier. She was a charming girl of sixteen, obviously passionately in love with him (he did not doubt that for an instant). Why should he not love her now, and even marry her, mused Rostov; but just at present he had so many other pleasures and interests before him! 'Yes, they have come to a wise conclusion,' he thought. 'I must remain free.'

'Well, that's all right then,' said he. 'We'll talk it over later on. Oh, how glad I am to be back with you!' he added. 'Well, and are you still true to Boris?' he asked.

'Oh, that's all nonsense!' cried Natasha, laughing. 'I don't think about him or anyone else, and I don't want to.'

'Oh, you don't, don't you! Then what are you up to now?'

'I?' queried Natasha, and a happy smile lit up her face. 'Have you seen Duport?'

'No.'

'Never seen Duport, the famous dancer? Well, then, you won't understand. That's what I'm up to.'

Curving her arms, Natasha held out her skirt in the way dancers do, ran back a few steps, turned round, executed a pirouette, brought her little feet sharply together and walked a few steps on the very tips of her toes.

'See, I'm standing on my toes! Look!' she said, but could not keep up on her toes. 'That's what I'm going to do. I'll never marry anyone: I'm going to be a dancer. Only don't tell anybody.'

Rostov laughed so loudly and merrily that Denisov in his room felt envious, and Natasha could not help joining in.

'No, but don't you think it a nice idea?' she kept repeating.

'Oh, quite. So you don't want to marry Boris now?'

Natasha flared up.

'I don't want to marry anyone. I'll tell him so myself when I see him.'

'Dear me!' said Rostov.

'But this is all nonsense,' Natasha prattled on. 'Is Denisov nice?' she asked.

'Very.'

'Well, good-bye for now. You go and dress. Is he a frightening person, Denisov?'

'Why should he be frightening?' asked Nikolai. 'No, Vasska's a capital fellow.'

'You call him Vasska? How funny! So he's very nice, is he?'

'Very nice.'

'Well, make haste now. We'll all have breakfast together.'

And Natasha rose on her toes and glided out of the room like a ballet dancer, but smiling as only happy girls of fifteen can smile. When Rostov met Sonya in the drawing-room he reddened. He did not know how to behave with her. Yesterday they had kissed in the first joyful moment of meeting again, but today they felt that out of the question. He felt that everybody, including his mother and sisters, was looking inquiringly at him and watching to see how he would behave with her. He kissed her hand and called her *you* and *Sonya*. But their eyes met and said *thou*, and exchanged tender kisses. Her eyes asked his forgiveness for having dared, through Natasha, to remind him of his promise, and thanked him for his love. His were thanking her for offering him his freedom, and telling her that one way or another he would never cease to love her, for it was impossible not to love her.

'But how funny it is,' said Vera, choosing a moment when all were silent, 'that Sonya and Nikolai meet as though they were strangers and call each other "you".'

Vera's remark was true enough, like all her observations, but like most of them it made everyone – not only Sonya, Nikolai and Natasha – feel uncomfortable, and the old countess, who feared lest her son's love for Sonya should stand in the way of his making a brilliant match, also coloured up like a girl.

To Rostov's surprise, Denisov pomaded and perfumed and in his new uniform, cut quite as dashing a figure in the drawing-room as on the field of battle, and showed himself more amiable to the ladies and gentlemen than Rostov had ever expected.

2

ON his return to Moscow from the army, Nikolai Rostov was welcomed by his home circle as the best of sons, a hero, their beloved Nikolai; by his relations as a charming, attractive and polite young man; by his acquaintances as a handsome lieutenant of hussars, a graceful dancer and one of the best matches in town.

The Rostovs knew everybody in Moscow. The old count had money enough that year, as all his estates had been remortgaged, and so Nikolai, acquiring a swift trotter of his own, very stylish riding-breeches such as no one else in Moscow yet had, and boots of the latest fashion with extremely pointed toes and small silver spurs, was able to spend his time very agreeably. After a short period of adapting himself to the old conditions of life, Nikolai found it very pleasant to be at home again. He felt that he had grown up and become very much a man. His despair at failing in a Scripture examination, the days when he had borrowed money from Gavrila to pay a sledge-driver, the secret kisses he had given Sonya he now looked back on as childishness which he had left immeasurably behind. Now he was a lieutenant of hussars in a jacket laced with silver and wearing the cross of St George (awarded to soldiers for bravery in action), and in the company of well-known racing men, elderly and respected persons, was training a trotter of his own for a race. There was a lady of his acquaintance on the boulevard whom he visited of an evening. He led the mazurka at the Arharovs' ball, talked about the war with Field-Marshal Kamensky, frequented the English Club, and was on intimate terms with a colonel of forty to whom Denisov had introduced him.

His passion for the Emperor had cooled somewhat in Moscow, since he did not see him and had no opportunity of doing so all that time. But still he often talked about him and his love for him, letting it be understood that he could say more and that there was something in his feelings for the Emperor which not everyone could understand; and with his whole soul he shared the adoration, general in that period in Moscow, for the Emperor Alexander Pavlovich, who was spoken of as the 'angel incarnate'.

During this brief stay in Moscow, before rejoining the army, Rostov did not draw closer to Sonya but, on the contrary, drifted away from her. She was very pretty and sweet, and obviously deeply in love with him; but he was going through that phase of young manhood when there seems so much to do that there is *no time* for that sort of thing, and the young man dreads to bind himself, and prizes his freedom which he needs for so much else. When he thought of Sonya during this stay in Moscow he said to himself, 'Ah well, I shall find plenty more like her, plenty whom I have not yet seen! There will be time enough to think about love when I want to, but now I am too busy.' Besides, it seemed to him that feminine society was somehow beneath his manly dignity. He went to balls and into

353

ladies' society with an affectation of doing so against his will. The races, the English Club, junketing with Denisov and visits to a certain house were another matter and quite the thing for a dashing young hussar.

At the beginning of March old Count Rostov was much occupied with the arrangements for a dinner at the English Club in honour of Prince Bagration. Walking up and down the hall in his dressing-gown, he gave directions to the club steward and to Feoktist, the famous head chef, concerning asparagus, fresh cucumbers, straw-berries, veal and fish for the dinner to the prince. From the day of its foundation the count had been a member of the club, and on the committee. To him had they entrusted the preparations for this ban-quet for Bagration, since few men knew so well how to organize a dinner on an open-handed, hospitable scale, and still fewer who would be so well able and willing to advance money, if funds were needed for the success of the fête. The chef and club steward listened to the count's orders with cheerful faces, aware that with no one else could it be so easy to extract a handsome profit for themselves out of a dinner costing several thousands.

'Well, then, mind and have scallops in the turtle soup, you know.'

'So there'll be three cold *entrées*, will there?' asked the chef.

The count pondered.

'I don't see how we can do with less – yes, three … the mayonnaise, that's one,' said he, bending down a finger.

'Then am I to order those large sterlets?' asked the steward.

'Yes, it can't be helped, we must take them if they won't knock the price down. Oh dear, I nearly forgot! Of course we must have another *entrée* on the table. Ah, goodness gracious!' he clutched at his head. 'Who's going to get me the flowers? Mitenka! Here, Mitenka! You sprint off to our country place' (this was just outside Moscow) 'and tell Maxim the gardener to set the serfs to work. Say that everything out of the hothouses is to come here, packed in felting. I must have a couple of hundred pots here by Friday,' he said to the factotum who appeared at his call.

Having given several further commands and directions, he was about to go to his 'little countess' to rest from his labours when he remembered something else of importance, turned back, summoned the chef and the club steward again, and began giving more orders. A light, masculine step and the jingling of spurs were heard at the door, and the young count came in, handsome and rosy, with his darkening moustache, visibly sleeker and in better trim for his easy life in Moscow.

'Ah, my dear boy, my head's in a whirl!' said the old man with a somewhat shamefaced smile at his son. 'You might come to my aid! There are still the singers to get. I shall have my own orchestra, but shouldn't we arrange for some gipsy singers as well? You military gentlemen like that sort of thing.'

'Upon my word, papa, I do believe Prince Bagration took less trouble preparing for the battle of Schön Graben than you are taking now,' said his son, smiling.

The old count pretended to be angry.

'Yes, you can talk, but just you try it yourself!'

And he turned to the chef, who with a shrewd and respectful expression looked observantly and sympathetically from father to son.

'What are the young people coming to, eh, Feoktist?' said the count. 'Laughing at us old fellows!'

'That's so, your Excellency, all they have to do is to eat a good dinner, but providing it and serving it all up – that's no affair of theirs!'

'True, true!' exclaimed the count, and gaily seizing his son by both hands he cried, 'Now I've got you, so take the sledge and pair at once, and go to Bezuhov's, and say your father has sent you to ask for strawberries and fresh pineapples. We can't get them from anyone else. If he's not at home himself, you'll have to go in and ask the princesses; and from there go on to the Gaiety – the coachman Ipatka knows the way – and look up Ilyushka, the gipsy who danced at Count Orlov's, you remember, in a white Cossack coat, and bring him along to me.'

'And am I to fetch some of the gipsy girls with him?' asked Nikolai, laughing.

'Now, now! ...'

At that moment Anna Mihalovna stepped noiselessly into the room with that air of meek Christianity mingled with practical and anxious preoccupation that never left her face. Though she came upon the count in his dressing-gown every day, he was invariably embarrassed and each time apologized for his costume.

'It does not matter at all, my dear count,' she said, modestly closing her eyes. 'But I'll go to Bezuhov's myself. Young Bezuhov has

355

arrived and now we shall get all we want from his hothouses. I have to see him in any case. He has forwarded me a letter from Boris. Thank God, Boris is now on the staff.'

The count was delighted to have Anna Mihalovna take upon herself one of his commissions, and ordered the small closed carriage to be brought round for her.

'Tell Bezuhov to come. I'll put his name down. Is his wife with him?' he asked.

Anna Mihalovna turned up her eyes, and an expression of profound sadness came over her face.

'Ah, my dear, he is very unfortunate,' she said. 'If all we hear is true, it is a dreadful business. Little did we dream of this when we were rejoicing so in his happiness! And such a lofty, angelic nature, that young Bezuhov! Yes, I pity him from the bottom of my heart, and shall try to give him what consolation I can.'

'Why, what has happened?' asked both Rostovs, old and young together.

Anna Mihalovna sighed deeply.

'Dolohov, Maria Ivanovna's son,' she said in a mysterious whisper, 'has, they say, compromised her completely. Pierre took him up, invited him to his house in Petersburg, and now ... she has come here and that scapegrace after her!' said Anna Mihalovna, meaning to show sympathy for Pierre but by the involuntary inflexions of her voice and the half-smile on her face betraying her sympathy for the 'scapegrace', as she called Dolohov. 'They say Pierre is quite broken up by the situation.'

'Well, anyway, tell him to come to the club. It'll all blow over. It will be a sumptuous banquet.'

On the next day, the 3rd of March, soon after one o'clock, the two hundred and fifty members of the English Club and their fifty guests were awaiting the guest of honour, the hero of the Austrian campaign, Prince Bagration. At first Moscow had been quite bewildered by the tidings of the battle of Austerlitz. The Russians at that period were so used to victories that news of a defeat made some people simply incredulous, while others looked for exceptional circumstances of some kind to explain so strange an event. At the English Club, where everyone of note and importance, everyone who had trustworthy sources of information foregathered, when the news began to arrive in December not a word was said about the war or the last battle, as though all were in a conspiracy of silence. The men who generally gave the lead in conversation – Count Rostopchin, Prince Yuri Vladimirovich Dolgoruky, Valuyev, Count Markov and Prince Vyazemsky – did not put in an appearance at the club but met privately together at each other's houses, and that section of Moscow society which took its opinions from others (to which, indeed, Count Rostov belonged) remained for a short time without leaders and without definite views in regard to the progress of the war. People in Moscow felt that something was wrong, and that it was difficult to know what to think of the bad news, and so better to be silent. But after a while, like jurymen emerging from the jury room, the bigwigs who guided opinion in the club reappeared, and a clear and definite formula was produced. Reasons were discovered to account for the incredible, unheard-of and impossible fact that the Russians had been beaten, all became plain and in every corner of Moscow one and the same story was current. The defeat was due, so people told each other, to the treachery of the Austrians, to a defective commissariat, to perfidy on the part of the Pole Przhebyzhewski and the Frenchman Langeron, to Kutuzov's inefficiency and (this in a whisper) to the youth and inexperience of the Sovereign, who had put faith in men of no character or ability. But the army, the Russian army, everyone declared, had been extraordinary and had performed miracles of valour. Soldiers, officers, generals were heroes to a man. But the hero of heroes was Prince Bagration, who had distinguished himself at the Schön Graben affair and in the retreat from Austerlitz, where he alone had withdrawn his column unbroken, and the livelong day had fought back an enemy of twice his strength. What also contributed to Bagration's selection for the rôle of popular hero in Moscow was the fact that he had no connexions in the city and was a stranger there. In his person, honour could be done to the ordinary Russian soldier who had won his way without influence or intrigue, and was still associated, through memories of the Italian campaign, with the name of Suvorov. And besides, paying such honour to Bagration was the best possible way of showing dislike and disapproval of Kutuzov.

'Had there been no Bagration somebody would have had to invent him,' said the wit Shinshin, parodying the words of Voltaire.

Kutuzov, no one spoke of, except those who whispered abuse, calling him the court weathercock and an old satyr.

All Moscow repeated Prince Dolgoruky's dictum: 'If you work with glue, sooner or later you're bound to get stuck,' which offered consolation for our defeat, in the reminder of former victories. Rostopchin, too, was quoted everywhere: 'The French soldier,' pronounced Rostopchin, 'has to be incited to battle by high-sounding phrases; the German must have it logically proved to him that it is more dangerous to run away than to advance; but the Russian soldier has to be held back and urged to go slowly!' Every day fresh stories were to be heard on all sides of individual feats of gallantry performed by our officers and the rank and file at Austerlitz. Here a man had saved a standard, another had killed half a dozen Frenchmen, a third had loaded five cannon single-handed. It was even related of Berg, by strangers, how when wounded in his right hand he had taken his sword in his left and gone forward. Nothing was said about Bolkonsky and only those who had known him intimately lamented that he had died so young, leaving a wife with child, and his eccentric old father.

3

On the 3rd of March all the rooms in the English Club buzzed with conversation, and, like bees swarming in spring, members and their guests wandered back and forth, sat, stood, met and separated, some in uniform, some in tailcoats and a few here and there with powdered hair and in Russian kaftans. Powdered and liveried footmen wearing buckled shoes and silk stockings stood at every door, anxiously trying to anticipate every movement of the guests and club members so as to proffer their services. The majority of those present were elderly and respected persons with broad, self-satisfied faces, plump fingers, and resolute gestures and voices. The guests and members of this class occupied certain habitual places and met together in certain habitual circles. A small proportion of those present were casual guests – chiefly young men, among them Denisov, Rostov, and Dolohov, now reinstated in the Semeonovsk regiment again. The faces of these younger men, especially the officers, bore that expression of condescending deference for their elders which seems to say to the older generation: 'We are ready to respect and honour you, but don't you forget that the future belongs to us.'

Nesvitsky was there too, as an old member of the club. Pierre, who at his wife's command had let his hair grow and abandoned his spectacles, walked about the rooms dressed in the height of fashion but looking sad and depressed. Here, as everywhere else, he was surrounded by an atmosphere of subservience to his wealth, and he treated the sycophants with the careless, contemptuous air of sovereignty that had become habitual with him.

In years, he belonged to the younger generation, but his fortune and connexions gave him a place among the senior and more influential set, and so he drifted from one group to another. Some of the most distinguished of the elder members formed the centres of circles which even strangers respectfully approached for the purpose of listening to the great. The largest groups were gathered round Count Rostopchin, Valuyev and Naryshkin. Rostopchin was describing how the Russians had been trampled underfoot by the fleeing Austrians, and had had to force their way through at the point of the bayonet.

Valuyev was confidentially informing his circle that Uvarov had been sent from Petersburg to ascertain what Moscow was thinking about Austerlitz.

In the third group Naryshkin was repeating the old story of the Austrian council of war at which Suvorov crowed like a cock in reply to the nonsense talked by the Austrian generals. Shinshin, who stood near, tried to make a joke, saying that Kutuzov had evidently not been able to learn from Suvorov even so simple a thing as the art of crowing like a cock, but the elder members looked sternly at the wag, giving him to understand that here and on this day it was out of place to speak so of Kutuzov.

Count Ilya Rostov, in his soft boots, hovered anxiously between dining-room and drawing-room, muttering hasty greetings to the important and unimportant alike, all of whom he knew, while every now and then his eyes sought out and feasted on the graceful, dashing figure of his young son, to whom he would send a wink of satisfaction. Young Rostov stood at the window with Dolohov, whose acquaintance he had recently made and greatly prized. The old count went up to them and shook hands with Dolohov.

'You will come and visit us, I hope. So you're a friend of my youngster's ... been playing the hero together out there. ... Ah, Vasili Ignatich ... How d'ye do, *mon vieux* ?' he said, turning to an old man who was passing them, but before he had finished his greeting there was a general stir and a footman came running in to announce with awe-struck countenance: 'He's arrived!'

Bells rang, the stewards rushed forward and the guests, who had been scattered about in the different rooms, congregated like rye shaken together in a shovel, and crowded at the door of the great drawing-room.

Bagration appeared in the doorway of the ante-room without hat or sword, which in accord with the club custom he had given up to the hall-porter. He had no astrakhan cap on his head, nor whip over his shoulder, as when Rostov had seen him on the eve of the battle of Austerlitz, but wore a tight new uniform with Russian and foreign orders, and the star of St George on his left breast. Evidently, with a view to the dinner, he had had his hair and whiskers trimmed, which did not change his appearance for the better. His face had a sort of naïvely festive expression which, in conjunction with his firm, virile features, gave him a rather comical look. Bekleshov and Fiodr Petrovich Uvarov, who had arrived with him, paused at the doorway to allow him, as guest of honour, to precede them. Bagration was embarrassed, and unwilling to avail himself of their courtesy: this caused some delay at the door, but finally Bagration did, after all, enter first. He walked shyly and awkwardly over the parquet floor of the reception-room, not knowing what to do with his hands: he would have been more at home and at his ease tramping over a ploughed field under fire, as he had at the head of the Kursk regiment at Schön Graben. The stewards met him at the first door and, expressing their delight at seeing such an illustrious guest, took possession of him, as it were, and, without waiting for his reply, surrounded and led him to the drawing-room. It was impossible to get into the room for the crowd of members and guests, jostling one another in their efforts to look over each other's shoulders at Bagration, as if he were some rare sort of wild animal. Count Ilya Rostov, laughing and repeating the words, 'Make way, *mon cher!* Make way, make way!' pushed through the throng more energetically than anyone, conducted the guests into the drawing-room and seated them on the sofa in the middle. The bigwigs, the most respected members of the club, beset the new arrivals. Count Ilya, again thrusting his way through the crowd, left the drawing-room and reappeared a minute later with another steward bearing a huge silver salver which he presented to Prince Bagration. On the salver lay some verses composed and printed in the hero's honour. At the sight of the salver

Bagration glanced about him in dismay, as though seeking help. But all eyes demanded that he should submit, and feeling himself in their power he resolutely took the salver in both hands and looked irately and reproachfully at the count who had brought it. Someone obligingly relieved Bagration of the tray (or he would, it seemed, have held it till nightfall and gone into dinner with it) and drew his attention to the ode. 'Well, I'll read it, then,' Bagration seemed to say, and fastening his weary eyes on the paper began to read with a concentrated and serious expression. But the author himself took the verses and started reading them aloud. Prince Bagration bowed his head and listened.

> Be thou the pride of Alexander's reign,
> Be of our Titus' throne the stern defender!
> Be thou our chieftain and our country's stay!
> At home a Rhipheus, a Caesar in the fray!
> Yea, e'en victorious Napoleon
> By sad experience has learned Bagration
> And dare not Herculean Russians trouble ...

But before he could finish, a stentorian major-domo announced that dinner was served. The door opened, and from the dining-room thundered the strains of the polonaise:

> Raise the shout of victory,
> Valiant Russia, now festive sing!

and Count Rostov, glancing angrily at the author who went on reading his verses, bowed Bagration in. All the company rose, feeling that dinner was of more importance than poetry, and Bagration, again preceding the rest, led the way into the dining-room. He was seated in the place of honour between two Alexanders – Bekleshov and Naryshkin (this was a delicate allusion to the name of the Sovereign). Three hundred persons took their places at the table, according to their rank and importance: those of greater consequence, nearer to the distinguished guest, as naturally as water flows to find its own level.

Just before dinner Count Ilya Rostov presented his son to Bagration, who recognized him and mumbled a few words, disjointed and awkward, as was everything else that he said that day. Count Ilya looked joyfully and proudly around at the assembled company while Bagration was speaking to his son.

Nikolai Rostov, with Denisov and his new acquaintance Dolohov, sat together almost at the middle of the table. Opposite them was Pierre, next to Prince Nesvitsky. Count Ilya Rostov and the other stewards sat facing Bagration and, as the very impersonation of Moscow hospitality, did the honours to the prince.

His labours had not been in vain. The fare – both for those who were keeping Lent and those who were not – was sumptuous, but still he could not feel perfectly at ease until the very end. He kept beckoning to the butler, whispered directions to the footmen and not without anxiety awaited each expected dish. Everything was excellent. With the second course, a gigantic sterlet (at the sight of which Ilya Rostov blushed with self-conscious pleasure), the footmen began popping corks and pouring out champagne. After the fish, which made a certain sensation, the count exchanged glances with the other stewards. 'There will be a great many toasts, it's time to begin,' he whispered, and glass in hand he got up. All were silent, waiting for what he would say.

'To the health of our Sovereign, the Emperor!' he cried, and at the same moment his kindly eyes grew moist with tears of joy and enthusiasm. The band immediately struck up 'Raise the shout of victory!' All rose from their seats and cheered 'Hurrah!' Bagration too shouted 'Hurrah', exactly as he had on the field at Schön Graben. Young Rostov's ecstatic voice could be heard above the three hundred others. He was on the point of tears. 'To the health of our Sovereign, the Emperor!' he roared, 'Hurrah!' and emptying his glass at a gulp he dashed it to the floor. Many followed his example, and the loud shouts continued for a long time. When the uproar subsided, the footmen cleared away the broken glass and everybody sat down again, smiling at the noise they had made and exchanging remarks. Then the old count rose again, glanced at a note that lay beside his place, and proposed a toast 'To the health of the hero of our last campaign, Prince Piotr Ivanovich Bagration!' and again his blue eyes were dimmed with tears. 'Hurrah!' cried the three hundred voices again, but this time instead of the band a choir began singing a cantata composed by a certain Pavel Ivanovich Kutuzov:

> No let can bar a Russian's way,
> Valour's the pledge of victory,
> For we have our Bagration
> And all our foes will be brought down ... etc.

As soon as the singers had finished, toast followed toast and Count Ilya Rostov became more and more moved, more glasses were smashed and the shouting grew louder. Healths were drunk to Bekleshov, Naryshkin, Uvarov, Dolgorukov, Apraksin, Valuyev, the stewards, the committee, all the club members and their guests, and finally and separately to the organizer of the banquet, Count Ilya Rostov. At this toast the count took out his handkerchief and hiding his face wept outright.

4

PIERRE was sitting opposite Dolohov and Nikolai Rostov. As usual he ate much and drank heavily. But those who knew him intimately noticed that a great change had come over him that day. He was silent all through dinner, and blinking and knitting his brows looked about him, or with fixed eyes and an air of complete absent-mindedness rubbed the bridge of his nose with his finger. His face was depressed and gloomy. He appeared to see and hear nothing of what was going on around him, and to be thinking of one thing only, that was painful and concerning which he had come to no conclusion.

This unresolved matter that tormented him arose out of hints from the princess in Moscow concerning Dolohov's close friendship with his wife, and an anonymous letter received that very morning, which in the vile facetious manner characteristic of anonymous letters told him that his spectacles were of little use to him and that his wife's intimacy with Dolohov was a secret to no one but himself. Pierre decidedly did not believe either the princess's hints or the letter but he flinched at the sight of Dolohov, who sat opposite him. Every time he chanced to meet Dolohov's handsome insolent eyes Pierre felt as though something hideous and awful was rising up in his soul, and he made haste to turn away. Involuntarily recalling his wife's past and her relations with Dolohov, Pierre saw clearly that what was said in the letter might well be true, or might at least appear to be the truth, if only it had nor referred to *his wife*. He could not help recalling how Dolohov, who had been completely reinstated after the campaign, had returned to Petersburg and come to him. Taking advantage of his friendship with Pierre as an old boon companion, Dolohov had made straight for Pierre's house and Pierre had put him up and lent him money. Pierre recalled how Hélène had smilingly expressed dissatisfaction at having Dolohov living under their roof; and how cynically Dolohov had praised his wife's beauty to him and from that day forth until they came to Moscow had never left their side.

'Yes, he is very handsome,' thought Pierre, 'and I know him. He would find it particularly alluring to besmirch my name and hold me up to ridicule after I had exerted myself on his behalf and befriended and helped him. I know, I understand what spice that would add to the pleasure of deceiving me, if it really were true. Yes, if it were true; but I don't believe it. I have no right to, and I can't believe it.' He remembered the expression on Dolohov's face in his moments of cruelty, as for instance when he had tied the policeman to the bear and dropped them into the water, or when without any provocation he challenged a man to a duel, or shot the post-boy's horse dead with a pistol. That expression often came over Dolohov's face when he was looking at him. 'Yes, he is a bully,' thought Pierre. 'It means nothing to him to kill a man. He must think that everyone is afraid of him, and find it pleasant. He must think that I am afraid of him too. And in fact I am afraid of him,' Pierre mused, and again felt something terrible and monstrous rising inside him. Dolohov, Denisov and Rostov were sitting opposite Pierre and seemed to be very lively. Rostov was chattering gaily to his two friends, one of whom was a dashing hussar and the other a notorious duellist and madcap, and every now and then he glanced ironically at Pierre, whose preoccupied, abstracted and solid appearance was very noticeable at this dinner. Rostov looked with disfavour upon Pierre, in the first place because Pierre in the eyes of the hussar was merely a millionaire civilian and husband of a beauty, and altogether an old woman, and secondly because Pierre in his preoccupation and absentmindedness had not recognized Rostov or responded to his bow. When the Emperor's health was drunk, Pierre, lost in thought, did not rise or lift his glass.

'What's the matter with you?' shouted Rostov, looking at him in an ecstasy of exasperation. 'Don't you hear – it's a toast to the health of his Majesty the Emperor?'

Pierre sighed and got submissively to his feet, emptied his glass and waiting till all were seated again turned with his kindly smile to Rostov.

'Why, I didn't recognize you!' he said. But Rostov was otherwise engaged, shouting 'Hurrah!'

'Aren't you going to renew the acquaintance?' said Dolohov to Rostov.

'Oh, confound him, he's a fool!' said Rostov.

'One should always be civil to the husbands of pwetty women,' remarked Denisov.

Pierre did not catch what they were saying, but he knew they were talking about him. He reddened and turned away.

'Well, now to the health of beautiful women!' proposed Dolohov, and with a serious expression, though a smile lurked at the corners of his mouth, glass in hand, addressed Pierre.

'Here's to the health of all lovely women, Peterkin – and their lovers!' he added.

Pierre with downcast eyes drank out of his glass, not looking at Dolohov or answering him. A footman, who was distributing copies of Kutuzov's cantata, laid a copy before Pierre as one of the principal guests. Pierre was just going to take it when Dolohov leaned across, snatched the sheet from his hand and began reading it. Pierre looked at Dolohov and his eyes dropped: the awful and hideous something that had been tormenting him all through the dinner rose up and took possession of him. He bent the whole of his ungainly person across the table.

'How dare you?' he shouted.

Hearing this cry and seeing to whom it was addressed, Nesvitsky and his neighbour on the right turned in haste and alarm to Bezuhov.

'Hush! Hush! What are you about?' they whispered in panic-stricken voices.

Dolohov stared at Pierre with clear, mirthful, cruel eyes, and that smile of his which seemed to say, 'Ah! This is what I like!'

'I am not giving it up!' he said, measuring his words.

Pale, with quivering lips, Pierre snatched the sheet of paper.

'You ... you ... blackguard! I challenge you!' he ejaculated, and pushing back his chair rose from the table.

At the very instant he did this and uttered these words Pierre felt that the question of his wife's guilt, which had been torturing him for the past twenty-four hours, was finally and incontestably answered in the affirmative. He hated her and was severed from her for ever. In spite of Denisov's entreaties that he should not get mixed up in the affair Rostov consented to act as Dolohov's second, and after dinner he discussed with Nesvitsky, Bezuhov's second, the arrangements for the duel. Pierre went home but Rostov, together with Dolohov and Denisov, stayed on at the club, listening to the gipsies and the other singers until late in the evening.

'Well, good-bye till tomorrow at Sokolniky,' said Dolohov, taking leave of Rostov on the club steps.

'And you're not worried?' asked Rostov.

Dolohov paused.

'Look here, in a couple of words, I'll let you into the whole secret of duelling. If you are going to fight a duel and the day before you make a will and write loving letters to your parents, and if you think you may be killed – you're a fool and as good as done for. But go with the firm intention of killing your man as quickly and surely as possible, then everything will be all right. As our bear-huntsman from Kostroma used to say to me: "A bear," he'd say, "sure, everyone's afraid of a bear – but once you set eyes on him your only fear is that he'll get away!" Well, that's how it is with me. *A demain, mon cher!*'

Next day at eight o'clock in the morning Pierre and Nesvitsky drove to the Sokolniky woods and found Dolohov, Denisov and Rostov already there. Pierre had the air of a man preoccupied with reflections in no way connected with the matter in hand. His haggard face was yellow. He had evidently not slept that night. He looked about him vaguely and screwed up his eyes as though dazzled by glaring sunshine. Two considerations absorbed him exclusively: his wife's guilt, of which after a sleepless night he had not a vestige of doubt, and the guiltlessness of Dolohov, who was certainly not called upon to protect the honour of a man who meant nothing to him. 'Maybe I should have done the same thing in his place,' thought Pierre. 'Indeed, I am sure I should. Then why this duel, this man-slaughter? Either I shall kill him, or he will put a bullet through my head, my elbow or my knee. Can't I get away from here, run off and disappear somewhere?' was the thought that passed through his mind. But at the very moments when such ideas occurred to him, he would be asking with a peculiarly calm and unconcerned face, which inspired the respect of the onlookers, 'Will it be long? Aren't we ready?'

When they were all set, with swords stuck in the snow to mark the limits to which they were to advance, and the pistols loaded, Nesvitsky went up to Pierre.

'I should not be doing my duty, count,' he faltered, 'or be worthy of your confidence and the honour you have done me in choosing me for your second, if at this grave moment, this very grave moment, I did not speak the whole truth to you. I consider this affair has not sufficient grounds, and does not warrant the shedding of blood. ... You were in the wrong, you lost your temper ...'

'Oh yes, it is horribly foolish ...' said Pierre.

'Then allow me to express your regrets, and I am sure our opposite numbers will agree to accept your apology,' said Nesvitsky (who like the other participants, and like all men in similar cases, did not believe even now that the business had actually come to a duel). 'You know, count, it is far more honourable to admit one's mistake than to let matters proceed to the irrevocable. There was no insult on either side. Allow me to confer ...'

'No, what is there to talk about?' said Pierre. 'It doesn't matter. ... Is everything ready then?' he added. 'Only tell me where I am to go, and where to fire,' he said with an unnaturally gentle smile. He took up the pistol and began to inquire about the working of the trigger, as he had never held a pistol in his hands before – a fact he was unwilling to confess.

'Oh yes, like that, of course. I know, I had only forgotten,' said he.

'No apologies, none whatever,' Dolohov was saying to Denisov (who on his side had been making an attempt at reconciliation), and he too went up to the appointed spot.

The place selected for the duel was some eighty yards from the road where the sledges had been left, in a small clearing in the pine woods, covered with melting snow after the thaw of the last few days. The antagonists stood forty paces from one another at the farther edge of the clearing. The seconds, in marking off paces, left tracks in the deep wet snow from the spot where they had been standing to the swords of Nesvitsky and Dolohov, which were stuck into the ground ten paces apart to mark the barrier. It was thawing and misty; forty yards away nothing could be seen. For three minutes everything had been ready, but still they delayed. Everyone was silent.

5

'WELL, let us begin!' said Dolohov.

'To be sure,' said Pierre, still with the same smile.

A feeling of dread was in the air. It was obvious that the affair that had begun so lightly could not now be averted in any way but was bound to run its course to the very end, irrespective of the will of men. First Denisov moved forward to the barrier and announced:

'Since the adve'sawies wefuse a weconciliation, may we not pwoceed? Take your pistols, and at the word *thwee* both of you advance. O-ne! T-wo! Thwee!' he shouted wrathfully, and stepped aside.

The combatants advanced along the trodden tracks, coming closer and closer, beginning to discern one another through the mist. They had the right to fire when they liked as they approached the barrier. Dolohov walked slowly, not raising his pistol, and fastening his bright sparkling blue eyes on his opponent's face. His mouth wore its usual semblance of a smile.

At the word 'three' Pierre moved quickly forward, missing the beaten path and stepping into the deep snow. He held the pistol at arm's length in his right hand, apparently afraid of shooting himself with it. His left arm he carefully kept behind his back because he felt inclined to use it to support his right arm, which he knew he must not do. Having gone half a dozen paces and strayed off the track into the snow, Pierre looked down at his feet, then glanced rapidly at Dolohov and, bending his finger as he had been shown, fired. Not at all expecting so loud a report, Pierre jumped at the sound, then smiled at his own sensations and stood still. The smoke, rendered denser by the mist, prevented him from seeing anything for a moment, but there was no second report as he had expected. All he could hear was Dolohov's hurried footsteps, and his figure came into view through the smoke. One hand was pressed to his left side, while the other clutched his drooping pistol. His face was pale. Rostov ran towards him and said something.

'No-o-o!' muttered Dolohov through his teeth. 'No, it's not over.' And struggling on a few staggering steps up to the sword he sank on the snow beside it. His left hand was covered with blood; he wiped it on his coat and leaned on it. His face was pale and frowning, and it trembled.

'Plea ... ' began Dolohov, but could not at first get the word out. 'Please,' he uttered with an effort.

Pierre, hardly able to restrain his sobs, started to run to Dolohov and would have crossed the space between the barriers when Dolohov cried: 'To your barrier!' and Pierre, grasping what was wanted, stopped by his sabre. Only ten paces divided them. Dolohov lowered his head, greedily sucked up a mouthful of snow, lifted his head again, straightened himself, drew in his legs and sat up, trying to find a firm centre of gravity. He gulped and swallowed the cold snow; his lips quivered but still smiled; his eyes glittered with strain and exasperation as he struggled to muster his remaining strength. He raised his pistol and aimed.

'Stand sideways! Cover yourself with your pistol!' ejaculated Nesvitsky.

'Covah you'self!' Denisov even shouted, in spite of himself for he was Dolohov's second.

With his gentle smile of compassion and regret, Pierre stood with legs and arms straddling helplessly, and his broad chest directly exposed to Dolohov, while he looked at him mournfully. Denisov, Rostov and Nesvitsky blinked. At the same instant they heard a report and Dolohov's angry cry.

'Missed!' howled Dolohov, and lay impotently face downwards in the snow.

Pierre clutched his temples and, turning round, walked away into the woods, plunging into the deep snow and muttering incoherent words.

'Folly ... folly! Death ... Lies ...' he repeated, with knitted brows. Nesvitsky stopped him and took him home.

Rostov and Denisov drove away with the wounded Dolohov, who lay silent in the sledge with closed eyes, answering not a word in reply to questions addressed to him. But as they entered Moscow he suddenly came to and, lifting his head with an effort, took Rostov, who was sitting beside him, by the hand. Rostov was struck by the totally transformed and unexpectedly exalted, tender expression on Dolohov's face.

'Well? How do you feel now?' he asked.

'Bad! But that is no matter. My friend,' said Dolohov in a gasping voice, 'where are we? In Moscow, I know. I don't count, but I have killed her, killed her.... She won't get over this. She won't get over ...'

'Who won't?' asked Rostov.

'My mother. My mother, my angel, my adored angel of a mother,' and Dolohov pressed Rostov's hand and burst into tears.

When he had grown a little calmer he explained to Rostov that he was living with his mother and if she were to see him dying she would not get over the shock. He begged Rostov to go on and prepare her.

Rostov went on ahead to carry out his mission, and to his immense surprise he learned that Dolohov the brawler, Dolohov the bully, lived in Moscow with an old mother and a hunchback sister, and was the most affectionate of sons and brothers.

6

PIERRE had of late rarely seen his wife alone. Both in Petersburg and Moscow their house was always full of guests. The night following the duel, instead of going to his bedroom, he remained, as he often did, in his huge study, the very room where old Count Bezuhov had died.

He stretched himself on the sofa with the idea of falling asleep and forgetting all that had taken place, but this he could not do. Such a tornado of thoughts, feelings, recollections suddenly arose inside him that, far from being able to sleep, he could not even keep still in one place but was compelled to leap up from the couch and pace the room with rapid strides. Now he seemed to see her in the early days of their marriage, with her bare shoulders and languid, passionate eyes, and then by her side he immediately saw Dolohov's handsome, insolent, hard, mocking face as he had seen it at the banquet, and then that same face pale, quivering and in agony as it had been when he reeled and sank in the snow.

'What has happened?' he asked himself. 'I have killed *her lover* – yes, killed my wife's lover. Yes, that was it. And why? How did I come to this?'

Because you married her, answered an inner voice.

'But how was I to blame?' he asked.

Because you married her without loving her; because you deceived both yourself and her. And vividly he recalled that moment after supper at Prince Vasili's, when he spoke those words he had found so difficult to utter: '*Je vous aime* – I love you.' 'It all started from that! I felt at the time' – he reflected – 'I felt at the time that it was wrong, that I had no right to do it. And so it has turned out.' He remembered their honeymoon and flushed at the recollection. Particularly vivid, humiliating and shameful was the memory of how one day shortly after his marriage he had come out of the bedroom into his study a little before noon in his silk dressing-gown, and found his head-steward there, who, with an obsequious bow, looked into his face and at his dressing-gown, and smiled faintly, as though to express by that smile respectful understanding of his master's happiness.

'And yet how many times I have been proud of her – proud of her majestic beauty, her social tact,' he reflected; 'been proud of my house in which she received all Petersburg, proud of her unapproach-ability and beauty. So this was what I prided myself on! I used to think then that I did not understand her. How often, pondering over her character, I have told myself that I was to blame for not under-standing her, for not understanding that everlasting composure and complacency and the absence of all preferences and desires, and the key to the whole riddle lies in the terrible word depravity: she is a depraved woman. Now that I have uttered the terrible word to myself everything has become clear.

'Anatole used to come to borrow money from her and kiss her on her naked shoulders. She didn't give him the money but she let herself be kissed. Her father in jest tried to rouse her jealousy: with a serene smile she would reply that she was not so stupid as to be jealous. "Let him do as he likes," she used to say about me. I asked once if she felt no symptoms of pregnancy. She laughed contemptuously and said she was not such a fool as to want children, and that *I* should never have a child by her.'

Then he recalled the coarseness and bluntness of her ideas, and the vulgarity of the expressions that were characteristic of her, though she had been brought up in the most aristocratic circles. 'Not quite such a fool,' 'Just you go and try it on,' 'Get out,' she would say. Often, watching her success with young and old, men and women, Pierre could not understand why it was he did not love her. 'Yes, I never loved her,' Pierre said to himself. 'I knew she was a dissolute woman,' he repeated, 'but I did not dare admit it to myself. And now Dolohov, sitting there in the snow and forcing himself to smile, dying maybe and meeting my remorse with some swaggering affectation!'

Pierre was one of those people who, in spite of an appearance of what is called weak character, do not seek a confidant in their troubles. He worked through his trouble alone.

'It is all, all her fault,' he said to himself; 'but what of that? Why did I bind myself to her? Why did I say "*Je vous aime*" to her, which was a lie, and worse than a lie? I am to blame and must endure ... what? The besmirching of my name? Unhappiness for life? Oh, that's all rubbish,' he thought. 'The disgrace to my name, my honour – all that's relative and apart from myself.

'Louis XVI was executed because they said he was dishonourable and a criminal' (Pierre developed the idea that came into his mind), 'and from their point of view they were right, just as were those who canonized him as a saint and died a martyr's death for his sake. Then Robespierre was guillotined for being a tyrant. Who is right, who is wrong? No one! But while you are alive – live: tomorrow you die, as I might have died an hour ago. And is it worth worrying oneself when one has only a second left to live, in comparison with eternity?' But at that moment when he believed himself soothed by such reflections he suddenly had a vision of *her* as she was at those moments when he had most violently expressed his insincere love for her, and he felt the blood rush to his heart, and had to jump up again and move about and break and tear to pieces whatever his hands came across. 'Why did I say to her "I love you"?' he kept asking himself. And as he repeated the question for the tenth time a phrase of Molière's came into his head: '*Mais que diable allait-il faire dans cette galère?* – But what the deuce was he doing in that mess?' and he began to laugh to himself.

In the night he called his valet and told him to pack up to go to Petersburg. He could not stay under the same roof with her. He could not imagine himself having anything more to say to her. He resolved that next day he would go away, leaving her a letter in which he would tell her of his intention of parting from her for ever.

In the morning when the valet came into the study with his coffee Pierre was lying on the ottoman, asleep with an open book in his hand.

He woke up and looked about him for a long while with a startled expression, unable to realize where he was.

'The countess sent to inquire if your Excellency was at home,' said the valet.

But before Pierre could decide what answer to send, the countess herself, in a white satin dressing-gown embroidered with silver and with her hair simply dressed (two immense plaits coiled twice round her exquisite head like a coronet), walked into the room, calm and majestic, except for a frown of fury on her rather prominent marble brow. With her imperturbable self-control she said nothing in front of the servant. She knew of the duel and had come to talk about it. She waited until the valet had set down the coffee and left the room. Pierre looked timidly at her through his spectacles, and like a hare surrounded by hounds who lays back her ears and continues to crouch motionless before her enemies so he tried to go on reading; but he was conscious that this was a senseless and impossible thing to do, and again he glanced timidly at her. She did not sit down but stood looking at him with a contemptuous smile while she waited for the valet to go.

'Well, what is this I hear? Now what have you been up to, I should like to know?' she said sternly.

'I – what have I – ?' stammered Pierre.

'Setting up as a hero, are you? Well, answer, what about this duel? What was it meant to prove? Eh? I am asking you.'

Pierre turned heavily on the sofa and opened his mouth but could not make a sound.

'If you won't answer, I'll tell you ...' continued Hélène. 'You believe everything you're told. You were told' – Hélène laughed, 'that Dolohov was my lover,' she said in French with her coarse plainness of speech, uttering the word *amant* as casually as any other word, 'and you believed it! Well, what have you proved? What did this duel show? Only that you're a fool, *que vous êtes un sot*, but everybody knew that before. What will be the outcome? That I'm made the laughing-stock of all Moscow; that everyone will say you were drunk and didn't know what you were doing, and challenged a man you are jealous of for no reason.' Hélène raised her voice and grew more and more excited. 'A man who's superior to you in every sense of the word ...'

'Er ... er ...' growled Pierre, frowning and neither looking at her nor stirring.

'And how came you to believe that he was my lover? ... Eh?

373

Because I like his company ? If you were more intelligent and agreeable I should have preferred yours.'

'Don't speak to me ... I beg of you,' muttered Pierre hoarsely.

'Why shouldn't I speak to you ? I can speak as I like, and I tell you bluntly – there are not many wives with husbands like you who would not have taken lovers (*des amants*), although I have not done so,' said she.

Pierre tried to say something, looked at her with strange eyes, the expression of which she did not understand, and lay down again. He was suffering physical pain at that moment: there was a weight on his chest and he could not breathe. He knew that he must do something to put an end to this agony, but what he wanted to do was too horrible.

'We had better part,' he murmured in a broken voice.

'By all means, on condition you provide for me,' said Hélène. 'Part! There's a threat to frighten me with!'

Pierre sprang up from the sofa and rushed staggering towards her.

'I'll kill you!' he shouted, and seizing a slab of marble from the table with a strength he had not known in himself till then he took a step towards her, brandishing it.

Hélène's face was dreadful to see. She shrieked and jumped back. His father's nature showed itself in Pierre. He felt the transports and fascination of frenzy. He flung down the slab, smashing it into fragments, and with outstretched arms advanced on Hélène, shouting 'Go!' in a voice so terrible that the whole house heard it with horror. God knows what he would have done at that moment had Hélène not fled from the room.

Within a week Pierre had made over to his wife the revenue from all his estates in Greater Russia, which constituted the larger half of his property, and had gone away alone to Petersburg.

7

Two months had elapsed since tidings of the battle of Austerlitz and of the fact that Prince Andrei was missing had reached Bald Hills, and in spite of all the letters sent through the Embassy, and the searches made, his body had not been found nor was he on the list of prisoners. What made it worst of all for his relatives was that there was still the possibility that he might have been picked up on the battlefield by the people of the country, and now be lying, recovering or dying, alone among strangers and incapable of sending word of himself. The newspapers from which the old prince first heard of the defeat at Austerlitz had, as usual, given the briefest and vaguest accounts of how the Russians had been obliged, after brilliant feats of arms, to retreat, and had made their withdrawal in perfect order. The old prince understood from this official report that our army had been defeated. A week after the newspapers had carried the news of Austerlitz a letter came from Kutuzov informing the prince of the fate that had befallen his son.

Your son [wrote Kutuzov] fell before my eyes, a standard in his hand and at the head of his regiment – like a hero worthy of his father and his Fatherland. To the regret of myself and of the whole army it has not been ascertained up to now whether he is alive or not. I comfort myself and you with the hope that your son is living, for otherwise he would have been mentioned among the officers found on the field of battle, a list of whom has been handed to me under flag of truce.

After receiving this letter, late in the evening when he was alone in his study, the old prince went for his regular walk next day, but he was silent with the bailiff, the gardener and the architect, and though he looked very grim he said nothing to anyone.

When Princess Maria went to him at the customary hour he was standing at his lathe and, as usual, did not look round at her.

'Ah, Princess Maria!' he said suddenly in an unnatural voice, throwing down his chisel. (The wheel continued to revolve from its own impetus. Princess Maria was long to remember the dying whirr of the wheel, which associated itself in her memory with what followed.)

She approached him, caught sight of his face, and something suddenly seemed to give way within her. Her eyes grew dim. By the expression on her father's face – not sad nor crushed but angry and working unnaturally – she saw that some terrible misfortune was hanging over her, about to crush her, the worst in life, a calamity she had not yet experienced, irreparable and incomprehensible – the death of one beloved.

'Father! Andrei?' said the ungainly, awkward princess with such an indescribable enchantment of grief and self-forgetfulness that her father could not bear to meet her eyes and turned away with a sob.

'I have had news! He is not among the prisoners, not among the killed. Kutuzov writes ...' he screamed shrilly, as though he would drive his daughter away with that shriek, 'he is killed!'

The princess did not sink down nor swoon. She was already pale but when she heard these words her face altered and a radiance shone from her beautiful, luminous eyes. It was as if joy, a supernatural joy independent of the joys and sorrows of this world, overlaid the great grief within her. She forgot all fear of her father, went up to him, took his hand and, drawing him to her, put her arm round his thin scraggy neck.

'Father,' she said, 'do not turn away from me: let us weep together.'

'Scoundrels! Blackguards!' screamed the old man, averting his face from her. 'Destroying the army, destroying men! And what for? Go – go and tell Lisa.'

The princess dropped helplessly into an arm-chair beside her father and wept. She could see her brother now as he looked when he said good-bye to her and Lisa with his tender and at the same time haughty expression. She could see him gentle and amused as he slipped the little icon round his neck. 'Did he believe now? Had he repented of his unbelief? Was he there now – there in the realm of eternal peace and blessedness?' she wondered.

'Father, tell me how it happened?' she asked through her tears.

'Go away, go away – he was killed in an action in which the finest men of Russia and Russia's glory were led out to slaughter. Go, Princess Maria. Go and tell Lisa. I will follow.'

When Princess Maria returned from her father the little princess was sitting at her work, and she looked up at her sister-in-law with that expression of happy inner serenity peculiar to women in her condition. It was evident that her eyes did not see Princess Maria but were looking within, deep into herself, at some joyful mystery being accomplished there.

'Marie,' she said, moving away from her embroidery-frame and leaning back, 'give me your hand.' She took the princess's hand and laid it on her belly.

Her eyes smiled, expectant, her little downy lip lifted and stayed so in childlike rapture.

Princess Maria knelt down before her and hid her face in the folds of her sister-in-law's dress.

'There – there – can you feel? I feel so strange. And do you know,

Marie, I am going to love him very much,' said Lisa, looking with shining, happy eyes at her husband's sister.

Princess Maria could not raise her head: she was weeping.

'What is the matter, Masha?'

'Nothing ... only I felt sad ... sad about Andrei,' she said, wiping away her tears against Lisa's knee.

Several times in the course of the morning Princess Maria attempted to prepare her sister-in-law, and each time began to cry. Unobservant as was the little princess in general, these tears, which she could not account for, agitated her. She said nothing but looked about uneasily as if in search of something. Before dinner the old prince, of whom she was always afraid, came into her room with a particularly restless and malign expression, and went out again without saying a word. She looked at Princess Maria with that appearance of attention concentrated within herself that is only seen in women with child, and suddenly burst into tears.

'Is there any news from Andrei?' she asked.

'No, you know it's too soon to hear anything, but Father is worried and I feel frightened.'

'So there's nothing?'

'Nothing,' answered Princess Maria, letting her lustrous eyes rest resolutely on her sister-in-law.

She had made up her mind not to tell her, and had persuaded her father to conceal the terrible tidings from Lisa, until after her confinement, which was expected before many days. Princess Maria and the old prince each bore and hid their grief in their own way. The old prince refused to cherish any hope: he decided that Prince Andrei had been killed, and though he sent an official to Austria to seek for traces of his son he ordered a monument from Moscow which he intended to erect in the garden to his son's memory, and told everybody that his son was dead. He tried to keep to his old routine but his strength started to fail him: he walked less, ate less, slept less, and every day he grew weaker. Princess Maria went on hoping. She prayed for her brother as though he were alive and was always expecting news of his return.

8

'DEAREST,' said the little princess after breakfast on the morning of the 19th of March, and her downy little lip was lifted as of old;

but as in that house since the terrible news had come smiles, tones of voice and even footsteps bore the stamp of mourning, so now the smile of the little princess, who was influenced by the general temper without knowing its cause, was such as to remind one still more of the general sorrow.

'Dearest, I'm afraid this morning's *fruschtique* (as Foka the cook calls breakfast) has disagreed with me.'

'What's the matter, sweetheart? You look pale. Yes, you do look very pale,' said Princess Maria in alarm, running up to her sister-in-law with her soft, ponderous tread.

'Shouldn't we send for Maria Bogdanovna, your Excellency?' said one of the maids who was present. (Maria Bogdanovna was the midwife from the neighbouring town who had been at Bald Hills for the last fortnight.)

'Oh yes,' assented Princess Maria, 'perhaps that's it. I'll go. Courage, my angel.' She kissed Lisa and was about to leave the room.

'No, no!' And, besides her pallor, the face of the little princess expressed childish terror at the inevitable physical suffering before her.

'No, it's only indigestion. ... Say it's only indigestion, say so, Marie, say ...' And the little princess began to cry and wring her hands in a capricious and even rather exaggerated fashion, like a child. Princess Maria hurried out of the room to fetch Maria Bogdanovna.

'*Mon Dieu! Mon Dieu!* Oh!' she heard behind her.

The midwife was already on her way to meet her, rubbing her small plump white hands with an air of significant composure.

'Maria Bogdanovna, I think it's beginning!' said Princess Maria, looking at the midwife with wide-open frightened eyes.

'Well, the Lord be praised, princess,' said Maria Bogdanovna, not hastening her step. 'You young ladies should not know anything about it.'

'But how is it the doctor from Moscow is not here yet?' said the princess. (In accordance with the wishes of Lisa and Prince Andrei it had been arranged for a doctor to come in good time from Moscow, and he was expected at any moment.)

'No matter, princess, don't be alarmed,' said Maria Bogdanovna. 'We shall manage quite well without a doctor.'

Five minutes later Princess Maria from her room heard something heavy being carried by. She peeped out. Footmen were for some reason moving the leather sofa from Prince Andrei's study into the bedroom. On their faces was a solemn and subdued look.

Princess Maria sat alone in her room listening to the sounds in the house, every now and again opening her door when anyone went along, and watching what was happening in the passage. A number of women made their way to and fro treading softly. They glanced at the princess and turned away. She did not venture to ask any questions, and going back into her room shut the door again and sat in an arm-chair, or took up her prayer-book, or knelt down before the icons. To her distress and surprise she found that prayer did not quiet her agitation. Suddenly the door opened softly and her old nurse, Praskovya Savishna, who hardly ever came into her room as the old prince had forbidden it, appeared on the threshold with a kerchief over her head.

'I've come to sit with 'ee a bit, dearie,' said the old nurse, 'and see, I've brought the prince's wedding candles to light before his saint, my angel,' she said with a sigh.

'Oh nurse, I'm so glad!'

'God is merciful, birdie.'

The old nurse lit the gilded candles before the icons and sat down by the door with her knitting. Princess Maria took a book and began reading. Only when they heard steps or voices did they look at one another, the princess anxious and inquiring, the old nurse reassuring. In every corner of the house everyone was dominated by the same feelings which Princess Maria experienced as she sat in her room. In accordance with the old superstition that the fewer people who know of the sufferings of a woman in labour, the less she suffers, everyone pretended to be ignorant of what was going on; no one mentioned it, but over and above the habitual staid and respectful good manners that obtained in the prince's household there was apparent a common anxiety, a mellowing of the heart and a consciousness that some great, unfathomable mystery was being accomplished at that very moment.

There was no laughter in the maids' large hall. In the men-servants' hall the men all sat in silence, as it were on the alert. In the serfs' quarters torches and candles were burning, and no one slept. The old prince walked about his study, treading on his heels, and sent Tikhon to Maria Bogdanovna to ask what news. 'Simply say, "The prince sends to inquire," and come back and tell me what she says.'

'Inform the prince that labour has commenced,' said Maria Bogdanovna, giving the messenger a significant look.

Tikhon returned and told the prince.

'Very good,' said the prince closing the door behind him, and Tikhon heard not the slightest sound from the study after that. Waiting a while, he went into the study on the pretext of attending to the candles. Seeing the prince lying on the sofa, Tikhon looked at him, observed his worried face, shook his head and dumbly going up to him kissed him on the shoulder, then went out without snuffing the candles or saying why he had come. The most solemn mystery in the world was in process of consummation. Evening passed, night wore on. And the feeling of suspense and softening of heart in the presence of the unfathomable did not wane but was heightened. No one slept.

It was one of those March nights when winter seems determined to resume its sway and lets loose a last desperate onslaught of howling winds and squalls of snow. A relay of horses had been sent to the high road to meet the German doctor from Moscow, who was expected every moment, and men were despatched on horseback with lanterns to the cross-roads to guide him over the ruts and snow-covered watery hollows.

Princess Maria had long since abandoned her book; she sat silent, her lustrous eyes fixed on her old nurse's wrinkled face, every line of which she knew so well, on the lock of grey hair that escaped from under the kerchief, on the baggy folds of skin under her chin.

Nurse Savishna, knitting in hand, was telling in low tones, scarcely hearing or following her own words, the story she had told hundreds of times before of how the late princess had been brought to bed of Princess Maria in Kishinyov, with only a Moldavian peasant woman to help instead of a midwife.

'God is merciful, doctors bain't needed,' she was saying.

Suddenly a gust of wind beat violently against one of the window-frames (by the prince's decree the double frames were always taken out of one window in each room as soon as the larks returned), and forcing open a carelessly fastened latch set the damask curtain flapping and blew out the candle with its chill snowy draught. Princess Maria shuddered; the old nurse laying down the stocking she was knitting went to the window and leaning out tried to catch the open casement. The cold wind fluttered the ends of her kerchief and the escaping locks of her grey hair.

'Princess, my dearie, there's someone driving up the avenue!' she said, holding the casement and not closing it. 'With lanterns – it must be the doctor …'

'Thank God, thank God!' cried Princess Maria. 'I must go and meet him: he does not know Russian.'

Princess Maria threw a shawl over her shoulders and ran to meet the stranger. As she was crossing the ante-room she looked through the window and saw a carriage with lanterns standing at the entrance. She went out on to the stairs. On a banister-post stood a tallow candle guttering in the draught. On the landing below was Philip the footman with another candle, looking scared. Still lower down, beyond the turn of the staircase, advancing footsteps were heard in thick overshoes, and a voice which seemed familiar to Princess Maria was saying something.

'Thank God!' said the voice. 'And father?'

'He has gone to bed,' answered the voice of the butler, Demyan, who was below.

Then the voice said something else and Demyan replied, and the footsteps in the thick overshoes approached more rapidly up the unseen part of the staircase.

'It's Andrei!' thought Princess Maria. 'No, it can't be, that would be too extraordinary,' and at the very moment she was thinking this the face and figure of Prince Andrei, in a fur cloak with a deep collar which was covered with snow, appeared on the landing where the footman stood with the candle. Yes, it was he, but pale and thin, and with an altered, strangely softened, agitated expression on his face. He came up the stairs and clasped his sister in his arms.

'You did not get my letter?' he asked, and not waiting for a reply which indeed he would not have received, for the princess was unable to speak – he turned back, and with the doctor who was behind him (they had met at the last post-station) he flew swiftly up the stairs again, and again embraced his sister.

'What a strange coincidence!' he cried. 'Dear Masha!' And flinging off his cloak and felt overshoes he went to his wife's apartment.

9

THE little princess lay supported by pillows, with a white night-cap on her head. (The pains had just left her.) Strands of her black hair curled about her hot perspiring cheeks; her rosy delightful little mouth with its downy lip was open and she was smiling joyfully. Prince Andrei entered and paused, facing her, at the foot of the couch on which she was lying. Her glittering eyes, staring in childish terror and excitement, rested on him with no change in their expression. 'I love you all,' they seemed to say, 'I have done no one any harm: why must I suffer like this? Help me!' She saw her husband but did not take in the meaning of his appearance before her just at this time. Prince Andrei went round to the side of the sofa and kissed her on the forehead.

'My darling!' he said. He had never called her this before. 'God is merciful ...'

She looked at him inquiringly, full of childish reproach.

'I expected help from you and none comes, none, even from you!' said her eyes. She was not surprised at his arrival: she did not realize that he was there. His coming had nothing to do with her agony or with its relief. The pains began again and Maria Bogdanovna advised Prince Andrei to leave the room.

The doctor came in. Prince Andrei left the room and meeting Princess Maria joined her again. They talked in whispers but kept breaking off. They were waiting and listening.

'Go, dear,' said Princess Maria.

Prince Andrei went to his wife's apartment again and sat waiting in the room next to hers. A woman ran out of the bedroom with a frightened face and was disconcerted when she saw Prince Andrei. He hid his face in his hands and sat thus for some minutes. Piteous, helpless, animal moans were heard through the door. Prince Andrei got up, went to the door and tried to open it. Someone was holding it shut.

'You can't come in! No!' said a terrified voice on the other side.

He began walking about the room. The moaning ceased; several seconds went by. Then suddenly a fearful shriek – it could not be her, she could not shriek like that – came from the bedroom. Prince Andrei ran to the door; the scream died away and he heard the wail of an infant.

'What have they taken a baby in there for?' wondered Prince Andrei for a second. 'A baby? What baby? ... Why a baby there? Or is the baby born?'

When he suddenly took in all the glad significance of that wail tears choked him, and leaning both elbows on the window-sill he began to cry, sobbing like a child. The door opened. The doctor with his shirt-sleeves tucked up and no coat on, came out of the room, pale, and lower jaw trembling. Prince Andrei turned to him but the doctor gave him a distracted look and passed by without a word. A woman rushed out and seeing Prince Andrei stopped, hesitating, in the door. He went into his wife's room. She was lying dead in the same position he had seen her in five minutes earlier, and despite the fixed eyes and the pallor of her cheeks there was the same expression as before on the charming childlike little face with its upper lip shaded with fine dark hair.

'I love you all, and have done no one any harm; and what have you done to me?' said the lovely, piteous, lifeless face.

In a corner of the room something red and tiny grunted and squealed in Maria Bogdanovna's shaking white arms.

*

Two hours later Prince Andrei stepped softly into his father's study. The old man knew everything already. He was standing near the door and as soon as it opened his rough old arms closed like a vice round his son's neck, and without a word he burst into sobs like a child.

*

Three days later the little princess was buried, and Prince Andrei stepped up to the side of the bier to take his last farewell of her. Even in the coffin the face was the same, though the eyes were closed. 'Ah, what have you done to me?' it still seemed to say, and Prince Andrei felt that something had broken away in his soul and that he was guilty of a wrong he could never set right nor forget. He could not weep. The old man also came up and kissed one of the waxen little hands lying peacefully crossed on her breast, and to him, too, her face said: 'Ah, what have you done to me, and why?' And the old man turned angrily away when he caught sight of this face.

*

In another five days there followed the christening of the young Prince Nikolai Andreich. The wet-nurse held back the swaddling-clothes with her chin while the priest with a goose feather anointed the baby's red and wrinkled little palms and soles.

His grandfather, who was his godfather, trembling and afraid of dropping him, carried the infant round the battered tin font, and handed him over to the godmother, Princess Maria. Prince Andrei sat in another room, his heart in his mouth lest they should let the child drown in the font, waiting for the conclusion of the ceremony. He looked up joyfully at the baby when the nurse brought him in, and nodded with satisfaction when she told him of the good omen that the bit of wax with the baby's hairs in it had floated and not sunk when it was thrown into the font.

10

ROSTOV's part in the duel between Dolohov and Bezuhov was hushed up by the efforts of the old count, and instead of being reduced to the ranks, as he expected, he was appointed an adjutant to the governor-general of Moscow. In consequence of this, he was unable to go to the country with the rest of the family but was kept in Moscow all the summer by his new duties. Dolohov recovered, and Rostov became very friendly with him during his convalescence. Dolohov lay in bed at his mother's house. Old Maria Ivanovna, who was tenderly and passionately devoted to her son, took a liking to Rostov on account of his friendship with her Fedya, and often talked to him about her son.

'Yes, count,' she would say, 'he is too noble and pure-souled for the corrupt society of our time. No one cares about virtue nowadays – virtue is a thorn in everybody's flesh. Come, tell me, count, was it right, was it honourable of Bezuhov? And Fedya, in his noble-hearted way, loved him and even now never says a word against him. Those pranks in Petersburg, when they played all those tricks on the policeman – they were in it together, weren't they? But there, Bezuhov got off scot-free while Fedya had to bear the whole brunt of it on his shoulders. What he has had to go through! True, he has been reinstated, but how could they help reinstating him? I don't suppose there were many other such gallant sons of the Fatherland out there! And now what? This duel! Have these people no feeling, no honour? Knowing he was an only son, to challenge him to a duel and then fire right at him! Fortunately God had mercy on us. And what was it all about? Who doesn't have love affairs nowadays? Why, if he was so jealous, as I see things he ought to have shown it sooner, but he lets it go on for twelve months. And then to call him out, reckoning on Fedya not fighting, because he owed him money! What baseness! What infamy! I know you understand Fedya, my dear count, and so, believe me, I feel deep affection for you. Few understand him. His is such a lofty, celestial nature!'

Dolohov himself during his convalescence often said things to Rostov which could never have been expected of him.

'People think me an ugly customer, I know,' said he, 'and they're welcome to. I don't give a damn unless I'm fond of a person; but I'd sacrifice my life for those I *am* fond of; the rest I'd throttle if they stood in my way. I have an adored and precious mother and two or three friends, of whom you are one; but as for everyone else – I only pay attention to them in so far as they are useful to me or mischievous. And most of them are mischievous, especially the women. Yes, my dear fellow,' he went on, 'I have met men who were tender, noble and high-minded; but I have never yet come across a woman – be she countess or cook – who could not be bought. I have yet to meet with the angelic purity and devotion which I look for in woman. If I found such a one I'd give my life for her! But those others! ...' He made a gesture of contempt. 'And you may not believe me but if I still set a value on life it is only because I still hope one day to meet such a heavenly creature who will regenerate me, purify me and elevate me. But you don't understand that.'

'On the contrary, I understand perfectly,' answered Rostov, who was very much under the influence of his new friend.

*

In the autumn the Rostovs returned to Moscow. Early in the winter Denisov, too, came back and stayed with them. The first half of this winter of 1806 which Nikolai Rostov spent in Moscow was one of the happiest, merriest periods for him and the whole family. Nikolai brought a lot of young men to his parents' house. Vera was a handsome girl in her twentieth year; Sonya, at sixteen, had all the charm of an opening flower; Natasha, half child, half grown-up, at one moment was droll and immature, at the next girlishly bewitching.

Love was in the air in the Rostov house at this time, as commonly happens in every household where there are very young and very charming girls. Every young man who came to the Rostovs and saw those impressionable, smiling young faces (smiling probably at their own happiness), and the eager bustle, and heard the young feminine chatter, so inconsequent but so friendly to everyone, so ready for anything, so full of hope, and the spontaneous bursts of singing and music, felt the same disposition to fall in love and live happily ever after which the young people of the Rostov household were feeling themselves.

Among the young men Rostov brought home one of the foremost was Dolohov, whom everyone in the house liked except Natasha. She almost had a quarrel with her brother over him. She insisted that he was a bad man, that in the duel with Bezuhov Pierre had been right and Dolohov wrong, and that he was disagreeable and affected.

'There's nothing for me to understand!' she would cry with self-willed obstinacy. 'He is spiteful and heartless. Now your Denisov I like, though he is a rake and all that, still I like him; so that shows I do understand things. I don't know how to put it ... everything *he* does is thought out beforehand, and I don't like that. But Denisov...'

'Oh, Denisov's another matter,' answered Rostov, implying that even Denisov was nothing compared to Dolohov. 'One must understand what a soul there is in Dolohov – you should see him with his mother. What a tender heart!'

'Well, I don't know anything about that, but he makes me uncomfortable. And he has fallen in love with Sonya – did you know that?'

'What nonsense ...'

'I'm certain of it, you'll see.'

Natasha proved to be right. Dolohov, who did not as a rule care for feminine society, began to be a frequent visitor, and the question for whose sake he came (though no one ventured to remark on it) was soon settled – he came because of Sonya. And Sonya, though she would never have dared to acknowledge it, knew, and she blushed scarlet every time Dolohov appeared.

Dolohov often dined at the Rostovs', never missed a play performance at which they were present, and attended Iogel's 'balls for young people', at which the Rostovs were always to be found. He paid marked attention to Sonya and looked at her in such a way that not only could she not bear his eyes on her without turning crimson but even the old countess and Natasha coloured when they saw that look of his.

It was evident that this powerful, strange man was falling under the spell of the dark, graceful girl, who was in love with another man.

Rostov noticed something new in Dolohov's relations with Sonya but he did not define to himself what these new relations were. 'Every one of them's in love with someone,' he said to himself, thinking of Sonya and Natasha. But he was not so much at ease with Sonya and Dolohov as before, and was less often at home.

In the autumn of 1806 everybody began to talk again about the war with Napoleon, and with even greater fervour than in the previous year. It was decreed that ten out of every thousand of the population should be recruited for the regular army, besides a further nine of the militia. Everywhere anathemas were heaped on Bonaparte, and the impending war was Moscow's only topic of conversation. For the Rostov family interest in these preparations for war entirely centred in the fact that Nikolai would not hear of remaining in Moscow, and was only waiting for the end of Denisov's furlough to rejoin their regiment with him after Christmas. His approaching departure, far from preventing him from enjoying himself, gave an added zest to his pleasures. He spent the greater part of his time away from home, at dinners, parties and balls.

II

ON the third day of the Christmas holidays Nikolai dined at home, a thing he had rarely done of late. It was a grand farewell dinner, as he and Denisov were leaving to join their regiment after Epiphany. About twenty people sat down at the table, including Dolohov and Denisov.

Never had love been so much in the air, and never had the amorous atmosphere made itself so strongly felt in the Rostovs' house as during these days of Christmas. 'Seize the moments of happiness – love and be loved! This is the only reality in the world: all else is fiddlesticks. And this is the one thing we are interested in here,' was the prevailing mood.

After exhausting two pairs of horses, as he did every day without having visited all the places he should have gone to or to which he had been invited, Nikolai returned home just before dinner. As soon as he went in he noticed, and felt, the tension of love about the house, and was conscious too of a curious embarrassment existing between certain of the company. Sonya, Dolohov and the old countess seemed particularly disturbed and in a lesser degree Natasha. Nikolai perceived that something must have happened before dinner between Sonya and Dolohov, and with his instinctive tact was very sympathetic and wary with both of them during the meal. That evening there was to be one of the dances that Iogel (the dancing-master) gave for all his pupils during the holidays.

'Nikolai darling, will you come to Iogel's? Please do!' said Natasha. 'He asked you specially, and Vasili Dmitrich' (this was Denisov) 'is coming.'

'Where would I not go at the young countess's wequest!' exclaimed Denisov, who at the Rostovs' had jestingly taken up the role of Natasha's knight. 'I'm even weady to dance the *pas de châle*.'

'I will if I can get away in time,' answered Nikolai. 'I promised to go to the Arharovs' – they're giving a party.'

'What about you?' ... he turned to Dolohov, but as soon as he had asked the question he saw that he should not have done so.

'Yes, possibly ...' Dolohov replied coldly and angrily, glancing at Sonya, and then, scowling, gave Nikolai just such a look as he had given Pierre at the club dinner.

'Something's wrong,' thought Nikolai, and he was still further confirmed in his surmise when Dolohov left immediately after dinner. He called Natasha and asked her what had happened.

'I was just looking for you,' said Natasha running out to him. 'I told you so but you wouldn't believe me,' she said triumphantly. 'He proposed to Sonya!'

Little as Sonya had occupied Nikolai's thoughts of late, he felt a sort of pang when he heard this. Dolohov was a suitable and in some respects a brilliant match for the dowerless orphan girl. From the old countess's point of view, and that of society, it was out of the question for her to refuse him. And so Nikolai's first feeling on hearing the news was one of indignation with Sonya. He had it on the tip of his tongue to say, 'Fine; of course she must forget her childish promises and accept the offer,' but before he could get it out Natasha went on:

'And fancy – she refused him! Definitely refused him! She told him that she loved another,' added Natasha after a pause.

'Yes, my Sonya could not have done otherwise,' thought Nikolai.

'Mamma begged her ever so many times not to, but she refused, and I know she will never change her mind once she has said a thing ...'

'And Mamma begged her not to refuse!' said Nikolai reproachfully.

'Yes,' said Natasha. 'Do you know, dearest Nikolai – don't be angry – but I know you won't marry her. I am sure of it, heaven knows how, but I know for certain that you won't marry Sonya.'

'Now you don't know anything about it,' said Nikolai. 'But I must go and talk to her. What a darling Sonya is!' he added, smiling.

'Indeed she is! I'll send her to you.' And Natasha kissed her brother and ran off.

A minute later Sonya came in, looking frightened, troubled and guilty. Nikolai went up to her and kissed her hand. This was the first time since his return that they had been alone together and talked of their love.

'Sophie,' he began, timidly at first but growing bolder as he went on, 'in case you are thinking of refusing not only a brilliant, an advantageous match – but he's a splendid, noble fellow ... he's my friend ...'

Sonya interrupted him.

'I have already refused him,' she said hurriedly.

'If you are refusing him for my sake, I am afraid that I ...'

Sonya again cut him short, giving him a frightened, beseeching look.

'Nicolas, don't say that to me!' she implored.

'No, I must. Perhaps it is conceited of me, but still it's better to speak out. If you are refusing him on my account, I ought to tell you the whole truth. I love you, I believe, more than anyone else ...'

'That is enough for me,' said Sonya, flushing crimson.

'No, but I have been in love a thousand times and shall fall in love again, though I don't feel for anyone else the friendship, trust and love that I do for you. Then I am young. Mamma does not wish it. Well – in fact – I can't make any promises. And I beg you to consider Dolohov's offer,' he said, finding it hard to bring out his friend's name.

'Do not say such things to me. I ask for nothing. I love you as a brother, and I shall always love you, and that's all I want.'

'You are an angel! I am not worthy of you, but I am only afraid of misleading you.' Nikolai once more kissed her hand.

Iogel's were the most enjoyable balls in Moscow. So the mammas said as they watched their daughters executing the steps they had lately learnt; so said the young people themselves as they danced till they were ready to drop; and so said the grown-up young men and women who came to these evenings in a spirit of condescension, and found them the greatest entertainment. That very year two matches had been made at the dances. The two pretty young princesses Gorchakov had found husbands there, which had further increased Iogel's fame. What distinguished these balls from others was the absence of host and hostess, and the presence of the kind-hearted Iogel, who fluttered about like a feather, scraping and bowing according to the rules of his art, as he collected their tickets from each of his pupils. Another feature was that only those came to these balls who really wanted to dance and enjoy themselves, in the way that girls of thirteen and fourteen do who are wearing long dresses for the first time. All with rare exceptions were pretty, or seemed to be, so rapturous were their smiles and so sparkling their eyes. Sometimes the best pupils, of whom Natasha, being exceptionally graceful, was the very best, even danced the *pas de châle*; but at this last ball only the *écossaise*, the *anglaise* and a mazurka which was just coming into fashion were danced. Iogel had taken a ballroom in Bezuhov's house, and the ball, as everyone said, was a great success. There were pretty faces by the dozen and the Rostov girls were among the prettiest. They were both particularly happy and gay. That evening, elated by Dolohov's proposal, her own refusal and the talk with Nikolai, Sonya had waltzed about her room at home so that the maid could hardly get her hair plaited, and now at the dance she was transparently radiant with impulsive happiness.

Natasha, no less elated by her first long skirt and at being at a real ball, was even happier. Both the girls wore white muslin dresses with pink ribbons.

Natasha fell in love the moment she walked into the ball-room. She was not enamoured of anyone in particular, but of everyone. She was in love with everyone on whom her eyes happened to fall for that moment.

'Oh, how lovely it is!' she kept saying, running up to Sonya.

Nikolai and Denisov strolled through the room, looking with kindly patronage at the dancers.

'How pwetty she is – she will be a waving beauty!' said Denisov.

'Who?'

'Countess Natasha,' answered Denisov.

'And how she dances! What gwace!' he said again after a pause.

'Who are you talking about?'

'Why, your sister,' cried Denisov testily.

Rostov smiled.

'My dear count, you were one of my best pupils – you must dance,' said little Iogel, coming up to Nikolai and speaking in French. 'Look at all these attractive young ladies.' He turned with the same request to Denisov, who was also a former pupil of his.

'*Non, mon cher*, I pwefer to be a wall-flower,' said Denisov. 'Don't you wecollect how ill I pwofited by your teaching?'

'Oh no!' said Iogel, hastening to reassure him. 'You were only somewhat inattentive, but you had talent – oh yes, you had talent.'

The band struck up the first notes of the newly-introduced mazurka. Nikolai could not refuse Iogel, and invited Sonya to dance. Denisov sat down by the elderly ladies and leaning on his sword and beating time with his foot he kept them in fits of laughter with his stories, while he watched the young ones dancing. Iogel with Natasha, his pride and his best pupil, were the first couple. Placing his little slippered feet lightly in position, Iogel flew across the room with Natasha – shy, but conscientiously executing her steps. Denisov did not take his eyes off her, and tapped his sword in time with the music with an air which made it plain that if he were not dancing it was because he did not care to and not because he could not. In the middle of a figure he beckoned to Rostov who was passing.

'This is not the weal thing at all,' he said. 'What sort of a Polish mazurka is this? But she does dance admiwably.'

Knowing that Denisov was celebrated even in Poland for his masterly dancing of the mazurka, Nikolai ran up to Natasha.

'Go and choose Denisov. There's a dancer for you – he's a miracle!' he said.

When it came to Natasha's turn to choose a partner, she got up and tripping across the hall in her dainty dancing-slippers trimmed with little knots of ribbon she timidly made her way alone to the corner where Denisov was sitting. She saw that everybody was looking at her and waiting. Nikolai noticed that Denisov and Natasha were smilingly disputing, and that Denisov was refusing though he grinned with delight. He ran up to them.

'Please, Vasili Dmitrich,' Natasha was saying. 'Do come.'

'Oh no, countess, weally and twuly,' Denisov replied.

'Now then, Vasska,' said Nikolai.

'They twy to coax me as if I were Vasska the cat,' laughed Denisov.

'I'll sing for you a whole evening,' said Natasha.

'The little enchantwess can do what she likes with me!' said Denisov, and he unhooked his sabre. He came out from behind the chairs, clasped his partner's hand firmly, threw back his head and put one foot forward, waiting for the beat. Only on horseback and in the mazurka was Denisov's short stature not noticeable and he looked the dashing fellow he felt himself to be. At the right beat of the music he glanced sideways with a triumphant and amused air at his partner, suddenly stamped with one foot, bounded from the floor like a ball and spun round the room, whirling his partner with him. Noiselessly he flew half across the hall on one foot and apparently not seeing the chairs ranged in front of him was dashing straight at them, when suddenly, clinking his spurs and spreading his legs, he stopped short on his heels, stood so for a second, with a clanking of spurs stamped with both feet, twisted rapidly round and striking his left heel against his right flew round in a circle again. Natasha divined what he meant to do, and abandoning herself to him followed his lead hardly knowing how. First he spun her round, holding her now with his right hand now with his left, then falling on one knee he twirled her round him, and again jumping up dashed so impetuously forward that it seemed as if he intended to race through the whole suite of rooms without drawing breath. Then he stopped suddenly again and executed some new and unexpected steps. When at last, after dexterously spinning his partner round in front of her chair, he drew up with a click of his spurs and bowed to her, Natasha did not even make him a curtsey. She fixed her eyes on him in amazement, smiling as if she did not recognize him.

'Whatever dance was that?' she brought out.

Although Iogel would not acknowledge this to be the proper mazurka, everyone was enthralled with Denisov's skill and he was continually being chosen as partner, while the old men, smiling, began to talk about Poland and the good old days. Denisov, flushed after the mazurka and mopping his face with his handkerchief, sat down by Natasha and would not leave her side for the rest of the evening.

<h2 style="text-align:center">13</h2>

FOR two days after this Rostov did not see Dolohov at his own or at Dolohov's home; on the third day he received a note from him.

As I do not intend to visit your house again for reasons you are aware of, and am going to rejoin the regiment, I am giving a farewell supper to my friends tonight – come to the English Hotel.

About ten o'clock that evening Rostov went to the English Hotel straight from the theatre, where he had been with his family and Denisov. He was at once shown to the best room in the place, which Dolohov had taken for the occasion.

Some twenty men were gathered round a table at which Dolohov was sitting between two candles. On the table lay a pile of gold and paper money, and Dolohov was keeping the bank. Rostov had not seen him since his proposal and Sonya's refusal, and felt uncomfortable at the thought of how they would meet.

As soon as Rostov entered the door Dolohov looked up with a clear cold glance, as though he had long been expecting him.

'We have not met for some time,' he said. 'Thanks for coming. I'll just finish dealing here, and Ilyushka will make his appearance with his chorus.'

'I called at your house once or twice,' said Rostov, reddening.

Dolohov made no reply.

'You might put down a stake,' he said.

Rostov at that instant recalled a singular conversation he had once had with Dolohov. 'Only a fool believes in gambling,' Dolohov had said then.

'Or are you afraid to play with me?' Dolohov asked, as though divining Rostov's thought, and he smiled.

Behind the smile Rostov saw the mood that Dolohov had been in at the club dinner and at various other times when, weary as it were of the monotony of daily life, he had felt the need to escape from it by some odd and usually cruel action.

Rostov felt ill at ease. He racked his brain without success for some repartee in reply to Dolohov's words. But before he could think of anything, Dolohov, looking straight into Rostov's face, said slowly and deliberately so that everyone could hear:

'Do you remember, you and I were talking about cards. ... He's a fool who trusts to luck: one should play a safe game, and I want to try.'

'Try what – your luck, or a safe game?' wondered Rostov.

'You're right, you'd better not play,' Dolohov added, and springing a new pack of cards said: 'Bank, gentlemen!'

Moving the money forward, Dolohov began to deal. Rostov sat down by his side and at first did not play. Dolohov kept glancing at him.

'Why don't you play?' said Dolohov. And strangely enough, Rostov felt impelled to take a card, stake a trifling sum on it and begin to play.

'I have no money on me,' said Rostov.

'I'll trust you!'

Rostov staked five roubles on a card and lost, staked again, and lost. Dolohov 'killed' – in other words, took Rostov's stake ten times running.

'Gentlemen,' said Dolohov after he had been holding the bank for some time, 'pray place your money on the cards or else I may get muddled over the reckoning.'

One of the players said he hoped that they could trust him.

'Yes, but I am afraid of getting the accounts mixed; so I beg you to lay the money on your cards,' replied Dolohov. 'Don't worry yourself, we'll settle up afterwards,' he added, turning to Rostov.

The game continued; a waiter kept bringing round champagne.

All Rostov's cards were beaten, and the sum of eight hundred was scored up against him. He was just writing '800 roubles' on a card, but while the waiter filled his glass he changed his mind and altered it to his usual stake of twenty roubles.

'Leave it,' said Dolohov, though he did not seem to be looking at Rostov at all, 'you'll win it back all the sooner. I lose to the others but win from you. Is it that you are afraid of me?' he asked again.

Rostov submitted, let the stake of eight hundred remain and laid down a seven of hearts with a torn corner, which he had picked up from the floor. Well he remembered that card afterwards. He placed the seven of hearts, on which he had written '800 roubles' with a broken bit of chalk in bold round figures; he emptied the glass of warm champagne that had been handed to him, smiled at Dolohov's words, and with sinking heart as he waited for the seven to turn up watched Dolohov's hands which held the pack. A great deal depended on Rostov's winning or losing on that seven of hearts. The previous Sunday the old count had given his son two thousand roubles, and although he never liked speaking of money difficulties had told Nikolai that this was the last money he could let him have till May, and so he begged him to be a little more careful this time. Nikolai had replied that it was enough and to spare, and gave his word of honour not to come for more before the spring. Now out of that sum only twelve hundred roubles was left, so on this seven of hearts hung not only the loss of sixteen hundred roubles but the necessity of going back on his word. Feeling sick and frightened, he watched Dolohov's hands and thought, 'Now then, make haste and deal me that card and I'll take my cap and drive home to supper with Denisov, Natasha and Sonya, and I'm sure I'll never touch a card again.' At that moment his home life – the jokes with Petya, his talks with Sonya, duets with Natasha, the games of picquet with his father, even his comfortable bed in the house in Povarsky street – rose before him with such force and vividness and attraction that it seemed like some long past, lost and hitherto unappreciated happiness. He could not conceive that a stupid chance, letting the seven be dealt to the right rather than to the left, might deprive him of all this newly-perceived, newly-comprehended happiness, and plunge him into the depths of unknown and undefined misery. That could not be, yet it was with dread in his heart that he waited for the movement of Dolohov's hands. Those broad, reddish hands with hairy wrists visible from under the shirt-cuffs laid down the pack of cards and took up a glass and the pipe that were passed to him.

'So you're not afraid to play with me?' repeated Dolohov; and as though he were about to tell a good story he leaned back in his chair, and began deliberately with a smile:

'Yes, gentlemen, I've been told there's a rumour going about Moscow that I'm too sharp with cards, so I advise you to be somewhat on your guard with me.'

'Come on, deal now!' said Rostov.

'Ugh, these Moscow rabbits!' said Dolohov, and with a smile he took up the cards.

'Aaah!' Rostov almost screamed, lifting both hands to his head. The seven he needed was lying uppermost, the first card in the pack. He had lost more than he could pay.

'Still, don't go ruining yourself,' said Dolohov with a passing glance at Rostov as he continued to deal.

14

AN hour and a half later most of the players were no longer seriously interested in their own play.

The whole game centred on Rostov. Instead of the sixteen hundred roubles, he had a long column of figures scored against him, which he had reckoned up to ten thousand but which he now vaguely supposed must have risen to at least fifteen thousand. In reality the sum already exceeded twenty thousand roubles. Dolohov was no longer listening to stories or telling them; he followed every movement of Rostov's hands and occasionally ran his eyes over the score against him. He had decided to play until that score reached forty-three thousand. He had fixed on this figure because forty-three was the sum of his and Sonya's ages. Rostov, supporting his head in both hands, sat at the table which was scrawled over with figures, wet with spilt wine, and littered with cards. One torturing sensation never left him – that those broad-boned reddish hands with the hairs visible under the shirt-cuffs, those hands which he loved and hated, held him in their power.

'Six hundred roubles, ace, a corner, a nine ... winning it back's out of the question! ... And how happy I should be if only I were at home! ... The knave, double or quits ... it can't be! And why is he doing this to me?' Rostov pondered and thought. Sometimes he put a higher stake on a card, but Dolohov refused it and fixed the stake himself. Nikolai submitted to him, and at one moment he was praying to God as he had prayed under fire on the bridge over the Enns; at the next it would occur to him that perhaps the first card that came to hand from the crumpled heap under the table would save him; then he reckoned up the rows of braiding on his jacket and tried staking the total of his losses on a card of that number; then he looked round for help from the other players, or stared at the now stony face of Dolohov and tried to read what was passing in his mind.

'He knows, of course, what this loss means to me. Surely he can't want to ruin me? Why, he was my friend. Why, I loved him. ... But it isn't his fault; what's he to do if he has all the luck? And it's not my fault either,' he thought to himself. 'I have done nothing wrong. Have I ever murdered or hurt anyone, or wished harm to anyone? Why, then, this horrible misfortune? And when did it begin? Such a little while ago I came to this table with the idea of winning a hundred roubles to buy that little casket for Mamma's name-day and then going home. I was so happy, so free, so light-hearted! And I did not realize then how happy I was! When did that end and when did this new, awful state of things begin? What outward sign marked the change? I have sat all the time in this same place at this same table, picking out cards and putting them down in the same way, and looking at those deft, broad-boned hands. Whenever did it happen, and what has happened? I am well and strong and just the same as I was, and in the self-same place. No, it cannot be! Surely it will all end in nothing.'

He was flushed and bathed in perspiration, though the room was not hot. And his face was all the more painful and piteous to see because of its futile efforts to seem calm.

The score against him reached the fateful figure of forty-three thousand. Rostov had just prepared a card by bending the corner, with which he meant to double the three thousand he had just won, when Dolohov, slapping the pack of cards down on the table, pushed them aside and taking a piece of chalk began rapidly adding up the total of Rostov's losses in his clear, firm hand, breaking the chalk as he did so.

'Supper, it's time for supper! And here are the gipsies!'

And a number of dark-skinned men and women were in fact coming in from the cold outside, saying something in their gipsy accent. Nikolai realized that all was over; but he said in an indifferent voice:

'What, won't you go on? And I had such a nice little card all ready,' as though what really interested him was the fun of the game itself.

'It's all over, I'm done for!' he thought. 'Now a bullet through my brains – that's all that is left to me!' And at the same time he said in a cheerful voice:

'Come now, just this one card.'

'All right!' said Dolohov, having completed the addition. 'All right! Make it twenty-one roubles then,' he said, pointing to the figure twenty-one, which was over and above the round sum of forty-three thousand; and taking up a pack he prepared to deal. Rostov submissively unbent the corner of his card and instead of the 6,000 he had intended to write carefully put 21.

'It's all the same to me,' he said. 'I only wanted to see whether you would win on this ten or let me have it.'

Dolohov gravely began to deal. Oh, how Rostov at that moment detested those hands with their short reddish fingers and the hairy wrists emerging from the shirt-bands, which held him in their power! ... The ten fell to him.

'Well, you owe me forty-three thousand, count,' said Dolohov, stretching himself and getting up from the table. 'One gets tired, though, sitting still so long,' he added.

'Yes, I'm tired too,' said Rostov.

Dolohov cut him short, as if to remind him that it was not for him to take a light tone.

'When do you propose to let me have the money, count?'

Rostov, flushing, drew Dolohov into the next room.

'I cannot pay it all immediately. Will you take an I.O.U.?' he asked.

'I say, Rostov,' exclaimed Dolohov, smiling brightly and looking Nikolai straight in the eye, 'you know the saying, "Lucky in love, unlucky at cards!" Your cousin is in love with you, I know.'

'Oh, how horrible to feel myself in this man's power,' thought Rostov. He knew the shock the news of his losses would be to his father and mother; he felt what happiness it would be not to have to confess to all this; and he was aware that Dolohov knew that he could set him free from this shame and sorrow, and now wanted to play cat and mouse with him.

'Your cousin ...' Dolohov was saying, but Nikolai cut him short.

'My cousin has nothing to do with this, and there is no need to mention her!' he cried with fury.

'Then when will you pay me?' demanded Dolohov.

'Tomorrow,' said Rostov, and left the room.

15

To say 'tomorrow' and maintain a dignified tone was not difficult, but to go home alone, see his sisters, brother, his mother and father, confess and ask for money he had no right to after giving his word of honour, was terrible.

At home they had not yet gone to bed. The younger members of the family after returning from the theatre had had supper and were now grouped round the clavichord. As soon as Nikolai entered the room he felt himself enfolded in the romantic atmosphere of love which pervaded the Rostov household that winter and now, after Dolohov's proposal and Iogel's ball, seemed to hang breathlessly around Sonya and Natasha, like the air before a thunderstorm. Sonya and Natasha in the light-blue dresses they had worn to the theatre, looking pretty, and conscious of it, were standing by the clavichord, happy and smiling. Vera was playing chess with Shinshin in the drawing-room. The old countess, waiting for her husband and son to come in, sat playing patience with an old gentlewoman who lived in the house with them Denisov, with shining eyes and ruffled hair, was sitting with one leg behind him at the clavichord, striking chords with his short fingers and rolling his eyes as he sang in his small, husky but true voice a poem of his own composition called *The Enchantress*, to which he was trying to fit music:

> Enchantress, say what magic fire
> Draws me to my forsaken lyre?
> What ardour sets my heart aglow?
> What rapture thrills my fingers slow?

he sang in passionate tones, his black agate eyes sparkling at the tremulous but happy Natasha.

'Splendid! Excellent!' cried Natasha. 'Now another verse,' she said, not noticing Nikolai.

'Everything's just the same with them,' thought Nikolai, peeping into the drawing-room, where he saw Vera and his mother and the old lady.

'Ah, and here's our Nikolai!' Natasha ran up to him.

'Is Papa home?' he asked.

'I am so glad you've come,' said Natasha, not answering his

question. 'We're having such a lovely time. Vasili Dmitrich is staying on another day for me, did you know?'

'No, Papa is not back yet,' said Sonya.

'Nikolai, my dearest, you in? Come here to me, dear boy,' called the old countess from the drawing-room.

Nikolai went to his mother, kissed her hand and without saying a word took a seat near her table and began to watch her hands as they laid out the cards. From the music-room he kept hearing the sound of laughter and merry voices trying to persuade Natasha to sing.

'All wight! All wight!' shouted Denisov. 'It's no good making excuses now! It's your turn to sing the ba'cawolle – I entweat you!'

The countess glanced at her silent son.

'What is the matter?' she asked.

'Oh, nothing,' said Nikolai, as if he were sick of continually being asked one and the same question. 'Will Papa be in soon?'

'I expect so.'

'Everything's the same for them. They know nothing about it. What am I to do with myself?' thought Nikolai, and he went back to the music-room where the clavichord was.

Sonya was sitting at the instrument playing the opening bars of Denisov's favourite barcarolle. Natasha was preparing to sing. Denisov was looking at her with enraptured eyes.

Nikolai began to pace up and down the room.

'Why do they want to make her sing? What can she sing? And there's nothing to be happy about,' thought Nikolai.

Sonya struck the first chord of the prelude.

'My God, I'm ruined – I'm a dishonoured man! A bullet through my brain is the only thing left for me – not singing!' his thoughts ran on. 'Could I go away? But where to? I don't care – let them sing!'

He continued to stride about the room looking gloomily at Denisov and the girls, avoiding their eyes.

'Darling Nikolai, what is the matter?' Sonya's eyes asked, looking intensely at him. She had seen at once that something had happened to him.

Nikolai turned away from her. Natasha too, with her quick instinct, had instantly noticed her brother's state of mind. She had observed it but felt in such high spirits at that moment, so far removed from sorrow, melancholy or self-reproach, that she purposely deceived herself (as young people often do). 'No, I am too happy

400

just now to spoil my happiness by having to sympathize with someone else's misery,' she felt; and she said to herself: 'Very likely it is
only my fancy, and he's really as happy as I am.'

'Now, Sonya,' she said, walking into the very middle of the room
where she considered the acoustics were best. Lifting her head and
letting her arms droop lifelessly as ballet-dancers do, Natasha, rising
energetically from her heels to her toes, took a turn about the centre
of the room and stood still.

'Behold me, here I am!' she seemed to say, in response to the rapt
gaze with which Denisov followed her.

'And what can she find to be so pleased about?' thought Nikolai,
looking at his sister. 'How is it she isn't bored to death, why has she
no conscience?'

Natasha took the first note, her throat swelled, her chest rose, her
eyes became serious. At that moment she was oblivious of everyone
and everything, and from her smiling lips flowed sounds which anyone may produce at the same intervals and hold for the same length
of time, yet a thousand times they leave one unmoved, and on the
thousand and first occasion set one thrilling and weeping.

Natasha that winter had for the first time begun to take her
singing seriously, mainly because Denisov had been so enthusiastic
over her voice. She no longer sang like a child, there was no longer
any of that comical, immature, painstaking effort which used to be
in her performance; but she did not yet sing well, pronounced the
musical connoisseurs who heard her. 'A beautiful voice. Not trained
though. It must be trained,' everyone said. Only they generally
said it some while after the sound of her voice had died away. While
they were actually listening to that untrained voice with its incorrect
breathing and labouring transitions even the connoisseurs said
nothing but only delighted in it and wanted to hear it again. Her
voice had a virginal purity, an unconsciousness of its own powers and
an unforced velvety tone, which so combined with its lack of
knowledge of the art of singing that it seemed as though nothing in
that voice could be altered without spoiling it.

'What is this?' thought Nikolai, listening to her and opening his
eyes wide. 'What has happened to her? How she is singing today!'
And suddenly the whole world centred for him on anticipation of
the next note, the next phrase, and everything in the world was
divided into three beats: *Oh mio crudele affetto* ... One, two, three ...

One, two, three ... One ... *Oh mio crudele affetto* ... One, two, three ... One. 'Ugh, this senseless life of ours!' mused Nikolai. 'All that misery, money, Dolohov, and anger, and honour – it's all trash ... but this is real. ... Now, Natasha, now darling! Now my girl! How will she take that top B? Yes, she's taken it, glory be to God!' And without being conscious that he was singing, to support her top B he sang seconds and gave her the third to her high note. 'Oh God, how fine! Did I really get that note? How glorious!' he thought.

Oh, how that chord vibrated, and how all that was best in Rostov's soul thrilled in harmony! And this best was something apart from everything else in the world, and above all else. What were gambling losses, Dolohovs and promises? ... All rubbish. One might murder and steal and yet be happy. ...

16

IT was a long time since Rostov had derived such enjoyment from music as he did that day. But no sooner had Natasha finished her barcarolle than reality again presented itself. Without a word he got up and went downstairs to his own room. A quarter of an hour later the old count came in from the club, cheerful and contented. Hearing him drive up, Nikolai went to meet him.

'Well, had a good time?' asked the old count, smiling gaily and proudly at his son.

Nikolai tried to say 'Yes', but found it impossible, and nearly burst into sobs. The count was lighting his pipe and did not notice his son's state.

'Well, I've got to do it!' thought Nikolai for the first and last time. And suddenly, in the most casual tone, which made him feel utterly ashamed of himself, he said to his father, as though he were asking for the carriage to drive into town:

'Papa, I have come on a matter of business. I was almost forgetting. I need some money.'

'What's that!' said his father who was in particularly good spirits. 'I told you it wouldn't be enough. Need much, do you?'

'Very much,' said Nikolai flushing and smiling a stupid careless smile for which he was long unable to forgive himself. 'I have lost a little at cards, I mean a good deal, a great deal – forty-three thousand.'

'What! To whom? ... You're not serious!' cried the count, flushing, as old people flush, an apoplectic red over his neck and the back of his head.

'I have promised to pay tomorrow,' said Nikolai.

'Well! ...' said the old count, spreading out his arms and sinking helplessly on the sofa.

'It can't be helped. It happens to everyone!' said the son in a free and easy tone, while in his heart he was feeling himself a worthless scoundrel whose whole life could not atone for his crime. He longed to kiss his father's hands, kneel and beg his forgiveness, while in a careless and even rude voice he was telling him that it happens to everyone!

The old count dropped his eyes when he heard these words from his son, and began to fidget about as though in search of something.

'Yes, yes,' he murmured, 'it will be difficult, I fear, difficult to raise ... happens to everybody! Yes, yes, it might happen to anyone ...' And with a furtive glance at his son's face the count went out of the room. Nikolai had been prepared for opposition, but had not at all expected this.

'Papa! Pa-pa!' he called after him, sobbing. 'Forgive me!' And clutching at his father's hand he pressed it to his lips and burst into tears.

*

While father and son were having this conversation, another and no less important one was taking place between mother and daughter. Natasha came running to her mother in great excitement.

'Mamma! ... Mamma! ... He has done it ...'

'Done what?'

'Made me – made me an offer. Mamma! Mamma!' she cried.

The countess could not believe her ears. Denisov had proposed. To whom? To this chit of a girl, Natasha, who not so long ago was playing with dolls, and who was still in the school-room?

'Don't, Natasha! What nonsense!' she said, hoping it was a joke.

'Nonsense indeed! I am telling you a fact,' said Natasha indignantly. 'I came to ask you what to do, and you call it "nonsense"....'

The countess shrugged her shoulders.

'If it is true that *Monsieur* Denisov has proposed to you, then tell him he is a donkey, that's all.'

'No, he isn't a donkey,' replied Natasha seriously, affronted.

'Well then, what do you want? You are all in love nowadays, it seems. Well, if you are in love, better go and marry him,' said the countess with a laugh of annoyance. 'Good luck to you!'

'No, mamma, I'm not in love with him. I suppose I'm not in love with him.'

'That's all right then, go and tell him so.'

'Mamma, are you cross? Don't be cross, dearest. It's not my fault, is it?'

'No, my dear, but what is it you want? Would you like me to go and tell him?' said the countess, smiling.

'No, I will do it myself, only tell me what to say. Everything comes easily to you,' said Natasha, responding to her smile. 'And you should have seen how he said it! You know, I am sure he did not mean to say it: it came out by accident.'

'Well, all the same, you must refuse him.'

'No, I mustn't. I am so sorry for him! He's so nice.'

'Then accept his proposal. It's high time you were married!' exclaimed the countess sharply and sarcastically.

'No, mamma, but I feel so sorry for him. I don't know how to tell him.'

'There's no need for you to tell him anything. I'll speak to him myself,' said the countess, indignant that anyone should dare to look upon her little Natasha as grown up.

'No you won't! I'll say it myself, and you listen at the door,' and Natasha ran across the drawing-room to the music-room, where Denisov was still sitting on the same chair by the clavichord with his face in his hands. He jumped up at the sound of her light step.

'Natalie,' he said, moving towards her with rapid steps, 'decide my fate. It is in your hands!'

'Vasili Dmitrich, I'm so sorry for you! ... No, but you are so nice ... but it cannot be ... not that ... but I shall always, always love you as a friend.'

Denisov bent over her hand and she heard strange sounds that she did not understand. She kissed his rough curly black head. At that moment they heard the hurried rustle of the countess's skirts. She came up to them.

'Vasili Dmitrich, I thank you for the honour you do us,' she said in an embarrassed voice, which sounded severe to Denisov, 'but my daughter is so young, and I should have thought that as my son's friend you would have addressed yourself to me first. In that case you would not have forced me to make this refusal.'

'Countess ...' began Denisov with downcast eyes and a guilty face. He tried to say more, but faltered.

Natasha could not see him in such a piteous plight, and remain calm. She began to sob aloud.

'Countess, I have acted w'ongly,' Denisov went on in an unsteady voice, 'but pway believe me, I so adoah your daughter and all your family that I would gladly sacwifice my life twice over....' He looked at the countess, and seeing her stern face said: 'Well, good-bye, countess,' and kissing her hand he left the room with quick resolute steps, without a glance at Natasha.

*

Next day Rostov saw Denisov off, as he was unwilling to remain another day in Moscow. All his Moscow friends gave him a farewell entertainment at the Gipsies', with the result that he had no recollection of how they got him into the sledge, or of the first three stages of his journey.

After Denisov's departure Rostov spent another fortnight in Moscow, waiting for the money which the old count was unable to raise all at once. He did not leave the house, and passed most of his time in the girls' sitting-room.

Sonya was more affectionate and devoted to him than ever. It seemed as if she were anxious to show that his gambling loss was an exploit for which she loved him all the more; but Nikolai now considered himself unworthy of her.

He filled the girls' albums with verses and music, and after having finally sent Dolohov the whole forty-three thousand roubles, and received his receipt he went away at the end of November, without taking leave of any of his acquaintances, to rejoin his regiment which was already in Poland.

PART TWO

I

AFTER the scene with his wife Pierre left for Petersburg. At the Torzhok post-station either there were no horses or the post-master was unwilling to supply them. Pierre was obliged to wait. Without undressing, he stretched himself on the leather sofa in front of a round table on which he put up his heavy feet in their thick over-boots and sank into thought.

'Will you have the portmanteaux brought in? And a bed got ready? Would you care for tea?' the valet kept asking.

Pierre did not answer, he heard and saw nothing. He had begun to reflect while at the last station and still pondered the same question – one so important that he took no notice of what went on around him. Far from being concerned whether he reached Petersburg earlier or later, or whether there would or would not be a place for him to rest in at this station, in comparison with the thoughts that engrossed him now it was a matter of indifference to him whether he spent a few hours or the rest of his life here.

The post-master, his wife, Pierre's valet, and a peasant woman selling Torzhok embroidery, came into the room offering their services. Without removing his feet from the table Pierre looked at them through his spectacles, unable to understand what they could want or how they managed to live without having decided the questions that so absorbed him. These same problems had occupied his mind ever since the day he had returned from the Sokolnik woods after the duel and had spent that first agonizing, sleepless night. But now in the solitude of the journey they seized on him with especial force. No matter what he began to think about, he always came back to these questions, which he could not answer, yet could not cease asking himself. It was as though the thread of the principal screw which held his life together had worn smooth. The screw would not go in or come out but went on twisting round in the same groove without catching, and it was impossible to stop turning it.

The post-master came in and began obsequiously begging his Excellency to wait just a little couple of hours, after which (come what might of it) he would let his Excellency have the horses reserved for the mail. It was plain that the man was lying and only wanted to get an extra tip out of the traveller. 'Was that good or bad?' Pierre wondered. 'For me good, for the next traveller bad, and for himself unavoidable because he needs the money for food. He tells me an officer once gave him a thrashing for letting a private traveller have the courier-horses. But the officer thrashed him because he was in a hurry. And I shot Dolohov because I considered myself injured. And Louis XVI was executed because they believed him to be a criminal, and a year later they executed those who had executed him – also for some reason. What is wrong? What is right? What should one love and what hate? What is life for, and what am I? What is life? What is death? What is the power that controls it all?' he asked himself. And there was no answer to any of these questions, except the one illogical reply that in no way answered them. This reply was: 'One dies and it's all over. One dies and either finds out about everything or ceases asking.' But dying, too, was dreadful.

The Torzhok pedlar-woman in a whining voice kept offering her wares, especially some goat-skin slippers. 'I have hundreds of roubles I don't know what to do with, and she stands there in her tattered cloak looking timidly at me,' thought Pierre. 'And what does she want the money for? As if it could add a hair's breadth to her happiness or peace of mind. Can anything in the world make her or me less enslaved to evil and death? Death which is the end of all things and must come today or tomorrow – at any rate in an instant of time as compared with eternity.' And again he twisted the screw with the stripped thread, and the screw still went on turning in the same place.

His servant handed him a half-cut novel in the form of letters by Madame de Souza. He began reading about the sufferings and virtuous struggles of a certain Amélie de Mansfeld. 'And why did she resist her seducer when she loved him?' he thought. 'God could not have put into her heart an impulse that was against His will. My wife – as she once was – didn't struggle, and perhaps she was right. Nothing has been discovered, nothing invented,' Pierre said to himself again. 'All we can know is that we know nothing. And that is the sum total of human wisdom.'

Everything within him and without seemed to him confused, meaningless and loathsome. But in this very repugnance to all his circumstances Pierre found a kind of tantalizing satisfaction.

'May I venture to ask your Excellency to make the least little bit of accommodation for this gentleman here,' said the post-master, coming into the room and introducing another traveller held up for lack of horses. The new-comer was a thick-set, large-boned, sallow, wrinkled old man with grey bushy eyebrows overhanging bright eyes of an indefinite grey colour.

Pierre took his feet off the table, stood up and went to lie down on the bed that had been made ready for him, occasionally glancing at the stranger, who with a tired, gloomy air, without paying any heed to Pierre, wearily allowed his servant to help remove his wraps, leaving him in a shabby nankeen-covered sheepskin coat with felt high-boots on his thin bony legs. The new-comer took a seat on the sofa, leant his large head with its broad temples and close-cropped hair against the back of it, and looked at Bezuhov. The stern, intelligent and penetrating expression of his gaze impressed Pierre. He felt a wish to speak to the new-comer, but by the time he had made up his mind to put a question about the state of the roads the traveller had closed his eyes and folded his shrivelled old hands, on one finger of which there was a heavy iron ring with a seal representing a skull. He sat without stirring, either resting or sunk, as it seemed to Pierre, in profound and calm meditation. The stranger's servant was also a sallow wrinkled old man without beard or moustache, evidently not because he was shaven but because they had never grown. The old servant was nimbly unpacking his master's canteen, preparing tea and bringing in a samovar of boiling water. When everything was ready the new-comer opened his eyes, moved up to the table, and after pouring out a tumbler of tea for himself filled another for the beardless old man and passed it to him. Pierre began to feel a sense of uneasiness, and the need, even the inevitability, of entering into conversation with this stranger.

The servant brought back his empty glass turned upside down with an unfinished bit of nibbled sugar beside it, and asked if anything more would be wanted.

'No. Give me my book,' said the stranger.

The servant handed him a book which Pierre took to be of a devotional character, and the traveller buried himself in his reading. Pierre looked at him. All at once the stranger laid down the book, put a marker in the page and closed it, and again, shutting his eyes and leaning back on the sofa, fell into his former attitude. Pierre looked at him, and had not time to turn away when the old man opened his eyes and fastened his severe, resolute gaze directly on Pierre's face.

Pierre felt confused, and tried to escape that searching look, but the brilliant old eyes drew him irresistibly.

2

'I HAVE the pleasure of addressing Count Bezuhov, if I am not mistaken,' said the stranger, in a loud deliberate voice.

Pierre looked silently and inquiringly at him through his spectacles.

'I have heard of you, my dear sir,' continued the stranger, 'and of the misfortune that has befallen you.' He seemed to lay special stress on the word *misfortune*, as much as to say: *Yes, misfortune! Call it what you please, I know that what happened to you in Moscow was a misfortune.* – 'I feel for you deeply, my dear sir.'

Pierre flushed, and hurriedly dropping his legs down from the bed leant forward towards the old man, with a forced and timid smile.

'I have not referred to this out of curiosity, my dear sir, but for graver reasons.'

He paused, still gazing at Pierre, and moved aside on the sofa by way of inviting Pierre to sit next to him. Pierre felt reluctant to enter into conversation with this old man, but involuntarily submitting he came over and sat by his side.

'You are unhappy, my dear sir,' the stranger continued. 'You are young, I am old. I should like, so far as lies in my power, to help you.'

'Oh yes,' said Pierre with an unnatural smile. 'Very much obliged to you. ... May I ask where you are travelling from?'

The stranger's face was not genial, it was even cold and severe, but in spite of this to Pierre both the speech and the face of his new acquaintance were irresistibly attractive.

'But if for any reason you feel averse from talking to me,' said the old man, 'say so, my dear sir.' And suddenly he smiled a quite unexpected, tender, fatherly smile.

'Oh no, not at all, on the contrary, I am very happy to make your acquaintance,' said Pierre, and glancing once more at the stranger's hand he examined the ring more closely. He perceived the skull on it – the symbol of Masonry.

'Allow me to inquire,' he said, 'are you a mason?'

'Yes, I belong to the Brotherhood of Freemasons,' said the stranger, looking more and more searchingly into Pierre's eyes. 'And in their name and my own I hold out a brotherly hand to you.'

'I am afraid,' said Pierre, smiling and hesitating between the confidence inspired in him by the personality of the freemason and his own habit of ridiculing the articles of the masonic creed – 'I am afraid I am very far from a comprehension – how shall I put it? – I am afraid my way of thinking in regard to the whole theory of the universe is so opposed to yours that we shall not understand one another.'

'I am familiar with your way of thinking,' said the freemason, 'and the outlook you mention, which seems to you the result of your own mental efforts, is the way of thinking of the majority of men, and is the invariable fruit of pride, indolence and ignorance. Forgive me, my dear sir, but if I had not been sure of it I should not have addressed you. Your way of thinking is a melancholy delusion.'

'In exactly the same manner I might take it for granted that you are in error,' said Pierre with a faint smile.

'I should never be so bold as to assert that I know the truth,' said the mason, impressing Pierre more and more with the precision and assurance of his speech. 'No one can attain truth by himself. Only by laying stone upon stone with the co-operation of all, through millions of generations from our forefather Adam to our own day, is the temple raised which is to be a worthy dwelling-place for the Most High God,' said the freemason, and closed his eyes.

'I ought to tell you that I don't believe … I do not believe in God,' said Pierre regretfully and with an effort, feeling it essential to confess the whole truth.

The mason looked intently at Pierre and smiled, much as a rich man holding millions in his hands might smile upon a poor wretch who told him that he, the poor man, was without the five roubles that would secure his happiness.

'Yes, you do not know Him, my dear sir,' said the freemason. 'You cannot know Him. You do not know Him, that is just why you are unhappy.'

'Yes, yes, I am unhappy,' assented Pierre; 'but what am I to do?'

'You do not know Him, my dear sir, and so you are very unhappy. You do not know Him, but He is here, He is in me. He is in my words – He is within thee, and even in those impious words thou hast just uttered!' pronounced the mason in a stern, vibrating voice.

He paused and sighed, evidently trying to master his emotion.

'If He did not exist,' he said quietly, 'you and I would not be speaking of Him, my dear sir. Of what, of whom have we been speaking? Whom hast thou denied?' he suddenly asked with triumphant austerity and authority in his voice. 'Who invented Him, if He does not exist? Whence came your hypothesis of the existence of such an inconceivable Being? How came you and all the rest of the world to postulate the existence of such an incomprehensible Being, a Being all-powerful, eternal and infinite in all His attributes? ...'

He stopped and remained silent for some time.

Pierre could not and had no wish to break this silence.

'He exists, but to understand Him is hard,' the freemason began again, looking not at Pierre but straight before him, while his old hands, which the fullness of his heart made it impossible for him to keep still, turned over the pages of his book. 'If it were a man whose existence thou didst doubt I could bring him to thee, I could take him by the hand and show him to thee. But how can I, an insignificant mortal, show all His omnipotence, all His infinity, all His goodness and mercy to one who is blind, or to one who shuts his eyes that he may not see or comprehend Him, and may not see or understand his own vileness and depravity?' He paused again. 'Who art thou? What art thou? Thou dost imagine thyself a wise man because thou could'st utter those blasphemous words,' he went on with sombre irony, 'while thou art more foolish and artless than a little babe playing with the parts of a cunningly-fashioned watch and, because he does not understand its use, dares to say he does not believe in the master who made it. To know Him is difficult. For centuries, from our forefather Adam to our own day, we have toiled after this knowledge and we are an infinity from the attainment of our aim; but in our lack of understanding we see only our own weakness and His greatness. ...'

Pierre listened with swelling heart, gazing into the freemason's face with shining eyes; he did not interrupt, nor ask questions, but with all his soul believed what this stranger was telling him. Whether he was convinced by the rational arguments contained in the freemason's words, or was persuaded, as children are, by the tone of authority and sincerity, or the tremor in the speaker's voice, which sometimes almost failed him, or those brilliant aged eyes grown old in that conviction, or the calm firmness and security of purpose which radiated from his whole being and which particularly impressed Pierre by contrast with his own desolation and hopelessness – at any rate Pierre longed with all his soul to believe, and he did believe, and experienced a joyous sense of comfort, regeneration, and return to life.

'It is not the mind that comprehends Him; it is life that makes us understand,' said the mason.

'I don't understand,' said Pierre, feeling with dismay the reawakening of doubt. He dreaded to detect any obscurity, any weakness in the mason's argument; he dreaded not being able to believe. 'I don't understand,' he said, 'how it is that human reason cannot attain the knowledge of which you speak.'

The freemason smiled his gentle, fatherly smile.

'Supreme wisdom and truth may be compared to the purest dew which we should like to imbibe,' said he. 'Can I receive this pure dew into an impure vessel and judge of its purity? Only by the inner purification of myself can I bring that dew contained within me to some degree of purity.'

'Yes, yes, that is so,' said Pierre joyfully.

'Supreme wisdom is not founded on reason alone, not on those worldly sciences of physics, history, chemistry and the like, into which intellectual knowledge is divided. The highest wisdom is one. The highest wisdom has but one science – the science of the All, the science which explains all creation and man's place in it. In order to absorb this science it is absolutely essential to purify and regenerate one's inner self, and so, before one can know, it is necessary to have faith and be made perfect. And for this purpose we have the divine light called conscience, which God has implanted in our souls.'

'Yes, yes,' cried Pierre.

'Turn thy spiritual gaze into thine inmost being and ask of thyself if thou art satisfied with thyself. What hast thou attained with no guide but the intellect? What art thou? You are young, you are rich, intelligent, well educated – what have you made of all the blessings vouchsafed you? Are you satisfied with yourself and your life?'

'No, I hate my life,' muttered Pierre, frowning.

'If thou hatest it, then alter it. Purify thyself, and as thou art purified thou wilt gain wisdom. Examine your life, my dear sir. How have you spent it? In riotous orgies and debauchery, taking everything from society and giving nothing in return. You have become the possessor of great wealth. How have you been using it? What have you done for your fellow-men? Have you ever given a thought to your tens of thousands of serfs? Have you done anything to help them physically and morally? No! You have profited by their toil to lead a dissipated life. That is what you have done. Have you tried to employ yourself for the good of others? No! You have eaten the bread of idleness. Then you married, my dear sir – took upon yourself the responsibility of guiding a young woman through life, and how did you do it? You did not help her to find the path of truth, my dear sir, but flung her into an abyss of deceit and misery. A man offended you and you shot at and might have killed him, and you say you do not know God and detest your life. There is nothing surprising about that, my dear sir!'

After these words the freemason again leant back on the sofa and closed his eyes, as though wearied by his long discourse. Pierre studied the stern, impassive, almost lifeless face of the old man, and moved his lips without uttering a sound. He wanted to say, 'Yes, I've led a vile, idle, vicious life!' but dared not break the silence.

The freemason cleared his throat huskily, as old men do, and called his servant.

'How about horses?' he asked, without looking at Pierre.

'Some have just come in,' answered the servant. 'Will you not rest here a little?'

'No, tell them to harness.'

'Can he really be going away and leaving me alone, without telling me everything and promising help?' thought Pierre, getting up and beginning to walk about the room with bowed head, occasionally glancing up at the freemason. 'Yes, I never thought of it before: I have led a contemptible, dissolute life, though I did not like it and did not want to,' mused Pierre. 'And this man knows the truth and if he liked he could disclose it to me.' Pierre longed but had not the courage to say this to the mason.

The traveller, having packed his things with his practised old hands, began buttoning up his sheepskin. When he had finished he turned to Bezuhov, and said in a tone of indifferent politeness:

'Where are you going now, my dear sir?'

'I? ... I'm going to Petersburg,' answered Pierre in a childlike, hesitating voice. 'I am very grateful to you. I agree with every word you said. But do not think me altogether bad. With my whole soul I have wished that I were what you would have me be; but I have never met with any help from anyone. ... Though I am myself most to blame for everything. Help me, teach me, and some day perhaps ...'

Pierre could not go on. He gulped and turned away.

There was a long silence: the freemason was evidently considering.

'Help is given from God alone,' he said, 'but such measure of aid which it is within the power of our Craft to give you will be afforded you, my dear sir. You are going to Petersburg. Hand this to Count Willarski' (he took out his note-book and wrote a few lines on a large sheet of paper folded in four). 'Allow me to offer you one piece of advice. When you reach the capital, first of all devote some time to solitude and self-examination, and do not return to your old manner of life. And now I wish you a good journey, my dear sir,' he added, seeing that his servant had come in, 'and all success. ...'

The traveller was Osip Alexeyevich Bazdeyev, as Pierre discovered from the post-master's register. Bazdeyev had been one of the most well-known freemasons and Martinists even in Novikov's time. For a long while after he had gone Pierre did not go to bed, or ask for horses, but paced up and down the room reviewing his evil past, and with the enthusiasm of regeneration pictured to himself a blissful, irreproachably virtuous future, which now appeared to him so easy of attainment. It seemed to him that he had gone wrong only because he had somehow forgotten how nice it was to be virtuous. Not a trace of his former doubts remained in his soul. He firmly believed in the possibility of the brotherhood of men united in the aim of supporting one another in the path of virtue, and Freemasonry he saw as such a brotherhood.

3

ON reaching Petersburg Pierre informed no one of his arrival, went nowhere, and spent whole days in reading Thomas à Kempis which some unknown person had sent him. One thing and one thing only he realized as he read: the hitherto unknown bliss of believing in the possibility of attaining perfection, and in the possibility of active brotherly love between men, which Osip Alexeyevich had revealed to him. A week after his arrival the young Polish Count Willarski, whom Pierre knew very slightly in Petersburg society, came into his room one evening with the same official and ceremonious air with which Dolohov's second had called on him. Closing the door behind him, and having satisfied himself that he was alone with Pierre, he addressed him:

'I have come to you with a message and a suggestion, count,' he said, not sitting down. 'A personage of very high standing in our Brotherhood has applied for you to be received into our Craft before the usual term, and has asked me to be your sponsor. I regard it as a sacred duty to fulfil this person's wishes. Do you desire to join the Fraternity of Freemasons under my sponsorship?'

Pierre was struck by the cold austere tone of this man, whom he had almost always seen before at balls, smiling amiably in the society of the most brilliant women.

'Yes, I do wish it,' said Pierre.

Willarski bowed his head.

'One more question, count,' he said, 'which I beg you to answer in all sincerity – not as a future mason but as an honest man (*galant homme*): have you renounced your former opinions? Do you believe in God?'

Pierre considered.

'Yes … yes, I believe in God,' he said.

'In that case …' began Willarski, but Pierre interrupted him.

'Yes, I do believe in God,' he repeated.

'In that case we can go,' said Willarski. 'My carriage is at your service.'

Throughout the drive Willarski sat silent. To Pierre's inquiries as to what he would have to do, and how he should answer, Willarski merely replied that brethren more worthy than he would prove him, and that Pierre had only to tell the truth.

They drove in at the gates of a large house where the lodge had its quarters, and passing up a dark staircase they entered a small lighted ante-room where they took off their overcoats without the assistance of a footman. From the ante-room they proceeded into another room. A man in strange attire appeared at the door. Willarski, stepping forward to meet him, said something to him in an undertone in French, and then went up to a small cupboard, where Pierre noticed apparel unlike any he had ever seen. Taking a handkerchief from the cupboard, Willarski put it over Pierre's eyes and tied it in a knot behind, catching his hair painfully in the knot. Then he drew his face down, kissed him and with a hand on his arm led him forward. Pierre's head hurt where the hair was caught in the knot, and he frowned with the pain and gave a shamefaced smile. His burly figure, with arms hanging down at his sides and face puckered up though smiling, moved after Willarski with timid, uncertain steps.

After leading him for about ten paces Willarski stopped.

'Whatever happens to you,' he said, 'endure bravely if you are determined to become one of us.' (Pierre nodded affirmatively.) 'When you hear a knock at the door, you will uncover your eyes,' added Willarski. 'I wish you good courage and success,' and pressing Pierre's hand Willarski went away.

Left alone, Pierre still continued to smile. Once or twice he shrugged his shoulders and put his hand to the handkerchief, as though he would have liked to take it off, but let it drop again. The five minutes he had spent with his eyes bandaged seemed to him an hour. His arms felt numb, his legs almost gave way, as if he were tired out. He was aware of the most complex and conflicting sensations. He was afraid of what they were going to do to him, and still more afraid of showing his fear. He felt curious to know what was coming, what would be revealed to him; but above all he was filled with joy that the moment had come when he would at last set out upon that path of regeneration and the actively virtuous life of which he had been dreaming ever since his meeting with Osip Alexeyevich. Loud knocks were heard at the door. Pierre took the bandage from his eyes and looked about him. The room was pitch dark, except in one spot where a small lamp was burning inside something white. Pierre went nearer and saw that the lamp stood on a black table on which lay an open book. The book was the Gospel, and the white thing in which the lamp was burning was a human skull with its eye-sockets and teeth. After reading the first verse of the Gospel: 'In the beginning was the Word, and the Word was with God,' Pierre wandered round the table and caught sight of a large open box filled with something. It was a coffin full of bones. He was not in the least surprised at what he saw. Hoping to enter on an entirely new life absolutely removed from the old one, he expected to meet with strange things, even more extraordinary than what he had already seen. A skull, a coffin, the Gospel - it seemed to him that he had been looking for all this, and indeed for still more. Trying to stir up a devotional feeling in himself, he peered around. 'God, death, love, the brotherhood of man,' he kept saying to himself, associating with these words vague but joyful conceptions of some kind. The door opened and someone came in.

By the dim light to which Pierre however had already become accustomed he saw a not very tall man. Evidently coming from light into darkness, the man paused, then with cautious steps approached the table and placed on it his small leather-gloved hands.

This short man was wearing a white leather apron which covered his chest and part of his legs; round his neck he had a sort of necklace and above that there was a high white ruffle, framing his oblong face, lighted from below.

'For what are you come hither?' asked the new-comer, turning in Pierre's direction at a faint rustle made by the latter. 'Why have you, who do not believe in the truth of the light, who have not seen the light, come here? What do you seek from us? Is it wisdom, virtue, enlightenment?'

At the moment the door opened and the unknown man came in Pierre felt a sense of awe and reverence such as he had experienced in his boyhood at confession; he felt himself in the presence of one who, in the routine of daily life, was a complete stranger, and yet his kin by the tie of human brotherhood. With bated breath and beating heart he moved towards the tyler (the term in Freemasonry for the brother who prepares a candidate for initiation into the Fraternity). Drawing nearer, he recognized the tyler as a man he knew, one Smolyaninov, and it jarred on him to think of the new-comer as a familiar figure: he would rather he were simply a brother and instructor in virtue. For a long time he could not utter a word, so that the tyler was obliged to repeat his question.

'Yes, I ... I ... seek regeneration,' Pierre got out with an effort.

'Very well,' said Smolyaninov, and went on at once. 'Have you any idea of the means by which our holy Order can help you to the attainment of your desire?' said the tyler quietly and rapidly.

'I ... hope ... for guidance ... help ... in regeneration,' said Pierre with a trembling voice and some difficulty in utterance, due to his excitement and to being unaccustomed to speak of abstract matters in Russian.

'What conception have you of Freemasonry?'

'I imagine that Freemasonry is the *fraternité* and equality of men with virtuous aims,' said Pierre, feeling ashamed, as he spoke, of the incongruity of his words with the solemnity of the moment. 'I imagine ...'

'Good!' said the tyler quickly, apparently quite satisfied with this answer. 'Have you sought the means of attaining your aim in religion?'

'No, for I thought religion contrary to truth, and so did not pursue it,' said Pierre, so softly that the tyler did not hear and asked him what he was saying. 'I was an atheist,' answered Pierre.

'You seek after truth for the purpose of observing its laws in your life; therefore you seek wisdom and virtue, do you not?' said the tyler, after a moment's silence.

'Yes, yes,' confirmed Pierre.

The tyler cleared his throat, crossed his gloved hands on his breast, and began to speak.

'It is now my duty to unfold to you the chief aim of our Craft,' he said, 'and if this aim harmonizes with yours you may with profit enter our Brotherhood. The first and principal object of our Order, the foundation on which it rests and which no human power can destroy, is the preservation and handing on to posterity of a certain important mystery ... which has come down to us from the most ancient times, and even from the first man – a mystery upon which perhaps the fate of the human race depends. But since this mystery is of such a nature that nobody can know or profit by it unless he be prepared by long and diligent self-purification, not everyone can hope to discover it speedily. Hence we have a secondary aim, that of preparing our brethren as far as possible to reform their hearts, to purify and enlighten their minds by those means which have been revealed to us by tradition through men who have striven to attain this mystery, and thereby to render them capable of receiving it. By purifying and regenerating our brethren we endeavour, thirdly, to improve the whole human race also, presenting in our brethren of the Craft an example of piety and virtue, and in this way we exert ourselves with all our might to combat the evil that is paramount in the world. Reflect on what I have said, and I will come to you again,' he concluded and went out of the room.

'To combat the evil that is paramount in the world ...' Pierre repeated, and a mental image of his future activity in that direction rose before him. He imagined men such as he had himself been a fortnight ago, and he mentally addressed an edifying exhortation to them. He pictured to himself vicious and unfortunate people, whom he would assist by word and deed; he saw oppressors whose victims he would deliver. Of the three aims enumerated by the tyler this last – the reformation of mankind – appealed particularly to Pierre. The great mystery mentioned by the tyler, though it excited his curiosity, did not seem to be of material importance; while the second aim, self-purification and regeneration, interested him very little since at that moment he was full of a blissful sense of already being completely cured of all his former vices, and geared to nothing but goodness.

Half an hour later the tyler returned to instruct the candidate in the seven virtues, corresponding to the seven steps of Solomon's Temple, which every freemason should cultivate in himself. These virtues were: (1) *discretion*, the keeping of the secrets of the Order; (2) *obedience* to those of higher rank in the Craft; (3) *morality*; (4) *love for mankind*; (5) *courage*; (6) *generosity*; (7) *the love of death*.

'Concerning the *seventh* of these,' said the tyler, 'by frequent meditation on death bring yourself to regard death not as an enemy to be dreaded but as a friend who sets free the soul, grown weary in the labours of virtue, from this miserable life, and leads it into the place of recompense and peace.'

'Yes, that's as it should be,' thought Pierre, when the tyler, after delivering himself of these words, again retired, leaving him to solitary reflection. 'It must be so, but I am still so weak as to love this life, the meaning of which is only now gradually opening before me.' But the other five virtues, which Pierre recalled, counting them on his fingers, he felt already in his soul: *courage*, *generosity*, *morality*, *love of mankind*, and, above all, *obedience* – which last seemed less a virtue to him than a pleasure. (He felt so glad now to be escaping from self-will and surrendering to those who knew the indubitable truth.) The seventh virtue Pierre had forgotten and he could not recall it.

The third time the tyler came back sooner, and asked Pierre if he were still firm in his intention to submit to everything that would be demanded of him.

'I am ready for anything,' said Pierre.

'I must inform you further,' said the tyler, 'that our Craft promulgates its teaching not by word only but makes use of certain other means which may perhaps have a more potent effect on the earnest seeker after wisdom and virtue than merely verbal explanations. This chamber with the objects you see therein must already, if you are sincere at heart, have told you more than any words could do; and in the course of your initiation it may be that you will be met with a like method of enlightenment. Our Craft follows the usage of ancient societies which explained their teaching through hieroglyphics. A hieroglyphic,' said the tyler, 'is the image of an abstract idea, embodying in itself the properties of the thing it symbolizes.'

Pierre knew very well what a hieroglyphic was, but he did not venture to speak. He listened to the tyler in silence, feeling from all he said that his ordeal was about to begin.

'If you are fully resolved, I must proceed to your initiation,' said the tyler, coming closer to Pierre. 'In token of generosity I request you to give me all your valuables.'

'But I have nothing with me,' replied Pierre, supposing that he was being asked to give up all his possessions.

'What you have with you: watch, money, rings ...'

Pierre made haste to get out his purse and his watch, and struggled for some time to remove the wedding ring from his fat finger. When this had been accomplished the tyler said:

'In token of obedience I ask you to undress.'

Pierre took off his coat, waistcoat and left boot according to the tyler's instructions. The mason drew the shirt back from Pierre's left breast, and stooping down pulled up the left leg of his trousers to above the knee. Pierre hurriedly began taking off his right boot and was going to tuck up the other trouser-leg to save this stranger the trouble, but the mason told him this was not necessary and gave him a slipper for his left foot. With a childlike smile of embarrassment, doubt and self-mockery, which would appear on his face in spite of himself, Pierre stood up, with his arms hanging by his sides, and legs apart, before the tyler, awaiting his next commands.

'And finally, in token of sincerity, I ask you to reveal to me your chief temptation.'

'My chief temptation! I *had* so many,' replied Pierre.

'The temptation which did more than all the rest to make you stumble on the path of virtue,' said the freemason.

Pierre paused, trying to think.

'Wine? Gluttony? Idleness? Laziness? Hasty temper? Anger? Women?' He went over his vices, mentally balancing them and not knowing to which to give preference.

'Women,' he said in a voice so low that it was scarcely audible.

The mason did not stir or speak for a long time after this reply. At last he moved up to Pierre, took the handkerchief lying on the table, and again blindfolded his eyes.

'For the last time I say to you – examine yourself thoroughly, put a bridle on your senses, and seek felicity not in your passions but in your heart. The fountain-head of happiness is not without but within us. …'

Pierre was already conscious of this refreshing fount of blessedness within him which now flooded his heart with joy and emotion.

4

SHORTLY after this there came into the dark chamber to fetch Pierre, not the tyler but Pierre's sponsor, Willarski, whom he recognized by his voice. To fresh inquiries as to the firmness of his resolve, Pierre answered:

'Yes, yes, I agree,' and with a beaming, childlike smile, his fat chest uncovered, stepping timidly and unevenly with one booted and one slippered foot, he advanced, while Willarski held a drawn sword against his bare breast. He was conducted out of the room along corridors that twisted backwards and forwards, and at last brought to the doors of the lodge. Willarski coughed, he was answered by a masonic rapping with hammers; the door opened before them. A bass voice (Pierre was still blindfolded) questioned him as to who he was, when and where he was born, and so on. Then he was again led away somewhere, the handkerchief still over his eyes, and as he went along they spoke to him in allegories of the toils of his pilgrimage, of sacred friendship, of the Eternal Architect of the Universe, and of the courage with which he must endure perils and labours. During these wanderings Pierre noticed that sometimes he was called the 'Seeker', sometimes the 'Sufferer' or the 'Candidate', and that at each new appellation they made various tapping sounds with gavels and swords. While he was being led up to some object he was aware of hesitation and uncertainty among his guides. He heard a whispered dispute, and one of the people round him insisting that he should be made to walk along a certain carpet. After that they took his right hand, laid it on something, while they bade him hold a pair of compasses to his left breast with his other hand, and repeat after someone who read the words aloud the oath of fidelity to the laws of the Order. Then the candles were extinguished and some spirit lighted, as Pierre guessed by the smell, and he was told that he would see the lesser light. The bandage was removed from his eyes and by the faint illumination of the spirit lamp Pierre saw as in a dream a number of men standing before him, all wearing aprons like the tyler's and holding swords pointed at his breast. Among them stood a man whose white shirt was stained with blood. On seeing this Pierre moved forward with his breast towards the swords, meaning them to pierce it. But the swords were drawn back and he was at once blindfolded again.

'Now thou hast seen the lesser light,' said a voice. Then the candles were relit and he was told that he had now to see the full light; and again the bandage was taken off, and ten or a dozen voices declaimed together: 'Sic transit gloria mundi.'

Pierre gradually began to recover himself and look about the room and at the people in it. Round a long table covered with black sat some twelve brethren in garments like those he had already seen. Several of them Pierre had met in Petersburg society. At the head of the table sat a young man he did not know, with a peculiar cross hanging from his neck. On his right sat the Italian abbé whom Pierre had seen at Anna Pavlovna's two years before. There were also present a very important dignitary, and a Swiss tutor who used to be in the Kuragin family. All preserved a solemn silence, listening to the words of the Worshipful Master, who held a gavel in his hand. Let into the wall was a star-shaped light. On one side of the table was a small carpet with various figures worked upon it; on the other was something resembling an altar on which lay the New Testament and a skull. Round the table stood seven large candlesticks of ecclesiastical design. Two of the brethren led Pierre up to the altar, placed his feet at right angles and bade him lie down, saying that he must prostrate himself at the gates of the Temple.

'He ought to receive the trowel first,' whispered one of the brethren.

'Oh, quiet, please!' said another.

Perplexed, Pierre peered about him with his short-sighted eyes, without obeying, and suddenly doubts rose in his mind. 'Where am I? What am I doing? They are making fun of me, surely? Will not the time come when I shall be ashamed of all this?' But these doubts only lasted a moment. He looked at the serious faces of those around him, thought of all he had just been through and realized that there was no stopping half-way. He was aghast at his hesitation, and trying to summon back his former feeling of devotion cast himself down at the gates of the Temple. And the devotional feeling did in fact return to him, and more powerfully than before. After he had lain there some little time he was told to get up, and a white leather apron such as the others wore was put on him, and he was given a trowel and three pairs of gloves. The Grand Master then addressed him. He told him that he must try never to stain the whiteness of that apron, which symbolized strength and purity; next, of the mysterious trowel, he said that Pierre was to toil with it to eradicate vice from his own heart and with forbearing patience smooth the hearts of his fellow-men. He was not to know the significance of the first pair of men's gloves, but must cherish them. The second pair, also men's, he would wear at the meetings of the lodge, and finally of the third pair – they were women's gloves – he said:

'Dear brother, these women's gloves are intended for you too. Give them to the woman whom you shall honour above all others. By this gift you pledge the purity of your heart to her whom you select to be your worthy helpmeet in Masonry.' Then after a pause he added: 'But beware, dear brother, that these gloves never deck hands that are unclean.'

Pierre fancied that the Grand Master was embarrassed as he said these last words. Pierre himself was even more embarrassed; he blushed to the point of tears, as children blush, looking about him uneasily, and an awkward silence followed.

The silence was broken by one of the brethren who led Pierre to the carpet and began reading to him, out of a manuscript book, an interpretation of all the symbols delineated upon it: the sun, the moon, the gavel, the plumb-line, the trowel, the untrimmed and four-square foundation stone, the pillar, the three windows, and so on. After this a place was assigned to Pierre, he was shown the masonic signs, told the password, and at last permitted to sit down. Then the Grand Master began reading the charges and regulations. They were very long, and Pierre, from joy, agitation and embarrassment, was not in a condition to understand what was being read. He managed to follow only the last words of the statutes and these impressed themselves on his memory.

'In our Temples we recognize no other degrees,' read the Grand Master, 'but those between virtue and vice. Beware of making any distinctions that may transgress against equality. Fly to a brother's aid whoever he may be, exhort him that goeth astray, raise him that falleth, and never harbour anger or enmity against thy brother. Be kindly and courteous. Kindle in all hearts the fire of virtue. Share thy happiness with thy neighbour, and may envy never dim the purity of this bliss.

'Forgive thine enemy, and avenge not thyself upon him, except by returning good for evil. Fulfilling in this wise the highest law, thou shalt recover traces of the ancient dignity which thou hast lost,' he concluded, and getting up he embraced and kissed Pierre.

Pierre looked round him with tears of joy in his eyes, not knowing what reply to make to the greetings and congratulations of acquaintances on all sides. He acknowledged no acquaintances: in all these men he saw only brethren, and he burned with impatience to set to work with them.

The Grand Master rapped with his gavel. All sat down in their places, and one of the masons read an exhortation on the necessity of humility.

The Grand Master proposed that the last duty be performed, and the important dignitary who bore the title of 'Collector of Alms' went round to all the brethren. Pierre would have liked to subscribe all the money he had in the world but the fear of being thought ostentatious checked him and he wrote down the same amount as the others.

The meeting was over, and it seemed to Pierre on reaching home that he had come back after a long journey of dozens of years' duration, completely changed and quite divorced from his former life and habits.

5

THE day following his initiation into the lodge Pierre was sitting at home reading a book and trying to fathom the significance of the Square, one side of which symbolized God, another the world of ethics, the third the physical world and the fourth a combination. Now and then his attention wandered from the book and the Square and in his imagination he began to formulate a new plan of life for himself. On the previous evening he had been told at the lodge that rumours of his duel had reached the Emperor's ears, and that it would be as well for him to leave Petersburg for a time. Pierre proposed to go to his estates in the south and there attend to the welfare of his peasants. He was dreaming joyfully of this new life when Prince Vasili suddenly walked into the room.

'My dear fellow, what have you been up to in Moscow? Why have you quarrelled with Hélène, *mon cher*? You are under a misapprehension,' said Prince Vasili, as he came in. 'I know all about it, and I can tell you positively that Hélène stands as innocent before you as Christ was before the Jews.'

Pierre was about to reply but Prince Vasili interrupted him.

'And why didn't you simply come straight to me as to a friend? I know how it was: I understand it all,' he said. 'You behaved as becomes a man who cares for his honour – a bit too hastily perhaps, but we won't go into that. But just consider the position you are placing her and me in, in the eyes of society and even of the court,' he added, lowering his voice. 'She is in Moscow, you are here. Remember, my dear boy,' and he drew Pierre down by the arm, 'this is simply a misunderstanding: I expect you feel it so yourself. Let us write her a letter together, now at once, and she'll come here and all will be explained. Otherwise, let me tell you, my dear boy, I am afraid you will live to repent of it.'

Prince Vasili gave Pierre a significant look.

'I have it from the best sources that the Dowager Empress is taking a keen interest in the whole affair. You know she is very graciously disposed to Hélène.'

Several times Pierre prepared himself to speak, but on one hand Prince Vasili would not give him the chance and on the other Pierre himself was loath to embark on the tone of determined refusal and dissent in which he was firmly resolved to answer his father-in-law. Moreover the words of the masonic precept, 'Be thou kindly and courteous,' recurred to his mind. He blinked, went red, got up and sank back again, struggling with himself to do what was for him the most difficult thing in life – to say something unpleasant to a man's face, to say the opposite of what the other, whoever he might be, expected. He was so much in the habit of submitting to Prince Vasili's accent of careless authority that he felt he would be unable to resist it even now; but he was also aware that on what he said now his whole future depended: what he said now would decide whether he continued along the same old road or advanced along the new path that had been so attractively pointed out to him by the masons, and where he firmly believed he would find regeneration.

'Come, dear boy,' said Prince Vasili playfully, 'just say "Yes", and I will write to her myself, and we'll kill the fatted calf.' But before Prince Vasili had time to finish his pleasantry, Pierre, not looking at him and with a flash of fury reminiscent of his father, exclaimed in a whisper:

'Prince, I did not invite you here. Go, please go!' He jumped up and opened the door for him. 'Go!' he repeated, amazed at himself and enjoying the expression of confusion and alarm that showed itself on Prince Vasili's face.

'What's the matter with you? Are you ill?'

'Go!' the quivering voice repeated once more. And Prince Vasili was obliged to withdraw, without receiving a word of explanation.

A week later Pierre, after taking leave of his new friends, the freemasons, and placing large sums in their hands for charity, set out for his estates. His new brethren gave him letters to the masons of Kiev and Odessa, and promised to write to him and guide him in his new way of life.

6

THE duel between Pierre and Dolohov was hushed up and, in spite of the Emperor's severity at that time in regard to duelling, neither the principals nor their seconds suffered for it. But the scandal of the duel, confirmed by Pierre's rupture with his wife, was the talk of society. Pierre had been looked upon with patronizing condescension when he was an illegitimate son, had been made much of and extolled for his virtues when he was the best match in Russia; but after his marriage – when marriageable daughters and their mothers had nothing to hope from him – he had fallen greatly in the esteem of society, especially as he had neither the wit nor the wish to court public favour. Now, all the blame for what had happened was thrown on him alone: he was said to be insanely jealous, and subject, like his father, to fits of bloodthirsty rage. And when, after Pierre's departure, Hélène returned to Petersburg she was received by all her acquaintances not only cordially but with a shade of deference that was a tribute to her misfortune. If the conversation turned on her husband Hélène, prompted by her characteristic *nous*, would assume a dignified expression, though she had no idea what impression it gave. This expression suggested that she had resolved to endure her troubles uncomplainingly, and that her husband was a cross laid upon her by God. Prince Vasili expressed his opinion more openly. He shrugged his shoulders when Pierre was mentioned, and pointing to his forehead remarked:

'A bit touched – I always said so.'

'I said from the first,' declared Anna Pavlovna, referring to Pierre, 'I said at once and before anyone else' (she always insisted on her priority) 'that he was a lunatic young man ruined by the dissolute notions of the age. I said so even at the time when everybody was in ecstasies over him, after he had just returned from abroad, and when, if you remember, he posed at one of my *soirées* as a sort of Marat. Well, and this is the result. I was against the marriage even then, and predicted what would come of it.'

On evenings when she was free Anna Pavlovna continued to give her *soirées* as before – *soirées* such as she alone had the gift of arranging – at which was to be found 'the cream of really good society, the flower of the intellectual essence of Petersburg,' to use her own words. Over and above this discriminating selection of society Anna Pavlovna's receptions were also distinguished by the fact that at each one she presented some new and interesting individual, and that nowhere else in Petersburg could the political thermometer reflecting the disposition of loyal court society be more accurately studied than in her drawing-room.

Towards the end of the year 1806, when all the melancholy details of Napoleon's destruction of the Prussian army at Jena and Auerstadt, and the surrender of the majority of the Prussian fortresses, had been received, when our troops had already entered Prussia and our second campaign against Napoleon was beginning, Anna Pavlovna gave one of her *soirées*. The 'cream of really good society' consisted of the fascinating and unhappy Hélène, deserted by her husband; of Mortemart; of the delightful Prince Hippolyte just home from Vienna; of two diplomats; of the old aunt; of a young man known simply as *un homme de beaucoup de mérite*; of a newly-appointed maid of honour and her mother, and several other less noteworthy persons.

The novelty of the evening on this occasion was Boris Drubetskoy, who had just arrived on a special mission from the Prussian army and was aide-de-camp to a very important personage.

What the political thermometer indicated at that *soirée* was something as follows:

'Whatever the rulers and commanders of Europe may do to countenance Bonaparte, with the object of causing *me* and *us* in general these annoyances and mortifications, our opinion in regard to Bonaparte cannot alter. We shall not cease to express our views on the subject in the plainest terms, and can only declare to the king of Prussia and others: "So much the worse for you. You made your bed, and now you must lie on it" – that is all we have to say!'

This was the reading of the political thermometer at Anna Pavlovna's that evening. When Boris, the choice morsel to be served up to the company, entered the drawing-room, almost all those invited had assembled, and the conversation, guided by Anna Pavlovna, turned on our diplomatic relations with Austria and the hope of an alliance with her.

Boris, elegantly dressed in the uniform of an aide-de-camp, looking fresh and rosy and grown to man's estate, came into the drawing-room with easy assurance, and was duly conducted to pay his respects to the aunt and then brought back to the general circle.

Anna Pavlovna held out her shrivelled hand for him to kiss, and introduced him to several persons whom he did not know, giving him a whispered description of each.

'Prince Hippolyte Kuragin – *charmant jeune homme*. Monsieur Krug, *chargé d'affaires* from Copenhagen – a man of great intellect'; and simply, of the young man always thus described, 'Monsieur Shitov – *un homme de beaucoup de mérite*.'

Thanks to his mother's efforts, his own inclinations and the peculiarities of his canny nature, Boris had with time succeeded in making a very snug place for himself in the service. He was aide-de-camp to a very eminent personage, had been sent on a most important mission to Prussia, and had only just returned from there as a special messenger. He had become thoroughly conversant with that unwritten code which had so pleased him at Olmütz, in virtue of which an ensign might rank incomparably higher than a general, and all that was needed to ensure success in the service was not exertion, not work, not courage or perseverance, but simply the art of knowing how to get on with the dispensers of promotions and awards; and he often marvelled himself at the rapidity of his own progress, and at the inability of others to grasp the secret. His whole manner of life, all his relations to former friends and acquaintances, all his plans for the future were completely transformed in consequence of this discovery. He was not well off but he would spend his last farthing to be better dressed than others, and would rather deprive himself of many pleasures than allow himself to be seen in a shabby carriage or appear in the streets of Petersburg in an old uniform. He cultivated the friendship and sought the acquaintance only of those who were above and could therefore be of use to him. He liked Petersburg and despised Moscow. He found it distasteful to look back on the Rostovs' house and his boyish passion for Natasha, and since the day of his departure for the army had not once been to see the Rostovs. To be in Anna Pavlovna's drawing-room he considered an important step up in the service, and he at once understood his rôle, and allowed his hostess to make the most of whatever interest he had to offer, while himself carefully scanning every face and appraising the advantages and possibilities of establishing intimacy with each of those present. He took the seat indicated to him beside the fair Hélène, and listened to the general conversation being carried on in French.

' "Vienna considers the bases of the proposed treaty so unattainable that not even a succession of the most brilliant victories would put them within reach, and she doubts the means we have of gaining them." Those are the actual words of the Vienna cabinet,' said the Danish *chargé d'affaires*.

'The doubt is flattering,' said the *man of great intellect* with a subtle smile.

'One should distinguish between the Cabinet in Vienna and the Emperor of Austria,' said Mortemart. 'The Austrian Emperor could never have thought of such a thing: it can only be the Cabinet who says that.'

'Ah, my dear *vicomte*,' put in Anna Pavlovna, 'Urope' (for some reason she pronounced it *Urope* as if that were a special refinement of French which she could allow herself in conversing with a Frenchman), 'Urope will never be a sincere ally of ours.'

After that, Anna Pavlovna led the conversation round to the courage and firmness of the king of Prussia, with the object of bringing Boris into action.

Boris listened attentively to each of the speakers, awaiting his turn, but every now and then he managed to glance in the direction of his neighbour, the beautiful Hélène, whose eyes several times met those of the handsome young aide-de-camp with a smile.

Speaking of the position of Prussia, Anna Pavlovna very naturally appealed to Boris to tell them about his journey to Glogau, and the state in which he found the Prussian army. Boris, without undue haste, in pure and elegant French, related a number of interesting particulars about the armies and the court, studiously abstaining from any expression of personal opinion in regard to the facts which he communicated. For some time he engrossed the general attention, and Anna Pavlovna felt that her guests appreciated the treat she had set before them. Hélène above all listened with the greatest concentration to what Boris had to say, asking him various questions about his expedition, and apparently much interested in the position of the Prussian army. As soon as he had finished, she turned to him with her habitual smile.

'You absolutely must come and see me,' she said in a tone which implied that certain considerations of which he could have no knowledge made it indispensable that he should call on her. 'Tuesday, between eight and nine. It will give me great pleasure.'

Boris promised to do so and was about to engage her in further conversation when Anna Pavlovna called him away, on the pretext that her old aunt wished to hear his story.

'You know her husband, of course?' said Anna Pavlovna, closing her eyes and indicating Hélène with a melancholy gesture. 'Ah, she is such an unfortunate, such an exquisite woman! Never mention him in her presence, I beg you. It is too painful for her!'

7

WHEN Boris and Anna Pavlovna returned to the others Prince Hippolyte had the ear of the company. Bending forward in his low chair he was saying:

'*Le roi de Prusse!*' and having said this he laughed. Everyone turned towards him. 'The king of Prussia?' repeated Hippolyte with another laugh, and then calmly and seriously settled himself in the depths of his arm-chair. Anna Pavlovna waited for him to go on, but as Hippolyte seemed quite decided to say no more she began to speak of how the impious Bonaparte had at Potsdam carried off the sword of Frederick the Great.

'It is the sword of Frederick the Great which I ...' she began, but Hippolyte interrupted her with the words: *'Le roi de Prusse ...'* and again, as soon as they turned towards him, excused himself and fell silent. Anna Pavlovna frowned. Mortemart, Hippolyte's friend, addressed him peremptorily.

'Come now, what about your *roi de Prusse*?'

Hippolyte laughed as though he were ashamed of laughing.

'Oh, nothing. I only meant ...' (He had intended to repeat a quip he had heard in Vienna which he had been trying all the evening to get in.) 'I only wanted to say that we are wrong to make war *pour le roi de Prusse* – the French idiom for having one's trouble for one's pains!'

Boris smiled discreetly, a smile that could be taken as ironical or appreciative, according to the way the pleasantry was received. Everybody laughed.

'Your pun is too bad! Very clever, but quite unjust,' said Anna Pavlovna, shaking her little shrivelled finger at him. 'We are not fighting *pour le roi de Prusse* but for right principles. Oh, that wicked Prince Hippolyte!' she said.

The conversation did not flag at all throughout the evening, dwelling chiefly on the political news. Towards the end of the *soirée* it became particularly eager, when the rewards bestowed by the Emperor were mentioned.

'You know, last year what's-his-name received a snuff-box with the portrait,' said the *man of great intellect*. 'So why shouldn't *X* get the same distinction?'

'I beg your pardon – a snuff-box with the Emperor's portrait is a reward, no doubt, but not an official distinction,' said one of the diplomats. 'Or rather, it's a present.'

'There have been precedents. I would instance Schwarzenberg.'

'It's impossible,' retorted another.

'Will you wager? The ribbon of the order, of course, is a different matter. ...'

When everybody rose to go, Hélène, who had spoken very little all the evening, turned to Boris again, graciously bidding him in a tone of pressing significance not to forget Tuesday.

'It is of great importance to me,' she said with a smile, looking round at Anna Pavlovna, and Anna Pavlovna, with the same melancholy expression with which she accompanied any reference to her royal patroness, gave her support to Hélène's wish. It appeared that from some words Boris had uttered that evening about the Prussian army Hélène had suddenly found it necessary to see him. Her manner seemed to convey that she would explain that necessity to him when he came on Tuesday.

But on Tuesday evening, in Hélène's magnificent salon, Boris received no clear explanation of the urgent reasons for his visit. Other guests were present, the countess talked little to him, and only as he kissed her hand on taking leave said unexpectedly and in a whisper, without any smile, which was strange for her:

'Come to dinner tomorrow evening. ... You must come. ... Do!'

During that stay in Petersburg Boris was constantly at the house of the Countess Bezuhov on a footing of the greatest intimacy.

8

THE war was blazing up and nearing the Russian frontier. Everywhere one heard curses on Bonaparte, 'the enemy of the human race'. Militiamen and recruits were being called out in the villages, and from the theatre of war came news of a conflicting character, as usual false and hence variously interpreted.

The life of old Prince Bolkonsky, Prince Andrei and Princess Maria had changed in many respects since 1805.

In 1806 the old prince had been appointed one of the eight commanders-in-chief created at that time to supervise recruiting all over Russia. Despite the infirmity of age, which had become particularly noticeable during the period when he supposed his son to have been killed, he did not think it right to refuse a duty assigned to him by the Sovereign in person, and this fresh opportunity for action gave him new energy and strength. He spent his time continually travelling about the three provinces entrusted to him; was pedantic in the performance of his duties, severe to the point of cruelty with his subordinates, and looked into everything down to the minutest details himself. Princess Maria had no more lessons in mathematics, and on mornings when he was at home only went to her father's study accompanied by the wet-nurse and little Prince Nikolai (as his grandfather called him). The baby Prince Nikolai lived with his wet-nurse and Nanny Savishna in the late princess's rooms, and Princess Maria passed most of the day in the nursery, doing all she could to take the place of mother to her little nephew. Mademoiselle Bourienne, too, appeared to be passionately fond of the child, and Princess Maria would often sacrifice herself to give her friend the pleasure of dandling and playing with the little *angel* (as she called the infant).

Near the chancel of the church at Bald Hills a small shrine had been made over the resting place of the little princess, and in the shrine was a marble monument brought from Italy, representing an angel with outspread wings ready to fly up to heaven. The angel's upper lip curled into the hint of a smile, and one day as Prince Andrei and Princess Maria were leaving the shrine they admitted to one another that the angel's face reminded them strangely of the little princess. But what was still stranger – though this Prince Andrei did not confess to his sister – was that in the expression the sculptor had chanced to give the angel's face Prince Andrei read the same gentle reproach which he had read on the face of his dead wife: 'Ah, why have you done this to me? ...'

Soon after Prince Andrei's return the old prince made over a large estate to him, Bogucharovo, twenty-five miles or so from Bald Hills. Partly because of the painful memories associated with Bald Hills, partly because Prince Andrei did not always feel equal to bearing with his father's idiosyncrasies, and partly because of a craving for solitude, Prince Andrei made use of Bogucharovo, began building, and spent most of his time there.

After the battle of Austerlitz Prince Andrei had firmly resolved to have done with the army, and, to escape active service when war broke out again and everybody had to serve, he placed himself under his father's orders and assisted in the levying of the militia. The old prince and his son seemed to have exchanged rôles since the campaign of 1805. The father, stimulated by activity, expected the best results from the new campaign, while Prince Andrei on the contrary, taking no part in the war and secretly regretting his inaction, saw only the dark side.

On the 26th of February 1807 the old prince set off on one of his circuits. Prince Andrei, as usual during his father's absences, was staying at Bald Hills. Little Nikolai had not been well for the last three or four days. The coachman who had driven the old prince to the next town returned bringing documents and letters for Prince Andrei. Not finding the young prince in his study, the valet went with the letters to Princess Maria's apartments, but he was not there either. He was told that the prince had gone to the nursery.

'If you please, your Excellency, Petrusha has brought some papers,' said one of the nursemaids to Prince Andrei, who was sitting in a child's small chair while, frowning and with trembling hands, he poured drops of medicine from a bottle into a wine-glass half full of water.

'What is it?' he said crossly, and his hand shaking he accidentally let too many drops fall into the glass. He tipped the contents on to the floor and asked for some more water. The maid handed it to him.

In the room were a child's cot, two chests, a couple of arm-chairs, a table, a child's table, and the little chair on which Prince Andrei was sitting. The curtains were drawn, and a single candle was burning on the table, screened by a bound volume of music, so that no light might fall on the cot.

'My dear,' said Princess Maria, turning to her brother from beside the cot where she was standing, 'better wait a bit ... later on ...'

'Oh, do stop, you don't know what you are talking about. You always want to put things off, and now see what comes of it!' said Prince Andrei in an exasperated whisper, with the manifest intention of wounding his sister.

'My dear, truly it would be better not to wake him – he's asleep,' implored the princess.

Prince Andrei got up and went on tiptoe to the little bed, wine-glass in hand.

'Perhaps we'd really better not?' he said, hesitating.

'Just as you please – really ... I think so ... but you must judge,' said Princess Maria, obviously intimidated and uneasy that her opinion should prevail. She drew her brother's attention to the maid, who was calling him in a whisper.

It was the second night that both of them had gone without sleep, watching over the baby who was feverish. These last days, lacking confidence in their own household doctor and expecting another who had been sent for from the town, they had spent trying a succession of remedies. Tired and overwrought, they vented their anxiety on each other, finding fault and quarrelling with one another.

'Petrusha is here with papers from your father,' whispered the maid.

Prince Andrei went out.

'What is it now?' he muttered angrily, and after listening to the verbal instructions his father had sent and taking the correspondence and his father's letter he returned to the nursery.

'How is he now?' queried Prince Andrei.

'Just the same. Wait, for heaven's sake. Karl Ivanich always declares that sleep is better than anything,' whispered Princess Maria with a sigh.

Prince Andrei went up to the baby and felt him. He was very hot.

'Confound you and your Karl Ivanich!' He fetched the glass with the medicine and came up to the cot again.

'André, you shouldn't!' said Princess Maria.

But he scowled at her spitefully, yet with a stricken look in his eyes, and bent over the child with the glass.

'But I wish it,' he said. 'Come, I beg you, give it to him.'

Princess Maria shrugged her shoulders but obediently took the glass and, calling the nurse, began giving the child the medicine. The baby screamed and choked. Prince Andrei winced and, clutching his head, went out and sat down on a sofa in the next room.

He was still holding the letters. Opening them mechanically, he began to read. The old prince in his large, oblong hand, now and then making use of abbreviations, wrote on blue paper as follows:

Have just this moment received by special messenger v. joyful news – unless it's a *canard*. Bennigsen seems to have obtained a complete victory over Bonaparte at Eylau. In Petersburg everyone's wild with delight, and innumerable awards have been sent to the army. Though he's a German – I congratulate him. I can't make out what that fellow in charge at Korchevo – one Handrikov – is up to: so far no reinforcements or stores have come from him. Gallop over at once and say I'll have his head off if everything's not here within the week. Have received a letter about the Preussisch-Eylau battle from Petenka too – he took part in it – it's all true. When people who have no business to don't meddle, even a German beats Bonaparte. They say he is retreating in great disorder. Mind you get off to Korchevo without delay and see to things!

Prince Andrei sighed and broke the seal of another envelope. This contained a closely-written letter covering two sheets from Bilibin. He folded it up without reading it, and re-read his father's letter, ending with the words: 'Get off to Korchevo without delay and see to things!'

'No, you must forgive me, I'm not leaving now till the child is better,' he thought, going to the door and looking into the nursery.

Princess Maria was still standing by the cot, gently rocking the baby.

'Yes, what in the name of goodness was the other disagreeable news he wrote about?' thought Prince Andrei, recalling his father's letter. 'Oh, I know: we have gained a victory over Bonaparte just when I'm not taking part. Yes, yes, he's always getting at me. ... Ah well, let him!' And he began reading the letter in French from Bilibin. He read without understanding half of it, read for the sake of diverting his mind, if only for a moment, from what it had been too long and too anxiously dwelling upon to the exclusion of everything else.

9

BILIBIN was now at the headquarters of the army, in a diplomatic capacity, and though he wrote in French with French jests and French turns of speech he described the whole campaign with fearless impartiality, in true Russian fashion, sparing his own side neither reproaches nor sarcasms. Bilibin wrote that the obligations of diplomatic *discrétion* were a torture to him, and that he was happy to have in Prince Andrei a trustworthy correspondent to whom he could pour out all the spleen that had been accumulating in him at the sight of what was going on in the army. The letter was dated some time back, before the battle of Preussisch-Eylau.

Since the day of our brilliant success at Austerlitz [wrote Bilibin] as you know, my dear prince, I have not left headquarters. I have acquired a decided taste for war, and it is just as well for me. What I have seen during the last three months is beyond belief.

I will begin *ab ovo* – at the very beginning. The 'enemy of the human race', as you are aware, attacks the Prussians. The Prussians are our faithful allies who have only betrayed us three times in three years. We take up their cause. But it turns out that the 'enemy of the human race' pays not the slightest heed to our fine speeches, and in his ill-mannered, savage way flings himself on the Prussians without giving them time to finish the parade they had begun, and hey presto! wipes the floor with them and installs himself in the palace at Potsdam.

'It is my most earnest desire,' writes the king of Prussia to Bonaparte, 'that your Majesty should be received and treated in my palace in a manner agreeable to your Majesty, and to this end I have hastened to take every step that circumstances allow. I hope I may have succeeded.'

The Prussian generals pride themselves on their politeness to the French, and lay down their arms at the first summons. The commander of the garrison at Glogau, with ten thousand men, asks the king of Prussia what he shall do if he is called upon to surrender.... Fact!

In short, hoping to settle matters by assuming a warlike attitude, lo and behold! we find ourselves at war in good earnest, and, what is worse, at war on our own frontiers with and for *le roi de Prusse*. Everything is all ready: we only lack one little item – a commander-in-chief. As it is now thought that our success at Austerlitz might have been more decisive had the commander-in-chief not been so young, all the octogenarians have been reviewed, and of Prozorovsky and Kamensky the choice is in favour of the latter, who arrives in a covered cart, *à la* Suvorov, and is received by us with acclamations of joy and triumph.

On the 4th *voilà*! – the first courier from Petersburg. The mails are taken to the field-marshal's room, for he likes to see to everything personally. I am called in to help sort the letters and take those meant for us. The field-marshal looks on and waits for the packages addressed to him. We hunt through – there isn't a single one. The field-marshal waxes impatient and sets to work himself, and finds letters from the Emperor to Count T., Prince V. and others. Then he flies into one of his wild furies. Blood and thunder right and left. He snatches the letters, tears them open and reads those from the Tsar addressed to others. 'Ah, so that's the way they treat me! No confidence in me! Ah, ordered to keep an eye on me! Very well then, get out, all of you!' And he writes the famous order of the day to General Bennigsen:

'I am wounded and cannot ride on horseback, and consequently cannot command the army. You have led your *corps d'armée* defeated to Pultusk: here it remains exposed, without fuel or forage, so something must be done, and, as you yourself reported to Count Buxhöwden yesterday, measures must be devised for retiring to our frontier. Proceed to do so this day.

'All my expeditions on horseback,' he writes to the Emperor, 'have given me a saddle-sore, which, coming on top of all my previous journeying, quite prevents me sitting a horse and commanding an army so widely scattered; and I have therefore handed over the said command to the general next in seniority, Count Buxhöwden, sending him my whole staff and appurtenances of the same, and advising him if he is short of bread to move farther into the interior of Prussia, seeing that only one day's ration of bread is left, and some regiments have none at all, as reported by division-commanders Ostermann and Sedmoretsky, and all that the local

437

peasants had has been eaten up. I shall myself remain in hospital at Ostrolenka till I recover. In most humbly submitting my report I would add further that if the army continues another fortnight in its present bivouac, by spring there will not be a healthy man left.

'Permit an old man to retire to the country who is already sufficiently disgraced by his inability to perform the great and glorious task for which he was chosen. I shall await your Majesty's most gracious permission here in hospital, that I may not have to play the part of *office clerk* rather than *commander* at the head of the army. My removal will make no more difference than would that of a man gone blind. Russia has thousands more where I came from!'

The field-marshal is vexed with the Emperor and punishes all of us; isn't that logical!

Thus ends the first act. Those that follow are naturally increasingly interesting and entertaining. After the field-marshal's departure it appears that we are within sight of the enemy and must give battle. Buxhöwden is commander-in-chief by right of seniority but General Bennigsen does not see it like that; more particularly as it is he and his corps who face the enemy and he wants to seize the opportunity to fight a battle 'on his own hand', as the Germans say. He fights it. This is the battle of Pultusk, which is considered a great victory but to my mind was nothing of the sort. We civilians, as you are aware, have a very undesirable way of deciding whether a battle was won or lost. The side that retreats after a battle has lost is what we say; and going by that, we lost the battle of Pultusk. In short, we retreat after the battle but we send a courier to Petersburg with news of a victory, and the general does not relinquish the command to Buxhöwden, hoping as a reward for his success to receive from Petersburg the title of commander-in-chief. During this interregnum we embark on a remarkably interesting and original series of manoeuvres. Our aim is no longer, as it should be, to avoid or attack the enemy, but solely to avoid General Buxhöwden, who by right of seniority should be our chief. We pursue this aim with so much energy that when we cross an unfordable river we even burn our bridges to cut off the enemy, who for the nonce, is not Bonaparte but Buxhöwden. General Buxhöwden was within an ace of being attacked and captured by superior enemy forces as a result of one of the pretty little manoeuvres by which we escaped him. Buxhöwden comes after us – we scuttle. No sooner does he cross to our side of the river than we cross back again. At last our enemy – Buxhöwden – catches up on us and attacks. Both generals lose their tempers. There is even a challenge to a duel on Buxhöwden's part and an epileptic fit on Bennigsen's. But at the critical moment the courier who carried the news of our Pultusk victory to Petersburg returns bringing our appointment as commander-in-chief, and our enemy number one – Buxhöwden – is done for: we can now turn our attention to number two – Bonaparte. But at this juncture what should happen but a third enemy rises against us – namely, the *Orthodox Russian* soldiery clamouring for bread, meat, biscuits, fodder and I don't know what else! The storehouses are empty, the roads impassable. The 'Orthodox' take to looting, and that after a fashion of which our last campaign can give you no idea. Half the regiments have formed themselves into free companies, scouring the countryside and putting everything to fire and sword. The inhabitants are ruined, root and branch; the hospitals overflow with sick, and famine is everywhere. Twice, bands of marauders have attacked headquarters, and the commander-in-chief has to ask for a battalion to drive them off. In one of these raids my empty trunk and my dressing-gown were carried away. The Emperor proposes to authorize all commanders of divisions to shoot marauders, but I very much fear this will oblige one half of the army to shoot the other.

At first Prince Andrei read with his eyes only but after a while, and in spite of himself, what he found (though he knew how much faith to put in Bilibin) began to interest him more and more. Having got thus far, he crumpled up the letter and threw it aside. It was not what he read that vexed him, but the fact that the life out there, in which he had no part, could still unsettle him. He shut his eyes, rubbed his forehead with his hand as though to rid himself of all interest in what he had been reading, and listened to the sounds in the nursery. Suddenly he fancied he heard a strange noise through the door. Panic seized him lest something should have happened to the child while he was reading the letter. He crossed on tiptoe to the nursery door and opened it.

Just as he went in he saw that the nurse was hiding something from him with a scared look, and Princess Maria was no longer beside the cot.

'My dear,' he heard what seemed to him his sister's despairing whisper behind him.

As often happens after sleepless nights and prolonged anxiety, he was overwhelmed by an unreasoning dread: the notion came into his head that the boy was dead. All that he saw and heard seemed a confirmation of his terror.

'It is all over,' he thought, and a cold sweat broke out on his forehead. He went to the cot, beside himself, convinced that he would find it empty, that the nurse had been hiding the dead baby. He opened the curtains and for a long while his frightened, wandering eyes could not find the baby. At last he saw him: the rosy-cheeked child had tossed about till he lay sprawled across the bed with his head lower than the pillow, in his sleep making a sucking noise with his lips and breathing evenly.

Prince Andrei was as rejoiced at seeing the child like that as if he had got him back from the dead. He bent down and as his sister had shown him tried with his lips whether the baby was still feverish. The soft forehead was moist. Prince Andrei passed his hand over the little head – even the hair was wet, so profusely had the child perspired. Not only was he not dead but, on the contrary, the crisis was over and he was on the mend. Prince Andrei longed to snatch up and hug and press this helpless little creature to his heart, but dared not do so. He stood over him, gazing at his head and at the little arms and legs that showed beneath the blanket. He heard a rustle at his elbow and a shadow appeared under the canopy of the cot. He did not look round, but still watching the infant's face listened to his regular breathing. The dark shadow was Princess Maria, who had come up to the cot with noiseless steps, lifted the cot-curtains and let them fall again behind her. Prince Andrei recognized her without looking round, and held out his hand to her. She pressed it.

'He is in a perspiration,' said Prince Andrei.

'I went to tell you so.'

The baby stirred faintly in his sleep, smiled and rubbed his forehead against the pillow.

Prince Andrei looked at his sister. In the dim shadow of the curtain her luminous eyes shone more than usually bright with the tears of happiness that stood in them. She leaned over to her brother and kissed him, slightly disturbing the curtains of the cot. Each made the other a warning gesture and stood quiet in the twilight under the canopy, as though unwilling to leave that seclusion where they three were alone, shut off from all the world. Prince Andrei was the first to move away, ruffling his hair against the muslin hangings.

'Yes, this is the one thing left me now,' he said with a sigh.

SHORTLY after his initiation into the Masonic Brotherhood Pierre set out for the province of Kiev, where most of his serfs were, taking with him the directions he had written for his own guidance in the management of his estates.

When he reached Kiev he summoned all his stewards and explained to them his intentions and wishes. He told them that steps would be taken shortly to complete the liberation of his serfs, and that till then they were not to be overburdened with labour, that women with young children were not to be sent to work, that assistance was to be given to the peasants, and punishments were to be admonitory instead of corporal, and that hospitals, alms-houses and schools were to be established on all the estates. A section of the stewards (there were some semi-literate foremen among them) listened in dismay, supposing the upshot of the young count's remarks to mean that he was dissatisfied with their management and embezzlement of his money. Others, after their first fright, found amusement in Pierre's lisp and the new words they had not heard before. Others, again, derived a simple satisfaction in hearing the sound of their master's voice; while the fourth and most intelligent group, which included the chief steward, divined from this speech how best they could handle the master for their own ends.

The chief steward expressed great sympathy with Pierre's projects; but observed that, these innovations apart, matters needed thoroughly going into, as they were in a bad way.

In spite of Count Bezuhov's enormous wealth Pierre, ever since he had inherited it and stepped into an annual income which was said to amount to five hundred thousand roubles, had felt himself much poorer than in the days when his father was making him an allowance of ten thousand roubles a year. He reckoned his budget pretty much as follows:

About 80,000 went in payments to the Land Bank; upkeep of the estate near Moscow and the town house, together with the allowance he made to the three princesses, accounted for 30,000; pensions took some 15,000, as did subscriptions to charitable institutions; the countess received 150,000 for her maintenance; about 70,000 were paid away in interest on loans; the building of a new church, which he had begun a couple of years before, was costing him a round 10,000; and the 100,000 that were left went, he did not know how, but so effectually that almost every year he was obliged to borrow. Moreover, every twelve months the chief steward wrote to inform him of fires and bad harvests, or of the necessity of rebuilding factories and workshops. And so the first task which confronted Pierre was one for which he had very little aptitude or inclination – practical business.

Every day Pierre *went into* things with his chief steward. But he felt that what he was doing did not advance matters one inch. He felt that what he was doing was somehow detached from reality, and did not link up with what was happening or advance it. On the one hand there was the chief steward picturing the state of affairs to him in the very worst light, pointing out to Pierre the absolute necessity of paying off his debts and undertaking new activities with serf-labour, to which Pierre would not agree. On the other hand, there was Pierre demanding that they should proceed to the work of liberating the serfs, which the steward countered by showing the necessity of first paying off the loans from the Land Bank, and the consequent impossibility of any early emancipation.

The steward did not say that this could not be done; he proposed to make it possible through the sale of forests in the province of Kostroma, the sale of some land lower down the river and of the Crimean estate. But all these operations according to the head steward entailed such complicated measures – the lifting of restrictive covenants and statutory provisions, the obtaining of licences and permits, etc. – that Pierre was lost in the labyrinth and confined himself to saying:

'Yes, yes, do that, then.'

Pierre had none of the practical tenacity which would have enabled him to attend to the business himself, and so he disliked the whole thing and merely tried in the steward's presence to keep up a pretence of activity. The steward for his part did his best to pretend to the count that he considered their consultations of great use to his master and a great inconvenience to himself.

In Kiev Pierre found some people he knew; others hastened to make his acquaintance and offer a warm welcome to the young man of fortune, the largest landowner of the province. Temptations to Pierre's besetting weakness – the one to which he had confessed at his initiation into the Lodge – were so strong that he could not resist them. Again, as in Petersburg, whole days, weeks and months of his life were busily filled with parties, dinners, lunches and balls, allowing him no time for reflection. Instead of the new life Pierre had hoped to lead, he still lived the old one, only in different surroundings.

Of the three precepts of Freemasonry Pierre had to admit that he was not fulfilling the one which enjoined every mason to set an example of moral uprightness; and that of the seven virtues he was entirely devoid of two – clean living and the love of death. He consoled himself with the thought that, on the other hand, he was fulfilling another of the precepts – the improvement of the human race – and had other virtues – love for his neighbour and generosity.

In the spring of 1807 Pierre decided to return to Petersburg. On the way he intended to visit all his estates and see for himself how far his orders had been carried out, and discover how the serfs whom God had entrusted to his care, and on whom he was doing his best to lavish benefits, were now faring.

The chief steward, who considered the young count's projects almost insane – unprofitable to himself, to his master and to the peasants – had made some concessions. While continuing to represent the liberation of the serfs as impracticable, he had arranged for the erection on all the estates of large schools, hospitals and alms-houses against the master's arrival. Demonstrations of welcome were organized – not on a sumptuous or magnificent scale, which he knew Pierre would not care for, but pious thanksgivings with icons and the traditional bread and salt, which knowledge of his master's character suggested would be more likely to affect him and pull the wool over his eyes.

The southern spring, the comfortable, rapid journey in his Vienna carriage and the solitude of the road all had a gladdening effect on Pierre. The estates, which he had not visited before, were each more picturesque than the other; the peasantry everywhere appeared prosperous and touchingly grateful for the favours conferred on them. He was met with such a welcome everywhere that, though he was embarrassed, Pierre's heart was overcome with a joyous sensation. At one place the peasants presented him with bread and salt and an icon of St Peter and St Paul, begging him to allow them, as a token of their love and gratitude for all that had been done for them to add a new chantry to the church at their own expense, in honour of his patron saints, Peter and Paul. In another place he was greeted by women with infants in arms who thanked him for releasing them from the obligation of heavy work. On a third estate the priest, bearing a cross, came to meet him, surrounded by children whom, through the count's generosity, he was instructing in reading, writing and religion. On all his estates Pierre saw with his own eyes brick buildings erected or in the course of erection, all to the same plan, for hospitals, schools and alms-houses, which were shortly to be opened. Everywhere he was shown the stewards' accounts, according to which the serfs' manorial labour had been cut down, and listened to the touching thanks of deputations of serfs in their full-skirted blue coats.

What Pierre did not know was that the village which had presented him with bread and salt and wanted to build a chantry in honour of St Peter and St Paul was a market village where a fair was held on St Peter's day, that the chantry had been begun long before by some well-to-do *muzhiks* of the village (the ones who formed the deputation), while nine-tenths of the peasants of that village lived in the utmost destitution. He did not know that since by his orders nursing mothers were not sent to work on his land they did vastly heavier work on their own bit of ground. He did not know that the priest who met him with the cross oppressed the peasants by his exactions, and that the pupils gathered round him had been yielded up to him with tears and were often ransomed back to their parents at a high price. He did not know that the brick buildings being raised according to plan were being built by serfs whose manorial labour was thus increased, and only lessened on paper. He did not know that where the steward had pointed out to him in the account-book that the serfs' payments had been reduced by a third their obligatory manorial work had been put up by a half. And so Pierre was in raptures with his visit to his estates and quite recovered the philanthropic frame of mind in which he had left Petersburg, and wrote enthusiastic letters to his 'brother-preceptor' as he called the Grand Master.

'How easy it is, how little effort is needed, to do so much good,' thought Pierre, 'and how little we trouble ourselves to do it!'

He was pleased at the gratitude shown him but felt ashamed at being the recipient of it. This gratitude reminded him of how much more he might do for these simple, kindly people.

The head steward, a thoroughly stupid sly man, quickly had the measure of the intelligent but naïve count, and played with him like a toy; and, seeing the effect produced on Pierre by the carefully arranged receptions, pressed him still harder with arguments proving the impossibility and, above all, the uselessness of emancipating the serfs, who were perfectly happy as they were.

Pierre in his secret soul agreed with the steward that it would be difficult to imagine more contented people, and that heaven only knew what would happen to them when they had their freedom, but he insisted, though reluctantly, on what he thought right. The steward promised to do all in his power to carry out the count's wishes, perceiving clearly that not only would the count never be in a position to verify whether every measure had been taken for the sale of the land and the forests to redeem the mortgage at the Land Bank, but in all probability would never even inquire, and would never find out that the newly-erected buildings were standing empty, and that the serfs continued to give in labour and money just what other people's serfs gave – that is to say, all that could be got out of them.

II

RETURNING from his southern tour, in the happiest frame of mind, Pierre paid a long-intended visit to his friend Bolkonsky, whom he had not seen for two years.

Bogucharovo lay in a flat, uninteresting part of the country among fields and forests of fir and birch, in parts cut down. The manor was at one end of the village, which stretched straight along the high road. In front was a pond recently dug and filled to overflowing, though the grass had not yet had a chance to grow over its banks. The house stood in the midst of a young copse having several large pines among the smaller trees.

The homestead consisted of a threshing-floor, out-buildings, stables, a bath-house, a lodge and a large stone house with a semicircular façade still in course of construction. Round the house was a garden recently laid out. The fences and gates were solid and new; two fire-pumps and a water-barrel painted green stood under a penthouse; the paths were straight, the bridges were strong and furnished with hand-rails. Everything gave the impression of having been done efficiently and with care. Some domestic serfs Pierre met, in answer to his inquiries as to where the prince lived, pointed to a small newly-built lodge at the very edge of the pond. Anton, an old servant who had looked after Prince Andrei in his boyhood, helped Pierre down from the carriage, said that the prince was at home and showed him into a neat little ante-room.

Pierre was struck by the unpretentiousness of this diminutive though scrupulously clean little house, after the brilliant surroundings in which he had last seen his friend in Petersburg. He quickly entered the tiny parlour, still unplastered and smelling of pine wood, and would have gone farther but Anton ran ahead on tiptoe and knocked at a door.

'Well, what is it?' came a sharp, forbidding voice.

'A visitor,' answered Anton.

'Ask him to wait,' and there was the sound of a chair being pushed back.

Pierre went with rapid steps to the door and suddenly found himself face to face with Prince Andrei, who came out frowning and looking older. Pierre threw his arms round him, and lifting his spectacles kissed his friend on the cheek and considered him intently.

'Well, this is a surprise! I *am* glad to see you,' exclaimed Prince Andrei.

Pierre said nothing; he could not take his eyes off his friend, so struck was he by the change in his appearance. His words were kindly, there was a smile on his lips and face, but his eyes were dull and lifeless in spite of the effort he made to give them a joyous, happy sparkle. It was not only that Prince Andrei had grown thinner, paler and more set: what disturbed and alienated Pierre till he got used to it was his friend's inertia, and the line on his brow which bore witness to continued preoccupation with some one thought.

As is usually the case when friends meet after a long separation the conversation took some time to settle down. They asked each other questions and gave brief replies about things they knew ought to be talked over at length. At last the conversation gradually came to rest on some of the topics previously touched upon only in passing, and the two discussed things that had happened in the past, their plans for the future, Pierre's travels and what he had been doing, the war, and so on. The preoccupied, crushed look which Pierre had remarked in Prince Andrei's eyes was still more noticeable now in the smile with which he listened to Pierre, especially when Pierre spoke with earnest delight of the past or the future. It was as though Prince Andrei wanted to interest himself in what his friend was saying, but was unable to, so that Pierre began to feel it was in bad taste to speak of his enthusiasms, dreams and hopes of happiness or goodness in Prince Andrei's presence. He felt shy of coming out with all his new masonic ideas, which the tour he had just made had in particular revived and strengthened. He restrained himself for fear of appearing naïve; at the same time he was bursting to show his friend that he was now an entirely different and much better Pierre than the one Prince Andrei had known in Petersburg.

'I can't tell you all I have gone through since then. I hardly recognize myself.'

'Yes, we have altered a great deal, a very great deal since those days,' said Prince Andrei.

'Well, and what of you?' asked Pierre. 'What are your plans?'

'Plans?' echoed Prince Andrei ironically. 'My plans?' he repeated, as if wondering at the word. 'Well, as you see, I'm building. I mean to move in here altogether next year. ...'

Pierre was silent, looking searchingly into Prince Andrei's face, which had grown so much older.

'No, I meant ...' Pierre began, but Prince Andrei interrupted him.

'But what is the use of talking about me. ... *You* must tell me – yes, tell me about your travels, and about all you have been doing on your estates.'

Pierre began describing what he had done on his estates, trying so far as he could to disguise his own share in the improvements that had been made. Prince Andrei several times finished Pierre's sentence for him, as though all that Pierre had done was an old familiar story, and listened not only without interest but even as if he blushed a little for what Pierre was telling him.

Pierre began to feel awkward and uncomfortable, and finally relapsed into silence.

'I know what, my dear fellow,' said Prince Andrei, who apparently also felt depressed and constrained with his visitor, 'I am only camping here – I just came over to have a look round. I am going back again to my sister today. I'll introduce you to her. But of course you know her already,' he added, evidently for the sake of saying something to a guest with whom he now found nothing in common. 'We'll set off after dinner. And now would you care to see my place?'

They went out and walked about till dinner-time, talking of the political news and mutual acquaintances, like people who are not very intimate. Only the new homestead and premises he was building produced any show of animation and interest in Prince Andrei, but even here, while they were on the scaffolding and he was in the middle of describing the plan of the house, he suddenly interrupted himself:

'However, this is very dull. Let us go and have dinner, and then we'll start.'

At the dinner-table the subject of Pierre's marriage came up.

'I was very much surprised when I heard of it,' said Prince Andrei.

Pierre coloured as he always did at any reference to his marriage, and said hurriedly:

'I'll tell you one day how it all happened. But you know it's all over and finished with for ever.'

'For ever?' said Prince Andrei. 'Nothing's for ever.'

'But you know how it all ended, don't you? You heard about the duel?'

'Yes, you had to go through that too!'

'The one thing which I thank God for is that I didn't kill the man,' said Pierre.

'Why so?' asked Prince Andrei. 'To kill a vicious dog is a very good thing really.'

'No, to kill a man is bad, wrong …'

'Why is it wrong?' pressed Prince Andrei. 'It is not given to man to judge of what is right or wrong. Men always did and always will err, and in nothing more than in what they regard as right or wrong.'

'What does harm to another is wrong,' said Pierre, pleased to see that for the first time since his arrival Prince Andrei was roused and had begun to talk, wanting to come out with what it was that had brought him to his present state.

'And who has told you what does harm to another man?' he asked.

'Harm? Harm?' exclaimed Pierre. 'We all know what harms ourselves.'

'Yes, we know that, but the harm I am conscious of in myself is something it would be impossible for me to inflict on others,' said Prince Andrei, growing more and more animated and evidently eager to express his new outlook to Pierre. He spoke in French. 'I know of only two real evils in life: remorse and illness. The only good is the absence of those evils. To live for myself so as to avoid those two evils: that's the sum of my wisdom now.'

'And how about love of one's neighbour, and self-sacrifice?' began

Pierre. 'No, I cannot agree with you. To live with the sole object of avoiding doing evil so as not to have to repent is not enough. I used to do that – I lived for myself and I spoilt my life. And only now, when I am living for others – or at least trying to –' (modesty impelled Pierre to correct himself) 'only now do I realize all the happiness life holds. No, I cannot agree with you, and indeed you don't believe what you are saying yourself.'

Prince Andrei looked at Pierre in silence, with an ironic smile.

'Well, you'll soon be seeing my sister, Princess Maria. You'll get on with her,' said he. 'Perhaps you are right for yourself,' he added after a brief pause, 'but everyone must live after his own fashion. You used to live for yourself, and you say that by doing so you nearly ruined your life and only found happiness when you began to live for others. But my experience has been exactly the opposite. I lived for honour and glory. (And, after all, what is honour and glory? The same love for others, the desire to do something for them, the desire for their praises.) In that way I lived for others, and not almost but quite spoilt my life. And only since I started living for myself have I found more peace.'

'But what do you mean when you say you live only for yourself?' asked Pierre, growing excited. 'What about your son, and your sister, and your father?'

'Ah, but they are part of myself – they are not other people,' explained Prince Andrei. 'But other people, one's *neighbour* – *le prochain* – as you and Princess Maria call them, are the great source of error and evil. One's neighbours are those – your Kiev peasants – whom one wants to do good to.'

And he looked at Pierre with a mocking, challenging expression. He obviously wished to draw him on.

'You are not serious,' replied Pierre, getting more and more worked up. 'What error or evil can there be in my wishing to do good (though I accomplished very little, and that badly)? But still, I tried and even met with some small success. What possible harm can there be in giving instruction to unfortunate people, our serfs – people just like ourselves – who were growing up and dying with no idea of God and truth beyond meaningless prayers and church ceremonies? How can it be wrong to teach them the consoling doctrines of a future life, where they will find recompense, reward and solace? Where is the evil and error in my providing people who were helplessly dying of disease, while material assistance could so easily be rendered, with a doctor, a hospital and asylum for the aged? And is it not palpably and unquestionably a good thing if a peasant, or a woman with a young baby, never knowing a moment's respite day or night, and I give them rest and leisure time?' said Pierre, talking fast and lisping. 'And that is what I have done, though badly and to a small extent, but I have made a start, and you cannot persuade me that it wasn't good, and, more than that, you can't make me believe that you do not think so yourself. And the great thing is,' he continued, 'I know – and know for certain – that the enjoyment of doing this good is the only sure happiness in life.'

'Oh, if you put the question like that it's quite a different matter,' said Prince Andrei. 'I build a house and lay out a garden, and you build hospitals. Either occupation may serve to pass the time. But as to what's right and what's good – you must leave that to Him Who knows all things: it is not for us to decide. Well, I see you want an argument,' he added, 'come on then.'

They got up from the table and sat out in the entrance-porch which served as a verandah.

'Come, let's argue the matter,' said Prince Andrei. 'You talk of schools,' he went on, crooking a finger, 'education, and so forth. In other words, you want to lift him' (he pointed to a peasant who passed by them taking off his cap) 'out of his animal existence and awaken in him spiritual needs, when in my opinion animal happiness is the only happiness possible, and you want to deprive him of it. I envy him, while you are trying to make him what I am, without providing him with my means. Then you say, "We must lighten his toil". But as I see it, physical labour is as essential to him, as much a condition of his existence, as intellectual activity is for you or me. You can't help thinking. I go to bed after two in the morning, thoughts come into my mind and I can't sleep but toss about till dawn, because I think and cannot help thinking, just as he can't help ploughing and mowing; if he didn't he would go to the tavern, or fall ill. Just as I could not stand his terrible physical labour, a week of which would kill me, so my physical idleness would be too much for him: he would put on weight and that would be the end of him. Thirdly – what was it now?' and Prince Andrei crooked a third finger. 'Oh, yes, hospitals, medicine. Our peasant has a stroke and is dying, but you have him bled and patched up. He will drag about, a cripple, for another ten years, a burden to everybody. It would be far easier and simpler for him to die. Plenty of others are being born to take his place. It would be different if you grudged losing a worker – which is how I look at him – but you want to cure him out of love for him. And he does not want that. And besides, what an illusion that medicine ever cured anyone! Killed them, yes!' said he, frowning sardonically and turning away from Pierre.

Prince Andrei gave such clear and precise utterance to his ideas that it was evident he had reflected on this subject more than once, and the words came out readily in quick succession, as happens when a man has not talked for a long time. His eyes became brighter, the more pessimistic the views he expressed.

'Oh, that is dreadful, dreadful!' said Pierre. 'What I don't understand is how you can live with such ideas. I had moments of thinking like that myself not long ago – it was in Moscow, and on a journey – but then I sink into such depths that I'm not really living at all. Everything seems hateful to me ... myself most of all. Then I don't eat, don't wash ... how is it with you? ...'

'Why not wash? That's not clean,' said Prince Andrei. 'On the contrary, one has to try to make one's life as pleasant as possible. I'm alive, and it's not my fault that I am, and so it behoves me to make the best of it, not interfering with anybody else until death carries me off.'

'But with such ideas what point is there for you in life? One would just sit without stirring, not embarking on anything ...'

'Life won't leave one in peace even so. I should be glad to do nothing, but here on the one hand the local Nobility did me the honour of selecting me to be their Marshal: it was all I could do to get out of it. They could not understand that I have not the required qualifications – the kind of busy, good-natured vulgarity – necessary for the position. Then there's this house here, which had to be built in order that I might have a nook of my own where I could be quiet. And now it's the recruiting.'

'Why aren't you serving in the army?'

'After Austerlitz?' said Prince Andrei gloomily. 'No, thank you very much. I vowed to myself I would never go on active service in the Russian army again. And I won't – not even if Bonaparte were here at Smolensk, threatening Bald Hills: even then I wouldn't serve in the Russian army. Well, as I was saying,' he continued, recovering his composure, 'now there's this recruiting. My father is chief in command of the 3rd circuit, and my only way of avoiding active service is to work with him.'

'So you are in the service after all ?'

'Yes.'

He paused a little.

'But why ?'

'I'll tell you why. My father is one of the most remarkable men of his time. But he is growing old, and though he is not exactly cruel he has too energetic a character. He is so accustomed to unlimited power that he is terrible, and now the Emperor has given him further authority as commander-in-chief over the recruiting. If I had arrived a couple of hours later a fortnight ago, he would have had the register-clerk at Yukhnovo hanged,' said Prince Andrei with a smile. 'And so I am serving, because no one but myself has any influence over him, and now and then I am able to save him from an act which would be a source of regret to him afterwards.'

'Ah, there, you see !'

'Yes, but it is not as you imagine,' Prince Andrei continued. 'It was not that I felt, or feel, kindly to the scoundrelly register-clerk who had been stealing boots or something from the recruits. Indeed, I should have been very glad to see him hanged, but I was sorry for my father – which means for myself again.'

Prince Andrei grew more and more eager. His eyes glittered fever-ishly as he tried to prove to Pierre that in his actions there was never any desire to do good to his neighbour.

'Look here, you want to liberate your serfs,' he went on. 'That is a very good thing, but not for you – I don't suppose you ever had any-one flogged or sent to Siberia – and still less for your peasants. If they are beaten, flogged, sent to Siberia, I dare say they are none the worse for it. In Siberia they can lead the same brute existence: the stripes on their bodies heal, and they are as happy as before. The men who would really benefit are those serf-owners whose moral nature is depraved, who bring remorse upon themselves, stifle that remorse and grow callous, all because of their power to inflict punishment justly and unjustly. It is such as they who have my pity, and for their sakes I should like to see the serfs liberated. You may not have come across it, but I have seen how good men brought up in those traditions of unlimited power grow more irritable with the years, turn cruel and harsh, and although aware of it cannot control themselves and daily add to the sum of their misery.'

Prince Andrei spoke so earnestly that Pierre could not help thinking that these ideas had been suggested to him by his father. He made no reply.

'So that is what I lament over: human dignity, peace of mind, purity, and not backs and heads, which remain the same backs and heads, beat and convict as you may.'

'No, no, a thousand times no! I shall never agree with you,' cried Pierre.

12

IN the evening Prince Andrei and Pierre got into an open carriage and drove to Bald Hills. Prince Andrei, glancing at Pierre, broke the silence now and then with remarks which showed that he was in good humour.

Pointing to the fields, he spoke of the improvements he was making in his husbandry.

Pierre preserved a gloomy silence, answering in monosyllables and apparently immersed in his own thoughts.

He was reflecting that Prince Andrei was unhappy, that he had gone astray and did not see the true light, and that it was his, Pierre's, duty to go to his aid, enlighten him and lift him up. But as soon as he began to deliberate on what he should say, and how he should say it, he foresaw that Prince Andrei by a single word, a single argument, would upset all his teaching, and he shrank from beginning, afraid of exposing everything he cherished and held sacred to the possibility of ridicule.

'No, but what makes you think so?' Pierre began all at once, lowering his head and looking like a bull about to charge; 'what makes you think so? You ought not to think so.'

'Think what?' asked Prince Andrei in surprise.

'About life, about man's destiny. It can't be so. I had the same ideas, and do you know what saved me? Freemasonry. No, don't smile. Freemasonry is not a religious sect, nor mere ceremonial rites, as I used to suppose. Freemasonry is something much better: it is the one expression of the highest, of the eternal in humanity.'

And he began to expound Freemasonry as he understood it to Prince Andrei.

He declared that Freemasonry was the teaching of Christianity freed from the fetters of State and Church: the doctrine of equality, fraternity and love.

'Our holy Brotherhood is the only thing that has real meaning in life; all the rest is a dream,' said Pierre. 'Understand, my dear fellow, that outside this fraternity all is falsehood and deceit, and I agree with you that an intelligent and good man has no alternative but, like you, to get through life trying only not to hurt others. But make our fundamental convictions your own, join our Brotherhood, give yourself heart and soul to us, let yourself be guided, and you will at once feel, as I did, that you are a link in a vast invisible chain, the beginning of which is hidden in the skies,' said Pierre.

Prince Andrei, looking straight before him, listened to Pierre's discourse in silence. More than once when he failed to catch a word owing to the rumble of the carriage wheels he asked Pierre to repeat it, and by the peculiar light that glowed in Prince Andrei's eyes, and by his silence, Pierre saw that he had not spoken without effect, and that Prince Andrei would not interrupt him nor laugh at what he said.

They reached a river that had overflowed its banks and which they had to cross by ferry. While the carriage and horses were being seen to, the two young men stepped on to the ferry-boat.

Leaning his elbows on the rail, Prince Andrei gazed silently at the flooding waters glittering in the setting sun.

'Well, what do you think of it?' Pierre asked. 'Why don't you speak?'

'What do I think? I was listening to you. It's all all right,' answered Prince Andrei. 'You say: join our Brotherhood and we will show you the purpose of life, the destiny of man, and the laws which govern the universe. But who are "we"? Men. How is it you know everything? Why am I the only one not to see what you see? You behold a reign of goodness and truth on earth, but I don't.'

Pierre interrupted him. 'Do you believe in a future life?' he asked.

'A future life?' Prince Andrei repeated, but Pierre gave him no time to reply, taking this echo of his words for a denial, the more readily as he knew Prince Andrei's atheistic views in the past.

'You say you can't see any reign of goodness and truth on earth. Nor could I, and it's impossible to, if we accept our life here as the end of all things. On *earth* – here on this earth' (Pierre pointed to the open country) 'there is no truth: it is all lies and wickedness. But in

454

the universe, in the whole universe, there is a kingdom of truth, and we who are now the children of earth are – in the eternal sense – children of the whole universe. Don't I feel in my soul that I am a part of that vast, harmonious whole? Don't I feel that I constitute one link, that I mark a degree in the ascending scale from the lower orders of creation to the higher ones, in this immense innumerable multitude of beings in which the Godhead – the Supreme Force, if you prefer the term – is manifest? If I see, see clearly the ladder rising from plant to man, why should I suppose that ladder breaks off with me and does not lead further and further? I feel not only that I cannot vanish, since nothing in this world ever vanishes, but that I always shall exist and always have existed. I feel that besides myself, above me, there are spirits, and that in their world there is truth.'

'Yes, that is Herder's theory,' commented Prince Andrei, 'but that won't convince me, my dear boy – life and death are what convince. What convinces is when you see a being dear to you, whose existence is bound up with yours, to whom you have done wrong that you had hoped to put right' (Prince Andrei's voice shook and he turned away), 'and all at once that being is seized and racked with pain, and ceases to exist.... Why? There must be an answer. And I believe there is. ... That is what can convince a man, that is what convinced me,' said Prince Andrei.

'Yes, yes, of course,' exclaimed Pierre. 'Isn't that the very thing I'm saying?'

'No. I only mean that one is not persuaded by argument that there must be a future life: it is when you are journeying through life hand in hand with someone, and suddenly your companion vanishes *there*, *into nowhere*, and you are left standing on the edge of the abyss, and you look down into it. As I have ...'

'Well, that's it then! You know there is a *there*, and there is a *Someone*? The *there* is the future life. The *Someone* is God.'

Prince Andrei did not reply. The carriage and horses had long ago been taken across to the other bank and reharnessed, and the sun was already half hidden and an evening frost was starring the puddles near the ferry; but Pierre and Andrei, to the astonishment of the footmen, coachmen and ferryhands, still stood on the ferry and talked.

'If there is a God and a future life, then there is truth and goodness, and man's highest happiness consists in striving to attain them. We must live, we must love, we must believe that we have life not only

455

today on this scrap of earth but that we have lived and shall live for ever, there, in the Whole,' Pierre was saying, and he pointed to the sky.

Prince Andrei stood leaning with his elbows on the rail of the ferry, and as he listened to Pierre he kept his eyes fixed on the red reflection of the sun on the blue waters. Pierre fell silent, and all was still. The ferry had long reached the other bank, and only the ripples of the current eddied softly against the bottom of the boat. It seemed to Prince Andrei that the water was lapping a refrain to Pierre's words: 'It's the truth, believe it.'

He sighed, and glanced with a radiant, childlike, tender look at Pierre's face, flushed and jubilant though still timidly conscious of his friend's superior intelligence.

'Yes, if only it were so!' said Prince Andrei. 'However, let us be going,' he added, and stepping off the ferry he looked up at the sky to which Pierre had pointed, and for the first time since Austerlitz saw those lofty eternal heavens he had watched while lying on the battlefield; and something long dormant, something better that had been in him, suddenly awoke with new and joyful life in his soul. The feeling vanished as soon as Prince Andrei fell back again into the ordinary conditions of life, but he knew that this feeling, which he was ignorant how to develop, lived within him. Pierre's visit marked an epoch in Prince Andrei's life. Though outwardly he continued to live in the same way, inwardly he began a new existence.

13

IT was growing dark by the time Prince Andrei and Pierre drove up to the main entrance at Bald Hills. As they approached, Prince Andrei, with a smile, drew Pierre's attention to the hubbub going on behind the house. An old woman bent with age, with a wallet on her back, and a short, long-haired young man in a black garment had returned hastily to the gate on seeing the carriage. Two women ran out after them, and all four, looking round at the *calèche*, with scared faces, hurried up the steps of the back porch.

'Those are some of my sister's "God's folk",' said Prince Andrei. 'They mistook us for my father. This is the one matter in which she disobeys him. His orders are to drive away these pilgrims, but she welcomes them.'

'But what are "God's folk"?' asked Pierre.

Prince Andrei had no time to answer. The servants came out to meet them, and he inquired where the old prince was and whether they expected him home soon.

The old prince was still in town, and expected back at any minute.

Prince Andrei led Pierre to his own apartments, which were always kept in perfect order and readiness for him in his father's house, and himself went to the nursery.

'Let us go and find my sister,' he said, rejoining Pierre. 'I have not seen her yet: she is hidden away somewhere, sitting with her "God's folk". It is her own fault – she will be embarrassed, and you will meet her "God's folk". A strange sight, I can tell you.'

'But who are these "God's folk"?' asked Pierre.

'You shall see.'

Princess Maria certainly was greatly disconcerted, and she coloured in red patches when they went in. In her cosy room, with lamps burning before the icon-stand, a young lad with a long nose and long hair, wearing a monk's habit. sat on the sofa beside her, behind a samovar. Near them in a low chair was a thin, shrivelled old woman with a meek expression on her childlike face.

'André, why didn't you let me know?' said the princess with mild reproach, standing up in front of her pilgrims like a hen protecting her chicks.

'Delighted to see you. I am very glad to see you,' she said to Pierre as he kissed her hand. She had known him as a child, and now his friendship with Andrei, his unhappy marriage, and above all his kindly, simple face disposed her favourably towards him. She looked at him with her beautiful luminous eyes as if to say: 'I like you very much, only, please, don't laugh at my flock.' After the first exchange of greetings they sat down.

'Ah, Ivanushka here too!' said Prince Andrei, with a smile indicating the pilgrim-lad.

'André!' said Princess Maria imploringly.

'It's a girl, you know,' Prince Andrei told Pierre in French.

'André, for pity's sake!' repeated Princess Maria.

It was plain that Prince Andrei's ironical tone towards the pilgrims and Princess Maria's unavailing championship had become a habit between them.

'But, my dear girl,' said Prince Andrei, still in French, 'on the contrary, you ought to feel obliged to me for giving Pierre some explanation of your bosom friendship with this young man.'

'Indeed?' said Pierre, gazing through his spectacles with curiosity and seriousness (for which Princess Maria was especially grateful to him) into Ivanushka's face, who perceiving that he was the subject under discussion considered them all with crafty eyes.

Princess Maria's embarrassment on her flock's account was quite unnecessary. They were not in the least abashed. The old woman, lowering her eyes but stealing sidelong glances at the new-comers, had turned her cup upside down in the saucer, placing her nibbled bit of sugar beside it, and sat quietly in her arm-chair, waiting to be offered another cup of tea. Ivanushka, sipping out of the saucer, peeped from under his brows with sly, womanish eyes at the young men.

'Where have you been? In Kiev?' Prince Andrei asked the old woman.

'I have, good sir,' answered the old woman garrulously. 'On the very Feast of Christmas it was given to me to partake of the holy, heavenly sacrament at the shrine of the saints. But now I'm from Kolyazin, sir, where a great and wonderful blessing has been revealed.'

'And was Ivanushka with you?'

'I take the road by myself, benefactor,' said Ivanushka, trying to make his voice sound deep. 'It was only at Yukhnovo that I fell in with Pelageya ...'

Pelageya interrupted her companion, evidently anxious to tell of what she had seen.

'In Kolyazin, master, a wonderful blessing has been revealed.'

'What was it? Some new relics?' asked Prince Andrei.

'Come, Andrei, that's enough,' said Princess Maria. 'Don't you tell him, Pelageya.'

'Nay ... why not, my dear, why shouldn't I? I like him. He's a good gentleman, one of God's elect, he's a benefactor, he once gave me ten roubles, I remember. When I was in Kiev, Crazy Kirill says to me (one of God's own, he is, goes barefoot winter and summer) – "Why aren't you going to the right place?" he says. "Go you to Kolyazin, there's a wonder-working icon revealed there, of the Holy Mother of God." So I took farewell of the saints and went. ...'

All were silent, only the pilgrim woman talked on in measured tones, breathing evenly.

'So I come, master, and folks say to me: "A great blessing has been vouchsafed, drops of holy oil trickle from the cheeks of the Most Holy Mother of God" ...'

'That will do, that will do, you can tell us another time,' said Princess Maria, flushing.

'Let me ask her something,' said Pierre. 'Did you see it with your own eyes?' he inquired.

'Oh yes, master, I was found worthy. Such a brightness was on her face, like light from heaven, and from the blessed Mother's cheeks first one drop, and then another ...'

'Of course it's a trick,' said Pierre naïvely, after listening intently to the pilgrim.

'Oh, master, whatever are you saying?' exclaimed Pelageya aghast, turning to Princess Maria for support.

'That's the way they impose on the people,' he repeated.

'Lord Jesus Christ!' cried the old woman, crossing herself. 'Oh, don't speak so, sir. There was a general once who didn't believe, and said he, "The monks are cheats," yes, and as soon as he said it he was struck blind. Well, and then he dreamed a dream, the Holy Virgin Mother of the Catacombs at Kiev comes to him and says: "Believe in me and I will make you whole." And so he kept beseeching, "Take me to her, take me to her." It's Gospel truth I'm telling you, I saw it with my own eyes. So they led him, stone blind as he was, straight to her, and he goes up and falls on his knees and says, "Make me whole," says he, "and I will give thee what I had from the Tsar." And, sir, I seen the star on her myself, just as he gave it to her. Well, and what do you think – he got back his sight. It's a sin to speak so. God will punish you,' she said admonishingly to Pierre.

'How did the star get into the icon?' Pierre asked.

'And was the Holy Mother promoted to the rank of general?' said Prince Andrei, smiling.

Pelageya suddenly turned pale and clasped her hands.

'Oh, master, master, what a sin! And you with a son too!' she began, turning from white to a vivid red. 'For what you have said, God forgive you.' She crossed herself. 'Oh Lord, forgive him! Dearie, what does it mean? ...' she asked Princess Maria. She got to her feet and, almost crying, began gathering up her wallet. Plainly she was both frightened and ashamed at having accepted charity in a house where such things could be said, and at the same time sorry that she must henceforth deprive herself of the bounty to be found there.

'Now what did you want to do this for?' said Princess Maria. 'Why did you come to my room? ...'

'No, Pelageya, I am not in earnest,' said Pierre. 'Princess, I give you my word I didn't mean to upset her,' he said in French. 'Forget it, I was only joking,' he said, smiling shyly and trying to efface his crime.

Pelageya paused doubtfully, but Pierre's face showed such sincere penitence, and Prince Andrei looked so meekly from her to Pierre and back again, that she was gradually reassured.

14

THE pilgrim-woman was appeased and, being encouraged to talk, told them a long story of Father Amphilochy, who led such a holy life that his dear hands smelt of incense, and of how on her last pilgrimage to Kiev some monks she knew let her have the keys to the catacombs, and of how, taking some dried bread with her, she had spent two days and two nights in the catacombs among the saints. 'I'd say a little prayer to one, read a passage from the Bible, and go on to another. Then I'd have a little nap, and once more go and kiss the holy relics; and such peace, dearie, such blessedness that a body has no wish to come out even into God's daylight again.'

Pierre listened to her gravely and attentively. Prince Andrei went out of the room. And leaving 'God's folk' to finish their tea, Princess Maria followed him with Pierre into the drawing-room.

'You are very kind,' she said to him.

'Ah, I truly did not mean to hurt her feelings. I understand them so well and have the greatest respect for them.'

Princess Maria looked at him without speaking, and a gentle smile played over her lips.

'I have known you a long time, you see, and am as fond of you as of a brother,' she said. 'What do you think of Andrei?' she asked hastily, not giving him time to respond to her expressions of affection. 'I feel very worried about him. His health in the winter was better, but last spring his wound reopened and the doctor said he ought to go away and have proper treatment. His state of mind makes me afraid too. His is not a nature that would let him weep away his suffering, in the way we women do. He carries it buried in him. Today he is cheerful and in good spirits, but that is thanks to your visit – he is not often like that. If you could only persuade him to go abroad! He needs activity, and this quiet regular life is very bad for him. Other people don't notice it, but I do.'

Soon after nine the footmen rushed to the front door, hearing the bells of the old prince's approaching carriage. Prince Andrei and Pierre also went out on to the steps.

'Who's that?' asked the old prince, alighting and catching sight of Pierre.

'Ah! Very glad! Kiss me,' he said, having learnt who the young stranger was.

Prince Bolkonsky was in high good humour and treated Pierre in the most cordial manner.

Before supper Prince Andrei, on returning to his father's study, found him disputing hotly with their visitor. Pierre was maintaining that a time would come when there would be no more war. The old prince chaffingly joined issue with him, but without getting angry.

'Drain the blood from men's veins and pour water in instead, and then there'll be no more war. Old women's nonsense, old women's nonsense,' he was saying, but still he patted Pierre affectionately on the shoulder as he went over to the table where Prince Andrei, evidently not caring to enter into the discussion, was glancing through the papers his father had brought from town. The old man began to talk of business.

'The marshal, a Count Rostov, hasn't sent half his contingent. Came to town and thought fit to invite me to dinner – I gave him dinner! ... And here, have a look at this. ... Well, my boy,' Prince Bolkonsky went on, addressing his son and clapping Pierre on the shoulder, 'your friend's a capital fellow – I like him! He wakes me up. Other people will talk sense but one has no wish to listen; whereas this fellow pours out rubbish and it does an old man good. Well, get along, get along! Perhaps I'll come and sit with ye at supper. We'll have another argument. Make friends with my little goose, Princess Maria,' he shouted after Pierre through the door.

It was only now on his visit to Bald Hills that Pierre appreciated fully the strength and charm of his friendship with Prince Andrei. This charm was not expressed so much in his relations with Prince Andrei himself as in his relations with all his family and household. With the stern old host and the gentle timid Princess Maria, though he scarcely knew them, Pierre at once felt like an old friend. They were all fond of him already. Not only Princess Maria, who had been won by his kindliness with the pilgrims, gave him her most radiant looks, but even the little yearling Prince Nikolai (as his grandfather called him) smiled at Pierre and let himself be taken in Pierre's arms, and Mihail Ivanich and Mademoiselle Bourienne watched him with happy smiles when he talked to Prince Bolkonsky.

The old prince came in to supper; this was evidently on Pierre's account. And during the two days the young man stayed at Bald Hills he was extremely genial with him, and told him to come and visit them again.

When Pierre had gone, and all the members of the household were together, they began to discuss him, as people always do after the departure of a new face, but, as rarely happens, no one had anything but good to say of him.

15

RETURNING from this furlough, Rostov for the first time felt and recognized how strong were the ties that bound him to Denisov and all the others in the regiment.

When he was approaching the Pavlograds he felt as he had on nearing his home in Moscow. At the first sight of a hussar, of his regiment, with uniform unbuttoned, at the sight of Dementyev's red head, and the picket-ropes of the roan horses, and when he heard Lavrushka gleefully shout to his master, 'The count has come!' and Denisov, who had been asleep on his bed, ran all dishevelled out of the mud hut to embrace him, and the officers gathered round to greet the new arrival, Rostov felt exactly as he had when his mother and father and sisters had hugged him, and tears of joy so choked him that he could not say a word. The regiment was home, too, and one as unalterably dear and precious as his parental home.

After reporting himself to his colonel and being reassigned to his former squadron, after taking his turn as officer for the day and going for forage, after getting back into the current of all the little interests of the regiment, after taking leave of his liberty and letting himself be nailed down within one narrow inflexible framework, Rostov experienced the same sense of peace, of moral support, and the same sense of being at home and in his right corner as he felt under the paternal roof. Here was none of that turmoil of the world at large in which he found himself out of his element and made mistakes in exercising his free will. There was no Sonya with whom he ought or ought not to reach a clear understanding. Here he did not have to make up his mind whether he would or would not go to this or that place. Here there were not twenty-four hours in the day which could be spent in such a variety of ways; here there was an end to that innumerable throng of individuals whose presence or absence was a matter of indifference to him; there was an end to those vague and undefined money-relations with his father, and nothing to remind him of that terrible loss to Dolohov. Here in the regiment everything was straightforward and simple. The whole world was divided into two unequal parts: one, our Pavlograd regiment; the other, all the remainder. And with that remainder one had no concern. In the regiment everything was definite: who was lieutenant, who captain, who was a good fellow, who was not, and, above all, who was a comrade. The canteen-keeper gave one credit, one's pay came every four months; there was nothing that had to be thought out and decided. One had only to behave honourably by the standards of the Pavlograd Hussars, and when given an order carry out what was clearly, distinctly, and unmistakably commanded – and all would be well.

Stepping back into these explicit conditions of regimental life, Rostov felt the delight and relief a tired man feels in lying down to rest. To Rostov army life was all the more agreeable during this campaign because after his gambling loss to Dolohov (for which, in spite of all his family's efforts to console him, he could not forgive himself) he had made up his mind to atone for his fault by serving not as he had done before but really well; by being a thoroughly admirable comrade and officer – in other words, a first-rate man, a thing which seemed so difficult out in the *world* but so possible in the regiment.

He had determined to repay his debt to his parents within five years. They were sending him ten thousand roubles a year, but now he resolved to take only two thousand and leave the rest towards repayment of the debt.

*

Our army, after various retreats, advances, and engagements fought at Pultusk and Preussisch-Eylau, was concentrated in the vicinity of Bartenstein, awaiting the Emperor's arrival and the beginning of a new offensive.

The Pavlograd regiment, belonging to that part of the army which had served in the hostilities of 1805, had been recruiting up to strength in Russia, and arrived too late for the first actions of the campaign. The Pavlograds had not been at Pultusk nor at Preussisch-Eylau, and when they reached the army in the field in the second half of the campaign were attached to Platov's division.

Platov's division was acting independently of the main army. Several times units of the Pavlograd regiment had exchanged shots with the enemy, had taken prisoners, and on one occasion had even captured Marshal Oudinot's carriages. In April the Pavlograd Hussars were stationed near a totally ruined and deserted German village, where they remained without stirring for several weeks.

A thaw had set in, it was muddy and cold, the ice on the river had broken, and the roads become impassable. For days neither provisions for the men nor fodder for the horses had been issued. As no transports could arrive, the men scattered about the abandoned and empty villages, searching for potatoes, but even these were few and far between.

Everything had been devoured and the inhabitants had all fled – if any remained they were poorer than beggars and there was nothing to be taken from them; even the soldiers, usually pitiless enough, instead of robbing them further often gave up the last of their rations to them.

The Pavlograd regiment had lost only two men wounded in action, but famine and sickness had reduced their numbers by almost half. In the hospitals death was so certain that soldiers suffering from fever, or the swelling caused by bad food, preferred to remain on duty, dragging their feeble legs to the front, rather than go to the hospitals. With the coming of spring the soldiers found a plant just showing above ground that looked like asparagus, which for some reason they called 'Molly's sweet-wort', and they wandered about the fields and meadows hunting for this 'Molly's sweet-wort' (which was very bitter), digging it up with their sabres and eating it, in spite of every injunction not to touch this noxious root. That spring a new disease broke out among the men, a swelling of the arms, legs and face, which the doctors attributed to this plant. But, orders notwithstanding, the soldiers of Denisov's squadron fed chiefly on 'Molly's sweet-wort', because this was the second week of eking out the last of the biscuits – half-pound rations being doled out to each man – and the last consignment of potatoes were frozen and sprouting.

The horses, too, had subsisted for a fortnight on straw from the thatched roofs; they had become shockingly thin and their winter coats still hung about them in tufts.

Despite this terrible destitution officers and men continued with the usual routine. Despite their pale, swollen faces and tattered uniforms, the hussars formed up for roll-call, attended to their duties, groomed their horses, polished their arms, tore down thatch from the roofs in place of fodder, and gathered round the cauldrons for their meals, from which they rose unsatisfied, joking about their vile food and their hunger. And just as usual during the hours when they were off duty they lit bonfires, stripped, and stood steaming themselves, smoked, picked out and baked sprouting rotten potatoes, while they told and listened to stories of Potemkin's and Suvorov's campaigns, or popular legends about Alyosha-the-artful-one or Mikolka who worked for the priest.

The officers also lived as usual in twos and threes in roofless, tumble-down houses. The seniors did what they could to get straw and potatoes and means of sustenance for the soldiers generally. The younger ones spent their time as they always did, some playing cards (money was plentiful if provisions were not), others with more innocent games such as quoits and skittles. The progress of the campaign as a whole was rarely spoken of, partly because they had no positive information of any sort and partly because of a vague feeling that in the main the war was going badly.

Rostov lived as before with Denisov, and the bond of friendship between them had become still closer since their furlough. Denisov never mentioned Rostov's family, but by the warmth of the affection his commander showed him Rostov felt that the elder hussar's luck-less passion for Natasha had something to do with the strengthening of their friendship. There was no doubt that Denisov tried to take care of Rostov and to expose him to danger as seldom as possible, and after an action greeted his safe return with undisguised joy. On one of his foraging expeditions in a deserted and ruined village where he had gone in search of provisions, Rostov found a Polish family consisting of an old man and his daughter with an infant at the breast. They were half-naked, starving, too weak to get away on foot, and had no means of obtaining transport. Rostov brought them to his quarters, installed them in his own lodgings, and kept them for several weeks while the old man was recovering. One of his comrades, talking of women, began chaffing Rostov, declaring that he was the slyest fellow of them all and that it would not be a bad thing if he introduced them to the pretty little Polish girl he had rescued. Rostov took the joke as an insult, flared up and was so disagreeable to the officer that it was all Denisov could do to prevent a duel. When the officer had gone away, and Denisov, who knew nothing himself of Rostov's relations with the Polish girl, began to upbraid him for his quick temper, Rostov said to him:

'But how could I help it ? ... she was like a sister to me, and I can't tell you how it offended me ... because ... well, because ...'

Denisov patted him on the shoulder, and took to walking rapidly up and down the room without looking at Rostov, a habit of his at moments of emotional disturbance.

'What a cwazy bweed you Wostovs are !' he muttered, and Rostov noticed tears in his eyes.

16

In the month of April the troops were cheered by news of the Emperor's arrival, but Rostov had no chance of being present at the review the Tsar held at Bartenstein: the Pavlograds were at the advance posts, a long way beyond Bartenstein.

They were bivouacking. Denisov and Rostov were living in a mud hut, dug out for them by the soldiers and roofed with branches and turf. The hut was made after a pattern then in vogue. A trench was dug three and a half feet wide, four feet eight inches deep, and eight feet long. At one end of the trench steps were cut and these formed the entrance, the approach. The trench itself was the room, in which the lucky ones such as the squadron commander had a plank lying on piles at the end opposite the entrance, to serve as a table. On each side of the trench the earth was hollowed out to a depth of about two and a half feet, and this did duty for bedsteads and couches. The roof was so constructed that one could stand upright in the middle of the trench, and even sit up on the beds if one leant over towards the table. Denisov, who fared luxuriously because he was popular with the soldiers of his squadron, had a board in the front part of the roof of his hut, with a piece of broken but mended glass in it for a window. When it was very cold embers from the soldiers' camp-fires were brought on a bent sheet of iron and put on the steps in the 'reception room' – as Denisov called that part of the hut – and this made it so warm that the officers, of whom there were always a number with Denisov and Rostov, could sit in their shirt-sleeves.

In April Rostov was on orderly duty. Returning between seven and eight one morning after a night without sleep, he sent for hot embers, changed his rain-soaked clothes, said his prayers, swallowed some tea, warmed himself, then tidied up the things on the table and in his own corner and, his face glowing from exposure to the wind, and with nothing on but his shirt, lay down on his back, his hands behind his head. He was pleasantly reflecting on the promotion which was likely to follow his last reconnoitring expedition, and was awaiting Denisov, who had gone out somewhere. He was anxious to have a talk with him.

Suddenly he heard Denisov shouting behind the hut in a voice vibrating with anger. Rostov moved to the window to learn whom he was speaking to, and saw the quartermaster Topcheyenko.

'I told you not to let them eat that Molly-woot stuff!' Denisov was roaring. 'And then with my own eyes I see Lazarchuk bwinging some fwom the field.'

'I did give the order, your Honour, over and over again, but they won't listen,' answered the quartermaster.

Rostov lay down again on his bed, and thought complacently: 'It's his turn now, let him look to things: I've done my day's work and now I'm having a lie-down – hurrah!' Through the wall he could hear Lavrushka, Denisov's smart rogue of a valet, talking as well as the quartermaster. Lavrushka was saying something about loaded wagons, biscuits and oxen he had seen when he had gone for provisions.

Then Denisov's voice from farther off was heard shouting: 'Second troop – to the saddle!'

'Where are they off to now?' wondered Rostov.

Five minutes later Denisov came into the hut, climbed with muddy boots on the bed, angrily lit his pipe, rummaged through his belongings, got out his riding-whip, buckled on his sabre and started out of the hut. To Rostov's 'Whither away?' he answered gruffly and vaguely that he had business to attend to.

'Let God be my judge afterwards, and our gweat monarch!' said Denisov as he went out, and next Rostov heard the hooves of several horses splashing through the mud. He did not even trouble to find out where Denisov had gone. Warm and comfortable in his corner, he fell asleep and stayed in the hut until late in the afternoon. Denisov had not returned. The weather had cleared, and near the next hut two officers and a cadet were playing *svayka*, laughing as they threw their pegs, which buried themselves in the soft mud. Rostov joined them. In the middle of a game the officers saw some wagons approaching with some fifteen hussars on their scraggy horses riding behind. The escorted wagons drove up to the picket-ropes and were surrounded by a crowd of hussars.

'There now, Denisov never left off worrying,' said Rostov, 'and here are the provisions.'

'So they are!' said the officers. 'Won't the men be pleased!'

A little behind the hussars came Denisov, accompanied by two infantry officers with whom he was discussing something. Rostov went to meet them.

'I warn you, captain,' one of the officers, a short thin man, evidently very angry, was saying.

'And I have told you that I am not weturning them,' replied Denisov.

'You will answer for it, captain. It's mutiny – carrying off transports from your own army! Our men have had no food for two days.'

'And mine have had nothing for two weeks,' retorted Denisov.

'It's highway robbery! You'll answer for this, sir!' repeated the infantry officer, raising his voice.

'Now what are you pestewing me for?' shouted Denisov, suddenly losing his temper. 'I am the one who is wesponsible, and not you, and you'd better not buzz about here till you get hurt. Be off!' he shouted at the officers.

'Very well then!' cried the little officer, undaunted and not budging. 'If you are determined on robbery, I'll …'

'Take yourself to the devil! Quick ma'ch, while you're safe and sound!' and Denisov rode his horse at the officer.

'Very good, very good!' muttered the officer threateningly, and turning his horse he trotted away, bouncing in the saddle.

'A dog astwide a fence! Vewily a dog astwide a fence!' Denisov called after him – the most insulting remark a cavalryman can make to an infantryman on horseback – and riding up to Rostov he broke into a guffaw.

'I appwopwiated 'em from the infantwy – I've taken their twans- ports by main force!' he said. 'Why, I can't let my men pewish of starvation.'

The wagons that had reached the hussars had been consigned to an infantry regiment, but learning from Lavrushka that the transport was unescorted Denisov with his hussars had forcibly seized it. The soldiers got as many biscuits as they wanted: there were even enough to share with other squadrons.

Next day the regimental commander sent for Denisov, and holding his fingers spread out before his eyes said:

'This is the way I look at the business: I know nothing about it and shall take no action, but I advise you to ride over to H.Q. and make matters right with the commissariat, and if possible sign a receipt for such and such stores received. If you don't, and the stuff is debited against the infantry regiment, there will be trouble and it may end unpleasantly.'

Denisov went straight from the colonel to headquarters with a sincere desire to act on this advice. In the evening he came back to his dug-out in a state such as Rostov had never seen him in before. He could not speak and was gasping for breath. When Rostov asked him what was wrong, he could only splutter incoherent oaths and threats in a faint voice.

Alarmed at Denisov's condition, Rostov suggested he should un- dress, and drink some water, while he sent for the doctor.

'Me to be twied for wobbewy – oh, some more water. ... Let them twy me, but I shall always thwash wascals, and I'll tell the Empewo' ... Give me some ice,' he kept muttering.

The regimental surgeon said it was necessary to bleed Denisov. A soup-plateful of black blood was taken from his hairy arm and only then was he able to relate what had happened.

'I get there,' began Denisov. '"Well, where are your chief's quar- ters?" I ask. They show me. "Will you be kind enough to wait?" "I've widden twenty miles, I have duties to attend to and no time to wait. Announce me." Vewy well: out comes the wobber-in-chief – he, too, thinks fit to lecture me: "This is wobbewy!" says he. "A wobber," I tell him, "is not a man who takes pwovisions to feed his soldiers but one who fills his own pockets!" "Will you please be silent?" Wight. "Go and sign a weceipt in the commissioner's office," says he, "but your affair will be weported to headquarters." I pwoceed to the commissioner's. I enter, and there at the table ... who do you suppose? No, think! ... Who is it that's starving us to death?' roared Denisov, banging the table so violently with the fist of his newly-bled arm that the board almost collapsed and the tumblers danced on it. 'Telyanin! "What," I shouted, "so it's you starving us to death, is it?" and I gave him one stwaight on the snout. ... "Ah, you unspeakable ... you ...!" and I started thwashing him. ... I enjoyed it, I can tell you,' cried Denisov with malignant glee, showing his white teeth under his black moustache. 'I'd have killed him if they hadn't pulled me away.'

'Here, here, what are you shouting for, keep quiet,' said Rostov. 'Now you've started your arm bleeding. Wait, we must tie it up again.'

Denisov was bandaged up once more and put to bed. Next morning when he woke he was in good spirits and unruffled.

But at noon the adjutant of the regiment appeared in Denisov's and Rostov's dug-out and with a grave and serious face regretfully showed them a formal communication addressed to Major Denisov from the regimental commander inquiring about the incidents of the previous day. The adjutant told them that the affair was likely to take a very ugly turn, that a court-martial had been convened, and that in view of the severity with which marauding and insubordination were now regarded he might think himself fortunate if he escaped with being reduced to the ranks.

The case as presented by the aggrieved parties was that Major Denisov, after seizing the transports, had appeared, unbidden and the worse for liquor, before the chief quartermaster, called him a thief, threatened to strike him and, when he was led away, had rushed into the office and given two officials a thrashing, dislocating the arm of one of them.

In reply to further inquiries from Rostov, Denisov laughed and said that it did certainly seem as though some other fellow had got mixed up in it, but that it was all stuff and nonsense, that he would not dream of being afraid of any court-martial, and that if those scoundrels dared to pick a quarrel with him he would give them an answer they would not easily forget.

Denisov spoke contemptuously of the whole matter, but Rostov knew him too well not to detect that at heart (though he hid it from the others) he feared a court-martial and was worried over the affair, which was obviously certain to have disastrous consequences. Forms to be filled in, and notices from the court, began to arrive daily, and on the 1st of May Denisov was ordered to hand his squadron over to the next in seniority and appear before the divisional staff to give an account of his violence at the commissariat office. On the previous day Platov made a reconnaissance of the enemy with two Cossack regiments and two squadrons of hussars. Denisov, as was his wont, rode out in front of the outposts parading his courage. A bullet fired by a French sharpshooter hit him in the fleshy upper part of the leg. Possibly at any other time Denisov would not have left the regiment for so slight a wound, but now he took advantage of it to excuse himself from appearing at headquarters, and retired into hospital.

17

In June the battle of Friedland was fought, in which the Pavlograds did not take part, and after that an armistice was declared. Rostov, who felt his friend's absence very keenly, having had no news of him since he left and feeling anxious about his wound and the progress of his affairs, took advantage of the truce to get leave to visit Denisov in hospital.

The hospital was in a small Prussian town which had twice been sacked by Russian and French troops. For the very reason that it was summer, when everything is so lovely out in the fields, the little town presented a particularly dismal appearance with its broken roofs and fences, its foul streets and ragged inhabitants, and the sick and drunken soldiers wandering about.

The hospital, which stood in a courtyard surrounded by the remnants of a wooden fence, had been established in a brick building with many of the window-frames and panes broken. A number of bandaged soldiers, with pale swollen faces, were walking about or sitting in the sunshine in the yard.

Directly Rostov entered the door he was enveloped by a smell of putrefaction, disease and disinfectant. On the stairs he met a Russian army doctor with a cigar in his mouth. The doctor was followed by a Russian assistant.

'I can't be everywhere at once,' the doctor was saying. 'Come this evening to Makar Alexeyevich, I'll be there.' The assistant asked some

471

further question. 'Oh, do as you think best! What difference will it make?' The doctor caught sight of Rostov coming upstairs.

'What are you doing here, sir?' said the doctor. 'What are you here for? Couldn't you meet with a bullet that you want to pick up typhus? This is a pest-house, my good sir.'

'What do you mean?' asked Rostov.

'Typhus, sir. It's death to come in these walls. Makeyev' (he pointed to the assistant) 'and I are the only two still hanging about. Half a dozen of our colleagues have been carried off. ... As soon as a new man comes it's all up with him within a week,' said the doctor with evident satisfaction. 'Prussian doctors have been invited here but our allies don't care for the idea at all.'

Rostov explained that he wanted to see Major Denisov of the Hussars, who was lying wounded there.

'I don't know, can't tell you, my good sir. You can imagine: I've got three hospitals on my hands – over four hundred patients! It's just as well the kind ladies of Prussia send us a couple of pounds of coffee and some lint each month or we should be lost!' He laughed. 'Four hundred, sir, and fresh cases arriving all the time. It *is* four hundred, isn't it? Eh?' he asked, turning to his assistant.

The assistant looked tired out. It was evident that he was in a hurry for the talkative doctor to be gone, and waited irritably.

'Major Denisov,' repeated Rostov. 'He was wounded at Moliten.'

'Dead, I fancy. Eh, Makeyev?' queried the doctor in a tone of indifference.

The assistant, however, did not confirm the doctor's words.

'Is he tall, with reddish hair?' asked the doctor.

Rostov described Denisov's appearance.

'Yes, there was someone like that,' exclaimed the doctor almost with glee. 'But I'm sure he's dead, but anyway I'll make inquiries. We had lists. Have you got them, Makeyev?'

'The lists are at Makar Alexeyevich's,' answered the assistant. 'But go to the officers' ward and you'll see for yourself,' he added, turning to Rostov.

'Ah, you'd better not, sir,' said the doctor, 'or you might find yourself having to stay here!'

But Rostov took leave of the doctor with a bow and asked the assistant to show him the way.

'Don't blame me, mind!' the doctor shouted up the stairs after him.

Rostov and the assistant entered a corridor. The hospital stench was so strong in this dark passage that Rostov held his nose and was obliged to pause and brace himself before he could go on. A door opened on the right, and an emaciated, sallow-looking man limped out on crutches, wearing his underlinen only and with nothing on his feet. Leaning against the doorpost, he gazed with glittering envious eyes at them as they passed. Glancing in at the door, Rostov saw that the sick and wounded were lying on the floor, some on straw, some on their greatcoats.

'May one go in and look?' asked Rostov.

'What is there to see?' said the assistant.

But just because the assistant was obviously disinclined to let him, Rostov went into the soldiers' ward. The foul air which he had already begun to get used to in the corridor was still stronger here. It was a little different, more pungent, and one felt that this was where it originated.

In the long room, brightly lit by the sun which poured in through the large windows, the sick and wounded lay in two rows with their heads to the walls, leaving a passage down the middle. Most of them were unconscious and paid no attention to the visitors. The others raised themselves or lifted their thin yellow faces, and all gazed intently at Rostov with the same expression of hope that help had come, and of reproach and envy of another's health. Rostov stepped into the middle of the ward, and looking through the open doors of the two adjoining rooms on both sides saw the same spectacle. He stood still silently looking round. He had never expected anything like this. Close to his feet, almost across the empty space down the middle, a sick man lay on the bare floor, a Cossack probably, to judge by the way his hair was cut. The man was lying on his back, with his huge arms and legs outstretched. His face was purplish-red, his eyes were rolled back so that only the whites were visible, and the veins in his bare legs and arms, which were still red, stood out like cords. He was beating the back of his head against the floor, hoarsely muttering some word which he repeated over and over again. Rostov tried to hear what he was saying and made out the word he kept repeating. It was 'drink – drink – a drink!' Rostov looked round in search of someone who would lay the sick man back in his place and give him water.

'Who looks after the sick here?' he asked the assistant.

Just at that moment an army service corps soldier, a hospital orderly, came in from the next room, marched up to Rostov and stood to attention.

'Good day, your Honour!' bawled this soldier, rolling his eyes at Rostov and evidently mistaking him for someone in authority.

'Get him to his place and give him some water,' said Rostov, pointing to the Cossack.

'Certainly, your Honour,' the soldier replied complacently, rolling his eyes more strenuously than ever and drawing himself up still straighter, but not stirring from the spot.

'No, there's nothing I can do here,' thought Rostov, lowering his eyes, and he was about to leave the room when he became aware of an intense look fixed on him from over on the right. Almost in the corner, sitting on a military overcoat, was an old soldier with a stern sallow face, thin as a skeleton's, and an unshaved grey beard. He was looking persistently at Rostov. The man next the old soldier was whispering something to him, pointing to Rostov. Rostov realized that the old man wanted to ask him some favour. He went closer and saw that the old man had only one leg bent under him, the other had been amputated above the knee. At some distance from him, his neighbour on the other side, lay the motionless figure of a young soldier with head thrown back. The pale waxen face with its snub nose was still freckled, the eyes were rolled up under the lids. Rostov looked at the snub-nosed soldier and a cold chill ran down his back.

'Why, that man seems to be ...' he began, turning to the assistant.

'We've begged and begged, your Honour,' said the old soldier with a quiver in his lower jaw. 'He's been dead since morning. After all, we're men, not dogs. ...'

'I'll send someone at once. He shall be taken away – taken away at once,' said the assistant hurriedly. 'Come, your Honour.'

'Yes, yes, let us go,' said Rostov hastily, and dropping his eyes and shrinking into himself, trying to pass unnoticed between the rows of reproachful, envious eyes fastened upon him, he went out of the ward.

18

Passing along the corridor, the assistant led Rostov to the officers' wards, consisting of three rooms opening into each other. Here there were bedsteads on which sick and wounded officers lay or sat. Others

474

were walking about in hospital dressing-gowns. The first person Rostov met in the officers' ward was a thin little man who had lost one arm. He was walking about the first room in a night-cap and hospital dressing-gown, with a stumpy pipe between his teeth. Rostov looked at him, trying to recall where he had seen him before.

'What a place for us to meet again!' said the little man. 'I'm Tushin, Tushin, don't you remember? – I gave you a lift at Schön Graben. They've lopped a bit off me, see …' he went on with a smile, showing the empty sleeve of his dressing-gown. 'Looking for Vasili Dmitrich Denisov, are you? A room-mate of mine!' he added when he heard who Rostov wanted. 'Here, this way,' and Tushin drew him into the second room, from which came the sound of loud laughter.

'How can they exist in this place, much less laugh?' thought Rostov, with the odour of the dead body which he had seen in the soldiers' ward still strong in his nostrils, and still seeing those envious glances fixed on him, following him out of the room, and the face of that young soldier with upturned eyes.

Denisov, with his head buried under the blanket, was sound asleep on his bed, though it was nearly noon.

'Ah, Wostov? How are you, how are you?' he called out, in exactly the same tone as in the regiment, but Rostov noticed sadly that for all his customary light-heartedness and swagger there was some new, sinister, smothered feeling which revealed itself in the expression of Denisov's face and the intonations of his voice.

His wound, though trifling, had still not healed even after a lapse of six weeks. His face had the same swollen pallor as all the other faces in the hospital. But it was not this that struck Rostov: what struck him was that Denisov did not seem pleased to see him, and his smile was forced. He did not ask about the regiment, nor about what was happening generally, and when Rostov spoke of the war he did not listen.

Rostov noticed that Denisov disliked even to be reminded of the regiment or of that other free life going on outside the hospital. He seemed to be trying to forget that old life, and was only interested in the affair with the commissariat officers. In reply to Rostov's inquiry as to how that matter stood, he at once produced from under his pillow a communication he had received from the commission and a rough draft of his answer to it. He brightened up as he began to read his own reply, and particularly drew Rostov's attention to the stinging rejoinders he made to his enemies. Denisov's fellow-patients, who had gathered round Rostov – a fresh arrival from the world outside – one by one drifted away as soon as Denisov began reading his answer. From their faces Rostov could tell that all these gentlemen had already heard the whole story more than once and were heartily sick of it. Only the man who had the next bed, a stout Uhlan, continued to sit on his bed, scowling gloomily and smoking a pipe, and little one-armed Tushin still listened, shaking his head disapprovingly. In the middle of the reading the Uhlan interrupted Denisov.

'But what I say is,' he broke in, turning to Rostov, 'he ought simply to petition the Emperor for pardon. They say that rewards and honours are to be rained on us now, so surely the mere matter of a pardon ...'

'Me petition the Empewo'!' exclaimed Denisov in a voice into which he tried hard to throw his old energy and fire but which sounded like an expression of impotent irritability. 'What for? If I were a highway wobber I might beg for mercy but I'm to be court-martialled for bwinging wobbers to book. Let them twy me, I'm not afwaid of anyone. I've served the Tsar and my countwy honouwably, and I am not a thief! And am I to be degwaded? ... Listen, I'm w'iting to them stwaight. This is what I say: "If I had wobbed the Tweasuwy ..."'

'It's neatly put, no question about that,' remarked Tushin, 'but that's not the point, Vasili Dmitrich,' and he too turned to Rostov. 'One has to submit, and that is what Vasili Dmitrich here won't hear of. You know, the auditor himself told you that it was a bad business?'

'Let it be a bad business, then,' said Denisov.

'The auditor wrote out a petition for you,' continued Tushin, 'and you ought to sign it and entrust it to this gentleman. No doubt he' (indicating Rostov) 'has connexions on the staff. You won't find a better opportunity.'

'Haven't I said I won't go cwinging and gwovelling?' Denisov interrupted him, and he went on reading his answer.

Rostov did not venture to try and persuade Denisov, though he felt instinctively that the course advised by Tushin and the other officers was the safest, and though he would have been glad to be of service to Denisov. He knew his friend's stubborn will and impetuous temper.

When Denisov had finished reading his venomous diatribe, which took over an hour, Rostov had nothing to say, and in the most dejected frame of mind spent the rest of the day in the society of Denisov's hospital companions who had gathered round again, telling them what he knew and listening to their stories. Denisov maintained a gloomy silence all the evening.

At length, when it was late and Rostov was about to leave, he asked Denisov whether there was anything he could do for him.

'Yes, wait a bit,' said Denisov glancing round at the officers, and taking his papers from under his pillow he went to the window where he had an inkpot, and sat down to write.

'It seems it's no use knocking one's head against a stone wall,' he said, coming from the window and handing Rostov a large envelope. It was the petition addressed to the Emperor which the auditor had drawn up for him, in which Denisov, making no reference to the shortcomings of the commissariat officials, simply asked for a pardon.

'Hand it in. It seems ...' He did not finish but forced his lips to a painfully unnatural smile.

19

HAVING returned to the regiment and reported to the commander the state of Denisov's affairs, Rostov rode to Tilsit with the letter to the Emperor.

On the 13th of June the French and Russian Emperors met at Tilsit. Boris Drubetskoy had asked the important personage on whom he was in attendance to include him in the suite appointed for the occasion.

'I should like to see the great man,' he said in French, alluding to Napoleon, whom hitherto he, like everyone else, had always called Bonaparte.

'You are speaking of Bonaparte?' the general said to him, smiling.

Boris looked at his general inquiringly, and immediately saw that he was being quizzed.

'I am speaking, *mon prince*, of the Emperor Napoleon,' he replied. The general patted him on the shoulder with a smile.

'You will go far,' he said, and took him to Tilsit with him.

Boris was among the few present at the Niemen on the day the two Emperors met. He saw the rafts with the royal monograms, saw Napoleon's progress past the French Guards on the opposite bank, saw the pensive face of the Emperor Alexander as he sat silent in the inn on the bank of the Niemen awaiting Napoleon's arrival. He saw both Emperors get into boats, and Napoleon, who was the first to

477

reach the raft, go forward with swift steps to meet Alexander and hold out his hand to him; then they disappeared together into the pavilion. Ever since he had begun to move in the highest circles Boris had made a practice of watching attentively all that went on around him, and noting it down. At Tilsit he inquired the names of those who had come with Napoleon and about the uniforms they wore, and listened carefully to the utterances of persons of consequence. At the moment the Emperors went into the pavilion he looked at his watch, and did not forget to look at it again when Alexander came out. The interview had lasted one hour and fifty-three minutes, an item which he recorded that evening among other facts which he felt to be of historic importance. As the Emperor's suite was a very small one, to be at Tilsit on the occasion of this interview between the two Emperors was a matter of great moment for a man who prized success in the service, and Boris, having succeeded in this, felt that henceforth his position was perfectly secure. He was not only known by name but people had grown accustomed to his presence and expected to see him. Twice he had executed commissions to the Emperor himself, so that the Sovereign knew his face, and the court, far from cold-shouldering him as at first, when they considered him a new-comer, would now have been surprised had he been absent.

Boris was lodging with another adjutant, the Polish Count Zhilinksy. Zhilinsky, a Pole brought up in Paris, was wealthy and passionately fond of the French, and almost every day of their stay at Tilsit French officers of the Guard and from the French High Command came to lunch or dine with him and Boris.

On the evening of the 24th of June Count Zhilinsky was giving a supper to his French acquaintances. The guest of honour was an aide-de-camp of Napoleon's. Others present included several French officers of the Guard and a page of Napoleon's, a young lad belonging to an old aristocratic French family. That same day Rostov, profiting by the darkness to pass unrecognized, arrived in Tilsit in civilian dress and went straight to the lodging occupied by Zhilinsky and Boris.

Rostov, in common with the whole army from which he rode, was as yet far from having undergone the change of feeling which had taken place at headquarters and in Boris towards Napoleon and the French – who had suddenly been transformed from foes to friends. In the army Bonaparte and the French were still regarded

478

with mixed feelings of animosity, contempt and fear. Only a short time back, in talking with a Cossack officer of Platov's Rostov had argued that if Napoleon were taken prisoner he would be treated not as a sovereign but as a criminal. Quite lately, falling in on the road with a wounded French colonel, Rostov had maintained with heat that no peace could be concluded between a legitimate sovereign and a criminal like Bonaparte. He was therefore strangely startled by the presence of French officers in Boris's rooms, wearing the uniform he had been accustomed to see with very different eyes from the line of pickets. The moment he saw a French officer, who thrust his head out of the door, that warlike feeling of hostility which always took possession of him at the sight of the enemy suddenly seized him. He stood still on the threshold and asked in Russian whether Drubetskoy lived there. Boris, hearing a strange voice in the ante-room, came out to meet him. A shade of annoyance crossed his face when he recognized Rostov.

'Ah, it's you! Glad to see you, very glad,' he said, however, coming forward with a smile. But Rostov had noticed his first reaction.

'I have come at a bad time, it seems. I shouldn't have come but it's a matter of business,' he said coldly.

'No, I was only surprised at your managing to get away from the regiment. I'll be with you in a moment,' he added in French to someone calling him from within.

'I see I'm intruding,' repeated Rostov.

By this time the look of annoyance had disappeared from Boris's face. Having evidently reflected and made up his mind how to act, with marked ease of manner he took Rostov by both hands and led him into the next room. His eyes, gazing serenely and unflinchingly at Rostov, seemed to be veiled by something – shielded as it were by the blue spectacles of conventional society. So it seemed to Rostov.

'Oh, please now! As if you could come at a wrong time!' said Boris, and he led him into the room where supper was laid and introduced him to his guests, mentioning his name and explaining that he was not a civilian but an officer of the hussars and his old friend.

'Count Zhilinsky – le Comte N.N. – le Capitaine S.S.,' said he, naming his guests. Rostov looked frowningly at the Frenchmen, bowed stiffly and said nothing.

Zhilinsky was obviously not pleased at the advent of this unknown Russian outsider into his circle, and did not speak to Rostov. Boris appeared not to notice the constraint produced by the new-comer and, with the same amiable composure and the same veiled look in his eyes with which he had welcomed Rostov, endeavoured to enliven the conversation. One of the Frenchmen, with characteristic Gallic courtesy, addressed the stubbornly-taciturn Rostov, remarking that the latter had probably come to Tilsit to see the Emperor.

'No, I came on business,' replied Rostov shortly.

Rostov's ill-humour had come on from the moment he detected the dissatisfaction on Boris's face, and as always happens with people who are in a bad temper he imagined they were all looking at him with hostile eyes, and that he was in everyone's way. And in fact he was in everyone's way, for he alone took no part in the conversation, which again became general. The glances the others cast on him seemed to say: 'And what is he sitting here for?' He rose and went up to Boris.

'I do really feel I'm embarrassing you,' he said in a low tone. 'Let me tell you my business, and I'll be off again.'

'Oh no, not at all,' said Boris. 'But if you are tired, come and lie down in my room and have a rest.'

'Yes, really ...'

They went into the little room where Boris slept. Rostov, without sitting down began at once, speaking irritably (as if Boris were in some way to blame), to tell him about Denisov's affair, asking him whether, through his general, he could and would intercede with the Emperor on Denisov's behalf, and get the petition for pardon to him. When they were alone together Rostov felt for the first time that he could not look Boris in the face without a sense of awkwardness. Boris, with one leg crossed over the other and stroking the slender fingers of his right hand with his left, listened to Rostov after the manner of a general listening to the report of a subordinate, now looking away now gazing straight at Rostov with the same veiled look. Each time he did so Rostov felt uncomfortable and cast down his eyes.

'I have heard of cases of this sort, and I know that his Majesty is very strict on such points. I think it would be best not to bring it to the Emperor's attention but to apply directly to the commander of the corps. ... But generally speaking, I believe ...'

'So you don't want to do anything? Well then, say so!' Rostov almost shouted, not looking at Boris.

Boris smiled.

'On the contrary, I will do what I can. Only I thought ...'

At that moment Zhilinsky's voice was heard at the door, calling Boris.

'Well, go along, go along, do ...' said Rostov, and refusing supper and remaining alone in the little room he walked up and down for a long time, listening to the light-hearted French chatter from the next room.

20

THE day on which Rostov arrived in Tilsit could not have been less favourable for proceedings on behalf of Denisov. It was out of the question for him to go himself to the general in attendance, since he was not in uniform and had come to Tilsit without permission, while Boris, even had he wished to, could not have done so on the day following Rostov's appearance. On that day, the 27th of June, the preliminaries of peace were signed. The Emperors exchanged decorations: Alexander received the *Légion d'honneur*, and Napoleon the Russian Order of St Andrew of the first degree; and that was the day arranged for the dinner to be given by a battalion of the French Guards to the Preobrazhensky battalion. The Emperors were to be present at this banquet.

Rostov felt so ill at ease and uncomfortable with Boris that when the latter looked in at him after supper he pretended to be asleep, and next morning left early to avoid another meeting. In a frock-coat and round hat he strolled about the town, staring at the French and their uniforms, and examining the streets and the houses where the Russian and French Emperors were staying. In the main square he saw tables being set up and preparations made for the dinner; in the streets he saw the Russian and French colours draped across from one side to the other, with the letters A and N in huge monograms. In the windows of the houses, too, there were flags and monograms.

'Boris doesn't care to help me, and I don't want to apply to him. That's settled,' thought Nikolai. 'All is over between us, but I'm not going away from here without having done everything I can for Denisov, and certainly not without getting his letter to the Emperor. The Emperor? ... He is here!' thought Rostov, who had unconsciously wandered back to the house occupied by Alexander.

Horses ready saddled were standing before the door and the suite were assembling, evidently preparing for the Emperor to come out.

'At any moment I may see him,' thought Rostov. 'If only I could give him the letter direct, and tell him all. ... Could they really arrest me for my civilian clothes? Surely not. He would understand on whose side justice lies. He understands everything, knows everything. Who can be juster and more magnanimous than he? Besides, even if they did arrest me for being here, what would it matter?' thought he, looking at an officer who was entering the house the Emperor occupied. 'Why, people are going in, I see. Oh, it's all nonsense! I'll go in and hand the letter to the Emperor myself: so much the worse for Drubetskoy who has driven me to it!' And suddenly, with a determination he would never have expected of himself, Rostov, fingering the letter in his pocket, went straight up to the house where the Emperor was staying.

'No, this time I won't miss my opportunity as I did after Austerlitz,' he thought, prepared every moment to meet the Monarch, and conscious of the blood rushing to his heart at the idea. 'I will fall at his feet and beseech him. He will lift me up, hear me out and even thank me. "I am happy when I can do good, but to remedy injustice is my greatest happiness,"' Rostov fancied the Emperor saying. And passing people who looked after him with curiosity, he entered the porch of the Emperor's house.

A broad staircase led straight up from the porch. On the right was a closed door. Below, under the stairs, was a door leading to the rooms on the lower floor.

'Who is it you want?' someone inquired.

'I have a letter, a petition, to hand to his Majesty,' said Nikolai, with a tremor in his voice.

'A petition? This way, please, to the officer on duty' (he was shown the door below). 'Only it won't be accepted.'

On hearing this indifferent voice Rostov grew panic-stricken at what he was doing; the thought of finding himself face to face with the Emperor at any moment was so alluring and consequently so terrifying that he felt like running away, but the attendant who met him opened the door to the officer's room for him, and Rostov went in.

A short stout man of about thirty, in white breeches, high boots and a batiste shirt which he had evidently only just put on, was standing in this room, while his valet buttoned on to the back of his breeches a pair of handsome new braces embroidered in silk that for some reason attracted Rostov's notice. The stout man was speaking to someone in the adjoining room.

'Devilish good figure and in her first bloom,' he was saying, but seeing Rostov he broke off and frowned.

'What do you want? A petition? ...'

'What is it?' asked the person in the other room.

'Another petitioner,' answered the man in the braces.

'Tell him to come back. He'll be out directly, we must go.'

'Come back another time, another time, tomorrow. It's too late. ...'

Rostov turned and was about to go but the man in the braces stopped him.

'Who is the petitioner? What's your name?'

'I come from Major Denisov,' replied Rostov.

'Who are you – an officer?'

'Lieutenant Count Rostov.'

'What audacity! Send it in through the proper channel. And go along with you ... go'; and he began putting on the uniform the valet handed him.

Rostov went back into the hall and noticed that by this time there were a great many officers and generals in full dress standing in the porch, and that he would have to pass through their midst.

Cursing his temerity, his heart sinking at the thought that he might at any moment meet the Emperor and be put to shame before him and placed under arrest, fully alive now to the impropriety of his conduct and repenting of it, Rostov with downcast eyes was making his way out of the house through the brilliant suite when a familiar voice called to him and a hand detained him.

'What are you doing here, sir, in a frock-coat?' demanded a deep voice.

It was a cavalry-general who had won the signal favour of the Emperor during this campaign, and who had formerly commanded the division in which Rostov was serving.

Rostov in dismay began to try and justify himself but, seeing the kindly, jocular face of the general, he drew him aside and in an excited voice explained the whole affair, begging him to intercede for Denisov, whom the general knew.

Having heard Rostov to the end, the general shook his head gravely.

'I'm sorry, very sorry for the gallant fellow. Give me the letter.'

Rostov had scarcely time to hand him the letter and finish telling him about Denisov's case before there were quick steps and the jingling of spurs on the stairs, and the general left his side to move to the porch. The gentlemen of the Emperor's suite ran down the steps and went to their mounts. Hayne, the same groom who had been at Austerlitz, led up the Emperor's horse, and on the stairs was heard the faint creak of a footstep which Rostov knew at once. Forgetting the danger of being recognized, Rostov made his way to the porch together with some inquisitive bystanders, and again after an interval of two years saw the features he adored: the same face, the same glance, the same walk, the same combination of majesty and mildness. ... And the feeling of enthusiasm and love for his Sovereign rose up again in Rostov's heart with all its old force. In the uniform of the Preobrazhensky regiment – white elk-skin breeches and high boots – and wearing a star Rostov did not know (it was the star of the *Légion d'honneur*), the Monarch came out on the steps, carrying his hat under his arm and putting on his glove. He paused and looked about him, brightening everything around by his glance. To one of the generals he spoke a few words, and also recognized Rostov's former commander, gave him a smile and beckoned to him.

All the suite drew back, and Rostov watched the general talking at some length to the Emperor.

The Emperor spoke a word or two in reply and took a step towards his horse. Again the crowd of the suite and the spectators in the street, with Rostov among them, moved closer to the Emperor. Stopping beside his horse with his hand on the saddle, the Emperor turned to the cavalry-general and said in a loud voice, evidently intended to be heard by all:

'I cannot do it, general. I cannot, because the law is mightier than I,' and he put his foot in the stirrup.

The general respectfully inclined his head, and the Monarch got into the saddle and rode down the street at a gallop. Beside himself with enthusiasm, Rostov ran after him with the crowd.

21

IN the public square to which the Emperor rode a battalion of the Preobrazhensky regiment was drawn up facing a battalion of the

French Guards in their bearskin caps, the Russians on the right, the French on the left.

As the Tsar rode up to one flank of the battalions, who presented arms, another group of horsemen galloped up to the opposite flank, and at the head of them Rostov recognized Napoleon. It could be no one else. He came at a gallop, wearing a small hat, a blue uniform open over a white vest, and the ribbon of St Andrew across his breast. He was mounted on a very fine thoroughbred grey Arab horse with a crimson gold-embroidered saddle-cloth. Riding up to Alexander, he raised his hat and as he did so Rostov, with his cavalryman's eye, could not help noticing that Napoleon sat neither well nor firmly in the saddle. The battalions shouted 'Hurrah' and *'Vive l'Empereur!'* Napoleon said something to Alexander. Both Emperors dismounted and took each other by the hand. Napoleon's face wore a disagreeably artificial smile. Alexander was saying something to him with an affable expression.

In spite of the kicking of the French gendarmes' horses which were keeping the crowd back, Rostov watched every movement of the Emperor Alexander and Bonaparte, never taking his eyes off them. It struck him with surprise that Alexander treated Bonaparte as an equal and that Bonaparte was perfectly at ease with the Russian Tsar, as if this proximity to a monarch were a natural everyday matter to him.

Alexander and Napoleon with the long train of their suites moved towards the right flank of the Preobrazhensky battalion, coming straight towards the crowd standing there. The crowd unexpectedly found itself so close to the Emperors that Rostov, in the front row, was afraid he might be recognized.

'Sire, I ask your permission to present the *Légion d'honneur* to the bravest of your soldiers,' said a harsh, precise voice speaking in French and articulating every letter.

It was the diminutive Bonaparte who spoke, looking up straight into Alexander's eyes. Alexander listened attentively to what was said to him and inclining his head smiled amiably.

'To the man who has conducted himself with the greatest courage in this last war,' added Napoleon, laying equal stress on each syllable and, with an assurance and composure revolting to Rostov, scanning the rows of Russian soldiers drawn up before him, all presenting arms and all gazing immovably at their own Emperor.

485

'Will your Majesty allow me to consult the colonel ?' said Alexander, and he took a few hasty steps towards Prince Kozlovsky, the commander of the battalion.

Bonaparte meanwhile began to draw the glove from his small white hand, tore it in so doing and threw it away. An aide-de-camp behind him rushed forward and picked it up.

'To whom shall it be given ?' the Emperor Alexander asked Kozlovsky in Russian, in a low voice.

'As your Majesty commands.'

The Emperor frowned with annoyance and glancing round said: 'But we must give him an answer.'

Kozlovsky ran his eyes over the ranks with a resolute air, including Rostov, too, in his scrutiny.

'Could he by any possibility choose me ?' thought Rostov.

'Lazarev!' the colonel called with a scowl; and Lazarev, the first man in the front rank, stepped briskly forward.

'Where are you off to ? Stand still!' various voices whispered to Lazarev, who did not know where he was to go. Lazarev stopped short, with a sidelong scared look at his colonel, and his face twitched, as often happens to soldiers called forward out of the ranks.

Napoleon slightly turned his head and stretched out his plump little hand behind him, as if to take something. The members of his suite, guessing at once what he wanted, whispered and stirred as they passed a small object from one to another, and a page – the same one Rostov had seen the previous evening at Boris's – sprang forward and, bowing respectfully over the outstretched hand and not keeping it waiting a single instant, laid in it an order on a red ribbon. Napoleon, without looking, pressed two fingers together and the badge was between them. Then he approached Lazarev, who stood rolling his eyes and still gazing obstinately at his own Monarch. Napoleon looked round at the Emperor Alexander to imply that what he was doing now he did out of consideration for his ally, and the small white hand holding the order touched one of Lazarev's buttons. It was as though Napoleon knew that it was enough for his hand to deign to touch the soldier's breast for that soldier to be for ever happy, rewarded and distinguished from everyone else in the world. Napoleon merely laid the cross on Lazarev's breast and, dropping his hand, turned towards Alexander as though sure that the cross must needs stay in position. The cross did, in fact, stick on.

Officious hands, Russian and French, instantly seized the cross and fastened it to the uniform. Lazarev glanced morosely at the little man with the white hands who had been doing something to him, and still standing rigidly, presenting arms, looked again into Alexander's eyes, as though he were asking whether he should continue to stand there, or was it his pleasure for him to go now, or perhaps do something else? But receiving no orders he remained for some time, motionless as a statue.

The Emperors remounted and rode away. The Preobrazhensky battalion, breaking ranks, began to mingle with the French Guards, and sat down at the tables prepared for them.

Lazarev was seated in the place of honour. Russian and French officers embraced him, congratulated him and pressed his hand. Crowds of officers and civilians flocked up simply to get a sight of him. A rumble of Russian and French voices and laughter filled the air round the tables in the square. Two officers with flushed faces, looking gay and happy, passed by Rostov.

'What do you say to the banquet, my boy? All served on silver plate,' remarked one of them. 'Seen Lazarev?'

'Yes.'

'Tomorrow, I hear, the Preobrazhenskys are to give them a dinner.'

'I say, but what luck for Lazarev! Twelve hundred francs pension for life.'

'How's this for a head-piece, lads!' shouted a Preobrazhensky soldier, donning a shaggy French cap.

'First-class! Suits you down to the ground!'

'Have you heard the password?' asked one Guards officer of another. 'The day before yesterday it was "*Napoléon, France, bravoure*"; yesterday was "*Alexandre, Russie, grandeur*". Our Emperor gives it one day and Napoleon the next. Tomorrow the Emperor will present a St George's cross to the bravest man in the French Guards. He can't help it. Must return the compliment.'

Boris and his friend Zhilinsky also came along to see the banquet to the Preobrazhensky regiment. On his way back Boris noticed Rostov standing by the corner of a house.

'Rostov! How are you? We missed each other,' he said, and could not refrain from asking what was the matter, so strangely dismal and troubled was Rostov's face.

'Nothing, nothing,' replied Rostov.

'You'll call round?'

'Yes, by and by.'

Rostov stood a long while at the corner, watching the feast from a distance. His brain was seething in an agonizing confusion which he could not work out to any conclusion. Horrible doubts were stirring in his soul. He thought of Denisov and the change that had come over him, and his surrender, and the whole hospital with those amputated legs and arms, and its dirt and disease. So vividly did he recall that hospital stench of putrefaction that he looked round to see where the smell was coming from. Then he thought of that self-satisfied Bonaparte with his little white hand, who was now an emperor, liked and respected by Alexander. For what, then, those severed arms and legs, why those dead men? Then his mind went to Lazarev rewarded and Denisov punished and unpardoned. He caught himself harbouring such strange reflections that he was terrified at them.

Hunger and the savoury smell of the Preobrazhensky dinner roused him from his reverie: he must have something to eat before going away. He went to an hotel he had noticed that morning. There he found so many people, among them officers who like himself had come in civilian dress, that he had difficulty in getting dinner. Two officers of his own division joined him at table. The conversation naturally turned on the peace. The two officers, Rostov's comrades, like most of the army, were dissatisfied with the peace concluded after the battle of Friedland. They declared that if we had only held out a little longer Napoleon would have been done for, as his troops had neither provisions nor ammunition. Nikolai ate and drank (chiefly the latter) in silence. He finished a couple of bottles of wine by himself. The conflict working within him still fretted him, and found no solution. He was afraid to give way to his thoughts yet could not rid himself of them. Suddenly, when one of his companions remarked that it was humiliating to see the French, Rostov began to shout with uncalled-for violence, and therefore much to the officers' surprise:

'And how, pray, can you judge what would have been best?' he cried, the blood rushing to his face. 'Why do you criticize the Emperor's actions? What right have we to sit in judgement on him? We cannot appreciate or understand the Emperor's aims or actions!'

'But I never said a word about the Emperor!' protested the officer, unable to find any other interpretation for Rostov's outburst than that he was drunk.

But Rostov did not heed him.

'We are not in the diplomatic service, we are soldiers and nothing more,' he went on. 'Command us to die – then we die. If we are punished, it means we're in the wrong; it's not for us to judge. If it's his Majesty the Emperor's pleasure to recognize Bonaparte as emperor and to conclude an alliance with him, it must be the right thing to do. If once we begin sitting in judgement and arguing about everything, there will be nothing sacred left. If we take that line we shall soon be saying there is no God, no nothing!' shouted Nikolai, banging the table with his fist. His outcry seemed utterly irrelevant to his listeners, but it was quite consistent with the train of his own thoughts.

'Our business is to do our duty, to fight, and not to think! And that's the sum of it!' he concluded.

'And to drink!' said one of the officers, who had no desire for a quarrel.

'Yes, and to drink!' agreed Nikolai. 'Hey, there!' he shouted. 'Another bottle!'

PART THREE

I

In the year 1808 the Emperor Alexander went to Erfurt for another interview with the Emperor Napoleon, and in the upper circles of Petersburg society there was much talk of the magnificence of this imperial occasion.

By 1809 the intimacy between 'the world's two arbiters', as Napoleon and Alexander were called, was such that when Napoleon declared war on Austria a Russian corps crossed the frontier in support of their former enemy, Bonaparte, against our former ally, the Austrian Emperor, and court circles speculated on a possible marriage between Napoleon and one of the Emperor Alexander's sisters. But besides considerations of foreign policy the attention of Russian society was at that time directed with keen interest on the internal changes taking place in every department of the administration.

Meanwhile life – actual everyday life with its essential concerns of health and sickness, work and recreation, and its intellectual preoccupations with philosophy, science, poetry, music, love, friendship, hatred, passion – ran its regular course, independent and heedless of political alliance or enmity with Napoleon Bonaparte and of all potential reforms.

*

Prince Andrei had spent two years uninterruptedly in the country. All the projects Pierre had attempted on his estates – and continually switching from one thing to another had never carried through – had been brought to fruition by Prince Andrei without display and without noticeable exertion. He possessed in the highest degree a quality Pierre lacked, that practical tenacity which without fuss or undue effort on his part gave impetus to any enterprise.

On one of his estates the three hundred serfs were transformed into free agricultural labourers (this was one of the first instances of the kind in Russia). On other estates the forced husbandry service was commuted for a quit-rent. At Bogucharovo a trained midwife was engaged at his expense to assist the peasant women in childbirth, and a priest paid to teach reading and writing to the children of the peasants and household servants.

Prince Andrei spent half his time at Bald Hills with his father and son, who was still in the nursery. The other half he passed at what his father called his 'Bogucharovo Hermitage'. Despite the indifference to the affairs of the world he had displayed to Pierre, he diligently followed all that went on, received many books, and was amazed to find that visitors arriving fresh from Petersburg, the very vortex of life, to see him or his father, lagged far behind himself – who never left the country – in knowledge of what was happening in home and foreign affairs.

In addition to looking after his estates and much general reading of the most varied kind, Prince Andrei was engaged at this time upon a critical survey of our last two unfortunate campaigns, and in working out a scheme of reform for our army rules and regulations.

In the spring of 1809 Prince Andrei set off to visit the Ryazan estates which his son, whose trustee he was, had inherited.

Warmed by the spring sunshine he sat in the *calèche*, looking at the new grass, the young leaves on the birch-trees and the first flecks of white spring clouds floating across the clear blue sky. He was not thinking of anything, but looked about him, carefree and absent-minded.

They crossed the ferry where he had talked with Pierre a year before. They drove through the muddy village, past threshing floors and green fields of winter rye, downhill by a drift of snow still lying near the bridge, uphill along a clay road hollowed into runnels by the rain, past strips of stubble land and a copse touched here and there with green, and into a birch forest extending along both sides of the road. In the forest it was almost hot; there was not a breath of wind. The birches, all studded with sticky green leaves, did not stir, and lilac-coloured flowers and the first blades of green grass lifted and pushed their way between last year's leaves. Dotted here and there among the birches, small fir-trees were an unpleasant reminder of winter with their coarse evergreen. The horses began to snort as they entered the forest and the sweat glistened on their coats.

The footman, Piotr, made some remark to the coachman; the coachman agreed. But apparently this was not enough for Piotr: he turned round on the box to his master.

'How mild it is, your Excellency!' he said with a respectful smile.

'What?'

'Mild, your Excellency.'

'What is he talking about?' wondered Prince Andrei. 'Oh, the spring, I suppose,' he thought, looking about him on either side. 'And indeed everything is green already. ... How early! And the birches and the wild cherry and alder too are all beginning to come out. ... But I don't see any sign of the oak yet. Oh yes, there's one, there's an oak!'

At the edge of the road stood an oak. Probably ten times the age of the birches that formed the bulk of the forest, it was ten times as thick and twice as tall as they. It was an enormous tree, double a man's span, with ancient scars where branches had long ago been lopped off and bark stripped away. With huge ungainly limbs sprawling unsymmetrically, with gnarled hands and fingers, it stood, an aged monster, angry and scornful, among the smiling birch-trees. This oak alone refused to yield to the season's spell, spurning both spring and sunshine.

'Spring, and love, and happiness!' this oak seemed to say. 'Are you not weary of the same stupid, meaningless tale? Always the same old delusion! There is no spring, no sun, no happiness! Look at those strangled, lifeless fir-trees, everlastingly the same; and look at me too, sticking out broken excoriated fingers, from my back and my sides, where they grew, just as they grew; here I stand, and I have no faith in your hopes and illusions.'

Prince Andrei turned several times to look back at this oak, as they drove through the forest, as though expecting some message from it. There were flowers and grass under the oak, too, but it stood among them scowling, rigid, misshapen and grim as ever.

'Yes, the oak is right, a thousand times right,' mused Prince Andrei. 'Others – the young – may be caught anew by this delusion, but we know what life is – our life is finished!'

A whole sequence of new ideas, pessimistic but bitter-sweet, stirred up in Prince Andrei's soul in connexion with that oak-tree. During this journey he considered his life as it were afresh, and arrived at his old conclusion, restful in its hopelessness: that it was not for him to begin anything new, but that he must live out his life, content to do no harm, dreading nothing and aspiring after nothing.

2

PRINCE ANDREI was compelled by his obligations as trustee of the Ryazan property to call upon the local Marshal of the Nobility. This was Count Ilya Rostov, and in the middle of May Prince Andrei went to see him.

It was by now the hot period of spring. The woods were already in full leaf. It was dusty, and so hot that the sight of water made one long to bathe.

Depressed and preoccupied with the business about which he had to consult the Marshal, Prince Andrei drove along the avenue leading to the Rostovs' house at Otradnoe. Behind some trees on the right he heard merry girlish cries, and caught sight of a bevy of young girls running to cross the path of his *calèche*. In front of the rest, and nearer to him, ran a dark-haired, remarkably slight, black-eyed girl in a yellow print dress, with a white pocket-handkerchief on her head from under which strayed loose locks of hair. The girl was shouting something, but then, seeing a stranger, ran back laughing, without looking at him.

Prince Andrei for some reason felt a sudden pang. The day was so lovely, the sun so bright, everything around so gay; but that slim pretty girl did not know or care to know of his existence, and was content and happy in her own life – foolish no doubt – but light-hearted and carefree and remote from him. 'What is she so glad about? What are her thoughts? Not of army regulations or Ryazan serfs and their quit-rents. What is she thinking of? Why is she so happy?' Prince Andrei asked himself with instinctive curiosity.

In 1809 Count Rostov was living at Otradnoe just as he had done in previous years; that is, entertaining almost the whole province with hunts, theatricals, dinner-parties and music. He welcomed Prince Andrei, as he did any new visitor, and insisted on his staying the night.

Several times in the course of a tedious day during which he was monopolized by his elderly hosts and the more distinguished of the guests (the old count's house was crowded on account of an approaching name-day), Prince Andrei found himself glancing at Natasha, laughing and amusing herself among the young people of the party,

493

and wondering each time, 'What is she thinking about? What makes her so happy?'

That night, alone in new surroundings, it was long before he could get to sleep. He read awhile, then put out his candle but afterwards relit it. It was hot in the room with the inside shutters closed. He was annoyed with the silly old man (as he called Rostov) who had detained him, declaring that the necessary documents had not yet arrived from town, and he was vexed with himself for having stayed.

He got up and went to the window to open it. As soon as he drew the shutters the moonlight flooded the room as though it had long been waiting at the window. He unfastened the casement. The still night was cool and beautiful. Just outside the window was a row of pollard-trees, looking black on one side and silvery bright on the other. Under the trees grew some sort of lush, wet, bushy vegetation with leaves and stems touched here and there with silver. Farther away, beyond the dark trees, a roof glittered with dew; to the right was a great, leafy tree with satiny white trunk and branches, and above it shone the moon, almost full, in a pale, practically starless, spring sky. Prince Andrei leaned his elbows on the window-ledge, and his eyes gazed at the heavens.

His room was on the first floor. Those above were also occupied, and by people who were not asleep either. He heard feminine voices overhead.

'Just once more,' said a girlish voice above him which Prince Andrei recognized at once.

'But when are you coming to bed?' replied a second voice.

'I shan't sleep – I can't, what's the use? Come, this will be the last time. ...'

Two girlish voices broke into a snatch of song, forming the final phrase of a duet.

'Oh, it's exquisite! Well, now let's say good-night and go to sleep.'

'You go to sleep, but I can't,' said the first voice, coming nearer to the window. She evidently thrust her head right out, for he could hear the rustle of her dress and even her breathing. Everything was hushed and turned to stone – the moon and her light, and the shadows. Prince Andrei, too, dared not stir, for fear of betraying his unintentional presence.

'Sonya! Sonya!' said the first voice again. 'Oh, how can you sleep? Just look how lovely it is! Oh, how glorious! Do wake up, Sonya!'

494

and there were almost tears in the voice. 'There never, never was such an exquisite night.'

Sonya made some reluctant reply.

'No, but do look what a moon! ... Oh, how lovely! Do come here. Darling, precious, come here! There, you see? I feel like squatting down on my heels, putting my arms round my knees like this, tight – as tight as can be – and flying away! Like this. ...'

'Take care, or you'll fall out.'

He heard the sound of a scuffle and Sonya's disapproving voice: 'Why, it's past one o'clock.'

'Oh, you only spoil things for me. All right, go to bed then, go along!'

Again all was silent, but Prince Andrei knew she was still sitting there. From time to time he heard a soft rustle or a sigh.

'O God, O God, what does it mean?' she exclaimed suddenly. 'To bed then, if I must!' and she slammed the casement.

'And for her I might as well not exist!' thought Prince Andrei while he listened to her voice, for some reason hoping yet dreading she might say something about him. 'And there she is again! As if it were on purpose,' thought he.

All at once such an unexpected turmoil of youthful thoughts and hopes, contrary to the whole tenor of his life, surged up in his heart that, feeling incapable of explaining his condition to himself, he made haste to lie down and fall asleep.

3

NEXT morning, having taken leave of no one but the count, and not waiting for the ladies to appear, Prince Andrei set off for home.

It was already the beginning of June when, on his return journey, he drove into the birch-forest where the gnarled old oak had made so strange and memorable an impression on him. In the forest the harness-bells sounded still more muffled than they had done six weeks before, for now all was thick, shady and dense, and the young fir-trees dotted about here and there did not jar on the general beauty but, yielding to the mood around, showed delicately green with their feathery young shoots.

The whole day had been hot. Somewhere a storm was gathering, but only a small rain-cloud had sprinkled the dust of the road and the sappy leaves. The left side of the forest lay dark in the shade, the right side gleamed wet and shiny in the sunlight, faintly undulating in the breeze. Everything was in blossom, the nightingales trilled and carolled, now near, now far away.

'Yes, that old oak with which I saw eye to eye was here in this forest,' thought Prince Andrei. 'But whereabouts?' he wondered again, looking at the left side of the road and, without realizing, without recognizing it, admiring the very oak he sought. The old oak, quite transfigured, spread out a canopy of dark, sappy green, and seemed to swoon and sway in the rays of the evening sun. There was nothing to be seen now of knotted fingers and scars, of old doubts and sorrows. Through the rough, century-old bark, even where there were no twigs, leaves had sprouted, so juicy, so young that it was hard to believe that aged veteran had borne them.

'Yes, it is the same oak,' thought Prince Andrei, and all at once he was seized by an irrational, spring-like feeling of joy and renewal. All the best moments of his life of a sudden rose to his memory. Austerlitz, with that lofty sky, the reproachful look on his dead wife's face, Pierre at the ferry, that girl thrilled by the beauty of the night, and that night itself and the moon and ... everything suddenly crowded back into his mind.

'No, life is not over at thirty-one,' Prince Andrei decided all at once, finally and irrevocably. 'It is not enough for me to know what I have in me – everyone else must know it too: Pierre, and that young girl who wanted to fly away into the sky; all of them must learn to know me, in order that my life may not be lived for myself alone while others live so apart from it, but may be reflected in them all, and they and I may live in harmony together.'

*

On reaching home Prince Andrei made up his mind to go to Petersburg in the autumn, and invented all sorts of grounds for this decision. A whole series of sensible, logical reasons showing it to be essential for him to visit Petersburg, and even to re-enter the service, kept springing to his mind. Indeed, it now passed his comprehension how he could ever have doubted the necessity of taking an active share in life, just as a month before he could not have believed that the idea of leaving the country could ever enter his head. It seemed clear to him that all he had experienced would be wasted and pointless unless he applied it to work of some kind and again played an active part. He could not understand how formerly he could have let such wretched arguments convince him that he would be lowering himself if after the lessons he had received from life he were to believe in the possibility of being useful or look forward to happiness and love. Now reason suggested quite the opposite. After his journey to Ryazan Prince Andrei began to tire of the country; his old pursuits ceased to interest him, and often when sitting alone in his study he got up, went to the looking-glass and contemplated his own face for a long while. Then he would turn away to the portrait of his dead Lisa, who, with her curls pinned up *à la grecque*, looked down at him tenderly and gaily out of the gilt frame. She no longer said those terrible words to him, but watched him with a simple, merry, quizzical look. And Prince Andrei, clasping his hands behind his back, would spend much time walking up and down the room, now frowning, now smiling, as he brooded over those preposterous, inexpressible ideas, secret as a crime, which were connected with Pierre, with fame, with the girl at the window, the oak, with woman's beauty, and love, which had altered his whole life. And if anyone came into his room at such moments he would be particularly short, severely decided and, above all, disagreeably rational.

'*Mon cher*,' Princess Maria might happen to say, entering at such a moment, 'little Nikolai can't go out today, it is very cold.'

'If it were hot,' Prince Andrei would answer his sister with peculiar dryness, 'he could go out in nothing but a smock, but as it is cold you will have to dress him in the warm clothes which were designed for that purpose. That is what follows from the fact that it is cold; not keeping a child indoors when it needs the fresh air,' he would say with exaggerated logicality, as it were punishing someone else for all that secret illogical element working within him.

On such occasions Princess Maria would think to herself how much intellectual activity dries up a man.

4

PRINCE ANDREI arrived in Petersburg in the August of 1809. It was the period when the youthful Speransky was at the zenith of his fame and his reforms were being pushed forward with the utmost vigour. That same August the Emperor was thrown from his carriage, injured his leg and was laid up for three weeks at Peterhof, seeing Speransky every day and no one else. At this period were elaborated the two famous decrees that so alarmed society – abolishing court ranks and introducing examinations to qualify for the grades of Collegiate Assessor and State Councillor. A complete imperial constitution was also under discussion, destined to revolutionize the existing order of government in Russia, legal, administrative and financial, from the privy council down to the district tribunals. Now those vague liberal dreams with which the Emperor Alexander had ascended the throne, and which he had tried to put into effect with the aid of Tchartorizhsky, Novosiltsov, Kochubey and Stroganov – whom he himself in jest had called his *comité du salut public* – were taking shape and being realized.

Now all these men were replaced by Speransky on the civil side and Arakcheyev on the military. Soon after his arrival Prince Andrei, as a gentleman of the chamber, presented himself at court and at a levée. The Emperor, though he met him twice, did not favour him with a single word. It had always seemed to Prince Andrei that he was antipathetic to the Emperor and that the latter disliked his face and general personality, and the cold repellent glance the Emperor gave him further confirmed this surmise. Courtiers explained to Prince Andrei that the Tsar's neglect of him was due to his Majesty's displeasure at Bolkonsky's not having served since 1805.

'I know myself that one cannot help one's likes and dislikes,' thought Prince Andrei, 'so it would be no use to present my proposal for the reform of the military code in person to the Emperor, but the project will speak for itself.'

He mentioned his memorandum to an old field-marshal, a friend of his father's. The field-marshal made an appointment to see him, received him graciously and promised to put the matter before the Emperor. A few days later Prince Andrei was notified that he was to call upon the minister of war, Count Arakcheyev.

At nine o'clock on the morning of the day appointed Prince Andrei entered Count Arakcheyev's waiting-room.

He did not know Arakcheyev personally and had never seen him; but what he had heard about him inspired but little respect for the man.

'He is minister of war, a person the Emperor trusts; his personal qualities are no concern of anyone's; it is his business to examine my project, consequently he alone could get it adopted,' reflected Prince Andrei as he waited among a number of important and unimportant people in Count Arakcheyev's ante-room.

During the period of his service – for the most part as an adjutant – Prince Andrei had seen the ante-rooms of many high dignitaries, and he was quick to recognize the various types. Count Arakcheyev's ante-room had quite a special character. The faces of the unimportant people awaiting their turn for an audience showed embarrassment and servility; those of higher rank gave a general impression of awkwardness concealed behind a mask of ease and ironical derision of themselves, their position, and the person they were waiting to see. Some walked thoughtfully up and down, others whispered and laughed, and Prince Andrei caught the nickname 'Strong-man Andreich' and 'We shall get it hot from the governor', referring to Count Arakcheyev. One general (a person of consequence), unmistakably chagrined at being kept waiting so long, sat crossing and uncrossing his legs and smiling disdainfully to himself.

But the moment the door opened all faces expressed one and the same sentiment – terror. Prince Andrei for the second time asked the adjutant on duty to take in his name, but he received a sarcastic stare and was told that his turn would come in due course. After several others had been shown in and out of the minister's room by the adjutant on duty, an officer whose abject, terrified air struck Prince Andrei was admitted to the fearful audience. The officer's interview lasted a long time. Suddenly a harsh bellowing was heard on the other side of the door, and the officer, pale and trembling, came out and clutching his head passed through the ante-room.

Immediately after this, Prince Andrei was conducted to the door and the officer on duty said in a whisper: 'To the right, at the window.'

Prince Andrei entered a plain, tidy study, and saw at the table a man of forty with a long waist, a long closely-cropped head, deep wrinkles, scowling brows over dull greenish-hazel eyes and a red drooping nose. Arakcheyev turned his head towards him without looking at him.

'What is your petition?' asked Arakcheyev.

'I am not … petitioning – for anything, your Excellency,' replied Prince Andrei quietly.

Arakcheyev's eyes turned to him.

'Sit down,' he said. 'Prince Bolkonsky?'

'I have no petition to make. His Majesty the Emperor has deigned to put into your Excellency's hands a project submitted by me ...'

'Allow me to inform you, my dear sir – I have read your project,' interrupted Arakcheyev, speaking the first words with a certain courtesy and then – without looking at Prince Andrei – gradually relapsing into a tone of querulous contempt. 'You are proposing new military laws? There are regulations in plenty and no one carries them out. Nowadays everyone's drawing up new regulations: it's easier to write 'em than to carry them out.'

'I have come at his Majesty the Emperor's wish to learn from your Excellency how you propose to deal with the memorandum I have presented,' said Prince Andrei politely.

'I have endorsed a resolution on your memorandum and forwarded it to the Committee. I do *not* approve of it,' said Arakcheyev, getting up and taking a paper from his writing-table. 'Here!' and he handed it to Prince Andrei.

Across the paper was scrawled in pencil, without capital letters or punctuation, and misspelt: 'unsound seeing its only an imitation of the french military coad and needlessly departing from our own articles of war.'

'To what Committee has the memorandum been referred?' inquired Prince Andrei.

'To the Committee on Army Regulations, and I have recommended your Honour being enrolled as a member. Only without salary.'

Prince Andrei smiled.

'I have no wish for one.'

'A member without salary,' repeated Arakcheyev. 'I wish you good day. Hey! Call the next one! Who else is there?' he shouted, bowing to Prince Andrei.

5

WHILE waiting for the formal notification of his appointment to the Committee, Prince Andrei looked up old acquaintances, especially those he knew to be in power and whose assistance he might need. He experienced now in Petersburg a sensation analogous to that which he had had on the eve of a battle, when he was fretted by restless curiosity and irresistibly attracted to those higher spheres where the future was being shaped, that future on which hung the fate of millions. From the angry irritability of the older generation, the inquisitiveness of the uninitiated, the reserve of the initiated, the hurry and preoccupation of everyone, and the innumerable committees and commissions – he heard of new ones every day – he felt that now, in the year 1809, here in Petersburg, some vast civil battle was in preparation, the commander-in-chief of which was a mysterious person whom he did not know but imagined to be a man of genius – Speransky. And this activity for reform, of which Prince Andrei had a confused idea, and Speransky its moving spirit, began to interest him so keenly that the matter of the army regulations very soon receded to a secondary place in his mind.

Prince Andrei found himself most favourably placed for securing a good reception in the highest and most diverse Petersburg circles of the day. The reforming party warmly welcomed and courted him, in the first place because he was said to be clever and very well read, and secondly because his emancipation of his serfs had gained him the reputation of being a liberal. The party of the dissatisfied older generation turned to him expecting his sympathy in their disapproval of the innovations, simply because he was the son of his father. The feminine world, *society*, received him gladly because he was rich, distinguished, a good match, and almost a new-comer, with a halo of romance on account of his supposed death in battle and the tragic loss of his wife. Moreover, the general opinion of all who had known him previously was that he had greatly improved during these last five years, having softened and grown more manly, lost his former affectation, pride and contemptuous irony, and had acquired the serenity that comes with years. People talked about him, were interested in him and eager to see him.

The day after his interview with Count Arakcheyev, Prince Andrei spent the evening at Count Kochubey's. He described to the count his interview with Strong-man Andreich (Kochubey spoke of Arakcheyev by that nickname with the same vaguely scoffing note in his voice which Prince Andrei had noticed in the minister of war's ante-room).

'*Mon cher*, even in this case you can't do without Mihail Mihailovich Speransky. He is the great factotum. I'll speak to him. He promised to come in this evening.'

'But what has Speransky to do with army regulations?' asked Prince Andrei.

Kochubey shook his head smilingly, as if wondering at Bolkonsky's simplicity.

'He and I were talking about you the other day,' Kochubey continued, 'about your free husbandmen. ...'

'Oh, so it was you, prince, who freed your serfs ?' said an old man of Catherine's time, turning disdainfully towards Bolkonsky.

'It was a small estate which brought in a very meagre income,' replied Prince Andrei, trying to minimize what he had done so as not to irritate the old man needlessly.

'Afraid of being late,' said the old man, looking at Kochubey. 'There's one thing I don't understand,' he continued. 'Who is to till the land if they are emancipated ? It is easy to write laws, but hard work to govern. In the same way now, I should like to ask you, count, who will be departmental heads when everybody has to pass examinations ?'

'Those who pass the examinations, I suppose,' answered Kochubey, crossing his legs and looking about him.

'Take Pryanichnikov now, one of my subordinates, a capital fellow, a priceless man, but he's sixty – is he to go up for examination ?'

'Yes, that is where the difficulty lies, since education is not at all general, but ...'

Count Kochubey did not finish. He got up, and taking Prince Andrei by the arm went to meet a tall, bald, fair-haired man of about forty with a large open forehead and a long face of strange and singular pallor. The new-comer wore a blue swallow-tail coat with a cross suspended from his neck and a star on his left breast. It was Speransky. Prince Andrei recognized him at once, and his heart thrilled, as happens at the great moments of one's life. Whether it was a thrill of respect, envy or anticipation, he did not know. Speransky's whole figure was of a peculiar type so that it was impossible to mistake him for a second. Never in any one of the circles in which Prince Andrei lived had he seen such calm, such self-possession allied to such awkward, ungainly movements; never had he seen so resolute yet gentle an expression as that in those half-closed, rather humid eyes, or such firmness as in that smile that meant nothing. Never had he heard a voice so delicate, smooth and soft; but what struck him most of all was the tender whiteness of face and hands – the hands, especially, which were rather broad yet extraordinarily plump, soft and white. Such whiteness and softness Prince Andrei had seen only in the faces of soldiers who had lain long in hospital. This was Speransky, Secretary of State, the Emperor's confidential adviser and his companion at Erfurt, where he had more than once met and talked with Napoleon.

Speransky did not shift his eyes from one face to another as people involuntarily do on entering a large company, and he was in no hurry to speak. He spoke slowly, sure of being listened to, and looked only at the person to whom he was talking.

Prince Andrei followed Speransky's every word and gesture with keen attention. As is often the case with men, particularly with those who judge their fellows severely, Prince Andrei, on meeting anyone new – especially anyone whom, like Speransky, he knew by reputation – always hoped to discover in him the perfection of human qualities.

Speransky told Kochubey he was sorry he had been unable to come sooner, as he had been detained at the palace. He did not say that the Emperor had kept him, and this affectation of modesty did not escape Prince Andrei. When Kochubey presented Prince Andrei, Speransky slowly transferred his eyes to Bolkonsky with the same smile on his face, and gazed at him in silence.

'I am very glad to make your acquaintance. I have heard of you, as everyone has,' he said.

Kochubey gave a brief account of Bolkonsky's reception by Arakcheyev. Speransky's smile broadened.

'The chairman of the Committee on Army Regulations is my good friend Monsieur Magnitsky,' he said, articulating every syllable and every word distinctly, 'and if you like I can put you in touch with him.' (He paused at the full stop.) 'I hope that you will find him sympathetic and willing to further anything that is reasonable.'

A little circle had immediately formed round Speransky, and the old man who had talked of his subordinate Pryanichnikov addressed a question to him.

Prince Andrei, taking no part in the conversation, watched Speransky's every gesture – Speransky, not long since an insignificant divinity student, who now held in his hands, those plump white hands, the fate of Russia, so Bolkonsky thought. He was struck by the extraordinarily scornful composure with which Speransky answered the old man. He appeared to drop him condescending words from an immeasurable height. When the old man began to speak too loudly

Speransky smiled and said that he could not judge of the advantage or disadvantage of what the Sovereign saw fit to approve.

Having talked for a little while in the general circle, Speransky rose and going over to Prince Andrei drew him away to the other end of the room. It was plain that he thought it necessary to interest himself in Bolkonsky.

'I have not had a chance to exchange two words with you, prince, thanks to the animated conversation in which that venerable gentleman involved me,' he said with a smile of bland contempt by which he seemed to imply that he and Prince Andrei were at one in recognizing the insignificance of the people with whom he had just been talking. This flattered Prince Andrei. 'I have known of you for a long time: to begin with from your action with regard to your serfs, the first instance of the kind among us, an example which it would be desirable to find generally followed; and secondly because you are one of those gentlemen of the chamber who have not considered themselves affronted by the new decree concerning the ranks allotted to courtiers, which is provoking so much discussion and cavil.'

'No,' said Prince Andrei, 'my father did not wish me to take advantage of the privilege. I began the service from the lower grades.'

'Your father, a man of the older generation, evidently stands far above our contemporaries who so condemn this measure, which merely re-establishes natural justice.'

'I think, however, that there is some ground for criticism,' said Prince Andrei, trying to resist Speransky's influence, of which he was beginning to feel conscious. It was distasteful for him to agree at every point: he felt a desire to contradict. Though he usually spoke easily and well, he now found some difficulty in expressing himself while talking with Speransky. He was too much absorbed in studying the personality of the famous man.

'The ground of personal ambition maybe,' Speransky put in quietly.

'And to some extent in the interests of the State too,' said Prince Andrei.

'How do you mean?' asked Speransky, mildly lowering his eyes.

'I am an admirer of Montesquieu,' replied Prince Andrei, 'and his idea that *le principe des monarchies est l'honneur* seems to me incontrovertible. Certain rights and privileges for the aristocracy appear to me to be the means of maintaining this sentiment.'

The smile vanished from Speransky's pallid face, which gained enormously from the change. Apparently Prince Andrei's thought interested him.

'If you regard the question from that point of view,' he began in French, which he pronounced with obvious difficulty, and speaking even more slowly than in Russian but with perfect composure. He went on to say that honour, *l'honneur*, cannot be upheld by privileges prejudicial to the working of the government service; that honour, *l'honneur*, is either a negative concept of not doing what is reprehensible, or it is a notorious source of the impulse which stimulates us to win commendation and rewards that bear witness to it.

His arguments were concise, simple and clear.

'An institution that upholds honour, that source of emulation, similar to the *Légion d'honneur* of the great Emperor Napoleon, is not prejudicial but helpful to the success of the service, but that is not true of class or court prerogatives.'

'I do not dispute that but it cannot be denied that court privileges have attained the same end,' returned Prince Andrei. 'Every courtier considers himself bound to fulfil his functions worthily.'

'Yet you do not care to avail yourself of your prerogatives, prince,' said Speransky, indicating by a smile that he wished to conclude amiably an argument embarrassing to his companion. 'If you will do me the honour of calling on me on Wednesday,' he added, 'I shall by that time have seen Magnitsky and have something to tell you that may interest you; and, moreover, I shall have the pleasure of a more circumstantial conversation with you.' Closing his eyes, he bowed and, trying to escape unnoticed, slipped from the room *à la française*, without saying good-bye.

6

DURING the first weeks of his stay in Petersburg Prince Andrei found all the habits of thought he had formed during his life of seclusion in the country entirely obscured by the petty preoccupations which engrossed him in that city.

Every evening on his return home he would jot down in his notebook four or five unavoidable visits or appointments for specified times. The mechanism of life, the arrangement of the day so as to be punctual everywhere, absorbed the greater part of his vital energy. He did nothing – he neither thought nor had time to think, and whatever he said in conversation, and he talked well, was merely the fruit of his meditations in the country.

He sometimes noticed with dissatisfaction that he repeated the same remark on the same day in different circles. But he was so busy for whole days together that he had no time to reflect that he was thinking of nothing.

As on their first meeting at Kochubey's, Speransky produced a strong impression on Prince Andrei on the Wednesday, when he received him *tête-à-tête* at his own house and talked to him long and confidentially.

To Bolkonsky so many people appeared contemptible and insignificant, and he had such a powerful longing to find in someone the living pattern of perfection towards which he was striving, that it was easy for him to believe he had discovered in Speransky his ideal of a perfectly rational and virtuous man. Had Speransky sprung from the same class in society to which Prince Andrei belonged, had he possessed the same breeding and moral traditions, Bolkonsky would soon have detected the weak and prosaically human side of his character; but as it was, Speransky's strange and logical turn of mind inspired him with respect the more because he did not altogether understand it. Besides this, Speransky, either because he appreciated Prince Andrei's abilities or because he considered it necessary to win him to his side, showed off his cool, easy wit before Prince Andrei and flattered him with that subtle flattery which goes hand in hand with conceit, and consists in a tacit assumption that one's companion is the only man besides oneself capable of understanding the folly of the rest of the world, and the sagacity and profundity of one's own ideas.

In the course of their long conversation on the Wednesday evening Speransky more than once remarked: '*We* regard everything that rises above the common level of rooted custom ...'; or, with a smile, 'But *our* idea is that the wolves should be fed and the sheep kept safe ...'; or '*They* cannot understand this ...'; and always with a tone and look that implied: '*We* – you and I – understand what *they* are and who *we* are.'

This preliminary long conversation with Speransky only served to strengthen the feeling produced in Prince Andrei at their first meeting. He saw in him a man of vast intellect and sober, accurate judgement who by his energy and persistence had attained power, which he was using solely for the welfare of Russia. In Prince Andrei's eyes Speransky was precisely the man he would have liked to be himself – able to find a rational explanation for all the phenomena of life, recognizing as important only what was logical, and capable of applying the standard of reason to everything. Everything seemed so simple, so lucid, in Speransky's exposition of it that Prince Andrei involuntarily agreed with him on every point. If he argued and raised objections it was for the express purpose of maintaining his independence and not submitting to Speransky's opinions entirely. Everything was right, everything was as it should be: only one thing disconcerted Prince Andrei. This was Speransky's cold, mirror-like eye which seemed to refuse all admittance to his soul, and his flabby white hands which Prince Andrei instinctively watched as one watches the hands of those who possess power. That mirror-like gaze and those delicate hands somehow irritated Prince Andrei. He was disagreeably struck too by the excessive contempt for others that he observed in Speransky, and the various shifts in the arguments he employed to buttress his ideas. He made use of every possible mental device, except analogy, and was too venturesome, it seemed to Prince Andrei, in passing from one to another. At one moment he would take his stand as a practical man and condemn visionaries; next as a satirist he was making ironical sport of his opponents; then he would become severely logical, or suddenly fly off into the domain of metaphysics. (This last resource was one he very frequently employed.) He would transfer a question to metaphysical heights, pass on to definitions of space, time and thought, and having deduced the refutation he needed descend again to the plane of the original discussion.

What impressed Prince Andrei as the leading trait of Speransky's mentality was his absolute and unshakable belief in the power and authority of reason. It was plain that it would never occur to him, as it did so naturally to Prince Andrei, that after all it is impossible to express the whole of one's thought; and that he had never known doubt, never asked himself, 'Might not everything I think and believe be nonsense?' And it was this very peculiarity of Speransky's mind that attracted Prince Andrei most.

During the first period of their acquaintance Bolkonsky conceived a passionate admiration for him akin to what he had once felt for

Bonaparte. The fact that Speransky was the son of a priest, which enabled many foolish persons to regard him with vulgar contempt as a member of a despised class, caused Prince Andrei to cherish his sentiment for him the more, and unconsciously to strengthen it.

On that first evening Bolkonsky spent with him, having mentioned the Commission for the Revision of the Legal Code, Speransky told Prince Andrei sardonically that the Commission had existed for fifty years, had cost millions and had done nothing except that Rosen-kampf had stuck labels on the corresponding paragraphs of the various articles.

'And that's all the State has got for the millions it has spent!' said he. 'We want to give the Senate new juridical powers but we have no laws. That is why it is a sin for men like you, prince, not to be in the government.'

Prince Andrei remarked that such work required legal training which he did not possess.

'But there is no one who does, so what are you going to do? It is a *circulus viciosus* which we must break out of by main force.'

Within a week Prince Andrei was a member of the Committee on Army Regulations, and – a thing he had never expected – was chairman of a sub-committee of the Commission for the Revision of the Legal Code. At Speransky's request he took the first part of the Civil Code that was being drawn up, and with the help of the *Code Napoléon* and the *Institutes of Justinian* set to work at formulating the section on Personal Rights.

7

NEARLY two years before this, in 1808, Pierre, on his return to Petersburg after visiting his estates, found himself by no design of his own in a leading position among the Petersburg freemasons. He organized memorial and dining lodge meetings, initiated new members and took an active part in uniting various lodges and acquiring authentic charters. He gave money for the building of masonic temples and did what he could to supplement the collection of alms, in regard to which the majority of the members were niggardly and irregular. He was almost alone in defraying the expenses of the alms-house the Order had founded in Petersburg.

His life meanwhile continued as before, with the same infatuations and dissipations. He liked to dine and drink well, and, though he considered it immoral and degrading to yield to them, he was unable to resist the temptations of the bachelor circles in which he moved.

Amid the hurly-burly of his activities and distractions, however, Pierre began to feel before a year was over that the more firmly he tried to rest upon it the more the ground of Freemasonry on which he stood slipped away from under his feet. At the same time he was conscious that the deeper the ground gave under him the more inextricably he was committed to it. When he had first entered the Brotherhood he experienced the sensations of a man who confidently steps on to the smooth surface of a bog. He puts down one foot and it sinks in. To convince himself of the firmness of the ground he puts his other foot down and sinks in farther, becomes stuck and must now wade knee-deep in the bog.

Osip Alexeyevich Bazdeyev was not in Petersburg. (He had of late stood aside from the affairs of the Petersburg lodges and now never left Moscow.) All the brethren, the members of the lodges, were men Pierre came across in everyday life and it was difficult for him to regard them merely as brothers in Freemasonry and not as Prince B. or Ivan Vasilyevich D., whom he knew in society mostly as people of weak and commonplace character. Under their masonic aprons and insignia he saw the uniforms and decorations which were their aim in ordinary life. Often after collecting alms, and reckoning up twenty to thirty roubles received for the most part in promises from a dozen members of whom half were as well-off as Pierre himself, he thought of the masonic vow whereby each brother bound himself to devote all his belongings to his neighbour; and doubts on which he tried not to dwell stirred in his soul.

He divided the brothers he knew into four categories. In the first he put those who took no active part in the affairs either of their lodges or of humanity but were exclusively occupied with the mystical science of the Order: with questions relating to the threefold designation of God, or the three primordial elements – sulphur, mercury and salt – or the meaning of the Square and all the various figures of the Temple of Solomon. Pierre respected this class of freemason, to which the elder brethren chiefly belonged, together, Pierre thought, with Osip Alexeyevich himself, but he did not share their interests. His heart was not drawn to the mystical side of Freemasonry.

In the second category he reckoned himself and brothers like him, seeking and vacillating, who had not yet found in Freemasonry a straight and comprehensible path but hoped to do so.

In the third category he placed the brethren (and they formed the majority) who saw nothing in Freemasonry but an external form and ceremonial, and prized the strict performance of these ceremonies, caring nothing for their purport or significance. Such were Willarski and even the Grand Master of the Supreme Lodge.

Finally, to the fourth category also belonged a great many brethren, particularly those who had entered the Brotherhood of late. These, so far as Pierre could observe, were men who had no belief in anything, nor desire for anything, but joined the freemasons simply for the sake of associating with the wealthy young members who were influential through their connexions or rank, and who abounded in the lodge.

Pierre began to feel dissatisfied with what he was doing. Freemasonry, at any rate as he saw it here, sometimes seemed to him to rest on externals. He never dreamed of doubting Freemasonry itself, but suspected that Russian masonry had got on to a false track and had deviated from its original principles. And so towards the end of the year he went abroad to devote himself to the higher mysteries of the Order.

*

It was in the summer of 1809 that Pierre returned to Petersburg. From the correspondence that passed between our freemasons and those abroad, it was known in Russia that Bezuhov had obtained the confidence of many highly placed persons, that he had been initiated into many mysteries, had been raised to a higher grade and was bringing back with him much that would be of advantage to the masonic cause at home. The Petersburg freemasons all came to see him, tried to ingratiate themselves with him, and all fancied that he had something in reserve that he was preparing for them.

A solemn meeting was convened of the lodge of the second degree, at which Pierre promised to communicate to the Petersburg brethren the message with which he had been entrusted by the highest leaders of the Order. The assembly was crowded. After the usual ceremonies Pierre got up and started on his address.

'My dear brethren,' he began, blushing and stammering, with a written speech in his hand, 'it is not enough to observe our mysteries in the seclusion of the lodge – we must act ... act. We are slumbering while we should be active.' Pierre took his manuscript and began to read.

For the propagation of pure truth and to secure the triumph of virtue, [he read], we must purge men of prejudice, diffuse principles in harmony with the spirit of the times, undertake the education of the young, unite ourselves by indissoluble bonds with the most enlightened men, boldly yet prudently contend with superstition, infidelity and folly, and form of men devoted to us a body linked together by singleness of purpose and possessed of authority and power.

To attain this end the scale must be weighted against vice and on the side of virtue; we must strive that the honest man may obtain his eternal reward even in this world. But in these great endeavours we are gravely hampered by the existing political institutions. What then is to be done in these circumstances? Are we to welcome revolutions, to overthrow society, oppose force with force? ... No! We are very far from that. All violent reforms are to be deprecated, because they can never do away with evil so long as men remain what they are, and also because wisdom has no need of violence.

The whole plan of our Order should be based on the idea of preparing men of character and virtue, bound together by unity of conviction – a conviction that it is their duty everywhere and with all their might to suppress vice and folly, and encourage talent and virtue, raising worthy men from the dust and attaching them to our Brotherhood. Not till then will our Order have the power imperceptibly to bind the hands of the promoters of disorder and to control them without their being aware of it. In a word, we must found a form of government holding universal sway, which would spread over the whole world without encroaching on civil ties or hindering other administrations from continuing their customary course and abandoning nothing except what stands in the way of the great aim of our Order – the triumph of virtue over vice. This aim is that of Christianity itself. Christianity taught men to be wise and good, and for their own profit to follow the example and precepts of the best and wisest men.

At that time, when all was plunged in darkness, preaching alone was of course sufficient: the novelty of truth endowed it with peculiar strength, but today we are obliged to have recourse to far more powerful means. Nowadays a man governed by his senses needs to find in virtue a charm palpable to those senses. The passions cannot be eradicated: we must strive to direct them to noble ends, and so it is necessary that everyone should be able to satisfy his passions within the limits of virtue. Our Order should provide means to that end.

So soon as we have a certain number of worthy men in every land, each of them in his turn training two others and all working in close co-operation, then all things will be possible for our Fraternity, which has already in secret accomplished so much for the welfare of mankind.

This discourse not only made a marked impression but caused agitation in the lodge. The majority of the brethren, affecting to see in it the dangerous doctrines of the German Illuminati, received it with a coldness that surprised Pierre. The Grand Master began to raise objections, and Pierre with growing heat went on to develop his view. It was a long time since there had been such a stormy session. The lodge split into parties, some accusing Pierre of Illuminism, others supporting him. At this meeting Pierre was for the first time struck by the endless variety of the human mind, preventing any truth from ever presenting itself in the same way to any two persons. Even those brethren who seemed to be on his side interpreted him after their own fashion with provisos and modifications to which he could not agree, since his chief desire was to convey his thought to others exactly as he himself understood it.

At the conclusion of the sitting the Grand Master reproved Pierre with irony and ill-will for his vehemence, and observed that it was not love of virtue alone but a liking for strife that had been his guide in the discussion. Pierre made no reply, and inquired briefly whether his proposal would be accepted. He was told that it would not, and without waiting for the usual formalities he left the lodge and went home.

8

AGAIN Pierre was overtaken by the despondency he so dreaded. For three days after the delivery of his speech at the lodge he lay on a sofa at home, seeing no one and going nowhere.

It was during this time that he received a letter from his wife, who implored him to see her, describing her sorrow at what had happened and her desire to devote her whole life to him.

At the end of the letter she informed him that in a day or two she would be arriving in Petersburg from abroad.

On top of the letter one of the masonic brethren whom Pierre respected least burst in upon his solitude, and, leading the conversation to the subject of Pierre's matrimonial affairs, by way of fraternal advice expressed the opinion that his severity to his wife was wrong, and that he was departing from the first principles of Freemasonry in not forgiving the penitent.

At the same time his mother-in-law, Prince Vasili's wife, sent to him beseeching him to call upon her, if only for a few minutes, in regard to a matter of supreme importance. Pierre saw there was a conspiracy, that they meant to reconcile him with his wife, and in the mood in which he then was he did not even dislike the idea. It was all the same to him. Nothing in life seemed to him of much consequence, and under the influence of the depression that engulfed him he no longer cared about his own freedom nor his obstinate determination to punish his wife.

'No one is right, no one is wrong, and so she, too, is not to blame,' he thought.

If he did not at once give his consent to a reconciliation with his wife it was only because in the despondent state into which he had lapsed he had not the energy to take any step. Had his wife come to him he would not have turned her away. In comparison with what preoccupied him was it not a matter of complete indifference whether he lived with his wife or not?

Vouchsafing no reply either to his wife or his mother-in-law, Pierre late one evening set out and drove to Moscow to see Osip Alexeyevich Bazdeyev. This is what he wrote in his diary.

Moscow, November 17th

I have just returned from seeing my benefactor, and hasten to note down all that I felt with him. Osip Alexeyevich lives in poverty, and for three years past has been suffering with a painful affection of the bladder. No one has ever heard him utter a groan or a word of complaint. From morning till late at night, except for the short while he gives up to his very frugal meals, he devotes himself to his scientific studies. He received me graciously and made me sit on the bed where he lay. I made him the sign of the Knights of the East and of Jerusalem, and he responded in the same manner, and with a gentle smile asked me what I had learned and gained in the Prussian and Scottish lodges. I told him everything as best I could, repeating to him the proposal I had laid before our Petersburg lodge and describing the unfriendly reception I had encountered, and the rupture which had occurred between myself and the brethren. After he had been silent and taken thought for some little time, Osip Alexeyevich put his view of the matter before me, so that all the past was immediately made plain to me, as well as the course that lies before me. He surprised me by asking whether I remembered the threefold aim of the Order: (1) the preservation and study of the Mystery; (2) the purification and reformation of oneself for its reception; and (3) the improvement of the human race through striving for such purification. Which, he asked, is the first and greatest of these three aims? Undoubtedly self-reformation and self-purification. It is only towards this aim that we can always strive, independently of whatever circumstances. But at the same time it is just this aim which requires of us the greatest effort, and so, led astray by pride, we let this aim drop, and occupy ourselves either with the Mystery which in our impurity we are unworthy to receive, or we seek the reformation of the human race while ourselves setting an example of depravity and abomination. Illuminism is not a pure doctrine precisely because it has been seduced by social activity and puffed up with pride. On this ground Osip Alexeyevich condemned my speech and all I had done. At the bottom of my heart I agreed with him. Talking of my domestic affairs, he said to me, 'The principal duty of a true mason, as I have told you, lies in perfecting himself. But we often think that by removing all the difficulties of our life we shall the more quickly attain our purpose; on the contrary, my dear sir,' he said to me, 'it is only in the midst of worldly cares that we can attain our three great aims: (1) self-knowledge – for man can only know himself by comparison with others; (2) greater perfection, which can only be obtained through struggle, and (3) the chief virtue – love of death. Only the vicissitudes of life can teach us the vanity of life and stimulate our innate love of death or rebirth into new life.' These words were all the more remarkable in that Osip Alexeyevich, in spite of grievous physical suffering, is never weary of life, though he loves death, for which – notwithstanding all his spiritual purity and loftiness – he does not yet feel himself sufficiently prepared. Next my benefactor explained to me the full significance of the Great Square of Creation and pointed out that the numbers three and seven are the basis of everything. He counselled me not to withdraw from the Petersburg brethren, and, while taking upon myself only the obligations of the second degree in the lodge, to endeavour to win the brethren from the seductions of pride, and try and turn them into the true path of self-knowledge and self-perfecting. Besides this, for myself personally, he advised me above all things to keep a watch over myself, and to that end he gave me a note-book, the one in which I am writing now, and in future I shall keep an account of all my actions.

Petersburg, November 23rd

I am living with my wife again. My mother-in-law came to me with tears in her eyes, and said that Hélène was back and implored me to hear her: she was innocent, and miserable that I had left her, and much besides. I knew that if I once let myself see her I should not have the strength to refuse her. In my perplexity I did not know where to turn for help and advice. Had my benefactor been here he would have told me what to do. I shut myself up in my room, read over Osip Alexey-evich's letters and recalled my conversations with him, and, taking all things together, I came to the conclusion that I ought not to refuse a suppliant and must hold out a helping hand to everyone – and especi-ally to the person so closely bound to me – and that I must bear my cross. But if I forgive her for the sake of doing right, then let my reunion with her have a spiritual aim only. That is what I decided, and what I wrote to Osip Alexeyevich. I told my wife that I begged her to forget the past, to forgive me whatever wrong I might have done her, and that I had nothing to forgive. It gave me joy to tell her this. May she never know how painful it was to me to see her again! I have installed myself on the upper floor of this great house, and am rejoicing in a pleasant sense of regeneration.

9

AT that time, as always indeed, the upper strata of society that met at court and at the grand balls was divided into a number of separate circles, each having its own particular tone. The largest of these was the French circle – supporting the Napoleonic alliance – the circle of Count Rumyantsev and Caulaincourt. In this group Hélène, as soon as she and her husband had resumed residence together in Petersburg, took a very prominent part. Members of the French Embassy fre-quented her drawing-room, and a great number of people distin-guished for their intellect and polished manners, and belonging to the same political persuasion.

Hélène had been at Erfurt during the famous meeting between the Emperors, and had there made the acquaintance of all the Napoleonic celebrities of Europe. At Erfurt she had enjoyed a most brilliant suc-cess. Napoleon himself had noticed her at the theatre, asked who she was and admired her beauty. Her triumphs as a beautiful and elegant woman did not surprise Pierre, for as time went on she had grown handsomer than ever. What did surprise him was that during these last two years his wife had succeeded in acquiring the reputation of being 'une femme charmante, aussi spirituelle que belle'. The distinguished Prince de Ligne wrote her eight-page letters. Bilibin saved up his epigrams to fire off for the first time in Countess Bezuhov's presence. To be received in Countess Bezuhov's *salon* was regarded as a certificate of intelligence. Young men read up books before one of Hélène's parties so as to have something to say in her drawing-room, and Embassy secretaries and even ambassadors confided diplomatic secrets to her, so that Hélène was a power in a certain way. Pierre, who knew she was very stupid, sometimes attended her receptions and dinner-parties, where politics, poetry and philosophy were discussed, and he listened with a strange feeling of perplexity and alarm. At these parties he felt as a conjurer must feel who is all the time afraid that at any moment his tricks will be seen through. But whether because stupidity was just what was needed to run such a *salon*, or because those who were deceived found pleasure in the deception, at any rate the secret did not come out and Hélène Bezuhov's reputation as a lovely and intelligent woman became so firmly established that she could say the most commonplace and stupidest things and still everybody would go into raptures over her every word and discover a profound meaning in it of which she herself had no conception.

Pierre was the very husband for this brilliant society woman. He was that absent-minded, eccentric, *grand seigneur* of a husband who got in no one's way and, far from spoiling the general impression of lofty tone in the drawing-room, he provided, by his contrast to his wife's elegance and *savoir faire*, an advantageous background for her. Pierre's constant absorption in abstract interests during the last two years, and his genuine contempt for everything else, gave him in his wife's circle, which did not interest him, that air of unconcern and indifference combined with benevolence towards all alike, which cannot be acquired artificially, and, for that reason, inspires involuntary respect. He would enter his wife's drawing-room as though it were a theatre, was acquainted with everybody, equally pleased to see everyone and equally reserved with them all. Sometimes he joined in a conversation which appealed to him and, regardless of whether any 'gentlemen of the Embassy' were present or not, mumbled out his opinions, which were by no means always in accord with those current at the moment. But society had grown so used to the queer husband of the 'most distinguished woman in Petersburg' that no one took his idiosyncrasies seriously.

Among the many young men who were daily to be seen in Hélène's house Boris Drubetskoy, who had already achieved marked success in the service, was, since Hélène's return from Erfurt, the most intimate friend of the Bezuhov household. Hélène called him 'mon page', and treated him like a child. The smile she gave him was the same as she bestowed on everybody, but sometimes it gave Pierre an unpleasant feeling. Boris behaved towards Pierre with a peculiar grave deference that was perfectly proper. This shade of deference also disturbed Pierre. He had suffered so painfully three years before from the mortification to which his wife had subjected him that he now protected himself from the danger of similar mortification, firstly by not being a husband to his wife, and secondly, by not allowing himself to be suspicious.

'No, now that she has become a *bas bleu* she has renounced her old inclinations for ever,' he told himself. 'There has never been an instance of a blue-stocking being carried away by affairs of the heart' – an axiom he had picked up somewhere and believed implicitly. Yet, strange to say, the presence of Boris in his wife's drawing-room (and he was almost always there) had a physical effect upon Pierre: it seemed to paralyse his limbs, to awaken all his self-consciousness and take away his freedom of movement.

'Such a strange antipathy,' thought Pierre, 'and yet at one time I really liked him very much.'

In the eyes of the world Pierre was a fine gentleman, the rather blind and ridiculous husband of a distinguished wife, a clever eccentric who did nothing but was no trouble to anyone, a good-natured, capital fellow – while all the time in the depths of Pierre's soul a complex and arduous process of inner development was going on, revealing much to him and bringing him many spiritual doubts and joys.

10

HE kept up his diary, and this is what he was writing in it at this time:

November 24th

Got up at eight, read the Scriptures, then proceeded to my duties –

(Pierre, on his benefactor's advice, had entered the service of the State and was on one of the government committees.)

Returned home for dinner and dined alone (the countess has a lot of guests I do not care for), ate and drank with moderation, and after dinner copied out some passages for the brethren. In the evening I went down to the drawing-room and told a funny story about B., and only bethought myself that I ought not to have done so when everybody was laughing loudly at it.

I go to bed with a happy tranquil mind. Lord God, help me to walk in Thy paths: (1) to conquer anger by gentleness and deliberation, (2) to vanquish lust by self-restraint and a turning away, (3) to shun the vanities of this world but without shutting myself off from (a) the service of the State, (b) family cares, (c) relations with my friends and (d) the management of my affairs.

November 27th

Got up late and lay a long while in bed after I was awake, yielding to sloth. O God, help and strengthen me that I may walk in Thy ways. Read the Scriptures but without proper feeling. Brother Urusov came and we talked about the vanities of the world. He told me of the Emperor's new projects. I was on the point of criticizing them but remembered my principles and my benefactor's words – that a true mason should be a zealous worker for the State when his services are required and a quiet onlooker when not called upon to assist. My tongue is my enemy. Brothers G.V. and O. visited me and we had a preliminary talk about the initiation of a new brother. They charge me with the duty of tyler. Feel myself weak and unworthy. Then we turned to the interpretation of the seven pillars and steps of the Temple, the seven sciences, the seven virtues, the seven vices, the seven gifts of the Holy Spirit. Brother O. was very eloquent. The initiation took place in the evening. The new decoration of the lodge contributed much to the magnificence of the spectacle. It was Boris Drubetskoy who was admitted. I nominated him and was the tyler. A strange feeling agitated me all the time I was alone with him in the dark chamber. I caught myself harbouring a feeling of hatred towards him which I vainly strove to overcome. For this reason I really wanted to save him from evil and lead him into the path of truth, but evil thoughts about him never left me. It seemed to me that his object in entering the Brotherhood was merely to be intimate and in favour with members of our Lodge. Apart from the fact that he had asked me several times whether N. and S. were members of our lodge (a question to which I could not reply), and that, so far as my observation goes, he is incapable of genuine respect for our holy Order and is too much occupied and too well satisfied with the outer man to care much for spiritual improvement, I had no grounds for doubting him; but he seemed to me insincere, and all the time I stood alone with him in the dark chamber I kept fancying that he was smiling contemptuously at my words, and I could gladly have stabbed his bare breast with the sword I held to it. I was unable to speak with any fluency, and I could not frankly communicate my misgivings to the brethren and the Grand Master. May the Great Architect of the Universe help me to find the true path out of the labyrinth of falsehood!

The next three pages in the diary were left blank, and then came the following:

Had a long and instructive private conversation with Brother V., who advised me to hold fast by Brother A. Much was revealed to me, though I am so unworthy. Adonai is the name of the creator of the world. Elohim is the name of the ruler of all. The third name, the name unutterable, means the *All*. Talks with Brother V. strengthen and refresh me, and confirm me in the path of virtue. In his presence there is no opportunity for doubt. I can see clearly the distinction between the poor doctrines of mundane science and our sacred, all-embracing teaching. Human sciences dissect in order to comprehend, and destroy in order to analyse. In the sacred science of our Order all is one, all is known, everything is known in its entirety and life. The trinity – the three elements of matter – are sulphur, mercury and salt. Sulphur is oil and fire; amalgamated with salt the fiery quality of sulphur arouses an appetite in salt by means of which mercury is attracted, seized, held and in combination produces other bodies. Mercury is the fluid, volatile, spiritual essence – Christ, the Holy Spirit, *He*.

December 3rd

Awoke late, read the Scriptures but was apathetic. Afterwards went down and walked to and fro in the large hall. Wanted to meditate but instead my imagination brought before me an incident which happened four years ago, when Dolohov, meeting me in Moscow after our duel, said he hoped I was enjoying complete peace of mind in spite of my wife's absence. At the time I made him no reply. Now I recalled every detail of the encounter and in my mind answered him with the most vindictive and biting retorts. I recovered myself and banished the subject only when I found I was burning with anger; but I did not sufficiently repent. After this Boris Drubetskoy came and began describing various adventures. From the first moment I was annoyed at his visit and made some contrary remark. He retaliated. I flared up and said a great deal that was disagreeable and even rude. He was silent, and I recollected myself only when it was too late. O God, I cannot get on with him at all. The fault lies in my own self-esteem. I set myself above him and consequently become a thousand times worse than he, for he condones my rudeness while I, on the contrary, nourish contempt for him. O God, grant that in his presence I may rather see my own vileness and behave in such fashion that it may profit him too. After dinner I had a nap and just as I was falling asleep I distinctly heard a voice saying in my left ear, 'Thine is the day'.

I dreamt that I was walking in the dark and was suddenly surrounded by dogs but I went on undismayed. Suddenly a smallish dog seized my left thigh with its teeth and would not let go. I began to strangle it with my hands. Scarcely had I succeeded in throwing it off when another, a bigger one, began biting me. I lifted it up but the higher I lifted it the bigger and heavier it grew. And suddenly Brother A. came along, and taking my arm led me to a building, to enter which we had to go along a narrow plank. I stepped on it but the plank bent and gave way, and I began clambering up a fence which I just managed to get hold of with my hands. After great efforts I dragged myself up so that my legs were hanging down on one side and my body on the other. I looked round and saw Brother A. standing on the fence and pointing me to a broad avenue and garden, and in the garden was a large and beautiful building. I woke up. O Lord, Great Architect of Nature, help me to tear from myself these dogs – my passions – especially the last, which unites in itself the violence of all the others, and aid me to enter that temple of virtue of which I was vouchsafed a vision in my dream.

December 7th

I dreamed that Osip Alexeyevich was sitting in my house, and I was very glad and eager to entertain him. But in my dream I kept chattering away to other people and all at once I bethought myself that this could not be to his liking, and I wanted to go up to him and embrace him. But as soon as I drew near I saw that his face had changed and grown younger, and in a low tone – so low that I could not hear – he was telling me something from the teachings of our Order. Then we all seemed to go out of the room and something strange happened. We were sitting or lying on the floor. He was telling me something. But in my dream I longed to let him see how moved I was, and not listening to what he was saying I began picturing to myself the condition of my inner man and the grace of God sanctifying me. And tears came into my eyes, and I was glad he noticed this. But he glanced at me with vexation and jumped up, breaking off his remarks. I was abashed and asked him whether what he had been saying did not concern me; he made no reply but gave me a kindly look, and then all of a sudden we found ourselves in my bedroom with a big double bed in it. He lay down on the edge of it and I burned with longing to caress him and lie down too. And in my dream he asked me, 'Tell me honestly, what is your chief temptation? Have you found out? I believe you have.' Put out of countenance by this question, I replied that sloth was my besetting sin. He shook his head incredulously. Still more disconcerted, I told him that though I was living with my wife, as he had counselled me, I was not living with her as a husband. To this he replied that a wife ought not to be deprived of her husband's embraces, and gave me to understand that this was my duty. But I answered that I should feel ashamed, and with this everything was gone. I awoke and in my mind was the Scripture text: 'The life was the light of men. And the light shineth in darkness; and the darkness comprehended it not.' Osip Alexeyevich's face had looked young and radiant. That day I received a letter from my benefactor in which he wrote of the obligations of the married state.

December 9th

I had a dream from which I awoke with my heart throbbing. I dreamt I was in my house in Moscow, in the big sitting-room, and Osip Alexeyevich came in from the drawing-room. I knew instantly that the process of regeneration had already taken place in him, and I rushed towards him. I embraced him and kissed his hands, and he said, 'Hast thou noticed that my face is different?' I looked at him, still holding him in my arms, and saw that his face was young but there was no hair on his head, and his features were greatly altered. And I said, 'I should have recognized you had we met by accident,' and at the same time I thought, 'Am I telling the truth?' And suddenly I saw him lying like a dead body; then he gradually came to himself again and went with me into the big study, carrying a folio book of cartridge paper. I said, 'I drew that,' and he answered me by an inclination of his head. I opened the book and on all the pages were drawings superbly done. And in my dream I knew that the drawings represented the adventures of the soul with her beloved. And among them I saw a beautiful picture of a maiden in diaphanous raiment and with a transparent body flying up to the clouds. And I seemed to know that this damsel was nothing else than a representation of the Song of Songs. And as I looked at the drawings in my dream I felt that I was doing wrong, yet could not tear myself away from them. O Lord, help me! O God if Thy forsaking me is Thy doing, then Thy will be done; but if I am myself the cause, teach me what I must do. I must perish from my corruption if Thou dost utterly abandon me.

THE Rostovs' monetary affairs had not improved during the two years they had spent in the country.

Though Nikolai Rostov had kept firmly to his resolution and was still serving quietly in an obscure regiment, spending comparatively little, the scale of life at Otradnoe – and particularly Mitenka's management of affairs – was such that debts increased like a snowball with every year. The old count saw but one way out of the difficulty, and that was to apply for some government appointment, so he had come to Petersburg to look for one and also, as he said, to let the lassies enjoy themselves for the last time.

Soon after their arrival in Petersburg Berg proposed to Vera and was accepted.

In spite of the fact that in Moscow the Rostovs moved in the highest society (without giving a thought to it one way or the other), in Petersburg their acquaintance was rather mixed. In Petersburg they were provincials, and the very people they had entertained in Moscow without inquiring to what set they belonged here looked down on them.

The Rostovs kept open house in Petersburg as in Moscow, and the most heterogeneous collection met at their suppers: country neighbours from Otradnoe, impoverished old squires with their daughters, Madame Peronsky, who was a maid of honour, Pierre Bezuhov, and the son of their district postmaster, who was in an office in Petersburg. Among the men who very soon became frequent visitors at the Rostovs' house in Petersburg were Boris, Pierre whom the count had met in the street and dragged home with him, and Berg who spent whole days at the Rostovs' and paid the elder daughter, Countess Vera, the attentions a young man pays when he intends to propose.

Not in vain had Berg shown everybody his right arm wounded at Austerlitz, and affected to hold his wholly unnecessary sword in his left hand. He related the episode so persistently and with so important an air that everyone had come to believe in the expediency and merit of his action, and he had received two decorations for Austerlitz.

In the Finnish campaign he had also succeeded in distinguishing himself. He had picked up a fragment of the grenade that had killed an aide-de-camp standing near the commander-in-chief, and had taken it to the commander. Again, as after Austerlitz, he talked to everyone about the incident at such length and so insistently that people ended up believing that it had been necessary to do this also, and the Finnish war brought him two more decorations. In 1809 he was a captain in the Guards, wore medals on his breast, and held some particular, lucrative posts in Petersburg.

Though there were some sceptics who smiled when Berg's merits were mentioned to them, it could not be denied that he was a painstaking and gallant officer, extremely well thought of at headquarters, and an upright young man with a brilliant career before him and enjoying an assured position in society.

Four years before, meeting a German comrade in the *parterre* of a Moscow theatre, Berg had pointed out Vera Rostov to him and said in German, 'There is the girl who shall be my wife,' and there and then had determined that he would marry her. Now in Petersburg, after duly considering the Rostovs' position and his own, he decided that the time had come to propose.

Berg's proposal was received at first with a hesitation by no means flattering for him. It seemed a strange idea at first that the son of an obscure Livonian gentleman should ask for the hand of a Countess Rostov; but Berg's most characteristic *trait* was an egoism so naïve and good-natured that the Rostovs found themselves thinking that it must be a good thing since he himself was so firmly convinced that it would be – and indeed that it would be even more than a good thing. Moreover, the Rostovs' affairs were in an embarrassing state, a circumstance of which the suitor could not but be aware; and above all, the chief consideration, Vera was now four-and-twenty, had been taken about everywhere, and, though she was undeniably good-looking and sensible, no one up to now had made her an offer. So consent was given.

'You see,' said Berg to his comrade, whom he called his friend only because he knew that everyone has friends. 'You see, I have weighed it all up carefully, and I shouldn't think of marrying if I had not considered it all round or if there were any difficulties. But now on the contrary, my papa and mamma are well provided for – I have made over to them the income from that land in the Baltic Provinces – and I can live in Petersburg on my pay, and with her little fortune and my careful habits we can get along nicely. I am not marrying for money –

I call that sort of thing dishonourable – but a wife ought to bring her share and a husband his. I have my position in the service, she has her connexions and some small means. That's something in these days, isn't it? But best of all, she's a handsome, estimable girl, and she loves me ...'

Berg blushed and smiled.

'And I love her, because she has plenty of sense and a nice nature. The other sister now, though they are the same family, is quite different – a disagreeable character and not the same intelligence. She is so ... you know? ... I don't like. ... But my betrothed. ... Well, you will be coming' – he was going to say 'to dine' but thought better of it and said – 'to take tea with us.' and hastily curling his tongue he blew a little round ring of tobacco smoke, the emblem of the happiness of which he dreamed.

After the first rather doubtful reactions of Vera's parents to Berg's proposal the family settled down to the festivity and happiness usual at such times, but the rejoicing was on the surface and not genuine. A certain awkwardness and constraint were perceptible in the feelings of the relations. It was as if their consciences smote them for not having been very fond of Vera and for being so ready now to get her off their hands. The old count was the most disturbed over this. He would probably have been unable to say what made him uncomfortable but his financial difficulties were at the root of the trouble. He had no idea how he stood or how much he owed, or what dowry he could give Vera. When his daughters were born he had assigned to each of them as a marriage portion an estate with three hundred serfs; but one of these estates had already been sold, and the other was mortgaged and the interest so much in arrears that they were bound to foreclose, so Vera could not have this estate either. Nor was there any money.

Berg had already been the accepted bridegroom for over a month, and only a week remained before the wedding, yet still the count had not decided in his own mind the question of the dowry, nor broached the subject to his wife. At one moment he considered giving Vera the Ryazan estate, then he thought of selling a forest or raising money on a note of hand. A few days before the wedding Berg entered the count's study early one morning and with a pleasant smile respectfully invited his future father-in-law to let him know what Countess Vera's dowry would be. The count was so disconcerted by this long-anticipated inquiry that without thinking he said the first thing that came into his head.

'I like your being businesslike about it, I like it. You will be quite satisfied. ...'

And patting Berg on the shoulder he got up, hoping to cut short the conversation. But Berg, smiling blandly, explained that if he did not know for certain how much Vera would have, and did not receive at least part of the dowry in advance, he would be obliged to withdraw.

'Because, consider, count – if I were to allow myself to marry now without knowing what I had to depend on to maintain my wife I should be acting abominably ...'

The conversation ended by the count, in his anxiety to be generous and to avoid further importunity, saying that he would give him a note of hand for eighty thousand roubles. Berg smiled sweetly, kissed the count on the shoulder and declared that he was very grateful but that he could not make his arrangements for his new life without receiving thirty thousand in ready money. 'Or at least twenty thousand, count,' he added, 'and in that case a note of hand for only sixty thousand.'

'Yes, yes, to be sure,' said the count hurriedly. 'Only you must allow me, my dear fellow, to give you twenty thousand and the note of hand for eighty thousand as well. Yes, that's it! Kiss me.'

12

NATASHA was sixteen and it was the year 1809, the year to which she had counted on her fingers with Boris after they had kissed four years ago. Since then she had not once seen him. With Sonya, and with her mother, if Boris happened to be mentioned, she would quite unconcernedly treat all that had gone before as childish nonsense, not worth talking about and long forgotten. But in the secret depths of her heart the question whether her engagement to Boris was a jest or a solemn, binding promise tormented her.

Ever since Boris had left Moscow in 1805 to join the army he had not been back to the Rostovs. Several times he had been in Moscow, and in travelling had passed within a short distance of Otradnoe, but not once had he gone to see them.

It sometimes occurred to Natasha that he did not want to see her, and this conjecture was confirmed by the sorrowful tone in which her elders referred to him.

'Nowadays it is the fashion to forget old friends,' the countess would say immediately Boris was mentioned.

Anna Mihalovna's visits too had been less frequent of late. There was a marked dignity in her manner and she never failed to allude rapturously and gratefully to her son's merits and the brilliant career on which he was embarked. When the Rostovs arrived in Petersburg Boris came to call upon them.

It was not without emotion that he drove to their house. His memories of Natasha were the most poetic memories Boris had. But at the same time he was going with the firm intention of making both her and her parents clearly understand that the childish vows between himself and Natasha could not be considered binding on either of them. He had a brilliant position in society, thanks to his intimacy with Countess Bezuhov; a brilliant position in the service, thanks to the patronage of an important personage whose complete confidence he enjoyed; and he was now busy begetting plans for marrying one of the richest heiresses in Petersburg, plans which might very easily be realized. When Boris entered the Rostovs' drawing-room Natasha was in her own room. On being told of his arrival she almost ran into the drawing-room, flushed and radiant with a more than friendly smile.

Boris remembered Natasha in a short dress, with dark eyes flashing under her curls and a wild childish laugh, as he had known her four years before; and so he was taken aback when a quite different Natasha came in, and his face expressed surprise and admiration. This expression on his face delighted Natasha.

'Well, do you recognize your mischievous little playmate?' asked the countess.

Boris kissed Natasha's hand, and said that he was astonished at the change in her. 'How pretty you have grown!'

'I should hope so!' replied Natasha's laughing eyes. 'And does Papa look older?' she asked.

Natasha sat down and, taking no part in Boris's conversation with her mother, silently and minutely studied her childhood's suitor. He felt the weight of that resolute and affectionate scrutiny, and now and again stole a glance at her.

Boris's uniform, his spurs, his cravat and the way his hair was brushed were all in the latest fashion and *comme il faut*. This Natasha noted at once. He sat a little sideways in the arm-chair next to the countess, with his right hand smoothing the most immaculate of gloves that fitted his left hand like a skin, while he spoke with a peculiar, delicate compression of the lips about the gaieties of high life in Petersburg, and with mild irony recalled the old days in Moscow and their Moscow acquaintances. It was not without design, Natasha felt sure, that in speaking of the flower of the aristocracy he alluded to an ambassador's ball that he had attended and to invitations that he had received from So-and-so and Such-and-such.

All this time Natasha sat silent, watching him from under her brows. This gaze disconcerted Boris and made him more and more uneasy. He kept turning to her and breaking off what he was saying. He did not stay above ten minutes, then rose and bowed his leave. Still the same inquisitive, challenging and rather mocking eyes looked at him. After his first visit Boris confessed to himself that Natasha attracted him just as much as ever, but that he must not yield to his feelings because to marry her – a girl almost without a dowry – would ruin his career, while to renew their former friendship without intending to marry her would be dishonourable. Boris determined that he would avoid seeing Natasha, but notwithstanding this resolution he appeared again a few days later, and began calling often and spending whole days at the Rostovs'. He told himself more than once that he must come to an understanding with Natasha and tell her that they must forget the old times, that in spite of everything ... she could not be his wife, that he had no means and they would never let her marry him. But he always failed to do so, and felt awkward about approaching the subject. Every day he became more entangled. Natasha, it seemed to her mother and Sonya, was in love with Boris as she had been before. She sang him his favourite songs, showed him her album, made him write in it, would not let him refer to the past, making him feel how delightful was the present; and every day he went away in a whirl without having said what he meant to say, not knowing what he was doing or why he kept going there, or how it would all end. He left off visiting Hélène, received reproachful notes from her daily, and yet still spent whole days together at the Rostovs'.

ONE night when the old countess, in night-cap and dressing-jacket, with her false curls and with her one poor little knob of hair showing under her white calico nightcap, knelt sighing and groaning on a rug and bowing to the ground in prayer, her door creaked and Natasha, also in dressing-jacket with slippers on her bare feet and her hair in curl-papers, ran in. The countess looked round and frowned. She was repeating her last prayer 'And if this pallet should be my deathbed.' Her devotional mood was dispelled. Natasha, flushed and eager, checked her rush when she saw her mother was praying, made a little bob and unconsciously put out her tongue at herself. Seeing that her mother still went on with her devotions, she danced on tiptoe to the bed, kicked off her slippers by quickly rubbing one little foot against the other, and sprang into the bed which the countess feared might become her bier. It was a high feather-bed with five pillows, each one smaller than the one below. Natasha skipped on to the bedstead, sank into the feather mattress, rolled over to the wall and began snuggling down under the quilt, tucking herself up, bending her knees up to her chin and then kicking out, and giving faintly audible giggles as she alternately hid her face under the counterpane and peeped out at her mother. The countess finished her prayers and came over to the bed with a stern face, but seeing that Natasha's head was hidden under the bedclothes she smiled her good-natured, weak smile.

'Come, come, come!' said she.

'Mamma, can we have a talk – may we?' said Natasha. 'There now, just one on your throat, and one more and that's all.' And she threw her arms round her mother's neck and kissed her under the chin. Natasha's manner with her mother appeared rough, but she was so dexterous and careful that however she hugged her mother she always managed to do it without hurting or upsetting her and making her feel annoyed.

'Well, what is it tonight?' said her mother, arranging her pillows and waiting until Natasha, who rolled over a couple of times, should cuddle down close to her under the quilt, drop her hands and become serious.

These visits of Natasha to her mother at night before the count came home from the club were one of the greatest joys of both mother and daughter.

'What is it tonight? And I want to talk to you about –'

Natasha put her hand on her mother's lips.

'About Boris. ... I know,' she said gravely. 'That's what I have come about. Don't say it – I know. No, do!' and she took away her hand. 'Go on, mamma. He's nice, isn't he?'

'Natasha, you are sixteen. At your age I was already married. You say Boris is nice. He is very nice, and I love him like a son, but what is it you're after? ... What is in your mind? You have quite turned his head, I can see that. ...'

As she said this the countess looked round at her daughter. Natasha lay staring straight before her at one of the mahogany sphinxes carved on the corners of the bedstead, so that the countess could only see her daughter's face in profile. She was struck by its serious, intent expression.

Natasha was listening and considering.

'Well, what then?' said she.

'You have completely turned his head, and what for? What do you want of him? You know you can't marry him.'

'Why not?' said Natasha, without altering her position.

'Because he is very young, because he is poor, because he is a relation ... because you yourself don't love him.'

'How do you know?'

'I know. It is not right, darling!'

'But if I want to ...' began Natasha.

'Leave off talking nonsense,' said the countess.

'But if I choose ...'

'Natasha, I am in earnest ...'

Natasha did not let her finish. She drew the countess's large hand to her, kissed it on the back and then on the palm, turned it over again and began kissing first one knuckle, then the space between the knuckles, then the next knuckle, whispering: 'January, February, March, April, May. Speak, mamma, why don't you say something? Speak!' said she, looking up at her mother, who was gazing tenderly at her daughter and in her contemplation had apparently forgotten what she had meant to say.

'It won't do, my love! Not everyone will understand that this friendship dates from the time when you were both children, and to see him on such intimate terms with you may prejudice you in the eyes of other young men who come to the house, and above all it is making him wretched for nothing. He may very likely have found a match that would suit him, some rich girl, and now he's going half out of his mind.'

'Out of his mind?' repeated Natasha.

'I'll tell you something that happened to me. I once had a cousin...'

'I know – Kirill Matveich, but he's old, isn't he?'

'He was not always old. But this is what I'll do, Natasha. I will have a talk with Boris. He must not come so often. ...'

'Why mustn't he, if he wants to?'

'Because I know it can't lead to anything.'

'How do you know? No, mamma, don't speak to him. What foolishness!' said Natasha in the tone of one being robbed of her property. 'All right, I won't marry him, but let him come if he enjoys it and I enjoy it.' Natasha smiled and looked at her mother. 'Not get married, but go on *as we are*,' she added.

'What do you mean, my pet?'

'Why, as we are, of course. I quite see I shouldn't marry him, but ... as we are.'

'As we are, as we are!' repeated the countess, and, shaking all over, she went off into a good-humoured, unexpected, elderly laugh.

'Don't laugh, stop!' cried Natasha. 'You're shaking the whole bed. You're awfully like me, just another giggler. ... Wait. ...' She snatched both the countess's hands and kissed a knuckle of the little finger, saying 'June,' and continued kissing – 'July, August' – on the other hand. 'Mamma, is he very much in love? What do you think? Was anybody ever so much in love with you? And he's very nice, very, very nice. Only not quite to my taste – he's so narrow, like the dining-room clock. ... Don't you understand? ... You know, narrow, pale grey, light-coloured. ...'

'What nonsense you do talk!' exclaimed the countess.

Natasha continued:

'Don't you really understand? Nikolai would ... Bezuhov, now, he's blue – dark-blue and red, and all square. ...'

'You flirt with him too,' said the countess, laughing.

'No, I found out he's a freemason. He's a jolly person, dark-blue and red. ... How can I make you see?'

'Little countess!' the count's voice called the other side of the door.

'Aren't you asleep?' Natasha jumped up, seized her slippers in her hand and ran off barefoot to her own room.

She could not get to sleep for a long while. She kept thinking that no one could ever understand all the things she understood, and what there was in her.

'Sonya?' she thought, glancing at that curled-up sleeping little kitten with her enormous plait of hair. 'No, how could she? She is all virtue. She's in love with Nikolai, and that's all she cares about. Even mamma doesn't understand. It is wonderful how clever I am and how ... charming she is,' she went on, speaking of herself in the third person and imagining that some very intelligent, extraordinarily intelligent and most superior man was saying this about her. 'She possesses everything, everything,' continued this man. 'She is unusually intelligent, charming and pretty too – uncommonly pretty – and graceful. She can swim, she rides horseback splendidly, and what a voice! One might really say a marvellous voice!'

She hummed a few favourite bars from a Cherubini opera, flung herself into bed, laughed happily at the thought that she would be asleep in a trice, called to Dunyasha to snuff out the candle, and before the maid was out of the room had already crossed into that other still happier world of dreams, where everything was as buoyant and lovely as in real life, and even more so because it was different.

*

Next day the countess sent for Boris and had a talk with him, after which he gave up going to the Rostovs'.

14

ON the 31st of December, on the eve of the new year 1810, an old grandee of Catherine's day was giving a ball to see out the old year. The diplomatic corps and the Emperor were to be present.

The grandee's well-known mansion on the English Quay blazed with innumerable lights. Police were stationed at the brilliantly-lit, red-carpeted entrance – not only gendarmes but the chief of police himself and dozens of officers. Carriages drove away, and new ones kept arriving with red-liveried footmen and grooms in plumed hats. From the carriages emerged men wearing uniform, stars and ribbons, while ladies in satin and ermine cautiously descended the carriage steps, which were let down for them with a clatter, and swiftly and noiselessly passed along the red baize into the porch.

Almost every time a new carriage drove up a whisper ran through the crowd and caps were doffed.

'The Emperor? ... No, a minister ... prince ... ambassador. Don't you see the plumes? ...' said the crowd among themselves. One man, better dressed than the rest, seemed to know who everybody was, and announced the names of all the most celebrated personages of the day.

Already a third of the guests had arrived, but the Rostovs, who were to be present, were still hurrying to get dressed.

There had been much discussion and numerous preparations for this ball in the Rostov family. Would the invitation arrive? Would their gowns be ready in time? Would everything turn out as it should?

Maria Ignatyevna Peronsky, an old friend and relative of the countess, was to accompany the Rostovs to the ball. She was a thin and sallow maid of honour at the Empress Dowager's court, who was acting as guide to her country cousins in their entry into Petersburg high society.

They were to call for her at ten o'clock at her house in the Tavrichesky gardens, but it was already five minutes to ten and the girls were not yet dressed.

Natasha was going to her first grand ball. She had got up at eight that morning and had been in a fever of excitement and energy all day. All her energies from the moment she woke had been directed to the one aim of ensuring that they all – herself, mamma and Sonya – should look their very best. Sonya and the countess put themselves entirely in her hands. The countess was to wear a dark red velvet gown; the two girls, white tulle dresses over pink silk slips, with roses on their bodices. Their hair was to be arranged *à la grecque*.

All the essentials had been done: feet, hands, neck and ears washed, perfumed and powdered, as befits a ball. The openwork silk stockings and white satin slippers with ribbons were already on; their hair was almost finished. Sonya was nearly ready, so was the countess; but Natasha, who had bustled about helping everyone, was less advanced. She was still sitting before the looking-glass with a *peignoir* thrown over her thin shoulders. Sonya, on the last stage, stood in the middle of the room fastening on a final bow and hurting her dainty finger as she pressed the pin that squeaked as it went through the ribbon.

'Not like that, Sonya, not like that!' cried Natasha, turning her head and clutching with both hands at her hair which the maid, who was dressing it, had not time to let go. 'That bow isn't right. Come here!'

Sonya sat down and Natasha pinned the ribbon differently.

'If you please, miss, I can't get on like this,' said the maid, still holding Natasha's hair.

'Oh, goodness gracious, wait then! There, that's better, Sonya.'

'Will you soon be ready?' came the countess's voice. 'It is nearly ten.'

'Coming, coming! What about you, mamma?'

'I have only my cap to pin on.'

'Don't do it without me!' cried Natasha. 'You won't do it right.'

'Yes, but it's ten o'clock.'

It had been agreed that they should arrive at the ball at half past ten, but Natasha had still to get her dress on before they called for Madame Peronsky.

When her hair was done, Natasha, in a short petticoat from under which her dancing-slippers showed, and her mother's dressing-jacket, ran up to Sonya, inspected her critically, and then flew on to her mother. Turning the countess's head this way and that, she fastened on the cap, gave the grey hair a hasty kiss and scurried back to the maids who were shortening her skirt.

The cause of the delay was Natasha's skirt, which was too long. Two maids were at work turning up the hem and hurriedly biting off the threads. A third, with her mouth full of pins, was running backwards and forwards between the countess and Sonya, while a fourth held the gossamer garment high on one uplifted hand.

'Hurry up, Mavra, darling!'

'Hand me that thimble, please, miss.'

'Aren't you ever going to be ready?' asked the count, coming to the door. 'Here are you still perfuming yourselves. Madame Peronsky must be tired of waiting.'

'Ready, miss,' said the maid, lifting up the shortened tulle skirt with two fingers, and giving it a puff and a shake to show her appreciation of the airiness and immaculate freshness of what she held in her hands.

Natasha began putting on the dress.

'In a minute, in a minute! Don't come in, papa!' she cried to her father at the door, her face eclipsed in a cloud of tulle. Sonya slammed the door to. But a moment later they let the count in. He was wearing a blue swallow-tail coat, stockings and buckled shoes, and was perfumed and pomaded.

'Oh, papa, how nice you look! Lovely!' exclaimed Natasha, as she stood in the middle of the room stroking out the folds of her tulle.

'If you please, miss, allow me,' said the maid, who was on her knees pulling the skirt straight, and shifting the pins from one side of her mouth to the other with her tongue.

'You can say what you like,' cried Sonya in despairing tones, as she surveyed Natasha's dress, 'you can say what you like, it is still too long!'

Natasha stepped back to see herself in the pier-glass. The dress *was* too long.

'Really, madam, it is not at all too long,' said Mavra, crawling on her knees after her young lady.

'Well, if it's too long we'll tack it up ... we can do it in a second,' said the determined Dunyasha, taking a needle from the kerchief she wore crossed over her bosom and, still on the floor, setting to work again.

At that moment the countess in her cap and velvet gown crept shyly into the room.

'Oo-oo, my beauty!' cried the count. 'She looks nicer than any of you!'

He would have embraced her but, blushing, she stepped back, for fear of getting her gown rumpled.

'Mamma, your cap wants to go more to one side,' said Natasha. 'I'll alter it for you,' and she darted forward so that the maids who were tacking up her skirt could not follow her fast enough and a piece of the tulle got torn off.

'Mercy, what was that? Really it was not my fault. ...'

'Never mind, I'll put a stitch in, it won't show,' said Dunyasha.

'My beauty – my little queen!' exclaimed the old nurse, coming in at the door. 'And little Sonya too! Ah, the beauties! ...'

At last at a quarter past ten they seated themselves in the carriage and were on their way. But they still had to call at the Tavrichesky gardens.

Madame Peronsky was all ready and waiting. In spite of her advanced age and absence of looks she had gone through the same process as the Rostovs, though with less flurry since to her it was a matter of routine. Her unprepossessing old body had been washed, perfumed and powdered in exactly the same way. She had washed just as carefully behind her ears, and when she had come down into the drawing-room in her yellow gown, wearing her badge as a maid of honour, her old maid had been just as enthusiastic in her admiration of her mistress's toilette as at the Rostovs'.

Madame Peronsky praised the Rostovs' dresses. They praised her taste and her attire, and at eleven o'clock, careful of their *coiffures* and their gowns, they settled themselves in the carriages and drove off.

15

NATASHA had not had a moment to herself since early morning, and not once had she had time to think of what was before her.

In the damp chill air, in the closeness and half dark of the swaying vehicle, she vividly pictured to herself for the first time what was in store for her there at the ball, in those brilliantly-lighted rooms – the music, the flowers, the dances, the Emperor, all the dazzling young people of Petersburg. The prospect was so splendid that she could hardly believe it would come true, so out of keeping was it with the cold outside and the stuffy darkness of the carriage. She only realized all that was in front of her when she walked along the red baize at the entrance into the vestibule, took off her fur cloak and, together with Sonya, preceded her mother between the flowers up the lighted staircase. Only then did she remember how she should behave at a ball, and tried to assume the dignified air she considered to be the proper thing for a girl on such an occasion. But, fortunately for her, she felt her eyes growing misty: she could not see anything clearly, her pulse was beating a hundred to the minute and the blood throbbed at her heart. It was impossible for her to put on the manner that would have made her ridiculous, and she moved on almost swooning with excitement and trying with all her might to hide it. And this was the very behaviour that became her best. Before and behind them other guests were mounting the stairs, also talking in low tones and wearing ball-dresses. The looking-glasses along the staircase reflected ladies in white, pale blue and pink gowns, with diamonds and pearls on their bare arms and bosoms.

Natasha looked in the mirrors and could not distinguish her reflection from the others. Everything intertwined into one brilliant procession. At the entrance to the ballroom the continuous hum of voices, footsteps and greetings deafened Natasha; and the light and glitter dazzled her still more. The host and hostess, who had already been standing at the door for half an hour repeating the same words of welcome – 'Charmé de vous voir' – to the various arrivals, greeted the Rostovs and Madame Peronsky in like manner.

The two young girls in their white dresses, each with a rose in her black hair, curtsied alike, but the hostess's eye involuntarily rested longer on the slender figure of Natasha. She looked at her and gave her a special smile for herself as well as her hostess smile. Looking at her, she was reminded perhaps of the golden days of her own girlhood, gone never to return, and of her own first ball. The host too followed Natasha with his eyes and asked the count which of the two was his daughter.

'Charmante!' said he, kissing the tips of his fingers.

In the ballroom guests stood crowding about the entry in expectation of the Emperor. The countess took up a position in one of the front rows of this crowd. Natasha heard and was conscious that several people were asking about her and looking at her. She realized that she was making a pleasant impression on those who noticed her, and this observation calmed her somewhat.

'There are some looking as nice as we do, and some not so nice,' she thought.

Madame Peronsky was pointing out to the countess the most interesting people in the ballroom.

'That is the Dutch ambassador, do you see? The grey-haired man,' she said, indicating an old man with a profusion of silver-grey curls, who was surrounded by ladies laughing at some story he was telling.

'Ah, and here comes the Queen of Petersburg, Countess Bezuhov,' she exclaimed, as Hélène made her appearance. 'How lovely she is! She quite holds her own beside Maria Antonovna –' (this was the Tsar's favourite) '– see how the men pay court to her, young and old alike. She's both beautiful and intelligent. They say a royal prince is head over heels in love with her. But look at those two – not a bit good-looking but even more run after.'

She pointed out a lady who was crossing the room followed by a very plain daughter.

'That girl's heiress to a million,' said Madame Peronsky. 'And look, here come her suitors. ... That's Countess Bezuhov's brother, Anatole Kuragin,' she said, indicating a handsome officer of the Horse Guards who passed by them, holding himself very erect and looking at something over the heads of the ladies. 'Handsome, isn't he? I'm told he is to marry the heiress. And your cousin, Drubetskoy, is very attentive to her too. They say she has millions. Oh yes, that is the French ambassador himself,' she replied in answer to the countess's inquiry as to the identity of Caulaincourt. 'He might be a king! All the same, the French are charming, very charming. No one more charming in society. Ah, here she is! Yes, after all, there is no one to compare with our Maria Antonovna! And how simply she is dressed! Exquisite! And that stout fellow in spectacles is the great freemason,' she went on, referring to Pierre. 'Set him beside his wife, and what a ridiculous creature!'

Swinging his portly figure, Pierre advanced through the throng, nodding to right and left as casually and good-naturedly as if he were making his way through crowds at a fair. He pushed forward, evidently looking for someone. Natasha was delighted to see the familiar face of Pierre, that 'ridiculous creature', as Madame Peronsky had called him, and knew it was they, and herself in particular, of whom he was in search. He had promised to be at the ball and find partners for her.

But before reaching them Pierre stopped beside a very handsome, dark man of medium height in a white uniform, who was standing by a window talking to a tall man wearing stars and a ribbon. Natasha at once recognized the shorter and younger man in the white uniform: it was Bolkonsky, who seemed to her to have grown much younger, happier and better looking.

'There's someone else we know – Bolkonsky, do you see, Mamma?' said Natasha, pointing out Prince Andrei. 'You remember, he stayed a night with us at Otradnoe.'

'Oh, do you know him?' said Madame Peronsky. 'I can't bear him. Everyone is crazy over him just now. And the conceit of him: it's beyond words! Takes after his father. And he's hand in glove with Speransky over some project or other. See how he treats the ladies! There's one talking to him, and he turns his back on her,' she said, pointing to him. 'I'd give him a piece of my mind if he behaved with me as he does with them.'

16

THERE was a sudden stir: a whisper ran through the assembly, which
pressed forward and then back, separating into two rows down the
middle of which walked the Emperor to the strains of the orchestra
which struck up at once. Behind him came his host and hostess. He
entered rapidly, bowing to right and left as if anxious to get through
the first formalities as quickly as possible. The band played the polonaise in vogue at the moment on account of the words that had been
set to it, beginning: 'Alexander, Elisaveta, our hearts ye ravish quite...'
The Emperor passed on into the drawing-room; the crowd
surged to the doors; several persons dashed backwards and forwards,
their faces transformed. The wave receded from the doors of the
drawing-room, where the Emperor appeared engaged in conversation with his hostess. A young man, looking distraught, bore down
on the ladies, begging them to move away. Several ladies, with faces
betraying complete disregard of all the rules of decorum, squeezed
forward to the detriment of their toilettes. The men began to select
partners and take their places for the polonaise.

Space was cleared, and the Emperor, smiling, came out of the
drawing-room leading his hostess by the hand but not keeping time
to the music. The host followed with Maria Antonovna Naryshkin;
and after them ambassadors, ministers and various generals, whom
Madame Peronsky diligently named. More than half the ladies had
partners and were taking up or preparing to take up their positions
for the polonaise. Natasha felt that she would be left with her mother
and Sonya among the minority who lined the walls, not having been
invited to dance. She stood with her slender arms hanging by her
sides, her scarcely defined bosom rising and falling regularly, and with
bated breath and glittering, frightened eyes gazed straight before her,
evidently equally prepared for the height of joy or the depths of
misery. She was not interested in the Emperor or any of the great
personages whom Madame Peronsky was pointing out – she had but
one thought: 'Can it be that no one will come up to me, that I shall
not be among the first to dance? Is it possible that not one of all these
men will notice me? They don't even seem to see me, or if they do
they look as if they were saying, "No, she's not the one I'm after, it's
no use looking at her!" No, it cannot be,' she thought. 'They must

know how I am longing to dance, and how splendidly I dance, and how much they would enjoy dancing with me.'

The strains of the polonaise, which had now lasted some little time, began to have a melancholy cadence in Natasha's ears, like some sad reminiscence. She wanted to cry. Madame Peronsky had left them. The count was at the other end of the ballroom. She and the countess and Sonya were as much alone in this crowd of strangers as though they stood in the heart of a forest: no one took any interest in them or wanted them. Prince Andrei passed with a lady, obviously not recognizing them. The handsome Anatole was smilingly talking to a partner on his arm, and he glanced at Natasha's face as one glances at a wall. Twice Boris passed them, and each time turned his head away. Berg and his wife, who were not dancing, came up to them.

Natasha was mortified at this family gathering here in the ball-room – as though there were nowhere else for family talk but here at the ball. She did not listen or look at Vera, who was telling her something about her own green dress.

At last the Emperor stopped beside his last partner (he had danced with three) and the music ceased. An officious aide-de-camp bustled up to the Rostovs requesting them to stand farther back, though as it was they were already close to the wall, and from the gallery came the precise, regular, enticing strains of a waltz. The Emperor glanced down the room with a smile. A minute passed – no one had as yet begun dancing. An aide-de-camp, the master of ceremonies, went up to Countess Bezuhov and asked her to dance.

Smiling, she raised her hand and laid it on his shoulder, without looking at him. The aide-de-camp, a master of his art, grasped his partner firmly round the waist, and with confident deliberation glided smoothly first round the edge of the circle, then at the corner of the room he caught Hélène's left hand and turned her, the only sound audible, apart from the ever-quickening music, being the rhythmic clicking of the spurs on his swift and agile feet, while at every third beat his partner's velvet skirts seemed to flash as she whirled round. Natasha watched them and was ready to weep that it was not she who was dancing that first round of the waltz.

Prince Andrei, in the white uniform of a cavalry-colonel, wearing silk stockings and buckled dancing-slippers, stood looking animated and in the best of spirits in the front row of the circle not far from the Rostovs. Baron Firhoff was talking to him about the preliminary sitting of the Council of State to be held next day. Prince Andrei, as one closely connected with Speransky and participating in the work of the legislative commission, could give reliable information in regard to the approaching session, concerning which there were many conflicting rumours. But he was not listening to what Firhoff was saying, and looked now at the Sovereign, now at the various gentlemen who were all ready but had not yet gathered courage to take the floor.

Prince Andrei was observing these gentlemen abashed by the Emperor's presence, and the ladies who were dying to be asked to dance.

Pierre came up to Prince Andrei and caught him by the arm.

'You always dance. I have a *protégée* here, the little Rostov girl. Do invite her,' he said.

'Where is she?' asked Bolkonsky. 'Excuse me, baron,' he added, turning to the man he had been talking to, 'we will finish this conversation elsewhere – at a ball one must dance.' He stepped forward in the direction Pierre indicated. Natasha's dejected, despairing face caught his eye. He recognized her, guessed her feelings, saw that it was her *début*, remembered the conversation he had overheard between her and Sonya at the window, and with an eager expression went up to Countess Rostov.

'Allow me to introduce you to my daughter,' said the countess, with heightened colour.

'I have the pleasure of her acquaintance already, if the countess remembers me,' said Prince Andrei with a low and courteous bow, quite belying Madame Peronsky's remarks about his rudeness; and approaching Natasha he started to put his arm round her waist even before he had completed his invitation to her to dance. He suggested that they should take a turn of the waltz. Natasha's face with the tremulous expression prepared for despair or rapture suddenly lighted up with a happy, childlike smile of gratitude.

'I have been waiting an eternity for you,' this frightened, happy little girl seemed to be saying with the smile that replaced the threatened tears, as she raised her hand to Prince Andrei's shoulder. They were the second couple to take the floor. Prince Andrei was one of the best dancers of his day. Natasha danced exquisitely. Her little feet in their satin dancing-shoes performed their rôle swiftly, lightly, as if they had wings, while her face was radiant and ecstatic with happiness. Her thin bare arms and neck were not beautiful – compared to

Hélène's her shoulders looked thin and her bosom undeveloped. But Hélène seemed, as it were, covered with the hard polish left by the thousands of eyes that had scanned her person, while Natasha was a girl appearing décolletée for the first time in her life, and who would certainly have felt very much ashamed had she not been assured by everyone that it was the proper thing.

Prince Andrei was fond of dancing, and wishing to lose no time in escaping from the political and intellectual conversations into which everyone tried to draw him, and anxious as quickly as possible to break through that burdensome barrier of constraint caused by the Emperor's presence, he danced, and had chosen Natasha for his partner because Pierre pointed her out to him and because she was the first pretty girl who caught his eye But he had no sooner put his arm round that slender supple figure, and felt her stirring so close to him and smiling up into his face, than her charm mounted to his head like wine, and he felt himself revived and rejuvenated when they stopped to get breath and he released her and stood watching the other couples.

17

AFTER Prince Andrei, Boris came up to ask Natasha for a dance, and he was followed by the aide-de-camp who had opened the ball, and several other young men, so that Natasha, flushed and happy, and passing on her superfluous partners to Sonya, did not miss a single dance throughout the rest of the evening. She noticed and saw nothing of what interested everyone else. Not only did she fail to remark that the Emperor had a long conversation with the French ambassador, that his manner was particularly gracious to a certain lady, or that Prince So-and-so and Monsieur So-and-so had done and said this and that, and that Hélène had a great success and was honoured by the special attentions of such-and-such a person, but she did not even see the Emperor, and was only aware that he had gone because the ball became livelier after his departure. For one of the jolliest cotillions before supper Prince Andrei was again her partner. He reminded her of their first encounter in the avenue at Otradnoe, and of how she had been unable to sleep that moonlight night, and told her how he had involuntarily overheard her. Natasha blushed at this reminiscence and tried to excuse herself, as if there had been something to be ashamed of in what Prince Andrei had accidentally listened to.

Like all men who have grown up in society, Prince Andrei enjoyed meeting someone not of the conventional society stamp. And such was Natasha, with her wonder, her delight, her shyness and even her mistakes in speaking French. His manner was particularly tender and careful. As he sat beside her talking of the simplest and most insignificant matters, he admired the radiance of her eyes and her smile which had to do with her own inner happiness and not with what they were saying. When Natasha was invited to dance, and got up with a smile and glided round the room, her shy grace particularly charmed him. In the middle of the cotillion, having completed one of the figures, Natasha, still out of breath, was returning to her seat when another cavalier importuned her. She was tired and panting, and evidently thought for a moment of declining, but immediately she put her hand on her partner's shoulder and was off again, with a smile to Prince Andrei.

'I would rather rest and stay with you, I'm tired,' said that smile; 'but you see how they keep asking me, and I'm glad of it, and happy, and I love everybody, and you and I understand all about it.' That and much more this smile of hers seemed to say. When her partner left her, Natasha flew across the room to choose two ladies for the figure.

'If she goes first to her cousin and then to another lady, she will be my wife,' Prince Andrei – greatly to his own surprise – caught himself thinking as he watched her. She did go first to her cousin.

'What nonsense enters one's head sometimes!' thought Prince Andrei. 'But one thing's certain – that girl is so sweet, so out of the ordinary, that she won't spend a month in the ballroom before she's married. ... Such as she are rare here,' he thought, as Natasha, readjusting a rose that was slipping on her bodice, settled herself beside him.

At the end of the cotillion the old count in his blue coat came up to the young people who had been dancing. He invited Prince Andrei to come and see them, and asked his daughter whether she was enjoying herself. Natasha did not answer at once: she only looked up with a smile that said reproachfully: 'How can you ask such a question?'

'It's the loveliest time I ever had in my life!' said she, and Prince Andrei noticed how her thin arms rose quickly as though to embrace her father, and instantly dropped again. Natasha had never been so happy. She was at that highest pitch of bliss when one becomes completely good and kind, and cannot believe in the existence or possibility of evil, unhappiness and sorrow.

*

Pierre at this ball for the first time felt humiliated by the position his wife occupied in court circles. He was morose and abstracted. A deep furrow ran across his forehead, and standing by a window he stared through his spectacles, seeing no one.

On her way to supper Natasha passed him.

Pierre's gloomy, unhappy face struck her. She stopped in front of him. She felt a desire to help him, to bestow on him the super-abundance of her own happiness.

'How delightful it is, count,' she said, 'don't you think so?'

Pierre smiled absent-mindedly, obviously not taking in what she said.

'Yes, I am very glad,' he replied.

'How can people not be pleased with anything?' thought Natasha. 'Especially anyone as nice as Bezuhov.' In Natasha's eyes all who were at the ball were alike good, kind, splendid people, full of affection for one another, incapable of harm – and so they all ought to be happy.

18

NEXT day Prince Andrei recalled the ball but it did not occupy his mind for long. 'Yes, it was a most brilliant ball. And then – oh yes, the little Rostov girl is very charming. There's something fresh, original, un-Petersburg-like about her that distinguishes her.' That was the extent of the thought he gave to the ball of the night before, and after his morning tea he set to work.

But either from fatigue or want of sleep he was ill-disposed for effort and could not get on. He was dissatisfied with what he did do, as was often the case with him, and was glad when he heard a visitor arrive.

The visitor was Bitsky, a man who served on various committees and frequented all the different cliques of Petersburg. He was a passionate devotee of the new ideas and of Speransky, and the most diligent purveyor of news in Petersburg – one of those men who select their opinions like their clothes, according to the prevailing fashion, and in consequence come to be regarded as the most eager

543

supporters of the latest trends. Scarcely giving himself time to remove his hat, he hurried busily into Prince Andrei's room and at once began talking. He had just heard all about that morning's sitting of the Council of State opened by the Emperor. He dilated with enthusiasm on the Sovereign's speech: it had been an extraordinary one – the sort of speech only constitutional monarchs deliver. 'The Sovereign said in so many words that the Council and the Senate are *estates* of the realm; he said that the government must rest not on arbitrary authority but on solid principles. The Emperor said that the fiscal system must be reorganized and the budgets made public,' recounted Bitsky, laying stress on certain words and opening his eyes significantly. 'Yes, today's events mark an epoch, the greatest epoch in our history,' he concluded.

Prince Andrei listened to the account of the opening of the State Council, to which he had so impatiently been looking forward and to which he attached so much importance, and was astonished that now that it was an accomplished fact he was not only unmoved but completely unimpressed. He listened with quiet irony to Bitsky's rhapsody. A very simple thought occurred to him: 'What is it to me and Bitsky – what is it to us what the Emperor is pleased to say in the Council? Can it make me any happier or better?'

And this simple reflection suddenly destroyed all the interest Prince Andrei had formerly taken in the impending reforms. That very day he was to dine at Speransky's – 'just a few of us', his host had said when inviting him. The idea of this dinner in the intimate home circle of the man he so admired had seemed very attractive to Prince Andrei, especially as he had not yet seen Speransky in his domestic surroundings, but now he had lost all desire to go.

At the appointed hour, however, he entered the modest residence in the Tavrichesky gardens. The little house, which was Speransky's own property, was remarkable for its extreme spotlessness (suggesting that of a monastery). In the parquet-floored dining-room Prince Andrei, who was rather late, found the friendly gathering of his host's intimate friends already assembled at five o'clock. There were no ladies present except Speransky's young daughter (who had a long face like her father's) and the child's governess. The other guests were Gervais, Magnitsky and Stolypin. From the vestibule Prince Andrei caught the sound of loud voices and a ringing, staccato laugh – a laugh such as one hears on the stage. Someone – it sounded like Speransky

– was giving vent to a distinct *ha-ha-ha*. Prince Andrei had never heard Speransky laugh before, and this shrill, ringing laugh from the great statesman made a strange impression on him.

He went into the dining-room. The whole party were standing between the two windows at a small table laid with hors-d'œuvre. Speransky, wearing a grey swallow-tail coat with a star on his breast, and evidently still the same white waistcoat and high white stock in which he had appeared at the famous meeting of the Council of State, stood at the table with a beaming countenance. His guests formed a ring round him. Magnitsky, addressing himself to Speransky, was relating an anecdote, and Speransky was laughing in advance at what Magnitsky was going to say. Just as Prince Andrei walked into the room Magnitsky's words were again drowned by laughter. Stolypin gave a deep bass guffaw as he munched a little square of bread and cheese. Gervais softly hissed a chuckle, and Speransky laughed his high-pitched staccato laugh.

Still laughing, Speransky held out his soft white hand to Prince Andrei.

'So glad to see you, prince,' he said. 'One moment ...' he went on, turning to Magnitsky and interrupting his story. 'We have agreed that this is a dinner for recreation, and not a word about business!' and giving his attention to the narrator again, he began to laugh afresh.

Prince Andrei looked at the hilarious Speransky with a sense of wondering and melancholy disillusion. This was not Speransky but some other man, it seemed to him. All that had formerly appeared mysterious and fascinating in Speransky suddenly became commonplace and unattractive.

At dinner the conversation never stopped for a moment, and seemed to consist of the contents of a book of funny stories. Before Magnitsky had finished his story someone else was anxious to tell them something even more amusing. Most of the anecdotes, if not confined to the world of officialdom, at least related to individuals in the service. It was as though in this company the nonentity of those people was so thoroughly taken for granted that the only possible attitude to them was one of good-humoured ridicule. Speransky described how at the Council that morning a deaf dignitary, on being asked his opinion, replied that he thought so too. Gervais gave a long account of an incident to do with the census, remarkable for the imbecility of everybody concerned. Stolypin, stuttering, broke in and began talking of the abuses that existed in the old order of things, with a warmth that threatened to give the conversation a serious turn. Magnitsky started making fun of Stolypin's vehemence. Gervais intervened with a pun, and the talk reverted to its former frivolous tone.

Evidently Speransky liked to rest after his labours and find amusement in a circle of friends, and his guests, knowing this, did their best to cheer him and divert themselves. But their gaiety seemed forced and mirthless to Prince Andrei. Speransky's shrill voice struck him unpleasantly, and his incessant laughter had a false ring that grated on him. Prince Andrei did not laugh and feared that the company would find him a kill-joy, but no one noticed that he was out of harmony with the general mood. They all appeared to be enjoying themselves greatly.

He made several attempts to join in the conversation, but each time his remarks were tossed aside like a cork flung back out of the water, and he could not bandy jokes with them.

There was nothing wrong or unseemly in what they said: it was witty, and might have been amusing but it lacked just that something which is the salt of mirth, and they were not even aware that such an element existed.

After dinner, Speransky's daughter and her governess rose. Speransky patted the little girl with his white hand and kissed her. And that gesture, too, seemed unnatural to Prince Andrei.

The men remained at table, sitting over their port after the English fashion. In the middle of a conversation that sprang up about Napoleon's Spanish affairs, which they all approved unanimously, Prince Andrei took it upon himself to disagree. Speransky smiled, and with the evident intention of changing the subject told a story which was totally irrelevant. For a few moments all were silent.

After they had sat for some time at table, Speransky corked up a bottle of wine, and remarking 'Good wine is expensive these days,' handed it to the servant and got up. All rose, and still talking noisily passed into the drawing-room. Two letters were brought in which had come by a courier, and Speransky took them to his study. As soon as he left the room the general merriment was abandoned and the guests began to talk sensibly together in low tones.

'Well, now for the recitation,' said Speransky, returning from his study. 'A wonderful talent!' he said to Prince Andrei. Magnitsky immediately threw himself into an attitude and began to recite some humorous verses he had written in French about certain well-known Petersburg people. Several times he was interrupted by applause. At the conclusion of the recitation Prince Andrei went up to Speransky and took his leave.

'Where are you off to so early?' inquired Speransky.

'I promised to be at a *soirée*. ...'

They said no more. Prince Andrei looked closely into those mirror-like, impenetrable eyes, and felt that it had been ludicrous of him to have expected anything from Speransky, or of any of his own activities connected with him, and marvelled how he could have attributed importance to what Speransky was doing. The measured mirthless laugh rang in Prince Andrei's ears long after he had left Speransky's.

When he reached home Prince Andrei began to live over his life in Petersburg during the last four months, as though it were something new. He recalled his exertions, the efforts he had made to see people, and the history of his project of army reform, which had been accepted for consideration and which they were trying to shelve for the sole reason that another scheme, a very inferior one, had already been prepared and submitted to the Emperor. He thought of the sittings of the committee of which Berg was a member. He remembered the conscientious and prolonged deliberations that took place at those meetings on every point relating to form and procedure, and how sedulously and promptly all that touched the substance of the business was evaded. He recalled his labours on the legislative reforms, and how painstakingly he had translated the articles of the Roman and French codes into Russian, and he felt ashamed for himself. Then he vividly pictured Boguecharovo, his pursuits in the country, his expedition to Ryazan; thought of his peasants and Dron the village elder, and mentally applying to them the section on Personal Rights, which he had classified into paragraphs, he was amazed that he could have spent so much time on such useless work.

19

THE next day Prince Andrei paid calls on various people whom he had not visited before, and among them on the Rostovs, with whom he had renewed his acquaintance at the ball. Apart from considerations of politeness which demanded the call, he also had a strong desire to see in her own home that original, eager girl who had left such a pleasant impression in his mind.

Natasha happened to be the first to receive him. She was wearing a dark blue everyday dress, in which Prince Andrei thought she looked even prettier than in her ball-gown. She and all the family welcomed him as an old friend, simply and cordially. The whole family, whom he had once criticized so severely, now seemed to him charming, simple, kindly folk. The old count's pressing hospitality and his good nature, particularly conspicuous and appealing here in Petersburg, were such that Prince Andrei could not refuse to stay to dinner. 'Yes,' he thought, 'they are excellent people, who of course have not the slightest idea what a treasure they possess in Natasha; but they are good people, who make the best possible background for this wonderfully poetical, delightful girl, so overflowing with life!'

In Natasha Prince Andrei was conscious of a strange world, completely remote from him and brimful of joys he had not known, that different world which even in the avenue at Otradnoe and on that moonlight night at the window had tantalized him. Now it mocked him no longer, and was no longer an alien world: he himself had stepped into it and was finding new satisfactions for himself.

After dinner Natasha, at Prince Andrei's request, went to the clavichord and began singing. Prince Andrei stood at the window talking to the ladies, and listened to her. Suddenly in the middle of a sentence he fell silent, feeling a lump in his throat from tears, a thing he would not have believed possible for him. He looked at Natasha as she sang, and something new and blissful stirred in his soul. He felt happy and at the same time sad. He had absolutely nothing to weep about, yet he was ready to weep. For what? For his past love? For the little princess? For his lost illusions? ... For his hopes for the future? ... Yes and no. The chief reason for his wanting to weep was a sudden acute sense of the terrible contrast between something infinitely great and illimitable existing within him and the narrow material something which he, and even she, was. The contrast made his heart ache, and rejoiced him while she sang.

As soon as Natasha finished her song she went up to him and asked him how she liked her voice. She asked the question and was then embarrassed, realizing that she ought not to have put it. He smiled, looking at her, and said he liked her singing just as he liked everything else she did.

It was late in the evening when Prince Andrei left the Rostovs. He went to bed from habit, but soon saw that he could not sleep. Having lit his candle he sat up in bed, then got up, then lay down again, not at all oppressed by his sleeplessness: his soul was so full of new and joyful sensations that it seemed to him as if he had just emerged from a stuffy room into God's fresh air. It did not enter his head that he was in love with the little Rostov girl, he was not thinking about her but only picturing her to himself, and in consequence all life appeared in a new light. 'Why do I struggle? Why am I toiling and moiling in this narrow, petty environment, when life, all life with its every joy, lies open before me?' he said to himself. And for the first time for a very long while he began making happy plans for the future. He decided that he must attend personally to his son's education, finding a tutor and putting the boy in his charge; then he ought to retire from the service and go abroad, see England, Switzerland, Italy. 'I must make the most of my freedom while I feel myself so overflowing with strength and energy,' he said to himself. 'Pierre was right when he said one must believe in the possibility of happiness in order to be happy, and now I do believe in it. Let the dead bury their dead; but while one has life one must live and be happy,' he thought.

20

ONE morning Colonel Adolf Berg, whom Pierre knew just as he knew everybody in Moscow and Petersburg, came to see him. Berg arrived in an immaculate brand-new uniform, with his hair pomaded and curled over his temples in imitation of the Emperor Alexander.

'I have just been calling on the countess, your wife. Unfortunately she could not grant my request, but I hope, count, I shall have better luck with you,' he said with a smile.

'What is it you wish, colonel? I am at your service.'

'I am now quite settled in my new quarters, count,' Berg informed him, evidently convinced in his own mind that this piece of news could not fail to be agreeable, 'and consequently I was hoping to arrange a little reception for my friends and those of my spouse.' (He smiled still more effusively.) 'I wanted to ask the countess and yourself to do me the honour of coming to us for a cup of tea and ... to supper.'

Only the Countess Hélène, considering it beneath her dignity to associate with nobodies like the Bergs, could have been cruel enough to refuse such an invitation. Berg explained so clearly why he wanted to gather a small but select company at his new rooms, and why this would give him pleasure, and why though he grudged money spent on cards and other disreputable occupations he was prepared to run to some expense for the sake of good society, that Pierre could not refuse, and promised to come.

'Only not too late, count, if I may venture to beg of you. About ten minutes to eight, if I may make so bold. We shall make up a rubber. Our general is coming. He is very kind to me. We will have a little supper, count. So do me the favour.'

Contrary to his usual habit of being late, Pierre that evening arrived at the Bergs' house not at ten but at fifteen minutes to eight.

The Bergs, having made every provision for the party, were ready for their guests to appear.

In their new, clean, light study, embellished with little busts and pictures and new furniture, sat Berg and his wife. Berg, tightly buttoned into his new uniform, sat beside his wife, explaining to her that one always could and should be acquainted with people above one in station, that being the only real satisfaction in having friends.

'You can always find something to imitate or ask for. Look at me now, how my life has gone since my first promotion.' (Berg measured his life not by years but by promotions.) 'My comrades are still nobodies, while at the first vacancy I shall be a regimental commander. I have the happiness of being your husband.' (He rose and kissed Vera's hand, but on the way he straightened a corner of the carpet which was rucked up.) 'And how did I accomplish all this? Principally by knowing how to select my acquaintances. It goes without saying, of course, that one must be conscientious and methodical.'

Berg smiled with the consciousness of his superiority over a weak woman, and paused, reflecting that this dear wife of his was after all but a feeble woman unable to appreciate the dignity of being a man— what it meant *ein Mann zu sein*. Vera meanwhile was smiling too with a sense of her superiority over her good, worthy husband, who nevertheless, like the rest of his sex, according to Vera's ideas of men, took an utterly wrong-headed view of the meaning of life. Berg, judging by his wife, considered all women weak and foolish. Vera, judging only by her husband and generalizing from her observation of him, supposed that all men believed that no one but themselves had any sense, though they had no real understanding and were conceited and selfish.

Berg rose and embracing his wife carefully so as not to crush her lace fichu, for which he had paid a round sum, kissed her full on the lips.

'The only thing is, we mustn't have children too soon,' he said, by a correlation of ideas of which he himself was unaware.

'No,' answered Vera, 'I don't at all want that. We must live for society.'

'Princess Yusupov was wearing one exactly like this,' said Berg, laying a finger on the fichu with a contented, happy smile.

Just then Count Bezuhov was announced. Husband and wife exchanged self-satisfied glances, each mentally claiming the credit for this visit.

'See the result of knowing how to make acquaintances,' thought Berg. 'This is what comes of possessing *savoir faire*!'

'Now I do beg of you,' said Vera, 'don't interrupt me when I am entertaining the guests, because I know very well what is likely to interest each of them and what to say to different people.'

Berg, too, smiled.

'Oh, but sometimes men must have their masculine conversation,' said he.

Pierre was shown into the brand-new drawing-room, where it was impossible to sit down without disturbing its symmetrical neatness and order; so it was perfectly comprehensible and not to be wondered at that Berg should magnanimously offer to sacrifice the symmetry of an arm-chair or of the sofa for his esteemed guest, and then, finding himself in a painful state of indecision on the matter, leave the visitor to decide the problem of where to sit. Pierre upset the symmetry by moving forward a chair for himself, and Berg and Vera immediately began their *soirée*, interrupting each other in their efforts to entertain their guest.

Vera, having decided in her own mind that Pierre ought to be entertained with conversation about the French Embassy, promptly embarked upon that subject. Berg, deciding that masculine conversation was required, cut in on his wife with some remarks on the war with Austria, and from general discussion involuntarily leapt to a personal review of the proposals made to him to take part in the Austrian campaign, and the reasons which had led him to decline them. Although the conversation was extremely desultory and Vera was indignant at the intrusion of this masculine element, both husband and wife felt with satisfaction that, even if only one guest was present, their *soirée* had begun very well and was as like as two drops of water to every other *soirée*, with the same conversation, tea and lighted candles.

Before long Boris, Berg's old comrade, arrived. There was a certain shade of patronage and condescension in his treatment of Berg and Vera. After Boris came the colonel and his lady, then the general himself, then the Rostovs, and now the party without a shadow of doubt began to resemble all other evening parties. Berg and Vera could not repress blissful smiles at the sight of all this stir in their drawing-room, at the sound of the disconnected chatter, and the rustle of skirts and of curtsies and bows. Everything was identically the same as it was everywhere else; especially so was the general, who admired the apartment, patted Berg on the shoulder, and with paternal authority superintended the setting out of the table for boston. The general sat down by Count Ilya Rostov, as the guest ranking next in precedence to himself. The elderly gathered near the elderly, the young people sat with the young, the hostess at the tea-table on which there were exactly the same kind of cakes in a silver cake-basket as the Panins had at their party. Everything was just as it was everywhere else.

21

PIERRE, as one of the most honoured guests, had to sit down to boston with Count Rostov, the general and the colonel. At the card-table he happened to be directly facing Natasha, and he was struck by the curious change that had come over her since the night of the ball. She scarcely spoke a word, and not only was she less pretty than she had been at the ball but would have looked positively plain but for the expression of gentle indifference on her face.

'What is the matter with her?' Pierre wondered, glancing at Natasha. She was sitting by her sister at the tea-table, making reluctant answers, without looking at him, to Boris who sat down beside her. After playing out a whole suit and to his partner's satisfaction taking five tricks, Pierre, hearing greetings and the steps of someone who had entered the room while he was picking up his cards, glanced again at Natasha.

'What has happened to her?' he asked himself with even more wonder than before.

Prince Andrei was standing before her, saying something with a look of tender solicitude. She had raised her head and was gazing at him with flushed cheeks, visibly trying to control her rapid breathing. And the radiance of some inner fire that had been extinguished before was alight in her again. She was completely transformed: instead of looking plain she was the beautiful creature she had been at the ball.

Prince Andrei went up to Pierre, and Pierre noticed a new and youthful expression in his friend's face.

Pierre changed places several times during the game, sitting now with his back to Natasha, now facing her, but during the whole six rubbers he watched her and his friend.

'There is something very important happening between them,' thought Pierre, and a mixed feeling of joy and bitterness agitated him and made him forgetful of the game.

After six rubbers the general got up, saying that it was no use playing like that, and Pierre was released. Natasha on one side was talking with Sonya and Boris. Vera, with a subtle smile, was saying something to Prince Andrei. Pierre went up to his friend and, asking whether they were talking secrets, sat down beside them. Vera, having observed Prince Andrei's attentions to Natasha, decided that a *soirée*, a real *soirée*, demanded some delicate allusions to the tender passion, and seizing an opportunity when Prince Andrei was alone, began a conversation with him about the emotions generally and her sister in particular. With so intellectual a guest as she considered Prince Andrei, she felt she must bring to bear all her art of diplomacy.

When Pierre joined them he noticed that Vera was being carried away by her own eloquence, while Prince Andrei seemed embarrassed – a rare thing with him.

'What do you think?' Vera was saying with an arch smile. 'You are so discerning, prince, and so quick at understanding people's characters. What do you think of Natalie? Is she capable of being constant in her attachments? Could she, like other women' (Vera meant herself) 'love a man once for all and remain faithful to him for ever? That is what I call true love. What is your opinion, prince?'

'I do not know your sister well enough,' replied Prince Andrei, with a sardonic smile behind which he hoped to hide his embarrassment, 'to be able to solve so delicate a question; and besides I have noticed that the less attractive a woman is the more constant she is likely to be,' he added, and looked up at Pierre who had just joined them.

'Yes, that is true, prince. In these days,' pursued Vera – speaking of 'these days' as people of limited intelligence are fond of doing, imagining that they have discovered and appraised the peculiarities of 'these days' and that human nature changes with the times – 'in these days a girl has so much freedom that the pleasure of being courted often stifles real feeling in her. And Natasha, it must be confessed, is very susceptible.' This return to the subject of Natasha caused Prince Andrei to contract his brows disagreeably. He made to rise, but Vera persisted with a still more subtle smile:

'Nobody, I imagine, has been so much run after as she has,' she went on, 'but till quite lately no one has ever made a serious impression on her. Of course, you know, count,' she turned to Pierre, 'even our charming cousin, Boris, who, between ourselves, journeyed very deep into the region of tenderness …' (she was alluding to a map of love much in vogue at that time).

Prince Andrei frowned and remained silent.

'You and Boris are friends, are you not?' asked Vera.

'Yes, I know him. …'

'I expect he has told you of his boyish love for Natasha?'

'Oh, so there was a romance between them, was there?' suddenly asked Prince Andrei, going unexpectedly red.

'Yes, you know close intimacy between cousins often leads to love. *Le cousinage est un dangereux voisinage.* Don't you agree?'

'Oh, undoubtedly!' said Prince Andrei, and with a sudden and unnatural liveliness he began chaffing Pierre, warning him to be very careful with his fifty-year-old cousins in Moscow, and in the midst of these jesting remarks he got up, and taking Pierre's arm drew him aside.

'Well?' asked Pierre, who had been watching in startled wonder his friend's strange excitement and had noticed the glance he turned upon Natasha as he rose.

'I must … I must have a talk with you,' said Prince Andrei. 'You know that pair of women's gloves?' (He was referring to the masonic gloves given to a newly-initiated brother to present to the woman he loved.) 'I … no, I will talk to you by and by …' and with a queer light in his eyes and a restlessness in his movements Prince Andrei crossed over to Natasha and sat down beside her. Pierre saw that Prince Andrei asked her something, and how she coloured as she replied.

But at that moment Berg came to Pierre and began insisting that he should take part in a discussion between the general and the colonel on affairs in Spain.

Berg was satisfied and happy. The blissful smile never left his face. The *soirée* was being a great success, exactly repeating every other *soirée* he had been to. Everything was similar: the ladies' refined conversation, the cards, the general raising his voice over the game, the samovar and the tea cakes; only one thing was lacking, which he had always seen at the evening parties he wished to imitate. There had not yet been a loud conversation among the men and argument over some grave intellectual concern. Now the general had started such a discussion and it was to this that Berg carried Pierre off.

22

NEXT day, having been invited by the count, Prince Andrei dined with the Rostovs and spent the rest of the day there.

Everyone in the house realized on whose account Prince Andrei came, and, making no secret of it, he tried to be with Natasha the whole time. Not only was Natasha, in her heart of hearts, frightened yet happy and enraptured, but all the household felt a sort of awe in the anticipation of a great and solemn event. With sad and sternly-serious eyes the countess gazed at Prince Andrei as he talked to Natasha, and timidly started some artificial conversation about trifles as soon as he looked her way. Sonya was afraid to leave Natasha and afraid of being in the way if she stayed with them. Natasha turned pale in a panic of expectation every time she was left for a moment alone with him. Prince Andrei surprised her by his bashfulness. She felt that he wanted to say something to her but could not bring himself to speak.

In the evening after Prince Andrei had gone the countess went up to Natasha and whispered:

'Well?'

'Mamma, for pity's sake, don't ask me any questions now! One mustn't talk about it,' said Natasha.

But that night Natasha, excited and scared by turns, lay a long time in her mother's bed, gazing straight before her. She told her how he had complimented her, how he had said he was going abroad, asked her where they were going to spend the summer, and then how he had asked her about Boris.

'But I never ... I never felt like this before,' she said. 'Only I feel afraid in his presence. I am always afraid when I'm with him. What does it mean? Does it mean that it's the real thing? Does it? Mamma, are you asleep?'

'No, my love; I am frightened myself,' answered her mother. 'Run along now.'

'I shouldn't sleep anyway. How silly to go to sleep! Mummy, mummy! Nothing like this has ever happened to me before!' she said, amazed and awed at the feeling she was aware of in herself. 'And could we ever have dreamed ...!'

It seemed to Natasha that she had fallen in love with Prince Andrei even when she first saw him at Otradnoe. It was as if she were terrified at the strange unexpected happiness of meeting again with the very man she had then chosen (she was firmly convinced that she had done so), and finding that he was apparently not indifferent to her.

'And it seemed as though it all had to happen – his coming to Petersburg while we are here. And our meeting at that ball. It was all fate. It's plain it was fate making everything lead up to this! Already *then*, directly I saw him, I felt something peculiar.'

'What else did he say to you? What are those verses? Read them to me ...' said her mother thoughtfully, referring to some verses Prince Andrei had written in Natasha's album.

'Mamma, it's nothing to be ashamed of that he's a widower?'

'Hush, Natasha. Pray to God – marriages are made in heaven,' said her mother, quoting the French proverb.

'Darling Mummy, how I love you! How happy I am!' cried Natasha, shedding tears of joy and excitement, and hugging her mother.

At that very same hour Prince Andrei was at Pierre's, telling him of his love for Natasha and his firm intention to make her his wife.

*

That evening Countess Hélène Bezuhov was holding an informal party. The French ambassador was there, and a prince of the blood, who of late had been a frequent visitor at the countess's, and a great number of brilliant ladies and gentlemen. Pierre had come down and wandered through the rooms, his preoccupied, absent-minded air of gloom attracting general attention.

Since the ball he had felt the approach of one of his attacks of nervous depression, and had been making desperate efforts to combat it. Since his wife's intimacy with the royal prince Pierre had unexpectedly been appointed a gentleman of the bedchamber, and from that time he had begun to feel a sense of weariness and shame in court society, and dark thoughts of the vanity of all things human came to him oftener than of old. At the same time the growing love he had noticed between his protégée Natasha and Prince Andrei aggravated his melancholy by the contrast between his own position and his friend's. He strove alike to avoid thinking of his wife and of Natasha and Prince Andrei. Once more everything seemed to him insignificant in comparison with eternity; again the question confronted him: 'What is the point of it all?' And days and nights together he forced himself to work at his masonic labours in the hope of warding off the evil spirit. Towards midnight he had withdrawn from the countess's apartments and was sitting in a shabby dressing-gown at a table in his own low-ceilinged room, which was cloudy with tobacco-smoke, and copying out the original transactions of the Scottish freemasons, when someone came in. It was Prince Andrei.

'Ah, it's you,' said Pierre vaguely, with a dissatisfied air. 'I'm hard at it, as you see.' He pointed to his manuscript-book in the way of unhappy people who regard their work as a means of salvation from the ills of life.

Prince Andrei, his face ecstatic with renewed life, came and stood in front of Pierre, and not perceiving his friend's wretched expression smiled down on him with the egoism of happiness.

'Well, my dear boy,' said he, 'I wanted to tell you about it yesterday, and now I have come to do so today. I have never experienced anything like it before. I am in love, my friend!'

Pierre heaved a sudden ponderous sigh and dumped his heavy person down on the sofa beside Prince Andrei.

'With Natasha Rostov, is it?' said he.

'Yes, yes, who else should it be? I would never have believed it, but the feeling is stronger than I. Yesterday I was in torment, in agony, but I would not exchange even that agony for anything in the world.

I have never lived till now. Only now am I alive, but I cannot live without her. But can she love me? ... I'm too old for her. ... Why don't you speak?'

'I? I? What did I tell you?' said Pierre suddenly, rising and beginning to walk about the room. 'I have always thought. ... That girl is such a treasure, such a ... She is a rare girl. ... My dear fellow, don't, I beseech you, stop to reason, do not have doubts – marry, marry, marry. ... And there will be no happier man on earth, of that I am sure.'

'But how about her?'

'She loves you.'

'Don't talk rubbish. ...' said Prince Andrei, smiling and looking into Pierre's eyes.

'She does, I know,' Pierre cried fiercely.

'No, do listen,' returned Prince Andrei, taking hold of him by the arm and stopping him. 'Do you know the state I am in? I must tell someone all about it!'

'Well, go on, talk away. I am very glad,' said Pierre, and indeed his face had changed; the frown had smoothed itself out, and he listened gladly to Prince Andrei. Prince Andrei seemed, and really was, an utterly different, new man. What had become of his *ennui*, his contempt for life, his disillusionment? Pierre was the only person to whom he could bring himself to speak frankly, and to him he revealed all that was in his heart, now gaily and boldly making plans reaching far into the future, saying he could not sacrifice his own happiness to the caprices of his father, declaring that he would either force his father to agree to the marriage, and like her, or dispense with his consent altogether; then marvelling at the feeling which had taken possession of him, as something strange and apart, independent of himself.

'I should never have believed it if anyone had told me I could love like this,' said Prince Andrei. 'It is not at all the same feeling that I had before. The whole world is split into two halves for me: she is one half, and there all is joy, hope and light: the other is where she is not, and there everything is gloom and darkness. ...'

'Darkness and gloom,' repeated Pierre; 'yes, yes, I understand that.'

'I can't help loving the light, it is not my fault. And I am very happy! You understand me? I know you are glad for my sake.'

'Yes, yes,' Pierre assented, looking at his friend with a touched and sad expression in his eyes. The brighter Prince Andrei's lot appeared to him, the more sombre seemed his own.

23

PRINCE ANDREI required his father's sanction for his marriage, and to obtain this he started for the country next day.

The old prince received his son's communication with outward composure but inward wrath. He could not comprehend how anyone could wish to alter his life, to introduce any new element into it, when his own was so near its close. 'Why can't they let me end my days as I want to, and then do as they please?' the old man said to himself. With his son, however, he employed the diplomacy he reserved for matters of serious import. Adopting a quiet tone, he went into the whole matter judicially.

To begin with, the match was not a brilliant one from the point of view of birth, fortune or rank. Secondly, Prince Andrei was not in his first youth and his health was poor (the old man laid special stress on this), while the girl was very young. Thirdly, he had a son whom it would be a pity to entrust to a chit of a girl. 'Fourthly, and finally,' the father said, looking ironically at his son, 'I beg of you to put it off for a year; go abroad, take a cure, have a look round, as you wanted to, for a German tutor for Prince Nikolai; and then if your love or passion or obstinacy – whatever you choose – is still as great, marry! And that's my last word on the subject. Make no mistake, the last!...' concluded the prince, in a tone which showed that nothing would get him to alter his verdict.

Prince Andrei saw clearly that the old man hoped that either his feelings or those of his prospective bride would not stand the test of a year, or else that he (the old prince himself) would die before then, and he decided to conform to his father's wish – to propose, and then postpone the wedding for a year.

Three weeks after his last visit to the Rostovs Prince Andrei returned to Petersburg.

*

On the morrow of her talk with her mother Natasha all day expected Bolkonsky, but he did not come. The next day, and the day after, it was the same. Pierre did not appear either and Natasha, unaware that Prince Andrei had gone away to see his father, did not know how to interpret his absence.

Three weeks passed in this way. Natasha had no desire to go any-where, and wandered from room to room like a ghost, listless and forlorn, weeping in secret at night and not going to her mother in the evenings. She was continually flushing and was very irritable. It seemed to her that everybody knew about her blighted hope, and was laughing at her and pitying her. In spite of all the intensity of her inward grief this wound to her vanity aggravated her misery.

Once she went to her mother, tried to say something and suddenly burst into tears. Her tears were the tears of an offended child who does not know why it is being punished.

The countess tried to comfort Natasha. At first Natasha listened to her mother's words, but all at once interrupted her.

'Stop, mamma! I am not even thinking about it, and I don't want to. He just came and then left off, left off. ...'

Her voice quivered, and she almost cried again but recovered her-self and went on quietly:

'And I don't want to be married at all. And I am afraid of him; I have quite, quite got over it now. ...'

The day after this conversation Natasha put on an old frock, which she knew always made her feel cheerful when she wore it in the mornings, and as soon as she was dressed began to resume her old occupations which she had dropped since the ball. After morning-tea she went to the ballroom, which she particularly liked for its loud resonance, and got to work on her sol-fa exercises. Having sung the first, she stood in the middle of the room and repeated a single musical phrase which pleased her specially. She listened with delight, as though it were new to her, to the charm of the notes ringing out, filling the empty ballroom and dying slowly away; and suddenly her heart felt lighter. 'What's the good of making so much of it? Things are nice as it is,' she said to herself; and she began walking up and down the room, not stepping naturally on the echoing parquet floor, but setting her little heels down first and then her toes (she had on a cherished pair of new slippers), and listening to the rhythmical tap of the heel and creak of the toe with as much pleasure as she had listened to the sounds of her own voice. Passing a looking-glass, she glanced into it. 'There, that's me!' the expression of her face seemed to say as she caught sight of her reflection. 'Well, and very nice too! I don't need anybody.'

A footman wanted to come in to clear away something in the room but she would not let him, and having closed the door behind him continued her promenade. That morning she had returned to her favourite mood of liking and being ecstatic over herself. 'What an enchanting creature that Natasha is!' she said, putting the words into the mouth of some third, generic male person. 'Pretty, a good voice, young, and in nobody's way if only they leave her in peace.' But however much they left her in peace she could not now be at peace, and was immediately aware of it.

In the vestibule the hall-door opened and someone asked: 'Are they at home?' and then footsteps were heard. Natasha was gazing in the looking-glass but she did not see herself. She was listening to the sounds in the hall. When she saw herself, her face was pale. It was *he*. She was sure of it, though she hardly caught his voice through the closed doors.

Pale and agitated, Natasha ran into the drawing-room.

'Mamma, Bolkonsky has come!' she cried. 'Mamma, it is awful, unbearable! I don't want ... to be tortured! What am I to do? ...'

But before the countess could answer, Prince Andrei entered the room with a grave and anxious face, which lit up as soon as he saw Natasha. He kissed the countess's hand and Natasha's, and sat down near the sofa.

'It is a long time since we had the pleasure ...' began the countess, but Prince Andrei interrupted her by answering her implied question, obviously in haste to say what he had on his mind to say.

'I have not been to see you all this time because I went to my father. I had to talk over an exceedingly important matter with him. I only got back last night,' he said, glancing at Natasha. 'I should be very glad if I might have a few words with you, countess,' he added after a moment's pause.

The countess lowered her eyes, sighing heavily.

'I am at your disposal,' she murmured.

Natasha knew that she ought to go away but was unable to do so: something gripped her throat and regardless of manners she stared straight at Prince Andrei with wide-open eyes.

'What at once? This minute? ... No, it can't be!' she was thinking.

He glanced again at her, and that glance convinced her that she was not mistaken. Yes, at once, this very minute, her fate was to be decided.

'Go, Natasha, I will send for you,' said the countess in a whisper.

With frightened, imploring eyes Natasha looked at Prince Andrei and her mother, and went out.

'I have come, countess, to ask for your daughter's hand,' said Prince Andrei.

The countess's face flushed hotly but she said nothing.

'Your offer ...' she began at last, sedately. He waited in silence, looking into her eyes. 'Your offer ...' (she hesitated in confusion) 'is agreeable to us, and ... I accept your offer. I am happy. And my husband ... I hope ... but it must rest with herself. ...'

'I will speak to her as soon as I receive your permission. ... Do you give it me ?' said Prince Andrei.

'Yes,' replied the countess. She held out her hand to him, and with mingled feelings of aloofness and tenderness pressed her lips to his forehead as he bent to kiss her hand. She wanted to love him as a son, but felt that he was a stranger who filled her with alarm.

'I am sure my husband will consent,' said the countess, 'but your father. ...'

'My father, whom I have apprised of my plans, has made an express stipulation that the wedding should not take place for a year. I wanted to tell you that too,' said Prince Andrei.

'True, Natasha is very young, but – that is a long time!'

'There is no alternative,' said Prince Andrei with a sigh.

'I will send her to you,' said the countess, and left the room.

'Lord have mercy upon us!' she murmured over and over again as she went in search of her daughter.

Sonya told her that Natasha was in her bedroom. She was sitting on her bed, pale and dry-eyed, gazing at the icons and whispering something as she rapidly crossed herself. When she saw her mother she jumped up and flew to her.

'Well, mamma ? ... Well ?'

'Go, go to him. He asks for your hand,' said the countess, coldly it seemed to Natasha. 'Go ... go,' murmured the mother mournfully and reproachfully with a deep sigh as her daughter ran off.

Natasha never remembered how she entered the drawing-room. As she opened the door and caught sight of him she stopped short. 'Can it be that this stranger has now become *everything* to me ?' she asked herself, and the reply came in a flash, 'Yes, everything: he alone is now dearer to me than all else in the world.' Prince Andrei approached her with downcast eyes.

'I have loved you from the first moment I saw you. May I hope?'

He looked at her and was struck by the grave impassioned expression of her face. Her face seemed to say: 'Why ask? Why doubt what you cannot help knowing? Why use words when words cannot express what one feels?'

She drew nearer to him and stopped. He took her hand and kissed it.

'Do you love me?'

'Yes, yes!' exclaimed Natasha, with something that seemed almost like vexation, and catching her breath more and more quickly she began to sob.

'What is it? What is the matter?'

'Oh, I am so happy!' she replied, smiling through her tears and, bending over closer to him, she hesitated for an instant, as if asking herself whether she might, and then kissed him.

Prince Andrei held her two hands in his, looked into her eyes and could find no trace in his heart of his former love for her. Some sudden transformation seemed to have taken place in him: the former poetic and mystic charm of desire had given way to pity for her feminine and childish weakness, fear at her devotion and trustfulness, and an oppressive yet sweet sense of duty binding him to her for ever. The present feeling, though not so bright and poetical as the former one, was stronger and more serious.

'Did your mother tell you that it cannot be for a year?' asked Prince Andrei, continuing to gaze into her eyes.

'Can this really be I – this "chit of a girl", as everybody calls me?' Natasha was thinking. 'Is it possible that from this time forth I am to be the *wife*, the equal, of this stranger – this dear, clever man whom even my father looks up to? Can it be true? Can it be true that there can be no more playing with life, that now I am grown up, that now a responsibility lies on me for my every word and action? Oh, what did he ask me?'

'No,' she replied, but she had not understood his question.

'Forgive me,' said Prince Andrei, 'but you are so young, and I have already had so much experience of life. I am afraid for you, you do not yet know yourself.'

Natasha listened with concentrated attention, doing her best but failing to take in the meaning of his words.

'Hard as this year will be for me, delaying my happiness,' continued Prince Andrei, 'it will give you time to be sure of your own heart. I ask you to make me happy at the end of a year, but you are free: our engagement shall remain a secret, and should you discover that you do not love me, or if you should come to love ...' said Prince Andrei with a forced smile.

'Why do you say that?' Natasha interrupted him. 'You know that from the very day you first came to Otradnoe I have loved you,' she cried, quite convinced that she was speaking the truth.

'In a year you will have learned to know yourself. ...'

'A who-ole year!' suddenly exclaimed Natasha, only now realizing that the wedding would have to wait a year. 'But why a year? Why a year? ...'

Prince Andrei began to explain to her the reasons for this delay. Natasha did not hear him.

'And can't it be helped?' she asked. Prince Andrei made no answer but his face expressed the impossibility of altering the decision.

'It's awful! Oh, it's awful, awful!' Natasha cried suddenly, and burst into sobs again. 'I shall die if I have to wait a year: it's impossible, it's awful!' She looked into her lover's face and saw that it was full of commiseration and perplexity.

'No, no! I'll do anything!' she said, immediately checking her tears. 'I am so happy.'

Her father and mother came into the room and gave the betrothed pair their blessing.

From that day Prince Andrei began to frequent the Rostovs' as Natasha's accepted suitor.

24

THERE was no betrothal ceremony and Natasha's engagement to Bolkonsky was not announced: Prince Andrei insisted upon that. He said that since he was responsible for the delay he ought to bear the whole burden of it. He declared that he considered himself irrevocably bound by his word but that he did not want to bind Natasha and would leave her perfectly free. If after six months she felt that she did not love him she would have every right to refuse him.

Naturally neither Natasha nor her parents would hear of this but Prince Andrei insisted. He was at the Rostovs' every day but did not behave with Natasha as though he were engaged to her: he addressed her with a certain formality and kissed only her hand. The day of the proposal saw the beginning of quite different, simple, friendly relations between Prince Andrei and Natasha. It seemed as though they had not known each other till then. Both liked to recall how they had regarded one another when they were *nothing* to each other; now they felt that they were entirely different beings: then they dissembled, now they were natural and sincere. At first the family felt awkward with Prince Andrei; he seemed like a man from another world and it took Natasha a long time to get them used to him, proudly assuring them all that he only appeared to be different but was really just like everybody else, and that she was not afraid of him and no one need be. After a few days they grew accustomed to him and fell back without constraint into their ordinary routine of life, in which he took his part. He could talk rural economy with the count, fashions with the countess and Natasha, and albums and embroidery with Sonya. Sometimes when they were by themselves, or even in his presence, the family would marvel at the way it had all happened, and how the prognostics of it all had been so apparent: Prince Andrei's coming to Otradnoe and their coming to Petersburg, and the resemblance between Natasha and Prince Andrei, which the old nurse had remarked on his first visit, and Nikolai's encounter with Andrei in 1805, and many other portents betokening that it was to be were observed by the family.

That atmosphere of romantic, silent melancholy which always accompanies a betrothed couple pervaded the house. Often they all sat in the same room without uttering a word. Sometimes the others would get up and go away, and the engaged pair, left alone, would remain as silent as before. They rarely spoke of their future life. Prince Andrei avoided it with dread, as well as from conscientious motives. Natasha shared this feeling as she did all his feelings, which she was always divining. Once she began to ask him about his son. Prince Andrei blushed, as he often did now – Natasha particularly liked it in him – and replied that his son would not live with them.

'Why not?' exclaimed Natasha, startled.

'I could not take him away from his grandfather, and besides. ...'

'How I should have loved him!' said Natasha, instantly guessing what was in his mind. 'But I know how it is, you are anxious that there should be no pretext for finding fault with us.'

The old count would sometimes come up, embrace Prince Andrei and ask his advice about Petya's education or Nikolai's advancement in the army. The old countess was apt to sigh as she looked at the lovers; Sonya was always afraid of being in their way, and constantly on the look out for excuses to leave them together, even when they had no desire to be alone. When Prince Andrei talked (he could tell a story very well) Natasha listened with pride; when she spoke, she noticed with fear and joy that he watched her with an intent and scrutinizing look. 'What does he hope to find in me?' she would ask herself in perplexity. 'What are his eyes probing for? Supposing I have not got what he is in search of?' Sometimes she fell into one of the mad, merry moods characteristic of her, and then it was an especial delight to see and hear him laugh. He seldom laughed but when he did he abandoned himself completely to his mirth, and after such laughter she always felt nearer to him. Natasha would have been utterly happy had not the thought of their parting, which was now near at hand, filled her with terror.

On the eve of his departure from Petersburg Prince Andrei brought Pierre with him. Pierre had not been to the Rostovs' once since the ball, and seemed bewildered and embarrassed. He devoted all his attention to the countess. Natasha sat down beside a little chess-table with Sonya, thereby inviting Prince Andrei to join them. He did so.

'You have known Bezuhov a long while, haven't you?' he asked. 'Do you like him?'

'Yes, he's a dear, but quite absurd.'

And she began, as people always did when speaking of Pierre, to tell anecdotes of his absent-mindedness, some of which were even pure invention.

'You know, I have confided our secret to him,' said Prince Andrei. 'I have known him since we were boys. He has a heart of gold. I beg you, Natalie,' Prince Andrei said with sudden seriousness, 'I am going away, and heaven knows what may happen. You may cease to'... all right, I know I am not to say that. Only this, then – whatever happens to you after I am gone. ...'

'What could happen?'

'If any trouble were to come,' pursued Prince Andrei, 'I implore you, Mademoiselle Sophie, if anything should happen, to go to him and no one else for advice and help! He may be the most absent-minded, ludicrous fellow, but he has a heart of gold.'

Neither her father nor her mother, nor Sonya, nor Prince Andrei himself, could have foreseen the effect of the parting on Natasha. Flushed and agitated, she wandered about the house that whole day, dry-eyed, busying herself with all sorts of trifling matters as though not understanding what was before her. She did not cry even when he kissed her hand for the last time. 'Don't go!' was all she said in a tone that made him wonder whether he really ought not to stay and which he remembered long afterwards. When he had gone, she still did not weep; but for several days sat in her room, not crying but taking no interest in anything and only saying from time to time: 'Oh, why did he go?'

But a fortnight after his departure, to the surprise of those around her, she just as suddenly recovered from her mental sickness and became her old self again, only with a change in her moral physiognomy, as a child's face changes after a long illness.

25

IN the twelve months following his son's departure abroad Prince Nikolai Bolkonsky's health and temper became much worse. He grew still more irritable, and it was Princess Maria who generally bore the brunt of his unprovoked outbursts of anger. It seemed as though he did all he could to seek out the vulnerable spots in her nature so as to inflict on her the cruellest wounds possible. Princess Maria had two passions and consequently two joys – her nephew, little Nikolai, and religion; and both were favourite themes for the old prince's attacks and jeers. Whatever was being talked about, he would bring the conversation round to the superstitiousness of old maids, or the petting and spoiling of children. 'You want to make him' (little Nikolai) 'into an old maid like yourself! A fine idea! Prince Andrei needs a son and not an old maid,' he would say. Or, turning to Mademoiselle Bourienne, he would ask her in Princess Maria's presence how she liked our village priests and icons, and make jokes about them.

He was constantly wounding Princess Maria's feelings, but it cost her no effort to forgive him. Could he be to blame where she was concerned? Could her father, who loved her, she knew in spite of it all, be unjust? Besides what is justice? Princess Maria never gave a thought to that proud word 'justice'. All the complex laws of mankind for her were summed up in the one clear and simple law of love and self-sacrifice laid down for us by Him, Who in His love had suffered for all humanity though He was Very God. What mattered to her the justice or injustice of men? All she had to do was to endure and love, and this she did.

In the course of the winter Prince Andrei had come to Bald Hills, had been gay, gentle and more affectionate than Princess Maria had known him for many years. She felt that something had happened to him, but he said nothing to his sister about his love. Before he left he had a long talk with his father, and Princess Maria noticed that they were ill-pleased with each other at parting.

Shortly after Prince Andrei had gone Princess Maria wrote from Bald Hills to her friend in Petersburg, Julie Karagin, whom she had dreamed – as all girls do dream – of marrying to her brother, and who was at that time in mourning for her own brother killed in Turkey.

Sorrow, it seems, is our common lot, my dear, sweet friend Julie.

Your loss is so terrible that I can only explain it to myself as a special providence of God Who, in His love for you, would chasten you and your incomparable mother. Ah, my dear, religion, and religion alone, can – I don't say comfort us – but save us from despair. Religion alone can interpret to us what, without its help, man cannot comprehend: why, for what purpose, kind and noble beings, able to find happiness in life, who have not only never injured a living thing but are indeed necessary to the happiness of others, are called away to God, while the wicked, the useless, or those who are a burden to themselves and other people, are left living. The first death I saw, and which I shall never forget – that of my dear sister-in-law – made just such an impression on me. Just as you ask fate why your splendid brother had to die, so I asked why that angel Lisa should be taken, who not only never wronged any one but never had a thought in her heart that was not kind. And what do you think, dear friend? Five years have passed since then, and already I with my humble intelligence begin to see clearly why she had to die, and in what way her death was but an expression of the infinite goodness of the Creator, Whose every action, though for the most part beyond our comprehension, is but a manifestation of His boundless love for His creature. Perhaps, so I often think, she was too angelically innocent to have the strength to perform all a mother's duties. As a young wife she was irreproachable: possibly she would not have been equally so as a mother. As it is, not only has she left us, and particularly Prince Andrei, with the purest memories and regrets, but in all likelihood there on the other side she will receive a place such as I dare not hope for myself. But, not to speak of her alone, that premature and terrible death has had the most blessed influence on me and on my brother, in spite of all our grief. At the time, at the moment of our loss, I could not have entertained such thoughts: I should have repelled them with horror, but now they are quite clear and incontestable. I write all this to you, dear friend, simply to convince you of the Gospel truth, which has become a principle of life for me: not one hair of our head shall fall without His will. And the one guiding principle of His will is His infinite love for us, and so whatever happens to us is for our good.

You ask if we are going to spend next winter in Moscow. In spite of all my desire to see you, I do not expect and do not wish to do so. And you will be surprised to hear that the reason for this is Bonaparte! I will tell you why: my father's health is noticeably worse – he cannot endure contradiction and is easily irritated. This irritability is, as you are aware, most readily aroused by political affairs. He cannot tolerate the idea that Bonaparte is negotiating on equal terms with all the sovereigns of Europe, and especially with our own, the grandson of the great Catherine! As you know, I am quite indifferent to politics, but from my father and his conversations with Mihail Ivanovich I am not ignorant of all that goes on in the world, and have heard in particular of the honours conferred on Bonaparte. It seems that Bald Hills is now the only spot on the terrestrial globe where he is not accepted as a great man - still less as emperor of France, the idea of which my father cannot stand. It appears to me that it is chiefly on account of his political views that my father feels reluctant to talk of going to Moscow. He foresees the clashes which would result from his habit of expressing his views regardless of anybody. All the benefit he would gain from medical treatment in Moscow would be undone through the inevitable quarrels about Bonaparte. In any case the matter will be decided very shortly.

Our home life continues as usual, except for my brother Andrei's absence. As I wrote to you before, he has greatly changed of late. It is only now, in this last year, that he has quite recovered his spirits after his grief. He has again become the way I remember him as a child: kind, affectionate, with that heart of gold to which I know no equal. He has realized, it seems to me, that life is not over for him. But, on the other hand, his health has deteriorated as his mind has mended: he is thinner and more nervous, and I feel anxious about him.

I am glad he is taking this trip abroad which the doctors recommended long ago. I hope that it will restore his health. You write that he is spoken of in Petersburg as one of the most energetic, cultivated and intelligent young men of the day. Forgive a sister's pride, but I have never doubted it. The good he did here to everyone – from his peasants to the local gentry – is incalculable. When he went to Petersburg he received only his due. I always wonder at the way rumours fly from Petersburg to Moscow, especially such false ones as the report you wrote to me about of my brother's betrothal to the little Rostov girl. I do not believe Andrei will ever marry again, and certainly not her. And this is why: in the first place, I know that though he rarely mentions his late wife he was too deeply afflicted by her loss ever to think of letting another fill her place in his heart, or of giving our little angel a stepmother. Secondly, because, so far as I know, that girl is not the kind of girl who would be likely to attract my brother. I do not think Andrei has chosen her for his wife; and I will frankly confess, I should not wish for such a thing. But I have been running on too long and am at the end of my second sheet. Farewell, dearest friend: God have you in His holy and almighty keeping. My dear companion, Mademoiselle Bourienne, sends you her fond love.

MARIE

26

IN the middle of the summer Princess Maria received an unexpected letter from Prince Andrei, from Switzerland, in which he gave her strange and surprising news. He informed her of his engagement to Natasha Rostov. The whole letter breathed ecstatic love for his betrothed, and tender and confiding affection for his sister. He wrote that he had never loved as he loved now, and that it was only now that he realized and understood the meaning of life. He begged his sister to forgive him for not having told her of his plans on his last visit to Bald Hills, though he had spoken of them to his father. He had not told her because Princess Maria might have tried to persuade their father to give his consent and, without attaining her object, would irritate him and draw all the weight of his displeasure upon herself. Besides, he wrote, the matter was not then so definitely settled as it was now.

At that time Father insisted on a delay of a year, and now *six months*, half of the period, have passed, and my resolution is firmer than ever. If it were not for the doctors keeping me here at the waters I should be back in Russia myself, but as it is I must put off my return for another three months. You know me and my relations with Father. I have need of nothing from him. I have been, and always shall be, independent; but to go against his will and incur his anger, when there may be so short a time left to him to be with us, would destroy half my happiness. I am writing a letter to him now about the same question, and beg you to choose a good moment to hand it to him, and then let me know how he receives it and whether there is any hope of his agreeing to reduce the term by three months.

After long hesitations, doubts and prayers Princess Maria gave the letter to her father. The next day the old prince said to her quietly:

'Write and tell your brother to wait till I am dead. ... It won't be long – I shall soon set him free.'

The princess tried to make some reply but her father would not let her speak, and raising his voice higher and higher went on:

'Marry, let the dear boy marry! ... Nice connexions! ... Clever people, eh? Rich, eh? Oh yes, a fine stepmother she'll make for little Nikolai! Write and tell him he may marry tomorrow if he likes. Nikolushka can have her for a stepmother, and I'll marry the little Bourienne! ... Ha, ha, ha! He mustn't be without a stepmother either! Only there's one thing, I won't have any more women-folk in my house: let him marry and go and live by himself. Perhaps you'd like to go and live with him too?' he added, turning to Princess Maria. 'You're welcome to, in heaven's name! Go – get out of my sight ... out of my sight ...!'

After this outburst the prince did not once refer to the subject again. But simmering chagrin at his son's poor-spirited behaviour found expression in his treatment of his daughter, and a fresh theme for irony was added to the old ones – allusions to stepmothers, and gallantries to Mademoiselle Bourienne.

'Why shouldn't I marry her?' he would say to his daughter. 'She'd make a splendid princess!'

And latterly, to her surprise and bewilderment, Princess Maria began to notice that her father was really associating more and more with the Frenchwoman. She wrote to her brother and told him how the old prince had taken the letter but comforted him with hopes of reconciling their father to the idea.

Little Nikolai and his education, Andrei, and her religion were Princess Maria's joys and consolations; but apart from these, since everyone must have some personal aspirations, Princess Maria cherished in the profoundest depths of her heart a hidden dream and hope that supplied the chief comfort in her life. This hope and consolation came to her through her 'God's folk' – the crazy prophets and pilgrims she continued to receive without her father's knowledge. The longer she lived, the more experience and observation she had of life, the more she wondered at the short-sightedness of men who seek enjoyment and happiness here on earth: toiling, aching, striving and doing evil to one another in their pursuit of that impossible, visionary, sinful happiness. Prince Andrei had loved his wife, she died, but that was not enough: he wanted to commit his happiness to another woman. Her father objected to this because he wanted a more distinguished and wealthier match for Andrei. And they all struggled and suffered and tormented one another, and injured their souls, their immortal souls, for the sake of winning some blessing that was gone in the twinkling of an eye. 'Not only do we know this ourselves, but Christ, the Son of God, came down upon earth and told us that this life is but a flash, a time of probation; yet we cling to it and think to find happiness in it. How is it no one realizes this?' thought Princess Maria. 'No one except these despised "God's folk", who come to me with wallets over their shoulders, climbing the back stairs, afraid of the prince catching them – not because they fear ill-usage at his hands, but to spare him the temptation to sin. To leave family and home, give up all thought of material blessings and, clinging to nothing, wander in hempen rags from place to place under an assumed name, never doing any harm but praying for people – praying alike for those who persecute them and those who shelter – there is no truth and life higher than that truth and life!'

There was one pilgrim, a quiet pock-marked little woman of fifty called Theodosia, who for over thirty years had gone about barefoot and wearing heavy chains. Princess Maria was particularly fond of her. One day when they were sitting together, in the dark except for the dim light of the lamp burning before the icons, and Theodosia was talking of her life, the feeling that Theodosia had found the only true path suddenly came over Princess Maria with such force that she resolved to become a pilgrim herself. After Theodosia had retired to sleep, Princess Maria pondered this for a long while, and at last made up her mind that, strange as it might seem, she must go on a pilgrimage. She confided her intention to no one but the monk who was her confessor, and Father Akinfi approved of her project. Pretending that she was getting presents for pilgrim-women, Princess Maria prepared for herself the complete outfit of a pilgrim: a coarse smock, bast shoes, a rough coat and a black kerchief. Many a time going up to the chest of drawers containing these treasures, Princess Maria would pause irresolute, wondering whether the moment had not arrived to carry out her plan.

Often as she listened to the pilgrims' tales she was so fired by their simple speech, natural to them but to her ears full of the deepest significance, that more than once she was on the point of abandoning everything and running away from home. In imagination she already saw herself with Theodosia, in rags, trudging along the dusty road with her staff and her wallet, going on her pilgrimage, free from envy, from earthly loves or desires, journeying from one shrine to another, and at last reaching that bourne where there is neither sorrow nor sighing, but everlasting joy and bliss.

'I shall stop at a place and pray there, and before I have time to grow used to it, become attached to it, I shall go on – on and on until my legs give way under me and I lie down and die somewhere. and find at last that eternal haven of peace where there is neither sorrow nor sighing ...' thought Princess Maria.

But afterwards at the sight of her father, and still more of little Nikolai, she wavered in her resolve, wept secretly and accused herself of being a sinner who loved her father and her little nephew more than God.

PART FOUR

I

THE Bible legend says that the absence of toil – idleness – was a circumstance of the first man's blessed state before the Fall. Fallen man, too, has retained a love of idleness but the curse still lies heavy on the human race, and not only because we have to earn our bread by the sweat of our brow but because our moral nature is such that we are unable to be idle and at peace. A secret voice warns that for us idleness is a sin. If it were possible for a man to discover a mode of existence in which he could feel that, though idle, he was of use to the world and fulfilling his duty, he would have attained to one facet of primeval bliss. And such a state of obligatory and unimpeachable idleness is enjoyed by a whole section of society – the military class. It is just this compulsory and irreproachable idleness which has always constituted, and will constitute, the chief attraction of military service.

Nikolai Rostov was experiencing this blissful condition to the full as after the year 1807 he continued to serve in the Pavlograd regiment, in command of the squadron that had been Denisov's.

Rostov had grown into a bluff, good-natured fellow, whom his Moscow acquaintances would have considered rather bad form but who was liked and respected by his comrades, subordinates and superiors, and who was well satisfied with his lot. Of late – in the year 1809 – he noticed that in her letters his mother lamented more and more frequently that their affairs were going from bad to worse, suggesting it was high time for him to return home to gladden and comfort his old parents.

Reading these letters, Nikolai felt a pang of dread at their wanting to drag him away from surroundings in which, fenced off from all the entanglements of existence, he was living so quietly and peacefully. He foresaw that sooner or later he would have to plunge back into that whirlpool of life, with its confusions and affairs to be straightened out, its steward's accounts, with its quarrels and intrigues, its ties, with society, with Sonya's love and his promise to her. It was all terribly difficult and complicated; and he replied to his mother in cold, formal letters in French, beginning, 'My dear Mamma' and ending 'Your dutiful son', which said nothing of any intention of coming home. In 1810 he received letters from his parents in which they told him of Natasha's engagement to Bolkonsky, and of the wedding having to wait for a year because the old prince did not approve. This letter vexed and mortified Nikolai. In the first place, he was sorry that Natasha, for whom he cared more than for all the rest of the family, should be lost to the home; and secondly, from his hussar point of view, he regretted not to have been there at the time to show that fellow Bolkonsky that it was by no means such an honour to be connected with him, and that if he loved Natasha he might dispense with his lunatic old father's consent. For a moment he wondered whether to apply for leave so as to see Natasha as an engaged girl, but then came the army manoeuvres, and he thought of Sonya and the difficulties at home, and once more he postponed it. But in the spring of that year he received a letter from his mother, written without his father's knowledge, and that letter decided him. She wrote that if Nikolai did not return and take matters in hand their whole estate would go under the hammer and they would be left destitute. The count was so weak, and trusted Mitenka so much, and was so good-natured, that everybody took advantage of him and things were going from bad to worse. 'For God's sake, I beg of you, come at once, if you don't want to make me and all the family wretched,' wrote the countess.

This letter had its effect on Nikolai. He possessed the common sense of the mediocre man which showed him what he ought to do.

The right thing now was, if not to retire from the service, at any rate to go home on leave. Why he had to go, he could not have said; but following his after-dinner nap he gave orders to saddle Mars, an extremely vicious grey stallion that he had not ridden for a long time, and when he returned with the horse in a lather he informed Lavrushka (Denisov's old servant who had remained with him) and his comrades who dropped in that evening that he was applying for leave and was going home. Difficult and strange as it was for him to reflect that he would go away without having heard from the Staff whether he had been promoted to a captaincy or would receive the order of St Anne for the last manoeuvres (a matter of the greatest interest to him); strange as it was to think that he would go away without having sold his three roans to the Polish Count Goluchowski, who was bargaining for the horses Rostov had wagered he would get two thousand roubles for; inconceivable as it seemed that the ball the hussars were giving in honour of the Polish Mademoiselle Przazdecki (to turn the tables on the Uhlans, who had just entertained their Polish belle, Mademoiselle Borzowski) would take place without him – he knew he must abandon this bright, pleasant existence and go where everything was upside-down and silly. A week later his leave came. His comrades – not only the hussars of his own regiment but the whole brigade – gave him a subscription dinner at fifteen roubles a head, at which there were two bands and two choruses. Rostov danced the *trepak* with Major Basov; tipsy officers tossed him in the air, embraced him and dropped him on the ground; the soldiers of the third squadron tossed him again, and shouted 'Hurrah!' Then they carried him to his sledge and escorted him as far as the first post-station.

For the first half of the journey, from Kremenchug to Kiev, as is always the way, all Rostov's thoughts were behind him, with the squadron; but after he had passed the half-way he began to forget his three roans and Dozhoyveyko, his quartermaster, and to wonder anxiously how things would be at Otradnoe and what he would find there. The nearer he got, the more intense – far more intense – were his thoughts of home (as though moral feelings, like gravity, were subject to the inverse square law). At the last post-station before Otradnoe he gave the driver a three-rouble tip, and ran breathlessly up the steps of his home, like a boy.

After the excitement of the first meeting and the odd feeling of disappointment at the reality falling short of expectation – the feeling that 'everything is just the same, so why was I in such a hurry?' – Nikolai began to settle down in the old world of home. His father and mother were just the same, only a little older. What was new in them was a certain uneasiness and occasional difference of opinion, which there used not to be, and which, as Nikolai soon found out, was due to the wretched state of their affairs. Sonya was now nearly twenty. She would grow no prettier: there was no promise in her of more to come; but she was pretty enough as she was. She exhaled happiness and love from the moment Nikolai returned, and this girl's faithful, steadfast devotion gladdened his heart. Petya and Natasha surprised Nikolai most. Petya was a big, handsome boy of thirteen, merry, mischievous and witty, with a voice that was already beginning to break. As for Natasha, it was a long while before Nikolai could get over his wonder, and he laughed whenever he looked at her.

'You're not the same at all,' he said.

'How? Am I uglier?'

'On the contrary, but what dignity – princess!' he whispered to her.

'Yes, yes, yes,' cried Natasha gleefully.

She told him all about her romance with Prince Andrei, and his visit to Otradnoe, and showed him his last letter.

'Well, are you glad?' Natasha asked. 'I am so at peace and happy now.'

'Very glad,' answered Nikolai. 'He is a splendid fellow. Are you very much in love then?'

'How shall I put it?' replied Natasha. 'I was in love with Boris, with our teacher, with Denisov; but this is quite different. I feel at peace and settled. I know there is not a better man in the world, and so I feel quite quiet and contented. It is not a bit like the other times ...'

Nikolai expressed his dissatisfaction at the marriage being delayed for a year; but Natasha fell on her brother with exasperation, proving to him that no other course was possible, that it would be a horrid thing to enter a family against the father's will, and that she herself wished it so.

'You don't understand in the least,' she kept saying.

Nikolai gave way and said no more.

Her brother often wondered as he looked at her. She did not seem at all like a girl in love and parted from her betrothed. She was even-tempered and serene, and quite as light-hearted as ever. This amazed Nikolai and even made him regard Bolkonsky's courtship rather sceptically. He could not believe that her fate was now sealed, especially as he had not seen her with Prince Andrei. It always seemed to him that there was something not quite right about this proposed marriage.

'Why the delay? Why no betrothal?' he thought. Once, when he started to talk to his mother about his sister, he discovered to his surprise and somewhat to his satisfaction that in the depths of her heart she too had doubts about the marriage.

'Here, you see,' said she, showing her son a letter of Prince Andrei's with that latent feeling of resentment a mother always has towards her daughter's future married happiness, 'he writes that he won't be coming before December. What can be keeping him? Illness, I suppose. His health is very delicate. Don't say anything to Natasha. And don't be surprised that she is so gay: these are the last days of her girlhood, but I know how she is every time she gets a letter from him. However, God grant, all may be well yet!' she concluded, adding as usual, 'He is an excellent man.'

2

At first after his return home Nikolai was grave and even depressed. He was worried by the impending necessity of going into the stupid business matters for which his mother had sent for him. To be rid of this burden as quickly as possible, on the third day after his arrival he marched off, angry and scowling and making no reply to inquiries as to where he was going, to Mitenka's lodge, and demanded an *account in full*. What he meant by an *account in full* Nikolai knew even less than the panic-stricken and bewildered Mitenka. The conversation and the examination of the accounts with Mitenka did not last long. The village elder, a spokesman from the peasants, and the village clerk, who were waiting in the passage, heard with awe and delight first the young count's voice roaring and snapping and getting louder and louder, and then terrible words of abuse following one upon another.

'You robber!... You ungrateful wretch! I'll thrash you like a dog! ... You're not dealing with my father this time!... Stealing everything we've got ...' and so on.

Then, with no less awe and delight, they saw the young count, his face purple with rage, his eyes bloodshot, drag Mitenka out by the scruff of the neck and with great dexterity apply his foot and knee to his rear whenever the pauses between his words gave him a convenient chance, as he shouted: 'Get out of here! Never let me see your face again, you blackguard!'

Mitenka flew headlong down the six steps and ran away into the shrubbery. (This shrubbery was a well-known haven of refuge for delinquents at Otradnoe. Mitenka himself was wont to hide there when he returned tipsy from town, and many of the residents of Otradnoe, anxious to keep out of Mitenka's way, were aware of its protecting powers.)

Mitenka's wife and her sisters, looking terrified, peeped into the passage from the door of their room, where a polished samovar was boiling and the steward's high bedstead stood with its patchwork quilt.

The young count paid no heed to them but, breathing hard, strode by with determined steps and went into the house.

The countess, who heard at once through the maids of what had happened at the lodge, was comforted by the reflection that now their affairs would certainly improve, though on the other hand she was uneasy as to the effect of the scene on her son. She tiptoed several times to his door and listened as he lighted one pipe after another.

Next day the old count drew Nikolai on one side and with a timid smile said to him:

'But you know, my dear boy, you got excited for nothing! Mitenka has told me all about it.'

'Of course,' thought Nikolai. 'I knew I should never make head or tail of anything in this idiotic place.'

'You were angry at his not having entered those seven hundred roubles. But they were carried forward, and you did not look on the other page.'

'Papa, he is a blackguard and a thief, I am sure of it. And what I have done, I have done. Still, if you don't wish it, I won't say any more to him.'

'No, my dear boy' (the count, too, felt embarrassed. He was conscious that he had mismanaged his wife's property and wronged his children, but he did not know how to remedy matters). 'No, I beg of you to take charge of things. I am old, I ...'

'No, papa. Forgive me if I have caused you unpleasantness. I understand less about it than you do.'

'Devil take them all – peasants and money matters, and carrying forward on the next page,' he thought. 'I used to know well enough how to score at cards, but this carrying over to the next page is quite beyond me,' said he to himself, and after that he did not meddle in the management of the family affairs. But once the countess called her son and told him that she had a promissory note from Anna

Mihalovna for two thousand roubles, and asked him what he thought should be done about it.

'This is what I think,' answered Nikolai. 'You say it rests with me. Well, I don't like Anna Mihalovna, and I don't like Boris, but they were our friends and are poor. This is what I should do!' and he tore the note in two, and by so doing caused the old countess to weep tears of joy. After that, the young Rostov took no further part in business of any sort, but devoted himself with passionate interest to what was to him a new pursuit – hunting – for which his father kept a large establishment.

3

WINTRY weather was already setting in; morning frosts hardened the earth saturated by the autumn rains. Already the grass was full of tufts and stood out bright green against the brownish strips of winter rye trodden down by the cattle, and against the pale yellow stubble of the spring sowing and the russet lines of buckwheat. The uplands and copses, which at the end of August had still been green islands amid black fields and stubble, had turned into golden and lurid crimson islands among the green winter corn. The hares had already half changed their summer coats, the fox-cubs were beginning to scatter, and the young wolves were bigger than dogs. It was the best time of the year for hunting. The hounds belonging to that eager young sportsman Rostov were not only in good condition but almost over-trained, so that at a common council of the huntsmen it was decided to give them three days' rest and then, on the 16th of September, to go off on a distant expedition, starting with the oak grove where there was a litter of young wolves.

Such was the position on September the 14th.

All that day the hounds were kept at home. It was frosty and the air was sharp, but towards evening the sky became overcast and it began to thaw. On the 15th, when young Rostov in his dressing-gown looked out of the window, he saw an unsurpassable morning for hunting: the sky seemed to be dissolving and sinking to the earth without a breath of wind. The only movement in the air was the soft downward drift of microscopic beads of drizzling mist. The bare twigs in the garden were hung with transparent drops which dripped down on to the freshly fallen leaves. The earth in the kitchen-garden gleamed wet and black like the heart of a poppy, and within a short distance melted into the damp grey shroud of fog. Nikolai stepped out into the wet and muddy porch. There was a smell of decaying leaves and dogs. Milka, a black-spotted bitch with broad hind-quarters and big prominent black eyes, got up when she saw her master, stretched her hind legs and lay down like a hare; then suddenly jumped up and licked him right on his nose and moustache. Another borzoi, a dog, catching sight of Nikolai from the garden path, arched his back and, rushing headlong to the steps with lifted tail, began rubbing himself against Nikolai's legs.

At the same moment a loud 'O-hoy!' rang through the air – the inimitable halloo of the huntsman, which unites the deepest bass with the shrillest tenor notes; and round the corner came Danilo, whipper-in and head huntsman, a grey, wrinkled old man with hair cut straight over his forehead, Ukrainian fashion, carrying a long bent whip in his hand. On his face was that expression of independence and scorn of everything which is only seen in huntsmen. He doffed his Circassian cap to his master and looked at him witheringly. This scorn was not offensive to Nikolai: he knew that, disdainful and superior as this Danilo seemed to be, he was, nevertheless, his devoted servant and huntsman.

'Oh, Danilo!' Nikolai said, shyly conscious at the sight of this perfect hunting weather, the hounds and the huntsman that he was being carried away by that irresistible passion for the chase which makes a man forget all his previous intentions, as a lover forgets everything in the presence of his mistress.

'What orders, your Excellency?' asked the huntsman in a bass voice deep as an archdeacon's and hoarse from hallooing, and a pair of flashing black eyes gazed from under their brows at the silent young master. 'Surely you can't resist it?' those two eyes seemed to be asking.

'It's a good day, eh? For a hunt and a gallop, eh?' said Nikolai, scratching Milka behind the ears.

Danilo made no reply but winked instead.

'I sent Uvarka out at daybreak to listen,' his bass voice boomed after a minute's pause. 'He says *she's* moved them into the Otradnoe enclosure. They were howling there.' (*She* meant the she-wolf, whom they both knew about, who had moved with her cubs to the Otradnoe copse, a small plantation a mile and a half from the house.)

'We ought to go after them, don't you think?' said Nikolai. 'Come to me and bring Uvarka.'

'Very good, sir.'

'Then put off feeding them.'

'Yes, sir.'

Five minutes later Danilo and Uvarka were standing in Nikolai's big study. Though Danilo was not a tall man, to see him in a room was like seeing a horse or a bear on the floor among the furniture, in domestic surroundings. Danilo felt this himself, and as usual stood just inside the door, trying to speak softly and not move for fear of breaking something in the master's apartment, and saying what he had to say as quickly as possible so as to get out into the open again, under the sky instead of a ceiling.

Having finished his inquiries and extracted from Danilo an opinion that the hounds were fit (Danilo himself was longing to go hunting), Nikolai ordered the horses to be saddled. But just as Danilo was about to go Natasha came hurrying in with swift steps, not yet dressed but wrapped in a big shawl of her old nurse's, and her hair not done. Petya ran in with her.

'You are going?' asked Natasha. 'I knew you would! Sonya said you wouldn't go, but I knew that today is the sort of day when you'd have to.'

'Yes, we are going,' replied Nikolai reluctantly, for he intended to hunt seriously that day and did not want to take Natasha and Petya. 'We are going, but only wolf-hunting: it wouldn't interest you.'

'You know I like that best of all,' said Natasha. 'How mean of him – going himself, and having the horses saddled, with never a word to us.'

'"No obstacles bar a Russian's path!" – we'll go!' shouted Petya.

'But you can't. Mamma said you mustn't,' Nikolai objected to Natasha.

'Yes, I'm coming. I shall certainly come,' said Natasha firmly. 'Danilo, have them saddle for us, and tell Mihail to come with my dogs,' she added, turning to the huntsman.

Danilo had found it irksome and unsuitable to be in a room at all, but to have anything to do with a young lady seemed to him quite impossible. He cast down his eyes and made haste to get away, as though it were no affair of his, and being careful as he went not to inflict any accidental injury on the young lady.

582

4

THE old count, who had always kept up an enormous hunting establishment but had now handed it all over to his son's care, being in excellent spirits on this 15th of September, prepared to join the expedition.

Within an hour the whole party was at the porch. Nikolai, with a stern and serious air betokening that he had no time to waste on trifles, walked past Natasha and Petya who were trying to tell him something. He saw to everything himself, sent a pack of hounds and huntsmen ahead to find the quarry, mounted his chestnut Don horse and, whistling to his own leash of borzois, set off across the threshing-floor to a field leading to the Otradnoe preserve. The old count's horse, a sorrel gelding called Viflyanka, was led by his groom, while the count himself was to drive in a light gig straight to a spot reserved for him.

Fifty-four hounds were led out under the charge of six hunt-attendants and whippers-in. Besides members of the family there were eight borzoi kennel-men and more than forty borzois, so that with the hounds in leashes belonging to the family there were about a hundred and thirty dogs and a score of riders on horseback.

Each dog knew its master and its call. Each man in the hunt knew his business, his place and what he had to do. As soon as they had passed the fence they all spread out evenly and quietly, without noise or talk, along the road and field leading to the Otradnoe covert.

The horses stepped over the field as over a thick carpet, now and then splashing into puddles as they crossed a road. The misty sky still seemed to be falling imperceptibly and steadily down to the earth; the air was still and warm, and there was no sound save for the occasional whistle of a huntsman, the snort of a horse, the crack of a whip, or the whine of a hound that had straggled out of place.

When they had gone about three-quarters of a mile, five more horsemen accompanied by dogs appeared out of the mist, approaching the Rostovs. In front rode a fresh-looking, handsome old man with a large grey moustache.

'Morning, Uncle!' said Nikolai as the old man drew near.

'That's the mark! Come on ... I was sure of it,' began 'Uncle'. (He was a distant relative of the Rostovs' and had a small property near them.) 'I knew you wouldn't be able to resist coming out, and it's a good thing you have. That's the mark! Come on!' (This was 'Uncle's' favourite expression.) 'Take the covert at once, for my Girchik says the Ilagins are out with their hounds at Korniky. That's the mark! Come on, or they'll snatch the litter from under your noses.'

'That's where I'm going. Shall we join forces?' asked Nikolai.

The hounds were united into one pack, and 'Uncle' and Nikolai rode on side by side. Natasha, muffled up in shawls which did not hide her eager face and shining eyes, galloped up to them, followed by Petya, who always kept close to her, and Mihail, a hunt-groom who had been told to look after her. Petya was laughing, and whipping and pulling at his horse. Natasha sat her black Arabchik with ease and confidence, and reined him in effortlessly with a firm hand.

'Uncle' looked round disapprovingly at Petya and Natasha. He did not like any frivolity mixed with the serious business of hunting.

'Good morning, Uncle. We are coming too!' shouted Petya.

'Good morning, good morning! but don't go overriding the hounds,' said 'Uncle' sternly.

'Nikolai darling, what a lovely dog Trunila is. He recognized me,' said Natasha of a favourite hound.

'In the first place Trunila is not a "dog" but a harrier,' thought Nikolai, and looked sternly at his sister, trying to make her feel the distance that ought to separate them at that moment. Natasha understood.

'You mustn't think we'll be in any one's way, Uncle,' she said. 'We'll stay in our places without budging.'

'And a good thing too, little countess,' said 'Uncle'. 'Only mind you don't fall off your horse,' he added, 'or you'll never get on again. That's the mark – come on! You've nothing to hold on to.'

The oasis of the Otradnoe covert came in sight a couple of hundred yards off, and the huntsmen were already nearing it. Rostov, having finally settled with 'Uncle' where they should set on the hounds, and shown Natasha her place – a spot where nothing could possibly run out – went round above the ravine.

'Well, nephew, you're after a big wolf,' said 'Uncle'. 'See she doesn't give you the slip now!'

'That depends,' answered Rostov. 'Karay, here!' he shouted, replying to 'Uncle's' remarks by this call to his borzoi. Karay was a shaggy, ugly, nondescript old dog famous for having tackled a big wolf un-aided. All took their places.

The elder Rostov, knowing his son's ardour in the hunt, hurried so as not to be late, and the huntsmen had hardly taken up their stand before the old count, cheerful, flushed and with quivering cheeks, drove up with his black horses over the winter rye to the position reserved for him where a wolf might come out. Having straightened his coat and fastened on his hunting-knives and horn, he mounted his glossy, well-fed Viflyanka, who was quiet and good-tempered, and as grey as himself. The horses with the trap were sent home. Count Ilya Rostov, though not a keen sportsman at heart, was well acquainted with the rules of the hunt, and rode to the fringe of bushes where he was to stand, arranged his reins, settled himself in the saddle and, feeling that he was ready, looked about him with a smile.

Beside him was his personal attendant, Semeon Tchekmar, a vet-eran horseman now somewhat stiff in the saddle. Tchekmar held in leash three formidable wolf-hounds, though they too had grown fat like their master and his horse. Two wise old dogs lay down un-leashed. Some hundred paces farther along the edge of the wood stood Mitka, the count's other groom, a reckless rider and passion-ate enthusiast. Before the hunt, in accordance with time-honoured custom, the count had drunk a silver goblet of mulled brandy, taken a snack and washed it down with half a bottle of his favourite Bordeaux.

Count Rostov was somewhat flushed with the wine and the drive. His eyes were inclined to be moist and they glittered more than usual. Sitting in the saddle wrapped up in his fur coat, he looked like a child taken out for a drive.

The lean, hollow-cheeked Tchekmar, having attended to every-thing, kept glancing at his master, with whom he had lived on the best of terms for thirty years, and perceiving that he was in good humour he anticipated a pleasant chat. A third person rode circum-spectly out of the wood – he had evidently learned by experience – and stopped behind the count. This individual was a grey-bearded old man in a woman's cloak with a tall peaked cap on his head. It was the buffoon, who went by a woman's name, Nastasya Ivanovna.

'Well, Nastasya Ivanovna,' whispered the count, winking at him, 'just you see what Danilo will do to you if you scare the beast away!'

'I wasn't born yesterday,' said Nastasya Ivanovna.

'Sssh!' hissed the count, and he turned to Tchekmar. 'Have you seen the young countess?' he asked. 'Where is she?'

'With young Count Piotr, behind the high grass yonder by Zharov,' answered Tchekmar, smiling. 'Though she be a lady she be very fond of hunting.'

'And you're surprised at the way she rides, Semeon, eh?' said the count. 'As good as any man!'

'Who wouldn't be? So bold she is, and sits so easy-like!'

'And Nikolai? By the Lyadov uplands, I suppose?' asked the count, still in a whisper.

'Yes, sir. He knows the best places. And there's naught he don't know about riding – times Danilo and me's struck of a heap,' said Tchekmar, knowing what would please his master.

'Rides well, eh? Fine fellow on a horse, eh?'

'A reg'lar picture! How he run that there fox out of the steppe Zavarzino way t'other day! Come flying out of them woods, 'twas a caution! Horse worth thousand roubles but nobody could set no price to the rider. Aye, a man'd need to go a long way to find the likes of him!'

'To find the likes of him ...' repeated the count, evidently sorry that Tchekmar had come to an end with his praises. 'To find the likes of him,' he said, turning back the skirt of his coat to get at his snuff-box.

'T'other day now, when he come out of church in his smart uniform, and Mihail Sidorych ...' Tchekmar broke off: in the still air he had distinctly caught the baying of a hound or two, signifying that the hunt was on. He bent his head and listened, shaking a warning finger at his master. 'They be on the scent of them cubs ...' he whispered, 'making straight to the Lyadov uplands.'

The count, forgetting to smooth out the smile on his face, looked into the distance, along the narrow open space, holding the snuff-box in his hand but not taking a pinch. After the cry of the hounds came the bass note of the hunting-call for a wolf, sounded on Danilo's horn; the pack joined the first three hounds and they could be heard in full cry with that peculiar howl which indicates that they are after a wolf. The whippers-in were no longer halloo-ing the hounds but had changed to the cry of 'Tally-ho!', and above all the others rose Danilo's voice, passing from a deep bass to piercing shrillness. His voice seemed to fill the whole wood, to ring out beyond it and echo far away in the open country.

After listening for a few seconds in silence the count and his groom felt convinced that the hounds had separated into two packs: one, the larger, was going off into the distance, in particularly hot cry; the other pack was flying along by the wood past the count, and it was with this pack that Danilo's voice was heard urging the dogs on. The sounds from both packs mingled and broke apart again, but both were becoming more distant. Tchekmar sighed and stooped down to straighten the leash in which a young borzoi had caught his leg. The count sighed too, and noticing the snuff-box in his hand opened it and took a pinch.

'Back!' cried Tchekmar to a borzoi that was pushing forward out of the wood. The count started and dropped the snuff-box. Nastasya Ivanovna dismounted to pick it up.

The count and Tchekmar were looking at him. Then in a flash, as so often happens, the sound of the hunt was suddenly close at hand, as though the baying hounds and Danilo's 'Tally-ho!' were right upon them.

The count glanced round and on the right saw Mitka staring at him with eyes starting out of his head. Lifting his cap, he pointed in front to the other side.

'Look out!' he shouted in a voice that showed the words had long been on the tip of his tongue, fretting for utterance, and, letting the borzois slip, he galloped towards the count.

The count and Tchekmar galloped out of the bushes, and on their left saw a wolf swinging easily along and with a quiet lope making for an opening a little to the left of the very thicket where they had been standing. The angry borzois whined and, tearing themselves free of the leash, rushed past the horses' hooves after the wolf.

The wolf paused in its course; awkwardly, like a man with a quinsy, it turned its heavy forehead towards the hounds, and still with the same soft, rolling gait gave a couple of bounds and disappeared with a swish of its tail into the bushes. At the same instant, with a cry like a wail, first one hound, then another, and another, sprang out helter-skelter from the wood opposite, and the whole pack flew across the open ground towards the very spot where the wolf had vanished. The hazel bushes parted behind the hounds, and Danilo's chestnut horse appeared, dark with sweat. On its long back sat Danilo, hunched forward, capless, his dishevelled grey hair hanging over his flushed, perspiring face.

'Tally-ho! Tally-ho! ...' he was shouting. When he caught sight of the count his eyes flashed lightning.

'You —!' he roared, threatening the count with his whip. 'You've let the wolf slip! ... Hunters indeed!' and as though scorning to waste more words on the startled, shamefaced count he lashed the heaving flanks of his sweating chestnut gelding with all the fury meant for the count and flew off after the hounds. The count, like a schoolboy that has been chastized, looked round with a smile of appeal to Tchekmar for sympathy in his plight. But Tchekmar was not there: he had galloped round to try to start the wolf again. The field too was coming up on both sides, but the wolf got into the wood before any of the party could head it off.

5

MEANWHILE Nikolai Rostov remained at his post, waiting for the wolf. By the way the hunt approached and receded, by the cries of the dogs whose notes were familiar to him, by the shouts of the whippers-in, advancing and retreating, he could form a good idea of what was happening at the copse. He knew that there were young and old wolves in the enclosure, that the hounds had separated into two packs, that in one place they were close on their quarry, and that something had gone wrong. He expected every second to see the animal come his way. He made a thousand different conjectures as to where and from what side the brute would appear, and how he should attack it. Hope alternated with despair. Several times he addressed a prayer to God that the wolf might come in his direction. He prayed with that sense of passionate anxiety with which men pray at moments of great excitement arising from trivial causes. 'Why not grant me this?' he said to God. 'I know Thou art great and that it's wrong to pray about this; but for God's sake make the old wolf come my way and let Karay spring at it – in front of "Uncle" who is watching from over there – and fix his teeth in its throat and finish it off!' A thousand times during that half-hour Rostov cast eager restless glances over the thickets at the edge of the wood, with the two scraggy oaks rising above the aspen undergrowth and the ravine with its waterworn side and 'Uncle's' cap just visible behind a bush on the right.

'No, no such luck for me,' thought Rostov. 'But wouldn't it be fine! No hope though. I'm always unlucky – at cards, in the war, everywhere.' Memories of Austerlitz and of Dolohov flashed vividly through his imagination, in rapid succession. 'Just once in my life to kill an old wolf: that's all I want!' he thought, straining eyes and ears and looking to left and right and listening to every tiny variation in the cries of the hounds. He looked to the right again and saw something running across the open ground towards him. 'No, it can't be!' thought Rostov, taking a deep breath as a man does at the coming of something long hoped for. The height of happiness was upon him – and so simply, without noise or flourish or display. Rostov could not believe his eyes and for over a second remained in doubt. The wolf ran forward and jumped heavily over a gully that lay across her path. It was an old wolf with a grey back and full reddish belly, running without haste, evidently feeling sure that no one saw her. Rostov held his breath and looked round at the borzois. They were standing and lying about, unaware of the wolf and not realizing the situation. Old Karay had turned his head and was angrily searching for a flea, baring his yellow teeth and snapping at his hind legs.

'Tally-ho!' whispered Rostov, pouting his lips. The borzois leaped up, jerking the iron rings of the leashes and pricking up their ears. Karay finished scratching his hind-quarters and got up, cocking his ears and faintly wagging his tail from which tufts of matted hair hung down.

'Shall I loose 'em or not?' Nikolai asked himself as the wolf moved away from the copse towards him. Suddenly the wolf's whole appearance changed: she shuddered, seeing what she had probably never seen before – human eyes fixed on her, and turning her head a little towards Rostov she paused, in doubt whether to go back or forward. 'Oh, no matter – forward ...' the wolf seemed to say to herself, and she continued on, not looking round, with a quiet, long, easy yet resolute lope.

'Tally-ho!' cried Nikolai in a voice not his own, and, unprompted, his good horse bore him at breakneck pace downhill, leaping over gullies to head off the wolf, and the hounds outstripped them, speeding faster still. Nikolai did not hear his own shout nor was he conscious of galloping. He did not see the borzois, nor the ground over which he was carried: he only saw the wolf who, quickening her pace, bounded on in the same direction along the hollow. The first to get close to her was Milka, the bitch with the black markings and powerful quarters. Nearer, nearer ... now she was level. But the wolf turned a sidelong glance upon her, and Milka, instead of putting on a spurt as she usually did, suddenly raised her tail and stiffened her forelegs.

'Tally-ho! Tally-ho!' shouted Nikolai.

The red hound, Lyubim, darted forward from behind Milka, sprang impetuously at the wolf and seized her by the hind-quarters, but immediately jumped aside in terror. The wolf crouched, gnashed her teeth, rose again and bounded forward, followed at a distance of a couple of feet by all the borzois, who did not try to come any closer.

'She'll get away! No, it's impossible!' thought Nikolai, still shouting in a hoarse voice.

'Karay! Tally-ho!...' he screamed, looking round for the old borzoi who was his only hope now. Karay, straining his old muscles to the utmost and watching the wolf intently, was running heavily alongside the beast to cut her off. But the swift lope of the wolf and the borzoi's slower pace made it plain that Karay had miscalculated. Nikolai could already see the wood not far ahead where the wolf would certainly escape if once she reached it. But in front dogs and a huntsman came into sight bearing almost straight down on the wolf. There was still hope. A long yellowish young borzoi, one Nikolai did not know, from another leash, rushed impetuously at the wolf from in front and almost knocked her over. But the wolf jumped up surprisingly quickly and gnashing her teeth flew at the yellowish borzoi, which with a piercing yelp fell with its head on the ground, bleeding from a gash in its side.

'Karay, old fellow!...' wailed Nikolai.

Thanks to this delay to the progress of the wolf, the old dog with the tufts of matted hair hanging from its haunches had now got within five paces of her. As though aware of her danger the wolf looked out of the corner of her eyes at Karay, tucked her tail yet farther between her legs and increased her speed. But here Nikolai saw that – wonder of wonders! – the borzoi was suddenly on the wolf, and the two had rolled head over heels into a gully just in front of them.

That instant when Nikolai saw the wolf struggling in the gully with the dogs, saw the wolf's grey coat under them, her outstretched hind-leg, her panting, terrified head with ears laid back (Karay was pinning her by the throat), was the happiest moment of his life. He had his hand on the saddle-bow ready to dismount and stab the wolf, when she suddenly thrust her head up from among the mass of dogs, and then her fore-paws were on the edge of the gully. She clicked her teeth (Karay no longer had her by the throat), gave a leap of her hind-legs out of the gully, and, having disengaged herself from the dogs, with tail tucked in again went forward. Karay, with bristling hair, apparently either bruised or wounded, crawled painfully out of the gully.

'Oh my God! Why?' cried Nikolai in despair.

'Uncle's' huntsman was galloping from the other side across the wolf's path, and his borzois stopped the animal's advance again. Again she was hemmed in.

Nikolai, his groom, 'Uncle' and his huntsman were all circling round the wolf, crying 'Tally-ho!', shouting and preparing to dismount whenever the wolf crouched back, and starting forward again every time she shook herself free and moved towards the copse where safety lay.

Right at the beginning of this onset Danilo, hearing the hunters' cries, had darted out from the wood. He saw Karay seize the wolf, and checked his horse, supposing the affair to be over. But, seeing that the horsemen did not dismount and that the wolf had shaken herself free and was making off, Danilo set his chestnut galloping not at the wolf but in a straight line for the copse, in the way Karay had done, to intercept the animal. As a result of this manoeuvre he came up with the wolf just when she had been stopped a second time by 'Uncle's' borzois.

Danilo galloped up silently, holding a drawn dagger in his left hand and thrashing the heaving sides of his chestnut with his riding whip as though it were a flail.

Nikolai neither saw nor heard Danilo until the chestnut, breathing heavily, panted past him, and he heard the sound of a falling body and saw Danilo lying on the wolf's back among the dogs, trying to seize her by the ears. It was obvious to the hounds, to the hunters and to the wolf herself that all was over now. The beast, her ears drawn back in terror, tried to rise but the borzois clung to her. Danilo half rose, stumbled and as though sinking down to rest rolled with his full weight on the wolf, snatching her by the ears. Nikolai was about to stab her but Danilo whispered: 'Don't, we'll string her up!' and shifting his position he put his foot on the wolf's neck. A stake was thrust between her jaws and she was fastened with a leash, as if bridled, her legs were bound together, and Danilo swung her over once or twice from side to side.

With happy, exhausted faces they laid the old wolf, alive, on a horse that shied and snorted in alarm, and, accompanied by the hounds yelping at her, took her to the place where they were all to meet. The hounds had killed two of the cubs and the borzois three. The huntsmen assembled with their booty and their stories, and everyone came to look at the wolf, who with her broad-browed head hanging down and the bitten stick between her jaws, gazed with great glassy eyes at the crowd of dogs and men surrounding her. When they touched her she jerked her bound legs and looked wildly yet simply at them all. Count Ilya Rostov also rode up and touched the wolf.

'Oh, what a formidable brute!' said he. 'An old one, eh?' he asked Danilo, who was standing near.

'That she be,' answered Danilo, hurriedly doffing his cap.

The count remembered the wolf he had let slip, and Danilo's outburst.

'Still, but you're a crusty fellow, my lad!' said the count.

Danilo said nothing but gave him a shy, sweet, childlike smile.

6

THE old count went home. Natasha and Petya promised to follow immediately. The hunting party went farther as it was still early. At midday they put the hounds into a ravine thickly overgrown with young trees. Nikolai, standing on stubble land above, could see all his whippers-in.

Facing Nikolai lay a field of winter rye, and there stood his own huntsman, alone in a hollow behind a hazel bush. The hounds had scarcely been loosed before Nikolai heard one he knew, Voltorn, giving tongue at intervals; other hounds joined in, now pausing and now again giving tongue. A moment later he heard from the ravine the cry that they were on the scent of a fox, and the whole pack rushed off together along the ravine towards the rye-field and away from Nikolai.

He saw the whips in their red caps galloping along the edge of the overgrown ravine. He even saw the hounds, and was expecting a fox to show itself at any moment in the rye-field opposite.

The huntsman standing in the hollow moved and loosed his borzois, and Nikolai caught sight of an odd, short-legged red fox with a fine brush scurrying across the field. The borzois bore down on it. Now they drew close to the fox which began to dodge between the field in sharper and sharper curves, trailing its brush, when suddenly a strange white borzoi dashed in followed by a black one, and all was confusion. The borzois formed a star-shaped figure, their bodies scarcely swaying and their tails all pointing outwards from the centre of the group. A couple of huntsmen galloped to the dogs, one in a red cap, the other, a stranger, in a green coat.

'What is the meaning of that?' wondered Nikolai. 'Where did that huntsman spring from? He's not one of "Uncle's" men.'

The huntsmen despatched the fox and stood on for a long time without strapping it to the saddle. Near by, bridled and with high saddles, were their horses, and the dogs lying down. The huntsmen were waving their arms and doing something to the fox. Presently from the same spot a horn sounded – the signal agreed upon in case of a dispute.

'That's Ilagin's huntsman having a row with our Ivan,' said Nikolai's groom.

Nikolai sent the groom back to fetch his sister and Petya, and rode at a walking pace to where the whips were getting the hounds together. Several of the field galloped to the scene of the squabble.

Nikolai dismounted and, with Natasha and Petya who had ridden up, stood near the hounds, waiting to see how the affair would end. Out of the bushes came the huntsman who had been disputing, and rode towards his young master with the fox tied to his crupper. While still some way off he took off his cap and tried as he came up to speak respectfully, but he was pale and out of breath, and his face was distorted with rage. One of his eyes was black, but of this he did not seem to be aware.

'What was the matter over there?' asked Nikolai.

'Why, he was going to kill the fox our hounds had hunted! And my bitch it was – the mouse-coloured one – that nipped her. Go and have me up for it! Snatching hold of the fox! I gave him one with the fox. Here she is on my saddle. Is it a taste of this you want?' said the huntsman, pointing to his hunting-knife and apparently imagining that he was still talking to his enemy.

Nikolai did not waste words on the man but, asking his sister and Petya to wait for him, rode over to where the rival hunt of the Ilagins was collected.

The victorious huntsman joined his fellows, and there, the centre of a sympathetic and inquisitive crowd, recounted his exploits.

The facts were that Ilagin, with whom the Rostovs had some quarrel and were at law, hunted over places that by custom belonged to the Rostovs, and on this occasion had, it would seem purposely, sent his party to the very 'island' the Rostovs were hunting, and had allowed his man to snatch a fox their hounds had put up.

Though he had never seen Ilagin, Nikolai, who knew no moderation in his opinions and feelings, accepted certain reports of violent and arbitrary behaviour on the part of this country squire, cordially detested him and considered him his bitterest foe. So now, excited and angry, he rode up to him, clenching his fist round his whip and fully prepared to take the most energetic and desperate measures to punish his enemy.

He had hardly passed an angle of the wood before his eyes fell on a stout gentleman in a beaver cap, riding towards him on a handsome raven-black horse, accompanied by two hunt-servants.

Instead of an opponent, Nikolai discovered in Ilagin a courteous gentleman of stately appearance, who was particularly anxious to make the young count's acquaintance. Ilagin raised his beaver cap as he approached Rostov, and said that he greatly regretted what had occurred and would have the man punished for daring to seize a fox hunted by someone else's borzois. He hoped to become better acquainted with the count and invited him to draw his covert.

Natasha, apprehensive that her brother might do something dreadful, had followed him in some excitement. Seeing the enemies exchanging friendly greetings, she rode up to them. Ilagin lifted his beaver cap still higher to Natasha, and with a pleasant smile declared that the countess was indeed a Diana both in her passion for the chase and her beauty, of which he had heard much.

To expiate his huntsman's crime Ilagin pressed Rostov to come to an upland of his about three-quarters of a mile away which he usually kept for himself and which, he said, was teeming with hares. Nikolai consented, and the hunt, its numbers now doubled, moved on.

The way to Ilagin's upland lay across country. The hunt-servants fell into line. The masters rode together. 'Uncle', Rostov and Ilagin kept stealing furtive glances at each other's hounds, trying not to be observed by their companions and searching anxiously for possible rivals to their own borzois. Rostov was particularly impressed by the beauty of a small thoroughbred, slender, black-and-tan bitch of Ilagin's, with muscles like steel, a delicate muzzle and prominent black eyes. He had heard of the sporting qualities of Ilagin's borzois, and in that beautiful bitch he saw a rival to his own Milka.

In the middle of a sedate conversation begun by Ilagin about the year's harvest Nikolai pointed to the black-and-tan bitch.

'A fine little bitch you have there!' he said in a careless tone. 'Full of go, is she?'

'That one? Yes, she's a good dog, gets what she's after,' answered Ilagin indifferently of his black-and-tan Yerza, for which the year before he had given a neighbour three families of house-serfs. 'So in your parts, too, count, the harvest is nothing to boast of?' he went on, continuing their previous conversation. And feeling it only polite to return the young count's compliment Ilagin scanned his borzois and picked out Milka, whose broad back caught his eye.

'Your black-spotted there's all right – a useful animal!' said he.

'Yes, she's fast enough,' replied Nikolai. ('Oh, if only a good big hare would cross the field now, I'd soon show you what sort of a borzoi she is!' he thought.) And turning to his groom he said he would give a rouble to anyone who unearthed a hare.

'I don't understand,' Ilagin went on, 'how it is some sportsmen can be so jealous about each other's game and packs. For myself, I can tell you, count, I enjoy the whole thing – riding, pleasant company – such as I have lighted on today, for instance ... what could be more delightful?' (He doffed his beaver cap to Natasha again.) 'But as for reckoning up pelts – I'm not interested in that.'

'Oh no!'

'Or being upset because someone else's borzoi and not mine gets on the scent first. All I care about is the chase itself, is it not so, count? Besides, I consider ...'

A prolonged halloo from one of the beaters interrupted him. The man was standing on a knoll in the stubble, holding his whip aloft, and now he repeated the long-drawn cry. (This call and the uplifted whip meant that he saw a sitting hare.)

'On the scent, I fancy,' said Ilagin carelessly. 'Well, let us course it, count!'

'Yes, we must ride up. ... Shall we go together?' answered Nikolai, looking intently at Yerza and 'Uncle's' red Rugay, the two rivals against which he had never as yet had a chance of pitting his own borzois. 'What if they outdo my Milka from the first!' he thought, as he rode with 'Uncle' and Ilagin towards the hare.

'A full-grown fellow, is it?' asked Ilagin, moving up to the beater who had sighted the hare – and not altogether indifferently he looked round and whistled to Yerza. 'What about you, Mihail Nikanorovich?' he said, addressing 'Uncle'.

The latter was riding with a sullen expression on his face.

'What's the use of my joining in? Why, you've given a village for each of your borzois. That's the mark – come on! They're worth thousands. No, I'll look on while you two compete against each other.'

'Rugay, hey, hey!' he shouted. 'Rugay, good dog!' he added, thus involuntarily expressing his affection and the hopes he placed on the red borzoi. Natasha could see and feel the anxious excitement which these two elderly men and her brother were trying to conceal, and was herself infected by it.

The huntsman on the hillock still stood with upraised whip and the gentry rode up to him at a walking pace. The hounds moving on the rim of the horizon turned away from the hare, and the whips, but not the gentlefolk, also moved off. Everything was done slowly and deliberately.

'Which way is it pointing?' asked Nikolai, after riding a hundred paces towards the whip who had sighted the hare.

But before the whip could reply the hare, scenting the frost coming next morning, could not stay still: he leapt up and was off. The pack on leash flew downhill in full cry after the quarry, and from all sides the borzois who were not tied rushed after the hounds and the hare. All the hunt, who had been advancing so unhurriedly, galloped across the field, getting the hounds together with cries of 'Stop!', while the whips directed their course with shouts of 'A-too!' The staid Ilagin, Nikolai, Natasha and 'Uncle' flew along, reckless of where or how they went, seeing nothing but the borzois and the hare, and fearing only lest they should for a single instant lose sight of the chase. The hare they had started turned out to be strong and swift. When he jumped up he did not immediately race off but pricked his ears, listening to the shouting and trampling that resounded from all sides at once. He made a dozen bounds, in no great haste, letting the borzois gain on him, and finally, having chosen his direction and realizing his danger, laid back his ears and was off like the wind. He had been lying in the stubble, but in front of him was the autumn-sowing where the ground was soft. The two hounds belonging to the huntsman who had sighted him, being the nearest, were the first to be on the scent and lay for him, but they had not gone far before Ilagin's black-and-tan Yerza passed them, got within a length, sprang upon the hare with frightful swiftness, aiming at his scut, and rolled over, thinking she had hold of him. The hare arched his back and bounded off more nimbly than ever. From behind Yerza rushed the broad-beamed, black-spotted Milka, and began rapidly gaining on the hare.

'Milka good dog, oh good dog!' rose Nikolai's triumphant cry. Milka looked as though she were just going to pounce on the hare, but her impetus carried her too far and she flew beyond, the hare having stopped short. Again the graceful Yerza came to the fore and paused close to the hare's scut as if measuring the distance so as not to make a mistake this time but seize him by the hind-leg.

'Yerza, my beauty!' urged Ilagin pathetically in a voice unlike his own. Yerza did not fulfil his hopes. At the very moment when she should have seized her prey, the hare swerved and darted along the ridge between the winter rye and the stubble. Again Yerza and Milka, running side by side like a pair of carriage horses, began to gain on their quarry, but it was easier for the hare to run on the ridge and the borzois did not overtake him so quickly.

'Rugay, come on, old man! That's the mark, come on!' another voice shouted this time, and 'Uncle's' thick-shouldered red borzoi, stretching out and curving his back, caught up with the two fore-most borzois, pushed ahead of them, put on speed with dreadful self-abandonment when close to the hare, knocked it off the ridge into the rye-field, again put on speed still more viciously, sinking half-way to his shoulders in the muddy field, until all that could be seen was the dog rolling over and over with the hare, the mud sticking to his back in large patches. The hounds formed a star-shaped figure round them. A moment later the whole party had drawn up round the crowding dogs. Only the radiantly happy 'Uncle' dismounted and cut off a pad, shaking the hare for the blood to drip off, and looking round excitedly with wandering eyes, unable to keep his feet and hands still. He kept speaking, not knowing what he said or whom he addressed. 'That's something like – come on! There's a dog for you. ... Outdid them all, whether they cost a thousand roubles or one! That's the mark, come on!' said he, panting and looking furiously about him as if he were berating someone, and as if they were all his enemies, who had insulted him, and he had only now at last succeeded in clearing himself. 'So much for your thousand-rouble animals – that's the mark, come on! Here, Rugay, here's a pad for you!' he cried, throwing down the hare's muddy pad, which he had just hacked off. 'You've earned it – that's the mark, come on!'

'She was all in – she ran it down three times all by herself,' Nikolai was saying, also not listening to anyone and regardless of whether he was heard or not.

'Cutting in sideways like that!' said Ilagin's groom.

'Once she had overshot and got it down any mongrel could catch it,' Ilagin was saying at the same moment, flushed and breathless from his gallop and the excitement. At the same time Natasha, without drawing breath, gave vent to her delight in a shriek so ecstatic and shrill that it set everyone's ears tingling. By that shriek she expressed what the others were expressing by all talking at once, and it was so strange that she must herself have been ashamed of so wild a cry, and the others would have been amazed at it at any other time. 'Uncle' himself twisted up the hare, hitched it neatly and smartly across his horse's back, as if by that gesture he would rebuke them all, and, with an air of not wishing to speak to anyone, mounted his bay and rode off. The others all followed, dispirited and outraged, and only much later were they able to recover their previous affectation of indifference. For a long time they continued to stare after the red dog, Rugay, who with his round back spattered with mud, rattling his chain, trotted along behind 'Uncle's' horse with the serene air of a conqueror. He looked to Nikolai as though he were saying:

'As you see, I'm like any other dog until it's a question of coursing a hare. But when there is work to be done, you had better look out!'

When, some while later, 'Uncle' rode up to Nikolai and addressed a remark to him, Nikolai felt flattered that, after what had happened, 'Uncle' was condescending enough to talk to him.

7

It was towards evening when Ilagin took leave of Nikolai, who found himself so far from home that he was glad to accept 'Uncle's' offer that the hunting-party should spend the night in his little village of Mihailovko.

'And suppose you put up at my place – that's the mark, come on!' said 'Uncle'. 'That would be better still. You see, the weather's wet. You could get a rest, and the little countess could be driven back in a trap.'

'Uncle's' invitation was accepted. A huntsman was sent to Otradnoe for a trap, while Nikolai rode with Natasha and Petya to 'Uncle's' house.

Four or five men-servants, big and little, rushed out to the front porch to meet their master. A score of women serfs, of every age and size, popped their heads out from the back entrance to have a look at the approaching cavalcade. The appearance of Natasha – a woman, a lady on horseback – aroused their curiosity to such a pitch that many of them came up and, unabashed by her presence, stared her in the face, making remarks as though she were some prodigy on show and not a human being who could hear and understand what was said about her.

'Arinka, look now, she sits sideways! Sitting on one side, while her skirt dangles. … And, see, she's got a little hunting-horn!'

'My goodness! And a knife too. …'

'A regular Tartar, isn't she!'

'How is it you don't tumble off head over heels?' asked the boldest of them, addressing Natasha directly.

'Uncle' dismounted at the porch of his little wooden house, which was buried in the middle of an overgrown garden, and after a glance at his retainers shouted peremptorily to those who were not wanted that they should take themselves off and that the others should see to the comfort and entertainment of the guests and the hunting-train.

The serfs ran off in different directions. 'Uncle' lifted Natasha from her horse and giving her his hand led her up the rickety wooden steps of the porch. Indoors, the house with its bare unplastered timber walls was not over-clean – there was nothing to show that the occupants were concerned to keep it spotless – but neither was it noticeably neglected. A smell of fresh apples pervaded the entrance, and the walls were hung with the skins of wolves and foxes.

'Uncle' conducted his guests through the vestibule into a small hall with a folding table and red chairs, then into the drawing-room with a round birch-wood table and a sofa, and finally into his study, where there was a tattered couch, a threadbare carpet, and portraits of Suvorov, of the host's father and mother, and of himself in military uniform. The study smelt strongly of tobacco and dogs.

'Uncle', after begging his visitors to be seated and make themselves at home, left them. Rugay, his back still covered with mud, came into the room and lay on the sofa, cleaning himself with his tongue and teeth. Leading from the study was a passage in which a partition with ragged curtains could be seen. From behind the screen came the sound of women laughing and whispering. Natasha, Nikolai and Petya took off their wraps and sat down on the sofa. Petya leaned on his elbow and was instantly asleep. Natasha and Nikolai sat without speaking. Their faces were burning, they were very hungry and in high good humour. They looked at one another – now that the hunt was over and they were indoors, Nikolai no longer considered it necessary to display his masculine superiority over his sister – Natasha winked at her brother, and neither of them could refrain for long from bursting into a ringing peal of laughter even before they had any pretext ready to account for it.

After a brief interval 'Uncle' came in wearing a Cossack coat, blue trousers and short top-boots. And Natasha felt that this very costume – which she had regarded with surprise and amusement when 'Uncle' wore it at Otradnoe – was just the right thing and in no respect inferior to a swallow-tail or frock-coat. 'Uncle' too was in the best of spirits and, far from taking offence at the brother's and sister's merriment (it could never enter his head that they might be laughing at his mode of life), he joined in their inconsequent mirth himself.

'Well, this young countess here – that's the mark, come on! – I never saw anyone like her!' said he, offering Nikolai a pipe with a long stem while with a practised motion of three fingers he filled another – a short broken one – for himself. 'She's been in the saddle the whole day, just like a man, and is still fresh as a daisy!'

Shortly after 'Uncle's' reappearance the door was opened – judging from the sound by a barefooted servant-girl – and a stout, rosy-cheeked, handsome woman of about forty, with a double chin and full red lips, entered carrying a huge loaded tray. She looked round at the visitors, her eyes and every movement expressing a dignified cordial welcome, and with a genial smile dropped them a respectful curtsey. In spite of her exceptional stoutness which obliged her to hold her head flung back while her bosom and stomach were thrust forward, this woman (who was 'Uncle's' housekeeper) stepped about with amazing agility. She went to the table, set down the tray and with her plump white hands deftly took and arranged the bottles and various hors-d'œuvre and other dishes. When she had finished, she moved back to the door and stood there with a smile on her face. 'Look at me! Now do you understand your little "Uncle"?' was what her bearing seemed to Rostov to imply. And how could one help understanding? Not only Nikolai but even Natasha realized the meaning of his furrowed brow, and the happy complacent smile which slightly curved his lips when Anisya Fiodorovna came into the room. On the tray were a bottle of herb-brandy, different kinds of vodka, pickled mushrooms, rye-cakes made with buttermilk, honey in the comb, still mead and sparkling mead, apples, plain nuts and roasted nuts, and nuts in honey. Later Anisya Fiodorovna brought in preserves made with honey and with sugar, a ham and a fowl that had just been roasted to a turn.

All this was the work of Anisya Fiodorovna's own hands, selected and prepared by her, and redolent of Anisya Fiodorovna herself, having a savour of juiciness, cleanliness, whiteness and pleasant smiles.

'Try a taste of this, my little lady-countess!' she kept saying, offering Natasha first one thing and then another.

Natasha ate of everything, and it seemed to her she had never seen or tasted such buttermilk-cakes, such delicious preserves, such nuts in honey, or such a chicken. Anisya Fiodorovna withdrew. After supper, over their cherry brandy, Rostov and 'Uncle' talked of hunts past and to come, of Rugay and Ilagin's dogs, while Natasha sat upright on the sofa, listening with sparkling eyes. She made several attempts to rouse Petya to eat something, but he only muttered incoherent words without waking. Natasha felt so gay and happy in these novel surroundings that her only fear was lest the trap should come for her too soon. After one of those fortuitous silences that are almost inevitable when one is entertaining acquaintances for the first time in one's own house, 'Uncle', responding to a thought that was in his visitors' minds, said:

'Yes, so you see how I am finishing my days. ... Death has to come.

Yes, that's the mark all right – you can't take anything with you. So where's the sense in being prudish?'

'Uncle' looked impressive and even handsome as he said this, and Rostov found himself remembering how highly his father and the neighbours always spoke of the old man. Throughout the whole province 'Uncle' had the reputation of being the most noble-hearted and unself-seeking of eccentrics. He was called in to arbitrate in family quarrels, he was chosen as executor. Secrets were confided to him; he was elected to be a justice and to fill other offices; but he always persistently refused all public appointments, spending the autumn and spring in the fields on his bay gelding, sitting at home in the winter, and lounging in his overgrown garden during the summer.

'Why don't you enter the service, Uncle?'

'I did once but gave it up. I'm not suited for it – that's the mark, come on! – I can't make head or tail of it. That's a matter for you – I haven't brains enough. But hunting is quite another thing – that's the mark, come on! Open that door there!' he shouted. 'What did you shut it for?'

The door at the end of the corridor (which word 'Uncle' always pronounced 'collidor') led to the huntsmen's room, as the sitting-room for the hunt-servants was called. There was a rapid patter of bare feet, and an invisible hand opened the door into the huntsmen's room. From the passage came the clear sounds of a balalaika being played by someone who was unmistakably a master. Natasha had been listening to the music for some time and now went out into the corridor to hear better.

'That's Mitka, my coachman. … I bought him a good balalaika, I'm fond of it,' said 'Uncle'.

It was the custom for Mitka to play the balalaika in the men's room when 'Uncle' returned from the chase. 'Uncle' liked that kind of music.

'How well he plays! It's really very nice,' said Nikolai with a certain unconscious superciliousness in his tone, as though he were ashamed to admit that the sounds pleased him very much.

'Very nice?' Natasha said reproachfully, noticing her brother's tone. 'Nice isn't the word – why it's absolutely lovely!'

Just as 'Uncle's' pickled mushrooms, honey and cherry-brandy had seemed to her the best in the world, so also did this tune at this moment strike her as the very perfection of musical delight.

'Go on playing, please, go on,' cried Natasha at the door as soon as the balalaika ceased. Mitka tuned up and began twanging away again at *My Lady*, with trills and variations. 'Uncle' sat listening with his head on one side, a faint smile on his lips. The refrain repeated itself again and again. The instrument had to be retuned more than once, after which the player would thrum the same air again, yet the listeners never wearied and their only desire was for ever the same tune. Anisya Fiodorovna came in and leaned her portly person against the doorpost.

'Listen to him now,' she said to Natasha, with a smile extraordinarily like 'Uncle's'. 'That's a good player of ours,' she added.

'He doesn't get that bit right,' exclaimed 'Uncle' suddenly, with a vigorous gesture. 'It ought to come spilling out – that's the mark, come on! – he ought to spill it out.'

'Can you play then?' asked Natasha.

'Uncle' smiled and did not answer.

'Anisya, go and see if the strings of my guitar are all right. It's a long while since I last touched it. That's the mark, come on! I'd quite given it up.'

Anisya Fiodorovna readily went off with her light step to do her master's bidding, and brought back the guitar.

Without looking at anyone 'Uncle' blew the dust off it, tapped the case with his bony fingers, tuned up and settled himself in his armchair. He grasped the guitar a little above the finger-board, with a somewhat theatrical gesture arching his left elbow, and, winking at Anisya Fiodorovna, struck a single chord, pure and sonorous. Then quietly, smoothly and confidently he began playing in very slow time not *My Lady* but the well-known air *Came a maiden down the street*. The hearts of Nikolai and Natasha thrilled in rhythm with the steady beat, thrilled with the sober gaiety of the song – the same sober gaiety which radiated from Anisya Fiodorovna's whole being. Anisya Fiodorovna flushed, and drawing her kerchief over her face went laughing out of the room. 'Uncle' continued to play correctly, carefully, energetically, while he gazed, transfigured and inspired, at the spot where Anisya Fiodorovna had stood. A faint smile lurked at one corner of his mouth, under the grey moustache, and grew broader as the song developed, as the rhythm quickened and a string almost snapped under the flourish of his fingers.

'Lovely, lovely! Go on, Uncle, go on!' cried Natasha as soon as he came to a stop. Jumping up from her place she hugged and kissed him. 'Oh, Nikolai, Nikolai!' she said, turning to her brother as though words failed her to describe the wonder of it all.

Nikolai too was greatly delighted with the performance, and 'Uncle' had to play the piece over again. Anisya Fiodorovna's smiling face reappeared in the doorway and behind her other faces. ...

At the crystal-flowing fountain
A maiden cries 'Oh stay!'

played 'Uncle' once more, running his fingers skilfully over the strings, and broke off with a shrug of his shoulders.

'Go on, Uncle *dear*,' wailed Natasha imploringly, as if her life depended on it.

'Uncle' rose, and it was as though there were two men in him, one of whom smiled a grave smile at the merry fellow, while the merry fellow struck a naïve, formal pose preparatory to a folk-dance.

'Now then, niece!' he exclaimed, waving to Natasha the hand that had just struck a chord.

Natasha flung off the shawl that had been wrapped round her, ran forward facing 'Uncle', and setting her arms akimbo made a motion with her shoulders and waited.

Where, how and when could this young countess, who had had a French *émigrée* for governess, have imbibed from the Russian air she breathed the spirit of that dance? Where had she picked up that manner which the *pas de châle*, one might have supposed, would have effaced long ago? But the spirit and the movements were the very ones – inimitable, unteachable, Russian – which 'Uncle' had expected of her. The moment she sprang to her feet and gaily smiled a confident, triumphant, knowing smile, the first tremor of fear which had seized Nikolai and the others – fear that she might not dance it well – passed, and they were already admiring her.

Her performance was so perfect, so absolutely perfect, that Anisya Fiodorovna, who had at once handed her the kerchief she needed for the dance, had tears in her eyes, though she laughed as she watched the slender, graceful countess, reared in silks and velvets, in another world than hers, who was yet able to understand all that was in Anisya and in Anisya's father and mother and aunt, and in every Russian man and woman.

'Well done, little countess – that's the mark, come on!' cried

'Uncle' with a gleeful laugh when the dance was over. 'Well done, niece! Now all we need is to pick you a handsome young husband—that's the mark, come on!'

'He's chosen already,' said Nikolai, smiling.

'Oho?' said 'Uncle' in surprise, looking inquiringly at Natasha, who nodded her head with a happy smile.

'And he's such a fine one,' she said. But as soon as the words were out a new train of thoughts and feelings arose in her. 'What did Nikolai's smile mean when he said "He's chosen already"? Is he glad or sorry? He seems to be thinking that my Andrei would not approve of or understand this jolly evening we're having. But he would understand it every bit. Where is he now, I wonder?' she thought, and her face suddenly grew serious. But this lasted only a second. 'Don't think about it – don't you dare think about it,' she told herself, and smilingly sat down again beside 'Uncle', begging him to play some more.

'Uncle' played another song and a valse; then after a pause he cleared his throat and struck up his favourite hunting song:

As the evening sun sank low
Fell the soft and lovely snow ...

'Uncle' sang as the peasant sings, with the full and naïve conviction that the whole meaning of a song lies in the words, and that the tune comes as a matter of course and exists only to emphasize the words. This gave the unconsidered tune a peculiar charm, like the song of a bird. Natasha was in raptures over 'Uncle's' singing. She determined to give up her harp lessons and play only the guitar. She asked 'Uncle' for his guitar and at once picked out the chords of the song.

Towards ten o'clock a carriage arrived to fetch Natasha and Petya, with a droshky and three men on horseback, who had been sent to look for them. The count and countess did not know what had become of them, and were in a great state of agitation, so one of the men said.

Petya was carried out like a log and deposited in the carriage, still sound asleep. Natasha and Nikolai got into the trap. 'Uncle' wrapped Natasha up warmly, and said good-bye to her with quite a new tenderness. He accompanied them on foot as far as the bridge – which they had to ride round, fording the river lower down – and sent huntsmen to ride in front with lanterns.

'Good-bye, my dear niece,' his voice called out of the darkness –

not the voice Natasha had known hitherto but the one that had sung *As the evening sun sank low*.

There were red lights in the village through which they drove, and a cheerful smell of smoke.

'What a darling "Uncle" is!' said Natasha, when they had come out on to the high road.

'Yes,' agreed Nikolai. 'You're not cold?'

'No, I'm quite all right, quite. I feel so happy!' answered Natasha, puzzled even by her sense of well-being. They were silent for a long while.

The night was dark and damp. They could not see the horses: they could only hear them splashing through the unseen mud.

What was passing in that receptive childlike soul that so eagerly caught and assimilated all the diverse impressions of life? How did they all find place in her? But she was very happy. As they were nearing home she suddenly hummed the air of *As the evening sun sank low* – the tune of which she had been trying to recapture all the way and had at last succeeded in remembering.

'Got it?' said Nikolai.

'What were you thinking about just now, Nikolai?' inquired Natasha.

They were fond of asking one another that question.

'I?' said Nikolai, trying to recollect, 'Let me see – at first I was thinking that Rugay, the red hound, was like "Uncle", and that if he were a man he would keep "Uncle" about him all the time, if not for hunting then for his harmony. What a peaceful being "Uncle" is! Don't you think so? Well, and what about you?'

'I? Wait a minute now. Yes, first I thought that here we are driving along and imagining that we are going home, but that heaven knows where we are really going in the darkness, and that all of a sudden we shall arrive and find we are not at Otradnoe but in fairyland. And then I thought ... no, that was all.'

'I know, I expect you thought about *him*,' said Nikolai, smiling, as Natasha could tell by his voice.

'No,' replied Natasha, though she certainly had been thinking about Prince Andrei at the same time, and how he would have liked 'Uncle'. 'And then I was saying to myself all the way, "How well Anisya carried herself – how beautifully she walked!"' And Nikolai heard her spontaneous, ringing, happy laugh. 'And do you know,' she suddenly added, 'I am sure I shall never again be as happy and at peace as I am now.'

'What rubbish – what silly nonsense!' exclaimed Nikolai, and he thought: 'What a darling this Natasha of mine is! I shall never find another friend like her. Why should she marry? I could drive like this with her for ever!'

'What a darling my Nikolai is!' Natasha was thinking.

'Ah, there's a light in the drawing-room still,' she said, pointing to the windows of the house which gleamed invitingly in the wet, velvety darkness of the night.

8

COUNT ILYA ROSTOV had resigned the office of Marshal of the Nobility because the position involved him in too much expense, but still his affairs showed no improvement. Natasha and Nikolai often found their parents engaged in anxious consultation, talking in low tones of selling the sumptuous ancestral Rostov house and estate near Moscow. Now that the count was no longer Marshal of the Nobility it was not necessary for them to entertain so extensively, and life at Otradnoe was quieter than in former years; but still the enormous house and the 'wings' were full of people, and more than twenty sat down to table every day. These were all dependants who had domiciled themselves almost like members of the family, or persons who were obliged, it seemed, to live in the count's house. Such were Dimmler, the musician, and his wife; Vogel, the dancing-master, with his family; an elderly maiden lady, Mademoiselle Byelov, who had her home there; and many others besides – Petya's tutors, the girls' former governess, and various people who simply found it preferable or more to their advantage to live at the count's than at home. There were not quite so many visitors as before, but the scale of living remained unchanged, for the count and countess could not conceive of any other. The hunting establishment was still there – indeed, Nikolai had even added to it – with fifty horses and fifteen grooms in the stables. Costly presents were still given on name-days, with formal dinner-parties to which the whole neighbourhood was invited. The count still played whist and boston, holding his cards spread out so that everyone could see them and thus allowing himself to be plundered of hundreds of roubles every day by neighbours, who looked upon the privilege of making up a rubber with Count Rostov as a most profitable source of income.

The count moved about in his affairs as though walking in a huge net, striving not to believe that he was entangled but becoming more involved at every step, aware that he had neither the strength to tear through the meshes that snared him, nor the patience and care required to set about unravelling them. The countess's loving heart told her that her children were being ruined, but she felt the count was not to blame, for he could not help being what he was, and that he was distressed himself (though he tried to hide it) by his knowledge of the disasters facing him and his family; and she tried to find means of remedying the position. Her feminine mind could see only one solution – for Nikolai to marry a rich heiress. She felt this to be their last hope, and that if Nikolai were to refuse the match she had found for him she would have to say good-bye to all idea of restoring their fortunes. The match she envisaged was Julie Karagin, the daughter of worthy, excellent parents, a girl the Rostovs had known from childhood, and who had lately come into a large fortune on the death of her last surviving brother.

The countess had written direct to Julie's mother in Moscow, suggesting a marriage between their children, and had received a favourable answer from her. Madame Karagin had replied that for her part she was agreeable, and everything would depend on her daughter's inclinations. She invited Nikolai to come to Moscow.

Several times the countess, with tears in her eyes, told her son that now that both her daughters were settled her only wish was to see him married. She declared that she would go to her grave content if this desire of hers were fulfilled. Then she would add that she happened to know of a splendid girl, and try to get from him his views on matrimony.

On other occasions she praised Julie and advised Nikolai to go to Moscow during the holidays to amuse himself. Nikolai guessed what was behind his mother's remarks, and during one of these conversations induced her to come out into the open. She told him frankly that their only hope of disentangling their affairs lay in his marrying Julie Karagin.

'But, mamma, suppose I loved a girl who was poor, would you really expect me to sacrifice my feelings and my honour for the sake of money?' he asked his mother, not realizing the cruelty of his question and simply wishing to show his noble-mindedness.

'No, you have not understood me,' said his mother, not knowing how to justify herself. 'You misunderstand me, Nikolai. It is your happiness I want,' she added, feeling that she was not telling the truth and had got into difficulties. She began to cry.

'Mamma, don't cry. You have only to tell me you wish it, and you know I will give my life, everything, for your peace of mind,' said Nikolai. 'I would sacrifice anything for you – even my feelings.'

But the countess did not want the question put like that: she did not want a sacrifice from her son, she would sooner have sacrificed herself for him.

'No, you have not understood me; don't let us talk about it,' she replied, wiping away her tears.

'Yes, maybe I am in love with a penniless girl,' said Nikolai to himself. 'But am I to sacrifice my feelings and my honour for money? I wonder how mamma could suggest such a thing. Does she think that because Sonya is poor I must not love her?' he thought. 'Must not respond to her faithful, devoted love? Yet I should certainly be far happier with her than with any doll of a Julie. I can always sacrifice my feelings for my family's welfare,' he went on to himself, 'but I cannot coerce them. If I love Sonya, then that for me is far more powerful and higher than everything else.'

Nikolai did not go to Moscow, and the countess did not renew her conversations with him about matrimony. But she saw with sorrow, and sometimes with exasperation, symptoms of a growing attachment between her son and the dowerless Sonya. Though she reproached herself for it, she could not refrain from grumbling and nagging at Sonya, often pulling her up without reason, and addressing her stiffly as 'my dear' and using the formal 'you' instead of the intimate 'thou' in speaking to her. What made the kind-hearted countess more irritated than anything with Sonya was that this poor, dark-eyed niece of hers was so meek, so good, so devotedly grateful to her benefactors, and so faithfully, unchangingly and unselfishly in love with Nikolai, that there were no grounds for finding fault with her.

Nikolai stayed on at home until the end of his leave. A fourth letter had come from Prince Andrei, from Rome, in which he wrote that he would long ago have been on his way back to Russia had not his wound unexpectedly reopened in the warm climate, which obliged him to defer his return till the beginning of the new year. Natasha was as much in love with her betrothed as ever, found the same comfort in her love, and was still as ready to throw herself into all the joys of life; but by the end of the fourth month of their separation she began to suffer from fits of depression against which she was unable to contend. She felt sorry for herself, sorry that she was being wasted all this time and of no use to anyone though she knew she had such capacity for loving and being loved.

Things were not cheerful at the Rostovs'.

9

CHRISTMAS came, and except for the solemn celebration of the Liturgy, the formal and wearisome compliments of the season from neighbours and servants, and the new gowns that everyone put on, there were no particular festivities to mark the holidays, though the perfectly still weather with the thermometer at thirteen degrees below zero, the dazzling sunshine by day and the wintry starlit sky at night seemed to call for some special celebration of Christmas-tide.

After midday dinner on the third day of Christmas week all the household dispersed to different rooms. It was the most tedious time of the day. Nikolai, who had been paying a round of visits in the neighbourhood that morning, was asleep on the sitting-room sofa. The old count was resting in his study. Sonya sat at the round table in the drawing-room, copying a design for embroidery. The countess was playing patience. Nastasya Ivanovna, the buffoon, with a woe-begone countenance, was sitting at the window with two old ladies. Natasha came into the room, went up to Sonya and glanced at what she was doing, and then crossed over to her mother and stood without speaking.

'Why are you wandering about like a homeless spirit?' asked her mother. 'What do you want?'

'*Him* – I want him ... now, this minute! I want *him*,' said Natasha, with glittering eyes and no sign of a smile.

The countess raised her head and gave her daughter a searching look.

'Don't look at me, mamma. Don't look, or I shall cry.'

'Sit down – come and sit here by me,' said the countess.

'Mamma, I must have him. Why should I be wasted like this,

mamma? ...' Her voice broke, the tears started to her eyes and in order to hide them she quickly turned away and left the room.

She went into the sitting-room, stood there for a moment lost in thought, and then continued into the maids' room. There an elderly housemaid was scolding a young girl who had just run in from the serfs' quarters, breathless with the cold.

'Give over playing,' said the old woman. 'There's a time for everything.'

'Let her be, Kondratyevna,' said Natasha. 'Run along now, Mavrushka, run along.'

And, having rescued Mavrushka, Natasha crossed the ballroom and went to the vestibule, where an old footman and two young lackeys were playing cards. They broke off and stood up as she entered.

'What shall I have them do?' thought Natasha.

'Yes, Nikita, please go. ... (Where can I send him?) Oh yes, go to the yard and fetch me a fowl, please, a cock, and you, Misha, bring some oats.'*

'Is it a handful of oats you want?' said Misha with cheerful readiness.

'Go on, make haste,' the old man urged him.

'And you, Fiodr, get me a piece of chalk.'

On her way past the butler's pantry she ordered the samovar to be put on, though it was not anywhere near the time for it.

Foka, the butler, was the most surly-tempered person in the house. Natasha liked to test her power over him. He could not believe his ears and went off to ask whether the samovar was really wanted.

'Oh dear, what a young lady!' said Foka, pretending to frown at Natasha.

No one in the house set so many feet flying or gave the servants so much trouble as Natasha. She could not see people without wanting to send them on some errand. It seemed as though she wanted to try whether one or another would not get cross or sulky with her; but no one's orders were so readily obeyed by the servants as Natasha's. 'Now what shall I do? Where can I go?' Natasha wondered, as she went slowly along the passage.

'Nastasya Ivanovna, what sort of children shall I have?' she asked the buffoon, who was coming towards her in his woman's jacket.

'Why, fleas, dragon-flies and grasshoppers,' answered the buffoon.

* Natasha had in mind to tell fortunes by making a pattern of oats on the floor for the fowl to pick up. — Tr.

'O Lord, O Lord, it's always the same: where shall I go? Oh, what shall I do with myself?' And tapping with her heels she ran quickly upstairs to see Vogel and his wife who lived on the top floor. Two governesses were sitting with the Vogels at a table spread with plates of raisins, walnuts and almonds. The governesses were discussing whether it was cheaper to live in Moscow or Odessa. Natasha sat down, listened to the conversation with a grave and thoughtful air, and then got up again.

'The island of Madagascar,' she said. 'Ma-da-gas-car,' she repeated, articulating each syllable distinctly, and without replying to Madame Schloss, who asked her what she was saying, she hastened from the room. Petya, her brother, was upstairs too: with his tutor he was preparing fireworks to let off that night.

'Petya! Petya!' she called to him. 'Carry me downstairs.'

Petya ran up and bent his back for her. She sprang on, putting her arms round his neck, and he pranced along with her.

'No, that's enough … the island of Madagascar!' she exclaimed, and jumping off his back she went downstairs.

Having as it were reviewed her kingdom, tested her power and made sure that everyone was submissive, but that all the same she was utterly bored, Natasha betook herself to the ballroom, caught up her guitar, sat down with it in a dark corner behind a bookcase and began to run her fingers over the strings in the bass, picking out a passage she recalled from an opera she had heard in Petersburg with Prince Andrei. For other listeners the sounds she drew from the guitar would have had no meaning, but in her imagination they called up a whole series of reminiscences. She sat behind the bookcase with her eyes fixed on a streak of light escaping from the pantry door, and listened to herself, turning over her memories. She was in a mood for brooding on the past.

Sonya passed to the pantry with a wine-glass in her hand. Natasha glanced at her, and at the crack in the pantry door, and it seemed to her that she remembered the light falling through that crack once before, and Sonya passing with a glass in her hand. 'Yes, and it was exactly the same in every detail,' thought Natasha.

'Sonya, what is this?' she cried, twanging a thick string.

'Oh, there you are!' said Sonya with a start, and she came closer to listen. 'I don't know. Is it a storm?' she ventured timidly, afraid of being wrong.

'There! That's just how she started, and came up with that same timid smile when all this happened before,' thought Natasha, 'and in just the same way I felt there was something lacking in her.'

'No, it's the chorus from the *Water-Carrier*, listen!' and Natasha hummed the air of the chorus so that Sonya might catch it. 'Where are you going?' she asked.

'To change the water in my glass. I am just finishing the design.'

'You always find something to do, but I can't,' said Natasha. 'And where's Nikolai?'

'Asleep, I think.'

'Sonya, go and wake him,' said Natasha. 'Tell him I want him to come and sing.'

She sat a little longer, wondering what the meaning of it all having happened before could be, and without solving the problem, or being in the least disturbed at not having done so, she drifted into reminiscence again, dreaming of the time when she was with *him* and he was looking at her with eyes of love.

'Oh, if only he would come quickly! I am so afraid it will never be. And worst of all, I am getting older, that's the trouble! Soon I shall no longer be what I am now. But perhaps he will come today – perhaps he is arriving this very moment. Perhaps he has come and is sitting in the drawing-room. Perhaps he arrived yesterday, and I have forgotten.' She rose, put down the guitar, and went to the drawing-room. All the domestic circle, tutors, governesses and guests, were already sitting at the tea-table. The servants stood behind – but Prince Andrei was not there and life was going on as before.

'Ah, here she is!' said the old count when he saw Natasha come in. 'Come and sit by me.'

But Natasha stayed by her mother, looking round as though in search of something.

'Mamma,' she murmured. 'Get him for me, get him, mamma – quickly, quickly!' and again she had difficulty in repressing her sobs.

She sat down at the table and listened to the conversation between the elders and Nikolai, who had also come in to tea. 'Oh Lord, always the same faces, the same talk, papa holding his cup and blowing on it just as he always does!' thought Natasha, to her horror feeling an aversion rising in her for the whole household because they were always the same.

After tea Nikolai, Sonya and Natasha went into the sitting-room, to their favourite corner, where their most intimate talks always began.

'Do you ever feel,' Natasha said to her brother when they were comfortably settled in the sitting-room – 'do you ever feel that there is nothing left to happen – nothing? As if everything nice is already in the past? And it's not so much that you are bored, as melancholy?'

'I should think so!' said he. 'Many a time when everything was all right and everybody in high spirits it has suddenly struck me that I'm sick of it all and that there's nothing left for us but to die. Once in the regiment, when I did not go to some jollification where there was music ... and all at once I felt so depressed. ...'

'Oh yes, I know, I know – I know that feeling,' Natasha interrupted him. 'It used to be like that with me when I was quite little. Do you remember that time when I was punished on account of those plums, and you were all dancing while I sat sobbing in the school room? I shall never forget it: I felt sad and sorry for everyone – sorry for myself and everyone in the world. And I hadn't done anything, that was the point,' said Natasha. 'Do you remember?'

'Yes,' said Nikolai. 'And I remember coming to you afterwards and wanting to comfort you, but, do you know, I felt shy about it. We were terribly ridiculous. I had a funny wooden doll then, and I wanted to give it to you. Remember?'

'And do you remember,' Natasha asked with a pensive smile, 'how once, long, long ago, when we were quite little, Uncle called us into the study – that was in the old house – and it was dark. We went in and all at once there stood ...'

'A Negro,' Nikolai finished for her with a smile of delight. 'Of course I remember! To this day I don't know whether there really was a Negro, or if we only dreamt it, or were told about him.'

'He had grey hair, remember, and white teeth, and he stood and stared at us. ...'

'Sonya, do *you* remember?' asked Nikolai.

'Yes, yes, I do remember something too,' Sonya answered timidly.

'You know, I've often asked papa and mamma about that Negro,' said Natasha, 'and they declare there never was a Negro. But you see, *you* remember about it.'

'Of course I do. I can see his teeth now.'

'How strange it is! As though it were a dream! I like that.'

'And do you remember how we rolled hard-boiled eggs in the ball-room, and all of a sudden two little old women appeared and began spinning round on the carpet? Was that real or not? Do you remember what fun it was?'

'Yes, and do you remember how papa in his blue overcoat fired a gun off in the porch?'

So, smiling with happiness, they went through their memories: not the melancholy memories of old age but the romantic reminiscences of youth – impressions from the most distant past in which dreams fuse with reality – and they laughed with quiet enjoyment.

Sonya, as usual, did not quite keep up with the other two, though they had grown up together.

Sonya had forgotten much that the others recalled, and what did come back to her failed to arouse the same romantic feeling as they experienced. She simply rejoiced in their enjoyment and tried to fit in with it.

She only really took part when they began to speak of her arrival in their home. She told them how afraid she had been of Nikolai be-cause he wore braid on his jacket, and her nurse had said that she too would be sewn up in braid.

'And I remember they told me that you had been born under a cabbage,' said Natasha, 'and I remember not daring to disbelieve it then, though I knew it wasn't true and I felt so uncomfortable.'

While they were talking a maid popped her head in at the door of the sitting-room.

'They have brought the cock, miss,' she said in a whisper.

'I don't want it now, Polya. Tell them to take it away,' replied Natasha.

In the middle of their talk in the sitting-room Dimmler came in and went up to the harp that stood in a corner. He took off the cover, and the harp gave out a jarring sound.

'Herr Dimmler, please play my favourite nocturne by Field,' cried the old countess from the drawing-room.

Dimmler struck a chord and, turning to Natasha, Nikolai and Sonya, remarked, 'How quiet you young people are!'

'Yes, we're philosophizing,' said Natasha, glancing round for a moment and then pursuing the conversation. They were now dis-cussing dreams.

Dimmler began to play. Natasha tiptoed noiselessly to the table,

615

took the candle, carried it away and returned, seating herself quietly in her former place. It was dark in the room, especially where they were sitting on the sofa, but through the lofty windows the silvery light of the full moon fell on the floor.

'Do you know,' said Natasha in a whisper, moving closer to Nikolai and Sonya (while Dimmler, who had finished the nocturne, sat softly running his fingers over the strings, apparently uncertain whether to stop or to play something else), '– do you know that when one goes on and on recalling memories, in the end one begins to remember what happened before one was in the world? ...'

'That's metempsychosis,' said Sonya, who had always been a good scholar and remembered what she learned. 'The Egyptians used to believe that our souls once inhabited the bodies of animals, and will return into animals again.'

'No, I don't believe we were ever in animals,' said Natasha, still in a whisper though the music had ceased. 'But I know for certain that we were angels once, in some other world, and we have been here, and that is why we remember. ...'

'May I join you?' said Dimmler, coming up quietly, and he sat down by them.

'If we have been angels, why should we have fallen lower?' said Nikolai. 'No, that can't be!'

'Not lower – who told you we were lower? ... Because I know what I used to be,' rejoined Natasha with conviction. 'You see, the soul is immortal ... therefore if I am to live for ever in the future I must have existed in the past, existed for a whole eternity.'

'Yes, but it is hard for us to imagine eternity,' remarked Dimmler, who had joined the young folk with a mildly condescending smile but now spoke as quietly and seriously as they.

'Why is it hard to imagine eternity?' demanded Natasha. 'After today comes tomorrow, and then the next day, and so on for ever; and there was yesterday, and the day before. ...'

'Natasha! Now it is your turn. Sing me something,' they heard the countess's voice. 'Why are you sitting there like conspirators?'

'Mamma, I don't feel a bit like it,' said Natasha, but she got up all the same.

None of them, not even the middle-aged Dimmler, wanted to break off their conversation and leave that corner of the sitting-room, but Natasha rose to her feet and Nikolai seated himself at the clavichord. Standing as usual in the middle of the room, and choosing the place where the acoustics were best, Natasha began to sing her mother's favourite song.

She had said she did not feel like singing, but it was long since she had sung, and long before she was to sing again, as she did that evening. The count, from his study where he was talking to Mitenka, heard her, and like a schoolboy in a hurry to run out and play, stumbled over his instructions to the steward, and at last stopped speaking, while Mitenka stood in front of him, also listening and smiling. Nikolai did not take his eyes off his sister, and drew breath in time with her. Sonya, as she listened, thought of the immense difference there was between herself and her friend, and how impossible it was for her to be anything like as bewitching as her cousin. The old countess sat with a blissful yet sad smile, and with tears in her eyes, ever and anon shaking her head. She was thinking of Natasha, and of her own youth, and of how there was something unnatural and dreadful in this impending marriage between Natasha and Prince Andrei.

Dimmler, who had seated himself beside the countess, listened with closed eyes.

'No, countess,' he said at last, 'this talent of hers is European: she has nothing to learn – what softness, what tenderness and strength. ...'

'Oh, how afraid I am for her, how afraid I am!' said the countess, not realizing to whom she was speaking. Her maternal instinct told her that Natasha had too much of something, and that because of this she would not be happy. Before Natasha had finished singing, fourteen-year-old Petya rushed into the room in great excitement to announce that some mummers had arrived.

Natasha stopped abruptly.

'Idiot!' she screamed at her brother, and running to a chair flung herself into it, sobbing so violently that it was a long while before she could stop.

'It's nothing, mamma, really it's nothing. Only Petya startled me,' she said, trying to smile; but the tears still flowed and the sobs still choked her.

The mummers (some of the house-serfs dressed up as bears, Turks, tavern-keepers and fine ladies – awe-inspiring or comic figures) at first huddled bashfully together in the vestibule, bringing in with them the cold and hilarity from outside. Then, hiding behind one another, they pushed into the ballroom, where, at first shyly but afterwards with ever-increasing merriment and zeal, they started singing, dancing and playing Christmas games. The countess, after identifying them and laughing at their costumes, went away to the drawing-room. The count sat in the ballroom with a beaming smile, applauding the players. The young people had vanished.

Half an hour later there appeared among the mummers in the ballroom an old lady in a farthingale – this was Nikolai. A Turkish girl was Petya. Dimmler was a clown. A hussar was Natasha, and a Circassian youth Sonya with burnt-cork moustaches and eyebrows.

After being received with well-feigned surprise, non-recognition or praise from those who were not mumming, the young people decided that their costumes were so good that they ought to be displayed somewhere else.

Nikolai, who had a strong desire to go out in his troika, the roads being in splendid condition, proposed that they should take with them a dozen of the house-serfs who were dressed up, and drive to 'Uncle's'.

'No, why disturb the old fellow?' said the countess. 'Besides, you wouldn't have room to turn round there. If you must go anywhere, go to the Melyukovs'.'

Madame Melyukov was a widow who lived with a host of children of various ages, and their tutors and governesses, about three miles from the Rostovs'.

'That's right, *ma chère*, an excellent idea,' chimed in the old count. 'I'll dress up at once and go with them. I'll make Pashette open her eyes.'

But the countess would not agree to let the count accompany them: his leg had been bad for several days. It was decided that the count must not go but that if Louisa Ivanovna (Madame Schoss) would act as chaperone, then the young ladies might visit the Melyukovs. Sonya, generally so reserved and timid, was more urgent than all the others in her entreaties to Madame Schoss not to refuse.

Sonya's costume was the best of all. Her moustaches and eyebrows were extraordinarily becoming to her. Everyone said how pretty she looked, and she was keyed up to an unusual pitch of energy and excitement. Some inner voice told her that now or never her fate would be decided, and in her masculine attire she seemed quite another person. Madame Schoss consented to go, and half an hour later four troikas, all jingling bells, drove up to the porch, their runners crunching and creaking over the frozen snow.

Natasha was the first to sound the note of Christmas gaiety, and this gaiety, spreading from one to another, grew wilder and wilder, reaching its climax when they all came out into the frosty air and, talking and calling to one another, laughing and shouting, got into the sledges.

Two of the troikas were the ordinary household sledges, the third was the old count's with a trotter from the Orlov stud as shaft-horse, the fourth was Nikolai's own troika with a short shaggy black horse between the thills. Nikolai, in his farthingale, over which he had belted his hussar's cloak, stood up in the middle of the sledge, holding the reins.

It was so light that he could see the metal of the harness shining in the moonlight, and the horses' eyes as they looked round in alarm at the noisy party gathered under the shadow of the porch roof.

Natasha, Sonya, Madame Schoss and two maids got into Nikolai's sledge. Into the old count's sledge went Dimmler and his wife, and Petya; while the rest of the mummers seated themselves in the other two sledges.

'You lead the way, Zahar!' shouted Nikolai to his father's coachman, so as to have the chance of racing past him on the road.

The old count's troika with Dimmler and his party started forward, its runners creaking as though they were frozen to the snow, its deep-toned bell clanging. The trace-horses pressed close to the shafts and, sinking in the snow, kicked it up, hard and glittering like sugar.

Nikolai followed the first sledge; behind him he heard the noise and crunch of the other two. At first they drove at a slow trot along the narrow road. As they passed the garden the shadows cast by the bare trees fell across the road and hid the bright moonlight, but as soon as they got beyond the fence the snowy plain, motionless and bathed in moonlight, stretched out before them, glittering like diamonds and dappled with bluish shadows. *Bump, bump!* went the first sledge over a cradle-hole in the snow; in exactly the same way the one behind dipped down and up again, and the others that followed; and then, rudely breaking the iron stillness, the troikas began to speed along the road, one after the other.

'A hare's track, a lot of tracks!' Natasha's voice rang out in the frost-bound air.

'How light it is, Nicolas!' came Sonya's voice.

Nikolai glanced round at Sonya, and bent down to look more closely into her face. It was quite a new, sweet face with black eyebrows and moustaches that peeped up at him from her sable furs – so close yet so distant – in the moonlight.

'That used to be Sonya,' thought Nikolai. He gave her a closer look and smiled.

'What is it, Nicolas?'

'Nothing,' said he, and turned to the horses again.

When they came out on to the beaten high road – polished by sledge-runners and cut up by rough-shod hooves, the marks of which were visible in the moonlight – the horses began to tug at the reins of their own accord, and quickened their pace. The near-side horse, arching his head and breaking into a short canter, strained at the traces. The shaft-horse swayed from side to side, pricking up his ears as though asking: 'Shall we go, or is it too soon?' In front, already a considerable distance ahead, the deep bell of the sledge rang farther and farther off, and the black horses driven by Zahar made a dark patch against the white snow. The shouts and laughter of his party of mummers could be clearly heard.

'Now then, my darlings!' cried Nikolai, pulling the reins to one side and flourishing the whip. And it was only the wind meeting them more sharply, and the tugging of the side-horses galloping faster and faster, that gave them an idea of how fast the sledge was flying along. Nikolai glanced behind. With screams and squeals and brandishing of whips, that caused even the shaft-horses to gallop, the other sledges speeded after them. The shaft-horse swung steadily beneath the shaft-bow over its head, with no thought of slackening pace but ready to increase it if need be.

Nikolai overtook the first sledge. They glided down a little slope and came out upon a broad trodden track that crossed a meadow near a river.

'Where are we?' wondered Nikolai. 'It must be the Kosoy meadow, I suppose. But no – this is a place I never saw before. It isn't the Kosoy meadow, nor Dyomkin hill – heaven only knows where we are. This is some new enchanted place. Well, no matter!' And, shouting to his horses, he began to gain on the first troika.

Zahar held back his steeds and turned his face, white to the eyebrows with hoar-frost.

Nikolai gave his team the rein, and Zahar, stretching out his arms, clucked his tongue and let his horses go.

'Steady there, master!' he cried.

Swifter still flew the two troikas, side by side, and swifter interwove the legs of the horses as they sped onward. Nikolai began to draw ahead. Zahar, arms still outstretched, raised one hand with the reins.

'You won't do it, master!' he shouted.

Nikolai urged his three to a gallop and passed Zahar. The horses kicked up the fine dry snow into the faces of those in the sledge – beside them sounded the jingle of bells and they caught confused glimpses of swiftly moving legs and the shadows of the sledge they were passing. From different sides came the whistle of runners on the snow and the voices of girls shrieking.

Checking his horses again, Nikolai looked around him. All about him lay the same magic plain bathed in moonlight and spangled with stars.

'Zahar's shouting that I'm to turn to the left, but why to the left?' thought Nikolai. 'Aren't we going to the Melyukovs? Is this the way to Melyukovka? Heaven only knows where we are going – the Lord knows what is happening to us, but whatever it is it is very peculiar and nice.' He looked round in the sledge.

'See, his moustache and eyelashes are all white!' said one of the strange, pretty, unfamiliar figures sitting by him – the one with the fine eyebrows and moustaches.

'I believe that was Natasha,' thought Nikolai. 'And that's Madame Schoss, but perhaps I'm wrong, and I don't know that Circassian with the moustache, but I love her.'

'Aren't you cold?' he asked.

They did not answer but began to laugh. Dimmler from the sledge behind shouted something – it was probably something funny – but they could not make out what he said.

'Yes, yes!' other voices laughed back.

'But here we are in a sort of magic forest with shifting black shadows, and a glitter of diamonds, a flight of marble steps and the silver roofs of fairy buildings, and the shrill yells of wild beasts. And if this really is the Melyukov place, then it's stranger than ever that after driving heaven knows where we should come to Melyukovka,' thought Nikolai.

It was, in fact, Melyukovka, and maids and footmen with beaming faces came running out to the porch, carrying candles.

'Who is it?' asked someone from the front door.

'Mummers from the count's. I know by the horses,' answered various voices.

II

PELAGEYA DANILOVNA MELYUKOV, a broadly-built, energetic woman wearing spectacles and a loose house-dress, was sitting in the drawing-room surrounded by her daughters whom she was doing her best to keep amused. They were quietly occupied in dropping melted wax into water and watching the shadows the wax shapes cast on the wall, when the steps and voices of the visitors began to echo through from the hall.

Hussars, fine ladies, witches, clowns and bears, clearing their throats in the vestibule and wiping the hoar-frost from their faces, came into the ballroom where candles were hurriedly lit. The clown – Dimmler – and the lady – Nikolai – opened the dance. Surrounded by shrieking children, the mummers hid their faces and, disguising their voices, bowed to their hostess and arranged themselves about the room.

'Dear me, there's no recognizing them! And Natasha there! Whoever is it she looks like? She really does remind me of someone. And there's Herr Dimmler – isn't he good! I didn't know him. And how he dances! And oh, my goodness, look at that Circassian! Why, how it suits dear little Sonya! And who is that? Well, you have cheered us up! Nikita, Vanya – clear away the tables. And we were sitting here so quietly. Ha, ha, ha! ... That hussar – that hussar over there! Just like a boy! And the legs! ... I can't look at him ...' various voices were exclaiming.

Natasha, who was a great favourite with the young Melyukovs, disappeared with them into rooms at the back of the house, where a burnt cork and sundry dressing-gowns and male garments were called for and received from the footmen by bare girlish arms from behind the door. Ten minutes later all the young Melyukovs were ready to join the mummers.

Madame Melyukov, having seen to it that space was cleared for the visitors, and arranged about refreshments for the gentry and the serfs, went about among the mummers with her spectacles on her nose, peering into their faces with a suppressed smile and failing to recognize any of them. It was not only Dimmler and the Rostovs that she failed to recognize: she did not even know her own daughters, or identify her late husband's dressing-gowns and uniforms which they had put on.

'And who can this one be?' she kept saying, addressing the governess and staring into the face of her own daughter disguised as a Kazan Tartar. 'I suppose it is one of the Rostovs. Well, Mr Hussar – what regiment do you belong to?' she asked Natasha. 'Here, give some fruit-jelly to that Turk,' she told the butler who was carrying round refreshments. 'Turkish law doesn't forbid jelly.'

Sometimes, as she looked at the strange and ludicrous capers cut by the dancers, who, having made up their minds once for all that no one would recognize them in their fancy dresses, were not at all shy, Madame Melyukov would hide her face in her handkerchief, and her fat body would shake from head to toe with irrepressible, good-natured, elderly laughter.

'My little Sasha! Look at my little Sasha!' she said.

After Russian country-dances and choruses Madame Melyukov made the serfs and gentry form into one large circle; a ring, a string and a silver rouble were fetched, and they all began playing games.

By the end of an hour every costume was crumpled and untidy. The burnt-cork moustaches and eyebrows were smudged over the perspiring, flushed and merry faces. Madame Melyukov began to recognize the mummers and compliment them on their clever dresses, telling them how very becoming they were, especially to the young ladies, and she thanked them all for having entertained her so well. The visitors were invited to supper in the drawing-room, while the serfs had something served to them in the ballroom.

'Now to tell one's fortune in the empty bath-house is a terrifying thing!' exclaimed an old maid who lived with the Melyukovs, during supper.

'Why?' asked the eldest Melyukov girl.

'You wouldn't go. It takes courage. …'

'I'll go,' said Sonya.

'Tell us what happened to that girl?' said the second Melyukov daughter.

'Well, this was the way of it,' began the old maid. 'A young lady went and took a cock, laid the table for two, all properly, and sat down. After a little while she suddenly hears someone coming ... a sledge drives up, harness bells jingling. She hears him coming! He walks in, precisely in the shape of a man, like an officer – and comes and sits down at the table with her.'

'Oh! Oh!' screamed Natasha, rolling her eyes in horror.

'Yes, and then? Did he speak?'

'He did, like a man. Everything was ordinary, and he began to try and win her over, and all she had to do was to keep him talking till the cock crowed; but she got frightened, just got frightened and hid her face in her hands. Then he clasped her in his arms. Luckily at that minute the maids ran in. ...'

'Come, what is the good of scaring them?' said Madame Melyukov.

'Why, mamma, you used to try your fortune that way yourself ...' said her daughter.

'And how does one tell one's fortune in a barn?' inquired Sonya.

'Well, say you went to the barn now, and listened. It depends on what you hear: if there's hammering and tapping, that's bad; but the sound of shifting grain is a good sign. And sometimes one hears ...'

'Mamma, tell us what happened to you in the barn.'

Madame Melyukov smiled.

'Oh, I've forgotten, it was so long ago ...' she replied. 'Besides, I'm sure none of you would go?'

'Yes, I will. Let me – I'll go,' said Sonya.

'Very well, then, if you're not afraid.'

'Madame Schoss, may I?' asked Sonya.

Whether they were playing the ring-and-string game, or the rouble game, or talking as now, Nikolai did not leave Sonya's side, and gazed at her with quite new eyes. It seemed to him that it was only now, thanks to those burnt-cork moustaches, that he really knew her. Indeed that evening Sonya was gayer, more animated and prettier than Nikolai had ever seen her before.

'So this is what she is like! And what a fool I have been!' he kept thinking, looking at her sparkling eyes and watching the happy, rapturous smile dimpling her cheeks under the moustache – a smile he had never seen before.

'I am not afraid of anything,' said Sonya. 'May I go at once?' She got up.

They told her where the barn was, and how she must stand silent and listen, and gave her a fur cloak, which she flung over her head with a glance at Nikolai.

'What an exquisite girl she is!' he said to himself. 'And what have I been thinking about all this time?'

Sonya went out into the passage to go to the barn. Saying that he felt too hot, Nikolai hurried to the front porch. It certainly was stuffy indoors from the crowd of people.

Outside there was the same still cold, and the same moon, except that it shone brighter than before. The light was so strong and the snow sparkled with so many stars that one's eye was not drawn to look up at the sky, and the real stars passed unnoticed. The sky was black and dreary; the earth was radiant.

'I'm a fool, an idiot! What have I been waiting for all this time?' thought Nikolai; and, running out from the porch, he turned the corner of the house and went along the path that led to the back door. He knew Sonya would come that way. Half-way to the barn lay some snow-covered stacks of firewood, and across and along them a network of shadows from the bare old lime trees fell on the snow and on the path leading to the barn. The log walls of the granary and its snow-covered roof, that looked as if they were hewn out of some precious stone, shone in the moonlight. A tree in the garden snapped with the frost, and all was silent and still again. Nikolai's lungs seemed to breathe in not air but an elixir of eternal youth and joy.

From the back porch came the sound of feet descending the steps. There was a ringing crunch on the last step which was thickly carpeted with snow, and the voice of an old maidservant was saying:

'Keep straight on along the path, miss. Only don't look round.'

'I am not afraid,' replied Sonya's voice; then along the path towards Nikolai came the sliding, squeaking sound of Sonya's little feet in her thin slippers.

Sonya came muffled up in her cloak. She was only a couple of paces away when she saw him, and to her too he was different from the Nikolai she had known and always slightly feared. He was in woman's dress, with tousled hair and a blissful smile new to Sonya. She ran quickly towards him.

'She's quite different and yet exactly the same,' thought Nikolai, looking at her face all lit up by the moonlight. He slipped his arms under the fur cloak that covered her head, embraced her, strained her to his heart, and kissed her on the lips which wore a moustache and smelt of burnt cork. Sonya kissed him full on the mouth, and disengaging her little hands pressed them to his cheeks.

'Sonya!' ... 'Nicolas!' ... was all they said. They ran to the barn and then back again to the house, which they re-entered, he by the front and she by the back porch.

12

WHEN they all drove back from Madame Melyukov's, Natasha, who always saw and noticed everything, arranged a change of seating, so that she and Madame Schoss should return in the sledge with Dimmler, while Sonya went with Nikolai and the maids.

On the way home Nikolai drove at a steady pace instead of racing, and kept gazing in the weird, all-transforming light into Sonya's face, trying to discover beneath the eyebrows and moustaches the Sonya of the past, and his present Sonya from whom he had resolved never to be parted again. He watched her intently, and when he recognized the old Sonya, and the new, and recalled the smell of burnt cork mingled with the sensation of her kiss, he drew in a deep breath of the frosty air and, looking at the ground gliding by and the sky shining above, felt himself in fairyland once more.

'Sonya, is it well with *thee*?' he asked from time to time.

'Yes,' Sonya would reply. 'And *thee*?'

When they were half-way home Nikolai handed the reins to the coachman and ran for a moment to Natasha's sledge and stood on the wing.

'Natasha,' he whispered in French, 'do you know, I have made up my mind about Sonya?'

'Have you told her?' asked Natasha, suddenly all radiant with joy.

'Oh, how strange you look with that moustache and those eyebrows, Natasha! Are you glad?'

'I am so glad, so glad! I was beginning to be vexed with you. I did not tell you, but you have been treating her badly. Such a heart she has, Nicolas! I'm horrid sometimes, but I was ashamed to be happy while Sonya wasn't,' continued Natasha. 'Now I am so glad! Well, run back to her.'

'No, wait a moment. ... Oh, how funny you look!' cried Nikolai, peering into her face and finding in his sister, too, something new,

626

unusual and bewitchingly lovely that he had never noticed in her before. 'Natasha, it's like fairyland, isn't it?'

'Yes,' she replied. 'You have done splendidly.'

'Had I seen her before as she is now,' thought Nikolai, 'I should have asked her long ago what to do, and have done whatever she told me, and all would have been well.'

'So you are glad, and I have done right?'

'Oh, quite right! I had a quarrel with mamma about it a little while ago. Mamma said she was angling for you. How could she say such a thing! I almost stormed at mamma. And I will never allow anyone to say or think anything bad of Sonya, for she is goodness itself.'

'Then it's all right?' said Nikolai, giving another searching look at the expression of his sister's face to see if she was in earnest. Then he jumped down and, his boots scrunching the snow, ran back to his own sledge. The same happy smiling Circassian, with moustaches and beaming eyes peeping up from under the sable hood, was still sitting there, and this Circassian was Sonya, and this Sonya was beyond a doubt to be his happy and loving wife in the days to come.

After they reached home, and told their mother how they had spent the evening at the Melyukovs', the girls went to their bedroom. They undressed, but without wiping off their burnt-cork moustaches sat a long time talking of their happiness. They talked of how they would live when they were married, how their husbands would be friends, and how happy they would be. On Natasha's table stood two looking-glasses which Dunyasha had put there earlier in the evening.

'Only when will it all happen? I fear me never. ... It would be too good!' said Natasha, rising and going over to the looking-glasses.

'Sit down, Natasha; perhaps you'll see him,' said Sonya.

Natasha lit the candles and sat down.

'I do see someone with a moustache,' said Natasha, seeing her own face.

'You shouldn't make fun, miss,' said Dunyasha.

With the help of Sonya and the maid Natasha got into the proper position before the glass. Her face assumed a serious expression, and she fell silent. She sat a long time looking at the receding line of candles reflected in the glasses and expecting (in accordance with the tales she had heard) to see a coffin, or else *him*, Prince Andrei, in that last dim indistinct square. But ready as she was to accept the slightest blur as the image of a man or a coffin, she saw nothing.

Her eyes began to blink and she moved away from the mirror.

'Why is it other people see things and I don't?' she said. 'Now you sit down, Sonya. Tonight you really must. Do it for me. ... I feel so full of dread today!'

Sonya sat down to the looking-glass, settled herself in the right position and began to look.

'Miss Sonya, now, is sure to see something,' whispered Dunyasha. 'You always make fun.'

Sonya heard this, and heard Natasha's whispered reply:

'Yes, I know she will: she did last year, you remember.'

For two or three minutes the three of them were silent. 'Of course she will!' murmured Natasha, and did not finish. ... Suddenly Sonya pushed away the glass she was holding, and covered her eyes with her hand.

'Oh, Natasha!' she cried.

'Did you see something? Did you? What was it?' exclaimed Natasha, supporting the looking-glass.

Sonya had not seen anything. She was just wanting to blink her eyes and get up when she heard Natasha say 'Of course she will!' She did not wish to disappoint either Dunyasha or Natasha, but she was tired of sitting there. She did not know herself how or why the exclamation had escaped her when she covered her eyes.

'Did you see him?' demanded Natasha, clutching her hand.

'Yes. Wait ... I ... saw him,' Sonya found herself saying, and not sure yet whether by *him* Natasha meant Nikolai or Andrei. ('Why not say I saw something? Other people see things. Besides, who can tell whether I saw anything or not?' flashed through Sonya's mind.)

'Yes, I saw him,' she said.

'How was he? How? Standing up or lying down?'

'No, I saw ... At first there was nothing. Then suddenly I saw him lying down.'

'Andrei lying down? Is he ill?' Natasha asked, looking at her friend with terrified eyes.

'No, on the contrary – on the contrary, his face was cheerful, and he turned round to me . . .' and as she was saying this she fancied she really had seen what she was describing.

'What next? Go on, Sonya.'

'I could not make out after that – there was something blue and red. ...'

'Sonya, when will he come back? When shall I see him? Oh God, how afraid I am for him and for myself, afraid for everything ...' Natasha began, and paying no heed to Sonya's attempts to comfort her she got into bed, and long after her candle was out lay open-eyed and motionless, gazing at the frosty moonlight through the frozen window-panes.

13

SOON after the Christmas holidays Nikolai told his mother of his love for Sonya and announced his firm intention to marry her. The countess, who had long ago noticed what was going on between Sonya and Nikolai, and was expecting this declaration, listened to him in silence, and then told her son that he might marry whom he pleased but that neither she nor his father would give their blessing to such a marriage. For the first time in his life Nikolai felt that his mother was displeased with him, and that, notwithstanding all her love for him, she would not give way. Coldly, without looking at Nikolai, she sent for her husband, and when he came in she tried, in a few chilling words to explain the situation to him, in Nikolai's presence, but she could not control herself, and bursting into tears of vexation left the room. The old count made a feeble appeal to Nikolai, begging him to give up his intention. Nikolai replied that he could not go back on his word, and his father, sighing and visibly embarrassed, very quickly cut short the conversation and went in to the countess. In all his encounters with his son the count was always aware of a sense of guilt for having squandered the family fortune, and so he could not feel angry with him for refusing to marry an heiress, and choosing the dowerless Sonya. On this occasion he was more vividly conscious than ever that if his affairs had not been in disorder no better wife than Sonya could have been wished for for Nikolai, and that no one but himself and his Mitenka and his incorrigible bad habits was to blame for the condition of the family finances.

The father and mother did not speak of the matter to their son again, but a few days later the countess sent for Sonya and, with a cruelty that surprised them both, upbraided her niece for enticing Nikolai, and accused her of ingratitude. Sonya listened in silence and with downcast eyes to the countess's bitter words, at a loss to understand what was required of her. She was ready to make any sacrifice for her benefactors. The idea of self-sacrifice was her favourite idea;

but in this case she could not see what she ought to sacrifice, or for whom. She could not help loving the countess and the whole Rostov family, but neither could she help loving Nikolai and knowing that his happiness depended on that love. She stood silent and dejected, and made no reply. Nikolai felt he could not endure the situation any longer, and went to have it out with his mother. He first implored her to forgive him and Sonya, and to consent to their marriage; then he threatened that if she persecuted Sonya he would instantly marry her in secret.

The countess, with an iciness her son had never seen in her before, replied that he was of age, that Prince Andrei was marrying without *his* father's consent, and he could do the same, but that she would never receive that *scheming creature* as her daughter.

Stung to fury by the words *scheming creature*, Nikolai, raising his voice, told his mother that he had never expected her to try and force him to sell his feelings, but that if this were so it was the last time he would ever ... but before he could speak the fatal word which the expression of his face caused his mother to await with terror, and which would perhaps have remained an agonizing memory to them both for ever, Natasha, who had been listening at the door, ran into the room with a pale, set face.

'Nikolai, my darling, you don't know what you are saying! Be quiet, be quiet, I tell you! Be quiet! ...' she almost screamed, so as to drown his voice.

'Mamma, dearest, he doesn't mean it at all ... my poor, sweet darling,' she said to her mother, who, conscious that they had been on the edge of a rupture, was gazing at her son in terror, yet because of her obstinacy and the heat of the quarrel could not and would not give way.

'Nikolai, I'll explain to you, you go away. And you, mamma darling, listen,' she entreated, turning to her mother.

Her words were incoherent but they achieved their purpose.

The countess, sobbing heavily, buried her face in her daughter's bosom, while Nikolai got up, clutching his head, and left the room.

Natasha set to work to effect a reconciliation, and so far succeeded that Nikolai received a promise from his mother that Sonya should not be ill-used, while he on his side pledged himself not to do anything without his parents' knowledge.

Firmly resolved to retire from the service as soon as he could wind up his military career, and return and marry Sonya, Nikolai, grave and melancholy and at variance with his parents but, as it seemed to him, passionately in love, left at the beginning of January to rejoin his regiment.

After Nikolai had gone the atmosphere in the Rostov household was more depressing than ever. The countess fell ill with the mental upset.

Sonya was unhappy at being parted from Nikolai, and still more so on account of the hostile tone the countess could not help adopting towards her. The count was more than ever taken up with the precarious state of his finances, which called for some decisive action. Their town house and estate near Moscow would have to be sold, and for this it was necessary to go to Moscow. But the countess's health obliged them to delay their departure from one day to the next.

Natasha, who had at first borne the separation from her betrothed lightly and even cheerfully, now grew more restless and impatient every day. The thought that the best time of her life, which might have been spent in loving him, was being wasted to no purpose fretted her continually. His letters for the most part irritated her. It hurt her to think that while she lived only in the thought of him he was living a real life, seeing new places and new people interesting to him. The more engaging his letters were the more they provoked her. Her letters to him, far from giving her any comfort, seemed to her a wearisome and artificial duty. She could not write, because she could not conceive of the possibility of expressing sincerely in a letter even a thousandth part of what she was accustomed to say by the tone of her voice, a smile and a look. The letters she wrote to him were dry and formal, all after one pattern. She attached no importance to these compositions, in the rough copies of which her mother corrected her spelling mistakes.

There was still no improvement in the countess's health, but the journey to Moscow could not be deferred any longer. Natasha's trousseau had to be ordered and the house sold. Moreover, Prince Andrei was expected in Moscow, where his father was spending the winter, and Natasha felt certain he had already arrived.

So the countess remained in the country, while the count, taking Sonya and Natasha with him, went to Moscow towards the end of January.

PART FIVE

I

AFTER Prince Andrei's engagement to Natasha, Pierre, without any apparent reason, suddenly felt it impossible to go on living as before. Firmly convinced as he was of the truths revealed to him by his benefactor, and happy as he had been in his first period of enthusiasm for the task of improving his spiritual self, to which he had devoted so much ardour – all the zest of such a life vanished with the engagement of Andrei and Natasha, and the death of Bazdeyev, the news of which reached him almost at the same time. Nothing but the empty skeleton of life remained to him: his house, a brilliant wife who now enjoyed the favours of a very important personage, acquaintance with all Petersburg, and his duties at court with all their tedious formalities. And this life suddenly began to fill Pierre with unexpected loathing. He ceased keeping a diary, avoided the company of the brethren, took to visiting the club again, drank a great deal and renewed his association with the gay bachelor sets, leading such a life that the Countess Hélène found it necessary to bring him severely to task. Pierre felt that she was right, and to avoid embarrassing her went away to Moscow.

In Moscow, as soon as he set foot in his enormous house with the faded and fading princesses and the swarm of servants; as soon as, driving through the town, he saw the Iversky chapel with innumerable tapers burning before the golden settings of the icons, the Kremlin square with its snow undisturbed by vehicles, the sledge-drivers and the hovels of the slum district; saw the old Moscovites quietly living out their days, with never a desire or a quickening of the blood; saw the old Moscow ladies, the Moscow balls and the English Club – he felt himself at home in a haven of rest. Moscow gave him the sensation of peace and warmth that one has in an old and dirty dressing-gown.

Moscow society, from the old ladies to the children, welcomed Pierre like a long-expected guest whose place was always ready waiting for him. In the eyes of Moscow society Pierre was the nicest, kindest, most intelligent, merriest and most liberal-minded of eccentrics, a heedless, genial Russian nobleman of the old school. His purse was always empty because it was open to everyone.

Benefit performances, wretched pictures, statues, charitable societies, gipsy choirs, schools, subscription dinners, drinking parties, the freemasons, the churches, and books – no one and nothing ever met with a refusal from him, and had it not been for two friends who had borrowed large sums from him and now took him under their protection he would have parted with everything. At the club no dinner or *soirée* was complete without him. The moment he sank into his place on the sofa after a couple of bottles of Margaux he would be surrounded by a circle of friends, and the discussions, the arguments and the joking began. Where there were quarrels his kindly smile and apt jests were enough to reconcile the antagonists. The masonic dinners were dull and dreary when he was absent.

When he rose after a bachelor supper and with his amiable, kindly smile yielded to the entreaties of the festive party to drive off somewhere with them the young men would make the rafters ring with their shouts of delight and triumph. At balls he danced if a partner was needed. Young women, married and unmarried, liked him because he paid court to no one but was equally agreeable to all, especially after supper. '*Il est charmant, il n'a pas de sexe,*' they said of him.

Pierre was one of those retired gentlemen-in-waiting, of whom there were hundreds, good-humouredly ending their days in Moscow.

How horrified he would have been seven years before, when he first arrived back from abroad, if anyone had told him there was no need for him to look about and make plans, that his track had long ago been shaped for him, marked out before all eternity, and that, wriggle as he might, he would be what everyone in his position was doomed to be. He would not have believed it! Had he not at one time longed with all his heart to establish a republic in Russia? Then that he might be a Napoleon? Then a philosopher, then a great strategist and the conqueror of Napoleon? Had he not seen the possibility of and passionately desired the regeneration of the sinful human race, and his own progress to the highest degree of perfection? Had he not established schools and infirmaries and liberated his serfs?

But instead of all that, here he was, the wealthy husband of a faithless wife, a retired gentleman-in-waiting, fond of eating and drinking, fond, too, as he unbuttoned his waistcoat after dinner, of abusing the government a bit, a member of the Moscow English Club, and a universal favourite in Moscow society. For a long while he could not reconcile himself to the idea that he was one of those same retired Moscow gentlemen-in-waiting he had so profoundly despised seven years before.

Sometimes he tried to console himself with the reflection that he was only temporarily leading this kind of life; but presently he was shocked by another reflection – how many men, like himself, with the same idea of its being temporary, had entered that life and that club in possession of all their teeth and a thick head of hair, only to leave it when they were toothless and bald?

In moments of pride, when he was reviewing his position, it seemed to him that he was quite different and distinct from those other retired gentlemen-in-waiting whom he had scorned in the past: they were vulgar and stupid, content and at ease with their position, 'while I am still dissatisfied – I still want to do something for mankind,' he would assure himself in moments of pride. 'But possibly all these comrades of mine struggled just as I do, trying to find some new and original path through life, and like myself have been brought by force of circumstances, by conditions of society and birth – that elemental force against which man is powerless – to the same point as I have,' he would say to himself in moments of humility; and after living for some time in Moscow he ceased to despise his companions in destiny, but began to grow fond of them, to respect and feel sorry for them as he was sorry for himself.

Pierre no longer suffered moments of despair, hypochondria and disgust with life, but the same malady that had formerly manifested itself in acute attacks was driven inwards and now never left him for an instant. 'What for? What is the use? What is going on in the world?' he asked himself in perplexity several times a day, involuntarily beginning to inquire into the meaning of the phenomena of life; but knowing by experience that there were no answers to these questions he made haste to put them out of his mind, and took up a book or hurried off to the club or to Apollon Nikolayevich's, to exchange the gossip of the town.

'Hélène, who has never cared for anything but her own body, and is one of the stupidest women in the world,' thought Pierre, 'is regarded by people as the acme of intelligence and refinement, and they pay homage to her. Napoleon Bonaparte was scorned by everybody while he was great, but since he became a pitiful buffoon the Emperor Francis seeks to offer him his daughter in an illegal marriage. The Spaniards, through their Catholic clergy, return thanks to God for their victory over the French on the 14th of June, while the French, through the same Catholic Church, offer praise because on that same 14th of June they defeated the Spaniards. My masonic brethren swear in blood that they are ready to sacrifice everything for their neighbour, but they don't give so much as one rouble to the collections for the poor, and the Astraea lodge intrigues against the "Manna Seekers", and fuss about getting an authentic Scottish carpet and a charter which nobody needs, and the meaning of which not even the man who copied it understands. We all profess the Christian law of forgiveness of injuries and love for our neighbour, the law in honour of which we have raised forty times forty churches in Moscow – but yesterday a deserter was knouted to death and a minister of that same law of love and forgiveness, the priest, gave the soldier the cross to kiss before his execution.' Thus mused Pierre, and this whole universal hypocrisy which everyone accepts, accustomed as he was to it, astonished him each time as if it were something new. 'I see this hypocrisy and muddle,' he thought, 'but how am I to tell them all that I see it? I have tried, and have always found that they, too, in the depths of their hearts know it as well as I do but are wilfully blind. Then so it must be, I suppose. But I – what am I to do with myself?' Pierre ruminated. He had the unlucky capacity many men, especially Russians, have of seeing and believing in the possibility of goodness and truth, but of seeing the evil and falsehood of life too clearly to be able to take any serious part in life. Every sphere of activity was, in his eyes, linked with evil and deception. Whatever he tried to be, whatever he engaged in, he always found himself repulsed by this knavery and falsehood, which blocked every path of action. Yet he had to live and to find occupation. It was too awful to be under the burden of these insoluble problems, and so he abandoned himself to the first distraction that offered itself, in order to forget them. He frequented every kind of society, drank much, purchased pictures, built houses, and above all – read.

He read, and read everything that came to hand. Returning home at night, he would pick up a book and begin to read even while his valets were taking off his things. From reading he passed to sleeping, from sleeping to gossip in drawing-rooms or the club, from gossip to carousals and women; from dissipation back to gossip, reading and wine. Drinking became more and more a physical and moral necessity alike. Though the doctors warned him that with his corpulence wine was dangerous to him, he drank heavily. He only felt quite comfortable when, having mechanically poured several glasses of wine down his capacious throat, he experienced a pleasant warmth in his body, an amiable disposition towards all his fellows, and a readiness to respond superficially to every ideal without probing it too deeply. Only after emptying a bottle or two did he feel vaguely that the terribly tangled skein of life which had appalled him before was not so dreadful as he had fancied. He was always conscious of some aspect of that skein, as with a buzzing in his ears he chatted or listened to conversation, or read his books after dinner or supper. But it was only under the influence of wine that he could say to himself: 'Never mind. I'll disentangle it. I have a solution all ready. But there isn't time now – I'll think it all out presently!' But that *presently* never came.

In the morning, on an empty stomach, all the old questions looked as insoluble and fearful as ever, and Pierre hastily picked up a book, and was delighted if anyone called to see him.

Sometimes he remembered having heard how soldiers under fire in the trenches, and having nothing to do, try hard to find some occupation the more easily to bear the danger. And it seemed to Pierre that all men were like those soldiers, seeking refuge from life: some in ambition, some in cards, some in framing laws, some in women, some in playthings, some in horses, some in politics, some in sport, some in wine, and some in government service. 'Nothing is without consequence, and nothing is important: it's all the same in the end. The thing to do is to save myself from it all as best I can,' thought Pierre. 'Not to see *it*, that terrible *it*.'

2

AT the beginning of the winter old Prince Bolkonsky and his daughter moved to Moscow. The fame of his past career, his wit and his eccentricity caused Moscovites to regard him with peculiar veneration; and as popular enthusiasm for the Emperor Alexander's régime was then cooling off, and a nationalist, anti-French tendency was all the vogue in Moscow, he became the centre of opposition to the government.

The prince had aged very much during the past year. Signs of senility showed themselves unmistakably in sudden naps, forgetfulness of quite recent events while his memory retained incidents of the remote past, and the childish vanity with which he accepted the rôle of leader of the Moscow opposition. In spite of this, when the old man came into the drawing-room for tea of an evening, in his old-fashioned coat and powdered wig, and incited by someone or other started on his abrupt observations on days gone by, or delivered still more abrupt and scathing criticisms of the present, he inspired in all his visitors a unanimous feeling of respectful esteem. For them the old-fashioned house with its huge pier-glasses, pre-Revolution furniture, powdered footmen, and the stern shrewd old man (himself a relic of a past century) with his gentle daughter and the pretty Frenchwoman, both so reverently devoted to him, presented a majestic and agreeable spectacle. But the visitors did not reflect that over and above the couple of hours during which they saw their hosts there were also twenty-two hours of the day and night during which the private and intimate life of the household continued its accustomed way.

Of late this private life had become very trying for Princess Maria. In Moscow she was deprived of her greatest joys – talks with the pilgrims, and the solitude which refreshed her at Bald Hills – and she had none of the advantages and pleasures of town life. She did not go out into society: everyone knew that her father would not allow her anywhere without him, and his failing health prevented his going out himself, so that she was not invited to dinners and evening parties. She had abandoned all hope of ever getting married. She saw the coldness and malevolence with which the old prince received and dismissed such young men as occasionally came to the house, and who might have been her suitors. She had no friends: since her arrival in Moscow she had been disappointed in the two who had been nearest to her. Mademoiselle Bourienne, with whom she had never been able altogether to open her heart, she now regarded with dislike, and for various reasons kept at a distance. Julie, with whom she had corresponded for the last five years, was in Moscow, but she seemed like a stranger when they met again. By the death of her brothers Julie had become one of the wealthiest heiresses in Moscow, and was at that time engrossed in a giddy whirl of fashionable amusements. She was surrounded by young men who, she believed, had suddenly learnt to appreciate her worth. Julie was at that stage in the life of a society woman past her first youth when she feels that her last chance of finding a husband has come, and that her fate must be decided now or never. With a mournful smile Princess Maria reflected every Thursday that she now had no one to send letters to, since Julie – Julie whose presence gave her no pleasure – was here in town and they met every week. Like the old French *émigré* who declined to marry the lady with whom he had spent all his evenings for years, she regretted that Julie was in Moscow and so there was no one to write to. In Moscow Princess Maria had no one to talk to, no one in whom to confide her sorrows, and many fresh sorrows fell to her lot just then. The time for Prince Andrei's return and his marriage was drawing near, but his mission to her to prepare his father was so far from having been successfully carried out that the whole thing seemed quite hopeless – any reference to the young Countess Rostov set the old prince beside himself (who in any case was almost always in a bad temper). Another trouble that weighed on Princess Maria of late arose out of the lessons she gave to her six-year-old nephew. In her relations with little Nikolai, to her consternation she detected in herself symptoms of her father's irritability. No matter how often she told herself that she must not lose her temper when teaching her nephew, almost every time that, pointer in hand, she sat down to show him the French alphabet, she so longed to hasten, to make easy the process of pouring her own knowledge into the child – who by now was always afraid that at any moment Auntie would get angry – that the slightest inattention on the part of the little boy would make her tremble, become flustered and heated, raise her voice, and sometimes even seize him by the arm and stand him in the corner. Having stood him in the corner, she would begin to shed tears over her spiteful, wicked nature, and little Nikolai, his sobs vying with hers, would come unbidden out of his corner to pull her tear-wet hands from her face, and try to comfort her. But the heaviest, far the heaviest of the princess's burdens was her father's irascibility, which was invariably directed against his daughter, and had of late reached the point of cruelty. Had he forced her to spend the night on her knees in prayer, had he beaten her or made her chop wood and carry water, it would never have entered her head that her lot was a hard one; but this loving despot – the more cruel from the very fact that he loved her, and for that very reason tortured both himself and her – knew not merely how to wound and humiliate her deliberately but how to make her feel that she was always and for ever in the wrong. Latterly he had exhibited a new trait, which caused Princess Maria more misery than anything. This was his ever-increasing intimacy with Mademoiselle Bourienne. The farcical notion, first suggested to his mind by the news of his son's intentions, that if Andrei got married he himself would marry the Bourienne evidently flattered his fancy, and of late he had persistently, and as it seemed to Princess Maria merely to give offence to her, lavished endearments on Mademoiselle Bourienne, and expressed his dissatisfaction with his daughter by demonstrations of affection for the Frenchwoman.

One day in Moscow, in Princess Maria's presence (she thought her father did it on purpose because she was there), the old prince kissed Mademoiselle Bourienne's hand and, drawing her to him, embraced and fondled her. Princess Maria flushed hotly and ran out of the room. A few minutes later Mademoiselle Bourienne came into Princess Maria's room smiling and making cheerful remarks in her agreeable voice. Princess Maria hastily wiped away her tears, went resolutely up to Mademoiselle Bourienne, and evidently unconscious of what she was doing began screaming at the Frenchwoman in furious haste, her voice breaking:

'It's loathsome, vile, inhuman to take advantage of weakness. …' She did not finish. 'Leave my room!' she cried, and burst into sobs.

The following day the prince did not say a word to his daughter, but she noticed that at dinner he gave instructions that Mademoiselle Bourienne should be served first. At the end of the meal, when the footman brought round the coffee and from habit began with the princess, the old prince flew into a sudden frenzy, flung his cane at Filipp, and instantly ordered that he should be sent off to the army.

'You disobey me … twice I told you! … You disobey me! She is the first person in this house, she's my best friend,' shouted the old prince. 'And if you,' he cried in fury, addressing Princess Maria for the first time, 'ever again dare, as you did yesterday, to forget yourself in her presence, I'll show you who is master in this house. Go! Get out of my sight! Beg her pardon!'

Princess Maria asked Mademoiselle Bourienne's pardon, and also her father's pardon for herself and Filipp the footman, who implored her to intercede for him.

At such moments a feeling akin to the pride of sacrifice gathered in her soul. And then all of a sudden the father whom she was criticizing would look for his spectacles, fumbling near them and not seeing them, or forget something that had just happened, or totter on his failing legs and turn to see if anyone had noticed his feebleness, or, worst of all, at dinner if there were no guests to keep him awake, would suddenly fall into a doze, letting his napkin drop and his shaking head sink over his plate. 'He is old and feeble, and I presume to criticize him!' she would think at such moments, revolted by herself.

3

In the year 1811 there was living in Moscow a French doctor called Métivier, who had rapidly become the fashion. He was enormously tall, handsome, polite and amiable as Frenchmen are, and, as everyone said, an extraordinarily clever doctor. He was received in the very best houses, not merely as a doctor but as an equal.

Old Prince Bolkonsky had always ridiculed medicine, but latterly on Mademoiselle Bourienne's advice had allowed this doctor to visit him, and had grown accustomed to him. Métivier came to see the old prince a couple of times a week.

On St Nikolai's day, the name-day of the prince, all Moscow drove up to the prince's front door, but he gave orders to admit no one. Only a select few, of whom he handed a list to Princess Maria, were to be invited to dinner.

Métivier, who arrived in the morning with his felicitations, considered himself entitled, as the old prince's doctor, to *forcer le consigne*, as he told Princess Maria, and went in to see the old man. It so happened that on that morning of his name-day the prince was in one of his very worst moods. He had been wandering about the house the whole morning, finding fault with everyone and pretending not to understand what was said to him, and not to be understood himself. Princess Maria well knew this mood of lowering querulousness, which generally culminated in an outburst of fury, and she went about all that morning as though facing a cocked and loaded gun, in expectation of the inevitable explosion. Until the doctor's arrival the morning had passed off safely. Having admitted the doctor, Princess Maria sat down with a book in the drawing-room near the door, through which she could hear all that passed in the study.

At first the only sound was Métivier's voice, then her father's, then both voices speaking at once. The door flew open, and on the threshold appeared the handsome figure of the terrified Métivier with his shock of black hair, followed by the prince in his skull-cap and dressing-gown, his face distorted with rage and the pupils of his eyes dilated.

'You don't see it?' shouted the prince. 'Well, I do! French spy, slave of Bonaparte, spy, get out of my house – get out, I tell you!' And he slammed the door.

Métivier, shrugging his shoulders, went up to Mademoiselle Bourienne, who had rushed in from the adjoining room on hearing the noise.

'The prince is not very well – bile and rush of blood to the head. Do not worry, I will look in again tomorrow,' said Métivier, and putting his fingers to his lips he hurried away.

Through the study door came the sound of slippered feet and the shouting of 'Spies, traitors, traitors everywhere! Never a minute's peace even in my own house!'

After Métivier's departure the old prince sent for his daughter, and the whole brunt of his fury fell on her. She was to blame that a spy had been admitted to see him. Had he not told her, told her to make a list, and not to let anyone in who was not on that list? Then why had that scoundrel been shown in? It was all her fault. With her, he said, he could not have sixty seconds' quiet to die in peace.

'No, ma'am! we must part, we must part, I tell you. Make up your mind to it! I cannot stand any more,' he said, and left the room. And then, as though afraid she might find some means of consolation, he returned and trying to appear calm added: 'And don't imagine I said that to you in the heat of the moment. No, I am perfectly calm, and I have weighed my words, and it shall be so – we must part. Find a home for yourself somewhere else! ...' But he could not restrain himself and, with the virulence which can only exist where there is love, obviously in anguish himself, he shook his fists at her and screamed:

'If only some fool would take her to wife!' After that he slammed the door, sent for Mademoiselle Bourienne and subsided in his study.

At two o'clock the six chosen guests assembled for dinner. These guests – the famous Count Rostopchin, Prince Lopuhin and his nephew, General Chatrov, an old comrade in arms of the prince's, and, of the younger generation, Pierre and Boris Drubetskoy – awaited their host in the drawing-room.

Boris, who had come to Moscow on leave a few days before, had been anxious to be presented to Prince Nikolai Bolkonsky, and he had so far succeeded in ingratiating himself that the old prince in his case made an exception to his rule of not receiving young bachelors.

The prince's house was not what was called 'fashionable', but it was the centre of a little circle into which, though not much talked about in town, it was more flattering to be admitted than anywhere else. Boris had realized this the week before, when he heard Rostopchin tell the commander-in-chief of Moscow, who had invited him to dine on St Nikolai's day, that he could not accept his invitation.

'On that day I always go and pay my devotions to the relics of Prince Nikolai Bolkonsky.'

'Oh yes, of course,' replied the commander-in-chief. 'How is he ? ...'

The little party that met together before dinner in the lofty, old-fashioned drawing-room with its ancient furniture resembled the solemn gathering of a court of justice. No one had much to say, and if they spoke it was in low tones. Prince Nikolai came in, grave and taciturn. Princess Maria seemed even quieter and more diffident than usual. The guests showed no inclination to address her, for they saw that she was not attending to what they said. Count Rostopchin alone kept the conversation going, now relating the latest news of the town, now the most recent political gossip.

Lopuhin and the old general occasionally put in a word. Prince Bolkonsky listened as a presiding judge listens to a report presented to him, only now and then, by his silence or some curt monosyllable, showing that he was taking cognizance of the facts laid before him. The tone of the conversation was based on the assumption that no one approved of what was being done in the political world. Incidents were related obviously confirming the opinion that everything was going from bad to worse; but in all their anecdotes and criticisms it was noticeable how each speaker came to a stop, or was brought to a stop, every time the point was reached beyond which his unfavourable opinions might reflect on the person of his Majesty the Emperor.

At dinner the talk turned on the latest political news: Napoleon's seizure of the possessions of the Duke of Oldenburg, and the Russian note – hostile to Napoleon – which had been sent to all the European courts.

'Bonaparte treats Europe the way a pirate treats a captured vessel,' said Count Rostopchin, repeating an epigram he had got off a number of times before. 'One only marvels at the long-suffering, or the blindness, of the ruling Sovereigns. Now it is the Pope's turn, and Bonaparte doesn't scruple to try and depose the head of the Catholic Church, and no one says a word. Our Emperor is the only one to raise a voice against the seizure of the Duke of Oldenburg's territory, and even …' Count Rostopchin paused, feeling that he was on the very borderline beyond which criticism was impossible.

'Other domains have been offered him in exchange for the Duchy of Oldenburg,' said Prince Bolkonsky. 'He shifts the dukes about as I might move my serfs from Bald Hills to Bogucharovo or my Ryazan estates.'

'The Duke of Oldenburg bears his misfortunes with admirable fortitude and resignation,' remarked Boris in French, putting in his word respectfully. He said this because on his journey from Petersburg he had had the honour of being presented to the duke. Prince Bolkonsky glanced at the young man as though he had it in mind to make some reply but thought better of it, evidently considering him too young to bother about.

'I read our protest about the Oldenburg affair and was surprised how badly the note was worded,' remarked Count Rostopchin in the casual tone of a man who knows what he is saying.

Pierre looked at Rostopchin in naïve wonder, unable to understand why he should be disturbed by the wretched style of the note.

'What difference does it make, count, how the note is written,' he asked, 'so long as the subject-matter is forcible?'

'*Mon cher*, with our army of five hundred thousand men it should be easy to have a good style,' returned Count Rostopchin.

Pierre perceived the point of Count Rostopchin's dissatisfaction with the wording of the note.

'I should have thought there were plenty of quill-drivers about,' said the old prince. 'In Petersburg they do nothing but write – not notes only, but even new laws. My Andrei there has written a whole volume of laws for Russia. Nowadays they're always at it!' and he laughed unnaturally.

The conversation languished for a moment. The old general cleared his throat to draw attention to himself.

'Did you hear what happened recently at the review in Petersburg? The way the French ambassador behaved!'

'What was that? Yes, I did hear something. He made some awkward remark in his Majesty's presence, I believe.'

'His Majesty drew his attention to the Grenadier division and the march past,' pursued the general, 'and it seems the ambassador took no notice and had the impudence to remark, "We in France do not trouble our heads over such trifles." The Emperor did not condescend to reply. At the next review, they say, the Emperor simply ignored his presence.'

All were silent. It was out of the question to pass any comment on this occurrence, since it related to the Monarch personally.

'Insolent rogues!' exclaimed the old prince. 'You know Métivier? I turned him out of my house this morning. He was here – they let him in to see me in spite of my request that no one should be admitted,' he went on, glancing angrily at his daughter. And he repeated from beginning to end his conversation with the French doctor, and his reasons for believing Métivier to be a spy. Though these reasons were very insufficient and obscure, no one made any rejoinder.

After the roast, champagne was served. The guests rose from their places to wish the old prince many happy returns. Princess Maria, too, went up to him.

He gave her a cold, angry look, and offered her his wrinkled, clean-shaven cheek to kiss. The whole expression of his face told her that he had not forgotten their conversation of that morning, that his mind was just as fully made up and only the presence of his guests prevented him from telling her so now.

When they went into the drawing-room for coffee, the old men sat together.

Prince Bolkonsky grew more animated, and began to express his views on the impending war.

He declared that our wars with Bonaparte would be disastrous so long as we tried to make common cause with the Germans and went meddling in European affairs, into which we had been drawn by the Peace of Tilsit. 'We had no business to fight either for or against

Austria. Our political interests are all in the east, and so far as Bonaparte is concerned the only thing is to have an armed force on the frontier and a firm policy, and he will never again dare to set foot in Russia, as he did in 1807!'

'How can we possibly make war against the French, prince?' asked Count Rostopchin. 'Can we arm ourselves against our teachers – our idols? Look at our young men, look at our ladies! The French are our gods, and Paris is our Kingdom of Heaven.'

He raised his voice, evidently so that all might hear him.

'Our fashions are French, our ideas are French, our sentiments are French! You sent Métivier packing because he is a Frenchman and a scoundrel, but our ladies crawl after him on their hands and knees. Yesterday I was at a party, and out of five ladies present three were Roman Catholics and had a dispensation from the Pope allowing them to do wool-work on Sundays. And there they sat, practically naked, like the sign-boards outside our public bath-houses, if you'll excuse my saying so. Ah, prince, when one looks at our young people, one would like to take Peter the Great's old cudgel out of the museum and break a few ribs in the good old Russian style. That would soon knock the nonsense out of them!'

All were silent. The old prince looked at Rostopchin with a smile and nodded his head approvingly.

'Well, good-bye, your Excellency, keep well!' said Rostopchin, getting up with his usual abruptness and holding out his hand to the prince.

'Good-bye, my dear fellow. ... His words are like music, I never tire of listening to him,' said the old prince, keeping hold of Rostopchin's hand and offering him his cheek. The others, too, rose when Rostopchin did.

4

PRINCESS MARIA, sitting in the drawing-room and listening to the old men's talk and fault-finding, understood not a word of what she was hearing; her one preoccupation was whether their guests had all observed her father's hostile attitude towards her. She did not even notice the marked attentions and amiabilities showed her all through dinner by Boris Drubetskoy, though this was his third visit to the house.

Princess Maria turned with an abstracted, inquiring look to Pierre who, hat in hand and with a smile on his face, was the last to come up to her after the old prince had retired and they were left alone in the drawing-room.

'May I stay a little longer?' he asked, letting his bulky person sink into a low chair beside Princess Maria.

'Oh yes,' she answered. 'You noticed nothing?' her eyes asked.

Pierre was in an agreeable, after-dinner mood. He looked straight before him and smiled softly.

'Have you known that young man long, princess?' he asked.

'What young man?'

'Drubetskoy.'

'No, not long. ...'

'Do you like him?'

'Yes, he's a pleasant young fellow. ... Why do you ask?' said Princess Maria, her mind still on the morning's conversation with her father.

'Because I have remarked that when a young man comes on leave from Petersburg to Moscow it is usually with the object of marrying an heiress.'

'You have observed that?' said Princess Maria.

'Yes,' continued Pierre with a smile, 'and this young man now so manages it that where there are wealthy heiresses – there he, too, is to be found. I can read him like a book. At present he is undecided whether to lay siege to – you or Mademoiselle Julie Karagin. He is very attentive to her.'

'He goes there then?'

'Yes, very often. And do you know the new-fashioned method of courting?' said Pierre with an amused smile, evidently in that gay mood of light-hearted raillery for which he had so often reproved himself in his diary.

'No,' replied Princess Maria.

'To please the Moscow girls nowadays one has to be melancholy. He is very melancholy with Mademoiselle Karagin,' said Pierre.

'Really?' said Princess Maria, looking into Pierre's kindly face and thinking all the time of her own trouble. 'It would ease my heart,' she thought, 'if I could make up my mind to confide what I am feeling to someone. And it is just Pierre I should like to tell it all to. He is so kind and generous. It would be a relief. He would give me advice.'

'Would you marry him?' asked Pierre.

'Oh heavens, count, there are moments when I would marry anybody!' exclaimed Princess Maria, to her own surprise and with tears in her voice. 'Ah, how bitter it is to love someone near to you and to feel that ...' she went on in a trembling voice, 'that you can do nothing but be a trial to him, and to know that you cannot alter it. Then there is only one thing left – to go away, but where could I go?'

'What is wrong? What is the trouble, princess?'

But without explaining further Princess Maria burst into tears.

'I don't know what is the matter with me today. Don't take any notice – forget what I said.'

Pierre's gaiety vanished completely. He questioned the princess anxiously, begged her to speak out, to confide her grief to him; but her only reply was to beseech him to forget what she had said, repeating that she did not remember it and that she had no troubles except the one which he knew about already – her fear lest Prince Andrei's marriage should cause a breach between father and son.

'Have you any news of the Rostovs?' she asked, to change the subject. 'I am told that they will be arriving soon. And I expect André too any day now. I should have liked them to meet here.'

'And how does he regard the matter now?' asked Pierre, by *he* meaning the old prince.

Princess Maria shook her head. 'But it can't be helped. A few more months and the year will be up. And it can't go on like this. I only wish I could spare my brother the first moments. I wish the Rostovs were coming sooner. I hope to get to be friends with her. ... You have known them a long time, haven't you?' said Princess Maria. 'Tell me truly, with your hand on your heart, what sort of a girl is she, and what do you think of her? But I want the whole truth, because, you see, André is risking so much in doing this against his father's will that I should like to know. ...'

A vague instinct told Pierre that these explanations and repeated requests to be told the *whole truth* betrayed some covert ill-will on Princess Maria's part towards her future sister-in-law, and a wish that he should not approve of Prince Andrei's choice; but in reply he said what he felt rather than what he thought.

'I don't know how to answer your question,' he said, blushing though he could not have told why. 'I really don't know what kind of girl she is. I can never analyse her. She is fascinating. But what makes her so, I can't tell you. That is all one can say about her.'

Princess Maria sighed, and the expression on her face said: 'Yes, that's what I expected and feared.'

'Is she clever?' she asked.

Pierre considered.

'I think not,' he said, 'and yet – yes. She does not think it worth while to be clever. ... Oh no, she is enchanting, and that's all about it.'

Princess Maria again shook her head disapprovingly.

'Ah, I do so want to like her! Tell her so, if you see her before I do.'

'I hear they are expected very soon,' said Pierre.

Princess Maria confided to Pierre her plan to become friends with her future sister-in-law as soon as the Rostovs arrived, and to try to get the old prince accustomed to her.

5

Boris had not succeeded in making a wealthy match in Petersburg, so with the same object in view he came to Moscow. Here he found himself hesitating between two of the richest heiresses, Julie and Princess Maria. Though Princess Maria, in spite of her plainness, seemed to him more attractive than Julie, without knowing why he felt uncomfortable about paying court to her. In his last conversation with her, on the old prince's name-day, she had met all his attempts to talk sentimentally with irrelevant replies, evidently not listening to what he was saying.

Julie, on the contrary, received his attentions eagerly, though she showed her readiness in a peculiar fashion of her own.

Julie was twenty-seven. At the death of her brothers she had become very wealthy. She was now decidedly plain, but believed herself to be not merely as pretty as before but far more captivating than she had ever been. She was sustained in this illusion firstly by the fact of having become an extremely wealthy heiress, and secondly because the older she grew the less dangerous she was to men, and the more freely could they gather round her and avail themselves of her suppers, her *soirées* and the lively company that frequented her house, without incurring any obligation. Men who, ten years ago, would have thought twice before going every day to a house where there was a young girl of seventeen, for fear of compromising her and en-tangling themselves, now appeared constantly and treated her not as a marriageable girl but as a sexless acquaintance.

That winter the Karagins' house was the most agreeable and hospitable in Moscow. In addition to the formal receptions and dinner-parties, every evening there was a numerous gathering, chiefly of men, who ate supper at midnight and stayed till three in the morning. Julie never missed a ball, a promenade or a play. Her gowns were always of the latest fashion. Nevertheless Julie pretended to be disenchanted with everything, and told everybody that she had no faith in friendship or in love, or any of the joys of life, and hoped for peace only 'beyond the grave'. She affected the air of one who has suffered a great disappointment, like a girl who has either lost her lover or been cruelly deceived by him. Though nothing of the kind had happened to her, it began to be thought that such was the case, and she herself came to believe that she had suffered a great deal in her life. This melancholy neither hindered her from enjoying herself nor prevented the young people who came to her house from passing their time very pleasantly. Each one of her visitors paid his tribute to the melancholy mood of his hostess, and then proceeded to enjoy himself with society gossip, dancing, intellectual games, and *bouts rimés* which were in vogue at the Karagins'. Only a few of the young men, among them Boris, entered more deeply into Julie's melancholy, and with these she had longer and more confidential conversations on the vanity of all worldly things, and to them she showed her albums, filled with gloomy sketches, maxims and verses.

Julie was particularly gracious to Boris. She mourned with him over his early disillusionment with life, offered him such consolations of friendship as she, who had suffered so much, could render, and opened her album to him. Boris sketched two trees in the album, and wrote under them in French: 'Rustic trees, your sombre branches shed darkness and melancholy upon me.'

On another page he drew a tomb and inscribed below it:

> Death gives us peace – 'tis death that brings release.
> 'Tis then alone our earthly sorrows cease!

Julie said this was exquisite.

'There is something so ravishing in the smile of melancholy,' she said to Boris, repeating word for word a passage copied from a book. 'It is a ray of light in the darkness, a *nuance* between sorrow and despair, heralding the possibility of consolation.'

Whereupon Boris wrote these lines for her in French:

Poisonous nourishment of a soul too sensitive,
Thou, the only joy my grieving spirit knows,
Tender melancholy, come! Thy consolation bring!
O come with respite from my solitary woes,
Mingle thy secret, soothing balm
With my tears that never cease to spring.

For Boris Julie played her most doleful nocturnes on the harp.
Boris read *Poor Liza* aloud to her, and more than once had to interrupt his reading because of the emotion that choked him. When they
met in society, Julie and Boris gazed at one another as if they were the
only two kindred souls in the world.

Anna Mihalovna, who often visited the Karagins, while playing
cards with the mother would make careful inquiries as to Julie's
dowry – which was to consist of two estates in Penza and the Nizhni
Novgorod forest lands. Anna Mihalovna looked on with emotion
and humble devotion to the will of Providence at the refined sadness
that united her son to the wealthy Julie.

'You are still as charming and melancholy as ever, my dear Julie,'
she would remark to the daughter. 'Boris says that here in your
house he finds repose for his soul. He has suffered so many disappoint-
ments, and is so sensitive,' said she to the mother. 'Ah, my dear, I
can't tell you how fond I have grown of Julie latterly,' she would say
to her son. 'But who could help loving her? She is such an angelic
being! Ah, Boris, Boris!' She paused for a moment. 'And how I pity
her mother,' she went on. 'Today she was showing me her accounts
and letters from Penza (they have enormous estates there), and she,
poor thing, with no one to help her. They do take such advantage
of her!'

Boris's face wore an almost perceptible smile as he listened to his
mother. He was quietly amused at her naïve diplomacy, but listened
to what she had to say and sometimes questioned her carefully about
the Penza and Nizhni Novgorod estates.

Julie had for some time been expecting a proposal from her melancholy adorer, and was fully prepared to accept it; but some secret
distaste for her, for her passionate desire to get married, for her affectation, and a feeling of horror at thus renouncing the possibility of
true love, still restrained Boris. The term of his leave was expiring.
He spent every day and all day at the Karagins', and each day, as he
thought the matter over, Boris told himself that he would propose

tomorrow. But in Julie's presence, looking at her red face and her chin (nearly always dusted with powder), her moist eyes, and her expression which betokened an ever-readiness to fly at a moment's notice from melancholy to unnatural ecstasies of wedded bliss, Boris could not bring himself to utter the decisive words, although in imagination he had long regarded himself as the master of those Penza and Nizhni Novgorod estates, and had more than once arranged how he would spend the income from them. Julie noticed Boris's hesitation and sometimes the thought occurred to her that he had an aversion for her; but her feminine vanity quickly restored her confidence, and she would assure herself that it was merely love that made him bashful. Her melancholy, however, was beginning to develop into irritability, and not long before Boris's departure she formed a definite plan of action. Just as Boris's leave of absence was drawing to a close Anatole Kuragin made his appearance in Moscow, and – it need hardly be said – in the Karagins' drawing-room, and Julie, abruptly abandoning her melancholy, became exceedingly gay and very attentive to Kuragin.

'My dear,' said Anna Mihalovna to her son, 'I hear from a reliable source that Prince Vasili has sent his son to Moscow to make a match with Julie. I am so fond of Julie that I should be very sorry for her. What is your opinion, my dear?'

The idea of being left to look a fool, and of having wasted that whole month in the arduous, melancholy service of Julie, and of seeing all the revenue from those Penza estates, which he had already assigned and put to proper use, fall into the hands of another, especially into the hands of that fool Anatole, outraged Boris. He drove off to the Karagins' with the firm intention of proposing. Julie met him in a lively, careless manner, casually mentioned how much she had enjoyed the ball the previous evening, and asked when he was leaving. Though Boris had come fully intending to speak of his love and was therefore resolved to take a tender tone, he began complaining irritably of feminine inconstancy, of how easily women could pass from sadness to joy, and how their moods depended solely on whoever happened to be paying court to them. Julie took offence at this, and replied that he was right: a woman needed variety, and the same thing over and over again would bore anyone.

'Then I should advise you …' Boris was about to retort, meaning to say something cutting; but at that instant the galling reflection occurred to him that he might have to leave Moscow without having attained his object and having wasted his efforts in vain (an experience he had never known yet). He stopped short in the middle of the sentence, lowered his eyes to avoid seeing the disagreeable look of annoyance and indecision on her face, and said:

'But it was not to quarrel with you that I came here. On the contrary. ...'

He glanced at her to make sure that he might go on. All her irritation had suddenly vanished, and her anxious, imploring eyes were fastened upon him in greedy expectation. 'I can always manage so as to see very little of her,' thought Boris. 'And the thing's been begun and must be finished!' He blushed hotly, raised his eyes to hers, and said:

'You know my feelings for you!'

There was no need to say more: Julie's face beamed with triumph and self-satisfaction; but she forced Boris to say all that is usually said on such occasions – to say that he loved her and had never loved any woman more. She knew that for her Penza estates and the Nizhni Novgorod forests she could demand that, and she received what she demanded.

The engaged couple, with no further allusions to trees that enfolded them in gloom and melancholy, laid plans for a brilliant establishment in Petersburg, paid calls, and made every preparation for a brilliant wedding.

6

COUNT ILYA ROSTOV, together with Natasha and Sonya, arrived in Moscow at the end of January. The countess was still unwell and unable to travel, but it was out of the question to wait for her recovery: Prince Andrei was expected in Moscow any day. Besides that, the trousseau had to be ordered, the estate near Moscow sold, and advantage taken of old Prince Bolkonsky's presence in Moscow to present his future daughter-in-law to him. The Rostovs' town house had not been heated that winter, and as, moreover, they had come only for a short time and the countess was not with them the count decided to stay with Maria Dmitrievna Ahrosimov, who had long been pressing her hospitality on the count.

Late one evening the Rostovs' four sledges drove into Maria Dmitrievna's courtyard in Old Konyusheny street. Maria Dmitrievna lived alone. She had already married off her daughter, and her sons were all in the service.

She still held herself as erect as ever, still gave everyone her opinion in the same loud, outspoken, blunt fashion, and her whole bearing seemed a reproach to other people for any weakness, passion or temptation – the possibility of which she did not admit. She was up early in the morning, wearing a loose jacket, to attend to her household affairs, after which she drove out – on saints' days to church, and thence to gaols and prisons; of what she did there she never spoke to anyone. On ordinary days, after she was dressed, she received everyone, whoever they were, who came to seek her aid. Then she had dinner, a substantial and appetizing meal at which there were always three or four guests. After dinner she played a game of boston, and at night had the newspapers or a new book read to her while she knitted. She rarely made any exception to her routine, and if she did it was only to visit the very important persons in the town.

She had not yet retired when the Rostovs arrived and the door in the hall creaked on its pulleys, admitting the travellers and their retinue of servants from the cold. Maria Dmitrievna, with her spectacles slipping down her nose and her head flung back, stood in the hall doorway looking at the newcomers with a stern, grim face. It might have been supposed she was really angry with them and ready to pack them off again at once, had she not at the same time been heard giving careful instructions to the servants for the accommodation of the visitors and their belongings.

'The count's things? Bring them this way,' she said, pointing to the portmanteaux and not stopping to greet anyone. 'The young ladies'? Take them over there, on the left. Well, what are you pottering about for?' she cried to the maids. 'Get the samovar ready! ... The girl's grown plumper and prettier,' she remarked, drawing Natasha towards her by her hood. (Natasha's cheeks were glowing from the cold.) 'Phoo! You *are* cold! Now take off your things, quick!' she cried to the count who was going to kiss her hand. 'You're frozen, I'll warrant. Bring some rum with the tea! ... Sonya, dear, *bonjour!*' she added, addressing Sonya and indicating by this French greeting her slightly contemptuous though affectionate attitude towards her.

When they came in to tea, having taken off their wraps and tidied themselves after their journey, Maria Dmitrievna kissed them all in turn.

'I'm heartily glad you have come and are staying with me. It was high time,' she said, giving Natasha a significant look. 'The old man is here, and his son is expected any day. You'll certainly have to make his acquaintance. Well, we'll talk about that later on,' she added, with a glance at Sonya as much as to say that she did not care to speak of that subject in her presence. 'Now, listen,' she said to the count. 'What are your plans for tomorrow? Whom will you send for? Shinshin?' She crooked one finger. 'That snivelling Anna Mihalovna – two. She's here with her son. That son of hers is getting married! Then Bezuhov, eh? He and his wife are here. He ran away from her, but she came galloping after him. He dined with me on Wednesday. As for them' – and she pointed to the girls – 'tomorrow I'll take them first to the Iversky chapel, and then to Suppert-Roguet's. I suppose you'll have everything new? Don't judge by me: sleeves nowadays are this size! Young Princess Irina Vasilyevna came to see me recently: she was an awful sight – looked as if she had put two barrels on her arms. Not a day passes now, you know, without some new fashion. And what business have you on hand?' she asked the count severely.

'Oh, a little of everything,' replied the count. 'The girl's rags to buy, and now a purchaser has turned up for the Moscow estate and the house. If you will be so kind, I'll fix a time and drive over to the estate for the day, leaving my lassies with you.'

'Very well. Very well. They'll be safe with me, as safe as in chancery! I'll take them where they must go, and scold them a bit and pet them too,' said Maria Dmitrievna, touching her god-daughter and favourite, Natasha, on the cheek with her ample hand.

Next morning Maria Dmitrievna bore the young ladies off to the Iversky chapel and then to Madame Suppert-Roguet, who was so afraid of Maria Dmitrievna that she always let her have gowns at a loss simply to get rid of her as quickly as possible. Maria Dmitrievna ordered almost the whole trousseau. When they got home she turned everybody out of the room except Natasha, and called her favourite to sit beside her arm-chair.

'Well, now we can have a talk. I congratulate you on your betrothed. You've hooked a fine fellow! I am glad for you: I've known him since he was so high.' (She put her hand a couple of feet from the floor.) Natasha coloured with pleasure. 'I like him and all his family. Now listen! You know, of course, that old Prince Nikolai is very much against his son's marrying. He's a crotchety old boy. Of course

Prince Andrei is not a child and can get on without him, but still it's not a very nice thing to enter a family against the father's will. One must act peaceably, with affection. You're a clever girl, you'll know how to manage. You must use your wits and your kind heart. Then all will be well.'

Natasha remained silent, not as Maria Dmitrievna supposed from shyness, but because she disliked anyone interfering where her love for Prince Andrei was concerned, which seemed to her so above and beyond all ordinary human matters that she did not believe anyone could enter into her feeling about it. She loved Prince Andrei, and only him, and knew only him; he loved her and was to arrive in a day or two and carry her off. She did not care about anything else.

'I have known him for a long time, don't you see, and I am very fond of Maria, your future sister-in-law. "With husbands' sisters – look out for blisters!" says the proverb, but this one wouldn't hurt a fly. She begs me to bring the pair of you together. Tomorrow you'll be going with your father to see her. Be very nice to her – you are younger than she is. When that young man of yours comes he'll find you already know his sister and father, and that they like you. Am I not right? Won't that be best?'

'Yes, I suppose so,' Natasha answered reluctantly.

7

NEXT day, on Maria Dmitrievna's advice, Count Rostov took Natasha to call on Prince Nikolai Bolkonsky. The count set out in anything but a happy frame of mind: at heart he felt alarmed, for he remembered only too vividly the last interview he had had with the old prince, at the time of the levying of the militia. He had invited the prince to dinner, and in reply had had to listen to an angry reprimand for not having furnished his full quota of men. Natasha, on the other hand, having put on her best gown, was in the highest spirits. 'They can't help liking me,' she thought. 'Everybody always does. And I am so willing to do anything they could wish for them, so ready to be fond of him for being *his* father and of her for being *his* sister that there can be no reason for them not to like me. ...'

They drove up to the gloomy old house in Vozdvizhenka street and entered the vestibule.

'Well, the Lord have mercy on us!' exclaimed the count, half in jest, half in earnest; but Natasha noticed that her father was flurried as he went into the ante-room and inquired timidly and softly whether the prince and the princess were at home. After they had given their names, some confusion was obvious among the servants. The footman who had hurried off to announce them was stopped by another footman at the drawing-room door, and the two stood whispering together. Then a maid ran into the hall and hurriedly said something, mentioning the princess. At last an elderly, cross-looking footman came and informed the Rostovs that the prince was not receiving but the princess would be glad to see them. The first person to come out to meet the visitors was Mademoiselle Bourienne. She greeted the father and daughter with effusive politeness, and conducted them to the princess's apartment. The princess, agitated and nervous, her face all crimson patches, hastened forward to welcome the visitors, treading heavily and endeavouring unsuccessfully to appear cordial and at ease. From the first she did not like Natasha. She thought her too fashionably dressed, too frivolous, too flighty and vain. Princess Maria had no idea that before having seen her future sister-in-law she was prejudiced against her through unconscious envy of her beauty, youth and happiness, as well as jealousy of her brother's love for her. Apart from this insuperable feeling of antipathy to her, Princess Maria was in a state of agitation at that moment because at the announcement of the Rostovs' visit the old prince had shouted at the top of his voice that he did not wish to see them, that Princess Maria might do so if she chose but they were not to be admitted to him. She had decided to receive them, but feared lest the prince might at any moment indulge in some vagary, as he seemed so upset by the Rostovs' arrival.

'Well now, princess, I have brought you my little songstress,' said the count with a bow and a scrape, and looking round uneasily as if he were afraid the old prince might appear. 'I am so glad that you are to get to know one another. ... Sorry, very sorry the prince is still ailing.' And after making a few more commonplace remarks he got up. 'If you'll allow me, princess, I will leave my Natasha in your hands for a little quarter of an hour, while I slip round to see Anna Semeonovna – in Dog's square, only a few steps from here. Then I'll come back for her.'

The count bethought himself of this diplomatic stratagem (as he told his daughter afterwards) to give the future sisters-in-law an opportunity to talk to one another freely, but also to avoid the possibility of meeting the prince, of whom he was afraid. He did not mention this to his daughter, but Natasha perceived her father's nervousness and anxiety, and felt mortified by it. She blushed for him, grew still more annoyed with herself for having blushed, and flung the princess a bold, defiant look which said that she was not afraid of anybody. The princess told the count that she would be delighted, and only begged him not to hurry away from Anna Semeonovna's, and he departed.

Despite the restless glances thrown at her by Princess Maria – who wanted to have a tête-à-tête with Natasha – Mademoiselle Bourienne would not leave the room, and persisted in keeping up a steady stream of chatter about the delights of Moscow, and the theatres. Natasha felt offended by the hesitation she had noticed in the ante-room, by her father's nervousness and by the unnatural manner of the princess who, she thought, was making a favour of receiving her. Consequently she was displeased with everything. She did not like Princess Maria, who seemed to her very plain, affected and unsympathetic. Natasha suddenly shrank into herself, and involuntarily assumed an off-hand manner which alienated Princess Maria still more. After five minutes of laboured, artificial conversation they heard the sound of slippered feet approaching rapidly. A look of terror came over Princess Maria's face. The door opened, and the old prince appeared, wearing a white night-cap and dressing-gown.

'Ah, madam,' he began. 'Madam, countess ... Countess Rostov, if I am not mistaken. ... I beg your pardon, pray excuse me. ... I did not know, madam. God is my witness, I did not know that you were honouring us with a visit. I came to see my daughter – which accounts for this costume. I beg you to excuse me. ... God is my witness, I did not know,' he repeated, stressing the word 'God' so unnaturally and so unpleasantly that Princess Maria stood with downcast eyes, not daring to look either at her father or at Natasha. Natasha, too, having risen and curtsied, did not know what to do. Only Mademoiselle Bourienne smiled agreeably.

'I beg you to excuse me, I beg you to excuse me! God is my witness, I did not know,' muttered the old man, and after looking Natasha over from head to foot he went out.

Mademoiselle Bourienne was the first to recover herself after this apparition, and she began to talk about the prince's indisposition.

Natasha and Princess Maria looked at one another in silence, and the longer they did so, without saying what they wanted to say, the more they were confirmed in their mutual antipathy.

When the count returned, Natasha made an ill-mannered display of relief, and immediately prepared to take her departure: at that moment she almost hated the stiff, elderly princess, who could place her in such an embarrassing position and spend half an hour with her without once mentioning Prince Andrei. 'Of course I couldn't be the first to speak of him in the presence of that Frenchwoman,' thought Natasha. A similar compunction was meanwhile tormenting Princess Maria. She knew what she ought to have said to Natasha, but she had been unable to say it both because Mademoiselle Bourienne was in the way and because – though she did not know why – she found it very difficult to speak of the marriage. The count was already leaving the room when Princess Maria hurried towards Natasha, took her by the hand and said with a deep sigh:

'Wait, I must ...'

Natasha gave her a mocking glance, though she could not have told what made her do so.

'Dear Natalie,' said Princess Maria, 'I want you to know how glad I am that my brother has found happiness. ...'

She paused, feeling that she was not telling the truth. Natasha noticed the pause and guessed the reason for it.

'I think, princess, this is not the time for speaking of that,' said Natasha coldly and with outward dignity, though she felt the tears rising in her throat.

'What have I said, what have I done?' she thought, as soon as she was out of the room.

They had to wait a long while for Natasha to come to dinner that day. She sat in her room crying like a child, blowing her nose and sobbing. Sonya stood beside her, kissing her hair.

'Natasha, what is there to cry about?' she asked. 'Why do you mind about them? It will all pass over, Natasha.'

'But if only you knew how insulting it was ... as if I ...'

'Don't talk about it, Natasha. It wasn't your fault, so why let it upset you? Kiss me now,' said Sonya.

Natasha lifted her head and, kissing her friend on the lips, pressed her wet face against her.

'I can't tell you. I don't know. No one's to blame,' said Natasha.

'It's my fault. But it all hurts terribly. Oh, why doesn't he come?'

She went down to dinner with red eyes. Maria Dmitrievna, who had heard how the prince had received the Rostovs, pretended not to notice Natasha's troubled face, and at table loudly and resolutely bandied jests with the count and her other guests.

8

THAT evening the Rostovs went to the opera, for which Maria Dmitrievna had taken a box.

Natasha did not want to go but could not refuse after Maria Dmitrievna's kindness, especially as it had been arranged expressly for her. Dressed and waiting for her father in the big hall, she surveyed herself in the tall looking-glass and when she saw how pretty, how very pretty she was, she felt even more melancholy than before, but it was a sweet, tender melancholy.

'Oh God, if he were here now I should not have that silly sort of shy feeling I had before. I would throw my arms round his neck and cling close to him, and make him look at me with those searching, inquiring eyes of his with which he has so often looked at me, and then I would make him laugh as he used to laugh then. And his eyes – how plainly I can see his eyes this very moment!' thought Natasha. 'And what do his father and sister matter to me? I love only him, him alone, him, with that dear face and his eyes and his smile – a man's smile and at the same time childlike. ... No, better not think of him, not think but forget. Better forget him altogether for the present, or I shan't be able to bear this waiting. I shall cry in a minute!' and she turned away from the looking-glass, making an effort not to weep. 'And how can Sonya love Nikolai so calmly and quietly, and wait so long and so patiently?' she wondered, seeing Sonya come in, dressed and ready with a fan in her hand. 'No, she's quite different from me. I can't be like her!'

Natasha at that moment felt so full of emotion and tenderness that it was not enough for her to love and know that she was loved: what she wanted now at this instant was to embrace her beloved, speak to him and hear from him the words of love that filled her own heart. As she rode along in the carriage, sitting beside her father and pensively watching the lights of the street lamps flickering on the frozen window, she felt still sadder and more in love, and forgot where she was going and with whom. The Rostovs' carriage fell into the line of carriages and drove up to the theatre, its wheels slowly creaking over the snow. Natasha and Sonya skipped down quickly, holding up their skirts. The count got out supported by the footmen, and making their way through the stream of ladies and gentlemen going in, and the programme-sellers, the three of them walked along the corridor to their box in the stalls. The sounds of music were already audible through the closed doors.

'Natasha, your hair!' whispered Sonya in French.

An attendant hurried up and slipped deferentially past the ladies to open the door of their box. The music sounded louder, and through the door they beheld the rows of brightly-lit boxes occupied by ladies with bare arms and shoulders, and the noisy stalls below, brilliant with uniforms. A woman entering the adjoining box shot a glance of feminine envy at Natasha. The curtain had not yet risen and the orchestra was playing the overture. Natasha, smoothing her gown, went forward with Sonya and sat down, gazing at the glittering tiers opposite. A sensation she had not experienced for a long time – that of having hundreds of eyes looking at her bare arms and neck – suddenly affected her with mixed pleasure and discomfort, and called up a whole swarm of memories, desires and emotions associated with that sensation.

The two remarkably pretty girls, Natasha and Sonya, with Count Rostov, who had not been seen in Moscow for some long while, attracted general attention. Moreover, everybody had heard vaguely of Natasha's engagement to Prince Andrei, and knew that the Rostovs had been living in the country ever since, and so gazed with curiosity at the girl who was to make one of the best matches in Russia.

Natasha's looks, as everyone told her, had improved in the country, and that evening, thanks to her agitation, she was particularly pretty. Her exuberance and beauty combined with her indifference to everything around her impressed all those who saw her. Her black eyes wandered over the crowd without seeking anyone, and her slender arm, bare to above the elbow, lay on the velvet edge of the box, while, evidently unconsciously, she opened and closed her hand in time to the music, crumpling her programme.

'Look, there's Alenina,' said Sonya, 'with her mother, isn't it?'

'Saints alive, Mihail Kirillich is fatter than ever!' exclaimed the old count.

'And do look at our Anna Mihalovna – what a head-dress she's got on!'

'The Karagins, Julie – and Boris with them. It's easy to see they're engaged.'

'Drubetskoy has proposed! Didn't you know? I heard today,' said Shinshin, coming into the Rostovs' box.

Following the direction of her father's eyes, Natasha saw Julie sitting beside her mother with a blissful look on her face and a string of pearls round her thick red neck – which Natasha knew was covered with powder. Behind them, wearing a smile and inclining his ear towards Julie's mouth, was Boris's handsome, smoothly-brushed head. He looked from under his brows at the Rostovs, and said something, smiling, to his betrothed.

'They are talking about us, about me and him!' thought Natasha. 'And she's jealous of me most likely, and he is trying to reassure her. They need not worry themselves! If only they knew how little they matter to me, any of them.'

Behind them sat Anna Mihalovna wearing a green head-dress, her face expressing resignation to the will of God but looking happy and festive. Their box was redolent of that atmosphere which hangs about an engaged couple and which Natasha knew and liked so much. She turned away and suddenly all the humiliation of that morning's visit came back to her.

'What right has he not to want to receive me into his family? Oh, better not think about it – not till *he* comes back,' she said to herself, and began looking about at the faces, some familiar, some unknown, in the stalls. In the front row, in the very middle, leaning back against the orchestra-rail, stood Dolohov in a Persian dress, his curly hair brushed up into an enormous shock. He was standing in full view of the audience, well aware that he was attracting the attention of the whole theatre, yet as much at ease as though he were in his own room. Around him thronged Moscow's most brilliant young men, whom it was obvious he dominated.

Count Rostov, laughing, nudged the blushing Sonya, pointing out to her her former admirer.

'Did you recognize him?' he asked. 'And where has he sprung from?' he inquired of Shinshin. 'I thought he had disappeared somewhere.'

'So he did,' replied Shinshin. 'He was in the Caucasus, and ran away

661

from there. They say he has been acting as minister to some ruling prince in Persia, and there killed the Shah's brother. Now all the ladies of Moscow have gone wild over him! "Dolohov the Persian" – that's what does it! Nowadays you hear nothing but Dolohov: they swear by him and invite you to meet him as if they were offering you a dish of choice sterlet. Dolohov and Anatole Kuragin have turned the heads of all our ladies.'

A tall, beautiful woman with a tremendous plait of hair and a great display of plump white shoulders and neck, round which she wore a double string of large pearls, entered the adjoining box, rustling her heavy silk gown and taking a long time to settle into her place.

Natasha found herself examining that neck and the shoulders, the pearls and the coiffure of the lady, and admired the beauty of the shoulders and the pearls. Just as Natasha was taking a second look at her, the lady glanced round, and meeting the count's eyes she nodded and smiled to him. It was Countess Bezuhov, Pierre's wife. The count, who knew everyone in society, leaned over and spoke to her.

'Have you been here long, countess?' he inquired. 'I'll call, I'll call to kiss your hand. I am in town on business and have brought my girls with me. They say Semeonova's acting is superb,' the count went on. 'Count Pierre never used to forget us. Is he here?'

'Yes, he said he would drop in,' answered Hélène, looking intently at Natasha.

Count Rostov resumed his seat.

'Handsome, isn't she?' he whispered to Natasha.

'Wonderful!' agreed Natasha. 'It would be easy to fall in love with her!'

At that moment the last chords of the overture were heard, and the conductor tapped with his stick. Some late-comers hurried to their places in the stalls, and the curtain rose.

With the rising of the curtain a hush fell on boxes and stalls, and all the men, old and young, in their uniforms and dress-coats, and all the women with precious stones on their bare flesh, concentrated their attention with eager expectation on the stage.

Natasha too began to look.

9

SMOOTH boards formed the centre of the stage, at the sides stood painted canvases representing trees, and in the background was a cloth stretched over boards. In the middle of the stage sat some girls in red bodices and white petticoats. One extremely fat girl in a white silk dress was sitting apart on a low bench, to the back of which a piece of green cardboard was glued. They were all singing something. When they had finished their chorus the girl in white advanced towards the prompter's box, and a man with stout legs encased in silk tights, a plume in his cap and a dagger at his waist, went up to her and began to sing and wave his arms about.

First the man in tights sang alone, then she sang, then they both paused while the orchestra played and the man fingered the hand of the girl in white, obviously waiting for the beat when they should start singing again. They sang a duet and everyone in the theatre began clapping and shouting, while the man and woman on the stage, who were playing a pair of lovers, began smiling, spreading out their arms and bowing.

To Natasha, fresh from the country, and in her present serious mood, all this seemed grotesque and extraordinary. She could not follow the opera, could not even listen to the music: she saw only painted cardboard and oddly dressed men and women who moved, spoke and sang strangely in a patch of blazing light. She knew what it was all meant to represent, but it was so grotesquely artificial and unnatural that she felt alternately ashamed and amused at the actors. She looked about her at the faces of the audience, trying to see if they felt as derisive and bewildered as she did; but all the faces appeared absorbed in what was happening on the stage, the while they expressed what seemed to Natasha to be an affected rapture. 'I suppose it has to be like this!' she thought. She kept looking in turn at the rows of pomaded heads in the stalls and then at the half-naked women in the boxes, especially at Hélène in the next box, who, quite uncovered, sat with a quiet, serene smile, not taking her eyes off the stage and basking in the bright light that flooded the theatre and the warm air heated by the crowd. Natasha little by little began to pass into a state of intoxication she had not experienced for a long time. She lost all sense of who and where she was, and of what was going on before her. As she gazed and dreamed, the strangest fancies flashed unexpectedly and disconnectedly into her mind. At one moment the idea occurred to her to leap over the footlights and sing the aria the actress was singing. Next she had an impulse to give a tap of her fan to an old gentleman sitting not far from her, or lean over to Hélène and tickle her.

At one time when there was a lull on the stage before the beginning of an aria a door leading to the stalls on the side nearest the Rostovs' box creaked, and the masculine steps of a belated arrival were heard. 'Here comes Kuragin!' whispered Shinshin. Countess Bezuhov turned, smiling, to the new-comer. Natasha, following the direction of the countess's eyes, saw an extraordinarily handsome adjutant approaching their box, with self-assured yet courteous bearing. This was Anatole Kuragin whom she had seen and noticed long ago at the ball in Petersburg. He was now in an adjutant's uniform with one epaulet and a shoulder knot. He moved with a discreet swagger, which would have been ridiculous if he had not been so good-looking and his comely features had not expressed such good-natured complacency and high spirits. Although the performance was in progress he sauntered down the carpeted gangway, accompanied by a slight jingling of sword and spurs, his perfumed, handsome head held high. With a glance at Natasha he went up to his sister, laid his finely-gloved hand on the edge of her box, nodded to her, and leaning forward asked her a question, with a gesture towards Natasha.

'Charming, charming!' said he, evidently referring to Natasha, who did not exactly hear the words but divined them from the movement of his lips. Then he took his place in the front row of the stalls, sitting beside Dolohov and giving a friendly, careless nudge with his elbow to the man whom most people treated so obsequiously. Anatole threw him a merry wink and a smile, and rested his foot on the orchestra screen.

'How alike brother and sister are!' remarked the count. 'And how handsome they both are!'

Shinshin, lowering his voice, began to tell the count some story of an intrigue of Kuragin's in Moscow, to which Natasha purposely listened just because he had called her charming.

The first act was over. In the stalls everyone stood up and began moving about, coming and going.

Boris arrived in the Rostovs' box, received their congratulations very simply and, with a lift of his eyebrows and an absent-minded smile, conveyed to Natasha and Sonya his fiancée's invitation to her wedding, and went away. Natasha, with a gay coquettish smile, had talked to him and congratulated him on his approaching marriage, though this was the very Boris she had once been in love with. In her present intoxicated, excited state everything seemed simple and natural.

The half-naked Hélène was sitting near her, smiling on all alike, and it was just such a smile that Natasha bestowed on Boris.

Hélène's box was filled and surrounded on the side of the stalls by the cleverest and most distinguished men, who seemed to be vying with one another in their desire to let everyone see that they knew her.

Throughout the *entr'acte* Kuragin stood with Dolohov in front of the footlights, never taking his eyes off the Rostovs' box. Natasha knew he was talking about her, and this afforded her gratification. She even turned so that he should see her profile from what she believed to be the most becoming angle. Before the beginning of the second act Pierre appeared in the stalls. The Rostovs had not seen him since their arrival. His face looked sad, and he had grown stouter since Natasha had seen him last. He walked to the front rows, not noticing anyone. Anatole went up to him and began saying something, with a look and a gesture towards the Rostovs' box. When he caught sight of Natasha, Pierre's face lighted up and he hurried along the row of stalls towards their box, where, leaning on his elbows and smiling, he talked to her for a long time. In the midst of her conversation with Pierre, Natasha heard a man's voice in Countess Bezuhov's box, and something told her it was Kuragin. She looked round and met his gaze. Almost smiling, he stared straight into her eyes with a look of such warmth and admiration that it seemed strange to be so near him, to look at him like that, to be so sure that he admired her, and yet not to be acquainted with him.

In the second act the stage was a cemetery, and there was a round hole in the back-drop to represent the moon. Shades were put over the footlights, and the horns and contra-bass began to play deep bass notes, while a number of people emerged from right and left, wearing black cloaks. These people began waving their arms, and in their hands they held things which looked like daggers. Then some other men ran in and began dragging away the maiden who had been in white but was now in light blue. They did not drag her away at once but spent a long while singing with her, until at last they did drag her off, and behind the scenes something metallic was struck three times, and everyone knelt down and sang a prayer. All these actions were repeatedly interrupted by the enthusiastic plaudits of the audience.

During this act every time Natasha looked towards the stalls she saw Anatole Kuragin, with an arm flung across the back of a chair, staring at her. She was pleased to see that he was so captivated by her and it did not occur to her that there could be anything amiss in it.

When the second act was over Countess Bezuhov stood up, turned towards the Rostovs' box – her whole bosom completely exposed – beckoned the old count with a small gloved finger, and paying no heed to those who had entered her box began talking to him with an amiable smile.

'Oh, you must introduce me to your lovely daughters,' said she. 'The whole town is singing their praises and I don't even know them.'

Natasha rose and curtsied to the magnificent countess. She was so delighted by praise from this brilliant beauty that she blushed with pleasure.

'I am determined to become a Moscovite too, now,' said Hélène. 'And aren't you ashamed of yourself for burying such pearls in the country?'

Countess Bezuhov had some right to her reputation of being a fascinating woman. She could say what she did not think – flattery especially – with perfect simplicity and naturalness.

'Now, my dear count, you must let me help to entertain your daughters. Though I am not here for long this time – nor are you either. But I'll do my best to amuse them. I heard a great deal about you when I was in Petersburg, and wanted to get to know you,' said she, turning to Natasha with her uniform lovely smile. 'I have also heard about you from my page, Drubetskoy – he is getting married, you know. And from my husband's friend, Bolkonsky, Prince Andrei Bolkonsky,' she went on with special emphasis, implying that she knew of his relation to Natasha. She asked that one of the young ladies should move into her box for the rest of the performance so that they might become better acquainted, and Natasha went over and sat next to her.

The third act took place in a palace in which a great many candles were burning and pictures of bearded knights hung on the walls. In the middle of the stage stood a man and woman – the king and queen, no doubt. The king was gesticulating with his right arm and, obviously nervous, sang something badly and sat down on a crimson throne. The damsel who had appeared first in white and then in pale blue now wore only a shift, and stood beside the throne with her hair hanging down. She sang something dolefully, addressing the queen, but the king peremptorily waved his hand, and men and women with bare legs emerged from the wings on both sides and began dancing together. Next the violins played very shrilly and merrily, and one of the women, with thick bare legs and thin arms, separated from the others, retired behind the scenes to adjust her bodice, then walked into the middle of the stage and began skipping into the air and kicking one foot rapidly against the other. Everyone in the stalls clapped and roared 'bravo!' Then one of the men was seen standing by himself at one corner of the stage. The cymbals and horns struck up in the orchestra, and this bare-legged man began leaping very high and making quick movements in the air with his feet. (This was Duport, who earned sixty thousand roubles a year for this accomplishment.) Everybody in the stalls, boxes and from up among the gods started clapping and shouting with all their might, and the man stopped and began smiling and bowing in all directions. Then other men and women with bare legs danced. Then one of the royal personages declaimed something in recitative and all the chorus replied. But suddenly a storm sprang up, chromatic scales and diminished sevenths were heard in the orchestra, and they all ran off, again dragging one of their number behind the scenes, and the curtain dropped. Once more there was a terrible uproar and tumult among the spectators, and the whole audience with rapturous faces began screaming:

'Duport! Duport! Duport!'

Natasha no longer thought this strange. She looked about her with a sense of satisfaction, smiling joyfully.

'Isn't Duport ravishing?' Hélène asked her.

'Oh yes,' answered Natasha.

10

DURING the *entr'acte* a draught of cold air blew into Hélène's box, the door was opened and Anatole came in, stooping and trying not to brush against anyone.

'Allow me to introduce my brother,' said Hélène, her eyes shifting uneasily from Natasha to Anatole.

Natasha turned her pretty little head towards the elegant young officer, and smiled at him over her bare shoulder. Anatole, who was as handsome at close quarters as he was from a distance, sat down beside her and told her he had longed for this pleasure ever since the Naryshkins' ball where he had had the happiness, which he had never forgotten, of seeing her. Kuragin was far more sensible and straightforward with women than he was in the society of men. He talked boldly and naturally, and Natasha was agreeably surprised at finding there was nothing formidable in this man, about whom so many stories were rife, but, on the contrary, the smile on his face could not have been more artless, jolly and good-natured.

Kuragin asked her what she thought of the performance, and told her how on a previous occasion Semeonova had fallen down on the stage.

'And do you know, countess,' said he, suddenly addressing her as though she were an old friend, 'we are getting up a fancy-dress ball. You ought to take part in it: it will be great fun. We are all assembling at the Arharovs'. Please come! Do – will you?'

As he was saying this he never took his smiling eyes off her face, her neck and her bare arms. Natasha had no doubt that he was enraptured by her. This pleased her, yet his presence somehow made her feel constrained and ill at ease. When she was not looking at him she felt that he was gazing at her shoulders, and she could not help trying to catch his eye, to divert it to her face. But looking into his eyes she was frightened, realizing that between her and him there was not that barrier of decorum she had always been conscious of between herself and other men. She did not know how it was that within five minutes she had come to feel terribly close to this man. When she turned away she feared he might seize her from behind by her bare arm, or kiss her on the neck. They talked of the most ordinary things, yet she felt that they were more intimate than she had ever been with any man. Natasha kept looking round to Hélène and her father, as though asking them what it all meant, but Hélène was engaged in conversation with a general and did not respond to her glance, while her father's eyes said nothing but what they always said: 'Enjoying yourself? I am so glad.'

In one such moment of awkward silence, during which Anatole's prominent eyes stared calmly and persistently at her, Natasha, to break the silence, asked him how he liked Moscow. She asked the question and blushed. She was feeling all the time that she was doing something improper by talking to him. Anatole smiled as though to encourage her.

'At first I wasn't particularly charmed – because what is it makes one like a town? It's the pretty women, isn't it? Well, but now I like it very much indeed,' he said, giving her a significant look. 'You'll come to the fancy-dress ball, countess? Do come!' and putting out his hand to her bouquet and dropping his voice he added in French, 'You will be the prettiest there. Do come, dear countess, and give me this flower as a pledge!'

Natasha did not understand what he was saying, any more than he did himself, but she felt that his uncomprehended words held some unseemly design. She did not know what to say, and turned away as though she had not heard his remark. But as soon as she turned away the thought came to her that he was there behind her, so close to her.

'What is he feeling now? Is he ashamed of himself? Angry? Ought I to mend matters?' she asked herself. She could not refrain from looking round. She looked straight into his eyes, and his nearness and self-assurance, and the simple-hearted warmth of his smile, vanquished her. She gave him an answering smile, looking straight into his eyes. And again she felt with horror that no barrier lay between him and her.

The curtain rose again. Anatole left the box, serene and gay. Natasha went back to her father in the other box, now completely under the spell of the world in which she found herself. All that was happening now seemed perfectly natural; while on the other hand all her previous thoughts concerning her betrothed, or Princess Maria, or her life in the country, had dissolved from her mind, as though all that belonged to a past that was far remote.

In the fourth act there was some sort of devil who sang and gesticulated until the boards were withdrawn from under him and he disappeared down below. That was all Natasha saw of the fourth act: she felt agitated and upset, and the cause of this agitation was Kuragin, whom she could not help watching. As they were leaving the theatre Anatole came up to them, called their carriage and helped them in. When it was Natasha's turn to take her seat he squeezed her arm above the elbow. Startled and flushed, she looked round at him. He was gazing at her with flashing eyes and a tender smile.

★

Not until she reached home was Natasha able to form any clear idea of what had happened, and suddenly, remembering Prince Andrei, she was horrified, and at tea, to which they all sat down after the theatre, she groaned aloud, flushed crimson and ran from the room.

'O God, I am lost!' she said to herself. 'How could I have let it go so far?' she wondered. For a long time she sat hiding her burning cheeks in her hands, trying to realize what had happened to her, but she could not grasp either what had happened or what she was feeling. Everything seemed dark, obscure and dreadful. There in that huge, brilliant auditorium, where Duport with his bare legs and his spangled jacket had capered about on the damp boards to the sounds of music, where young girls and old men, and the nearly naked Hélène, with her proud, serene smile, had cried 'Bravo!' till they were hoarse – there in the protecting shadow of that Hélène it had all seemed simple and natural; but now, alone by herself, it was past comprehension.

'What does it mean? What was that terror I felt of him? What is the meaning of these stings of conscience which I feel now?' she asked herself.

Only to the old countess could Natasha have talked, at night in bed, of all she was feeling. She knew that Sonya, with her strict and single-minded outlook, would either not understand at all or would be horrified at such a confession. So Natasha accordingly had to try, by her own unaided efforts, to solve the riddle that tormented her.

'Have I really forfeited Prince Andrei's love or not?' she asked herself, and laughed reassuringly. 'What a fool I am to wonder that! What did happen? Nothing. I have done nothing. I didn't lead him on at all. Nobody will know and I shall never see him again,' she told herself. 'So it's plain that nothing happened, that there is nothing to repent of, and that Andrei can love me still. But why "still"? O God, O God, why isn't he here?'

For a moment Natasha felt comforted, but again some instinct told her that though it was all true, and though nothing had happened, yet the former purity of her love for Prince Andrei was lost. And again in imagination she went over the whole conversation with Kuragin, and saw the face, the gestures and the tender smile of that handsome, impudent man as he squeezed her arm.

ANATOLE KURAGIN was living in Moscow because his father had sent him away from Petersburg, where he had been spending over twenty thousand roubles a year in ready money, besides running up bills for as much more, for which his creditors were dunning his father.

Prince Vasili informed his son that he would, for the last time, pay one-half of his debts, but only on condition that he went to Moscow as adjutant to the commander-in-chief – a post his father had managed to procure for him – and finally made up his mind to try to contract a good match there. He suggested either Princess Maria or Julie Karagin.

Anatole consented and went to Moscow, where he took up residence at Pierre's house. Pierre at first received him unwillingly, but got used to him after a while, occasionally accompanied him on his carousals and gave him money in the guise of loans.

Shinshin spoke truly when he said that Anatole had begun the moment he arrived to turn the heads of all the ladies in Moscow, mainly by the fact that he treated them with nonchalance, and openly preferred gipsy-girls and French actresses – with the most prominent of whom, Mademoiselle Georges, he was said to be on terms of close intimacy. He never missed a drinking-party given by Danilov or any other member of Moscow's fast set, drank whole nights through, leaving all his companions under the table, and was at every *soirée* and ball in the best society. Rumours were widespread of his intrigues with married ladies, and at balls he flirted with a few of them. But he fought shy of young girls, especially the wealthy heiresses, who were most of them plain. He had good reason for this, having been married a couple of years before – a fact known only to his closest friends. Two years previously, when his regiment had been stationed in Poland, a Polish landowner of small means had forced Anatole to marry his daughter. Anatole had lost no time in abandoning his wife, and in consideration of a sum of money which he agreed to send periodically to his father-in-law he was allowed by the latter to pass himself off as a bachelor.

Anatole was always very well satisfied with his position, with himself and with the rest of the world. He was instinctively and thoroughly convinced that he could not possibly live otherwise than in the way he did live, and that he had never in his life done anything evil. He was incapable of considering how his behaviour might affect others, or what the consequences of this or that action of his might be. He believed that just as a duck is so created that it must live in water, so he was created by God for the purpose of spending thirty thousand roubles a year and occupying the highest pinnacle in society. He was so firmly grounded in this opinion that others, looking at him, were persuaded of it too, and refused him neither the exalted position in society nor the money, which he borrowed right and left with obviously no notion of ever repaying it.

He was not a gambler – at least he was never interested in winning money at cards. He was not vain. He did not mind what people thought of him. Still less could he be accused of ambition. More than once he provoked his father by injuring his own prospects, and he laughed at honours of all kinds. He was not tight-fisted, and never refused anyone who asked of him. All that he cared for was 'a good time' and women, and as according to his ideas there was nothing ignoble about these tastes, and as he was incapable of considering the effect on others of the gratification of his desires, he was sincere in his opinion of himself as a man of unimpeachable character and in his contempt for rogues and wrong-doers, and with a tranquil conscience carried his head high.

Rakes, those male Magdalens, cherish a secret belief in their own innocence similar to the feeling women Magdalens have, and which is based on the same hope of forgiveness. 'All will be forgiven her, for she loved much, and all will be forgiven him because he enjoyed himself much.'

Dolohov, back again in Moscow that year after his exile and his Persian adventures, and once more leading a dissipated life of luxury and gambling, renewed his friendship with his old Petersburg comrade Kuragin, and made use of him for his own ends.

Anatole was genuinely fond of Dolohov for his cleverness and audacity. Dolohov, who needed Anatole Kuragin's name, renown and connexions as a bait to ensnare rich young men into his gambling circle, made use of him and amused himself at his expense without letting him suspect it. Apart from these interested motives for which he required Anatole, the very process of dominating another man's will was in itself an enjoyment, a habit and a necessity for Dolohov.

Natasha had made a deep impression on Kuragin. At supper after the opera he described to Dolohov, in the manner of a connoisseur, the attractions of her arms, shoulders, feet and hair, and expressed his intention of paying court to her. The possible consequences of such a flirtation Anatole was incapable of considering, just as he never had any notion of what might be the outcome of any of his actions.

'Yes, she's pretty, my lad, but she's not for us,' Dolohov said to him.

'I'll tell my sister to ask her to dinner,' said Anatole. 'How would that be?'

'You'd do better to wait till she's married. …'

'You know I adore little girls,' pursued Anatole. 'They lose their heads at once.'

'You've already come to grief once over one "little girl",' replied Dolohov, who knew of Anatole's marriage. 'Take care!'

'Well, one can't get caught a second time! What?' said Anatole, with a good-humoured laugh.

12

THE day after the opera the Rostovs stayed at home, and nobody came to call. Maria Dmitrievna had a private conversation with the count to discuss something which they kept from Natasha. Natasha guessed they were talking about the old prince and concocting some scheme, and this made her feel uneasy and humiliated. Every minute she expected Prince Andrei, and twice that day sent a man-servant to Vozdvizhenka street to find out whether he had arrived. He had not. She was having a more difficult time now than during her first days in Moscow. To her impatience and pining for him were now added the unpleasant memory of her interview with Princess Maria and the old prince, and a fear and anxiety of which she did not understand the cause. She was continually fancying either that he would never come or that something would happen to her before he came. She could no longer day-dream about him by herself for hours on end. As soon as she turned her mind to him recollections of the old prince, of Princess Maria, of the theatre and of Kuragin began to intrude on her thoughts. Once more she asked herself whether she had not done something wrong, whether she had not already broken faith with Prince Andrei, and again she found herself going over in the minutest detail every word, every gesture, every shade in the play of expression on the face of the man who had been able to arouse in her such incomprehensible and terrifying feelings. To the eyes of those about her Natasha seemed livelier than usual, but she was far from being as serene and happy as before.

On Sunday morning Maria Dmitrievna invited her guests to come to the service at her parish church – the Church of the Assumption.

'I don't like those fashionable churches,' she said, evidently priding herself on her independent ideas. 'God is the same everywhere. Our parish priest is an excellent man: he conducts the service decently and with dignity, and the deacon is the same. Where is the holiness in giving concerts in the choir? I don't like it: it's mischievous nonsense!'

Maria Dmitrievna liked Sundays and knew how to celebrate them. On Saturday her house was scrubbed and polished from top to bottom, and on the Lord's Day neither she nor her servants did any work, but wore their best clothes and went to church. She had some extra dishes for dinner in the dining-room, and there was vodka and roast goose or a sucking-pig in the servants' hall. But nowhere in the whole house was the influence of the day more distinctly legible than on the broad, severe face of Maria Dmitrievna herself which on Sundays wore a fixed expression of solemn festivity.

After church, when they had finished their coffee in the dining-room, where the loose covers had been removed from the furniture, a servant announced that the carriage was ready, and Maria Dmitrievna rose with a stern air. She wore her best shawl in which she paid calls, and announced that she was going to see Prince Nikolai Bolkonsky to have it out with him concerning Natasha.

After she had gone, a dressmaker from Madame Suppert-Roguet's waited on the Rostovs, and Natasha, very glad of this diversion, having shut herself in a room adjoining the drawing-room, began trying on her new dresses. Just as she had put on a bodice basted together, with the sleeves not yet tacked in, and was turning her head to see in the looking-glass how the back fitted, she heard her father's voice in eager conversation with another voice, a woman's voice, which made her flush red. It was Hélène's voice. Before Natasha had time to take off the bodice she was trying on, the door opened and in walked Countess Bezuhov, dressed in a velvet gown of dark heliotrope with a high collar, her face alive with amiable, friendly smiles.

'Oh my enchantress!' she cried to the blushing Natasha. 'Charming! No, this is really beyond anything, my dear count,' she said to Count Rostov, who had followed her in. 'The idea of being in Moscow and not going anywhere! No, I shall not let you off! This evening Mademoiselle Georges is to recite for me at my house, and I am having a few friends in. If you don't bring your lovely girls – who are much prettier than Mademoiselle Georges – I shall positively have to quarrel with you. My husband is away in Tver or I would send him to fetch you. You must come. You positively must! Between eight and nine.'

She nodded to the dressmaker, who knew her and was curtseying respectfully, and seated herself in an arm-chair beside the looking-glass, draping the folds of her velvet gown picturesquely about her. She kept up a flow of good-humoured, light-hearted chatter, and repeatedly expressed her admiration of Natasha's beauty. She examined the new dresses and praised them, as well as one of her own, *en gaze métallique*, which had just arrived from Paris, and advised Natasha to have a copy of it.

'However, anything suits you, my charmer!' she remarked.

The smile of pleasure on Natasha's face never left it. She felt happy, as if she were blossoming out under the praises of this nice Countess Bezuhov, who before had seemed so grand and unapproachable and was now so kind to her. Natasha's spirits rose, and she felt almost in love with this woman, who was so beautiful and so gracious. Hélène for her part was sincere in her admiration of Natasha and in her wish that she should enjoy herself. Anatole had more than once begged her to bring him and Natasha together, and it was with this object that she had come to the Rostovs. The idea of throwing her brother and Natasha together amused her.

Though at one time, in Petersburg, Hélène had been annoyed with Natasha for drawing Boris away from her, she did not think of that now and in her own way wished Natasha nothing but good. As she was leaving the Rostovs she called her *protégée* aside.

'My brother was dining with me yesterday, and we nearly died of laughter – he eats nothing and can only sigh for you, my charmer! He is madly, quite madly in love with you, my dear.'

Natasha flushed crimson when she heard this.

'How she colours up, how she colours up, *ma délicieuse!*' pursued Hélène. 'You must be sure to come. Though you are in love, that is no reason for shutting yourself up like a nun. And even if you are betrothed, I cannot think your fiancé would not wish you to go into society rather than be bored to death.'

'Then she knows I am engaged,' thought Natasha. 'So she and her husband Pierre – that good, upright Pierre – must have talked and laughed about this. So there can be no harm in it.' And again under Hélène's influence what had struck her before as terrible now seemed simple and natural. 'And she is such a *grande dame*, so kind, and has obviously taken a great fancy to me. And why shouldn't I enjoy myself?' thought Natasha, gazing at Hélène with wide-open, wondering eyes.

Maria Dmitrievna returned in time for dinner, silent and grave-faced, having evidently suffered a rebuff at the old prince's. She was still too agitated by the encounter to be able to describe the interview calmly. To the count's inquiries she replied that everything was all right and that she would tell him about it next day. On hearing of Countess Bezuhov's visit and the invitation for that evening Maria Dmitrievna remarked:

'I don't care to associate with Countess Bezuhov, and I should advise you not to. However, go, since you have promised. It will be a little amusement for you,' she added, addressing Natasha.

13

COUNT ROSTOV took the girls to Countess Bezuhov's. There were a fair number of people present, nearly all strangers to Natasha. Count Rostov was displeased to see that the company consisted almost entirely of men and women notorious for the freedom of their conduct. Mademoiselle Georges was standing in a corner of the drawing-room surrounded by young men. There were several Frenchmen there, among them Métivier, who had been a constant visitor at Countess Bezuhov's ever since her arrival in Moscow. The count decided not to sit down to cards or let his girls out of his sight, and to get away as soon as Mademoiselle Georges' performance was over.

Anatole was at the door, evidently on the look-out for the Rostovs. Having exchanged greetings with the count, he immediately went up to Natasha and followed her into the room. The moment Natasha saw him she was overcome by the same feeling she had had at the opera – a mixed feeling of gratified vanity at his admiration for her,

676

and terror at the absence of any moral barrier between them.

Hélène welcomed Natasha with delight, and was loud in admiration of her loveliness and her dress. Soon after their arrival Mademoiselle Georges went out of the room to change her costume. In the meantime chairs were arranged in the drawing-room and the guests began to take their seats. Anatole found a chair for Natasha and was about to sit down next to her, but the count, keeping a sharp eye on his daughter, took the seat beside her himself. Anatole sat behind.

Mademoiselle Georges, with bare, plump, dimpled arms, and a red shawl flung across one shoulder, came into the empty space left for her between the chairs, and assumed an unnatural pose. A murmur of enthusiasm hailed her.

Mademoiselle Georges gazed round her audience with theatrical gloom, and began to declaim a long soliloquy in French describing her guilty passion for her son. In places she raised her voice, in others she dropped to a whisper, solemnly lifting her head; sometimes she broke off or spoke huskily, rolling her eyes.

'*Adorable!*' ... '*Divin!*' ... '*Délicieux!*' was heard on all sides.

Natasha's eyes were fastened on the fat actress, but she neither saw nor heard nor understood anything of what went on before her. She was only aware of being borne irrevocably away again into that strange and senseless world so remote from her old one, a world in which there was no knowing what was good and what was bad, what was sensible and what was folly. Behind her sat Anatole, and conscious of his proximity she experienced a frightened sense of expectancy.

After the first monologue the whole company rose and crowded round Mademoiselle Georges, rapturously expressing their admiration.

'How beautiful she is!' Natasha remarked to her father, who had got up with the rest and was moving through the throng towards the actress.

'I don't think so when I look at you,' said Anatole, following Natasha. He said this at a moment when only she could hear him. 'You are enchanting ... from the first moment I saw you I have never ceased. ...'

'Come along, Natasha, come along!' said the count, turning back for his daughter. 'How pretty she is!'

Making no reply, Natasha stepped up to her father with a dazed look in her eyes.

After several more recitations Mademoiselle Georges took her departure, and Countess Bezuhov invited her guests into the ballroom.

The count would have liked to go home, but Hélène besought him not to spoil her impromptu ball. The Rostovs stayed on. Anatole asked Natasha for a valse and as they danced together he pressed her waist and her hand, and told her she was bewitching and that he loved her. During the *écossaise*, which she also danced with him, Anatole said nothing when they happened to be by themselves but merely gazed at her. Natasha wondered whether she had not dreamed what he said to her during the valse. At the end of the first figure he pressed her hand again. Natasha lifted frightened eyes to him, but there was such confident tenderness in his fond expression and smile that she found it impossible to look at him and say what it was she had it on her tongue to say. She lowered her eyes.

'Do not say such things to me. I am betrothed and I love another,' she murmured rapidly. She glanced up at him. Anatole was neither disconcerted nor hurt by what she had said.

'Don't speak to me of that. What is that to do with me ?' said he. 'I tell you I am madly, madly in love with you. Is it my fault if you are irresistible ? ... It's our turn to lead.'

Natasha, excited and agitated, looked about her with wide, scared eyes, and seemed gayer than usual. Afterwards she remembered almost nothing of what took place that evening. They danced the *écossaise* and the *gross vater*. Her father suggested that they should go but she begged to remain. Wherever she was, whoever was talking to her, she felt *his* eyes upon her. Later she recalled how she had asked her father to let her go to the dressing-room to rearrange her dress, that Hélène had followed and spoken laughingly of her brother's passion for her, and that she again met Anatole in the little sitting-room. Hélène vanished somewhere, leaving them alone, and Anatole had taken her hand and said in a tender voice:

'I cannot come to call upon you, but is it possible that I am never to see you ? I love you to distraction. Can I never ... ?' and, barring her way, he brought his face close to hers.

His large, shining, masculine eyes were so close to hers that she saw nothing but them.

'Natalie ?' he whispered inquiringly, and she felt her hands being squeezed till they hurt. 'Natalie ?'

'I don't understand. I have nothing to say,' her eyes replied.

Burning lips were pressed to hers, and at the same instant she felt herself set free, and Hélène's footsteps and the rustle of her gown were heard in the room. Natasha looked round at her, and then, crimson and trembling, threw a frightened look of inquiry at Anatole and moved towards the door.

'One word, just one, for God's sake!' cried Anatole.

She paused. She so wanted a word from him that would explain to her what had happened, and to which she could find an answer.

'Natalie, just one word ... only one!' he kept repeating, evidently not knowing what to say, and he repeated it till Hélène came up to them.

Natasha returned with Hélène to the drawing-room. The Rostovs went away without staying for supper.

When they got home Natasha lay awake all night, tormented by the problem she could not solve: which did she love – Anatole or Prince Andrei? She loved Prince Andrei – she remembered distinctly how deeply she loved him. But she loved Anatole too: of that there was no doubt. 'Otherwise, how could all that have happened?' she said to herself. 'If, after that, I could return his smile when we said good-bye; if I could let things go so far, it means that I fell in love with him at first sight. So he must be kind, noble and splendid, and I could not help loving him. What am I to do if I love him and the other too?' she asked herself, and was unable to find an answer to those terrible questions.

14

MORNING came with its daily cares and bustle. Everyone got up and began to move about and talk, dressmakers came again, Maria Dmitrievna appeared and they were summoned to breakfast. Natasha kept looking uneasily at everybody with wide-open eyes, as though she wanted to intercept every glance directed towards her, and did her utmost to seem exactly as usual.

After breakfast (this was always her favourite time), Maria Dmitrievna settled herself in her easy chair and called Natasha and the count to her.

'Well now, my friends, I have thought the whole matter over and this is my advice,' she began. 'Yesterday, as you know, I went to see Prince Bolkonsky. Well, I had a talk with him. ... He thought fit to scream at me, but I am not one to be shouted down. I said what I had to say!'

'And he – what did he say?' asked the count.

'He? He's an old fool … will not listen to anything. But what is the use of talking? As it is, we have worn this poor girl out,' said Maria Dmitrievna. 'My advice to you is, finish your business and go back home to Otradnoe … and wait there.'

'Oh no!' exclaimed Natasha.

'Yes, go back,' said Maria Dmitrievna, 'and wait there. If your betrothed comes here now, there'll be no escaping a quarrel; but alone with the old man he will talk things over and then come to you.'

Count Rostov approved of this suggestion, seeing the sound sense of it at once. If the old man were to come round, it would be all the better to visit him in Moscow or at Bald Hills later on; and if not, then the wedding, against his wishes, could only take place at Otradnoe.

'That is perfectly true,' said the old count. 'I am only sorry I went to see him and took her.'

'No, why be sorry about that! Being here, you had to pay your respects. But if he won't have it … that is his affair,' said Maria Dmitrievna, searching for something in her reticule. 'Besides, the trousseau is ready, so there is nothing to keep you; and what isn't ready yet I will send on. Though I don't like to lose you, it's the best way, and God bless you.' Finding what she was looking for in her reticule she handed it to Natasha. It was a letter from Princess Maria. 'She has written to you. What a state she is in, poor thing! She's afraid you might think she does not like you.'

'Well, and she doesn't like me,' said Natasha.

'Don't talk nonsense!' cried Maria Dmitrievna.

'I shall accept no one's word for that: I know she doesn't like me,' replied Natasha boldly as she took the letter, and an expression of such resolute, cold anger came over her face that Maria Dmitrievna looked at her more intently and frowned.

'Don't you contradict me like that, my good girl,' she said. 'What I say is true! You answer that.'

Natasha did not reply, and retired to her room to read Princess Maria's letter.

Princess Maria wrote that she was in despair at the misunderstanding that had arisen between them. Whatever her father's feelings might be, she begged Natasha to believe that she could not fail to love her, as the girl chosen by her brother, for whose happiness she was ready to make any sacrifice.

'Do not believe, however,' she wrote, 'that my father is ill-disposed towards you. He is ailing and old, and one must make excuses for him; but he is good-hearted and generous, and will come to love the woman who makes his son happy.' Princess Maria went on to ask Natasha to fix a time when she could see her again.

After reading the letter Natasha sat down at the writing-table to pen a reply.

'*Chère Princesse*,' she began, writing rapidly and mechanically, and then paused. What more could she write after all that had happened the evening before? 'Yes, yes! All that did happen, and now everything is different,' she thought as she sat before the letter she had started. 'Must I break off with him? Must I really? This is frightful!...' and to escape these dreadful thoughts she ran in to Sonya and began looking through embroidery designs with her.

After dinner Natasha went to her room and again took up Princess Maria's letter. 'Can it be that all is over?' she thought. 'Can all this have happened so quickly and have destroyed everything that went before?' She recalled in all its former strength her love for Prince Andrei, and at the same time felt that she loved Kuragin. She vividly pictured herself as Prince Andrei's wife, remembered the dreams of happiness with him which her imagination had so often painted, and at the same time, aglow with emotion, went over every detail of yesterday's meeting with Anatole.

'Oh why may I not love them both at once?' she kept asking herself in the depths of bewilderment. 'Only so could I be perfectly happy; but now I have to choose, and I can't be happy if I let either of them go. One thing is certain,' she thought, 'to tell Prince Andrei what has happened, or to hide it from him, is equally impossible. But with the *other* nothing is spoilt. But must I really part for ever from the happiness of Prince Andrei's love, which I have been living in for so long?'

'Please, miss!' whispered a maid, entering the room with a mysterious air. 'A man told me to give you this —' and she handed Natasha a letter. 'Only, for mercy's sake ...' the girl went on, as Natasha, without thinking, mechanically broke the seal and began reading a love-letter from Anatole, of which, without taking in a word, she understood only that it was a letter from him – from the man she loved. Yes, she loved him. Otherwise how could what had happened have happened? How could a love-letter from him be in her hand?

With trembling hands Natasha held that passionate love-letter, composed for Anatole by Dolohov, and as she read she found in it an echo of all that she imagined herself to be feeling.

'Since yesterday evening my fate is sealed: to be loved by you or to die. There is no other alternative for me,' the letter began. Then he went on to say that he knew her parents would never consent to her marriage to him, Anatole, for various secret reasons which he could reveal to her alone, but that if she loved him she need only say the word *Yes*, and no human power could hinder their bliss. Love would conquer all. He would spirit her away and carry her off to the ends of the earth.

'Yes, yes, I love him!' thought Natasha, reading the letter for the twentieth time and looking for some peculiarly deep meaning in every word.

That evening Maria Dmitrievna was going to the Arharovs' and proposed taking the girls with her. Natasha pleaded a headache and stayed at home.

15

ON her return late in the evening Sonya went to Natasha's room, and to her surprise found her still dressed and asleep on the sofa. Open on the table beside her lay Anatole's letter. Sonya picked it up and read it.

As she read she glanced at the sleeping Natasha, trying to discover in her face some key to the mystery of what she was reading, but found none. Natasha's face was calm, gentle and happy. Clutching at her breast to keep herself from choking, Sonya, pale and trembling with fright and agitation, sat down in a low chair and burst into tears.

'How is it I noticed nothing? How can it have gone so far? Can she have left off loving Prince Andrei? And how could she have let Kuragin go to such lengths? He is a deceiver and a scoundrel, that's plain! What will Nicolas, dear noble Nicolas, do when he hears of it? So that was the meaning of her excited, determined, unnatural look the day before yesterday, and yesterday and today,' thought Sonya. 'But it's impossible that she can care for him! She probably opened the letter without knowing who it was from. Most likely she feels insulted by it. She could not do such a thing!'

Sonya wiped away her tears and went up to Natasha, scrutinizing her face again.

'Natasha!' she murmured, hardly audibly.

Natasha awoke and saw Sonya.

'Ah, you're back?'

And impulsively, as often happens at the moment of awakening, she gave her friend a tender hug. But noticing Sonya's look of embarrassment her own face became troubled and suspicious.

'Sonya, you read that letter?' she demanded.

'Yes,' answered Sonya softly.

Natasha smiled ecstatically.

'No, Sonya, I can't any longer –' she said, 'I can't hide it from you any longer! You know, we love one another! Sonya, darling, he writes ... Sonya ...'

Sonya stared wide-eyed at Natasha, unable to believe her ears.

'But Bolkonsky?' she asked.

'Ah, Sonya, if you only knew how happy I am!' cried Natasha. 'You don't know what love ...'

'But, Natasha, do you mean to say the *other* is all over?'

Natasha stared at Sonya with her large eyes, as though she could not grasp the question.

'What, are you breaking it off with Prince Andrei?' said Sonya.

'Oh, you don't understand a thing! Don't talk nonsense. Listen!' exclaimed Natasha with a flash of temper.

'No, I can't believe it,' insisted Sonya. 'I don't understand. How can you have loved one man for a whole year and suddenly.... Why, you have only seen him three times! Natasha, I don't believe you, you're joking. In three days to forget everything and be like this. ...'

'Three days?' interrupted Natasha. 'It seems to me as if I'd loved him a hundred years. It seems to me as if I had never never loved anyone before. You can't understand. Sonya, wait – sit here.' Natasha threw her arms round her and kissed her. 'I have heard of this happening – and so have you too, surely? But it's only now that I feel such love. It's not what I felt before. As soon as I saw him I felt he was my master and I his slave, and that I could not help loving him. Yes, his slave! Whatever he bids me, I shall do. You don't understand that. What am I to do? What am I to do, Sonya?' cried Natasha with a blissful yet frightened face.

'But just think what you are doing,' said Sonya. 'I can't leave it like

683

this. This secret correspondence. . . . How could you let him go so far?' she asked, with a horror and disgust she could with difficulty conceal.

'I told you, I have no will,' Natasha replied. 'Why can't you understand? I love him!'

'Then I won't let it go on. ... I shall tell!' cried Sonya, bursting into tears.

'What do you mean? For God's sake. ... If you tell, you are my enemy,' declared Natasha. 'You want me to be miserable, you want to see us separated. ...'

When she saw Natasha's alarm Sonya wept tears of shame and pity for her friend.

'But what has passed between you?' she asked. 'What has he said to you? Why doesn't he come to the house?'

Natasha did not answer.

'For God's sake, Sonya, don't tell anyone; don't torture me,' implored Natasha. 'Remember, you oughtn't to interfere in such matters. I have confided in you. ...'

'But why this secrecy? Why doesn't he come to the house?' Sonya persisted. 'Why doesn't he ask for your hand straight out? You know Prince Andrei left you perfectly free, if anything like this happened; but I don't believe it. Natasha, have you considered what these *secret reasons* can be?'

Natasha fixed wondering eyes on Sonya. Evidently this question had not occurred to her before and she did not know how to answer it.

'I don't know what his reasons are. But there must be reasons!'

Sonya sighed and shook her head distrustfully.

'If there were reasons ...' she began.

But Natasha, divining her doubts, interrupted her in dismay.

'Sonya, one can't doubt him! One can't, one can't! Don't you understand?' she cried.

'Does he love you?'

'Does he love me?' repeated Natasha with a smile of pity at her friend's stupidity. 'Why, you have read his letter, haven't you? You've seen him.'

'But supposing he's not an honourable man?'

'*He!* ... Not an honourable man? If you only knew!' exclaimed Natasha.

'If he is an honourable man he should either declare his intentions or give up seeing you; and if you won't tell him, I will. I'll write to him. I'll tell papa!' said Sonya resolutely.

'But I can't live without him!' cried Natasha.

'Natasha, I don't understand you. And what are you saying? Think of your father, of Nicolas.'

'I don't want anyone, I love no one but him. How dare you say he's dishonourable? Don't you know that I love him?' screamed Natasha. 'Sonya, go away! I don't want to quarrel with you; go away, for God's sake, go! You see how wretched I am,' Natasha cried angrily, in a voice of repressed irritation and despair. Sonya burst into sobs and ran from the room.

Natasha went to the table and without a moment's reflection wrote the answer to Princess Maria which she had been unable to write all the morning. In her letter she briefly informed Princess Maria that all their misunderstandings were at an end; that availing herself of the magnanimity of Prince Andrei, who when he went abroad had given her her freedom, she begged Princess Maria to forget everything and forgive her if she had been at fault in any way; but that she could not be his wife. At that moment this all seemed so easy, simple and clear to Natasha.

*

The Rostovs were to return to the country on Friday, but on Wednesday the count departed with the prospective purchaser to his estate near Moscow.

On the day the count went out of town Sonya and Natasha were invited to a big dinner-party at the Karagins', whither they were chaperoned by Maria Dmitrievna. At that party Natasha again met Anatole, and Sonya noticed that she said something to him, trying not to be overheard, and that all through dinner she was more worked up than ever. When they got home Natasha was the first to embark on the subject Sonya was waiting for.

'There, Sonya, you said all sorts of silly things about him,' Natasha began in a meek voice – the voice in which children speak when they want to be praised for being good. 'I have had it all out with him today.'

'Well, what happened? What did he say, then? Natasha, how glad I am you're not angry with me. Tell me everything. What did he say?'

Natasha pondered.

'Oh, Sonya, if you knew him as I do! He said. ... He asked me what promise I had given Bolkonsky. He was so glad I was free to refuse him.'

Sonya sighed miserably.

'But you haven't refused Bolkonsky, have you?' she said.

'Perhaps I have! Maybe all is over between me and Bolkonsky! Why do you have such hard thoughts of me?'

'I don't think anything, only I don't understand this. ...'

'Wait a little while, Sonya, you'll understand everything. You'll see the sort of man he is! Don't think hard thoughts of me, or of him either.'

'I don't think hard thoughts of anyone: I love and am sorry for everybody. But what am I to do?'

Sonya would not let herself be won over by the affectionate tone Natasha used with her. The more tender and ingratiating grew Natasha's face, the more serious and stern was Sonya's expression.

'Natasha,' said she, 'you asked me not to speak to you of all this, and I haven't, but now you yourself have begun. Natasha, I don't trust him. Why this secrecy?'

'There you go again!' interrupted Natasha.

'Natasha, I am afraid for you!'

'Afraid of what?'

'I am afraid you are rushing to your ruin,' declared Sonya resolutely, herself horrified at what she had said.

A spiteful look showed on Natasha's face again.

'Then I'll go to my ruin, so I will, and the sooner the better! It's not your business! It won't be you, but I, who'll suffer. Leave me alone, leave me alone! I hate you!'

'Natasha!' moaned Sonya, aghast.

'I hate you, I hate you! You're my enemy for ever!' And Natasha ran out of the room.

Natasha did not speak to Sonya again, and avoided her. With the same agitated expression of astonishment and guilt she wandered about the house, trying one occupation after another and instantly abandoning them.

Hard as it was for Sonya, she kept watch on her friend and never let her out of her sight.

The day before the count was to return, Sonya noticed that Natasha sat by the drawing-room window all the morning, as if expecting something, and that she made a sign to an officer who drove past, whom Sonya took to be Anatole.

Sonya began watching her friend still more attentively, and observed that at dinner and throughout the evening Natasha was in a strange and unnatural state, quite unlike herself. She answered questions at random, began sentences and did not finish them, and laughed at everything.

After they had drunk tea Sonya noticed a housemaid at Natasha's door timidly waiting for her to pass. She let the girl go in, and then listening at the door learned that another letter had been delivered. And all at once it became clear to Sonya that Natasha had some dreadful plan on foot for that evening. Sonya knocked at the door. Natasha would not let her in.

'She is going to run away with him!' thought Sonya. 'She is capable of anything. There was something particularly piteous and determined in her face today. And she cried when she said good-bye to papa,' Sonya remembered. 'Yes, that's it, she means to elope with him – but what am I to do?' she wondered, recalling all the incidents that so clearly betokened some terrible intention on Natasha's part. 'The count is away. What am I to do? Write to Kuragin, demanding an explanation? But who is to make him answer? Write to Pierre, as Prince Andrei asked me to in case of trouble? ... But perhaps she really has already refused Bolkonsky – she sent a letter to Princess Maria yesterday. And Uncle is not here!'

To tell Maria Dmitrievna, who had such trust in Natasha, seemed to Sonya a fearful step to take.

'But one way or another,' thought Sonya as she stood in the dark corridor, 'now or never the time has come for me to show that I am mindful of the family's goodness to me and that I love Nicolas. Yes, if I have to stay awake for three nights running I'll not leave this passage and will hold her back by force, and not let the family be disgraced,' she said to herself.

16

ANATOLE had lately moved to Dolohov's house. The plan for abducting Natasha had been suggested and arranged by Dolohov a few days before, and on the day that Sonya, after listening at Natasha's door, resolved to safeguard her, it was to have been put into execution. Natasha had promised to come out to Kuragin at the back porch at ten o'clock in the evening. Kuragin was to get her into a troika he would have waiting, and drive with her forty miles to the village of Kamenka, where an unfrocked priest was prepared to perform a marriage ceremony over them. At Kamenka a relay of horses was to be in readiness which would take them as far as the Warsaw high road, and from there they would hasten abroad by means of post-horses.

Anatole had a passport and an order for post-horses, ten thousand roubles borrowed from his sister and another ten thousand raised with Dolohov's assistance.

The two witnesses for the mock marriage – Hvostikov, a retired petty official whom Dolohov made use of in his gambling transactions, and Makarin, once a hussar, a weak, good-natured fellow who had an unbounded affection for Kuragin – were sitting in Dolohov's front room taking tea.

In his large study, the walls of which were hung to the ceiling with Persian rugs, bearskins and weapons, sat Dolohov in a travelling tunic and high boots in front of an open bureau on which lay an abacus and some bundles of paper money. Anatole, with uniform unbuttoned, was walking to and fro, from the room where the witnesses were sitting through the study into a room behind, where his French valet and other servants were packing the last of his things. Dolohov was counting the bank-notes and jotting down various amounts.

'Well,' he said, 'Hvostikov must have a couple of thousand.'

'Give it him then,' said Anatole.

'Makarka –' (their name for Makarin) 'now he would go through fire and water for you for nothing. So here are our accounts all settled,' said Dolohov, showing him the memorandum. 'Is that right?'

'Yes, of course,' answered Anatole, evidently not attending to Dolohov and looking into space with a smile that did not leave his face.

Dolohov banged down the lid of his desk, and turned to Kuragin, smiling sardonically.

'But see here, now – you'd really better drop the whole business. There's still time!'

'Fool!' retorted Anatole. 'Don't talk rubbish! If you only knew... the devil only knows what!'

'No, really, throw it all up,' urged Dolohov. 'I'm speaking in earnest. It's no joking matter, this plot of yours.'

'What, teasing again? Go to the devil with you! Eh?...' said

Anatole, frowning. 'Really, I'm in no humour for your stupid jokes.'
And he left the room.

Dolohov smiled a contemptuous, supercilious smile when Anatole
had gone.

'Wait now,' he called after Anatole. 'I'm not jesting, I'm talking
sense. Come here, come here!'

Anatole returned and looked at Dolohov, trying to concentrate his
attention and evidently submitting to him against his will.

'Listen to me. I'm speaking for the last time. Why should I joke?
Have I ever done anything to thwart you? Who is it made all the
arrangements for you? Who found the priest and got the passport?
Who raised the money? I did.'

'Well, and I am very much obliged to you. Do you suppose I am
not grateful?' Anatole sighed and embraced Dolohov.

'I have been helping you, but all the same I must tell you the truth:
this is a dangerous game and, if you think about it, a stupid one.
You carry her off – well and good. Do you imagine they'll let it stop
at that? It will come out that you are already married. Why, they'll
have you up on a criminal charge. ...'

'Oh, rubbish, rubbish!' ejaculated Anatole again, scowling. 'Haven't
I explained to you again and again?' And Anatole, with the peculiar
infatuation of the dull-witted for any deduction they have arrived at
by their own reasoning, repeated the argument he had put to Dolohov
a hundred times already. 'I have told you time after time – I see it
like this: if this marriage turns out to be invalid,' he went on, crooking one finger, 'then it follows I have nothing to answer for. But if
it is valid, no matter! Abroad no one will ever know anything about
it. Isn't that so? So don't, don't, don't talk to me!'

'Seriously, you'd better drop it! You'll only get yourself into a
mess. ...'

'Go to the devil!' cried Anatole and, clutching at his hair, left the
room, but returned at once and sank into an arm-chair facing Dolo-
hov, with his legs doubled up under him. 'It's the very devil! What?
Feel how it beats!' He took Dolohov's hand and placed it on his heart.
'Ah, what an ankle, my dear fellow! What eyes! She's a goddess!
What?'

Dolohov, with a cold smile and a gleam in his handsome, insolent
eyes, looked at him, obviously disposed to get some more amusement
out of him.

'Well, and when your money's gone, what then?'

'What then? Eh?' repeated Anatole, with genuine perplexity at the thought of the future. 'What then? I don't know what then. … But what is the use of talking nonsense!' He glanced at his watch. 'It's time!'

Anatole went into the back room.

'Hurry up there! Dawdling about!' he shouted to the servants.

Dolohov put away the money, called a footman and, telling him to bring them something to eat and drink before the journey, went into the room where Hvostikov and Makarin were sitting.

Anatole lay on the sofa in the study, leaning on his elbow and smiling dreamily as he murmured softly to himself.

'Come and eat something. Here, have a drink!' Dolohov called from the next room.

'I don't want anything!' replied Anatole, continuing to smile.

'Come, Balaga is here.'

Anatole rose to his feet and went into the dining-room. Balaga was a famous troika-driver who had known Dolohov and Anatole some six years and had given them good service with his troikas. More than once when Anatole's regiment was stationed at Tver he had started out with him from Tver in the evening, set him down in Moscow before daybreak and driven him back again the next night. More than once he had enabled Dolohov to escape when pursued. More than once he had driven them about the town with gipsies and 'ladykins' as he called the *cocottes*. More than once in their service he had run over pedestrians and upset vehicles in the streets of Moscow, and always 'his gentlemen' as he called them had protected him from the consequences. He had ruined more than one horse in their service. They thrashed him now and again, and many a time they had made him drunk on champagne and madeira, which he loved; and he knew of more than one exploit of each of them which would long ago have condemned any ordinary man to Siberia. They often called Balaga into their orgies and made him drink and dance at the gipsies', and many a time thousands of roubles of their money had passed through his hands. In their service he risked his skin and his life twenty times a year, and wore out more horses than the money they gave him would ever pay for. But he was fond of them, liked driving at the mad pace of twelve miles an hour, liked upsetting a driver or running down a pedestrian, and flying full gallop through the Moscow streets.

He liked to hear those wild, tipsy shouts behind him, urging him on when it was impossible to go any faster. He liked giving a painful lash round the neck to some peasant who was already hurrying out of his way more dead than alive. 'Real gentlemen,' he thought them.

Anatole and Dolohov were fond of Balaga too, for his spirited driving and because he liked the things they liked. With other people Balaga haggled and bargained, charging twenty-five roubles for a couple of hours' excursion, and rarely went himself, generally sending one of his young men. But 'his gentlemen' he always took personally, and never demanded payment for the job. Only when he happened to know through the valets that there was cash in the house he would turn up of a morning two or three times a year, quite sober, and with a deep bow would ask them to help him out. The gentlemen always made him sit down.

'Please give me a helping hand, Fiodr Ivanich, sir,' or 'your Excellency,' he would say. 'I am right out of horses. Spare me what you can to go to the fair.'

And Anatole and Dolohov, when they were in funds, would let him have a thousand or two.

Balaga was a flaxen-haired, squat, snub-nosed peasant of around seven-and-twenty, with a red face and a particularly red, thick neck, little twinkling eyes and a small beard. Now he wore a fine dark-blue, silk-lined coat over a sheepskin.

He turned to the corner where the icons hung and crossed himself before going up to Dolohov and holding out a small black hand.

'Fiodr Ivanich – my respects!' said he, bowing.

'Good-day to you, my good fellow. Well, here he comes!'

'Good-day, your Excellency!' he said, again holding out his hand, this time to Anatole who was just entering.

'I say, Balaga,' exclaimed Anatole, clapping his hands on the man's shoulders, 'have you a soft spot for me or not, eh? Now's the time to do me a service. ... What horses have you come with, eh?'

'The ones your man ordered – your favourites,' replied Balaga.

'Now see here, Balaga! Drive all three to death, but get me there in three hours, understand?'

'If we kill them, how shall we get there?' said Balaga with a wink.

'None of your jokes now, or I'll smash your snout for you!' cried Anatole suddenly, his eyes glaring.

'Who's joking?' laughed the driver. 'As if I'd grudge my gentle-

691

men anything! We'll drive as fast as ever the horses can gallop.'

'Ah!' grunted Anatole. 'Well, sit down.'

'Yes, sit down!' said Dolohov.

'I'll stand, Fiodr Ivanich.'

'Nonsense! Sit down! Have a drink,' said Anatole, and poured him out a large glass of madeira.

The driver's eyes lit up at the sight of the wine. After refusing it at first for manners' sake, he tossed it off and wiped his mouth with a red silk handkerchief which he took out of his cap.

'And when are we to start, your Excellency?'

'Let me see. ...' Anatole looked at his watch. 'We must set off at once. Mind now, Balaga! You'll get us there in time, eh?'

'That depends on our luck at the outset. If we get off well, why shouldn't we do it in time?' said Balaga. 'Didn't we get to Tver in seven hours once? I'll warrant you remember that, your Excellency!'

'Do you know, one Christmas I drove from Tver,' said Anatole, smiling at the recollection and turning to Makarin, who was gazing at him adoringly. 'Would you believe it, Makarka, we went so fast we could hardly breathe. We ran into a train of loaded sledges and jumped right over two of them. How's that, eh?'

'What horses those were!' Balaga took up the tale. 'I'd put a couple of young horses in the traces with the bay in the shafts,' he went on, turning to Dolohov, 'and just fancy, Fiodr Ivanich, those beasts galloped forty miles! There was no holding 'em. My hands were numb with the frost, and I flung down the reins. "Hold on, your Excellency!" thinks I, and I rolls over backward into the sledge and lays there sprawling. No need of driving 'em. Why, we couldn't hold 'em in till we reached the place. Those devils got us there in three hours! Only the near one died of it.'

17

ANATOLE left the room and returned a few minutes later wearing a fur coat girdled with a silver belt, and a sable cap jauntily set on one side and very becoming to his handsome face. Having glanced in the looking-glass and then standing before Dolohov in the same attitude he had assumed for the mirror, he took up a glass of wine.

'Well, Fiodr, good-bye, and thanks for everything – farewell!' said Anatole. 'Now, companions and friends ...' – he considered for a moment – '... of my youth ... farewell!' he said, turning to Makarin and the others.

Although they were all going with him, Anatole evidently wished to make something touching and solemn out of this address to his comrades. He spoke in a loud, deliberate voice, squaring his shoulders and swinging one leg.

'All of you take your glasses. You, too, Balaga. Well, comrades, friends of my youth, we have had jolly good times together, we've lived and had our fling, what? And now when shall we meet again? I am going abroad. We have had a good time together – so farewell, lads! Here's to our health! Hurrah! ...' he cried, draining his glass and flinging it on the floor.

'Here's to your good health!' said Balaga, who wiped his mouth with his handkerchief when he too had emptied his glass.

Makarin embraced Anatole with tears in his eyes.

'Alas, prince, how it grieves my heart to part from you,' he said.

'Come, let us be off!' cried Anatole.

Balaga was about to leave the room.

'No, stop!' said Anatole. 'Shut the door. We must sit down for a moment first. That's the way.'

They closed the door and all sat down.*

'Now, quick march, lads!' said Anatole, rising.

Joseph, his valet, handed him his sabretache and sabre, and they all went out into the vestibule.

'But the fur cloak – where is it?' asked Dolohov. 'Hey, Ignatka! Run in to Matriona Matveyevna and ask her for the sable cloak. I've heard what happens at elopements,' continued Dolohov with a wink. 'She's sure to come skipping out more dead than alive, wearing indoor things. Delay for an instant and there'll be tears and "dear papa" and "dear mamma", and next minute she's frozen and for going back again – but you wrap her up in the fur cloak right away and carry her to the sledge.'

The valet brought a woman's fox-lined pelisse.

'Fool, I told you the sable. Hey, Matriona, the sable!' he shouted, so that his voice rang out through the room.

A handsome, slim, pale-faced gipsy-girl with brilliant black eyes

* For the sake of the traditional Russian custom of pausing to reflect before setting out on a journey. – Tr.

and purple-black curls, wearing a red shawl, ran out with a sable mantle on her arm.

'Here, I don't grudge it – take it!' she said, visibly afraid of her master and regretful of the cloak.

Dolohov, making her no answer, took the cloak, threw it over Matriona and wrapped her up in it.

'That's the way,' said Dolohov. 'And then like this!' and he turned the collar up round her head, leaving only a small opening for her face. 'That's how to do it, see?' and he moved Anatole's head forward to meet the opening left by the collar, from which Matriona's flashing smile peeped out.

'Well, good-bye, Matriona,' said Anatole, kissing her. 'Ah me, my follies here are over. Remember me to Stioshka. There, good-bye! Good-bye, Matriona, wish me luck!'

'The good God now grant you great happiness, prince!' said Matriona with her gipsy accent.

Outside before the porch two troikas were standing, with two stalwart young drivers holding the horses. Balaga took his seat in the foremost, and holding his elbows high slowly and carefully arranged the reins in his hands. Anatole and Dolohov got in with him. Makarin, Hvostikov and the valet seated themselves in the other sledge.

'All ready?' asked Balaga. 'Off!' he shouted, twisting the reins round his hands, and the troika flew at breakneck speed down the Nikitsky boulevard.

'Grrrh! ... Look out there! Hi! ... Grrh!' yelled Balaga and the sturdy young fellow seated on the box. In Arbatsky square the troika knocked against a carriage: there was a cracking sound, shouts were heard, and the troika flew off along Arbat street.

After driving the length of Podnovinsky boulevard a couple of times, Balaga began to rein in, and turning back drew up at the crossing by Old Konyusheny street.

The smart young fellow on the box jumped down to hold the horses by their bridles, while Anatole and Dolohov strode along the pavement. When they reached the gate, Dolohov whistled. The whistle was answered, and a maidservant ran out.

'Come into the courtyard, or you'll be seen. She'll be here directly,' she said.

Dolohov stayed by the gate. Anatole followed the maid into the courtyard, turned the corner, and ran up into the porch.

He was met by Gavrilo, Maria Dmitrievna's gigantic footman.

'Kindly walk this way to the mistress,' said the footman in his deep bass, blocking all retreat.

'What mistress? And who are you?' asked Anatole in a breathless whisper.

'Kindly step in. My orders are to bring you in.'

'Kuragin! Come back!' shouted Dolohov. 'Treachery! Come back!'

Dolohov, at the little wicket-gate where he had waited, was struggling with the yard-porter who was trying to lock it and keep Anatole in. With a last desperate effort Dolohov shoved the porter aside, and grabbing Anatole by the arm as he came running back pulled him through the gate and made off with him to the troika.

18

MARIA DMITRIEVNA, coming upon Sonya weeping in the corridor, had forced her to confess everything. Intercepting Natasha's note to Anatole and reading it, she marched into Natasha's room with the note in her hand.

'You shameless hussy!' she said to her. 'I won't hear a word!'

Pushing back Natasha, who looked at her with amazed but tearless eyes, she locked her in her room, and having given orders to the yard-porter to admit the persons who would be coming that evening but not to let them out again, and having instructed the footman to show these persons up to her, she seated herself in the drawing-room to await the abductors.

When Gavrilo came to inform her that the persons who had come had run away again, she rose frowning, and, with her hands clasped behind her back, for a long while paced to and fro through the rooms, pondering what she should do. Towards midnight she went to Natasha's room, fingering the key in her pocket. Sonya was sitting sobbing in the corridor.

'Maria Dmitrievna, for God's sake let me in to her!' she pleaded.

Making no reply, Maria Dmitrievna unlocked the door and went in.

'Disgusting! Abominable! ... In my house. ... Shameless wench! Only I'm sorry for her father!' thought she, trying to restrain her wrath. 'Hard as it may be, I'll tell them all to hold their tongues, and keep it from the count.'

Maria Dmitrievna walked into the room with resolute steps. Natasha was lying on the sofa, her head hidden in her hands, and she did not stir. She was lying in the same position in which Maria Dmitrievna had left her.

'Pretty conduct, pretty conduct, indeed!' exclaimed Maria Dmitrievna. 'Making assignations with lovers in my house! It's no use dissembling: you listen when I speak to you!' And Maria Dmitrievna shook her by the arm. 'Listen when I speak. You've disgraced yourself like any common hussy. I don't know what I wouldn't do to you, but I feel for your father, so I will keep it quiet.'

Natasha did not change her position, but her whole body began to heave with noiseless, convulsive sobs which choked her. Maria Dmitrievna glanced round at Sonya and sat down on the edge of the sofa beside Natasha.

'It's lucky for him he escaped; but I'll catch up with him!' she said in her rough voice. 'Do you hear what I say?'

She put her large hand under Natasha's face and turned it towards her. Both Maria Dmitrievna and Sonya were startled when they saw how Natasha looked. Her eyes were dry and glittering, her lips tightly compressed, her cheeks sunken.

'Let me be. ... What do I care? ... I shall die!' she muttered, wrenching herself free from Maria Dmitrievna's grasp and falling back into her former position.

'Natalie!' said Maria Dmitrievna. 'I wish for your good. Lie still, stay like that then, I won't touch you. But listen ... I am not going to tell you how wrongly you have acted. You know that yourself. But when your father comes back tomorrow – what am I to say to him? Eh?'

Again Natasha's body shook with sobs.

'Suppose he hears of it, and your brother, and your betrothed?'

'I have no betrothed. I have refused him!' cried Natasha.

'That makes no difference,' pursued Maria Dmitrievna. 'If they hear of this, will they let it pass? There's your father, I know him ... if he challenges him to a duel, will that be all right? Eh?'

'Oh, leave me alone! Why did you have to spoil everything? Why? Why? Who asked you to interfere?' screamed Natasha, raising herself on the sofa and glaring spitefully at Maria Dmitrievna.

'But what was it you wanted?' cried Maria Dmitrievna, losing patience again. 'You weren't kept under lock and key, were you?

696

Who hindered him from coming to the house? Why carry you off like some gipsy singing-girl? ... And if he had carried you off – do you suppose they wouldn't have found him? Your father, or your brother, or your betrothed? He's a scoundrel, a knave – that's a fact!'

'He's better than any of you!' shrieked Natasha, sitting up. 'If you hadn't meddled. ... O my God, why has it come to this? What does it mean? Sonya, how could you? Go away!'

And she burst into a passion of tears, sobbing with the despairing vehemence of those who feel that they are the instruments of their own misery. Maria Dmitrievna was about to speak again, but Natasha cried out:

'Go away! Go away! You all hate and despise me!' And she flung herself back on the sofa.

Maria Dmitrievna continued for some time to admonish her, insisting that it must all be kept from the count and assuring her that nobody would know anything about it if only Natasha herself would undertake to forget it all and not let it be seen that anything had happened. Natasha did not answer. She ceased to sob, but grew cold and was seized with a fit of shivering. Maria Dmitrievna put a pillow under her head, covered her with two quilts, and herself fetched some lime-flower water, but Natasha had nothing to say to her.

'Well, let her sleep,' said Maria Dmitrievna, as she went out of the room, supposing Natasha to be asleep.

But Natasha was not asleep: her fixed, wide-open eyes stared straight before her out of her pale face. All that night she did not sleep or weep, and did not speak to Sonya who got up and went to her several times.

On the following day Count Rostov returned from his estate near Moscow, in time for lunch as he had promised. He was in capital spirits. The purchaser and he were coming to terms very nicely and there was nothing to keep him in Moscow any longer, away from the countess whom he missed. Maria Dmitrievna met him and told him that Natasha had been very unwell the day before and they had sent for the doctor, but that now she was better. Natasha did not leave her room that morning. With compressed, parched lips and dry, staring eyes she sat at the window, uneasily watching the people who drove past, and hurriedly glancing round at anyone who entered the room. She was obviously expecting news of him – expecting that he would either come himself or write to her.

When the count went in to see her she turned round nervously at the sound of a man's footstep, and then her face resumed its cold, almost vindictive expression. She did not even get up to greet him.

'What is it, my angel? Are you ill?' asked the count.

Natasha was silent for a moment.

'Yes, ill,' she answered.

To the count's anxious inquiries as to why she was so dejected and whether anything had happened with her betrothed she protested that it was all right and begged him not to worry. Maria Dmitrievna confirmed Natasha's assurances that nothing had befallen. From the pretended illness, from his daughter's distress and the troubled faces of Sonya and Maria Dmitrievna, the count saw clearly that something had gone wrong during his absence; but it was so terrible for him to imagine anything discreditable occurring in connexion with his beloved daughter, and he so prized his own cheerful tranquillity, that he avoided asking questions and did his best to persuade himself that there was nothing very much out of the way, and his only regret was that her indisposition would delay their return to the country.

19

FROM the day of his wife's arrival in Moscow Pierre had been intending to go away somewhere, so as not to be with her. Then, soon after the Rostovs came to the capital, the impression made upon him by Natasha hastened the carrying out of his intention. He went to Tver to see Bazdeyev's widow, who some time since had promised him her deceased husband's papers.

On his return to Moscow Pierre was handed a letter from Maria Dmitrievna asking him to come and see her on a matter of great importance concerning Andrei Bolkonsky and his betrothed. Pierre had been avoiding Natasha. It seemed to him that his feeling for her was stronger than a married man's should be for his friend's betrothed. And some fate was continually throwing them together.

'What can have happened? And what do they want with me?' he wondered as he dressed to go to Maria Dmitrievna's. 'If only Prince Andrei would hurry up and come home and marry her!' thought he on his way to the house.

On the Tverskoy boulevard someone hailed him.

'Pierre? Been back long?' called a familiar voice. Pierre raised his head. In a sledge drawn by a pair of grey trotting-horses that were bespattering the splashboard with snow Anatole and his constant companion Makarin dashed by. Anatole was sitting bolt upright in the classic pose of the stylish army officer, the lower part of his face muffled in a beaver collar and his head bent a little forward. His face was fresh and rosy, his white-plumed hat was set jauntily on one side, displaying his curled and pomaded hair besprinkled with powdery snow.

'Yes, there goes a true sage,' said Pierre to himself. 'He sees nothing beyond the enjoyment of the moment. Nothing worries him and so he is always cheerful, satisfied and serene. What wouldn't I give to be like him!' he thought enviously.

In Maria Dmitrievna's ante-room the footman who helped him off with his fur coat told him that the mistress asked him to come to her in her bedroom.

Opening the ballroom door Pierre caught sight of Natasha sitting at the window, looking pale, thin and bad-tempered. She glanced round at him, frowned and with an expression of frigid dignity walked out of the room.

'What has happened?' asked Pierre, going on to Maria Dmitrievna.

'Fine doings!' answered Maria Dmitrievna. 'Fifty-eight years have I lived in this world – and never have I witnessed anything so disgraceful!'

And having exacted from Pierre his word of honour not to repeat a syllable of what he should hear from her, Maria Dmitrievna informed him that Natasha had broken her engagement with Prince Andrei without the knowledge of her parents; that the cause of her doing so was Anatole Kuragin into whose society Pierre's wife had thrown her, and with whom Natasha had attempted to elope during her father's absence, in order to be secretly married.

Pierre, with hunched shoulders, listened open-mouthed to what Maria Dmitrievna was saying, hardly able to believe his ears. That Prince Andrei's dearly-loved betrothed – that the hitherto charming Natasha Rostov should throw over Bolkonsky for that fool Anatole, who was already married (Pierre was in the secret of the marriage), and should be so enamoured of him as to agree to run away with him, was more than Pierre could comprehend or imagine.

699

He could not reconcile the agreeable impression he had of Natasha, whom he had known since her childhood, with this new picture of baseness, folly and cruelty. He thought of his wife. 'They are all alike,' he said to himself, reflecting that he was not the only man whose unhappy fate it was to be tied to a worthless woman. But at the same time he could have wept for Prince Andrei and his wounded pride. And the more he grieved for his friend, the deeper was the contempt and even disgust he felt for that Natasha who had just passed him with such icy dignity in the ballroom. He could not know that Natasha's soul was overflowing with despair, shame and humiliation, and that she was not to blame if her face happened to express cold dignity and severity.

'Married?' exclaimed Pierre, catching at Maria Dmitrievna's last words. 'He could not marry her: he already has a wife.'

'Worse and worse!' ejaculated Maria Dmitrievna. 'A nice youth! What a scoundrel! And there she sits waiting for him. These two days she's been expecting him. That at least must stop: we must tell her.'

When she had learned from Pierre the details of Anatole's marriage, and poured out the vials of her wrath against Anatole in abusive words, Maria Dmitrievna explained to Pierre why she had sent for him. She was afraid that the count or Bolkonsky, who might arrive at any moment, might hear of the affair (though she hoped to conceal it from them), and challenge Anatole to a duel. She therefore begged Pierre to tell his brother-in-law in her name to leave Moscow and never dare to let her set eyes on him again. Pierre – only now realizing the risk to the old count, Nikolai and Prince Andrei – promised to do as she desired. After briefly and precisely expounding to him her wishes, she let him go to the drawing-room.

'Mind, the count knows nothing. Behave as if you knew nothing either,' she said. 'And I will go and tell her it's no use expecting him! And do stay to dinner if you care to,' she called after Pierre.

Pierre met the old count, who seemed nervous and upset. That morning Natasha had told him that she had broken off her engagement to Bolkonsky.

'Trouble, trouble, *mon cher*!' he said to Pierre. 'Nothing but trouble with these girls away from their mother! I am only sorry I ever came. I'll be plain with you. Have you heard that she has broken off her engagement without consulting any of us? True, the engagement never was much to my liking. Of course he's a fine man and all that, but there you are – with his father against it they wouldn't have been happy, and Natasha will never want for suitors. Still, it has been going on for so long – and then to take such a step without a word to her father or mother! And now she's ill, and God knows what it is! Yes, it's a bad thing, count, a bad thing for girls to be away from their mother. ...'

Pierre saw that the count was deeply disturbed, and he tried to bring the conversation round to some other subject, but the count kept returning to his troubles.

Sonya entered the drawing-room, looking agitated.

'Natasha is not very well: she's in her room and would like to see you. Maria Dmitrievna is with her and she too asks you to come.'

'Yes, of course you are a great friend of Bolkonsky's, no doubt she wants to give you some message for him,' said the count. 'Oh dear, oh dear, how happy it all was before this!' And clutching the spare grey locks on his temples the count left the room.

Maria Dmitrievna had told Natasha that Anatole was married. Natasha had refused to believe her, and demanded confirmation from Pierre himself. Sonya told Pierre this as she led him along the corridor to Natasha's room.

Natasha, pale and unbending, was sitting beside Maria Dmitrievna, and the moment Pierre appeared at the door she met him with feverishly glittering, imploring eyes. She did not smile or nod. She simply looked hard at him, her look asking only one thing: was he a friend, or, like the others, an enemy in regard to Anatole? Pierre as himself obviously did not exist for her.

'He knows all about it,' said Maria Dmitrievna, indicating Pierre and addressing Natasha. 'Let him tell you whether I was speaking the truth.'

Natasha glanced from one to the other as a hunted and wounded animal watches the approaching dogs and sportsmen.

'Natalia Ilyinichna,' Pierre began, dropping his eyes with a feeling of pity for her and loathing for the thing he had to do, 'whether it is true or not should make no difference to you . ...'

'Then it is not true that he is married?'

'Yes, it is true.'

'Has he been married long?' she asked. 'On your word of honour?'

Pierre gave his word of honour.

'Is he still here?' she asked quickly.

'Yes, I have just seen him.'

She was obviously incapable of speaking, and made a sign with her hands that they should leave her alone.

20

PIERRE did not stay for dinner, but left the room and went away at once. He drove about the town in search of Anatole, the mere thought of whom now made his blood boil and his heart beat till he could hardly breathe. He was not on the ice-hills, nor at the gipsies', nor at Comoneno's. Pierre drove to the club. At the club everything was going on as usual: the members who had dropped in for dinner were sitting about in groups. They greeted Pierre, and talked of the news of the town. The footman, after welcoming Pierre, told him, knowing his friends and his habits, that there was a place left for him in the small dining-room, that Prince Mihail Zakarich was in the library, but Pavel Timofeich had not arrived yet. One of Pierre's acquaintances in the middle of a remark about the weather asked him if he had heard of Kuragin's abduction of the young Countess Rostov which was talked of in the town, and was it true? Pierre laughed and said it was nonsense, for he had just come from the Rostovs'. He asked everyone about Anatole. One man told him he had not come in yet, another that he would be there for dinner. It gave Pierre an odd sensation to see this calmly indifferent crowd of people who had not the slightest inkling of what was passing in his mind. He walked about the hall, waiting till everyone had arrived, and then, as Anatole had not turned up, did not stay for dinner but drove home.

Anatole, for whom Pierre was looking, dined that day with Dolohov, consulting him as to ways and means of achieving the exploit that had miscarried. It seemed to him essential to see Natasha. In the evening he went to his sister's to discuss with her how to arrange a meeting. When Pierre returned home after vainly ransacking all Moscow his valet told him that Prince Anatole was with the countess. The countess's drawing-room was full of guests.

Pierre, without greeting his wife whom he had not seen since his return to Moscow – at that moment she seemed to him more utterly detestable than ever – entered the drawing-room and catching sight of Anatole walked straight up to him.

'Ah, Pierre,' said the countess, approaching her husband. 'You don't know what a plight our poor Anatole is in. ...'

She stopped short, seeing in the forward thrust of her husband's head, in his flashing eyes and resolute tread, the terrible indications of that fury and might which she knew and had herself experienced after his duel with Dolohov.

'Wherever you are, depravity and evil are to be found,' said Pierre to his wife. 'Anatole, come with me, I want a word with you,' he added in French.

Anatole glanced round at his sister and got up obediently, prepared to follow Pierre.

Pierre took him by the arm, pulled him to him and was leading him out of the room.

'If you dare in my drawing-room ...' muttered Hélène in a whisper, but Pierre walked out of the room without replying.

Anatole followed him with his usual jaunty swagger. But his face betrayed uneasiness.

Reaching his study, Pierre shut the door, and addressed Anatole without looking at him.

'You promised Countess Rostov to marry her? You were about to elope with her? Is that so?'

'*Mon cher*,' returned Anatole (the whole conversation proceeded in French), 'I consider myself under no obligation to answer questions put to me in that tone.'

Pierre's face, already pale, became distorted with fury. With his great hand he seized Anatole by the collar of his uniform, and shook him from side to side till Anatole's features registered a sufficient degree of terror.

'When I tell you that I *want a word with you* ...' insisted Pierre.

'Well, what? This is ridiculous, what?' said Anatole, fingering a button of his collar that had been wrenched off together with a bit of the cloth.

'You are a scoundrel and a blackguard, and I don't know what restrains me from the pleasure of cracking your skull with this,' said Pierre, expressing himself so artificially because he was speaking French. He took up a heavy paper-weight and lifted it threateningly, but at once hurriedly put it back in its place.

'Did you promise to marry her?'

'I – I – I didn't think ... in fact I never promised because ...'

Pierre interrupted him.

'Have you any letters of hers? Have you any letters?' he demanded, advancing upon Anatole.

Anatole cast him one look and immediately thrust a hand into his pocket and drew out his pocket-book.

Pierre took the letter Anatole handed him, and pushing aside a table that stood in his way plumped down on the sofa.

'I shan't do anything to you, don't be afraid,' said Pierre in response to Anatole's gesture of alarm. 'The letters – that's one,' he continued, as if repeating a lesson to himself. 'Two – ' he went on after a moment's silence, getting to his feet again and beginning to pace up and down the room, 'tomorrow you leave Moscow.'

'But how can I? ...'

'Three – ' pursued Pierre, not heeding him, 'you are never to breathe a word of what has passed between you and Countess Rostov. I know I can't prevent your doing so, but if you have a spark of conscience ...' Pierre took several turns about the room in silence. Anatole sat at the table, scowling and biting his lips.

'You must surely understand that besides your pleasure there is such a thing as other people's happiness, other people's peace of mind; that you are ruining a whole life for the sake of a little amusement for yourself. Amuse yourself with women like my wife – with such you are within your rights: they know what it is you want of them. They are armed against you by a similar experience of depravity; but to promise an innocent girl to marry her ... to deceive, to kidnap. ... Don't you see that it's as low-down as hitting an old man or a child! ...'

Pierre paused and glanced at Anatole, with a look of inquiry now in place of anger.

'I don't know about that, what?' said Anatole, growing bolder in proportion as Pierre mastered his wrath. 'I don't know about that, and don't want to,' he said, not looking at Pierre and with a slight tremor of his lower jaw, 'but you have used words to me – talked about being low-down, and so on – which as a man of honour I can't allow from anyone.'

Pierre stared at him in amazement, unable to understand what he was after.

'Though it was only tête-à-tête,' Anatole went on, 'still I can't. ...'

'Is it satisfaction you want?' said Pierre ironically.

'At least you can retract what you said, what? If you want me to do as you wish, what?'

'I will! I'll take it back!' exclaimed Pierre. 'And I beg you to forgive me.' Pierre involuntarily glanced at the torn button. 'And if you require money for your journey ...'

Anatole smiled. That base, cringing smile which Pierre knew so well in his wife revolted him.

'Oh you vile, heartless breed!' he exclaimed, and walked out of the room.

Next day Anatole left for Petersburg.

21

PIERRE drove to Maria Dmitrievna's to report to her that her wishes had been carried out and Kuragin banished from Moscow. The whole house was in a state of alarm and commotion. Natasha was very ill, having, as Maria Dmitrievna told him in confidence, poisoned herself the night she had heard that Anatole was married, with some ratsbane procured by stealth. After swallowing a little she had been so frightened that she woke Sonya and confessed what she had done. The necessary antidotes had been administered in time and she was now out of danger, though still so weak that there could be no question of moving her to the country, and the countess had been sent for. Pierre saw the distracted count and Sonya, red and swollen with weeping, but he was not allowed to see Natasha.

Pierre dined at the club that day and heard on every side gossip about the attempted abduction of the young Countess Rostov. He strenuously denied these rumours, assuring everyone that nothing had happened except that his brother-in-law had proposed to her and been refused. It seemed to Pierre that it was his bounden duty to conceal the whole affair and re-establish Natasha's reputation.

He was awaiting Prince Andrei's return with dread, and called daily on the old prince for news of him.

Prince Bolkonsky had heard all the stories flying about the town from Mademoiselle Bourienne, and had read the note to Princess Maria in which Natasha had broken off her engagement. He seemed in better spirits than usual and looked forward with impatience to his son's home-coming.

A few days after Anatole's departure Pierre received a note from

705

Prince Andrei announcing his arrival and asking him to come to see him.

Directly Prince Andrei reached Moscow his father had handed him Natasha's note to Princess Maria breaking off her engagement (Mademoiselle Bourienne had purloined it from Princess Maria and given it to the old prince), and from his father's lips Prince Andrei heard the story of Natasha's elopement, with various supplementary details.

Prince Andrei arrived in the evening and Pierre came to see him the following morning. Pierre expected to find Prince Andrei almost in the same state as Natasha, and was therefore surprised on entering the drawing-room to hear him in the study loudly and eagerly discussing some intrigue going on in Petersburg. The old prince's voice and another interrupted him from time to time. Princess Maria came out to meet Pierre. She sighed, turning her eyes towards the door of the room where her brother was, obviously wanting to make a show of sympathy with his sorrow; but Pierre saw by her face that she was both glad at what had happened and at the way her brother had taken the news of Natasha's faithlessness.

'He says he expected it,' she remarked. 'I know his pride will not let him express his feelings, but still he has borne up under it better, far better, than I expected. Evidently it had to be. ...'

'But is everything really all over between them?' asked Pierre.

Princess Maria looked at him in astonishment. She could not understand how anyone could even ask such a question. Pierre went into the study. Prince Andrei, greatly altered and apparently restored to health, but with a new and perpendicular line between his brows, was standing in civilian clothes facing his father and Prince Meshchersky, arguing hotly and making forceful gestures.

They were talking about Speransky, news of whose sudden banishment and alleged treachery had just reached Moscow.

'Now he is being criticized and accused by the very men who a month ago were lauding him to the skies,' Prince Andrei was saying, 'and were incapable of appreciating his aims. It is very easy to find fault with a man when he's out of favour, and throw upon him the blame for everybody else's mistakes; but I maintain that if anything good has been accomplished in the present reign it has been done by him – by him alone. ...' He caught sight of Pierre and paused. His face quivered and immediately assumed a malicious expression. 'And posterity will vindicate him,' he wound up, and at once turned to Pierre.

'Well, how are you? Still getting stouter?' he said in an animated tone, but the newly-formed furrow on his forehead deepened. 'Yes, I am very well,' he replied in answer to Pierre's inquiry, and smiled. It was clear to Pierre that his smile meant: 'Yes, I am well, but my health is of no use to anyone now.'

After a few words to Pierre about the awful roads from the Polish frontier, about people he had met in Switzerland who knew Pierre, and about Monsieur Dessalles, whom he had brought back from abroad to be his son's tutor, Prince Andrei warmly took part again in the conversation about Speransky which was still going on between the two elderly men.

'If there had been any treason, or if there were any proofs of secret relations with Napoleon, they would have been made public,' he said, speaking hurriedly and excitedly. 'I personally don't like and never have liked Speransky, but I do like justice!'

Pierre was now beginning to realize that his friend was labouring under that necessity, with which he himself was only too familiar, of getting thoroughly worked up and argumentative over some irrelevant topic for the purpose of stifling thoughts too painful and too near the heart to be endured.

When Prince Meshchersky had gone, Prince Andrei took Pierre's arm and invited him into the room that had been prepared for him. A bed had been made up there, and some open portmanteaux and trunks stood about. Prince Andrei went to one and took out a small casket, from which he drew a packet wrapped in paper. All this he did in silence and with speed. He stood up and cleared his throat. His face was gloomy and his lips set.

'Forgive me for troubling you. ...'

Pierre perceived that Prince Andrei was going to speak of Natasha, and his broad countenance expressed pity and sympathy. This expression on Pierre's face irritated Prince Andrei. He went on in a clear, resolute, disagreeable voice:

'I have received my dismissal from Countess Rostov, and reports have come to my ears that your brother-in-law has been seeking her hand, or something of the kind. Is that true?'

'Both true and untrue,' began Pierre; but Prince Andrei interrupted him.

'Here are her letters and her portrait,' he said. He took the packet from the table and handed it to Pierre.

'Give this to the countess … if you happen to see her.'

'She is very ill,' said Pierre.

'Then she is here still?' inquired Prince Andrei. 'And Prince Kuragin?' he asked quickly.

'He left some time ago. She has been at death's door. …'

'I am very sorry to hear of her illness,' said Prince Andrei with a disagreeable smile – a cold, spiteful smile like his father's.

'So Monsieur Kuragin has not honoured Countess Rostov with his hand?' said Prince Andrei. He snorted several times.

'He could not have married her, for the reason that he is married already,' said Pierre.

Prince Andrei laughed unpleasantly, again reminding one of his father.

'And where is your brother-in-law now, if I may ask?' he said.

'He has gone to Peters. … But I don't really know,' replied Pierre.

'Well, that's no matter,' said Prince Andrei. 'Tell Countess Rostov from me that she was and is perfectly free, and that I wish her all happiness.'

Pierre took the packet. Prince Andrei, who seemed to be considering whether he had said everything he wanted to say, or was waiting to see if Pierre would say anything, looked fixedly at him.

'Listen. You remember our discussion in Petersburg?' said Pierre. 'About …'

'I remember,' returned Prince Andrei hastily. 'I said that a fallen woman should be forgiven, but I did not say I could forgive her. I can't.'

'But how can you compare …?' said Pierre.

Prince Andrei cut him short. He cried harshly:

'Yes, ask her hand again, be magnanimous, and so on? … Yes, that would be very noble, but I'm not equal to following where that gentleman has walked. If you wish to remain my friend never speak to me of that … of all this business! Good-bye now. So you'll give her the packet?'

Pierre left the room, and went to the old prince and Princess Maria. The old man seemed livelier than usual. Princess Maria was the same as always, but beneath her sympathy for her brother Pierre could see that she was delighted that the engagement had been broken off. Looking at them, Pierre realized what contempt and animosity they all felt for the Rostovs, and that it was hopeless in their presence even to mention the name of the girl who could give up Prince Andrei for anyone in the world.

At dinner the conversation turned on the war, of the imminence of which there could now be no doubt. Prince Andrei talked incessantly, arguing now with his father, now with the Swiss tutor Dessalles, and displaying an unnatural animation, the cause of which Pierre so well understood.

22

THAT same evening Pierre went to the Rostovs' to fulfil the commission entrusted to him. Natasha was in bed, the count at the club, and Pierre, after giving the letters to Sonya, went to Maria Dmitrievna, who was greatly interested to know how Prince Andrei had taken the news. Ten minutes later Sonya came to Maria Dmitrievna.

'Natasha insists on seeing Count Bezuhov,' said she.

'But how? Are we to take him up to her? Why, your room is all in a muddle,' protested Maria Dmitrievna.

'No, she is dressed and has come down to the drawing-room,' said Sonya.

Maria Dmitrievna could only shrug her shoulders.

'If only her mother would come! The girl has worried me to death! Now mind, don't go telling her everything,' she said to Pierre. 'One hasn't the heart to scold her, she is such a piteous object, poor thing!'

Natasha was standing in the middle of the drawing-room, looking much thinner, and with a pale set face (though not in the least overcome with shame as Pierre had expected). When he appeared in the doorway she hesitated, flustered and evidently undecided whether to go to meet him or wait for him to come to her.

Pierre hastened forward. He thought she would offer her hand as usual; but stepping near him she stopped, breathing hard, her arms hanging lifelessly, in exactly the same pose in which she used to stand in the middle of the ballroom to sing, but with an utterly different expression on her face.

'Count Bezuhov,' she began rapidly, 'Prince Bolkonsky was your friend – is your friend,' she corrected herself. (It seemed to her that everything was in the past, and now all was changed.) 'He once told me to turn to you if ...'

Pierre choked dumbly as he looked at her. Till then he had in his heart reproached her and tried to despise her, but now he felt so sorry for her that there was no room in him for reproach.

'He is here now: tell him ... to for ... forgive me!' She paused and her breath came still faster, but she shed no tears.

'Yes ... I will tell him,' murmured Pierre; 'but ...' He did not know what to say.

Natasha was evidently dismayed at the thought that might occur to Pierre.

'Of course I know all is over between us,' she said hurriedly. 'No, that can never be. I am only tortured by the wrong I have done him. Only tell him that I beg him to forgive, to forgive – forgive me for everything. ...' Her whole body trembled and she sat down on a chair.

A feeling of compassion such as he had never known before flooded Pierre's heart.

'I will tell him, I will tell him everything once more,' said Pierre. 'But ... I should like to know one thing. ...'

'Know what?' Natasha's eyes asked.

'I should like to know, did you love ...' Pierre did not know what to call Anatole, and flushed at the thought of him – 'did you love that vile man?'

'Don't call him vile!' said Natasha. 'But I – I don't know – I don't know at all. ...'

She began to cry again, and Pierre was more than ever over-whelmed with pity, tenderness and love. He felt the tears trickling under his spectacles and hoped they would not be noticed.

'We won't speak of it any more, my dear,' said Pierre, and it suddenly seemed so strange to Natasha to hear his affectionate, gentle, sympathetic tone.

'We won't speak of it, my dear – I'll tell him everything. But one thing I beg of you: look on me as your friend, and if you need help, advice, or simply to open your heart to someone – not now, but when your mind is clearer – think of me.' He took her hand and kissed it. 'I shall be happy if I am able. ...'

Pierre grew confused.

'Don't speak to me like that. I am not worthy of it!' cried Natasha, and she would have left the room but Pierre held her hand. He knew he had something more to say to her. But when he had spoken he was amazed at his own words.

'Hush, hush! You have your whole life before you,' he said to her.

'Before me? No! All is over for me,' she replied, in shame and self-abasement.

'All over?' he echoed. 'If I were not myself, but the handsomest, cleverest, best man in the world, and if I were free I would be on my knees this minute to beg for your hand and your love.'

For the first time for many days Natasha wept soft tears of gratitude, and giving Pierre one look she fled from the room.

Pierre, too, when she had gone almost ran into the ante-room, restraining the tears of tenderness and happiness that choked him, and without stopping to find the sleeves of his fur coat, flung it over his shoulders and got into his sledge.

'Where to now, your Excellency?' asked the coachman.

'Where to?' Pierre wondered. 'Where can I go now? Surely not to the club or to pay calls?' All men seemed to him so pitiful, such poor creatures in comparison with this feeling of tenderness and love in his heart – in comparison with that softened, grateful last look she had turned upon him through her tears.

'Home!' said Pierre, and despite the twenty-two degrees of frost he threw open the bearskin coat from his broad chest and joyously inhaled the air.

It was clear and frosty. Above the dirty ill-lit streets, above the black roofs, stretched the dark starry sky. Only as he gazed up at the heavens did Pierre cease to feel the humiliating pettiness of all earthly things compared with the heights to which his soul had just been raised. As he drove out on to Arbatsky square his eyes were met with a vast expanse of starry black sky. Almost in the centre of this sky, above the Prichistensky boulevard, surrounded and convoyed on every side by stars but distinguished from them all by its nearness to the earth, its white light and its long uplifted tail, shone the huge, brilliant comet of the year 1812 – the comet which was said to portend all manner of horrors and the end of the world. But that bright comet with its long luminous tail aroused no feeling of fear in Pierre's heart. On the contrary, with rapture and his eyes wet with tears, he contemplated the radiant star which, after travelling in its orbit with inconceivable velocity through infinite space, seemed suddenly – like an arrow piercing the earth – to remain fast in one chosen spot in the black firmament, vigorously tossing up its tail, shining and playing with its white light amid the countless other scintillating stars. It seemed to Pierre that this comet spoke in full harmony with all that filled his own softened and uplifted soul, now blossoming into a new life.

END OF VOLUME ONE

MORE ABOUT PENGUINS
AND PELICANS

Penguinews, which appears every month, contains details of all the new books issued by Penguins as they are published. From time to time it is supplemented by *Penguins in Print*, which is our complete list of almost 5,000 titles.

A specimen copy of *Penguinews* will be sent to you free on request. Please write to Dept EP, Penguin Books Ltd, Harmondsworth, Middlesex, for your copy.

In the U.S.A.: For a complete list of books available from Penguin in the United States write to Dept CS, Penguin Books, 625 Madison Avenue, New York, New York 10022.

In Canada: For a complete list of books available from Penguin in Canada write to Penguin Books Canada Ltd, 41 Steelcase Road West, Markham, Ontario.